Jeff Shaara is the New York Times bestselling author of *The Glorious Cause*, *Rise to Rebellion*, and *Gone for Soldiers*, as well as *Gods and Generals* and *The Last Full Measure* – two novels that complete the Civil War trilogy that began with his father's Pulitzer Prize–winning classic *The Killer Angels*. Shaara was born in 1952 into a family of Italian immigrants in New Brunswick, New Jersey. He grew up in Tallahassee, Florida, and graduated from Florida State University. He lives in Missoula, Montana.

Visit the author online at www.JeffShaara.com

Praise for To the Last Man:

"A gripping account of World War I—from tactics to strategy. The reader feels the horror of the trenches in France and is drawn into the maneuvering of political and military leaders on both sides of the battle. Jeff Shaara shows the dominance of the U.S. military in the context of coalition warfare—as relevant today as it was in 1918."
General Tommy R. Franks

"A sweeping, searching look at World War I. Jeff Shaara's novel rings with authenticity, from the feelings of frontline soldiers to the challenges of high-level command."
General Wesley Clark

"[*To the Last Man*] is first-rate storytelling that aptly describes aspects of a conflict that continues to shape our world today."
Booklist

"Exciting glimpses into some of the less familiar aspects of World War I show that with *To the Last Man* Jeff Shaara has successfully graduated from his Civil War novels."
The Washington Post

Also by Jeff Shaara
(published by The Random House Publishing Group)

GODS AND GENERALS
THE LAST FULL MEASURE
GONE FOR SOLDIERS
RISE TO REBELLION
THE GLORIOUS CAUSE

To the Last Man

A Novel of the First World War

Jeff Shaara

BANTAM BOOKS

LONDON • TORONTO • SYDNEY • AUCKLAND • JOHANNESBURG

TO THE LAST MAN
A BANTAM BOOK : 055381740X
9780553817409

First publication in Great Britain
This edition published by arrangement with Ballantine Books,
a division of Random House Publishing Group, a division of
Random House Inc.

PRINTING HISTORY
Bantam edition published 2006

5 7 9 10 8 6 4

Set in 10/12pt Sabon by
Falcon Oast Graphic Art Ltd.

Bantam Books are published by Transworld Publishers,
61–63 Uxbridge Road, London W5 5SA,
a division of The Random House Group Ltd

Addresses for companies within The Random House Group Limited
can be found at:
www.randomhouse.co.uk/offices.htm.

Printed and bound in Great Britain by
Cox & Wyman Ltd, Reading, Berkshire.

The Random House Group Limited makes every effort to ensure
that the papers used in its books are made from trees that
have been legally sourced from well-managed and credibly
certified forests. Our paper procurement policy can be found at:
www.randomhouse.co.uk/paper.htm.

There must be no course but to fight it out.
Every position must be held to the last man.
There must be no retirement. With our backs
to the wall and believing in the justice of our
cause each one of us must fight on to the
end.

—Field Marshal Sir Douglas Haig
Commander in Chief,
British Expeditionary Force
April 12, 1918

Contents

TO THE READER

No conflict in human history has brought about greater change to our world than the First World War. In no other war were so many nations so transformed, from the borders drawn on maps to the rulers whose empires fell to dust. In no other war was the horror so utterly surprising, and so graphically visible to the entire world. And in no other war did the outcome so completely pave the way for an even more tragic war that would follow only two decades later.

As the twentieth century dawned, philosophers and social scientists were trumpeting the arrival of the Modern Age, a breathless optimism that the thundering stampede of new technology would radically improve the quality of life for people the world over. Overlooked was that human nature had not evolved along with its machines. Humanity's worst instincts—for conquest, domination, aggression, jealousy, and barbaric cruelty—would become plainly evident. The killing machines had improved as well.

It might be best that I describe this book by defining what it is not. This is not a comprehensive, blow-by-blow history of the First World War. This book does not take the reader to every corner of the immense war. This is not a history book at all, certainly not in the way that you may be familiar with that term from high school. This is the story, primarily, of four men, told through their points of view, as they might have told the story themselves. They are four distinctly different characters, who are involved in the war from four very different perspectives. This is a novel, by definition, because you are in their minds, hearing their words, and experiencing the war, and their world, as they saw it. The events, and each character's participation or observation of those events, are as accurate as I could make them, an accuracy to which I am fiercely dedicated.

This story does not always focus on those characters who are the most familiar, or the most legendary. If this diminishes the book for you, I apologize. What I have tried to construct is a story that will carry the reader through this time alongside the more familiar as well as the virtually unknown. Many of the characters (and events) in this book are household names; many definitely are not.

If you are familiar with my previous books, then you know that typically I have followed the points of view of commanders, the people at the top. Such an approach here would simply not work. The more modern the war, the farther the commanders are from what is happening in front of them. However, I do not ignore the men who were responsible for engineering what took place in the field, and thus one of the principal characters in this story is General John J. Pershing. The other characters are Baron Manfred von Richthofen (far better known as the "Red Baron"), Raoul Lufbery of the Lafayette Escadrille, and Private Roscoe Temple, United States Marine Corps. Though these men do not share the same experiences, they have one thing distinctly in common. Each man's life is radically changed by his experience, and each one provides an insight into his time. And each one is very much a hero.

In all my stories, I hold tightly to the rule of avoiding anachronisms, both in vocabulary and in speaking styles. While the language of the early twentieth century was not so radically different from that of today, differences do exist, and I have made every effort to be true to the time.

In addition, it is obvious to anyone reading this story that the German characters spoke German, and most (but not all) of the French characters spoke French. Indeed, many of the conversations between General Pershing and various French commanders took place in French. I have purposely avoided most references to interpreters, and I have made no attempt to differentiate what language is being spoken in each passage of dialogue. Only occasionally do I mention a character's accent. It has always been my feeling that emphasizing the obvious accent or inflections of speech is a distraction, interrupting the flow of the story, and, frankly, shows disregard for the intelligence of the reader.

It is my hope that this story will both surprise and entertain you. If occasionally you find the images uncomfortable, or the story line unexpectedly tragic, I can offer no apology for that. The story is true; the images are real. And we must never forget.

—Jeff Shaara
June 2004

ACKNOWLEDGMENTS

I have often been told that novels require no acknowledgment. In this case, I disagree. One enormous benefit that has come to me in the preparation of this story is the input I have received from descendants of soldiers who fought in the war. In addition, since I am frequently asked about the kinds of research materials I use, I thought it appropriate to list many of the primary sources.

For their generous gifts of materials, I offer my sincere thanks to:

    Jeff and Colleen Clenard, Scottsdale, Arizona
    Walt Diffenderfer, New Cumberland, Pennsylvania
    Patrick Falci and Joan McDonough, Rosedale, New York
    Dr. William B. Gallagher, Tucson, Arizona
    Colonel Keith Gibson, Lexington, Virginia
    John M. Kennedy, Shelby, Ohio
    Fredrick Landesman, Walnut Creek, California
    Jack Smith, Pleasanton, California

The following is a partial list of the historical figures whose original source materials, memoirs, or collections of letters were used in the rescarch for this book:

General John J. Pershing, USA
General George S. Patton, USA
General George C. Marshall, USA

General John A. Lejeune, USMC
General James Harbord, USA
Captain Edward Rickenbacker, 94th Aero Squadron
Lieutenant Edwin "Ted" Parsons, Lafayette Escadrille
Lieutenant Bert Hall, Lafayette Escadrille
Lieutenant Roland Richardson, 213th Aero Squadron
Captain (Dr.) Marshall C. Pease, USA
President Woodrow Wilson
Private Carl Heterius, 137th Infantry Regiment
Private Arthur G. Empey, BEF
Lieutenant Harvey L. Harris, USA
Lieutenant John Thomason, USMC
Captain Manfred von Richthofen, Imperial German
Flying Service
General Erich Ludendorff, Imperial German Army
Field Marshal Paul von Hindenburg, Imperial German
Army
Sergeant Karl McCune, USMC
Private Fitch L. McCord, USMC
Corporal John Aasland, USMC
Prime Minister David Lloyd George
Marshal Ferdinand Foch

List of Maps

INTRODUCTION

At the beginning of the twentieth century, Europe has enjoyed nearly three decades of peace. But the complacency of its people masks a dark shadow growing beneath the various governments that maintain an uneasy hold on their relationships with their neighbors. The Franco-Prussian War in 1871 was an overwhelming victory for Germany, and a crushing humiliation for France, a result of centuries of bitter feuding between two distinctly different cultures. With their victory, the Germans take control of the regions of Alsace and Lorraine, which lie along their mutual border. As sorely as the French feel the loss of that territory, there is a final humiliation that plants an even more bitter seed. To celebrate their victory, the Germans stage a triumphant march of their soldiers down the Champs-Élysées, through the core of Paris—a symbolic assault on French pride that only deepens the unhealing wounds of the war.

In Germany, Kaiser Wilhelm II rules a country whose pride is in its military. The great beloved heroes of the German Empire are its soldiers, most notably Otto von Bismarck. Bismarck begins to emphasize German preparedness for a war he believes to be inevitable. For him, "a generation that has taken a beating is always followed by a generation that deals one." His philosophy spreads through German military consciousness, hardening into a firm belief that France is most certainly planning to take its revenge on Germany by starting another war. Most German militarists accept completely the notion that in order to prevent such a potential catastrophe, Germany must strike first. The most pressing question is not why, but how.

The strategy is named for its architect, Count Alfred von

Schlieffen, the German military's chief of staff. The Schlieffen Plan calls for a preemptive strike into France that flows first across Belgium, and slices into France from the North, a massive unstoppable wave that will wrap around and consume Paris. Von Schlieffen discounts any problems dealing with France's ally, Russia, nor does the plan consider any real threat from a French counterattack through Alsace-Lorraine. As designed, the Schlieffen Plan would deploy nearly all of Germany's available troop strength, and drive them so rapidly to their objective that no reaction from France or its allies will come quickly enough to prevent Germany's rapid victory. The war would be over virtually as soon as it begins.

But von Schlieffen does not carry out his own plan. He retires from service in 1906, and dies in 1913. Germany's military planning falls into the hands of Field Marshal Helmuth von Moltke, the nephew of one of Germany's great heroes of the Franco-Prussian War. The younger von Moltke is not the leader his uncle was, however, and he immediately begins to find fault with certain elements of the Schlieffen Plan. Von Moltke lacks the confidence of so many of his predecessors, and his cautious nature causes him to amend the plan so that a significant percentage of Germany's strike force is stripped away and placed defensively along the Alsace-Lorraine border. But neither von Moltke nor the kaiser has the confidence to order the final go-ahead. They require some spark, some specific incentive to justify the order. It comes in Sarajevo, Bosnia, on July 28, 1914.

Austrian archduke Franz Ferdinand, the heir apparent to the throne of the Austria-Hungarian Empire, parades through the city, accompanied by his wife, Sophie. The archduke is keenly aware that throughout the Balkans there is considerable unrest and anger at Austria and its rulers, fueled by centuries-old feuds between the various ethnic factions in the region, most notably the Serbs. His vain and lavish show for the crowds in Sarajevo is obviously dangerous. But the archduke ignores his advisers and insists that the adoring crowds justify any danger. It is a catastrophic error in judgment. Both the archduke and his wife are gunned down by a Serbian nationalist. The outcry in Austria is predictable, and the Austrian military sees the opportunity to eliminate the annoyance of what they see as Serbian interference in Austria's rightful dominance of the region. The Austrians make blusterous demands and ultimatums, knowing that their military is far superior to the Serbians'. The Serbians, in a desperate effort to avoid war, make every effort to accept the often ridiculous demands. Frustrated by Serbian compliance, and seeking the excuse to launch a crushing blow that would add Serbia's resources to her own, the Austrians finally demand that the Serbs allow the Austrian army to occupy Serbia as a means of rounding up Serbian troublemakers. The line has been crossed. Serbia refuses, and the Austrians have their excuse.

A regional dispute between a large power and one who is very much weaker suddenly takes on a life that has consequences few can predict. The Serbians have a treaty of alliance with the French and also with the Russians, who face the Austrians along an enormous common border. The Austrians, in order to counter the Russian threat, gain assurances from Kaiser Wilhelm that Germany will come to Austria's aid, should Russia attack. Any open conflict with Russia will trigger a response from the French, who have their own alliance with Russia. The Germans have their spark.

There is still one piece of the puzzle left to chance. In order to invade France, German troops will march through neutral Belgium. Belgium has a formal alliance with England, who has pledged to secure Belgian sovereignty. The kaiser does not believe the British will enter a war against Germany, just for what he sees as the relatively minor concerns of the Belgians. Germany does not intend to occupy Belgium, merely pass through the country. The German navy, however, sees a war with England as an opportunity. For more than a century, the British have dominated the seas, something the ambitious German admirals would like to change. Germany's coastline is limited, and the navy's proponents are eager to find some way to expand Germany's influence on the oceans, thus opening new doors economically, as well as militarily. If England enters a war on behalf of the Belgians, so be it.

The dominoes are set to fall. In the capitals of Europe, furious

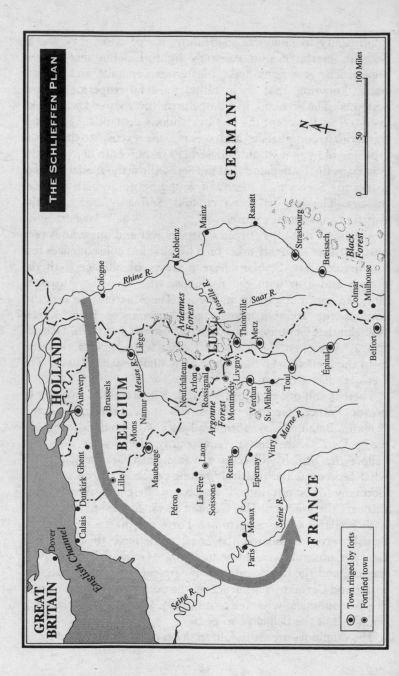

THE SCHLIEFFEN PLAN

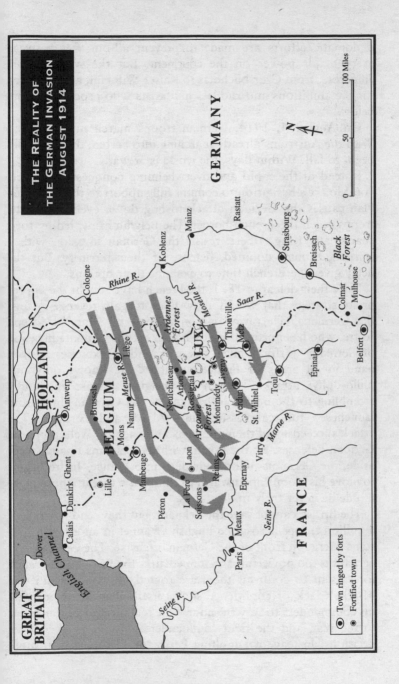

THE REALITY OF
THE GERMAN INVASION
AUGUST 1914

GREAT BRITAIN

HOLLAND

BELGIUM

GERMANY

FRANCE

LUXEMBOURG

Black Forest

English Channel

Rhine R.

Meuse R.

Moselle R.

Saar R.

Marne R.

Seine R.

Seine R.

Dover

Calais

Dunkirk

Ghent

Antwerp

Brussels

Lille

Mons

Maubeuge

Péron

Laon

La Fère

Soissons

Reims

Epernay

Vitry

Meaux

Paris

Liège

Namur

Neufchâteau

Arlon

Rossignol

Montmédy

Verdun

St. Mihiel

Longwy

Toul

Thionville

Metz

Épinal

Belfort

Colmar

Mulhouse

Strasbourg

Breisach

Rastatt

Mainz

Koblenz

Cologne

Ardennes Forest

Argonne Forest

N

⊙ Town ringed by forts
● Fortified town

0   50   100 Miles

diplomatic efforts are made to prevent all-out war between every major power on the continent. But the weak-minded emperors, from Czar Nicholas to Kaiser Wilhelm, are no match for the ambitious and ruthless militarists who prod them from below.

On August 4, 1914, German troops march into Belgium. With the Austrians already marching into Serbia, the dominoes begin to fall. Within days, the world is at war.

Instead of the rapid and overwhelming conquest of France, von Moltke's hesitation to commit full support to the Schlieffen Plan causes the German attack to bog down even before the troops reach the French border. The Belgian army, led by their charismatic King Albert, resists the German invasion with a spirited, though doomed, defense of their territory. But the delay gives the French time to examine their options.

Since their defeat in 1871, the French have sought the appropriate strategy that would allow them to gain revenge against the Germans. The army is commanded by Marshal Joseph Joffre, who has nurtured his own plan for the ultimate invasion of Germany. Joffre is given free rein, and he exercises an iron hand in all areas of France's military. He knows only one philosophy: attack. Though the Belgian defense is rapidly crumbling to the north, Joffre ignores the German threat and launches a full-scale assault into Alsace and Lorraine. The attack succeeds, and then grinds to a halt against well-prepared German defenses. To the north, with the Belgians finally swept aside, the Germans make their push into France. Joffre begins to move his troops northward, to confront a threat whose magnitude he never truly understands.

The British cannot save the Belgians, but they send nearly half a million troops across the English Channel in an effort to put some barrier in front of the German offensive. The German juggernaut is too powerful, and immediately the British and French forces sent to confront them are routed. But once again von Moltke's lack of confidence shows itself. Instead of ordering his commanders to stay the course, he remains out of touch, far to the rear, and the field commanders must make their own decisions. Instead of engulfing Paris, the Germans turn more toward the west, in an attempt to surround the French army. But in the field, the Germans have extended beyond their own ability to feed and supply their army, something the original Schlieffen Plan had failed to address. What von Moltke fails to realize is the opportunity that still rests in his hands. With the war less than a month old, the Belgians are conquered, the French are facing utter defeat, and the British are nearly eliminated before they can fully mobilize their army.

What follows is called the (First) Battle of the Marne. With the power of the German thrust wavering, cracks begin to appear in the German position, and on September 7, 1914, Joffre seizes the advantage and attacks. The Germans are without effective communications to their commander, and uncertain of his troops' precise situation, von Moltke makes his final error. Once more he hesitates. With their position in jeopardy, and no one available to give a definitive order, the German field commanders believe they have no alternative but to pull back. The exhausted French and British troops cannot follow up their success, can only follow the German withdrawal, until both sides reach a safe defensive position. All along a ninety-mile front, the attacks have ground down into paralysis. Both sides have their northern flanks exposed, and thus begins a race to the sea, with both German and British troops seeking to turn the other's flank. But neither side succeeds, and the northernmost point of the front is thus anchored firmly against the English Channel. With troops furiously fortifying their defenses, a no-man's-land is created that eventually stretches from Flanders, in western Belgium, to the Swiss border, south of Alsace-Lorraine. The Western Front has come into existence. As both sides prepare for what surely must follow, the extraordinary cost of the first great battle becomes known. Both sides suffer twenty-five percent casualties. Driven by the shock of just what kind of horror they face, the armies turn the Western Front into a fortress of defensiveness. Mammoth networks of underground trenches extend all along both sides of the line.

Stung by the enormity of their failure, the kaiser blames von Moltke's timidity, and replaces him with General Erich von Falkenhayn. Joffre responds to the catastrophic carnage by blaming his generals, and he replaces numerous field commanders all along the line. Ultimately, both sides spend the rest of the year licking their wounds, planning what, if anything, they can do next.

In the East, the Russians respond as expected, and they begin a campaign along an enormous front of the German/Austrian border. The fighting there is as bloody and, ultimately, as inconclusive.

In November 1914, the Germans are gratified to learn that the Ottoman Empire of Turkey has decided to join the war on the German side. The centuries-old influence of the Ottoman Turks has waned across the region, a vast empire that once included most of North Africa and the Middle East. Their chief rival in specific areas such as Egypt and Mesopotamia is the British, and the Turkish rulers recognize an opportunity to reclaim both land and past glory. The Turks strike at their Russian neighbors as well, where, along their mutual borders, a variety of tribal and ethnic cultures have waged violent confrontations for centuries. Throughout the Balkans and Arabia the ethnic violence takes a horrific toll, including the slaughter of nearly six hundred thousand Armenians. The war ignites old ethnic differences into full-scale confrontations, and those on the weaker side of a dispute are often the victims of unspeakable abuses.

Germany provides considerable economic and military assistance to the Turks, the kaiser recognizing the importance of Turkish control of the Straits of the Dardanelles. The straits, bordered by the Gallipoli Peninsula, are Russia's only outlet from the Black Sea to the Mediterranean, and thus a powerful economic artery for one of Germany's primary enemies. In February 1915, the British launch a furious assault on the Gallipoli Peninsula. British colonial troops from New Zealand and Australia (Anzac) are sent ashore only to find that no specific plan has been made for them to proceed inland, and almost no reconnaissance has been made of the countryside they are supposed to attack. The inept leadership causes enormous casualties to the Anzac, who are finally withdrawn without gaining any of their objectives. England's catastrophic failure is symbolic in that no nation can rely on its past glories to win battles in this new, horribly modern war.

Across the Atlantic Ocean, one great variable remains. President Woodrow Wilson declares immediately that his nation shall follow a course of neutrality. Wilson's principles are born of his own personal, somewhat pacifist philosophy, as well as the political reality that the United States is indeed a melting pot of cultures and ethnicities that includes significant numbers of citizens (and voters) sympathetic to every side of the war. Throughout the country, the propaganda wars heat up and violence breaks out between ethnically diverse groups fiercely loyal to their homelands. But many Americans are simply bystanders, intently watching from afar what is unfolding in Europe. Most Americans want no part of what they see as a European problem, and they support Wilson's declaration of neutrality. But the public perceptions begin to shift, the result of the intense propaganda campaigns waged by both sides. It is the British who prove to be more effective at stating their case. Americans also have difficulty accepting German rationalizations for their unprovoked invasion of Belgium, made worse by the German army's crushing blow to the Belgian army's attempts to defend their own territory. Then, the Germans make a monumental strategic mistake. On May 7, 1915, a German submarine off the Irish coast fires two torpedoes at the opulent ocean liner *Lusitania*, which sinks in twenty minutes. Nearly twelve hundred people lose their lives, including one hundred twenty-four Americans. Though the Germans claim, with some accuracy, that the *Lusitania* was carrying arms as well as passengers, the attack is seen as an unjustifiable atrocity. For the first time, the war has struck directly and blatantly at American interests.

Though most Americans are still opposed to active involvement in the war, some have already taken a stand, and they travel to Europe to make some direct contribution to a cause they feel is worth fighting for. In the American military, there is a blossoming awareness that if the United States should join the war, there is a desperate need for modernization and preparation of an army that, for a generation, has had little to do but chase banditos in Mexico.

John J. Pershing

Born 1860, in Laclede, Missouri. While still in his late teens, he shows a passion for teaching and passes the required examinations that grant him a teaching certificate. Though younger than some of his students, he gains their respect as a young man of discipline, who will tolerate no bullying and no one's laziness toward his studies. At age twenty-one, he takes the examination for the United States Military Academy at West Point, believing that a West Point education will give him the foundation he will need to build a solid career in teaching. Though he has no expectations of becoming a soldier, at West Point he is surprised to find himself drawn to a career in the military. He finds enormous inspiration from the study of military history and heroes, most notably Ulysses Grant, and graduates Class of 1886, thirtieth in his class, out of seventy-seven.

Pershing accepts the most sought-after route available to a young officer, that of cavalry. His first assignment is with the Sixth Cavalry, which places him at Fort Bayard, New Mexico—Indian country—and instead of the romantic notions he had imagined, he finds the post unspeakably dull. In 1890, he moves with the Sixth to the Dakotas, and eventually commands a group of Sioux Indians who have been recruited as scouts. He gains unexpected insight into and tolerance for his former "enemy."

Still yearning to teach, in 1891, he accepts a position as professor of military science at the University of Nebraska, and moves to Lincoln. He brings West Point discipline to what is regarded as a poor military school. Within a year, he transforms the academy into a respected replica of West Point. Despite the satisfaction he receives from his work with young cadets, he continues to look to his own education, and in 1893, he earns a law degree. But he decides against a career in law, accepting the advice of a good friend, who tells him, "Better lawyers than you are starving in Nebraska. Your [army] pay may be small, but it comes very regularly."

Promoted to first lieutenant, Pershing accepts a challenging assignment with the Tenth Cavalry, a Negro unit stationed at Fort Assiniboine, Montana. Pershing thrives in the command and earns the respect of his troops, as well as an affinity for their status as second-class soldiers. It is this command that gives him the nickname "Black Jack."

In 1896, he catches the eye of army commander General Nelson Miles, and is invited to join Miles as a staff officer in Washington. But Pershing chafes at life in the capital, and in 1897, he seeks, and is granted, a post as an instructor at West Point. With the winds of war blowing toward a serious conflict with Spain, Pershing requests reassignment with the Tenth Cavalry, and in 1898, when war is declared, Pershing travels to meet the regiment at Tampa, Florida, to prepare for the invasion of Cuba. He participates in what becomes known as the Battle of San Juan Hill, where he meets and befriends Teddy Roosevelt.

One key spoils of the war is the Philippines, which is consumed by factional and civil war. Pershing arrives in Manila in November 1899, and becomes adjutant general, and governor of Mindanao. Here he successfully juggles the particular differences that inspire bloodshed between Moslem, Chinese, and native Filipino interests. The lessons learned in dealing with both Indian and Negro concerns provide Pershing with an enormous advantage in bridging the wide cultural gaps, and surprising to his fellow officers, he is held in high esteem among the Moro (Moslem) tribes.

He is recalled to Washington in 1903, to serve on the newly created War Department General Staff. He reluctantly settles into the social scene and meets Frances Warren, the daughter of Senator Francis Warren of Wyoming. Their romance is the stuff of gossip, and on January 26, 1905, they are married in what is considered to be a major social event, attended by many in Congress, as well as Teddy (now president) Roosevelt. Roosevelt so admires Pershing that the president exercises this authority somewhat excessively, and he promotes Pershing from captain to brigadier general, which does not endear Pershing to many ranking officers in the army.

Pershing returns to the Philippines with his wife and newborn daughter, and they remain there for seven more years, during which time Frances gives birth to three more children, two girls and a boy.

In 1913, he receives a new assignment and moves his family to the Presidio in San Francisco. He is almost immediately ordered to Fort Bliss, near El Paso, Texas, to command the army's Eighth Brigade, confronting the crisis that is blossoming with Mexico. The crisis is the result of a general chaos south of the border due to Mexico's revolution and power struggle, which spills over the border in the form of raids and banditry that the American government cannot ignore. He observes from a great distance the war that roars to life in Europe, but his duty in Texas is tedious and isolated, and Pershing can focus only on his own command.

On August 27, 1915, he receives the devastating news that his home in San Francisco has burned, and that his wife and three daughters have been killed; only his young son has survived. The tragedy numbs him so severely that he can function only by performing his duty with fanatical dedication. The job is frustrating beyond tolerance for many of the soldiers under his command, but Pershing persists, only occasionally allowing his emotions to surface. Driven deeper into bored despair, he cannot help casting an eye toward the events in Europe. Despite his president's calls for neutrality, Pershing understands the world through a soldier's eye. The wider the war, and the longer it lasts, the less likely it is that anyone can remain neutral.

Roscoe Temple

Born 1898, near the thriving farm community of Monticello, in northern Florida. His father dies when he is an infant, and he has no recollection of the man. He is raised by a stern mother and an affectionate grandfather. The family farms the land, and his mother's unwillingness to remarry puts her squarely in what is typically a man's role as the overseer of a difficult life. Temple observes his mother's love for her land, but more, he learns to appreciate all that nature has provided them. From an early age, he follows his grandfather through the winding paths that carry him deep into woods and swamplands, all the places that attract the imagination of a boy.

Temple, a voracious consumer of books, reads as many novels and histories as can be found in his rural community, and travels to the closest larger town, Tallahassee, to find more. He focuses on a study of the Civil War, inspired mainly by his grandfather's stories of life as a Confederate soldier. But Temple seeks more than fantasy, and he begins to wonder about a career in the military. With tales of the Spanish-American War flowing across the land, and with the ebullient Teddy Roosevelt inspiring the nation to think of America as a place that gives birth to men of action, Temple's fantasies jell into ambition. The spring after the outbreak of the war in Europe, he graduates from the rural high school, with a total of three classmates. He counts the days until his eighteenth birthday, and though he has spoken of little else than becoming a soldier, his mother is stunned when he announces that he intends to join the Marine Corps. Despite the needs of the farm, she will not stand in the way of her only child's dream, and in 1917, he travels to Quantico, Virginia. Though the country seems twisted into turmoil and disagreement about the meaning of the war, whether or not the nation should imperil its youth in a foreign conflict, Temple nurtures the dream, and by the end of 1917, he is a Marine.

Raoul Lufbery

Born 1885, in Clermont-Ferrand, France, the youngest son of an American chemist. His mother dies before Lufbery is a year old, and when his father remarries and returns to America, Lufbery and his brothers remain in France in the care of relatives.

Lufbery grows up an independent and undisciplined young man and leaves France at age nineteen. Having no notion of what he wants to do with his life, he begins to travel. He finds his way to North Africa, Germany, Turkey, among many other stops, and survives by accepting any work he can find. In 1906, he and an older brother sail for New York, hoping to visit his father, who lives in Wallingford, Connecticut. But unknown to either of them, the elder Lufbery happens to leave New York by ship the same week his sons arrive. Lufbery will never see his father again. For two years he labors at a silver factory in Connecticut. In 1908, he begins another search for some kind of future, and he travels first to Cuba, then to New Orleans, and on to San Francisco, again working any odd jobs he can find.

He enlists in the army and serves in the Philippines under Pershing, where he pursues the paperwork required to become a naturalized American citizen. When his enlistment expires, Lufbery leaves the army and begins to travel again, sailing to Japan, China, and then to India.

In 1912, in Calcutta, he meets Frenchman Marc Pourpe, who is an accomplished and celebrated pilot. Pourpe travels throughout the world performing aerobatic exhibitions for astonished audiences. Lufbery sees an opportunity and applies himself to the art of aircraft mechanics. When Pourpe is satisfied that Lufbery is a qualified mechanic, he hires him to accompany the exhibition. In 1914, he tours with Pourpe through Asia and North Africa, and when Pourpe learns of the availability of a new aircraft, Lufbery accompanies him to France. Lufbery has now completed a journey that has taken him completely around the world.

While they are in France the war breaks out, and, to Lufbery's distress, Pourpe hears the call of his native country and joins the fledgling French Air Service. Lufbery responds by joining the French Foreign Legion, the home to a growing number of Americans who have come to Europe in search of adventure, or simply to participate in the war. Pourpe's influence helps Lufbery make the transfer to the Air Service, a move sought by hundreds of foreigners who would rather explore the new adventure of aviation instead of life in the infantry. Lufbery never stops fine-tuning his mechanical skills, and learns as much as he can about every new aircraft motor in production, while continuing to serve as Pourpe's personal mechanic.

On December 2, 1914, Marc Pourpe is killed while attempting to land his plane in inclement weather. Lufbery is devastated. Though he can easily find a place as a mechanic with any number of pilots, he begins to see a new mission in his life. He blames Germany and the war for the death of his one close friend, and driven by a need for revenge, Lufbery requests transfer to the French pilot school at Chartres. He completes his training in October 1915, and is assigned to a French bomber squadron. But he finds the work boring and seeks recertification as a fighter pilot. In May 1916, he receives certification to fly the French Nieuport, that country's finest front-line weapon against the growing threat of the German Air Service. Despite his perfect fluency in French, as an American citizen, the Aeronautique Militaire feels justified in assigning him to a recently organized squadron of American pilots. Lufbery knows that, now, he will have his opportunity to face the enemy in the air.

Baron Manfred von Richthofen

Born 1892, in Breslau, Lower Silesia, the oldest son of a professional soldier. At age nine, his family moves to Schweidnitz, where Richthofen becomes enamored of the woodlands that ring his family's estate. He immediately develops a love of guns and hunting, and when given an air rifle by his father, he engages in his first safari by killing three of his grandmother's domestic ducks.

At age eleven, he is sent by his father to the Wahlstatt Military School in Berlin, the tradition for sons of Prussian officers. Richthofen hates the rigidity of the school, spends far more time engaging in athletics than in his studies in the classroom. He is punished constantly for climbing the many trees that surround the school, and on one occasion he climbs to the highest point in the area, a church steeple, where the view of the world from above captivates him. He spends six miserable years at Wahlstatt, but at age seventeen, the tedium concludes. He is enrolled at the Senior School, Lichterfelde, south of Berlin, which proves far more enjoyable. Instead of the mundane rules of discipline, Lichterfelde is dedicated to the instruction of soldiers, and Richthofen takes to his studies with a passion. He reads the complete works of Clausewitz, the definitive volumes on the science and philosophy of war, impressing not only his teachers, but his father as well. He graduates Lichterfelde in 1910, and enters the Berlin War Academy, the final step for a young man's leap into a career as a military officer. For the first

31

time he receives detailed instructions on modern political thinking, including the prevailing winds that blow through Germany at the time. But Richthofen is bored by the talk of politics and intrigue, and focuses on his final graduation, which will open the door to his career in his chosen field, the cavalry. He enlists in the First Regiment of Uhlans, a mobile, light cavalry unit, and in 1912 is given his commission as lieutenant. He continues to train as a cavalry officer, and in the summer of 1914, he is stationed close to the eastern border with Russian-occupied Poland. The young lieutenant is oblivious to the whirlwind swirling around him. During a particularly festive dinner, Richthofen and his fellow officers are startled to receive word that the border has suddenly become a war zone.

He leads his cavalry on various missions, probing into Russian territory, and has several close brushes with units of Cossack cavalry that never amount to any significant action, neither side seeming to believe that they are actually supposed to fight. But the war finds him, and in mid-August, he is transferred to the northernmost sector of the Western Front. Richthofen is assigned to patrol a region of the Argonne Forest, and he leads fifteen men into an ambush by an alert patrol of French infantry. He loses ten men in the attack and barely escapes himself. The ambush is an embarrassment for the young lieutenant, but more, it convinces him that men on horseback have no place in this new, modern war. He is assigned to service in the Signal Corps, finds himself crawling through mud to lay telephone line between trenches. As he witnesses firsthand the men doing the actual fighting, Richthofen begins to feel as though the real war is passing him by.

While he sits dejectedly in a frozen dugout, waiting for the order to return to his command post, he hears a sound like none he has heard before, drawing his eye skyward. He has no idea what the black crosses on the wings signify, or what the mission of the aircraft is. But he realizes that if he is to join the war, he might have to volunteer for duty where opportunity is still available. In May 1915, his transfer is granted, and he is sent to Cologne, to the Air Service Replacement Center. There, he will learn to fly an aeroplane.

PART I

TO TOUCH THE SKY

Imagine how thrilling it will be tomorrow marching toward the front with the noise of battle growing continually louder. I go into action with the lightest of light hearts!

—ALAN SEEGER, American poet
French Foreign Legion, 1914

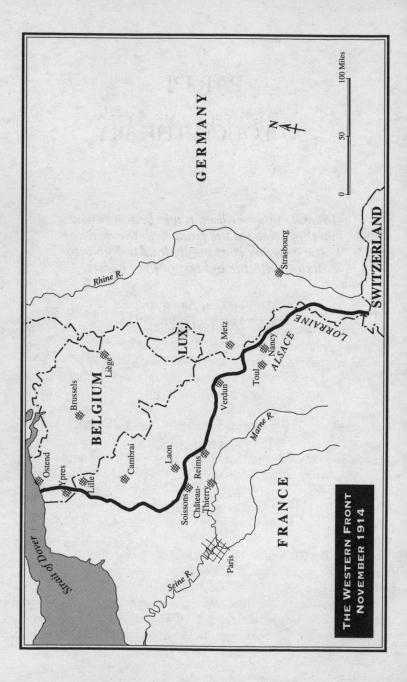

THE WESTERN FRONT
NOVEMBER 1914

GERMANY

SWITZERLAND

Rhine R.

Strasbourg

LUX.

Metz

LORRAINE

Nancy

Toul

ALSACE

Verdun

BELGIUM

Liège

Brussels

Ypres

Ostend

Lille

Cambrai

Laon

Reims

Soissons

Château-Thierry

Marne R.

FRANCE

Paris

Seine R.

Strait of Dover

N

0   50   100 Miles

1

THE REPLACEMENT

The British Lines, Near Ypres,
Western Belgium—Autumn 1915

The darkness was complete, a slow march into a black, wet hell.
He was the last man in the short column, one part of a line of
twenty men, guided by the low sounds in front of him, soft
thumps, boots on the sagging duckboards. There were voices,
hard whispers, and, close to him, a hissing growl from the
sergeant: "Keep together, you bloody laggards! No stopping!"

No one answered, no protests. Each man held himself tightly
inside, the words of the sergeant swept aside by the voices in
their own minds, a tight screaming fear, the only response they
could have to this march into the black unknown.

They had come as so many had come, crossing the Channel
on small steamers, filing through the chaos of the seaports, and
after a few days, they had boarded the trains. There was
singing, bands playing along the way, the raucous enthusiasm of
young recruits. They had stared curiously at the French and
Belgian countryside, returning the smiles of the people who
greeted them at every stop, and few noticed that as the trains
moved farther inland, closer to the vast desolation of the
Western Front, the villagers were quieter, the faces more grim.
Then the trains stopped, and the men were ordered out onto
roads that had seen too much use, repaired and repaired again.
They would march now only at night, hidden from the eyes in
the air, the aeroplanes that sought out targets for German
artillery. If the roads were bad, the small trails and pathways
were worse, men stumbling in tight files, moving closer still to
the front. The fire in the recruits was dampened now, by the
weather, the ever-present mud, the soggy lowlands of Flanders.

Then came the first sounds, low rumbles, louder as they marched forward. Even in the darkness, both sides threw a nightly artillery barrage at the other, some firing blind, some relying on the memory of the daytime, a brief glimpse of movement on the road, convoys of trucks and horse-drawn carts. Some had the range, knew every foot of the road that stretched out behind the enemy's lines. Throughout the night, the targets might be unseen, but they were there, and every man at every big gun knew that in the darkness, each road, each small path might be hiding great long lines of men, new recruits, the replacements who marched quietly to the front.

His guts were a twisted knot, his arms pulled to his sides, one hand tightly curled around his rifle, his eyes straining at the unseen man in front of him. The soft wood beneath him was bouncing now, sagging low, and his knees buckled, trying to match the rhythm of the footing. There were more soft sounds, splashes, the duckboards spread across some chasm of black water. His mind tried to focus, one foot in front of the other, keeping his boots on the narrow wooden boards. He imagined a great pond, inky and deep, the duckboards some kind of bridge, but the image was not complete, his mind shouting at him, to the front, focus to the front. The man in front of him made a low grunt, water splashing, the man stepping hard, trying to catch himself.

"Bloody hell!"

He stumbled as well, his boots down in the water, the duckboards sagging too low, and he felt the man suddenly beneath him. He fought for his balance, falling now, one hand pushing down hard on the man's back.

"Get off me, you bloody bastard!"

"Shut up, Greenie! On your feet!" It was the sergeant again, and rough hands grabbed his arm, jerking him upright. Beneath him, the other man pulled himself to his feet, both of them gripped hard by the sergeant.

"Stay awake! Keep moving!"

He wanted to whisper something to the man in front, an apology, but the march was on again, the rhythm of his boots blending with the others, soft sounds of water and wood. He felt the wetness in his socks now, the chill of the water adding to the cold hard stone in his chest.

The replacements had been called *greenies* from their first moment on the march, green troops, sent forward to rebuild the front-line units, fill the gaping holes in the British regiments. Their training had been rapid, some said far too rapid, a nation scrambling to find new soldiers, more soldiers than anyone had thought they would need. They had been parceled out into small squads by a system none of them understood, led by unfamiliar sergeants, hard, angry men who had done this work before, the men who knew the trails, who could find their way in the dark.

He had joined with many of his friends from the village, a small farming town near the Scottish border. No one had thought the army would be away from home through Christmas, but the newspapers spoke of great battles, a new horror for the world, words and places that seemed foreign and fantastic. In the village, there had been talk of young men who would not come home, strangers mostly, sons of farmers barely known, word of families in mourning. His friends spoke of the adventure of it all, that if any of them missed it, or worse, avoided it, they would be called shirkers, traitors to the king. No matter the accounts in the newspapers, a massive and bloody war that had swallowed the whole of Europe, few who lived in the small village could resist the call, to march in song and parade to join a war the likes of which Britain had not seen since Napoleon.

He tried to adjust his massive backpack, the darkness broken by a small clink of metal, his canteen rattling against the trenching tool that hung down the side of his pack. He had become used to the weight, the clumsy mass just part of the rhythm of the march, bouncing with him on the duckboards.

The ground beneath him was hard now, the wood not moving, no water, and the boots were louder, echoes in the darkness. He heard voices to one side, a group of men, still unseen, and the voices hushed as they passed. He stared through the darkness, wondering, officers perhaps, speaking of plans and tactics. He glanced up, no stars, the night still thick and black. A soft breeze swept past him, a wave of sharp odor. He hunched his shoulders, fought off the smell, but it was all through him, burning his nose, then harder still, sharp and sickening. The man in front of him made a choking sound, others as well, hard coughs, curses.

"Keep moving! That's just the roses, you bloody greenies! Plenty more to come!"

The smell was settling dull in his mind, his brain numbing to it. The breeze seemed to stop, but the smells were still there, all around him, and the man in front of him said, "A horse. A bloody horse!"

He moved past the shape, could hear the hard buzz of flies, was grateful now for the dark. He squinted his eyes, fought through the worst of the smell, stared down for a long while. The march continued, more hard odor, different, unseen decay, and he focused on his footsteps, tried not to think of what lay rotting in the deep mud around him. He could see the faint outline of his boots, the motion steady, constant, realized he could see. He looked ahead of him, could see a shape, the man in front of him outlined in a dark gray mist. He glanced to the side, more shapes, low hulks, movement. The duckboards began to sag again, more splashes, and he looked down, each step pushing the water out in low ripples. He stared ahead, past the shadow of the man, tried to see beyond, to see where they were going, what the land looked like. The sergeant moved past him now, another hard whisper.

"The first trench line is just ahead. We'll be at the guard post in a minute. Step down easy. We're close. No talking. None! Old Fritz is just out there a ways!"

He could hear something new, a slight quiver in the sergeant's voice. There was none of the profane anger, the mindless screaming at men who had done nothing wrong. He thought of the word, *close*. How close? Close enough that the sergeant is afraid? He felt his legs turning cold, the hard chill in his chest spreading. There was another low voice, unfamiliar, the words barely reaching him. He could see another man, a gray shape, an officer, speaking in low tones to the sergeant, the man's words finding him through the heavy mist.

"Sergeant Cower . . . you're late . . . daylight . . . heads low."

Behind the two men there was another low, fat hulk. But the soft dawn was spreading, and he could see a shape, a fat round barrel. His heart jumped, hard tightness—of course, a cannon. A big one. The carriage was hidden, buried in the wet muddy ground, the barrel pointing out in the direction of the march. The sergeant was moving toward them again, waving his arm, a downward motion, words coming now, but there was a new sound, a hard whistle, ripping the air above them. The ground in front of him erupted, a mass of earth and men, and he felt himself pushed back, rolling down, his face hitting the mud, his backpack lurching up over his shoulders. There was another great scream, another shell landing a few yards to his left, the ground under him rising up in one great gasp, then settling back down. More dirt fell on him, heavy, a sharp punch into his backpack, nearly rolling him over. He gripped the ground, his hands clawing into the mud, but the sounds kept rolling over him, thunderous bursts, the ground still bouncing beneath him. He tried to breathe, blew a sharp breath out, his face buried in water, tried to raise his head, another great blast, lifting him up, dropping him again hard in the mud. He gasped for air, turned his face to the side, saw only smoke, no men, no great gun. He forced a breath, his throat seared by the heat. He looked for the sergeant, tried to shout, something, not words, fought for air, another scream above him, another great blast behind him, other sounds now, more screams. Men. The dirt settled on him again, and he thought of the sergeant, the man's words, trench line, *close*. He raised his head up, saw motion, a man running, then another blast, the man disappearing, swept away. He tried to stand, the backpack nearly falling over his head, the weight pulling him over. He tried to run, his legs useless, soft jelly, felt a hand now, a hard grip under his arm.

"Let's go! Move!"

The hand released him, and he reached down for his rifle, saw only water, the voice again.

"*Move!*"

The man was running out ahead, and he followed, pumped his legs through the churned-up mud, the backpack bouncing wildly. He saw the man drop down, a large round hole, more black water, and he followed, stumbled down, splashed hard, water up to his waist.

"*Down!*"

He rolled to one side, the backpack sinking beneath him, could sit now, water to his chest, the muddy rim of the hole above him, protection. The shells still came over them, but fell farther back now, the impact jarring him in hard rumbles. He wiped at his eyes, but the mud on his hands made it worse, and he blew hard through his nose, dislodging mud and water. His hands were empty, a new burst of fear, so many days of drill, of screaming sergeants, the routine pounded hard into every man, the punishment. *Never lose your rifle*. . . .

"My rifle . . . I dropped it! I have to go back. . . ."

The hand clamped hard on his shoulder again, and he saw the face of the sergeant.

"Stay put! There's more rifles to be found. You wounded?"

The question confused him, and he looked down, saw only water, said, "I don't know. I don't know."

"You better check, Greenie. But keep down."

He moved his hands along his sides, was suddenly terrified of what he would find. He felt for his legs, his hands probing slowly beneath the dark water, said, "I don't know. It doesn't hurt."

The sergeant did not laugh, said, "Roll over. Let me have a look. You could bloody well have a hole somewhere. There's no pain, sometimes. Just a piece . . . goes missing."

He turned, the backpack rising up beneath him. Now there was a short laugh, and the sergeant said, "No, don't appear you been hit. But the quartermaster's gonna be mighty ticked. You let Fritz blow the hell out of your pack."

He slid the pack off, moved it around, saw shreds of cloth, the contents, his clothes, food rations, ripped to small bits of cloth and metal. He stared at the useless mass, pushed it away from him, watched it disappear into the water.

"Say a prayer, Greenie. Probably saved your neck."

He probed again, his hands feeling his chest, stomach, and the sergeant was serious now.

40

"Naw, Greenie, you're fine. If I hadn't gotten you into this shell hole, you might have joined your mates. Direct hit . . ." The sergeant paused, looked up into the thick gray sky. "Shelling's stopped. For now. You best get moving. Trenches should be ahead, if there's still anything left. Chances are, those boys fared better than you greenies. Take a look. See if anyone's moving."

He slid to one side of the shell hole, adjusted his helmet, eased his head up slowly, and the sergeant said, "Go on, there's nothing to fear now. Fritz can't see you back this far. If they start shelling again, you know where to find me."

He glanced up out of the hole, saw low drifting smoke, mounds of dirt, duckboards scattered, splintered. "I don't see anything." He turned, saw the sergeant staring at him, saw the man shivering, the water around him moving in low ripples.

"You best go on. They're waiting for the greenies up ahead. You'll see the trenches, a hole bigger'n this one, pile of sandbags. Tell the guards you're a replacement for B Company. They'll know where to put you." He paused, took a long breath, spit something out into the black water. "Double-time it, though. Fritz could start his guns again."

"I don't know the way. I'll wait for the others. You have to lead the way!"

He felt a small cold panic rising, stared at the sergeant, who said, "Go! I'll be staying here."

"But the others!"

He was angry now, furious at this man, this bully, the big man with the temper and the hard hands, quick to punish, quick in his abuse of the replacements. From the beginning of the march, the sergeant had been on them, cursing them, finding fault with every step. He moved through the water, closer to the sergeant, said, "Damn you! You cannot just order me. . . . I cannot just go alone! We must find the others!"

The sergeant closed his eyes for a moment, said softly, "Direct hit. The first shell . . . there are no others."

"You're mad! Twenty men!"

He scrambled to the edge of the shell hole, eased his head up, searched the dull gray. His heart was pounding again, the cold

41

returning. He climbed up farther, pulled himself out of the hole, crawled slowly away. The smoke was mostly gone, the air now thick with wet mist, a light rain beginning to fall. He paused, listened, tried to hear voices, heard only the faint hiss of the rain. He glanced beyond the shell hole, toward the front lines, the place where the trenches were supposed to be. He raised his head up farther, felt suddenly naked, no rifle, nothing in his hands, no heavy mass on his back. He felt light, like an animal, stood up slowly, bent low, began to move back, followed the shattered trail of the duckboards. He could see the muddy ground broken into round patches of water, shell holes in every direction. He crouched low, saw a rifle, thought, mine . . . but the butt was missing, useless. He eased close to a shell hole, said in a low voice, "Anyone . . . ?"

He peered over the edge, saw an arm in the water, fingers curled in a loose grip around a rifle. He fought the sickness rising inside him, reached down, pulled at the rifle, the hand giving way, the arm now rising slowly, the man's body pulled free of the mud below. He tried not to look, but the face turned up in the water, familiar, the name digging into him, Oliver. He turned away, pulled the rifle close to him, held it for a long moment, fought the tears, the panic. He tried to breathe, his throat tight, said in a low voice, "Sorry, old chap. I've lost my Enfield. Don't expect you'll tell the captain."

He felt his belt, the ammunition pouches still full, his bayonet still in the scabbard, his gas mask there as well. He could hear a hard thump in the distance, more artillery, and he crouched low, ignored the mud beneath him, the rain dripping from the rim of his helmet. He searched through the mist, saw the cannon now, the big gun still hunched low in the mud, but the barrel was pointing straight up, the carriage a shattered mass of steel. The cold panic began to rise again, and he shouted, "Anyone?"

The cannon in the distance had quieted again, and the steady hiss of the rain filled the air around him. He stood again, looked for his own shell hole. The ground was a maze of craters and ragged holes, but he could see his own tracks, still fresh in the deep mud. He kept low, followed them to the great wide hole, could see down, the sergeant still perched against the side, head and shoulders above the water. He felt relief, the sight of the big man, the professional, reassuring. He knelt, said, "No one else! We have to go! The trenches . . ."

The sergeant looked up slowly, soft tired eyes, said, "You made it, Greenie. The rest . . . direct hit. Tell them up front. They're expecting you. Company B."

He waited for the sergeant to move, to crawl up out of the hole, but the man closed his eyes again, a long deep breath. He understood now, slid back down into the water, moved closer to the man, said, "You're wounded! Let me help. . . ."

The sergeant's hand came up, pushed against his chest, holding him back.

"Get out of here, Greenie. They need you up front." The hand dropped, disappeared into the black water.

"Let's go, sir. I'll carry you." He reached around the sergeant's back, tried to grip his shirt, pull him up out of the mud. He looked up toward the edge of the shell hole.

"I can pull you up here. Come on."

He felt his grip loosening, the shirt tearing free, and he grabbed again, tried to hold the sergeant from behind. His hand touched something soft, hot, and he released the grip, raised his hand out of the water, saw a strip of cloth, a piece of shirt, soaked with thick red blood, darkened by the muddy water.

"God! Oh God! We'll get help!"

The sergeant slid back against the soft wall of the shell hole, said, "Get out of here, Greenie. Now! Nothing you can do for me."

The sergeant slid down lower in the water, one long hard breath.

"What do I do, Sergeant?"

The sergeant looked at him, then closed his eyes, his head falling back against the soft dirt, a soft whisper. "You're a soldier, Greenie. You *fight*."

The guard led him through a maze of mud and water, a deep snaking ditch that led finally to an opening in the side of a low hill, and then, wooden steps, leading down into wet stinking darkness. His guide pointed the way, then followed him down. The steps made a sharp turn to one side, and he was surprised to see a large room, a cave, carved into the dirt, timbers over his head, wood planks on the floor. The room was lit by a small flicker from a candle on a low wooden table, two men sitting, officers. One said, "Who's he, Corporal?"

His guide was still behind him, up on the steps, said, "Greenie, sir. Sergeant Cower's squad. Only one made it through. No sign of Cower."

"Damn!"

He could see the officer clearly, a captain, a small man, thin moustache, staring at him. The captain motioned to the guide, said, "All right, Corporal. After breakfast, find me some more, if you can. Half of them probably lost in the mud. Not like Cower to lose his way."

"Yes, sir."

"Sir . . . I was with Sergeant Cower. He was badly wounded. He ordered me . . . I don't believe he survived, sir."

"Damn! Cower knew better than to try to come forward that close to daybreak. Fritz throws his artillery at us every morning like an alarm clock. Anyone else make it, Private?"

"I don't believe so, sir. I didn't see anyone else. The Germans hit a cannon."

"Just one?" The captain laughed, unexpected. "He's losing his touch. Those Heinie gunners know every inch of that ground back there."

The older man moved papers on the table, handed one to the captain. He could see a map spread on the table, looked beyond into dark corners, saw a narrow bed, a small stove, a black tin smokestack, leading up through the timbers above. He studied the older officer, realized he was a colonel. He was surprised, straightened himself, reflex, had never been so close to a high-ranking officer. The captain scanned the paper, said, "Yes, here he is. Appears he's the only one left out of a couple dozen. Christ." The captain paused, looked at him. "Welcome to our piece of heaven, Private. This is your lucky day, in more ways than one. Company B is down to twelve men. You're number thirteen. You will report to Lieutenant Graves. Where's your backpack, your mess?"

"I'm sorry, sir. I lost most of my equipment in the attack."

"It wasn't an attack, Private. Just a little fireworks show. You'll learn the difference. Corporal, take this man to his post."

He saluted, waited, seemed to be ignored, and after a long moment, the captain glanced up, returned the salute, said nothing, returned to his papers. His guide said, "This way, Greenie."

The corporal moved away, up the dark wooden steps. He followed, heard a voice behind him, the colonel, "Dammit, they're dying faster than we can get them into line."

The lieutenant was a young man, not much older than he was, a surprise, a boyish face staring at him with a discomforting mix of anger and fear.

"One man! One damned replacement! We're at one-tenth strength, and they send me one damned greenie. No word on when we might get more, I suppose?"

He realized it was a question, said, "I don't know, sir."

Graves seemed disgusted by his answer, and he felt suddenly to blame.

"No, of course you don't know! I'm betting you don't know much else either. Did they actually train you, Private?"

He felt his patience giving way, could feel himself sagging into the mud under his feet.

"Yes, sir. Four months—"

"Yes, fine, four months. A seasoned veteran. Let me explain something to you, Private. You are one more rifle. We needed fifty. They expect me to hold this part of the line. . . ." The lieutenant stopped, looked down.

He could see a difference in the officer's face now, the fear growing, erasing the anger.

Graves pointed down the trench line. "Go on, there. Around the curve, then turn left. There's a row of dugouts. Find one for yourself. With all that training they gave you, you should know what happens next. If not, just ask. You had breakfast?"

He shook his head, "No, sir. My backpack was lost—"

"There's food up there. There's always something. The one

thing they won't let us do is starve." Graves turned away, disappeared down a dark hole in the side of the trench.

He looked where Graves had pointed, more narrow duckboards bridging black muddy water, then looked up, saw a gray sky, framed by the sandbags along the top of the trench. He stepped carefully, followed the curve in the trench, saw another deep ditch branching off to the left, turned, could see a half dozen men now, a wide flat space, sloping ground, water deep on one side. Three men were squatting low, perching like filthy birds on the dry side of the trench floor. The other three were standing up above them on a shelf of boards and hard dirt, leaning up beside tall narrow openings in the fat sandbags. Farther down the trench, there were holes cut into the dirt walls, the dugouts, no more than three feet high, and just as wide, but deeper, extending back into the dark earth. Some had feet sticking out, mud-caked boots, men lying motionless. Faces began to look his way, dark eyes appearing under the rims of rag-covered helmets.

One of the sitting men said, "Who the hell are you?"

"Is this . . . Company B?"

"That's a military secret. One more time. Who the hell are you?"

"Lieutenant Graves told me to come this way. I'm reporting to B Company. I'm a replacement."

"A replacement for what?"

A pair of boots began to move, the legs withdrawing, then a bare head emerging from one of the dugouts, and the man said, "How many of you?" The man dragged himself out, stood up slowly, stretching his back, his shirt carrying a corporal's stripes.

"Just me. I'm the only one who made it. We were attacked by artillery."

The corporal moved closer to him, appraising, said, "Cower's group? He told me last night we were getting the next bunch."

"Sergeant Cower did not survive. We took a direct hit. No one else survived." The words came out easily, surprising him.

"Except you."

"I suppose so."

The faces stared at him, were motionless, and one man said, "Windy, I'll bet. You run, Greenie? You leave your buddies out there? Looking for your mama down here in this hole?"

He realized the man was calling him a coward. But there was no energy, no emotion in the words, and he had none himself, said only, "I didn't run. I was last in line. The sergeant said my backpack saved me. Before he died."

The corporal glanced at the man who spoke, said, "Leave it be, Snake. He's here in one piece, and we'll take what we can get. So, Greenie, you got no pack? You look like you spent the night in a shell hole. Maybe Snake's right. Maybe you're windy, eh? We've had a few, little boys who run like hell when the shooting starts. Advice for you, Greenie. They don't run far. Fritz has a special talent for killing cowards. Safest place for you is right here in this hole."

He looked at the others, heard small laughs, the man called Snake still staring at him with hard unsmiling eyes. Another man stood now, said, "Where you from?"

"Alston, west of Newcastle. Farm town . . ."

"Yeah, I know it. Got family near there. You need something to eat?"

"Anything you can spare."

The corporal turned away, moved back to his dugout, said, "There's plenty, Greenie. They still send rations up here for men who were carried outta this hole days ago. All right, Duke, he's yours. Feed him, show him where to sleep. Make sure his rifle's not full of crud. He'll be on the line tonight. Give him the drill."

He looked again at the man called Duke, now standing in front of him, tall, thin, a ragged beard, and the man said, "This way, Greenie. Watch your step. That water's about four feet deep."

He followed, the others now ignoring him, all except Snake.

"You go windy on us, and I'll stick you."

The man's cold stare cut into him, and Duke said, "Leave him be, Snake. He'll be all right. C'mon, Greenie."

They eased around a curve in the trench, and he saw more dugouts, but no signs of men.

"Take any of these. Make it your own. Mine's right here.

47

Château Duke." Duke sat, reached back into the small cave, pulled out a heavy backpack, then leaned farther inside the dugout, dragged out a wooden crate. "Here you go. Duke's Fine Eatery. Used to be Duke's Pub, but the rum's been scarce for a while."

He sat, watched as Duke picked through the crate, all sizes of metal tins, some with labels, some unmarked.

"Only have what comes in the tin cans. Rats get everything else. I'd offer you a spare backpack, but the rats chew those up too. We lose a man and before he's even to the ambulance, the rats have cleaned up any sign of him. Supply pretty good about replacing equipment though. I'll make sure the lieutenant sends word back."

"Thank you. Your name really Duke?"

The man kept searching, examining the tins, said, "Doesn't matter. The only man who needs to know names is the lieutenant, so your mama can get her letter." He shoved the crate back into the dugout, spread the variety of food on the ground in front of him. "Take your pick. Bully beef, jam, canned biscuits. More bully beef. Never run out of that. Great factories all over England devoted to turning a perfectly respectable cow into this bloody swill."

He was suddenly very hungry, reached for a tin of the beef. Duke said, "We can heat it up. Got a Tommy cooker back here somewhere."

"No, it's all right. This'll do."

Duke laughed, said, "If you say so. You passed your first test, Greenie. A rare display of courage."

He felt around his belt, drew his bayonet, stabbed at the tin. The thick brine sprayed out, the pickle smell now overpowering. He kept cutting the tin, finally ripped a large hole in the top, stabbed at the dense wad of meat, held it up, the salty liquid dripping down the dull blade of the bayonet. He took a large bite, and Duke laughed again, said, "Slow down, Greenie. This isn't Blighty. They trained us to eat a whole meal in ten seconds. Out here, you have all day. If Fritz hasn't attacked us by now, we have the rest of the day off."

He could feel Duke watching him, felt genuine warmth in the

man, not like any of the others. He took a long drink from his water bottle, felt a dent in the tin, realized now the bottle had been hit by shrapnel. Duke saw him fingering the dent, said, "The bloke who led you up here, Cower. A good man, you know. He'd volunteer to bring up the replacements every time. Finally, the captain stopped asking the rest of us, just gave him the job for the whole battalion. He used to fetch a hundred at a clip, but lately, we might see a couple dozen. Or . . . one." Duke paused, gathered up the empty food tins. "Supply will probably refit you, new backpack and all. Could take a while. I can loan you a few things." Duke pointed. "You still got the important things: bayonet, gas mask." Duke ran his fingers down both sides of his stomach, scratched hard, dug fingers into his filthy shirt, made a small grunt. "Got him. Little bastard. They got to you yet? Too soon, I bet. Give 'em a day. One thing about cooties: you'll never worry about being alone."

He had heard all the stories about cooties, that every man in every trench was infested. It was unavoidable, some kind of lice that found its way into your clothes, and multiplied until it tormented every part of a man's body. At Blighty, they had issued each man a small container of Insect Powder, and the sergeants were quick to point out the description on the label: *Good for Body Lice*, with the assurance that indeed, it was. The cooties loved the stuff.

"You best clean your rifle. I've some oil here, a pull-through. Digger says you're going up on the line tonight. Your rifle better be clean. Only thing that makes Digger mad."

"The corporal?"

"Digger. Word of advice. When they issue you a new pack, store the gun oil with the cheese ration. Makes the cheese taste like sardines. You smoke?"

"Uh, no."

"You will. I have a good bit of shag here. Not sure where the army gets this stuff. Package says imported. I'm pretty sure it's imported from some Irishman's barnyard. Got some antifrost-bite grease here. Works like a charm for waterproofing boots. Your boots leak?" Duke looked at the thick mud caked on his boots. "No, too late for that. Digger's right. You look like you

49

spent some time in a shell hole. Don't take 'em off though."

He tried to flex his toes, felt them gripped tightly in a block of muddy cement.

"Why not?"

"Once they've been soaked like that, you'll never get them back on again. Just wait a while, they'll dissolve. Your socks'll hold out a while longer. Last pair had to be cut out of my feet, a damned nurse picking at the pieces with a tweezers. Grew right into my skin. Inside of your boot just like some kind of chemistry lab. All manner of biology goes on in there. Best we don't know. Ah . . . underwear. Different story. Can't spare that. Don't worry, the army's good about delousing and generous with the underwear. We get pulled out of here, they won't let us near civilization until we get stripped down and scrubbed. Amazing how a man's dreams can narrow down to such simple luxury. Clean underwear."

He was impressed with the man's obvious experience, was feeling overwhelmed.

"How long have you been here?"

"This hole? Hell, I don't know. One hole or another. Five, six months. They keep calling this a stalemate. Pretty damned stale, that's for sure. Winter was pretty quiet, so we just stayed put. The lieutenant said they forgot about us. Could be. They sure as hell ought to forget about *him*. Green replacements are one thing. Green officers just get people killed. Graves showed up here sometime around Christmas, replaced Lieutenant Dunnigan. Good officer, that man. Killed on a night patrol. Right next to me." He paused, knocked a piece of mud from his boot. "So then young Lieutenant Graves arrives in the middle of a snowstorm, and right away wants us to fall into formation, do some kind of drills, show him we're real soldiers. Captain had to talk some sense into him, probably kept him alive." He stopped, the smile gone. "Bother you, Greenie? Disrespecting my lieutenant? They don't teach you anything about that in Blighty. They tell you all officers are geniuses, from Marshal Haig all the way down to this bloody jackass Graves. Here's a military secret, Greenie. They lied." He gathered his pack together, slid it back into the dugout. "Anything you need, let me know."

50

The man's words had filled him with curiosity, his mind filling with questions.

"You just stay right here? This trench? Seems mighty temporary."

"It is, actually. This particular corner of hell has only been here for a month or so. We have to move every so often. Damned things just fill up with water. No way to drain them. This whole part of the world is just one big swamp. The water's gotta go somewhere. You dig a hole, it's gonna fill up. Some engineer finally figured out if you slope the bottom, the water might stay on one side. Works for a while, like right now. Won't last. A good hard rain and this thing'll fill up about waist-deep. Then they'll move us again, if Fritz cooperates. We get pulled out of here every couple of months, spend a week in a rest area. Red Cross, YMCA centers. Actual women. God's gift to the army. When I came up, the regiment was near full strength, never knew half the people in the company. Lieutenant Dunnigan had a full command, though about the time he got hit, we started losing men pretty regular. Fritz started this little artillery display every dawn, and damned if he didn't drop at least one down our throats every damned time. Graves and the captain been screaming at the rear for replacements. The whole regiment is weak. Each company gets whatever they can send us. That's where you come in." He scratched at his stomach, seemed to drift away for a long moment, pinched hard at another tormenter under his shirt. "No more strangers in Company B. Know them all now. All twelve." He looked up. "Thirteen."

He had chosen one of the dugouts at random, and Duke had given him a waterproof sheet to cover the damp ground. He spread it over the hard dirt, slid himself inside as far as he could. His feet still hung out into the trench, and he thought of the man whose work had created this small sanctuary, shorter, he supposed. The dugout grew narrow and shallow in the back, and he lay with his helmet as a pillow, his face only inches from the dirt above him. He wasn't usually afraid of tight spaces, but had to fight it now. He kept his eyes closed, annoyed that sleep had not come quickly. The dugout was deathly quiet, the earth around him shielding him from anything that might be happening aboveground. Of course, likely nothing was happening up there. No one would be aboveground in daylight. They had taught him that much at Blighty. This network of trenches faced no-man's-land, and Duke had told him that the Germans were only three hundred yards away, the only barrier vast thick coils of barbed wire, and, of course, the rifles of the lookouts. There hadn't been a major assault against these lines in months, and no one seemed afraid that the Germans would suddenly start something. The daily ritual of the shelling was all the war these men were facing now, and yet they were still vulnerable, holed up like rats, dying in their protected places, victims of bad luck. He opened his eyes, stared up into the dark earth. Right here. A perfect tomb.

Every part of him was stiff exhaustion, but still the sleep would not come. He could not avoid thinking about the night before, the awful march, made terrifying by the shelling. The men who had died didn't seem real to him anymore, names forgotten already. Well, of course. No names. These men don't want to know, because if you die, they'll forget you anyway. They didn't teach that at Blighty: make no friends. Duke seems different. Something in his character, a teacher maybe, eager to help. But how many has he helped, and how many of those has he forgotten? Except for Sergeant Cower. He remembers him, they all do, even the officers. I thought he was such a bastard, loudmouthed and mean. But he was no bastard at all. Just did his job, leading greenies like me to the front. He knew he was dying, and still did his job, sent me off in the right direction. Don't forget him.

A shock woke him, and he rose up, his face smacking the dirt above him, a small cave-in filling his eyes and nose.

"What? What?"

"Wake up, Greenie. Sun's going down. It's your watch."

He felt hands around his legs, pulling him out of the dugout, blinked through the dirt, saw Duke and the corporal. Behind them, Graves stood with his hands clasped behind him. He said, "Good. Get him up on the parapet. Give him the drill. No mistakes, Private. You learn quickly out here. I'll be in my quarters."

The young lieutenant was gone, and Duke pointed back into the dugout, said, "Your rifle, Greenie. Be needing that, you know."

He retrieved the rifle, followed the two men to the larger space, where the shelf was, sandbags stacked high on one side of the trench. The corporal pointed, and Duke said, "Up you go. I'll be right next to you." Both men stepped up onto the parapet, a stiff wide board, three feet above the bottom of the trench. Duke glanced at the nearest opening in the sandbags, said, "Keep your face away from here until it's full dark. When the snipers can't see, we'll put the rifles up into the slots. We hung a few bells out on the barbed wire this week. Some genius at headquarters actually had a good idea. Should let us know if Fritz is trying to do something nasty."

The corporal was down behind them, said, "You have two hours' watch, starting at full dark, about a half hour from now. I'll relieve you for two hours' rest, then you're back up again."

He felt an icy chill, held tight to his rifle, hoped no one could see he was shaking. Duke looked back toward the corporal, said, "Don't worry. He'll be all right." Duke looked at him now, no smile on his bearded face. "Right, Greenie?"

He nodded, his throat tight, and Duke reached down, helped another man up onto the parapet. "Evening, Cutter." The other man said nothing, leaned back against the sandbags, lit a ragged cigarette.

He looked up, saw fading daylight, the sky still a dull gray. He focused his eyes, fought against the last bit of dirt, pulled his helmet down snugly on his head. Something grabbed his foot, and he jumped, startled, saw a man down below.

The man jumped with him, cursed, said, "For God's sake, man. It's just the bombs. I cleaned 'em off. Jesus, Duke, what's his problem? Afraid he might die?" The man laughed now, disappeared down the trench.

Duke said, "I assume they taught you how to throw a Mills bomb."

He stared at the half dozen steel balls beside his feet, each one with a small handle, the round ring of its pin protruding from the top.

"I can throw them. He just . . . surprised me." He reached down, held one in his hand, the heavy steel that fit his grip perfectly. He recalled the training, dozens of drills, pull the pin, hold, count to three, the proper method of throwing. He glanced up again, measured the height of the sandbags, taller than what they had used at Blighty. Duke said, "If Fritz makes a dash for us, don't just depend on the rifle. They teach you that?"

He nodded.

"Once we know he's out there, we start throwing these things at him as fast as we can. They'll bring us more pretty quick. Fritz doesn't care for Mr. Mills."

Cutter was on the far end of the parapet, saying, "Dark enough, Duke."

"Yep."

They raised their rifles, slid them into the sandbags, the guns resting, balanced perfectly.

"Give it a minute, Cutter. I bet Billy Boche is on duty tonight."

The two men leaned back against the sandbags, faced toward the rear of the trench, seemed to be waiting for something. He mimicked their every move, waited as they waited, and suddenly there was a loud whack against the sandbags, then another. Duke laughed, said, "There's one sniper over there, knows we start manning these lookouts at dark. He's probably had his rifle sighted in on these slits for hours. Hasn't gotten us yet. We used to post bets, whether or not he'd actually hit the center opening, had a wood target set up across the trench in case his shot made it through. He never did. Then one night a seventy-seven shell hit the target. Took four men with it." He paused. "Took some of the fun out of the game."

Cutter lit another cigarette, said, "I'd give a bottle of Highland brew to the bastard who could stick that bloody Boche bastard."

"Cutter, if you ever found a bottle, you wouldn't share it with Marshal Haig himself."

"I would if he'd go over there and stick Billy Boche."

He tried to share the humor, the low laughter, but couldn't take his eyes from the opening in the sandbags. They waited for several minutes, and Duke said, "All right, blokes. All quiet."

They moved closer to the sandbags, stared out through the opening, and he could see a low squat mass, spread all along the ground in front. *The barbed wire.* It was the first time he had seen no-man's-land, but there was really nothing to see. He held his eyes wide, tried hard not to blink, heard nothing but the quick thumping in his ears, his own heartbeat. He took a deep breath, tried to calm himself, every part of him straining to see and hear something, anything. Long minutes passed, the anticipation eating at him, his hands gripped tightly around the rifle. His foot moved slightly, touched the row of Mills bombs at his feet, and he rehearsed it in his mind, the sound of the bell, watching a large hulking shadow moving close, waiting for Duke to move first, to be sure. Then, one motion, reach down, grip the bomb, pull the pin, fling the bomb up and over the sandbags. His heart was racing again, come on! I can do this! I'm ready! He felt as awake as he had ever been, his eyes like two searchlights, probing the dark, any movement, his ears catlike, ready for any small sound. He could hear breathing, not his own, and his heart jumped, his body frozen, focused, realized now it was Duke, only a few feet away. He let out a long breath, spoke silently to himself, the teacher lecturing the recruit. Calm down. Focus to the front. His eye flicked, caught some movement, and he froze again, the voice in his head silent. He stared again, the shadows dancing, then motionless, a trick of the eye. He tried to see the barbed wire, cursed silently. How can I see anything? Dammit! They could be pouring through, a hundred men, right in front of me. If they're quiet, I won't know until they're right here, crawling over the sandbags! He held tight to his breathing, the voice in his head again: Barbed wire, you bloody idiot. Bells. You'll hear the bells. He blinked hard, his eyes suddenly watering. No! He wiped with his sleeve, fought the blurriness. His eyes locked on the blackness again, the strain now slicing through his skull, dull pain working up the back of his neck. He massaged the ache with his hand, blinked again, could feel cramps creeping into his feet, his legs. He tried to flex his knees, ease the tightness, the voice shouting at him: Greenie! Do your duty! Behind him, another voice, soft, and he ignored it, thought, All right! I can do this! Now a touch on his leg, and he jumped, a sharp sound bursting out, "AHH!"

"Jesus, Greenie. Get hold of it, man. Time's up. Two hours. Take a break."

He looked at the voice, a hard whisper, could see nothing in the trench, then dull movement below him. It was the corporal.

"Sorry. Yes, all right. I'm coming down."

He heard a soft voice close to him, and Duke said, "Not so bad, eh, Greenie? You survived your first watch. Most greenies start shooting at something, swear they see Fritz coming. Must give those boys across the way a good chuckle."

He followed Duke down from the parapet, and immediately the corporal climbed up, then two more men, moving into position. Cutter sat down, lit a cigarette, then said in a low voice, "You'll learn, Greenie. Get some rest. Two hours and we do it again."

He could see the shadow of Duke moving away, followed, heard a harsh sound, stopped. He listened for a moment, realized Duke was coming back toward him, grabbing him by the sleeve. They were at the parapet again, and he heard a voice, not a whisper, the lieutenant.

"Everyone but the watch, follow me back toward my quarters."

The rest of the men seemed to emerge from the darkness, some sliding out of dugouts, no one talking. He was curious, followed the line of men, turning right, out of the front trench, then right again, duckboards and water. He felt his way, his hand reaching out to the man in front of him, saw a sudden flicker of light, the glow of a candle. Graves, on the far side of the light, said, "Gather up. When we're done here, take word back to the watch, fill them in." He paused, seemed to gather himself, stared down into the candlelight. "We have received orders. Apparently, there has been something in the works for a while. It is not customary that junior officers be informed until the last minute. Tomorrow morning, at four hundred hours, the artillery will commence a bombardment of the enemy trenches. They will sustain fire for ninety minutes, and then cease. During the bombardment, you will be escorted to the regimental embarkation parapet. Ladders are being put in place now. You, or rather we, will await the sound of a single whistle, and, along with the rest of the regiment, we will commence an advance toward the enemy. By all estimates, the artillery should destroy any obstacle, including the barbed wire, and any opposition that would otherwise await us on the other side. Command has every confidence that we will achieve our purpose, and capture the enemy's defenses, then advance into his artillery. Command has apparently suffered enough of the enemy's nightly barrage. I am told one shell came perilously close to division headquarters." He looked at the faces, said, "Is the corporal here? . . . I don't see you."

"No, sir, he's on the watch."

"Inform him of these details. You are dismissed."

The candle disappeared into the dugout, and he stood blindly, felt a hand on his arm, heard the low voice of Duke, "Well, now, you are one lucky bloke, Greenie. On the line for one whole day, and by God, you will share the privilege of going over the top!"

He completed three shifts on the parapet, had seen nothing, heard no sounds but the hard pounding in his chest. He had two more hours of rest before the artillery would begin, lay in his dugout, staring sleeplessly into the black dirt above him. Then the order came, Graves himself coming for them, the young lieutenant wearing his own helmet, carrying a rifle. It was the first time he realized that the lieutenant was, after all, a soldier just like the rest of them. The lessons of Blighty had come back. Of course, lieutenants lead their men into the fight.

They moved through the trench, past more rows of sandbags, the darkness above them matched by the black silence of the men. He followed the man in front of him, his feet bouncing on duckboards, the routine so familiar now. Then they were halted, and he could feel the presence of more men, the trench thick with smells and small sounds, belts and bayonets, rifles and

Mills bombs, each man preparing for what was to come. He had thought Duke was close to him, wasn't sure now, could see no faces, only the dark shapes. A whisper, passed down the line, "Muddy your bayonets. Muddy your helmets."

He heard the sound of metal, then men digging into the trench wall, another lesson from Blighty. Bayonets reflect light. And if your helmet has no cloth covering, it will shine as well, a deadly beacon for an enemy rifleman. He reached out, felt for the side of the trench, grabbed a handful of soft dirt, ran it along his bayonet, then put a hand flat on his helmet, the thin shredded canvas barely holding. He grabbed another handful, spread it out on his helmet. He had done this at Blighty, drill after drill, the lessons taught day after day: the shrapnel-proof helmet, a first in modern times, essential in modern combat, and the bitter sarcasm of the sergeants: shrapnel-proof unless it's actually hit by a piece of shrapnel.

Another hard whisper: "Fix bayonets!"

He felt for the muzzle of his rifle, his hands shaking, fingers not working, stiff and cold. He rattled the bayonet into place, gave a hard tug, held the rifle straight up in front of him, tight against his chest, the bayonet pointing skyward, no accidents in the trenches. There was a long silent moment, and then a hard clap of thunder rolled into the trench, startling them all, followed by a great long roar, unbroken, the ground shaking beneath him. He put a hand out, felt himself rocking, unsteady, the roar louder, deafening, filling his brain, his bones. He dropped down to his knees, pulled his head low into his shoulders, the top of his helmet tight against the rifle. He wanted to look up, had heard you could see the artillery shells as they passed over, streaks of red and white light whistling overhead. But the roar was pressing him down, curling him into one tight hard ball.

After long minutes, the sounds had a rhythm, his mind absorbing the noise, growing used to it. His knees ached, his feet crushed into his boots, his hands throbbed, gripping his rifle, but he was held tight in the grasp of the shelling, no movement, no relief. His mind began to wander, out into the darkness, what was happening over there, beyond the wire. He realized now that there were no explosions around them. Of course, the artillery is all ours. They're not firing back, at least not at us, not here. Does that mean we're winning? He was deathly curious, wondered if anyone was up on the parapets, if anyone could see the impact of the shelling on the enemy lines. Fritz. Heinie. The Boche. He had never seen a German, wondered if he would see one now, or if the lieutenant was right, the artillery would do the work, sweeping away any opposition. If that's true, why are we doing this? Fight the war with cannon. No one has to use the bayonet. The thought froze him. Another lesson from Blighty: cold steel to the enemy's throat. A line of recruits, running wildly, screaming and cursing and driving bayonets into straw dummies. It had been unreal then, a game, men with brave talk, all the stuff of bad novels, Englishmen and savages, redcoats securing the glory of the empire. The instructors, so matter-of-fact: "Insert your bayonet firmly into the enemy, then withdraw. If the bayonet will not come out, fire your rifle. The recoil will remove it." *Insert*. My God, please. Let them be gone.

The great roar began to quiet, then hushed, deafening silence, and around him, a groan rose from the huddled men.

"Up, to the ladders!"

There were no more whispers now, voices rising, the officers moving quickly through the men, lifting them up, prodding them forward, words of encouragement. He straightened himself up, worked the pain out of his legs, felt his gut twist into a hot swirl. The men began to move, shuffling slowly, and now, from somewhere out beyond the trench, a new sound, high and shrill, familiar this time. It was a whistle.

"Up! Over the top! *Give them hell!*"

The men kept moving, and now he was climbing short steps, rungs of a narrow ladder. He reached the top, stepped through a row of sandbags, followed the man in front of him, men pushing him from behind. He was surprised that he could see, low gray shadows, the first faint light of a misty dawn. He was on flat ground now, thick and wet, could see the shadows of men spread all along in front of the trenches. There were more whistles, and somewhere down the line, close by, a shout, "Go! Advance!"

The men were moving in one wave, and he moved with them, blindly, probing with his boots, the ground suddenly falling away, his boots filling with water. He fought through it, could see he was in a small shell hole, climbed up the other side, stared ahead, the rifle pointing out, the bayonet leading the way. Shouts flew all along the line, meaningless words, some men swarming past him, some falling in the mud, rising again, the wave unbroken. His legs carried him with automatic rhythm, his boots pulling him into the mud, then out again. In front of him, men were slowing, gathering, precut gaps in their own wire, men filing through quickly. He was carried along with them, streams of men, guided through narrow paths. Now they were in the open again, broken, hilly ground, shell holes old and new, churned-up dirt, bursts of awful smell gagging him. He moved faster, clean air, but the smells returned, hard and thick, would not go away. He pushed himself forward, could see now, huge shadows, great fat mounds of barbed wire. There was no order to the coils, wire piled on wire, and he felt a hard tug on his leg, a piece of wire grabbing him. He pulled free, his pants torn, tried to see down in front of him, thought, There is no path. This is German wire!

Men were gathering again, but there were no guides, no easy way through. Men were probing, some stepping high, trying to find a way, and he could see that the barbed wire was a shattered heap, piled around shell holes. He stopped as the men around him stopped, some men pulling at the wire in their clothes. He could hear words, close by, a man giving orders, an officer waving his arms, shouting into the face of another man, "Go to the wireless station! The barbed wire is uncut! The bloody guns didn't destroy it, just blew it to hell, scattered it all over the damned place! We'll have to pick our way through. Tell the artillery to be ready in support. This will take some time!"

Men were moving all along the mounds of wire, some pushing into gaps in the great fat coils, then retreating, their paths closed. He followed one man into a gap, the ground an uneven

60

mound of mud and wire, the man shouting, "This way! I found an opening!"

He could see dark flat ground beyond the wire, a clear area, men now gathering behind him, moving as he moved, a mass of soldiers walking, some running, toward the one narrow place in the line. He felt his chest heaving, slipped down into a shell hole, his ankle twisting, more water in his boots. He pulled himself up, the wire behind him, could see that the way was clear now, and he ran again, wide stretch of ground, slowed, thought, How much farther? Few were running now, the lines of men drawing closer, the massed power now ready to strike, all eyes searching, trying to see the German works. He glanced up at the starless sky, the darkness still disguising the land, saw something move far out in front of him, reflection of metal, a light, cigarette perhaps, one man's deadly mistake. Others had seen it as well, and men began to shout.

"This way!"

He ran slowly, deliberately, looked again for the flicker of light, didn't have to look back, could feel the strength behind him, pushing on toward the enemy. There was nothing of Blighty in this, no lesson from bitter sergeants, no way to train a man to feel the energy that drove him forward, raw and savage. He searched the ground in front of him, thought, Where? It must be close! He heard a dull pop, then another, ignored the sounds, and suddenly the sky exploded into bright light, bursting rockets, hissing torches floating slowly to the ground. All along the line, bright lights hovered overhead, some finding the ground, spewing up sparks and flame, the wave of men silhouetted in perfect detail. There was a new sound now, flickers of light ahead of him, like a long thin row of sparks. The sounds grew, rolling over him, the chatter and rattle of rifle fire, and another new sound, strangely familiar, a flash of memory, a child holding a piece of wood against the turning spokes of a wagon wheel. But the memory was shattered by the flashes of light, and the cries of the men around him. Machine guns.

The air around him was alive, men falling, punched and jerked down, some tumbling forward, others turned and twisted. Behind him, the opening in the barbed wire was gone, seeming to close, disappear behind all of them. He looked for an officer, someone in command, someone to tell him what to do. Men were spread on the ground around him, others firing their rifles, then cut down as well. He searched the ground for a shell hole, but the ground was flat and undisturbed, and he saw the face of the sergeant, Cower, the man they would all remember, the man who had called him a soldier. He turned toward the machine guns, held the bayonet high, and moved forward.

The officers studied the map, teacups spread on the table. Questions were asked and answered, an aide standing ready with a pointer. There were pins on the map, blue and red, undulating rows in two parallel lines. The room was busy, staff officers moving in and out, reports read, orders dictated to aides who wrote quickly on pads of paper. One man, a colonel, studied the pins, heard words of encouragement from the others, shared their smiles. He said something to an orderly, who obeyed quickly, took his tea away, brought him a fresh cup. Now more aides appeared, more dispatches, and the officers read each one, much talk, the smiles giving way to concern, and then, the smiles were gone. The room was quiet now, and the colonel stared at the map for a long moment, reached out across the wide table, pulled a blue pin out of the map, and tossed it aside.

Outside, the reporters held their daily vigil, newspapermen, waiting for the official posting of the day's events, something to send home to readers already weary of bad news. An aide appeared, tacked a paper to a board, the reporters gathering, expectant, then disappointed. The paper read, *"Minor activity along Ypres front. Engagements of no importance."*

2

RICHTHOFEN

Döberitz, Germany—December 1915

He sat straight upright in the front seat, waited, could hear the pilot behind him fiddling with controls, the cables groaning slightly as the pilot worked and tested. Richthofen watched another man standing out front, his hand on the prop, impatient, annoyed with the pilot's careful appraisal of the plane. Finally the pilot said, "Now!"

The man at the propeller gave one strong pull, the prop jerking into motion, the engine coughing black smoke. Richthofen jumped in his seat, smiled—finally, the adventure would begin! The pilot revved the engine, and the black exhaust and the wind from the prop hit Richthofen full in the face, and suddenly his leather helmet was swept up and behind his head, jerking at his goggles, blinding him. He tried to control the helmet, the chin strap too loose, fumbled with the small buckle. He pulled the goggles back around his eyes, tried to shout to the pilot, but the roar from the spitting engine was too loud. He blinked the smoke from his eyes, grabbed at his helmet, jerked it back down on his head, tightened the chin strap. He was breathing heavily, the exhaust burning his throat, choking him, and he could feel the plane bumping along the ground, rolling out toward the takeoff area. Richthofen fought through the misery, tried to see all that was happening around him, but now the scarf around his neck was whipping behind him, unwrapping from his collar, the silk sliding free. He grabbed for it, but the sharp blast of wind stripped it away, the scarf now gone. He called out again, could not hear his own words, remembered the notepad in his pocket, the advice from the instructor, the only way to communicate. He retrieved the stub of pencil, wrote a single word, *wait!* He reached his hand over his shoulder, expected the pilot to take the paper from his hand, but the paper was ripped away, gone as well. The plane bumped along, and he tried to turn in the seat, impossible, stared ahead through the whirl of the prop, pulled again at the chin strap, tightening it further. The pilot revved the engine, the roar growing louder still, the wind pressing Richthofen's head back. Now the plane was rolling faster, the bumps more severe. The excitement was gone, replaced by cold terror, and he felt his flight jacket inflating, his body swelling into a fat sausage, thought, My God, I'm going to explode! He imagined himself catapulted up and away, thrown far behind the plane like his scarf, and he punched at his chest, realized now it was only air forced inside the jacket, his failure to close it completely. He worked his fingers frantically, fastened it tightly at his neck. He gripped the leather trim that lined the edge of the cockpit, held tight with his leather gloves, his mind screaming at him to end this madness.

"Stop! Enough!"

His voice was swept away by the prop, and the plane kept rolling, faster, the jerking motions fewer, one hard bounce, punching him into the small wood seat, then a long floating feeling. He felt his stomach rising, a wave of queasiness, tried to breathe, and the plane settled back down, another bounce, and up again. Suddenly the jerkiness was gone, the plane cutting through the air in a smooth rush. He stared ahead, his stomach calming. He glanced over the side of the plane, saw the ground falling away, the airfield gone, trees now, another open field, drifting past. He still held tightly to the sides of the plane, looked out the other side, but the terror was replaced by the sheer wonder. Yes, I am flying! He could not help a laugh, the plane continuing to climb, the trees growing smaller, a farmhouse, animals, doll-like, the ground now a patchwork of greens and browns.

Richthofen ignored the deafening roar, stared out at the horizon, could see a cluster of odd shapes, realized it was Cologne, the great cathedral rising above the town. He was smiling now, turned as much as he could in the seat, tried to see in every direction. He was growing used to the wind, looked again at the magnificent cathedral, tall spires reaching up to God. Yes, this is what God sees, this is how He moves above us. He saw a flock of birds far below, rising up out of an open field, like so many small insects. There was a farmer, a team of mules, the man waving up at him, and Richthofen had not stopped smiling, thought of returning the greeting, but no, not a good idea. Keep your arms inside the plane. There was a tap on his shoulder now, and he tried to turn, but of course, he could not move that far, realized what the pilot was asking him . . . and the smile was erased. It flooded over him, the job he was supposed to do, the purpose of the flight. He focused, looked out to one side, Cologne, a road, the farms. He was supposed to navigate, to find a point several miles distant, guide the pilot by hand signals, and then, once the target was reached, guide the pilot back to the aerodrome. He searched the horizon, angry at himself now: You are lost, you fool!

The pilot made wide turns, first one way, then the other, trying to help him locate the landmarks. Richthofen was miserable now, shook his head, the only signal he could muster. The plane made one wide sweeping turn, and after several minutes, he could feel them dropping down, his stomach rising again. To one side he could see the familiar aerodrome, a small crowd of pilots, the instructors, all watching him. The plane swung down to the far end of the field, lower still, the bushes and trees a few feet below them, then open grass, and now the pilot cut the motor, the prop jerking to a stop. Richthofen felt a cold shock, something terribly wrong, expected the plane to simply fall, held tightly to the sides, braced for the crash. The plane bounced once, then settled onto the grass, slowed quickly, the seat jarring him. They rolled to a stop, the instructor walking slowly toward the plane, Richthofen feeling a hot burn of embarrassment.

"So, Lieutenant, did you accomplish your mission?"

He stared down for a moment, said, "I did not, sir."

Behind him, the pilot said, "He had rather a good time of it, though."

The instructor stood stiffly, his hands clasped behind him,

said, "We do not have time for sightseeing, Lieutenant. There are others in this squadron who understand why they are here."

"Sir, I have no excuses. It was my first time . . . I have not flown before."

"Well, Lieutenant, if you intend to fly again, I suggest you pay more attention to your duty."

"Yes, sir. I will, sir." The instructor began to move away, and Richthofen could see the faces of the others, some of the students laughing quietly. The pilot rose up behind him, climbed out of his seat. Richthofen still sat, stared at the controls in front of him, ran his hands over the edge of the small cockpit, said, "Sir!"

The instructor stopped, turned toward him, and Richthofen said, "I would like to try again, sir."

"You will have another opportunity, Lieutenant."

"Uh, sir, how about . . . right now?"

Richthofen had finally passed the tests, had been sent first to the Western Front as an observer, little more than a helpless passenger in the large bombers, assisting the pilots to "lay their eggs" on targets that varied from troop barracks to factories to bridges. The men he flew with enjoyed their work, celebrated each night with real and imagined tales of the vast destruction of their enemy. But Richthofen chafed at being a passenger. In some of the large bombers the observers sat behind the pilot, and he had passed the idle time watching as the pilots worked their controls, studied every move, every turn and dip of the plane corresponding to some action by the man at the controls. It had not taken him long to lose patience with being an observer. By December 1915, he was enrolled at the pilot training school at Döberitz, near Berlin. Within weeks, he had mastered those examinations as well, and he would finally sit at the controls of his own bomber, while someone else searched for targets.

Throughout 1915, the Western Front had been locked mostly into a quiet stalemate, but in the East, the Russian campaign against Germany's eastern borders had spread all across the Eastern Front. Despite a catastrophic defeat for the Russians at

Tannenberg, which effectively ended their invasion of German territory, Russian forces had begun to launch attacks against what they believed to be the more vulnerable Austrians. With the enormous resources of manpower the Russians could bring to their front lines, the German High Command was forced to send aid to their Austrian allies, and shift German troop strength away from France.

With so much of the fighting now away from the West, Richthofen's squadron had been moved to the Russian front. The Russians had few modern aeroplanes, and fewer pilots to fly them, and the Germans had complete control over the airspace. The Russians offered only one obstacle, a talent for antiaircraft fire, but their guns were too few, and it was a simple matter for the German pilots to route their missions through vast areas of empty countryside. Though Richthofen treasured every moment in the air, the routine was numbing and as the weeks passed, he began to pursue targets of a different kind, cavalry and infantry. Few Russian soldiers had ever experienced an assault from the air, and Richthofen discovered that entire regiments could be sent into panic by the machine-gun fire from one German plane. This was hardly sport. For Richthofen the marvelous joy of climbing into the cool air each day was dulled by the utter sameness of the duty he was to perform. The skills had become second nature: finding his way by map or by landmark, another *basket of eggs* dropped on some target whose importance had no meaning to him. He thought too often now of the Eindeckers, the single-winged, single-seat planes whose pilots needed no observer, planes unencumbered by bombs. When the weather kept him on the ground, he passed his time dreaming of flying alone, no orders, no maps, nothing on the ground to distract him. The passion and the instincts were the same that he had carried into the forests, but there was a difference. In the clouds, your prey was seeking you as well, two hunters stalking each other. He could not imagine it without feeling a sharp surge of raw excitement. The perfect hunt.

3

LUFBERY

Near Bar-le-Duc, France—May 24, 1916

The ride had been typical misery, the old French bus seeming to roll on wheels of iron, the flat bench seats no better. The bus was jammed with soldiers, and Lufbery was pressed against the window, could only stare out, another man's shoulder digging deep into his back. He suffered in silence, but the other passengers were a raucous group. He could tell from their talk and their youth that the men were new recruits, this bus one of hundreds that bounced and rattled their way toward the fighting around Verdun.

It had begun in mid-February 1916, a carefully constructed plan by the German High Command to break the yearlong stalemate in the West by seizing the ancient French fortress. The capture of Verdun, and the French defenses that surrounded it, would strike a blow against a powerful position that stood squarely between the southern flanks of the German army and the open roadways to Paris. But Verdun's strategic importance was overshadowed by the symbolic meaning of the place, a defensive site that had defended the plains along the Meuse River since the time of the Romans. German planners knew well that the loss of Verdun would be catastrophic to French morale, and could possibly cause the French government to lose their backbone for continuing the war. But as precise as the planning had been, the execution was marred by delays, bad weather, and bad timing, and when the German troops finally launched their assault, the French were aware of what was coming. Though the German push had obliterated the front-line French defenses, the fortress itself had been held by a valiant defense the Germans could not destroy. What the German High Command had predicted would be a quick and decisive blow stretched instead into month after month of futile attacks. The combined loss of men was staggering, more than a million casualties, an incomprehensible human disaster, the most costly battle in the history of war.

Lufbery had learned of this convoy of buses passing near the pilot training center, their route carrying the troops through the village of Bar-le-Duc, close to the airfield at Behonne. He had been given a seat only at the insistence of an officer at the airfield, the passengers grumbling as they made space for him, a narrow slot against the window, the worst seat on the bus. He didn't know their unit, didn't know if the men even knew each other at all. But they were sharing the adventure now, had passed the time with bawdy songs, bad voices and guilty laughter, wearing the innocent smiles of young men who do not yet know what awaits them. When the songs stopped, the talk began, and Lufbery could feel the men were energized by their nervousness, sharing their dreams for glory, or the sweet stories of the romances they had left behind. As the stories passed through the crowd, he had stayed quiet, had heard so much of this before. He passed the time inside his own mind, staring out the window scanning the dull gray sky, searching for aeroplanes. But the boisterous talk had begun to exhaust itself, and finally they turned to him, this stranger with the different uniform. Lufbery saw the man on the bench in front of him standing, facing him now.

"What of you, *Poilu*? Someone waiting for you, eh?"

The name belonged to all of them, every man in the French army referring to himself and everyone else as *poilu*. Lufbery saw the young man's smile fading as he saw the age on Lufbery's face. "You're not one of us, eh?"

"I am not a recruit, no."

The man's eyes widened.

"A veteran, then!"

The others seem to savor the word, all faces looking to him now. The voices began to trample each other, but the questions were the same: "What have you seen?

Where did you fight? Have you been to Verdun?"

He let the questions pour over him, held up a hand, said, "Sorry, I am not infantry. I am a pilot."

The word seemed to puzzle them, the man in front of him leaning close. "You fly aeroplanes?"

The man laughed, the joke spreading through them all. One man slapped him on the back, nearly jarring Lufbery's hat off his head. "A pilot! More like a dreamer! Tell me, *Poilu*, have you seen the angels?"

He did not understand their reaction, said, "I have been assigned to Escadrille Américaine, at Bar-le-Duc."

The man in front of him seemed genuinely curious now, waved a hand in the air, tried to quiet the others. "American? You don't sound like an American, *Poilu*."

Lufbery felt their innocence, their teasing coming only from their ignorance. These were men who had certainly never seen an aeroplane, or anyone who flew one. But if they were going to Verdun, they would learn much more. Every available flying squadron was relocating closer to the fighting, and the skies above the battlefields were already growing crowded, bombers and observers, and now, the fighter planes that would try to shoot them down.

"I was born in France. My father was American."

But the young men had no real interest in explanations, and the jokes began again, birds and balloons, men calling out to the bus driver, a small man with dark skin.

"Driver! Take me to Bar-le-Duc as well! I wish to fly with the hawks!"

The jokes faded away, and they were mostly ignoring him now. Lufbery felt the pressure in his back again, pushing him into the window. The bus was silent for a long moment, the men suddenly trapped by the thoughts of the journey, the destination, the fear energizing another round of noise, any distraction to wipe those thoughts away. The bus swerved, stopped abruptly, the man beside Lufbery leaning hard against him, crushing him. The curses began, every man shouting something obscene to the driver, who stood, faced them, his voice barely audible.

"Bar-le-Duc!"

Lufbery strained to stand, and the man beside him leaned away again, silence spreading through the bus. He moved toward the aisle, said, "Permit me. I must get off here."

The driver broke the silence. "Bar-le-Duc! Now!"

Lufbery reached the front of the bus, saw angry impatience on the driver's face. He ignored the talk, the laughter around him. But they did not all laugh, and he saw some of them staring at him, innocent curiosity. He was older than any of them by ten years, and as he reached the door he saw the freckled face of a boy, too young to be here, to wear the uniform. But the boy was looking at him with genuine respect.

"Good luck, sir."

Sir. He wanted to correct the young man, *sir* is for officers. I am merely a corporal.

"Good luck to you as well, *Poilu*."

Another man reached out, surprised Lufbery by taking his arm.

"Sir, what is it like to fly?"

There was honesty in the young man's face, and Lufbery heard the angry voice of the driver, "Now! Hurry! I must go!"

"I'm sorry," Lufbery said. "There is no time to explain. Perhaps you will fly one day."

"I would be afraid. Why do you do it?"

It was the one question Lufbery could answer, and he moved past the driver, stepped down through the doorway, said, "To kill Germans."

Lufbery had become qualified first in the bombers, had already served for more than six months with the French Escadrille 106. But he shared the ambitions of many who piloted the clumsy two-seaters, and was able to persuade his commanding officer to send him to the fighter training field at Plessis-Belleville. It had been his first experience in the Nieuports, the petite biplane that was France's answer to the German single-wing Fokker Eindeckers. The Nieuports were the first fighter planes that could effectively compete with the Fokker, but what the French required most were capable pilots to fly them. It was not a skill that Lufbery came by naturally, and the training had been a struggle. Finally, in early May, he had earned his certificate, and his new assignment.

The American Escadrille had been founded by a small group of pilots, aided by the energy and finances of several influential Americans in Paris. One of the most influential was Dr. Edmund Gros, a physician from California, who had established an American hospital in Paris, as well as organizing an American ambulance corps. The strict letter of American law made it illegal for an American to fight under the flag of another nation, and with the American government's insistence on a neutral status in the war, the men who volunteered for service to France were forced to walk a tightrope with the French government. Some had joined the French Foreign Legion, the catchall for misfits and soldiers of fortune from all over the world. But several Americans had other ambitions. They wanted to fly. The meetings had begun, private affairs between Dr. Gros and French government officials, eager to find a way to bring much-needed American assistance to the French air service without setting off alarms in Washington, Paris, or Berlin. After lengthy and delicate discussions, the French ministers nervously rationalized that it was no violation of American law if the American participants had not been recruited in the United States. The loophole had been found, and Dr. Gros now began to assemble the first American unit to be officially allowed to fight for the French army. There were seven men, most already familiar with flight training. Among them, Bill Thaw and Norman Prince were the sons of wealthy American financiers, the kind of men whose influence carried weight in the government ministries in Paris. Through their efforts, other Americans of great wealth were encouraged to contribute to the funding of the American Escadrille, including men with the familiar names of Vanderbilt and Morgan. Despite the American government's official stance of neutrality, the American businessmen understood the economic value of the Allied cause. To the financiers, President Woodrow Wilson's policy of neutrality was a naïve political mistake that might result in a German victory. Should the French and English lose the war, the cost to the financial interests in the United States could be catastrophic, since far more trade existed with those nations than with nations aligned with Germany. If this small group of American pilots were successful against the Germans, their exploits could inspire thousands more to take up the cause, putting pressure on Wilson to acknowledge America's crucial economic link to the Allies.

Regardless of the political wrangling, for the pilots, the American Escadrille offered them the opportunity to fly as a single unit. The French government insisted that the Americans grant some concessions to soothe the continuing uneasiness in Paris about the direct participation of American fighting men, and so, the escadrille would be designated as Escadrille N-124, would be commanded by a French officer, would be part of a larger French air wing, and would take its orders from the French Air Service. To the seven pilots themselves, these were merely details. All they really needed were aeroplanes.

Lufbery walked along the single-lane road, could see a row of odd buildings, barnlike structures, massive sheets of canvas for walls. He stepped out onto a wooden bridge, crossed over a wide ditch, a trickle of muddy water flowing underneath. He was close to the soft-sided structures now, could see that out in front, the ground was a flat grassy plain, and beyond, there were trees and low hills. He listened, expected to hear something of motors, heard only silence, and the dull tramp of his boots on the hard dusty road.

He moved between two of the canvas buildings, heard voices now, French. He stepped out in front of the buildings, was surprised to see they weren't buildings at all. The front side of each canvas shelter was open, and he realized, Of course, these are hangars. He walked out in front of one, empty and cavernous, saw a puddle of grease, the familiar debris of aeroplanes. He kept moving, followed the voices toward the great open maw of another hangar. He saw the men gathered in the center of the hangar, surrounding a plane, a ragged Nieuport 11. They saw him now, one man pulling a pistol from his belt.

"You! What are you doing here?"

He held one hand in the air, eased the bag from his shoulder, let it drop to the ground.

"I am Corporal Raoul Lufbery. I have orders to report here. Is this the American Escadrille?"

He scanned their uniforms, five men, no officers, dirty hands and greasy shirts. One man stepped away from the plane, moved toward him, appraising.

"Lufbery? They've been expecting you. I'm LeBlanc, chief mechanic. Welcome to the One twenty-four."

The man was matter-of-fact, still appraising him, and Lufbery saw the pistol disappear. He looked at the plane now, ripped fabric, broken wing struts, a pool of oil spreading beneath the motor.

"What happened to this one?"

LeBlanc backed away, waved him forward, said, "See for yourself. You flown the fighters before?"

Lufbery moved closer to the plane, could see more than rips in the cloth, saw small round holes punched through, both wings, down the side, the tail shredded, one side barely attached.

"Bombers. I flew the Nieuports in training."

"Well, Corporal, this is something you didn't see in training. Shot to pieces, this one. He was lucky to make it back. Damned Boche bullet shattered his windscreen, busted up his face pretty bad. He'll be in hospital for a few days."

Lufbery had memorized the names, the first seven pilots of the American Squadron. He was the eighth. He saw jagged glass in front of the cockpit, all that was left of the windscreen.

"Who? May I know?"

LeBlanc was down on one knee, running his hand beneath the motor housing.

"No hole. Can't find the oil leak. We'll have to take her apart. Dammit." He looked up at Lufbery now, said, "Corporal Rockwell. He made our first kill, you know."

"I had heard, yes."

"Made another one too, but he couldn't get confirmation. The Boche bastard made it back behind his own lines."

Kiffin Rockwell's success had come just four days earlier, the first confirmed victory for the American Squadron, and in Paris, the newspapers had already shouted the story. But the lack of confirmation was something all the fighter squadrons had to contend with. Early in the war, pilots on both sides were claiming victories every time they flew, every puff of smoke from an enemy plane counting as a kill. Now, the victory had to be confirmed by another source, usually an infantry observation post, someone on the ground who had actually witnessed the enemy plane going down. Even if a pilot had watched his adversary crash, his word alone, or even the word of his fellow pilots, would not do.

Lufbery moved closer to the damaged Nieuport, ran his hand over the fabric, put a finger into one of the holes. Beside him, LeBlanc cursed, slid under the nose of the plane, stared up into the motor. "Excuse us, Corporal. We have some work to do here."

"If I may ask . . . where are the pilots?"

Another man looked up from the far side of the plane, said, "Flying. Where else might they be?"

At the tail, a man was taping the fabric. "They've been out about an hour," he said, glancing at a watch. "Should be another hour or so."

LeBlanc was ignoring Lufbery now, said, "Dent in the fuel tank. No hole though. No sign of a bullet hole in the cowling. Where the hell is the leak?"

Lufbery knelt down beside him, said, "Mind if I have a look?"

"With all respect, Corporal, I've never met a pilot yet who didn't just get in the way. You do your work, and we'll do ours. We'll fix this bird if we have to take the whole damned motor apart."

Lufbery ignored the insult, said, "I agree with you about pilots. Most of them won't get their hands dirty. However, I have considerable experience with motors. I was a mechanic before I was a pilot."

"That so? All right then, Corporal Mechanic, five of us can't find a hole in this damned motor, maybe you can. We figure a fragment of a Boche shell made its way in somehow. The oil drained right out of her."

"How long did it take?"

LeBlanc looked up at him.

"Couple days. What the hell does that matter? There still has to be a hole. We came out here this morning to patch up the body, and there was a puddle."

Lufbery bent low, turned over on his back, slid himself beside LeBlanc. He reached up, closed his eyes, worked his fingers up and around, felt his way through the motor's shell.

"Well, Corporal? Where's the hole?"

Lufbery eased his hand out of the motor, slid out from under the plane. He saw a rag, wiped his hands, said, "There isn't one."

There were low laughs, LeBlanc emerging from beneath the plane.

"Feel free to assist us again, Corporal, anytime."

"The oil isn't leaking from a hole. The motor's been jarred. The gasket seals have cracked."

LeBlanc looked at the others, then at Lufbery, said, "Cracked? Corporal, every one of us has checked the bolts. That motor's sealed up tight as a drum."

"No, actually, it isn't. Each cylinder has been jarred." He looked at the prop now, one blade with a long thin gash. "There. The imbalance in the prop caused the motor to jar, to shake just enough that it cracked the gaskets. The bolts are tight, but the oil is seeping right through the gaskets. That's why it took two days to make a puddle. You'll have to pull the cylinders, put new gaskets in."

They stared at him in silence, and he wiped his hands again with the rag, said, "I should find my quarters. Are the pilots billeted here?"

LeBlanc pulled himself up now, said, "Um, no. There's a château on the way to the village, number forty-five. A short walk. Lieutenant DeLaage should be there. He's the second in command. Do you need help with your baggage?"

Lufbery moved toward the bag, hoisted it up on his shoulder, said, "No. I'll find it. Thank you."

He walked out toward the open field, stopped, thought a moment, then turned, saw the mechanics still watching him.

"I do not wish to offend, but if it is acceptable to you, I should like to assist with the preparation of any aeroplane that I fly."

LeBlanc shrugged his shoulders, said, "By all means, Corporal."

"Thank you."

Lufbery turned again, moved out into the gray sunlight, pulled his bag up higher on his shoulder. He rounded the corner of the hangar, moved back toward the one-lane road, could hear the talk again, the brusque voice of LeBlanc, "All right, let's pull these cylinders. I believe it's the gaskets. . . ."

Lufbery could not help a smile.

He did not expect a handshake, Lieutenant DeLaage greeting him with a wide smile, and perfect English. DeLaage was a younger man, a neat cropped moustache, common among the French officers.

"Corporal Lufbery! Welcome! Most delighted to meet you! I trust your journey was not difficult."

Lufbery held a salute, and DeLaage waved it aside, said, "Nonsense. I don't hold to such formality here. Captain Thenault a bit more, perhaps. But I assure you, I am no different than any one of you. We are all here to fly, yes?"

The man's smile was infectious, and Lufbery responded with a smile of his own, didn't know what to say. He watched as DeLaage opened a small cabinet, retrieved a bottle of brandy.

"Not so much during the day, mind you, but . . . well, no one else is here." He winked at Lufbery now. "If they were, this bottle would quickly disappear. It is a curious thing. You Americans have an astounding capacity for alcohol."

The glasses were filled, and Lufbery sipped the powerful tonic, felt his face curling from the aroma. DeLaage laughed, said, "My own private stock. Quite a treat, I promise you. Most of these fellows seem happy with anything the villagers provide. A Frenchman should take pride in his country's spirits. Regrettably, it requires more than patriotism to swallow some of what inhabits the cellars hereabout. Have you received word of your promotion?"

Lufbery did not expect the question.

"Um, no, sir."

"Soon, I promise. Once this unit was established, it was merely a formality before all of you were granted the rank of sergeant. A small token of appreciation. Some would say very small. However, there are other rewards as well. Bill Thaw is already a sergeant, his papers coming through this morning. He doesn't know yet. Mr. Rockwell should be as well. Headquarters is determined to reward success. With Mr. Rockwell's confirmed kill, he will soon receive promotion to adjutant, the equivalent to your, um, sergeant-major, I suppose."

Lufbery could sense that DeLaage knew far more of what was happening around him than the mechanics.

"Is Mr. Rockwell all right? Are his injuries severe?"

"Oh, you heard! No, far worse in appearance. Cut up his face rather badly. The doctors spent some time just picking glass out of him. The captain ordered him to the hospital, but I am confident Mr. Rockwell will return quickly."

Lufbery glanced down at his bag, said, "Is there room for me here in this house?"

"Oh, certainly! You will room with Norman Prince. Fine fellow. Top of that stairway, to the right."

Lufbery glanced up the narrow stairs, reached down for his bag, and DeLaage said, "Your record says that you were born in France."

"Yes, Clermont-Ferrand."

"Ah yes, beautiful down there."

"My father is American. I became an American citizen several years ago. Is there anything else, sir?"

"Forgive me for mentioning this, Mr. Lufbery, but I was quite familiar with Marc Pourpe. He was an inspiration to many young men, including myself. Flying was something new to this world, and I was in awe of his skills. You were close, eh?"

Lufbery did not speak of Pourpe often, chose his words, said, "He taught me how to fly. He taught me everything I know about aeroplanes. His death was very . . . difficult."

"I apologize, Mr. Lufbery. It is not my place to open such a wound."

"He is the reason I am here, sir. There is no apology for that. The finest man I ever knew is dead because of this war."

"He is your inspiration, then? How fortunate that you hold something positive from his loss. Tragedy destroys some men, steals their will to fight. I have seen it in this army, from the beginning of the war. When a man loses a friend, he has a choice to make. He can lose himself in mourning, or he can fight on."

"I have every intention of fighting on. It is all I care about."

DeLaage studied him, nodded slowly. "Revenge can be a powerful tonic." He held up his glass. "Like the strongest brandy."

Lufbery thought a moment, did not like the word. "I would not call it revenge. Marc Pourpe was a man who had a passion for life. He never wasted a single day with mundane concerns; he never complained about the trivial. Every sunrise meant the start of some new adventure. Even this war . . . when he learned of it, he was scheduled to begin a new flying tour of the Orient. But of course, he would not turn his back on his country, so he volunteered immediately with the Aeronautique Militaire."

"Yes, I recall. It was in the newspapers."

"The newspapers. When he was killed, they came to me, his mechanic, had to know every detail. I had nothing to tell them. His death had meaning to me that they would not understand." He paused, saw quiet concern on DeLaage's face. "I have worked hard to become a good pilot, Lieutenant. I cannot bring him back. But I intend to do what I can to make the Germans regret they started this war."

"And you shall have your opportunities, Mr. Lufbery. All that is required of you here is that you fly well, that you fight hard, and that you behave like a man. I understand your desire to kill the enemy, but I must mention that Captain Thenault and I require absolute obedience when we are on patrols." He laughed now. "Some of you Americans seem convinced you can take on all of Germany in your one little Nieuport. I promise you, if you allow us to lead you, this squadron will enjoy a great deal of success."

Lufbery downed the last bit of brandy, looked down at his

bag again, and DeLaage said, "Of course! You are probably tired. Go up to your room. The others should return from their patrol at any time. I know that Captain Thenault is anxious to meet you."

"Thank you, sir."

Lufbery picked up the bag, began to climb the steps, heard the clatter at the front door, a breathless voice, "Sir! They're back! Sergeant Thaw is down! He did not return! They say he crashed in the combat area!"

"Did he survive?"

"We don't know, sir. The captain is already driving to the front!"

DeLaage followed the man out the door, the house suddenly empty, silent. Lufbery stood on the steps, stared down at the empty foyer, the front door open slightly, swinging slowly closed. He turned, moved slowly up the stairs, thought, So, it has begun.

He had thought of waiting at the house, but the silence was awful. Once his bag was emptied, he could not just sit. After several long minutes of staring out the window, his patience snapped shut. In one quick motion, he was down the stairs, out into the dusty road, and on his way to the airfield.

He moved up behind the canvas hangars, heard many voices this time, could already smell the exhaust, the spent gasoline of the returning planes. He moved out in front, saw a crowd of men, some of them mechanics. But there were others as well, a tight circle of men, animated, the voices growing louder. Lufbery moved closer, could hear the words now, one man, the uniform of a captain, a heavy French accent.

"Do you wish to fly? It is that simple! I will not have this!"

The captain's fury was directed at one man, the others standing back just a step, allowing the man to endure the full brunt of the officer's rage. There was silence for a long moment, and Lufbery could see the captain's face now, the color of Bordeaux wine.

"Well, Mr. Chapman?"

"Sir, I believed you did not see the enemy. I could not allow them to pass without a look."

"A look! Mr. Chapman, you broke formation against my orders! You attacked a squadron of enemy planes without any investigation! Your outrageous behavior nearly cost the life of your comrade!"

Lufbery stayed back, could see the face of the guilty pilot, recognized the name, Chapman. Victor Chapman was young, early twenties, and far taller than any of the men around him. He seemed to bend under the weight of the captain's dressing-down. Behind him, the other men were silent, no one even suggesting a smile. They began to notice Lufbery now, one man pointing, the perfect excuse to interrupt the captain's relentless lecture.

"Sir. The new man."

The captain turned abruptly, and Lufbery could see he was about his own age, wore the same tight moustache as DeLaage. Lufbery felt the stares from all of them, said, "Sorry to interrupt. I am Raoul Lufbery. I was assigned—"

"Good!" The captain moved close to him, glanced back to the others. "Yes, good! He should hear this as well! Mr. Lufbery, I am Captain Georges Thenault, your commanding officer. Some of these men do not yet seem to recognize my authority. We nearly lost a man today because one of your fellow pilots decided to play cowboy. The fight he got us into could have sent us all to the ground."

Lufbery could see the guilt on Chapman's face, the man clearly aware of what he had done. Chapman seemed to welcome Thenault's change of attention, said, "Raoul, is it? Welcome. Victor Chapman. Not my finest day, as you might have noticed."

The name flowed into Lufbery's mind now, and he said, "Bill Thaw?"

Chapman nodded. "Yep. He was wounded, was able to pancake his plane near the French lines. He's all right, should be back here tonight."

Thenault had said his piece to Chapman, held a hand out to Lufbery now, said, "Forgive my temper, Mr. Lufbery. We experienced a problem today." He looked at Chapman. "I believe it is solved, yes?"

Chapman glanced at the others, said, "Yes. Very sorry."

The others began to move toward Lufbery, a few sympathetic hands patting Chapman on the back. The introductions began, the names all familiar to Lufbery, the roster he had studied. He felt the warmth of their greetings, saw smiles on each face, even Thenault. DeLaage was there, emerging from the hangar, and Lufbery could see the row of Nieuports behind him, the mechanics tending to each one.

"Ah, Mr. Lufbery! So you have met your comrades. Have you explained your particular talent? Quite unusual, certainly for this group."

Lufbery wasn't sure what DeLaage meant.

"No? Well, Mr. Lufbery here is quite the mechanic, isn't that right?"

Lufbery was embarrassed now, had never thought of himself as having talent at all.

"I was first trained to be a mechanic, before I learned to fly."

"So, you're handy with a wrench, eh?"

The voice belonged to Norman Prince, one of the men responsible for the squadron's birth. Prince was younger than Lufbery had expected, but unlike the baby-faced Chapman, he wore the French-style moustache. Prince laughed now, said, "Don't tell Kiffin Rockwell. He hates mechanics. Thinks they're all witches or something."

The others laughed, obviously agreeing with Prince's odd description. Lufbery wasn't sure how to respond, and Prince seemed to read him, said, "He'll be back here in a couple days. Only man in the squadron who speaks English worse than the captain. Has to be because he's from Tennessee. Must have learned how to shoot when he was three years old, with some damned squirrel gun or something. He took down our first Boche plane. Our first hero."

"Yes, I heard."

Prince continued, seemed to enjoy his own story.

"Rockwell's a genuine Confederate. I think he believes Germans are just Yankees in disguise. Hates the Boche more than any man alive." He glanced at Thenault, seemed to test the captain's mood. "But if the captain here doesn't let him back in the air before much longer, old Kiffin might begin to hate Frenchmen too. Hell, I have to keep quiet about going to Harvard. He might take a shot or two at me."

Even Thenault laughed, surprising Lufbery. He could feel the humor in all of them, something shared, could feel the openness extending toward him as well. Prince said to Thenault, "We have a Nieuport for our new man yet?"

Thenault shook his head, said, "Mr. Lufbery, we have only five aeroplanes thus far. We had six." He glanced at Chapman. "But I have been promised more in a few days. In the meantime, we shall patrol in shifts. Mr. Lufbery, you shall accompany me tomorrow morning." He looked at the others. "Mr. Prince, Mr. Hall, Mr. Cowdin. We will make the first patrol. Six o'clock is typical for us, Mr. Lufbery."

"Yes, sir."

Prince moved close to him, one arm around Lufbery's shoulders.

"You ready to kill some Germans?"

Lufbery didn't answer, could see DeLaage looking at him, quiet concern in the Frenchman's eyes.

DeLaage said, "Mr. Prince, Mr. Lufbery may teach us all how to do that."

4

LUFBERY

Behonne Airfield, France—June 18, 1916

He brought the plane in slowly, settled on a clear strip of grass, could see DeLaage's plane already moving toward the hangar. Bert Hall was behind him, circling, and Lufbery eased the nose down, felt the Nieuport settling beneath him in a sinking glide. He flicked the toggle, cut the gasoline to the motor, the prop still spinning, washing him with warm air. The plane now dropped the last couple of feet, bouncing gently over tufts of soft grass. He flipped the switch again, the motor engaging, and he pushed the rudder pedal with his foot, turned to follow DeLaage.

His flexed his feet, the numbness just now wearing off. He was still not used to the bone-chilling cold of the air at high altitude, something Pourpe had once cautioned him about. Pourpe had rarely flown higher than a few thousand feet, had to stay within clear sight of his audience. Lufbery had watched alongside the awestruck spectators as Pourpe performed, dancing the plane in loops and spins and all manner of acrobatics. Even after so many months the show itself was unnerving to Lufbery, watching his friend stretch aircraft to the limit of their engineering, and sometimes beyond.

Lufbery's fear had evolved into curiosity, and on a tour of Egypt, Pourpe had secured use of a two-seater, would finally allow his mechanic to experience the heights for himself. Pourpe knew what every pilot knows, that the first time a man feels himself leave the ground, there are two possibilities: he will be terrified, or he'll feel the greatest thrill of his life. It did not surprise Pourpe that Lufbery had no fear at all. Instead, the mechanic marveled at the sights, as much as he marveled at the engineering that kept the plane in the air. It was a strange new experience for Lufbery, how the higher you flew, the thinner the air. He experienced the struggle to breathe, discovered with amazement how every little movement became an effort, the brain floating in some kind of stupor. Pourpe had warned him, if you weren't careful, you might lose your senses completely. When Lufbery began to fly on his own, he experimented, testing his own limits, flying as high as the primitive planes would allow. It was pure fun at first, feeling his mind dissolve, testing how high he could go before dropping back down to heavier air. But the cold had been a shock, and despite Pourpe's warning, Lufbery had been totally unprepared, had thought his feet would freeze completely away. Now, he wore the fur-lined boots, the same boots all the American pilots wore. No one else in the squadron seemed to complain. After every patrol, every pilot hopped down from his Nieuport with the same exhilaration. He had watched the others, listened to the talk as the heavy flying suits were peeled away, the boots yanked off. They wore nothing special inside the boots, the same thick wool socks he wore, and it had begun to infuriate him that they kept silent about the frozen agony of their toes. After three weeks in the squadron, he assumed it was his agony alone, some weakness that he dare not admit. He had witnessed too much of their teasing already, these pilots clearly a rowdy group, inspired to relentless taunting of any weakness any one of them might reveal. They might all have frozen toes, but if they weren't going to admit it, he wouldn't either.

He had been out on the early patrol, had followed DeLaage alongside Cowdin, and the new man, Charles Johnson. But with the patrol completed, the planes would not stay on the ground any longer than the mechanics required to refuel the tank, and, if necessary, reload the machine gun.

The Nieuport 11 was the smallest aeroplane Lufbery had ever flown. The French had nicknamed it the *bébé*, the pronunciation barely acceptable to men who considered themselves fighter pilots. No one wanted to fly anything called a baby. What the Nieuport 11 lacked in size, it made up for in power and maneuverability, the small craft capable of speeds over a hundred miles per hour, matching her with both the single wing

Fokker Eindecker, as well as the new German two-winged Albatros. If the Nieuport had a weakness, it was firepower. Though the Germans had not invented the interrupter gear, they were perfecting it. Previously, it was impractical to mount a machine gun on the nose of the plane, since firing the gun would eventually destroy the plane's own propeller. The French pilot Roland Garros had attempted to solve the problem by attaching steel plates to the inside of the prop, which would deflect those bullets that actually struck the blades. But Garros had been shot down, and both he and his plane had been captured. His secret had been revealed, but to the German engineers, his plane's odd technology caused more amusement than concern. While the two-seater planes had a machine gun mounted in the back, no danger to the prop, if the single-seat aeroplane was to become an effective fighter, something more sophisticated was required. The concept of the interrupter gear had been available to both sides at the start of the war, but only the Germans had accurately predicted how valuable a weapon the single-seat aeroplanes might become. The Fokkers had the gear now, which connected the motor to the mechanism of the machine gun, interrupting the firing of the gun when the blade of the prop was in the bullet's path. German pilots could aim their guns by aiming the nose of their plane. A skilled pilot was automatically becoming a skilled marksman.

The Nieuport's one Lewis machine gun was mounted on the plane's top wing, so as to fire above the blades of the prop. In an engagement, the pilot had to concentrate on flying the plane while reaching up over his head to fire the gun, two distinctly separate skills. Worse, the Lewis guns carried their ammunition in a round drum that fastened directly to the gun itself. The drum held exactly forty-seven bullets, which could be exhausted in a few seconds. Each pilot carried spare drums, fastened to the inside of the cockpit. But changing the drum while being pursued by an enemy aircraft could be a nightmare. The pilot usually had to stand up, holding the plane's stick between his knees. The mechanism for freeing the drum was clumsy and awkward, often too difficult to manage for stiff fingers and gloved hands. Worse still, the Lewis gun jammed so easily that often it wouldn't fire at all.

*　*　*

The second patrol was on the move, and Lufbery stood at the entrance to the hangar, watched as Thenault led Prince and Rockwell, and another new man, Clyde Balsley, out onto the grassy plain. Balsley was young, barely twenty-three, had arrived at the end of May. He was said to be a Texan, and the jokes had begun immediately, that the squadron's Confederate forces had doubled. Kiffin Rockwell had returned to the squadron after a week's recuperation, his face still scarred and bruised from the destruction of his windscreen. Rockwell learned immediately that he had no ally after all. Though Balsley had grown up in San Antonio, he was in fact from Pennsylvania, much to the delight of the squadron's other Pennsylvanian, Bill Thaw.

Balsley had yet to fly, had been forced to wait on the arrival of new aircraft, a delay that had driven Captain Thenault to red-eyed fury. Finally, Thenault decided Balsley had waited long enough, and had assigned him to a patrol. Lufbery had watched Balsley scramble up into the Nieuport with undisguised glee. Thenault had seen it as well, had waited until Balsley was tight in his plane before walking up to the Nieuport, saying something to Balsley that no one else could hear. Lufbery knew what was said, had heard the same thing on his first patrol, knew the order by heart. *Do not break formation unless I give the signal.* Every new man was given the lecture the first day at the field, the same lesson Lufbery had witnessed being drilled into Victor Chapman.

The Nieuports were gone now, disappearing into the morning sun. Lufbery could still hear the drone of the motors, turned, saw Bill Thaw, and Thaw said, "Coffee? I fired up the cooker in the hangar. The mechanics'll polish it off pretty quick. I saved you a cup."

Lufbery flexed his toes, could still feel the cold stiffness, moved toward Thaw, said, "Thanks, yes. Chilly this morning."

Thaw laughed, said, "It's June, Luf. Has to be eighty degrees. Problems with your feet again?"

He saw the smile, understood now why Thaw was so popular

with the others. There was no sarcasm in the man's voice, nothing to embarrass Lufbery.

"Didn't think anyone knew. I'll get used to it. Maybe thicker socks."

They moved into the hangar, and Lufbery saw the mechanics gathered around the naked fuselage of a Nieuport, propped up on a row of sawhorses, the frame of the new plane just delivered. It was another source of annoyance to Thenault, that the Aeronautique Militaire was shipping the new planes to the airfield in pieces, the mechanics having to assemble them bit by bit, some of the parts often not arriving for several days.

Thaw emptied the steaming remains of the pot into a thick clay cup, handed it to Lufbery. He put the scalding coffee to his lips, caught the sharp smell of oil, held the cup away. Thaw said, "What? Something wrong?"

Lufbery offered the cup, and Thaw smelled, said, "Damn!" He looked around toward the mechanics, and Lufbery saw the men turning away, heard low laughter. Thaw poured the coffee on the ground, said, "Not funny. Not one bit."

One man looked up, feigning innocence, said, "Ah, but Monsieur Thaw, if the castor oil is good for the Nieuport motors, it is good for your motor as well, eh?"

Thaw looked at Lufbery, said, "Third time this week. I made the mistake of telling them that the motor oil they use here is the same junk my mother gave me when I was a baby. Bad enough we have to smell that stuff when we fly." He shouted to the mechanic now, "That's the last time! The next man puts castor oil in the coffee will test my Lewis gun from the unfriendly end!"

The mechanic waved at him, still smiling, no one believing Bill Thaw would stay angry for long. Thaw said, "Let's go to the house. Chapman will want some coffee too. I'll make more there." Lufbery looked at the fat bandage around Thaw's left elbow, said, "Still hurt?"

Thaw shrugged. "Only in the morning. Which is now. Wakes me up early. Damned shame. I have all this vacation time, and my arm acts like an alarm clock." He glanced at the sky. "They'll be gone for at least another hour. We should go. I'd like to be here when they get back."

88

Lufbery knew it was Thaw's particular quirk, that he would always be at the field when the planes came in from a patrol. It was becoming that way with all of them: Rockwell, Thaw, and now Chapman, who sat confined to the resident quarters with a fat white bandage on his head. The wounds to the pilots had not been life threatening, the injury to Thaw's arm the worst, but every wound had forced each man to stay on the ground until the captain cleared him to fly again. Regardless of their injuries, Lufbery could sense that each man regarded his ground time as a sort of punishment.

They walked to the house, Thaw leading the way. Lufbery was by far the shortest man in the squadron, had learned to scramble to keep up with the others, especially when they were as energized as Bill Thaw. Thaw was only twenty-three, but he wore a fat walrus moustache that made him seem much older. With his stocky trunk, thick arms, and big dark eyes, some said he looked like some sort of Mexican *bandito*.

They were on the main road now, kept to the grassy edge, suffered through the dust of a train of trucks and buses, more French troops and their equipment rolling toward Verdun. The convoy passed, and Lufbery brushed dirt from his uniform, said, "Poor devils."

Thaw stopped, seemed surprised.

"Who? The *poilus*? They're the lucky ones. They get to fight and die for their mother country. No better way to go. Not like the Boche. They're fighting to conquer. Not much spiritual fulfillment in that."

Lufbery had rarely heard any of the pilots mention religion, was curious now.

"Is that important? You believe we're being judged by God?"

Thaw shook his head. "Never give it much thought. Most of the Frenchmen are good Catholics though. You ever seen one after a cathedral's been blown to hell? They cry more for a building than they do for each other. How 'bout you? You're born here, right?"

Lufbery nodded, started walking again. "Don't think my father cared much if I was a Catholic or not. My mother died when I was a baby. Don't know what she would have thought.

I've been to so many places—the Orient, Arabia, Cuba, most every big city in America. So many different ways people talk about God. Not sure how anyone can claim they know the one true way."

Thaw laughed now, said, "That's not a conversation you want to have with Kiffin Rockwell. I don't fault him for it, certainly. The man grew up with very strict beliefs. You get taught how to see the world through one set of eyes, makes some people downright passionate about it. I envy that sometimes. Like the French. Soldiers crying over a busted-up statue of the Virgin Mary. They're inspired by that, makes them better fighters, some kind of fire deep down."

"So, why are you here?"

Thaw shrugged. "Same reason as the rest of us, I guess. It felt like the right thing to do. When the Boche invaded Belgium, it really bothered me. I don't know any Belgians, don't know that I ever met one. But look how they fought back, this little pissant country standing up to the strongest army in the world. Surprised the hell out of Kaiser Bill. The Boche thought they had a clear path into France. The Belgian king, what's his name, Albert. Led his army himself, stood right up to the Boche guns and said, *Hell no you don't*. Not without a fight. He knew he didn't have a chance in hell, but he fought them anyway. Guts. Gotta admire that. Really made me think. These Boche bastards think they can just march into France and take over, like it's their Divine Right. There's your religion for you. I guarantee you Kaiser Bill thinks God's on his side."

They walked in silence for a minute, the house visible now. Thaw looked at him, said, "Okay, what about you? Why'd you sign up?"

Lufbery didn't hesitate. "To kill Germans."

Thaw absorbed the answer, laughed now. "Good a reason as any."

They finished the coffee, the maid cleaning up Thaw's mess in the kitchen. Lufbery had settled into a soft chair in the narrow parlor, surrounded by bookshelves, dusty volumes that seemed to have been untouched for years. Chapman sat across from him, his arms crossed, staring at the floor. Lufbery could not help staring at the bandage on the man's head, and Chapman noticed him, said, "It's nothing. A damned scratch. If Thenault doesn't let me fly tomorrow, I may steal a plane and do it anyway."

Thaw came in now, said, "If you go anywhere, you better tell them to put a bigger windscreen on your Nieuport. How the hell you get those long damned legs into a cockpit is a mystery to me anyway."

Chapman laughed, and Lufbery smiled as well, could see now that Thaw had a talent for disarming anyone's anger. Chapman swung his knees from side to side, said, "Took me a while to figure it out. Damned French aeroplanes are made for short stubby little Frenchmen." He looked at Lufbery. "No offense, Luf."

Lufbery laughed. "I'm not French. Just stubby. But I'm not the one with the bandage on my head. Maybe you do need a bigger windscreen."

"You see Kiffin's face? Sure, that's all I need, more glass in front of me to cut me to hell. Nope. Gotta maintain my good looks. Keep these mademoiselles coming back for more. They like these old long legs. Makes 'em curious about . . . the rest."

Thaw laughed now, and the maid appeared, said, "Monsieur Thaw. My son has returned with the equipment you requested."

Thaw hooted, followed her out of the room, and Lufbery said, "What equipment?"

Chapman shook his head. "No telling. But he's been harassing that poor woman ever since we got here. She's had her boy running all over the town trying to find God knows what."

They could hear Thaw shouting now, and Chapman said, "All right, I guess we gotta go see."

Lufbery followed him out through the rear door of the house. Thaw was in the yard, a long thin pole in his right hand, whipping it back and forth above him.

"Yee hee! Perfect!"

He reached in his pocket now, pulled out what seemed to be money, handed it to the boy, a gangly twelve-year-old. The boy made a bow, stared at Thaw as he continued to whip the pole.

Lufbery saw a wooden box on the ground beside Thaw, and Chapman said, "What the hell? You bought a bull whip?"

Thaw was all smiles, set the pole down, picked up the box, opened the lid.

"Look! A spool of line, some wooden lures, the whole works!"

Lufbery understood now, said, "Fishing pole."

Thaw dumped the contents of the box on the ground, and Chap-man sniffed, turned, moved back toward the door, said, "Fishing? In a war?"

Thaw ignored him, and Chapman was back inside the house now. Lufbery moved closer, saw strange pieces of wood, some carved and painted, and Thaw held one up, said, "See? Looks damned near like a Johnstown mule-bug. Caught a pile of trout on one just like it."

Lufbery studied the jumble of assorted tackle, said, "Where would you fish around here?"

"Hah! Plenty of streams a little west of here. One good-sized one, empties into a swamp, small ponds all over the place. I could see the damned fish in every hole."

Lufbery felt his own enthusiasm building, said, "A swamp? Muddy ground?"

"Not too bad. The woods are pretty thick, but there's trails, probably made by farmers. You fish? You're welcome to come along."

"No, I don't fish. But, thank you, yes, I would like to come along. It sounds like the perfect place to pick mushrooms."

He had returned to the airfield with Thaw and Chapman, watched as Thenault brought the patrol home. But Thenault did not make his usual slow circle around the field, brought his Nieuport straight in, a hot, fast landing. He taxied quickly toward the hangar, and the others landed behind him. Lufbery knew now what they all knew. There were only three of them. The mechanics were out quickly, the usual routine, and Lufbery saw Thenault rip off his goggles, toss the helmet to the ground. He pulled himself up and out of the plane, jumped to the ground, shouted, "Balsley is down!" He pounded his fists into his thighs. "I should not have allowed him . . . it was too soon!"

Chapman was close to him now, said, "What happened? Is he alive?"

Thenault shook his head. "Don't know yet. He was being pursued, but he was staying ahead of them. We dove into an attack. . . . I think his gun jammed."

Thenault was pacing now, and Lufbery could see the man was furious with himself.

Chapman was close to Thenault, his voice rising as well. "Where? Verdun?"

Thenault tried to get control of himself, seemed to calm in the presence of the tall man. "Verdun, yes. He was headed back this way. I lost sight of him south of the fortress."

"Then he could be on our side of the lines. I'll telephone the infantry outposts. They must know something."

Thenault nodded silently, stared at the ground. Chapman was gone quickly, jogged toward the rear of the hangar, toward the telephone station. Thaw moved out past Thenault, waited for Rockwell and Prince to climb out of their planes. Both men were talking to Thaw in low voices, and Lufbery saw heads shaking. Thenault looked at Lufbery, said, "His first patrol. How can that be?"

Lufbery had never seen Thenault show this kind of emotion.

"Captain, he was trained as well as any of us. Did he break formation?"

Thenault shook his head.

"No. We all made the attack together. He was close to a two-seater, and I thought the Boche was finished, but then, Balsley spun away. It must have been his gun. Once the Boche knew that he was vulnerable . . . there was nothing we could do about it."

There was a shout, from the rear of the hangar, and they all turned, saw Chapman waving. "They have him! He crashed in between the lines! They're taking him to the evacuation hospital! He's alive!"

Thenault rushed past Lufbery, everyone in the hangar now letting go of his own emotion, shouts of relief. Lufbery followed Thenault, and Chapman put down the telephone, said, "Let me go to him! I'll find him!"

Lufbery could see Thenault hesitating, and Chapman leaned close to Thenault now. "Dammit, Captain, if you won't let me fight, at least let me go to him!"

Thenault was surrounded by the pilots now, and Lufbery saw the calm returning to the captain's face.

"We can do no good for him today. We must allow the hospital to do their work. Tomorrow, Mr. Chapman, you may find the location. You may offer our profound relief at his survival."

Chapman had found Balsley, came back to Behonne with word that Balsley's wounds were serious enough that the young man would probably not return to the squadron. Lufbery had listened as intently as the others, as Chapman conveyed word of the horror of Balsley's condition. The young man was housed in a bloody awful facility, close to the front lines and under the constant threat of German bombardment. But the horror was worse for Balsley himself, the young man already having endured several operations to remove shrapnel from a gaping, infected wound in his hip. Lufbery had known Balsley only as well as any of them could, but now, Lufbery felt he didn't know Chapman at all. Chapman was cocky, even arrogant at times, but his arrogance came from his roots, the New York–bred child of an aristocratic family, a direct descendant of John Jay, America's first chief justice. Lufbery had known this kind of arrogance before, had seen it as well in some of the others in the squadron. But now, Chapman had become obsessed with Balsley, as though the health of the entire squadron depended on the health of this one unfortunate young pilot.

June 23, 1916

Lufbery was suited up, waited while the mechanics rolled the Nieuport out onto the grassy plain. Thenault and Prince were close by, each man adjusting his suit, pulling on the heavy fur boots.

Chapman's head wound was still wrapped tightly with the fat bandage, but Thenault had allowed him to fly on short practice runs, keeping close to the airfield. Chapman had complained every time, but Thenault had been firm. Chapman was still injured, would take to the air in small strides. But when Thenault was not around, Chapman allowed his anger to show, and Lufbery knew that Chapman planned to confront Thenault this morning, insisting that his convalescence was complete. He heard the man's voice now, a jovial greeting to the mechanics, Chapman suddenly appearing around the side of the hangar, already in his suit. Thenault watched him approach, and Chapman held out a cloth bag, said, "I found some oranges! The doctors say it's the only thing they'll allow Balsley to eat. They won't even let him drink water, but I convinced the doctor to give him these. This should brighten him up a bit!"

Thenault watched as Chapman tossed the bag into the cockpit of one of the newly assembled planes.

Chapman forced the smile, said, "I'm fit and ready to fly, sir!"

Lufbery saw the hard frown fixed on Thenault's face, and Thenault said, "You would join us then?"

"Certainly, sir! And, on the way home, I can deliver the oranges to the hospital."

Thenault seemed to ponder his decision, said, "No. You will not accompany the patrol just yet. You may, however, deliver the oranges. It is a very kind gesture, Mr. Chapman."

Lufbery waited for the explosion, watched the smile disappear from Chapman's face. "Sir, I insist. I am fit to fly. . . ."

"Mr. Chapman, it is not a discussion. You will deliver the oranges to Mr. Balsley. Perhaps, in a day or two, you can again join the patrols."

Chapman walked slowly over to the new aeroplane, leaned against the side of the plane, said nothing. Thenault climbed into his Nieuport, said, "Gentlemen. Let us proceed."

Lufbery still watched Chapman, saw hard disappointment on the man's face, said, "Maybe tomorrow, Victor. Rest today. It can't hurt. It's a nice thing you're doing . . . the oranges."

Chapman glanced at him, nodded, said nothing. Lufbery felt a twinge of nervousness in his stomach, said, "Take it easy today, Victor."

Lufbery moved to his plane, climbed up, the propman standing at the front, ready for his signal to crank the motor. Lufbery
saw Thenault's Nieuport already rolling out across the grass. He
wanted to talk to Chapman again, but there was no time, and
there was, after all, nothing more he could say. He flipped the
fuel switch, motioned to the propman, who gave a hard pull,
the motor of the Nieuport coughing, roaring to life.

Chapman boarded the Nieuport a few minutes later, spoke to
no one but the propman, held his anger at the captain tightly
inside. He flew the Nieuport along the same route as the patrol
he had wanted to join, but was far behind them, alone, climbing higher than the patrol would normally fly. As the sun rose
higher, he could see reflections, small dots of light, manic movement, the chaos of a confrontation far out in front of him. He
kept the plane above the action, was soon close enough to see
Nieuports swirling around a squadron of German biplanes. But
the Nieuports were outnumbered, and Chapman watched as
they broke off the fight, maneuvering under the skilled hand of
their captain, seeking the safety of the clouds, possibly returning to their own field. But Chapman would not turn away,
Thenault's angry lecture long gone from his mind. He dove the
Nieuport hard, pushed downward toward the formation of five
German planes, believing that none of them had seen him, none
were aware of the deadly surprise. As he moved in behind the
formation, he caught more reflections, could see now that there
were more German planes, two-seaters, the squadron larger
than he had thought. The observers had spotted him, the entire
enemy formation now spreading out, planes looping and
swirling to intercept him. In seconds, he was surrounded,
fought with his plane and his machine gun, the sky around him
a cascading swirl of black crosses on fabric wings, machine-gun
bullets ripping the air. The fight was brief, one bullet now finding him, a sharp jolt to his head, the tall man falling forward
against the windscreen, the Nieuport tumbling in a violent spin
to the earth below.
In minutes the German soldiers reached the crumpled
wreckage, some grabbing for souvenirs, one man snatching the

mangled Lewis gun from the plane's shattered wing. They pulled the body free now, stood aside as an officer moved close, the man reaching into the dead man's pockets, retrieving letters addressed to someone named Balsley. The officer would give the letters to the Red Cross, would assume that they belonged to the pilot. The officer would not give the man's name another thought, had no reason to think the letters were for another man who lay desperately wounded a few miles away. The only mystery lay scattered on the ground around the wreckage, the soldiers now picking them up, sniffing them, tossing them to each other, an impromptu game. The officer allowed them their sport, carried the letters back to his shelter, wondered why anyone would fly with a bag of oranges.

5

LUFBERY

The death of Chapman weighed heavily on all of them, and Lufbery could see the changes in every man. Some openly mourned, DeLaage and Kiffin Rockwell most of all. Others, like Bill Thaw, had tried to defuse the pain, putting a smiling face on their sadness. But even Thaw was not immune, had escaped the sadness of the residence by disappearing with his fishing pole into the nearby forests. Lufbery had finally asked Thaw if he could come along. The request had been met with Thaw's familiar smile, and now Lufbery followed him as Thaw tramped off through the dark swamps. With the stifling heat of the summer, the streams were clear and shallow, the muddy swamps not so difficult to cross. The air was thick with flying and buzzing pests, and he had slapped at the bugs, drawing Thaw's immediate attention. The fisherman would study them, comparing the squashed insects in Lufbery's clothing to whatever small fuzzy lure he had in his tackle. Lufbery tried to understand Thaw's enthusiasm, the man happily engaged for long minutes tying a simple knot in his fishing line. While Thaw eased along the streams, Lufbery scouted the soft ground for the precious mushrooms, was delighted to find a variety he had not expected. By the time the sun had begun to set, both men were successful. As they made their way over the increasingly familiar trails, Lufbery marveled at Thaw's ability to recall every detail of every victory over the fish he carried home. Lufbery's victory was his own, Thaw having no understanding why any man would spend time in the outdoors just to dig up fungus.

The maid watched from the doorway as both men found new

98

ways to create utter chaos in her kitchen. But the results were promising, the smells rolling through the house, inspiring the others to demand faster service, their rowdy impatience fueled by generous amounts of wine.

Lufbery was impressed as he watched Thaw prepare the fish, a sizzling pan awash in generous amounts of butter and garlic. Lufbery had completed his work with the mushrooms as well, more garlic and more butter, the maid silently fuming that the two amateur chefs had wiped her larder clean. When they were finally ready to make their presentation, she had followed, surprised in spite of herself that even though these two Americans had left her kitchen in complete shambles, the dinner they had prepared was actually edible.

The men had gathered, and Lufbery held the platter of mushrooms in one hand, removed empty bottles of wine from the table with the other. He set his platter down now, waited while Thaw did the same. The groans and murmurs grew, and Thaw beamed at him from the far end of the long table, said, "See? I told you they would approve! The French aren't the only ones who can cook!"

More wine was poured, and Lufbery sat, waited for the inevitable congratulations, saw forks ripping into Thaw's heaping mound of fish. Beside him, Rockwell leaned close to the dark steaming mass of mushrooms, said, "Uh . . . what we got here?"

Lufbery puffed up, said, "France's finest bounty. Enjoy!"

"Hmm. Nope, I'll just have the fish."

Lufbery tried to ignore Rockwell's lack of southern graciousness, moved the platter toward Prince, who seemed to recoil.

"Thanks, Luf, but I try not to take unnecessary risks. You sure these are the, um, eating kind?"

Rockwell seemed pleased to have some support for his doubts, said, "I knew a fellow once. Ate a mushroom and dropped dead, facedown into his soup."

Lufbery saw the faces of the others now, the frowning insults to his skill, had not expected to be questioned.

"I assure you . . . I am quite capable of identifying—"

DeLaage reached out, grabbed the platter, said, "I have

confidence, Mr. Lufbery. Gentlemen, what you decline I shall enjoy."

The portions were divided, the Americans diving into the fish, the Frenchmen spooning out great heaps of Lufbery's mushrooms, while behind him, the maid mumbled low curses in the kitchen.

They had discussed adding some adornment to the planes, something appropriate for the American Escadrille, something to distinguish them from the French. There had been only one good suggestion, and they had all agreed it was the perfect American symbol. Once the planes were adorned, every other squadron, friend or enemy, would know that these Nieuports belonged to the Americans.

They had found the painter in Bar-le-Duc, an old man whose shaking hands had stilled with the grasp of his brushes. Now his job was done, and the old man stood back, waited for the compliments. Each pilot studied the old man's work, the perfectly crafted portrait of an Indian chief in full headdress on the fuselage of each plane. They moved closer now, eyeing the careful attention to detail. Thenault said, "Anyone have any objections?"

They all shook their heads, and Rockwell reached out, probed with his finger, said, "When will it be dry? Can we fly now?"

Thenault translated the question to the man, who shrugged, and Thenault said, "Once you fly, the paint will dry quickly. Perhaps we should find out, eh?"

July 30, 1916

The patrol had gone out, DeLaage leading four of them in an escort mission to protect a squad of French observers. Lufbery sat on the ground near his plane, wiped sweat from his eyes with his sleeve, ran his fingers through the metal box of bullets. He plucked one out, looked at it closely, thought, *Rust*. Damn it all. He tossed it aside into a growing pile beside him, retrieved another. Rockwell was there now, said, "What are you doing?"

Lufbery didn't look up, wiped a bullet with a polishing cloth, slipped it gently into the Lewis drum.

"These damned guns jam too easily. I'm finding out why. Some of these bullets are junk. Look here." He pointed to the pile of rejects. "Some of them have bulges, some are showing rust. Some are just plain bent."

Rockwell knelt down, watched as Lufbery wiped another shell, slid it into the drum.

"You . . . polishing them too?"

"Damned right." He stopped now, looked at Rockwell, saw a smile. "Laugh if you want. Until they give us a better machine gun, we have to make do with these. Damned if I'm going get shot to pieces because my gun jams. It happened to Balsley, could happen to any of us."

Rockwell moved close, reached into the metal box, pulled out a handful of the shiny brass, said, "Hmm. I figured it was the gun, not the shells."

Lufbery always enjoyed Rockwell's southern drawl, shook his head now. "Nope. Some of those shells are just garbage. Same problem I have with the motors. I've seen parts that wouldn't work in a child's toy, and they're sending 'em to us to keep us in the air."

Rockwell sat back now, said, "I watched you fiddle with your motor. I always figured it was best not to know about such things."

Lufbery wiped another bullet with the cloth.

"So they tell me."

"No, I mean, I think it's all fine that you know how to fix things. These mechanics seem to appreciate it and all. I figure if I know too much about what keeps these things up in the air, it just gives me something else to worry about. If I hear some strange noise, I tell the mechanic about it. If I'm at ten thousand feet, and I know that the noise means something bad, well, it'll just scare me."

Lufbery slid another shell into the drum, leaned back against the wheel of the Nieuport.

"Ignorance is bliss?"

Rockwell smiled. "Suppose so. I'd rather leave it all in God's hands. If it's my time, not much I can do about it anyway."

Lufbery looked again to the metal box, pulled out another shell.

Rockwell stood, said, "The captain said you were going up a little later. By yourself?"

"I want to test my gun, work on some ground targets maybe."

"Keep an eye out up top. You know what can happen."

Rockwell moved away, and Lufbery wiped at his brow again, the sweat soaking the collar of his shirt. He examined another shell, tossed it aside, thought, God's hands. If that makes you happy, not much I can say. I'd rather worship the well-tuned motor and the well-oiled machine gun.

He rose up through a dense haze, a swirling wind that rocked and bounced the plane. The wind was from the north and east, unusual, and the clouds of dust and smoke rose from the great expanse of desolate ground around Verdun. There had been a brief lull in the fighting, and though Lufbery knew nothing of tactics and strategy, he had guessed that both sides were probably drained as much by the heat of the sun as by the heat of the fight.

He headed north, had expected to fly low, but the smoke and glare was blinding him through the goggles. He circled, drove the plane higher, could feel the updrafts from the heat, the plane still rocking, dipping into air pockets made worse by the heat. After a long few minutes, the air was cooler, the motion of the plane smoothing out, the smoke now below him. The sky above was sharp and blue, no clouds anywhere, and he circled again, thought, Hardly the time to test the guns. Not much to shoot at up here.

Lufbery glanced at the altimeter, had passed twelve thousand feet, the chill finding him again, his feet already turning numb. He curled his toes, flexed them, anything to keep the circulation going. As much as he loved flying, the frustration had become constant, so many patrols, with nothing to show for it. He banked hard to the right, could barely see the ground, caught a glimpse of fire, something burning, a narrow stream of black

102

smoke extending westward. It had always been an odd sensation flying over the combat zones, so far removed from so much that was happening below. Even today, he thought, this hot insufferable day, and someone must die, some artilleryman still doing his job, taking aim at what was probably a truck. And some poor jerk, thinking it was safe to drive around in the daylight, that everyone was, what? Taking a holiday? He stared down at the black smoke, shook his head, no, you don't know what happened, and it's not for you to ridicule the dead. You're just in a damned foul mood.

He was heading south now, back toward Behonne, dropped the nose slightly, thought, Well, hell, might as well go home. He scanned the sky above him, instinct, then looked below, the sun slightly behind him. He saw a single reflection, far below, his heart suddenly leaping in his chest. He nosed the plane down steeper, a single aeroplane, moving west. Could be French, an observer, heading home, he thought. Not much to see today.

He turned the Nieuport to move in directly behind the plane, could see now it was large, thought, It's an observer, certainly. Two-seater. The wings were flecked in camouflage, and his heart jumped again. In the midst of the camouflage were two black crosses.

He was still nosing downward, gaining rapidly on the larger plane, both of them now moving through the smoky haze. He gripped the stick with one tight fist, glanced up at the Lewis gun, the drum of bullets, polished and perfect. He focused on the man in the back, the observer, could see a machine gun hanging to one side, the man not seeing him, never suspecting anyone else was up here with him. The Nieuport was straight behind the two-seater now, and he tried to measure the distance, a hundred yards, less, closer still. His heart was rattling hard in his chest, and he reached up, felt for the Lewis gun, pulled up just slightly on the stick, the Nieuport rising, then he brought the nose back down, the observer standing, seeing him now, reaching for the machine gun. Lufbery squeezed the trigger, the Lewis gun chattering above him. The observer was down in the cockpit, the German plane twisting to one side now, and Lufbery stayed close, his finger hard on the trigger, emptied the drum, the number in his mind, forty-seven, forty-seven. . . .

The two-seater was coming apart in front of him, began to spin, black smoke trailing in a corkscrew behind it. Lufbery followed, but the plane was falling rapidly. He pushed the Nieuport into a steep dive, could see nothing but smoke and haze, glanced at the altimeter, the plane now dropping below four thousand feet. He eased up on the stick, then banked hard, could still see the twist of black smoke, the German pilot out of control. He dove again, and now he saw it, the bright flash on the ground, and he brought the Nieuport into a wide circle, saw thick woods, flames erupting through the tops of the trees.

He leveled the plane, realized his hands were shaking. He stared at the fire, tried to see something else, anything, some details. He stared ahead now, began to feel sick, thought, There is nothing to see. You killed two men. I will never know if they died from the bullets, or from the fire. Should it matter? I hope it was the bullets. Forty-seven. Should have been enough. They were so close. The voice in his mind was manic, trying to distract him from what he had seen. He took a long deep breath, let the sharp wind from the prop push him back against the seat. The stirring in his gut was calmer now, and he focused on his job, looked at the compass, turned the plane to the south. He searched for landmarks, suddenly felt a cold shock. He looked up, searched the sky above him, turned as far as he could in the seat, looked behind him, banked the plane hard, as if to catch the surprise of the enemy on his tail. But there was no one, the sky above him empty. His hands were shaking again, and he said aloud, "Thank God."

The ground was familiar now, a small shattered village beside a muddy river, a broken and battered church. He knew Behonne was ten miles to the southwest. He began to climb up toward the smoother air, watched the compass turn as he turned. Two of them. I killed two of them.

The sickness had passed, and he began to feel something else, wanted to get back to the field, to see them all, tell them what had happened. It will be a celebration, he thought. Unless they don't believe me. They must. Surely they know I would not lie. But no one else was here; no one else saw.

He stared ahead, searched the smoky horizon for the field. He was angry now, thought of the teasing, the smiling faces, Thaw and Rockwell, Prince, all the rest. Well, to hell with them. They don't have to believe me at all. I know what happened today.

He simmered for a long few minutes, stared ahead at the spires of Bar-le-Duc, banked the plane in the familiar landing pattern. He brought the Nieuport straight in, bounced hard, a sloppy landing. He felt defiant, was ready for them, was surprised to see them coming, pilots and mechanics, hands in the air. He looked for Thenault, saw him now, expected some sort of tirade. Hell, you told me I could go. I don't want to hear any damned dressing-down. He shut off the motor, the plane rolling to a stop, and they were around him now, smiles and cheers, men slapping the sides of the plane. Thenault ran up beside him, shouted, "They saw you! The plane fell inside our lines! You are confirmed!"

He pulled the helmet off, stood up in the cockpit, "What? Who?"

"The infantry observers. They saw the German go down in the woods. They saw the whole thing! They identified you from the Indian on the aeroplane! They telephoned just a few minutes ago!"

Thaw was there now, held out a beefy hand.

"Congratulations, Luf!"

Rockwell was smiling at him, said, "I told them about your bullets. I bet you didn't misfire a one of them!"

Thenault stepped back, made room for Lufbery to climb from the plane. He jumped down, and they were on him now, hands on his back, cheers and smiling faces. He moved with them toward the hangar, heard all the congratulations, the questions, knew he would tell the story all night long, thought, Hell, I killed two Germans. After all, isn't that the point?

In the next week, Lufbery's fortunes changed dramatically, wiping away the months of frustration. The day after his first confirmed kill, he scored again, another two-seater. Within a week he had shot down two more. The Aeronautique Militaire was quick to reward the sudden success of the American pilot, and Lufbery was astonished to receive the French Croix de Guerre, and the Médaille Militaire. If the American Escadrille hoped to receive attention back home, some recognition that might inspire more Americans to take up the cause, Lufbery had opened the door. In a few short weeks, a copy of *The New York Times* was sent to Bar-le-Duc, a headline that regaled its readers with all manner of heroic exploits, some of them embarrassingly exaggerated. Lufbery had suddenly put them on the map. But the pilots always welcomed the excuse to tease one of their own. To their gleeful delight the *Times* had referred to him as "Loveberry."

6

RICHTHOFEN

Near Kovel, Russia—August 1916

His bombs had missed the bridge, but he had not thought of blaming the observer. His attention had been drawn instead to the chaos that spread below him, and he watched in amazement as an entire regiment of Cossack cavalry scattered away from the river. Men were tumbling from horses, their mounts running wildly to escape the strange horror of this great terrifying machine. His observer was patting him on the back, and Richthofen nodded, waggled the wings, the signal that the supply of bombs had been exhausted, the machine gun nearly empty. He swung the plane around in a wide arc, one last look at the Cossacks below, a crowd of Russian infantry gathering upriver, some of the men uselessly firing their rifles in his general direction. He paid more attention to the bridge, untouched, his bombs either splashing harmlessly in the river, or punching black smoking holes in the riverbanks. It didn't matter if the fault lay with the observer, or with his own flying. The target had been missed. He clenched his fist, would probably not come out this way for a while, knew he had missed his one opportunity. It would be the observer's job to make the report to headquarters, and the man would certainly paint a glowing portrait: hundreds of enemy troops sent into panic. Headquarters would be pleased, would judge the mission a success. But Richthofen had missed the bridge. The hunter had failed to find his prey.

He had been a hunter all his life, had spent most of his youth in the woods that were a part of his family's estate. Even now, when his friends in the squadron would take advantage of the tempting distractions of Berlin, Richthofen would go instead to the forests, would seek out the homes of those who enjoyed the land as he did. It was a treat for the local gentry to host this new kind of soldier, the man who flew the wondrous aeroplanes. He would spend long days stalking the deer and wild boar that filled the forests, but then, would surprise his hosts by not sharing the feast afterward. He rarely ate meat, saw nothing of reward in consuming the animal he had shot. He had always been an exceptional marksman, had no patience for sloppiness, for the men who shot at every movement, who would empty their rifles at a running beast. As his hosts soon learned, if he wasn't close enough to bring the hunt to a perfect conclusion, he wouldn't shoot. There was always tomorrow.

The sun was setting in front of him, and in the distance he could see a thick red fog, signs of some fight, artillery perhaps, or even other bombers. The smoke had spread skyward, shading the landscape beneath him, and he spent long minutes studying the ground for some glimpse of the fields where the fighting had been. It was always a curiosity to him, the networks of trenches, rows of barbed wire, so much confusion and chaos to those on the ground, so clearly defined and even beautiful from the air. It was an observation made by many others long before he had flown, and the sky over every battlefield was flecked with aircraft, many with no more weaponry than the simple camera. From the first days of the war, the aeroplanes had been used as a new and invaluable set of eyes, the observer's job to photograph every square foot of ground, to give the commanders a view that no general could ever see. Some were used by the artillery commanders, to locate targets, signaling the men who aimed the great guns, guiding them to a perfect kill. But as the value of the cameras became known, so too did the urgency of killing the cameramen, and the observation planes had soon become equipped with machine guns of their own, to ward off the certain attack by the new squadrons of fighter planes. The use of aeroplanes was quickly becoming a war of its own, separate from the awful destruction that spilled out over the ground beneath them.

Even on the most routine missions, Richthofen had thoroughly enjoyed the godlike serenity, the strange feeling of dominance over all that was below. But all of that had become routine, and he wondered about the fighter pilots, the men who flew the new single-wing Fokker Eindecker, or the sturdy, tough Albatros, planes that were designed for only one purpose, to seek and destroy the enemy in the air. The names of the pilots were becoming familiar, the men who not only survived the new kind of war, but flourished, who consistently sent enemy planes out of the sky in fiery crashes. The legends grew first in the trenches, the foot soldiers who stared up in fascination at the spinning and swirling fights above them, who cheered the victor, even if they had no idea which side had prevailed. But headquarters knew, and the newspapers were given the names, and now every pilot of the war had learned of the men who were a new kind of hero.

The first had been Max Immelmann, the first German to conceive of the aeroplane as a bayonet in the air, who had mastered the maneuvers that had changed the way air battles were fought. They called his method the "Immelmann Turn," pulling the plane up and over in a loop, then rolling upright, so that the pursued was suddenly face-to-face with his pursuer. Immelmann had shot down an astonishing fifteen enemy planes, but in June, Immelmann himself had been shot down by the British, and the Fatherland had lost its first great warrior of the air.

Richthofen eased the plane into a slow circle, aimed for the leading edge of the wide, flat field. He knew the observer was terrified, the man comfortable with every part of the flight except the landing. Richthofen smiled, dipped the nose of the plane, the ground coming up quick, then he pulled back on the stick just so, the nose coming up, the plane settling down gently. He reached for the switch, cut the engine, the prop jerking to a stop, the plane dropping the last couple of feet to the ground with a spongy bounce. He nodded, thought, How was that one, old boy?

He took pride in his flying, had come to feel each plane as a part of himself, adjusting to each craft's own personality. They were all different, each one an individual. The pilots were loud in their opinions, which planes were better, but Richthofen was comfortable in either the Fokker or the Albatros. He had listened with silent impatience to the pilots who complained about their "boxes," had believed more often than not that if a man had difficulty flying his plane, it was his own fault. But when the beer loosened the tongues, and the pilots competed with each other over the right to complain, Richthofen would remember why he preferred the solitude of the forests.

The plane rolled to a stop, and he was surprised to see several men running toward him, some waving. He raised his goggles, lifted himself up, one leg swinging out onto the side of the plane. They were close now, excited voices, "Manfred! Captain Boelcke's coming! He'll be here tonight! Boelcke himself!"

The name shot through him and he said, "Boelcke? Here? Why?"

"He's visiting his brother, wants to share dinner with the squadron. You will come, yes?"

He jumped down from the plane, unstrapped his helmet, looked at the faces, suspected a joke. "Oh, certainly, I will be there. I am positive the great Boelcke has come to this odd corner of nowhere *just* to have a meal with his brother."

The men seemed unaware of his sarcasm, began to move away, flowing back toward the barnlike hangar. The mechanics were there now, hovering around the plane like two bees at a flower.

"Any problems with her, Lieutenant?"

He glanced back. "I smelled a bit more oil than usual. Nothing else."

He followed the others, knew there would be heat and much beer in their quarters, saw his observer already telling his friends of the great victory over the fleeing Russian cavalry. Richthofen would make his own report, matter-of-fact, the enemy regiment diverted, delayed in their crossing of the river, certainly something the commanders would appreciate. He did not think of the bridge now, knew that no one would care except him.

His quarters were simple and crude, and they prompted much talk behind his back. He had pitched a large tent in the thick

110

woods that ran up to the edge of the aerodrome, preferred to sleep to the sounds of the night. There had been jokes of course, the man who hated the indoors, but it was old now, the others used to his lack of social enthusiasm. It was not the men who drove him to the tent, something they had not understood at first. He was not rude or unfriendly, was happy to accept their invitations to dinner, would even share a beer afterward. But the other pilots seemed too willing to use the nighttime as the excuse for celebration, and he placed much more value on sleep. For him, the day began well before the first light, and he would be airborne before the sun rose. It was the most glorious time of day, the soft red glow spreading out before him as he prowled the air near the Russian lines. It was different in the West, the French and Belgian countryside so often obliterated by fog. It had been maddening to him, to be forced to sit and wait beside his plane, staring into thick gray soup. No pilot could risk flying above the fog, the vast blanket that would hide not only your target, but the route home, and, possibly, the aerodrome itself. The pilots all knew that if the fog surprised them, rolled in at sunset, there could be nowhere to go, nothing to do but wait helplessly as you exhausted your fuel. It wasn't the thought of the crash that bothered him. He had already smashed up more than one training craft, had walked away sheepishly from broken aeroplanes that had stood up on their noses, victims of his mistakes. The mishaps were a part of every pilot's training, so many hours in the air, but those days were far behind him. He was far more terrified of dying with no meaning, some foolish error, or a mechanical problem that would bring the ground rushing up to kill you for no good reason. He could not imagine a worse way to die.

He had made some effort to understand the workings of the planes, from the delicate temperament of the machine guns to the motors themselves. Too often, the pilots seemed to treat the low-ranking men with disdain, had casual disrespect for the men who dirtied their hands. But no matter how many times he had studied the manuals or put his hands into black grease, it was not a talent Richthofen would ever master. To him, the mechanics were the most important members of the squadron.

The men of the squadron began to move through the hangar area, toward their quarters. They were housed in a row of railroad cars, brought up close to the aerodrome, the most rapid and efficient means of moving the squadron should the need arise. The planes themselves were often carried by train, an odd bit of illogic that Richthofen didn't question. The men had simply made the railcars their home, shared their meals in a dining car. He was still skeptical of their enthusiasm, could hear the men rehearsing their questions, all the guidance they would seek from the great Boelcke. He stepped out past the train, hopped across the tracks, followed the familiar trail to his tent. He wiped at the black grime on his face, thought, Well, of course, if he really is coming, I suppose I should clean up a bit.

Oswald Boelcke had replaced Max Immelmann as Germany's most prolific flying ace. The two men had been in competition until Immelmann's death, and Boelcke had continued his amazing string of victories, downing more than two dozen enemy planes. Richthofen had followed his exploits, had memorized every account he could find in the papers. He thought of Boelcke as more than some sort of national hero, had imagined himself often in Boelcke's place, envied the man who must surely be the finest pilot of the war. All the pilots spoke of Boelcke with reverence, and not even the loud talkers dared to compare themselves to Germany's great ace.

It was the kaiser who seemed to understand Boelcke's value to Germany beyond his accomplishments in his plane. Not long after Immelmann's death, Boelcke had been ordered out of the sky, was thought to be far more useful as an inspiration to troops and pilots on every front. Boelcke had been sent to aerodromes in nearly every theater of the war, and Richthofen had read about the man's recent journey to Turkey. Richthofen had wondered about Boelcke's reaction to all of that, the great fighter suddenly reduced to an instrument of public relations. You don't teach men how to be efficient pilots by holding up one man as an example. Boelcke would surely know that. It's simply propaganda. It must be driving him mad.

He reached his tent, stepped inside, looked toward the small table, a shallow metal bowl filled with soapy water, the washcloth folded neatly to one side. There was a burst of motion from under the bed, his dog exploding into a slobbering welcome. He smiled, caught the dog as the huge front paws came up onto Richthofen's chest.

"Very good, Moritz! You wait for me like I instructed! Now, sit down!"

The dog obeyed reluctantly, and Richthofen moved toward the soapy water. He had not seen his orderly, but the man had done his work, a fresh bowl of water for Moritz, and the soapy one for himself. He wiped the oily crust from his face, the cold water refreshing, waking him. The dog sat up, whimpered slightly, and Richthofen turned toward him, said, "You cannot fool me, my friend. I know that Corporal Menzke has fed you. Now, sit quietly."

The dog seemed to understand Richthofen's command, sank down to its belly.

He had purchased the dog as a puppy, and though he knew the breed, he had not quite expected the young Great Dane to grow into such an enormous beast. Dogs did not serve well as mascots, some of them wandering tragically into the propeller of their master's plane. Moritz had been among those, but he survived the encounter, had lost only half of one ear. Richthofen had simply clipped the other one to match. The dog slept in his tent every night, and when Richthofen was not flying, the dog stayed close to him nearly everywhere he went. When Moritz had been much smaller, Richthofen had even carried him on board a two-seater, the dog enjoying the flight as much as Richthofen himself. But Moritz' days as copilot had ended. The dog was simply too big to fit in the plane.

Moritz rolled over now, hopeful of a brisk rub, and Richthofen leaned down and obliged him. It was their ritual, the dog begging for the undeserved meal, Richthofen rewarding him only with a playful rub of the dog's upturned belly.

He noticed a clean uniform on the narrow bed, polished boots below, more good work from his orderly. He stood up, pointed, the dog moving obediently to the far corner of the tent. Well, more evidence that everyone around here believes Boelcke is coming. All right then, we shall see.

* * *

"A toast to the Fatherland's finest air warrior!"

"A salute!"

Boelcke had indeed arrived, and all evening long, the wine had flowed freely. Richthofen had watched Boelcke carefully, could see the man was growing weary of the celebration. He glanced toward Boelcke's brother, Wilhelm, the senior pilot in the squadron, wondered if Wilhelm was jealous of his younger, far more famous brother. Wilhelm was raising his glass with the others, seemed to share their revelry, and Richthofen obliged as well, his glass in the air.

It was typical to assume that a great war hero carried some age with his experience, but Boelcke was only twenty-five, and he seemed younger still, a clean-cut boyishness that gave no hint of his extraordinary talent for killing the enemy. Richthofen could see fatigue on Boelcke's face, the smiles and appreciation forced now, and Richthofen wondered if the attention and endless toasting had become tediously commonplace. Richthofen had not been as boisterous as some of the other men, and he could feel that the evening was nearly concluded. If he was to speak to Boelcke it would have to be soon. He had fought for the courage all evening, wanted to ask what the man knew that made him so very good at what he did.

"Allow me, um. Excuse me."

The faces turned to him, some of the men surprised that he had spoken up at all.

"My apologies, Captain Boelcke, but I have wanted . . . perhaps we have all wanted to inquire. Can you offer this gathering some gift of your skill, some instruction we might follow?"

He was immediately embarrassed, the room suddenly dead silent. Of course, it was the question they all wanted to ask. Boelcke smiled, surprising him, said, "Very simple, Lieutenant. I get close to my prey, aim well, and when I shoot him, he falls down."

The others laughed, wineglasses raised, but Richthofen did not share the humor. Boelcke nodded toward him, the smile gone, and Richthofen understood. It was not a joke.

* * *

The party continued long after Richthofen had retired. He was expecting to rise early, another mission toward the Russian lines. He sat on his cot in the darkness, pulling on his boots, knew that his observer would be up as well, would be waiting for him beside the plane. He heard voices, listened, heard Menzke, his orderly, and another man. He stood, moved to the opening in his tent, raised the flap, peered out. There was lantern light, and, walking beside Menzke, a man in uniform. It was Boelcke.

"Excuse me, Lieutenant. I regret the early hour, but then I am told that you are often in the air at daybreak. I share the habit. May I speak with you?"

It was the first time Richthofen had been embarrassed that his quarters was a tent.

"By all means, Captain. Please, um, if you would like, come inside."

He backed into the tent, unsure, but Boelcke seemed not to notice the humble surroundings. Menzke handed Richthofen the lantern, said simply, "Sir." The orderly disappeared into the darkness. Boelcke looked toward the huge hulk sleeping in the corner of the tent, seemed to hesitate, and Richthofen said, "My dog, sir. He will not disturb us. Please, sit."

"I will not occupy your time more than necessary, Lieutenant. As you know, I am on my way back to Berlin. It has become part of my job to visit aero squadrons along the way. I thought it especially important to come here."

"Yes, sir. Your brother is a fine officer. It is a pleasure to serve with him."

Boelcke smiled. "Yes, I enjoy visiting with Wilhelm. But that is not entirely the reason for my visit. I have been urging Berlin to allow me to return to flying. I am not comfortable being some sort of symbol. I believe that I may best serve my country by fighting the enemy. My wishes have finally been heard, and I am delighted that my plans have been approved."

Richthofen felt an odd sense of relief, said, "I am pleased for you, sir. Though it is not my place to question the wishes of the High Command."

Boelcke smiled, held up a hand. "Please be at ease,

Lieutenant. Are you aware that in the West, the enemy is rapidly gaining superiority over our air forces?"

Richthofen was surprised at Boelcke's frankness. "No, sir. I have not heard anything of that."

"No, it is not something the High Command discusses with newspapers. However, it is true. I have been authorized to confront the problem directly. It is my intention to form an elite fighter squadron whose sole purpose is to hunt down enemy planes, be they fighters, bombers, or observers. Berlin has given me a free hand in selecting those pilots I consider worthy of the job." Richthofen felt a stirring in his stomach, and Boelcke continued. "I have had considerable discussion with my brother about the pilots in this command. What I require are men who have a natural ability to control their aeroplane, whose performance in the air is not injured by their behavior on the ground. I am not interested in men who are prone to speak loudly of their accomplishments. This has nothing to do with glory and newspapers. I require men of discipline and focus and aggressive spirit. We will have one mission, Lieutenant: Kill the enemy. Shoot his planes out of the air."

Richthofen felt his own excitement growing, matching the fire in Boelcke's words.

"Sir, is there an opportunity for a pilot of my abilities? I believe I have the experience. . . . I would prefer nothing more—"

"The decision has already been made, Lieutenant. Prepare your baggage. We leave immediately."

7

RICHTHOFEN

Near Lagnicourt, France—September 17, 1916

His job was to stay in formation, close on Boelcke's right. There were four planes in the patrol, the number decided by Boelcke himself, the mission, the technique all determined by the captain. Boelcke had continued his amazing string of successes, had used his mastery of the air not only to decimate the British air forces he encountered, but to educate the young men who were still very much his students. He had shot down nearly thirty aircraft. The lessons were being learned by his students firsthand.

At dinner the night before, Richthofen had been chosen for today's squadron, had been surprised and enormously relieved. He had observed Boelcke sitting in quiet judgment of his students, more than once caught Boelcke staring at him, appraising his responses to the lessons. It was quickly obvious to all of the young pilots that the captain placed a high priority on their mechanical aptitude, that a pilot's survival might depend on his ability to repair his plane. It had always been Richthofen's primary weakness, and beyond the mechanics of the plane itself, Richthofen still didn't completely grasp the working of the machine guns. The Albatroses were equipped with two Maxims, the latest incarnation of the efficient weapon used with such deadly skill by German infantrymen. The guns' ammunition was fed by a continuous cloth belt, the number of shells determined only by how much weight the Albatros could carry. Richthofen had been impressed when he saw the belts being folded into the boxes beside the motor, a thousand shells at a time.

The new planes also used the ingenious technology of the

interrupter gear, which to Richthofen was a mechanical wonder. But he knew that Boelcke was not pleased that this one lieutenant could barely figure out how to unjam his guns.

They flew near ten thousand feet, and as the sun rose behind them, Richthofen looked frequently to his left, could see Boelcke's head always in motion, studying every part of the sky around them. The mission was simple: find enemy planes and shoot them down. Richthofen stared ahead, a few low clouds just now catching the first glow from the rising sun. He looked out to the right, into empty space, more clouds, frowned, saw no one else, nothing to disturb the tranquillity of the morning sky.

The Albatros hummed beneath him, the motor tuned flawlessly, the cables tight, no rattles, no vibration. It was another result of Boelcke's influence, this time on the mechanics. Boelcke gave them all a strong sense of the team, every man's job crucial. No plane left the airfield without a thorough grooming.

Richthofen glanced up, more empty sky, felt a clenching emptiness in his stomach. There must be someone out here. Perhaps they know we are coming. Surely there are spies. He smiled at the thought; well, it could be so. Captain Boelcke is well known on both sides now. Perhaps today the British will stay home. Fortunate for the British.

He knew Boelcke had no patience for boastfulness, but Richthofen was inside his own mind now, enjoyed an unusual moment of playfulness, could not help feeling the strength of the man who flew beside him, the pure power of the man's skill. Certainly that must affect those men out there, those men who know that if they take to the air, today might be the day they meet the great Boelcke.

The lessons had been drilled and drilled again, from the formation they flew in now to Boelcke's rules of engaging the enemy. Richthofen had never been a good student, despised classrooms and lecturing, but he had grasped at every word that came from Boelcke. They learned every detail about the planes they flew, and those of the British and French, their strengths and weaknesses, comparisons in maneuverability and speed.

Boelcke focused on the pilots, the skills each man must have, coordination, dexterity, quick reflexes. Only when a pilot understood his own limitations, and those of his plane, would Boelcke impart the most difficult lesson to teach: how to make the kill. The rules rolled through Richthofen's thoughts: Do not be seen, come in from behind, use the sun to hide yourself, wait for the enemy to focus his attentions elsewhere. Don't waste your ammunition by shooting at him from too great a distance. Surprise is everything: see him before he sees you.

Richthofen stared out to the horizon again, thought of the emphasis Boelcke placed on eyesight, clarity of vision. Well, of course, you must be able to see. And right now, I don't see anything.

Boelcke was suddenly in motion beside him, rocking his plane, tilting his wings. Richthofen's heart jumped, and he saw Boelcke point, a gloved hand motioning to the right. He stared that way, the sun reflecting off a low, fat cloud, and then, a brief flicker of light, then more, and now Richthofen could see a mass of dark specks, tried to count, eight, ten, then more. He looked back toward Boelcke, who moved his plane out in front of the others, and Boelcke made a hand signal, up, gain altitude. Richthofen was confused for a moment, looked again toward the distant planes, counted again . . . more than a dozen, clearly visible now. *Fourteen*. Boelcke's Albatros was already rising above him, and Richthofen followed, thought, Why do we wait? He ran Boelcke's rules through his mind, the sun is behind us, surely they do not see us . . . but Boelcke was higher still, and Richthofen silenced the questions in his mind. Just follow him, Lieutenant.

They circled to gain altitude, rose up far above the British planes, and Boelcke led them in a sweeping arc, kept a wide distance from the enemy. Richthofen waited for the sign, saw Boelcke motioning now, ordering them to straighten out. The four Albatroses were now in line directly behind and above the British squadron, simply following them. Richthofen kept in formation as precisely as he could, his Albatros responding perfectly to his subtle commands. He kept looking toward Boelcke, and the captain seemed to sense the excitement of his students, more hand signals. Wait. Richthofen stared down, tried to see details of the British planes. Boelcke's lessons echoed in his head again, and he could see the different sizes and configurations, a cluster of eight in the center of the formation, much larger planes. The other six seemed to surround them, and now it was clear to him: bombers, and their fighter escorts. The British formation did not waver, completely unaware of the pursuers above them, and Boelcke repeated the hand signals, stay back, no fight.

They followed the British squadron deeper into German territory, and Richthofen's curiosity was digging at him. He pulled out a small stiff map from a pocket beside him, then glanced at the compass. They are heading for . . . Marcoing. There is a railway depot there. He glanced down, searched for smoke, a plume of gray always to be found somewhere. He spotted one now, spreading out in a low fan toward the east. They had a tailwind. He smiled, looked over at Boelcke, who ignored him now, the captain staring straight at the enemy far down in front of them. Richthofen followed Boelcke's gaze, understood the routine of the British mission. They will drop their bombs, and then return to their bases. But they will face a strong headwind. They will consume their fuel, and so they will not be able to maneuver away from us for very long. Even if the fighters could escape, the bombers are slow and clumsy and cannot be left behind. He smiled, a hard grip on the controls. And then we will have them.

The bombers began to change formation, a maneuver Richthofen knew well. They were beginning their bombing run. He could see Marcoing now, partially hidden by low clouds, saw the larger planes dropping away, disappearing as they made their dives toward their targets. The air around the British was speckled with white dots now, antiaircraft fire coming from the ground. He began to think of the railroad depot and the men who worked there. What must be happening there? We could have attacked them before they reached Marcoing, stopped their mission. He looked over toward Boelcke, saw him concentrating on the action below them, and Richthofen thought, It was his decision. We could have attacked them before, but then we might not have had the advantage we will have now. He stared down, could see nothing of bombs and bullets, of the men dying. He scolded himself, Stop this! You have your mission. It is likely that the bombers missed their targets. He remembered Russia, that damned bridge, the panicking Cossacks. That day, he had no antiaircraft guns to contend with, and below, he could see that the gunners at Marcoing were pouring out a heavy fire. That will make the bombers lay their eggs too quickly, no time to be precise.

He realized now that the signs of the fight were out behind him, Boelcke leading them out to the east of the British bombardment. Boelcke waggled his wings, and Richthofen focused on the hand signals: circle. And wait.

They banked the planes into wide arcing turns, guided by the direction of the sun, and the blanket of smoke drifting above Marcoing. Now Boelcke straightened them out again, and the sun was behind them. Richthofen strained to see below, gray smoke rising higher through the low clouds. The British should be returning home now. It doesn't take long to complete this kind of mission. He glanced at Boelcke, saw him waving, pointing, and then, one last signal. *Dive*.

Richthofen pushed the stick forward, clamped his jaw tight, the wind ripping at him, the goggles pressed hard against his face. He searched the clouds below, could see what Boelcke saw now, a ragged formation coming together, the fighters gathering up the bombers, herding their flock, their mission complete. The British planes were all moving west, the sun at their back, blinding them to what might be behind them. Richthofen saw one fighter, out to the right of the squadron, eased his hand to the single trigger that would unleash the Maxims. The Albatros was closing the distance rapidly, and he could see the British plane in detail now, a two-seater, thought, A Vickers! His heart danced in his chest, his hand shaking, the cold slicing through his gloves, his finger hovering just off the trigger. The plane's insignia was clearly visible now, the rainbow circles on the wings, two blind eyes staring up at him. He could see the two brown dots behind the top wing, the pilot and the man behind him, the observer. There was a machine gun mounted on the edge of the observer's seat, hanging limply over the side of the plane, the men still with no idea of their fate. The Albatros screamed downward, and the Vickers seemed to grow, wide and fat, a great slow bird hanging in front of him. He tried to judge the distance, but he was close enough now, less than a hundred meters, then closer still, and he knew it was time. He pulled the trigger, the Maxims chattering in front of him, a rain of spent shells whistling past him. He expected the Vickers simply to drop, but the observer stood up quickly, turned toward him, the machine gun now in the man's hands. Richthofen could see the flashes from the muzzle, the Albatros still gaining rapidly on the British plane. He stared for one frozen moment, the Vickers within thirty meters, closer, the gunner firing straight at him. His hands jerked at the stick, the Albatros spinning to one side, the Vickers now above him, turning about, the gunner still firing at him. Richthofen dropped the plane into a cloud, his hands shaking, the sounds of his heart tearing through his head. Damn! He stared at the white blindness for a long moment, took a deep breath. He thought of Boelcke, the others, had no idea what they were doing. He was embarrassed, thought, Thirty meters! And you missed! He tried to guess how much ammunition he had used, how much was left, thought, It was very fast, surely, not many shots. He banked the plane hard, said aloud, "It is not yet over!"

He emerged from the cloud, was amazed to see planes in every part of the sky, smoke and streaks of fire. The bombers were in a dense crowd below him, self-protection, their escorts darting above, fending off their attackers. He stared at the bombers, an easy target, thought of the pilots, terrified men, wondering if their protection would survive. The bombers had observers as well, probably the same mounted machine gun, but they were too slow, would be easy prey for the Albatros. He pushed his hand against the stick, the nose easing down, the bombers right below him. He could see the pilots and their observers, staring up at the great war in the sky above them. He glanced up, realized now, the Vickers was still above him, was turning away, seeking some new target. The bombers were forgotten now, and he gripped the stick, the nose coming back up, and he laughed, nervous, excited. He did not see me. He doesn't know I'm here!

He was surprised how much slower the Vickers was, one of Boelcke's lessons coming back to him. It was the great advantage of both the Fokkers and the new Albatroses, the larger and more efficient motor. He held the nose up, kept beneath the tail, out of sight of the British observer. He eased closer still, the Maxims pointing up into the motor of the Vickers, then back, just a bit . . . the cockpit . . . fifty meters, thirty. Now! The Maxims made a long burst, the underside of the Vickers ripped in two long tears. He was nearly into the tail of the British plane, pulled hard to the side, rolled away, a tight banking turn, was quickly out of range. But he pushed the Albatros forward, easing up closer again, expected to see the observer firing, but the machine gun was hanging limp, the man not visible at all. He could see one small round lump, the head of the pilot, low in the cockpit. He kept closing, and suddenly, the Vickers seemed to freeze in the air, the propeller coming to an abrupt stop. Richthofen raised the nose of the Albatros, streaked by the Vickers, a brief glimpse of the pilot, the man still holding tight to his controls. The Vickers fell away now, cutting sideways through the air, losing altitude rapidly. He turned the Albatros, dove down, followed. Boelcke's words came to him, Beware the trick. The British pride themselves on aerobatics, will spin their plane as though they are dead, then bring her back to life far below you. And if you are not aware, then you will be the prey! He followed the Vickers down, could see the pilot moving, the wings jerking wildly, the man clearly struggling to keep it in the air. Richthofen noticed the ground now, surprising him, the first time he had thought of that. He eased the nose of the Albatros up slightly, looked at the altitude gauge, six hundred meters, pulled up into a shallower dive. The Vickers kept falling, but then the plane seemed to level out, slowing, then suddenly it was on the ground, a sliding cascading wreck, the plane breaking into pieces, pancaking on smooth ground, spinning slightly, then coming to a stop. He wanted to shout, something, words not coming, the sudden thrill overwhelming him, a moment of pure joy. He punched his fist in the air, then eased the Albatros around in a wide circle, studying the wreckage. He was surprised to see troops emerging from a thick row of brush, gray uniforms. German troops! They began to wave at him, some running for the wreckage, and he eyed the open field, smooth grass, slipped the Albatros lower, flew closer to the ground, only a few feet above the wreckage. The troops backed away now, scrambling to the edge of the open field. He was laughing, still punched at the air, eyed the field, thought, Grass, no stumps or, please God, no holes. He moved out beyond the end of the field, eased the plane around, aimed the nose toward the wrecked Vickers. He cut the motor, the plane easing down the last few feet, the wheels bumping hard, the plane tilting to one side, the wingtips nearly hitting the ground. He pulled at the stick, bounced again, and the plane was rolling now, then stopped a few yards from the wreckage. He was up and out of the plane as the soldiers swarmed around him, some cheering him, others surrounding the wrecked Vickers. He jumped down into soft grass, ran with them, reached the Vickers, stopped, saw a man on the ground crawling from the wreckage, pushing himself with one leg, the other dragging behind him. His clothes were bloody, one arm shattered, barely attached to his body. Richthofen shouted to the soldiers, some of the men already up on the wreckage, "Stop! Get back!"

The hard authority in his voice halted them, the soldiers backing away. The man still struggled toward him, dragging his leg, his helmet ripped, goggles gone, and the man looked up at him now, said something Richthofen couldn't understand, seemed to point behind him. Richthofen stepped past him, saw another man's hand, a sleeve, protruding from beneath the wreck. He motioned to the soldiers, "Lift, here!"

The men obeyed, the plane tilting, and he could see the observer now, the man crumpled low in his cockpit, his goggles still in place, his clothing soaked in blood, the man shot through several times. He looked at the pilot again, the man now lying in the soft grass, staring up at him, blinking through the red crust in his eyes. Richthofen said, "Get a litter. This man is still alive."

He backed away, the soldiers moving forward, some probing

and pulling at the wreckage. He walked slowly back to his plane, could see the undercarriage bent and twisted, his Albatros nearly wreckage itself. He thought of Boelcke. I should not have come down here; this was foolish. But it is my first. Surely he will understand. He leaned against his plane, the image of the British observer in his mind. I suppose a man should know what he has done, he thought. There is responsibility here. One of us was to die today. He thought of the observer emptying his machine gun toward him. Yes, one of us was to die today. If you had been a better shot, calmer perhaps, if I had given you more time . . . but it was not to be. This day was mine.

He looked up, could see streaks of smoke in the air, some of the fighting still going on above him. He had the sudden image of horses in his mind, the cavalry, facing your enemy, and leading your men straight into the fight. As a boy he had always hoped to be a cavalryman, but there was a new reality now. Horses do not make good charges into barbed wire and machine-gun fire. He had left the cavalry believing it to be obsolete, a relic of another time. But if the weapons had changed, the art of war had not. He ran his hand along the side of the plane, simply another kind of horse, the obedient servant.

He could see soldiers carrying the litter out of the field, others still milling around the wrecked British plane. He thought, The pilot will die, no doubt. He is too badly wounded. So I killed two men today. The sight of the wounded man had been unexpected, but he was surprised at himself, that he had not really felt any emotion. He looked again at the wreck, could not deny the thrill that still ran through him. He wondered about that now, Am I supposed to feel some kind of sorrow, some regret? No, you have hunted too much, have seen too many wounded animals. A wounded man is no different. The pilot will die soon, and the observer did not suffer at all. Remember that. It is part of the successful hunt. That is, after all, the most important thing.

The dinner that night had been a boisterous affair. All four of Boelcke's planes had claimed a victory. Throughout the evening, the wine had flowed, and Boelcke insisted that each one share every detail of his own engagement with the British fighters. As the students crowed about their accomplishments, Boelcke sat back quietly, allowing them their special moment. Richthofen understood. They were being graded. As the evening drew to a close, Richthofen retired to his small room, expected to rise again before the first light. He was surprised that Boelcke followed him.

Boelcke sat in a small chair, pointed at the bed, a silent command for Richthofen to sit.

"We will not fly tomorrow. The weather in the autumn is usu-ally poor in this part of France." Boelcke paused, and Richthofen still didn't know why he was here. Boelcke rubbed his chin, stared down for a moment, said, "From what I observed, and from your description of your engagement with the enemy, it appears your approach was more aggressive than discreet. When I gave the command to dive, I did not anticipate that you would attempt to devour the enemy plane with your propeller. You claim he didn't see you until you opened fire?"

"Yes, sir." Richthofen felt a burn in his cheeks, realized now that Boelcke had come to admonish him.

"You had sufficient time to prepare a careful and precise attack. Yet you overtook your enemy with such haste that you could not make the fatal shot. When you see a man shooting his gun at you, you can be sure that you have made a mistake. An experienced gunner can kill you with every bullet he fires, every one. You were fortunate he did not shoot well. You were also fortunate that you made your escape into a cloud, that the enemy was not simply waiting for you to emerge from your cover. It was to your advantage that the fighting was all around you. Did you consider that another of the enemy planes might have fallen in behind you?"

Richthofen weighed every word, felt foolish now for his pride. It had never occurred to him that another British fighter might have been coming up behind him. Boelcke stood slowly, moved toward the window, stared out into darkness.

"Why did you land? You caused severe damage to the

undercarriage of your plane. And you abandoned your comrades. Did you consider that your own glory was more important than the lives of the rest of us?"

He could not look at Boelcke now. "Sir, you are correct."

Boelcke spun around, said, "That does not excuse you, Lieutenant. On this day, *we* all returned home. *We* may drink our wine and slap our backsides, and brag about our great skill. Right now, not so many miles from here, the British are mourning their losses. Men died, their aerodrome is quiet. Today belonged to us. Tomorrow . . . who is to say, Lieutenant? But there is one perfect truth to what we do. Not one of us, not me and not you, can hold ourselves up as invincible. We bloodied our enemy today. Tomorrow, he will carry vengeance in his heart, and the memory of fallen comrades. It will drive him and inspire him and make him a better fighter. And if you are not better as well, he will kill you. *He* will circle you as you fall from the sky; *he* will land beside you and gloat over your death. I do not expect you to let that happen."

8

LUFBERY

Paris—September 1916

The squadron had been ordered to leave their hangars at Behonne, and relocate to Luxeuil-les-Bains, closer to the Swiss/German border. Luxeuil was the field where the American Escadrille had first organized, and as a base of flying operations, it was far more sophisticated and much larger than Behonne. The takeoff area was nearly two miles long, and because of the sheer size of the open ground, Luxeuil accommodated several flying squadrons, including a number of British units. But there would be an even more significant change. When the Americans vacated Behonne, they left their Nieuport 11s behind. At Luxeuil, they received their new aircraft, the Nieuport 17. The new plane was larger than the Eleven, with a more powerful motor, thus could climb higher and faster than the tiny *bébés*. Except for Lufbery, most of the pilots paid less attention to the mechanical specifics than to the armament the new planes carried. Finally, they would have the interrupter gear. Even though Lufbery was happily anticipating dirtying his hands with the grease of the new motors, he knew, as they all did, that the antiquated Lewis gun had been replaced by a weapon that could match what they faced from the Germans. And the new guns were belt-fed. Lufbery had every intention of continuing his rigid inspection of his bullets, would still clean and polish every one. But he shared the grateful relief of every man in the squadron, that the nightmare of struggling with the ridiculous drum of the Lewis gun was a thing of the past.

The road to Luxeuil led southward out of Bar-le-Duc, but the squadron first traveled west, to Paris. The holiday had been granted them by the Aeronautique Militaire, in recognition of their fine work, but was also to allow time for the final preparation and delivery of the Nieuport 17s. Once in the city, each man began to explore his desired form of recreation, most of it in the enormous variety of bars and nightclubs that surrounded their hotel. After a week that seemed far too brief, they gathered together again, bleary eyes and vacant smiles, some already talking of their adventures, others struggling in the fog of a deadly hangover to recall exactly what it was they had done.

Lufbery spotted a chair on the far side of the hotel lobby. He moved that way, tried not to step in rhythm to the sharp pounding in his head. He reached the chair, sat slowly, stared blindly at the people who passed. The hotel was busy, but Paris could not hide from the effects of the war, and Lufbery had noticed that many of the guests were foreigners, diplomats and various government types. The uniforms were there as well, and they caught his eye now, brought him into focus. He watched a small gathering, engulfed in a cloud of cigar smoke, saw older men whose chests were blanketed by the adornments of their nations' prestige. Most every uniform he had seen had been accompanied by medals, a great many medals. Lufbery studied the men, heard bits of a language he had not heard in a long time, thought, Greek perhaps. Wouldn't be Turkish. Not here. His brain was weaving in a nonsensical dance, and he lost interest in the costumes of the dignitaries, saw Rockwell suddenly appear, looking as unsteady as Lufbery. Rockwell saw him now, made a feeble wave, crossed the lobby.

"Good morning. It is morning, right?"

Lufbery shook his head, had not thought to look at his watch. "No idea."

Lufbery thought of offering Rockwell his chair, but no part of his body seemed willing to move. Rockwell simply sat on the floor beside him, said, "Where is everybody?"

Lufbery fought through the headache, said, "I heard singing. Think it was Prince."

Rockwell stared down between his knees, said, "I didn't hear anything." He looked up now, took a deep breath. "I am

129

somewhat embarrassed, Luf. Have to admit I never did anything like this before."

"Like what? Have fun?"

Rockwell looked up at him, a goofy, crooked smile. "It was fun, wasn't it? Did you see that girl? The one who kept buying me champagne?"

"The nurse. Yep, I remember her. From New York, she said. Loves all us heroes."

Rockwell's head dropped again, and Lufbery put a hand on his shoulder. "You okay?"

"Not sure I can come back to Paris. Dangerous place."

Lufbery managed a small laugh. "Why? You paid your bill, didn't you?"

Rockwell looked up again. "There was a bill?" He laughed as well, said, "No, well, that's not what I meant. I don't think my folks would have been too proud of their boy last night. Not the sort of thing they taught us at VMI."

Lufbery patted Rockwell's shoulder. "They didn't teach you how to shoot down German aeroplanes either. Nobody can teach you what to expect in a war." Lufbery leaned forward now, rubbed his neck, probed the headache. "I had no idea how badly I needed this. Probably everybody in the squad feels the same way. We've been at it for five months, without a break. It takes a toll. Look what happened to Cowdin."

"I know. A shame. Just couldn't handle it."

Lufbery had tried to stay clear of Elliot Cowdin, a combative, disagreeable man who had been one of the original members of the Escadrille. Cowdin had responded to the pressures of confronting the enemy by drinking himself into a cold stupor nearly every night. Every man in the squadron enjoyed a good party, but Cowdin took it a step further, had gone missing more than once. By midsummer, Captain Thenault had endured enough, and Cowdin was quietly transferred out of the Escadrille.

Lufbery said, "I'm surprised more of us don't fall apart like that."

Rockwell looked up at him. "You have to love it."

"Love what? Flying? Or killing? Or how about dying? How do you love one part of it and pretend the rest doesn't happen?"

130

Rockwell still looked at him, said, "I don't know, Luf. It's what a soldier does. I can't explain that. Shouldn't have to. You're maybe the best flyer we have. Even the captain says so, says you ought to be on every patrol, to keep us all straight."

Lufbery was surprised. "He really said that?"

"I don't understand you, Luf. I thought you came here to kill Germans. That's why I'm here, for certain. When I'm not trying to get on the tail of one of those Boche bastards, I'm thinking about it. When I'm asleep, I'm dreaming about it."

"How often you dream about one of them getting on *your* tail?"

Rockwell smiled. "Luf, every time I climb into that Nieuport, my guts turn upside down." He paused. "Any man who says he's not afraid is either a liar or he's nuts."

Lufbery sat back again, said, "Thanks, Kiffin. I thought maybe I was the only one who needed to get puke-faced drunk."

"I told you, Luf, this week ain't the kind of thing I can write home about. But you know what? A few months from now, I'll be ready to do it all over again. Did you see that nurse?"

Lufbery laughed, heard a commotion outside the hotel, a burst of singing. He looked toward the front entrance, saw Prince and Thaw burst through the door. The two men stopped, put their arms out wide, began to sing, their voices anchored in distinctly separate keys.

> *"Two valve springs you'll find in my stomach,*
> *Three spark plugs are safe in my lung,*
> *The prop is in splinters inside me,*
> *To my fingers the joystick has clung.*
> *Pull the cylinders out of my kidneys,*
> *The connecting rods out of my brain,*
> *From the small of my back get the crankshaft,*
> *And assemble the motor again!"*

They waited, obviously expecting an ovation. The lobby seemed to return to normal, and Lufbery pulled himself up from the chair, Rockwell standing as well. They applauded, each clap of Lufbery's hands sending a jolt through his head.

Thaw made a deep bow, appraised the indifference of the crowd. "Apparently, the French have no taste for music."

Lufbery could see something tied to Thaw's wrist, a leather strap hanging down, the end still dangling beyond the doorway. People were moving past Thaw now, and suddenly a woman screamed outside the entranceway. Prince rushed out, and Thaw said, "Oh, for crying out loud. It's just a big kitty."

Prince returned now, held a large tan animal in his arms, its collar attached to the strap on Thaw's wrist. The two men moved closer, and Rockwell said, "What in God's name is that?"

The two men were beaming now, and Thaw said, "Gentlemen, allow me to introduce our newest member. Only four months old, and already he has seen the world, traveled all the way from Africa, where he was destined to spend his adult life confined to the cell of some Parisian circus cage. But for five hundred measly francs, we have rescued him."

Prince leaned close to Lufbery, bathing him in the smell of sour champagne. "We decided his name should be Whiskey."

Lufbery stared at the animal, thought, Entirely appropriate.

Rockwell inched closer, put a hand out, the animal sniffing his fingers. "What the hell is it?"

Thaw feigned offense, said, "Sir, have you no appreciation for Mother Nature's most profoundly respected beast?"

Prince said, "He's our new mascot."

Lufbery could not help a laugh, said, "I'll be damned. It's a lion cub."

He put his finger out, the lion licked it, and Rockwell said, "Careful, Luf. That thing's got teeth."

Lufbery rubbed the lion's nose, and the cub suddenly took the finger in its mouth, began softly sucking. Thaw looked at Lufbery with surprise, said, "Well, hello. You must be his mother!"

Luxeuil, France—September 18, 1916

Kiffin Rockwell had been right about the captain's respect for Lufbery's flying ability. Thenault began an experiment, positioned

Lufbery several thousand feet above the rest of the formation, to keep watch and act as a reserve weapon should the squadron find itself in a sudden disadvantage. For Lufbery it was a different experience to fly alone, above it all, to see the patrols below you swirling around each other, each side seeking the advantage. If any one of the Escadrille pilots got in trouble, Lufbery could dive in quickly, turning the tide of the battle. The Germans had perfected the ambush, using their slow two-seat observers as bait. The German observers would fly low, under ten thousand feet, tempting prey for any fighter patrol. The trap would be sprung from above, the new Albatroses suddenly diving out of the sun onto anyone foolish enough to ignore the skies above them. Thenault's strategy was for his patrol to attract the complete attention of any enemy fighters. No one would search the clouds for one straggler high above. Lufbery had always respected the birds of prey, the soaring majesty of the eagle and the falcon. Now, he had become one. Of course, his increased altitude had one very definite disadvantage. The higher he flew, the colder his feet would get.

The clouds around him were tall and gray, and he struggled to keep the patrol in sight below him. The larger clouds could be a godsend in a fight, could offer sanctuary, and a means to turn back on the enemy before he could respond. But now, they were simply in his way. He looked at the altimeter, had kept the Nieuport just above fifteen thousand feet. The sun broke through now, a mile-wide gap in the tall gray pillars beside him. Lufbery turned the Nieuport slightly, kept close to the cloud wall on his right, leaned out to the left to scan the air below him. He could see the patrol again, five planes, the open V formation that Thenault preferred. He tried to flex his toes, shifted his feet in the tight space above the rudder pedals, thought, Why should this be such a torment? He clenched his arms against him, the thick warm coat keeping away the cold. They can make a damned coat that works. Why not boots? He rapped his feet against the sides of the cockpit, flexed his ankles. No use. If I'm lucky, I'll still have feet when I land. They might break off inside these damned boots. He tried to distract himself from the one source of misery, found the patrol again, saw that nothing was happening to change their formation. His mind began to drift, and he thought of the lion cub, smiled. When the train brought the bleary-eyed pilots to Luxeuil, they had expected to hear some grief from Thenault, some restriction about animals in the hangars. Dogs and cats were everywhere, and Thaw had already rehearsed his speech that they had earned the right to whatever mascot they chose. But Thenault had surprised them, ordered only that the cub be kept outdoors. Lufbery had seen the look of resignation on Thenault's face, and DeLaage had agreed with him that these pilots had already demonstrated such an odd variety of personal habits, the young lion's presence was just another American quirk.

Whiskey had begun to follow Lufbery around like the gentle pet no one else had expected it to be. The lion's devotion to Lufbery had created a good-natured jealousy among its rescuers, particularly Nimmie Prince, who seemed offended by the cub's indifference to him. Lufbery had no good explanation for Whiskey's behavior. He had never owned a cat, had never lived anywhere long enough to have a pet at all. It didn't take long for Lufbery to realize that the lion asked for little or nothing in return. Lufbery's guard had begun to come down, and very quickly, the affection was mutual. Now, when Whiskey wanted to play, Lufbery obliged him. The cub was particularly adept at surprise attacks, something that visitors to the airfield found unnerving. It had become Lufbery's favorite sport, luring the annoying newspaperman or highbrow visitor into the hangar, knowing Whiskey was lurking in expectation of the game. The cub would always respond to the short command, leaping out suddenly to terrify the various stuffed-shirted visitors. As much as everyone in the hangar enjoyed the spectacle, it was the one part of the cub's behavior they thought necessary to hide from Captain Thenault. Lufbery wondered about taking Whiskey aloft with him, whether the big cat might actually help to keep his feet warm. But the space was far too confined, and Whiskey was, after all, a cat. It would not do for some act of feline unpredictability to occur at fifteen thousand feet.

The planes beneath him disappeared beneath another cloud,

and Lufbery guided the Nieuport through a narrow gap, the sun in his eyes now. It was the wrong tactical position to be in, but he was unconcerned, thought, A few seconds, just ease around to the left—

He caught the flash behind him, heard the hard thump, saw a rip in the wing. He turned in the seat, said aloud, "What the hell . . . ?"

He saw the plane moving up close to his tail, and he jerked at the stick, twisted and dove straight into the cloud. His heart was racing now, and he stared into white fog, thought, Who would be up here?

He emerged from the far side of the cloud, banked hard around, waited, searched every inch of the sky. Now he saw the plane, but it had turned as well, had climbed above him, and he thought, Damn! Smart fellow.

He banked, aimed again for the cloud, saw the other plane turning as well, could see the plane's white belly, and on the wings, the two distinct black crosses. The Nieuport plunged into the cloud again, and his mind raced. Should I climb? No, drop, come around the other way. He pulled hard on the stick, emerged again from the cloud, spun the plane over on its back, pulled back on the stick, the plane now facing back into the cloud. Where are you, you Boche bastard?

He saw the other plane now, flying the opposite direction, a hundred yards away, and he could see the distinct shape of the Albatros. The pilot was staring at him, the Albatros dipping down, turning to move underneath him. No you don't, you son of a bitch. He banked toward the Albatros, the German plane sliding beneath him, no time for either man to shoot. He dove now, put the nose nearly straight down, then turned in a tight spiral, brought the Nieuport back around. He expected to see the Albatros coming around as well, searched frantically, saw him now, off to the side again, out of range. Damn! He jerked the stick, began to loop around the German's tail, focused on his gun sights, close, closer, but the Albatros seemed to jump up, rolled above him, spun down, trying to get behind him. No, you don't! Lufbery repeated the looping spin, the Albatros repeating the same move. They were clear of the clouds now, and Lufbery tried to spot the patrol below him, but there was no time, the Albatros matching his every move, darting up and over, as Lufbery spun to keep the German off his tail. They were circling now, both men seeking to close on the other, neither man gaining the advantage, each move either high or low matched by the other. Lufbery stared out toward the German, saw black goggles, the man looking back at him. They continued to circle, and his heart was racing in his chest. He scanned the Albatros, saw every detail, two machine guns on the motor housing, the black cross on the plane's fuselage, the plane's nose painted bright red. He thought of fuel, ran the time through his mind, how many minutes had it been? Thirty, forty before I saw him. More, perhaps. And the wind, blowing out of the west. So, we are moving your way, eh, Boche? You think I'll just keep up this carousel ride until it's too late? He ran tactics through his mind, the distance to the cloud bank, no, too far. If I straighten out, he'll have me. He glanced down, the ground below him rotating slowly, no sign of the patrol, of anyone else. Where the hell are you? I could use a little assistance up here! He looked again at the German, thought, How much fuel do *you* have, Boche? How much longer before you are in trouble? Perhaps we should just wait and see.

The German suddenly waved at him, and Lufbery could see hints of a smile beneath the man's goggles. Lufbery ignored the gesture, thought, So, you're enjoying this little dance? He was losing patience now, glanced again toward the ground, thought, Someone see me up here? Dammit, all it will take is one of you to come up here. He looked again at the Albatros, was surprised to see the plane's belly again, the Albatros suddenly falling away in a sharp dive. Damn! He pushed the Nieuport down hard, turned to follow, but the Albatros had a head start, was already dropping far below him. He glanced at the compass, saw the German was heading east. Why, you bastard. You're going home. Well, I suppose you answered my question. You were obviously low on fuel. No wonder you were watching me so carefully. You were waiting for me to look away, just that one brief second. Smart fellow. Perhaps next time I won't let you get away.

He pulled the Nieuport level, scanned the air beneath him, still no sign of the patrol. He looked at his watch, thought, Better find your way home. He began to drop, searched the ground for details, could see a snaking smear of wide brown earth, the familiar sign of no-man's-land. He was east of the line, German territory, thought of the Albatros again. It had to be his fuel. Otherwise, the bastard had the advantage. Lufbery moved toward a low line of clouds, dropped the nose again, the clouds shielding him from any antiaircraft fire on the ground. He thought of the German pilot waving to him. What was that? Arrogance? I'm letting you go home this time. Or else, what, Boche, you trying to be my friend? He ran the confrontation through his mind, the details, the turns he had made, the cleverness of the German. He scolded himself: you assumed no one else would be up here. Hell, he might have assumed the same thing. Perhaps we were both fools.

"A red nose? An Albatros with a red nose? You certain?"

"He was less than seventy-five yards from me for fifteen minutes. How sure do I have to be?"

DeLaage clenched his fists, shook them. "Do you know who that was?"

Lufbery shrugged. "No idea. New aeroplane though. Clean belly. Two machine guns."

The others had gathered, drawn by DeLaage's unusual volume.

"Mr. Lufbery, it is clear to me that your opponent today was Oswald Boelcke. The description of his Albatros was provided by the British. He used to fly only the Eindeckers, but the Tommies believe the Albatros is a better aeroplane, so it follows that Boelcke would change. The red nose was always Boelcke's signature. You sure what you saw was solid red?"

"Yes. The entire cowling. Boelcke? Really?"

The others began to hoot and cheer, Rockwell slapping his back.

"Luf, you almost had yourself a day! Imagine, shooting down Boelcke!"

Lufbery didn't share their joy, said, "I didn't shoot down anything. Never came close."

DeLaage shouted out to them all now, "A duel with the great Boelcke!"

Rockwell said, "He waved at you? He actually waved?"

"Well, hell, any closer, and we coulda kissed."

He had a crowd now, all the mechanics gathering as well. He saw Thenault, the captain making his way through the others.

"Congratulations, Mr. Lufbery. You fought a duel with the Boche's finest air flyer!"

Rockwell slapped Lufbery's arm again, said, "And, not only that, Captain, but Boelcke even waved at him."

Thenault said, "A salute! He honored you. It was the proper thing to do. You showed him you were his equal. Even the Boche know of chivalry! It is said that pilots are so very much like the knights of old times. This is proof, yes?"

Lufbery would say nothing to dampen the party that was enveloping him. He tried to share the mood, to smile with them, felt Rockwell's hand on his back, thought, Of course, a southern gentleman, would identify with all this talk of knighthood. He glanced at Rockwell, at Thenault, the beaming congratulations still pouring from DeLaage. He looked toward the Nieuport, saw one mechanic at the wing, already patching the rip. He wanted to object: Leave it there; let me see it every time I fly. But the man's work was done, the plane whole again. He heard a cheer, some words from Thenault, "Tonight, we shall drink a toast to our American knight!"

Lufbery could not look at them, turned, stared out to the open field, felt annoyed by the word, thought, I don't ride a damned horse. Killing the enemy has nothing to do with chivalry. If that was really Boelcke, then the only thing that happened today was that one of us missed an opportunity.

September 20, 1916

The vicious fighting along the Verdun front had settled into what the generals were describing as a lull, and what the men in the front-line trenches referred to as a brief rest from the fires of hell. The French had taken advantage of the relative quiet to put a plan into action to damage or even destroy the German

138

munitions works at Oberndorf. The Mauser plant there was responsible for much of Germany's production of rifle and machine-gun parts, and the only means the French had of accomplishing the mission was a bombing raid by air. For the first time, the Americans understood that the escadrille's relocation to Luxeuil had a strategic purpose. For days prior to the planned attack, the fighter squadrons would rehearse their role in the raid by serving as bomber escorts, each pilot learning the routine of shepherding enormous flights of French and British bombers on what the Aeronautique Militaire believed would be their most important raid of the war. For their part of the preparation, the bombers were sent aloft to dump their payloads on targets closer to home, ammunition dumps or truck and artillery parks just across the German lines. Thenault had been told that the attack would take place sometime in the near future, the exact date a closely guarded secret. For now, there was only one job for the Americans to perform: when the weather would allow, they would climb above the formations of bombers and make every effort to keep the enemy fighters away.

Only the officers spoke of the Oberndorf raid, the rest of them pretending not to dwell on a mission that was different from anything they had done before. They all knew that the raid would take them deep into German territory. Despite all the talk of secrecy, no one believed the Germans would ever be caught off guard; the fighters would lead their sheep through every fighter squadron the Germans could throw at them.

With the grim rumors flowing around them, the squadron needed little excuse for a party, anything to take their thoughts away from the duty that loomed in front of them. On this night, the excuse was easy. It was Kiffin Rockwell's twenty-fourth birthday.

Luxeuil was famed for its grand spa, and the spa had become famed among the pilots for its spacious party rooms and well-stocked supply of alcohol. By midnight, Lufbery was working the bar, a concession from the usual bartender, Bert Hall, the only man among the squadron who rarely drank. Even Rockwell himself had accepted that in France, polite hospitality usually included some variation of the grape.

* * *

Rockwell was steadier than most of the others, moved toward the bar bearing an empty glass. Lufbery put down his own champagne glass, and Rockwell said, "What's this? The bartender drinking his own wares?"

"French tradition. What you need?"

Rockwell seemed to think for a moment, said, "Champagne, I suppose. Wish I felt more like a party. This has been very nice of you. Most of you."

Lufbery could hear the tone of Rockwell's words, said, "What's the problem?"

Rockwell shook his head.

"Not the time, Luf. It's my birthday."

"Hey, it's your party. Somebody giving you grief?"

Rockwell took a sip of his champagne, set the glass down.

"I'm just getting tired of the blowhards. There's some here who think that if they actually fly over German territory, they get to claim a victory."

"Prince?"

Rockwell looked at him. "Not for me to say."

"Look, Kiffin, I know you been having some problems with ole Nimmie. He's different from you and me. If we were that rich, we'd be different too."

Rockwell leaned close, tried to hush his own voice. "Luf, being different doesn't give you the right to claim glory that's not yours to claim. Bert Hall's no different. You know as much as any man here how tough it is to shoot down a Boche plane. But listen to them strutting about; you'd think they were shooting pigeons out of a barn."

"Kiffin, they can claim anything they want to. There's no official confirmation, and without confirmation, it doesn't matter. Hell, you knocked those two Boche down a few weeks ago, couldn't count them officially. I've sent down one or two behind their lines. What difference does it make? A dead German is a dead German."

"It seems Prince has been putting the pressure on Thenault to put him in for a medal. Thenault approved it. Is that fair?"

"So, rich boys measure their success with medals. Kiffin,

140

when this is over, there'll be medals enough to go around."

There was a sudden burst of singing from across the room, DeLaage showing off his talents at an old piano. Lufbery slid Rockwell's glass toward him.

"Here. Go join them. It's your damned party."

Rockwell picked up the glass, stared at it.

"Thanks, Luf. I'm glad I met you. You're one of the good guys. You know, I been meaning to tell somebody. If anything happens to me, I want to be buried right where I fall. Right in the spot."

"What the hell are you talking about?"

"Oh, come on, Luf, you can't tell me you don't think about this stuff. I got some money, too. Haven't spent much here. If the Boche don't steal it, I want you to take whatever's left and have a party with it. Bigger than this one. Invite the British even. Thaw wants to know how much they can drink."

"Jesus, Kiffin. What's gotten into you? It's your birthday, for crying out loud."

Rockwell raised the champagne glass, smiled. But Lufbery saw sadness in the young man's eyes. Rockwell moved away toward the men gathered at the piano. Lufbery saw Prince on the far side of the room, the man keeping space between him and Rockwell. Lufbery wiped a damp rag on the bar, thought, Damned shame we can't all get along. Too many differences.

Thaw crossed the room now, weaved slightly as he reached the bar. "Somebody die? Bartenders are supposed to make people laugh."

"Sorry. Just thinking."

Thaw followed his stare, said, "Prince? Yeah, I know. A big damned mouth. I get damned tired of hearing him talk about the honor we're bringing to our country. What the hell is honor anyway? History is full of men who do some pretty dishonorable things, all in the name of honor."

"Profound, Bill. Obviously, you need more to drink."

"If you say so. You're the bartender."

"Brandy. It needs more brandy." Thaw stood in front of him,

141

leaned heavily on the thick wooden bar, and Lufbery stared at the goblet, saw the thin lines of bubbles rising.

"Maybe. Gotta mix this quicker. The champagne's getting flat."

"Can't have flat champagne."

"Nope."

Thaw had assumed the role of cocreator, most of the others immobile, spread out on various flat surfaces around the large room. Lufbery raised a squat black bottle, squinted at the label. "Napoleon Brandy."

Thaw said, "Use that. He won't mind."

"Who?"

"Napoleon."

"Nope." Lufbery poured the brandy into the goblet, a near equal blend with the champagne. He held it out to Thaw, who took the goblet, swirled it in a meaningless ceremony, took a drink. "Ooooo. Yep. That's it."

Lufbery slapped his hand on the bar. "Success!" He leaned close to Thaw now, said in a low voice, "The secret is the proportions. Half. Double. Equal. The same."

Thaw drank from the goblet again, pointed at Lufbery. "Mighty impressive. What'll we call it?"

"What? The drink?"

"It's gotta have a name. We invented it."

Lufbery tried to think for a moment, nothing at all running through his brain. "It's up to you."

Thaw stood straight, his hands supporting him against the bar. "Thank you. All right then. In honor of the French. And the Americans." He winked at Lufbery. "And of course the French-Americans. We should call this . . . um . . . the Lafayette Cocktail."

Lufbery rolled the words through his brain, nodded. "On behalf of General Lafayette, I accept. What about Napoleon?"

Thaw shook his head. "Hell with him. He shoulda made better brandy."

September 23, 1916

It was to be a two-man patrol, Lufbery and Rockwell going up together to escort a small squad of bombers along the lines east of Luxeuil. They had begun just after sunrise, a perfect cloudless day, the kind of weather that was becoming rare now with the change of seasons. Lufbery had purchased a new pair of thick wool socks, knitted for him by an old woman in the town. He was surprised that anyone noticed, had drawn some quiet satisfaction when several of the others had asked for the woman's name, some of them admitting finally that they were tired of cold feet.

He followed Rockwell, the Nieuports rocking from the sharp breeze that blew in from the north. It was habit now to test the machine guns, a luxury given them by the long belts of ammunition. Lufbery still cleaned his bullets, still tossed out the imperfect rounds, had noticed that Rockwell had begun to follow his example, and some of the others as well.

Rockwell banked to the right, waved at him, and Lufbery followed, could hear a brief burst of chatter from Rockwell's guns. Lufbery pressed the trigger button on the stick, one shot ringing from the gun, then silence. He pressed again, no response from the gun, and he leaned forward, tried to see what was wrong. He reached over the windscreen, rapped on the gun with his gloved fist, a solution that had never worked. He saw Rockwell looking at him, his Nieuport drifting close alongside, and Lufbery pointed to the gun, said aloud, "Damn it all!"

Rockwell seemed to understand, pointed down, and Lufbery nodded, thought, Nothing else to do. I have to fix whatever the hell is wrong. He motioned to Rockwell, *go on ahead*. No reason for both of us to waste time. He knew the bombers were waiting, knew as well that Rockwell could hold his own against any German intruders, at least long enough for Lufbery to clear his gun. He pulled the stick to the right, peeled away from Rockwell, who waved a brief farewell. Lufbery searched the familiar ground, could see the Luxeuil spa on the horizon. In a few short minutes, he was over the airfield, dropped down, and eased the Nieuport to the ground. The mechanics emerged from

143

the hangar, surprised, and he waved at them, pointed at the gun. He released the waist strap, climbed up, saw LeBlanc, a smirk on the man's face. LeBlanc said, "Ah, Sergeant. A problem with the bullets, eh? Too much polish?"

Lufbery ignored him, had heard enough teasing remarks about his special care for both his motor and his gun. He stood up in the cockpit, leaned out over the windscreen, said, "If you don't mind, I could use some help. Find out what the hell's wrong with this thing."

LeBlanc was serious now, knew by the tone of Lufbery's voice that the teasing could wait. Lufbery pulled on the bolt at the side of the gun, but the mechanism was frozen, and LeBlanc moved up close, pulled out a small hammer, said, "A moment. Let me try." He rapped the side of the gun, and Lufbery pulled again, the bolt suddenly giving way, ejecting a bullet out to the side. LeBlanc picked it up, showed it to Lufbery, said, "Still shiny."

Lufbery took the shell, studied it, saw nothing wrong, tossed it into the grass.

"Damned guns. What do I have to do?"

"Well, Sergeant, it's like the motors. Sometimes they just want a lit-tle . . . affection."

"Right."

Lufbery pulled the bolt again, the action smoother now. LeBlanc pulled a small can of oil from his sagging pocket, squirted a stream into the gun, said, "That should help. But be nice to her."

"Pull the prop, please."

LeBlanc moved to the front of the plane, grabbed the prop, gave a hard pull, and the motor roared to life, LeBlanc waving at him, *all clear*. Lufbery jabbed at the rudder, spun the plane around, aimed for a fat tree to one side of the field. He moved the plane up to within fifty yards, pressed the trigger, the gun springing to life, a short blast into the bark of the tree. He spun the plane again, aimed for the long open field, saw LeBlanc walking back to the hangar.

Lufbery was airborne again, looked out across the vast expanse of blue, turned to follow the course he and Rockwell

144

had begun a half hour before. I'll probably never find him now. Bomber pilots are a nervous lot. They won't dally about. They may have dropped their loads already.

He continued to climb, searched the sky, could see puffs of smoke on the horizon, the familiar signs of antiaircraft fire. Well, somebody's over there. Best take a look. He moved toward the smoke, caught the reflection of a single plane, aimed the nose of the Nieuport to intercept it. He was within a half mile of the plane now, could see it was a two-seater, flying a low straight course along the French lines. The plane drew a steady pattern of antiaircraft fire, the smoke dotting the air around it, drawing a perfect line in the air for anyone to follow. Lufbery banked around, looked high above the plane, smiled. Oh yes, Mr. Boche, I have seen this little game before. Now, where are your friends? He scanned the blue above him, continued to turn the Nieuport in a slow sweeping arc. He saw the reflections now, a thin line of specks. He looked at the altimeter, eight thousand feet. He estimated the height of the other planes, thought, Twelve, at least. They're not coming yet, don't see me. If I can climb quick enough, I could give them a hell of a surprise. The sun was behind him now, and he continued to turn, pushing the Nieuport higher. He stared at the formation of German fighters, said to himself, You bastards just keep going. Don't be looking around too much just yet.

Suddenly two of the planes broke away, turning and dropping, moving in his direction. Damn! He leveled out, looked at the gun, thought of LeBlanc. All right, you, um, beautiful piece of machinery. Oh hell, I was never good with mush like that. He pressed the trigger button on the stick, the gun responding with a short burst. Well, it worked. I'll buy you a drink for that, LeBlanc.

The fight was long and frustrating, neither German pilot good enough to find Lufbery's weakness, and both of them just careful enough to keep him from finding theirs. The Germans threw as much fire at him as he threw back, but there was never a clear shot, all three pilots trusting to luck. Though Lufbery knew he had struck both of the enemy planes, there had not been enough damage to send either pilot out of the fight. Finally, Lufbery had to break it off himself. He was running out of both ammunition and fuel. The Germans did not pursue, and he could only guess that they had shortages of their own, or possibly, they had seen enough of this Nieuport that carried the strange insignia of the screaming Indian.

He was not yet ready to return to Luxeuil, could see more antiaircraft fire, new bursts from another section of the line. The fine weather had brought the airfields alive, and he knew there would be more targets and more opportunity. He scanned the ground, saw the familiar ruins of what had once been someone's village. He knew the area, knew of an airstrip, where a squadron of Nieuports was based, a small town called Fontaine. He dropped down, looked for the familiar landmarks, saw three Nieuports in formation passing below him. He saw the field now, two more Nieuports just leaving the ground. Very good. Perhaps you gentlemen can spare some ammunition, and a bit of gasoline?

They met him as he taxied to the lone hangar, and he saw men pointing at the insignia on the plane. It was customary now, the Indian head becoming familiar to every squadron in the area. He switched off the motor, readied his greeting, was surprised to see so many men gathering. There was an officer now, and Lufbery released the belt, raised himself up. He was prepared to climb down from the plane, but he saw that the man was moving toward him quickly, waving.

"You are of the Americans, yes?"

There was nothing friendly in the man's words, no smile.

"Yes. I was hoping you could provide some fuel—"

"Very sorry. Very sorry, indeed. We just heard."

"Heard what?"

"Your man. American. Fell near here. The infantry retrieved his body before the Boche artillery destroyed his aeroplane."

"What man? *Who?*"

The words had come out in a hard shout, and the officer said, "I don't know his name. I'm very sorry."

Lufbery sat down in the cockpit, stared blindly at the

146

instruments in front of him. Men were moving around the plane now, and he caught the smell of gasoline. He looked up, saw the officer close beside the plane.

"I am very sorry. Please, allow me to offer my sympathy. France is grateful for such men as you."

Lufbery had no words, saw the mechanics backing away, their job complete, one man standing beside the prop. He felt the officer's hand on his shoulder, said the only thing he could think of. "Thank you."

Lufbery nodded to the propman, the plane sputtering to life. He turned the Nieuport back out toward the open field, his movements coming from instinct. The Nieuport rolled ahead, left the ground, carrying him up into the great open blue.

They were waiting for him at Luxeuil, had received a telephone message from the officer at Fontaine. He rolled the plane to a stop, saw their faces, the mechanics standing together, LeBlanc crying. The pilots moved toward the Nieuport, and Lufbery saw tears in DeLaage's eyes, saw a grim stare from Thaw. Lufbery said, "Was it Kiffin?"

DeLaage nodded, said, "Shot in the chest. The infantry said he was already dead when he crashed. A blessing."

Lufbery looked at the gun on the cowling of his plane, his mind filling with dark rage. He wanted to rip the gun from the plane, tear it to small pieces of scrap metal. He stood up in the cockpit, tore the helmet from his head, his hands shaking.

DeLaage was up on the side of the plane, seemed to read him, said, "Nothing for you to do now. Come."

Lufbery felt the hand on his sleeve, wanted to slap it away, stared at the machine gun through a teary fog in his eyes.

DeLaage said, "Captain Thenault has taken an auto to pick up his body. The infantry recovered him."

"What happened to him?"

Thaw was there now, said, "Come on down, Luf. I'll tell you as much as we know."

Lufbery stood frozen, blinked at the tears. The anger was hard inside of him, and he reached down for the stick, pressed the trigger. The gun barked, a short burst that startled them all.

147

"I need ammunition. I should go back up."

DeLaage still had his sleeve, said, "Not just yet. Collect yourself. We will all do what we must."

"C'mon, Luf." He looked down at Thaw, the soft kindness in the man's face calming the anger. "We'll get those bastards yet. But not just now."

Lufbery felt himself growing weak, every part of him sinking into the sadness. He climbed down, jumped to the ground, felt DeLaage's hand under his arm.

"Mr. Lufbery, there was nothing any of us could have done. He was struck by an exploding shell. It was his time."

Lufbery looked at Thaw, who nodded to him.

"That's right, Luf. Nothing you could have done."

Lufbery turned, put his hand on the plane, stared at the gun for a long moment. He saw the face of the young southerner, heard the soft drawl, the man's embarrassment at his own human frailties. He thought of DeLaage's words, *his time*. Something Kiffin would say. You would know more about that than I would, my friend. And if that is true, if that is what God is about, then I suppose you are at peace. But there is no *peace* here, and my *time* has not yet come.

9

RICHTHOFEN

October 28, 1916

He had continued to fly beside Boelcke, had watched his captain destroy the enemy with remarkable consistency, an astounding record of forty kills. Boelcke had chosen his fights carefully, singling out a vulnerable enemy, a lone flyer, perhaps, or a pilot who had allowed himself too much distance from his support. It was not merely that he sought the easy prey. The sky had become his classroom, each combat a lesson for his students. The captain had led his squadron to each engagement, but held them back, commanding his students not to participate, but to learn. The lessons were succeeding. Within a few weeks after Richthofen's first kill, as Boelcke allowed him to join in the fighting again, Richthofen had shot down six more enemy planes. One more would total eight, the milestone that would qualify him for the Order Pour le Mérite, Germany's highest award for its fighting aces.

Richthofen no longer took the foolish risks, would confirm that his victim was destroyed, but now he would return to the fight, follow each engagement to its conclusion. He would still visit the wreckage of his opponents, but later, usually driven to the site by car, guided by infantry. He learned that he was not alone, many of the pilots seeking some memento of their enemy's last fight. Richthofen began to remove and retrieve the serial numbers from the British planes, providing not only the unquestionable authentication of his victory, but a record of the specific aircraft he had shot down.

Boelcke had led them on patrols throughout the day, returning to Lagnicourt to refuel, then up in the sky again. Boelcke's description of the weather during the autumn months was

149

accurate, and they had flown through dark clouds and misting rain for most of the day. Richthofen had seen a change in Boelcke, a silent determination to remain in the sky, regardless of the absence of enemy planes. Richthofen knew that the pressure was coming from Berlin, an insatiable appetite from the High Command for exploits they could print in the newspapers. As this dismal day had begun, Richthofen had stood beside his plane enduring a rain shower, had assumed they would be ordered back inside. But Boelcke had climbed into his Albatros, had barked the order for five others to join him. They had made five patrols, even going far into British territory, something the German fighters rarely had to do. But the British had stayed in their hangars.

The prop was billowing Richthofen with a thick wet mist, his overcoat soaking wet, the chill cutting all the way through him, down into his legs. After one miserable flight in the morning, it had occurred to him to carry along a dry cloth, protecting it in the map pocket, using it to wipe the smear of greasy wetness that coated his goggles. He wiped again, the cloth nearly useless, his vision clouded by the fading daylight as well, darkness now spreading out over the east. The day was finally coming to a cold, soggy conclusion.

He hunched his shoulders up, but the cold was all through his clothes, and he glanced over toward Boelcke, saw him waving, pointing straight ahead. He looked that way, was surprised to see two small dots, outlined against dull gray clouds. Boelcke began to climb, the others following, and Richthofen shook off the cold, thought, Finally! What fools would be out here this late in the day? They are heading west. It is obvious they believe their day has concluded. We shall change their minds.

Boelcke led them closer, six Albatroses now above and behind the two British planes. Richthofen could see the details of the planes now, single-seaters. Six against two. If the British pilots did not see them in time, it would be over quickly. Boelcke pointed toward him, and Richthofen understood. Boelcke would pursue one, Richthofen the other, with the other four planes in support. Richthofen glanced to the other side, caught the nod from the man on his right. He would be close behind should Richthofen need him.

The dive began, the Albatroses gaining quickly on the two British fighters. But the British were vigilant and immediately began to turn away, dodging the oncoming assault. Richthofen tried to follow the enemy's tight turn, was close enough to fire, but the British pilot spun back the other way, Richthofen turning to keep pace. His target climbed up in front of him, then banked again, and Richthofen caught sight of the other planes, Boelcke in close pursuit, Boelcke's wingman just behind him. Richthofen's prey cut right in front of Boelcke, and Richthofen saw Boelcke's plane lurch up, then slip sharply to the side, his wingman now right on top of him. The two planes seem to touch, then separate, and Richthofen felt a cold horror, turned, followed Boelcke, saw his plane dipping, lurching in the air. Small pieces of Boelcke's plane ripped free, fluttered away into the clouds, the plane itself circling slowly downward. Richthofen scanned the sky above him, searched frantically for the enemy planes; but there was no sign of them, the British pilots making good their escape. The German pilots now brought their planes into a loose formation, all following Boelcke down. Richthofen watched in cold horror, shouted to Boelcke, the words useless, the man's plane falling into a cloud, out of sight. He stabbed at the con-trols, circled the cloud, waited for Boelcke to appear, saw it now, the plane emerging below, twisting in an ugly spiral, the top wing now gone, ripped completely free. Richthofen was suddenly in a cloud now, unexpected, and he stared ahead, the wetness blinding him, closed his eyes for a long moment, the hard cold emptiness filling him. The cloud gave way, the sky in front of him empty, the darkness covering them all.

Cambrai, France—November 3, 1916

The procession took them into the cathedral, a vast crowd of silent observers standing motionless as they passed. Six pilots from Boelcke's squadron bore the coffin, while Richthofen carried a velvet pillow, which held Boelcke's extraordinary

151

collection of medals. As he stepped in rhythm to the solemn procession around him, Richthofen held tightly to his emotions, stared at the medals, various shapes, different colored ribbons. But he stared hard at the one medal that topped the display, the one that mattered above all the others, the Order Pour le Mérite. He knew Boelcke would scold him for such thoughts, that no man should care so about medals and decorations, but Richthofen understood that it was not about glory or anything that would be in the newspapers. That one medal meant that you had bested your enemy, and had done it consistently. There was no recognition that could equal that, not to a fighter.

The air was thick with scent, great wreaths and displays of flowers, sent from all over Germany. Of course, the German people would pour out their sorrow for their great hero, and newspapers were already spilling over with headlines that made Richthofen cringe, that Boelcke would find ridiculous, praise and farewells to "the mighty ace who taught all of Germany to fly."

But there had been one extraordinary surprise, an unexpected farewell, and as Richthofen followed Boelcke to his final rest, the words echoed through his mind. The day before the funeral, he had heard the low hum of a motor, had rushed outside the hangar to watch a single British plane circling low over the aerodrome. The men had scrambled to the antiaircraft guns, but it was not an attack, no bombs, simply a wreath dropped into the wide field, black ribbon trailing a tightly wound gathering of flowers. It was a message, a salute that would mean more to the fallen soldier than any headline, a show of respect that fighting men had shared on this same land for a thousand years:

To the Memory of Captain Boelcke, Our Brave and Chivalrous Foe

Command of Boelcke's flying squadron was given to Lieutenant Stephan Kirmaier, a capable veteran pilot, who made no attempt to change Boelcke's methods. Richthofen was pleased with Kirmaier's disciplined approach, and the squadron had continued its successful dominance over the airspace near Lagnicourt. In only three weeks, Kirmaier and his young pilots had shot down another two dozen British planes. But the squadron would not enjoy the luxury of celebration. Less than a month after Kirmaier had taken command, he went down himself, a victim of the increasing accuracy of the British gunners. Kirmaier's successor was named quickly, another veteran, Lieutenant Stephan Walz. But Walz was more of an administrator than a fighter, and though Richthofen had not thought of himself as commanding anything but his own plane, the young flyers of the newly named "Boelcke Squadron" increasingly looked to him to lead them into combat. It was a responsibility he accepted.

November 23, 1916

It had been another intense fight, a flurry of swirls and dives, more than a dozen planes involved, the British pilots responding with surprising skills. As the fight spread out over the vast landscape of the combat zone below them, Richthofen had engaged a single-seater, a de Haviland, the distinctly odd "pusher" design with the motor and prop behind the wings, the pilot's seat jutting out in front. The "DH" was a much more maneuverable fighter than the Vickers, but it could still not outrace the Albatros. There had been no surprise attack for either pilot, no chance for Richthofen to make his careful approach from the de Haviland's blind side. The British pilot had dueled Richthofen for more than thirty minutes, loops and banking turns, the two men circling each other in tight spirals, until, finally, the westerly wind and the DH's lack of fuel had forced the British pilot to break off the engagement. But Richthofen would not let him go and continued the pursuit. The DH continued to dodge and weave in front of him, Richthofen amazed at the dexterity of the British plane and its pilot. The DH led Richthofen down close to the ground, the two planes finally racing barely a hundred feet over the astonished faces of the German troops below. But the Albatros was simply too fast, and Richthofen kept his craft moving in as straight a line as possible, knowing that each dip and turn of the DH slowed it down, allowing the gap to close between them. Before the British pilot could reach the safety of his own antiaircraft guns, Richthofen had closed within range. The burst from the Maxims had been fatal to the pilot, and the DH dropped heavily, slid and tumbled into a heap of wreckage near the German trenches. It was Richthofen's eleventh kill.

He sat alone in his room, scratched the dog's ears, the huge animal spread out across the single bed. Richthofen was simply passing time, expected to hear from his orderly at any moment. He had sent a customary request to the infantry commander where the DH had gone down. If Richthofen could not go to the plane himself, he would ask someone in command there to retrieve some piece of the enemy fighter, remove the fabric serial number if possible. The infantry was usually happy to oblige him, his name now becoming known to most of the senior officers in his sector of the front. Since Boelcke's death he had begun to decorate the walls of his small room with the distinct souvenirs, mostly the serial numbers, printed on rectangles of cloth cut from the planes' fuselages. There were other scraps, bits of propeller, fragments of iron from a destroyed motor, some personal effect from the pilot.

He had adopted another habit as well, something that began with his first kill. He left the dog on the bed, stood now in front of the small glass cabinet, looked intently at a line of silver cups. Each cup was barely two inches high, was engraved with the details of a particular kill, the date and type of plane, how many men had died. The cups were in a neat row, spread across one shelf of the cabinet. After each new victory was confirmed, he would send word to a silversmith in Berlin, and a few days later, the newly engraved cup would arrive. He did not discuss the trophies with anyone in the squadron, knew it was something that Boelcke would frown on. It was, after all, a demonstration of self-praise.

He picked up the cup engraved with the number "8," felt a slight rush of familiar anger. He had so counted on receiving the Order Pour le Mérite, had worked hard to keep that ambition tightly hidden. He really didn't know himself how much the medal would mean to him, until suddenly it was withheld. Berlin understood the importance of the medal, and many of Germany's pilots were quickly rising to the challenge, the number of their kills growing at an enormous rate, and that was exactly the problem. The more pilots who received the medal, the less significant it would become. Word came directly from General von Hoeppner, the commander of the entire German Air Service. In order to qualify for the Order Pour le Mérite, a pilot now had to claim sixteen victories, not eight. Richthofen knew better than to complain about the order, but had responded with a rare outburst of anger. Berlin had certainly perceived the sudden shock to the morale of the pilots, and within days, a brief explanation had been sent to the aerodromes: before his death, Max Immelmann had shot down fifteen enemy planes. In order to qualify for the medal, one must surpass Immelmann. The explanation had seemed to satisfy the pilots. Even in Berlin, the Order Pour le Mérite was beginning to be referred to now as the "Blue Max."

The dog had moved up close to him, seemed to follow Richthofen's every mood, staring into the glass cabinet with him, watching as Richthofen returned the cup to the shelf, lining it up evenly with the others.

Since Boelcke's death, Richthofen found it harder to be social, could not escape the question: Which one of them would be next? Boelcke had been right: *none* of them was invincible. None of . . . *us*. He ran his finger lightly over the rim of each cup, thought, At least, if that time ever comes, someone, my family perhaps, can have these small treasures, a way to remember my own accomplishments. If they know little else about me, they will know I did . . . this. It may be all that I can give them.

There was a knock at the door, and Richthofen carefully closed the glass panel on the cabinet. He pointed to the bed, and the dog obeyed, jumping up out of the way.

"You may enter."

He expected Corporal Menzke, was surprised to see pilots and mechanics; the hallway was packed with smiling men. Lieutenant Walz stepped forward, said, "Lieutenant, I have confirmation of the plane you bested today. It was a DH-Two."

"Yes, sir, I am aware of that. I saw it from quite close up. Forgive me, sir. What is this? I don't understand."

Walz was smiling, said, "No, I don't expect you do. There is no way for you to know, of course." Walz glanced at the crowd packed in behind him, said, "Lieutenant, despite your distaste for seeing your name in the newspapers, I'm afraid that this time, it is not to be avoided. Are you familiar with the British ace Major Lanoe Hawker?"

"Certainly, we all are, sir. Some say he is the enemy's finest fighter."

"In fact, Lieutenant, some say that he is the enemy's equivalent of Oswald Boelcke."

The name dug into him, and Richthofen nodded, said quietly, "I have heard something of that, yes."

"Lieutenant, you still do not understand, do you? Your victim today, the DH-Two you brought down, according to the infantry, the pilot was killed instantly. That pilot was Major Lanoe Hawker."

At the end of May 1916, the German navy had sailed from its ports along the North Sea to confront a mighty British fleet, resulting in what was now known as the Battle of Jutland. Nearly three hundred warships had engaged in a confusing series of attacks and retreats, made worse by poor weather and sloppy seamanship on both sides. The results had slightly favored the Germans, but both sides were severely crippled, so much so that the German fleet returned to its ports and, except for the widespread submarine patrols, abdicated control over the North Sea to the British navy. The British had responded by securing a blockade of Germany's seacoast. The German High Command was very much aware that the German people were beginning to feel the shortages that resulted. As supplies of meat and grain and fuel began to diminish, loud voices emerged, first in the cities, young Germans who saw the kaiser and his ministers as corrupt relics of the past, who viewed the war as reckless and destructive to the working people of Germany. Many of these voices began to speak of a new order, recited the writings of a man named Karl Marx, took their energy from similar unrest that was spreading throughout Russia. To a military command whose hands were fully occupied with maintaining a war on several fronts, a collapse in German morale had to be avoided at all costs. The German people needed a fresh burst of hope: if not great victories, then, of course, great heroes. A handsome young flying ace fit the role perfectly. Richthofen's victory over the celebrated Lanoe Hawker was trumpeted throughout Germany. With the High Command's blessing, the German people had their new hero.

Richthofen continued to improve as a fighter, and, so, continued to destroy enemy planes. As a quiet winter settled over the shell-shocked ground of the Western Front, the planes still flew, the duels and raids continued. Within weeks after the death of Hawker, Richthofen was surprised to receive another order from Air Service headquarters in Cologne. He had not only achieved the success required for his Order Pour le Mérite, but his sixteenth kill elevated him above every other surviving German pilot. The rewards came quickly. Lieutenant Manfred von Richthofen was ordered out of Squadron Boelcke and was given a command of his own.

10

LUFBERY

On October 15, the long-awaited bombing raid over the Mauser Works had finally been launched. Of the dozens of bombers participating, only a fraction actually found their targets, and the minor damage they inflicted on the armament factory caused a work stoppage of less than three days. Even with the protection of two dozen fighter escorts, including four from the American Escadrille, ten French and British bombers had been shot down by German fighters. Despite the extreme attention to the planning and execution, the raid had been a miserable failure. Most of the blame lay with the bombers themselves. The primary lesson learned was that in a daylight raid, there was no perfect solution to the vulnerability of the slow and clumsy planes, especially as they bore their heavy payloads. While the French and British were embroiled in the controversy, passing blame back and forth, the Americans were occupied with another calamity of their own.

Three days before the raid, Norman Prince had crashed his Nieuport, tangling with electrical wires as he approached the airfield. His injuries were severe, and, like Clyde Balsley, he was confined for what could be a lengthy stay in the hospital. The conflicts and ruffled feathers Prince had caused were forgotten, every man in the squadron carrying his own despair for Prince's condition. When Lufbery and the others returned exhausted and frustrated from the disaster of the Mauser raid, they landed at Luxeuil only to learn that Norman Prince had died. Of the seven original founders of the American Escadrille, only three were still flying.

November 23, 1916

He had allowed the lion cub to follow him, against the advice of Thenault. But the forest was quiet, the distractions few, and Lufbery had felt an aching need for the solitude.

He carried the small basket, poked the soft clusters of leaves, peered around the old stumps. The change of seasons had made his search for mushrooms more difficult, the forest floor now carpeted with the fading colors that had painted the trees around him. He glanced back, thought it was a good idea to keep a close watch on Whiskey's adventures, making sure the cub didn't simply disappear. Lufbery didn't have to be told that some local farmer might not find it amusing if a lion cub suddenly appeared in his chicken coop.

The cub seemed content to nose its way along behind him, sniffing and pawing the soft ground. Lufbery bent low, searched beneath a fat dead tree, and close beside him, Whiskey suddenly launched himself into a small hole, digging furiously. The movement startled Lufbery, the cub's playfulness shattering the silence.

"What the hell . . . ?"

Lufbery stood, observed the commotion, thought of scolding the cub, watched as Whiskey began to bounce around a fat stump.

"Now look, my friend. I didn't bring you out here to go hunting. I don't need you chasing some damned varmint all over hell and gone. Maybe Thenault was right. This might be a mistake."

The cub abandoned his pursuit, scampered up beside him, rolled over onto Lufbery's boots, the usual request for attention. Lufbery smiled, could feel his dark mood swept away. He reached down, a quick rub of the cat's exposed belly, then withdrew his hand quickly. It was a routine painfully learned; the cub would offer his underside, but if your hand lingered, the cat would curl up around your arm, biting and clawing at your shirtsleeve. It was all play, of course, but Lufbery knew that Whiskey would soon be six months old. Though he was still a kitten, the animal's strength and power was increasing. Sooner or later, the games might actually become dangerous.

The basket was still empty, and he scanned the woods around him, watched as the cub bounced away to some new adventure, plunging headfirst into a boggy pile of moss. Lufbery had made these trips more often lately, had felt the need to escape from the company of the other pilots, if only for an hour or two. They had all done the same, each in his own way—Thaw with his fishing pole, some by making themselves familiar to the local barmaids. The parties at the Luxeuil spa had become regular affairs, DeLaage doing his best to boost their morale with his piano playing. It was a distraction to be sure, the songs and the steady flow of alcohol waltzing the men into a gentle stupor. There was nothing of celebration to it, no one launching them into gales of laughter, the kind of spirit that had once brought them together. There were simple friendships now, the cama-raderie of men who share the common experience. But the grand stories were few, most of the men content to keep their day's combat to themselves. Even among the newer men, there was nothing to share, no new sensation or thrill that they had not all experienced by now. What had become more prominent in each man was something Lufbery had done his best to hide, to stuff down into some dark corner of his mind. As the months had passed, and the familiar faces had begun to disappear, the enthusiasm and the sense of adventure had been replaced by fear. He would never acknowledge it, knew that he had built a reputation for being utterly fearless, the one man among them who could stare into the face of the enemy and not blink. But he shared the certainty with all of them, that if this war went on, the question was not if they would survive, but when they would die.

He moved away from the thick brush, found the main path, led the cub back toward the road to Luxeuil. The search for mushrooms had been futile, and he knew the maid would scold him for not looking hard enough. It was their game, humorless and routine, the old woman insisting that no American could master the art of gathering the *champignon*. Even on those days when his basket was full, she would find some other excuse to scold him. But it was a game with rules, and he would defuse her scolding with a deep apologetic bow, then plant a

160

kiss on her cheek, which would end her lecture and the game, and would bring the old woman a satisfied smile.

He glanced back, saw the cub bounding up behind him. It stopped abruptly, leapt off the trail, plunged into a boggy mud hole, began slurping the dark water noisily. Lufbery laughed, thought, Life's simple pleasures. Drinking mud. He kept moving, glanced up at the fading sunlight, felt the chill in the air. He glanced at his watch, aware of the late hour. There would be a celebration tonight, another party of sorts, inspired by the energy of the French officers. The party was for Lufbery, the inevitable presentation that meant far more to the French than to him. But he would comply, would not do anything to appear ungracious.

On the same day that Prince had crashed, Lufbery had shot down an enemy three-seater, a clumsy hulk of a plane that was almost too easy a target. But there was more to the event than the downing of another enemy plane. The kill had been confirmed as Lufbery's fifth victory. The number was significant for only one reason. It meant that Raoul Lufbery was the first man in the American Escadrille to be recognized officially as an *ace*.

The party had unfolded as usual, the ceremony first, Thenault presenting Lufbery with the certificate from the Aeronautique Militaire, the men congratulating him with their handshakes, their eyes focused squarely on the bar. He had been surprised by their enthusiasm, could not help feeling that the men were trying just a bit too hard. But then the bottles were passed, and according to the routine they all expected, DeLaage launched his assault on the piano. In minutes, the men had settled into their accustomed chairs, waiting for the wine to unroll the blessed fog over their brains.

Thenault had left the festivities, not unusual, but Lufbery was surprised to see him returning now, holding a piece of paper. The captain moved quickly toward the piano, and DeLaage responded to a silent order, the room suddenly quiet. Thenault had their attention, and Lufbery could not help eyeing the others, the reflex now, checking each man, making a silent roll call. But everyone was there, and the news could not be as horrible as what they had learned to fear. Thenault said, "Excuse me, gentlemen. I had thought this could wait until tomorrow, but, as you are all assembled, I should tell you. I have received an order from the Aeronautique Militaire, which was passed to them from Army General Headquarters." Thenault paused, seemed to choose his words carefully. "There is one disadvantage to America. You live in a country that allows anyone to speak out. Even . . . the Boche. It seems that your government has been receiving consider-able pressure from the German representatives in Washington. According to head-quarters, the German ambassador has been aggressively protesting to your President Wilson, that since America professes to be neutral, it is an . . . *outrage* to the kaiser that Americans are fighting in the air for France."

The voices began to rise, and DeLaage stood now, said, "*Outrage?* Shall we talk about the butchery—"

Thenault held up his hands, shouted the order: "Quiet!"

Lufbery saw the hard impatience on Thenault's face, and the room was silent again. Thenault said, "This is not the time for protest. It should be no surprise to you that my government has been told by your secretary of state that the existence of the Escadrille Américaine is a violation of your country's neutrality. However, I am pleased that the Aeronautique Militaire has not gone so far as to order you to stop flying."

DeLaage stepped closer to Thenault, said, "Then, what do they want us to do?"

Thaw rose from a chair, looked around at the others, said, "I'm guessing, Captain, that they want us to change the damned name."

Thenault smiled now, surprising Lufbery.

"Mr. Thaw, you are a wise man. I have been ordered that the designation of this squadron eliminate any reference to America. The official correspondence from the Ministry of War in Paris has suggested that Escadrille N-One twenty-four now refer to itself as the Escadrille des Volontaires."

The hum of protest filled the room and DeLaage said, "Ridiculous! Every flying squadron in France can claim to be made up of volunteers!"

Thenault held up a hand. "I said the name was *suggested*. I just spoke with Dr. Gros by telephone. He offers a suggestion of his own. If we must change our name, how do you feel about honoring the man who is a hero to both our countries? I am speaking of course of the marquis de Lafayette."

There was a hum of approval, and Lufbery looked at Thaw, who shrugged, said, "The Lafayette Escadrille? Sounds all right to me. Hell, we named a drink after him."

With the debacle of the raid on the Mauser Works behind them, the Aeronautique Militaire began to examine ways to make better use of its fighter squadrons. As the fighting around Verdun had settled into slow strangling exhaustion, the focus of the air commanders shifted northward, to the activity along the Somme River. With the weather growing colder, the newly named Lafayette Escadrille was ordered to relocate again, this time north of Paris, closer to the Belgian border. The village was called Cachy, and to the pilots who had grown accustomed to the comforts of Luxeuil, the change was a shock. The Americans began to experience what the British already knew, that autumn meant rain, and that any airfield was just as likely as the no-man's-land along the front lines to become a muddy lake. On those days when the planes could fly at all, the Americans also learned that along this part of the Western Front, the Germans spent as much time bombing airfields as they did troops. If any pilot among the escadrille had thoughts of belonging to the elite, that the men who flew the aeroplanes should be immune from facing the same misery and horror as the infantryman, at Cachy, that illusion was swept away. As the infantry huddled in the perfect misery of their trenches, the pilots suffered as well. The Germans were perfecting the art of night bombing, and the Americans shared the new terror of the unseen enemy: the sudden shattering blast that shook them from their beds, that destroyed hangars and the planes within them. Lufbery understood that there could be no sanctuary now, no peaceful escape through the gentle forests. This was a war that had no end.

11

LUDENDORFF

By the autumn of 1916, Germany's monumental effort to capture the French fortress of Verdun had bogged down into a bloody tit for tat, both sides continuing to launch attacks against their enemy without accomplishing any lasting success. With so much of Germany's resources aimed at Verdun, to the north, across the flatlands and low hills of Flanders, the British sensed an opportunity. Their commander, Field Marshal Sir Douglas Haig, assumed that the German strength in front of him had been weakened, that the German High Command must surely have shifted enormous amounts of manpower southward in their efforts to envelop Verdun. In July, Haig had ordered his own attack, three-quarters of a million men surging across the fields of Flanders. The British command was confident that a weakened German front might allow the British to sweep the enemy out of northern France and Belgium, driving the kaiser's troops all the way back into Germany. But the German lines were far more formidable than Haig's intelligence had realized, and the British found themselves embroiled in another quagmire, any hope of a quick breakthrough shattered by massive amounts of artillery and thousands of machine guns hidden behind the thick concrete of the German defenses. It was called the Battle of the Somme, and by November, the cost was nearly as devastating as the awful fights to the south. It was a shock for which the British High Command, and the British people, were not prepared. Another million men had gone down, neither side gaining the advantage, either in ground or in numbers.

As the seasons began to change, the specter of the coming

winter threw a shroud over the commands of both sides. Winter would mean immobility, would increase the suffering of the men who had already suffered more losses than any army that ever crossed a battlefield. The British were the first to concede, and on November 19, the assaults along the Somme front were halted. For all their losses, the British had gained barely seven miles of ground. To the south, the battles still erupted around Verdun, but any major gains the Germans had made in the spring had been erased by French counterattacks in the fall. After nine months of fighting, neither side had the spirit or the resources to gain any advantage at all.

Along the Western Front, the great battles of 1916 had added another two million casualties to what had already become an incomprehensible number of dead and dying. The legacies of the past were forgotten, replaced by the stunning horror of the present. From Flanders to the Swiss border, the Western Front had become one massive graveyard, a generation of young men trampled into the muddy fields by the new realities of war.

In Germany, there were other changes as well. The attack at Verdun had been the strategy of the German commander Erich von Falkenhayn, who had replaced Field Marshal von Moltke after the failures of 1914. With the failure of the Verdun offensive, Falkenhayn had sealed his own fate. The kaiser was forced to look to the east, to the Russian front, the one campaign where Germany's commanders had shown the intelligence and aggressiveness that produced success. In late August 1916, the two men responsible for securing Germany's eastern borders were called to the kaiser's palace. By the first of September, Falkenhayn was demoted, and in his place Kaiser Wilhelm named Field Marshal Paul von Hindenburg to overall command. Von Hindenburg was Germany's beloved old soldier, an aging veteran of the Franco-Prussian War, a kindly and bearlike grandfather who inspired both soldier and civilian. But the kaiser understood that the success in the East could not be laid solely on von Hindenburg's shoulders. The kaiser had been convinced by his closest advisers, including his son, Crown Prince Wilhelm, that the tactics and operations against Russia had actually been carried out by von Hindenburg's deputy, Erich Ludendorff. Ludendorff's official rank was first quartermaster general, but everyone in the High Command accepted that Ludendorff was in fact the man who formed the strategy. Though the kaiser had an intense dislike for Ludendorff and his methods, Ludendorff had his supporters in the High Command, men who understood that this fierce man possessed the brutal efficiency that the German war effort required. Despite his misgivings, the kaiser was forced to accept that von Hindenburg and Ludendorff were a team. Von Hindenburg may have been in command, but Ludendorff was in charge.

He was a stocky bull of a man, with short-cropped hair that emphasized his thick round face, and a massive neck that filled the collar of his starched uniform. At fifty-one, Ludendorff was younger than the most senior officers of the High Command, but Verdun had proven that experience could be a curse, that the nature of war had changed faster than the men who fought it. On both sides the old veteran commanders were falling away, victims of their own inefficiency or incompetence. But Ludendorff had not sat idly by hoping for recognition, did not have the patience to wait for Falkenhayn to collapse on his own. Ludendorff had begun his own campaign with the High Command, chopping away at Falkenhayn's support at every opportunity, a carefully engineered campaign to elevate himself and von Hindenburg in the eyes of the kaiser, and to everyone who mattered in Berlin. Though many in the army had been surprised by Ludendorff's rapid rise, to Ludendorff himself it was simply part of the plan.

Near Fort Douaumont, France—
November 23, 1916

They led him through the captured earthworks, over freshly laid duckboards, while above him, on the firing line, nervous riflemen scanned the ground to the west. It was Ludendorff's second inspection trip to the lines of the Western Front, as close to the enemy positions as any commanding general should ever go.

He had arrived from the East at the end of August, had made his first inspection up north, to the lines that faced the British. But that fight was over now, and no one expected the exhausted British to do anything at all for the rest of the winter. But here, the French had made headway, had counterattacked with surprising success, pushing the Germans back from their gains earlier in the year. Ludendorff was not a man to lounge in the comforts of his headquarters and study maps, did not know his subordinates well enough yet to trust the accuracy of every report. There were hard decisions to be made about the ongoing turmoil of Verdun. Before he would make his recommendations to von Hindenburg, he would see the situation for himself.

Ludendorff followed his guides through a snaking ditch, the dirt walls rising high on both sides of him. The trenches had been built by the French, had been captured and lost and captured again. He stepped through soft mud now, the duckboards blasted away, one side of the trench caved in, the officer in front of him stopping, offering a hand. Ludendorff ignored him, stepped up on the mound of earth, peered out to the side, could see the open ground in front of the trench, shattered barbed wire, a desolate landscape of churned and burned earth. He stepped back down, ignored the concern on the faces of the other men, followed them through more of the filth and smells. He saw troops moving toward him in line, and he stopped, moved to the side, let them pass, caught the glances in his direction, but there was no recognition, and he saw their eyes darting forward again, men trained not to stare at a high-ranking officer. He looked at them all, measured and inspected, saw clean uniforms and bright faces. Some of them were very young, replacements called up from the dwindling manpower of home, boys ordered to become men. In front of him, an officer turned, whispered, "Reinforcements, sir. They will be relieving the men who captured this ground."

There was a patronizing tone to the man's voice, and Ludendorff said, "I am familiar with reinforcements, Major Baum. Shall we move on?"

The smells were filling him now, unavoidable, Baum glancing

back nervously. The major stopped, whispered again, "Sir, perhaps this is far enough."

"Keep moving, Major. I want to see an observation post."

The officers escorting him seemed uncomfortable now, nervous glances to the top of the trenches, some of them looking to him, expecting, what, he wondered, relief from this *terrifying* ordeal? Ludendorff felt his impatience rising, had little use for officers who did not have the stomach for the front lines. Baum commanded the battalion, and Ludendorff had sensed hesitation in the man from their first meeting. He had seen too much of this before, thought, Another clerk who has found his way to command of a combat unit. Send your men up here to do the dirty work, while you stay safe in your concrete shelter. No wonder this campaign has failed.

He looked up to the parapet, saw riflemen all along the firing line, some sitting, leaning against the soft dirt, others standing, dull black eyes watching him pass. Baum seemed not to notice them, and Ludendorff slowed for a moment, absorbed their stares, could feel the strength of these men, the veterans, men who had made the fight, who had driven their bayonets into the enemy. His escort continued to move forward, heads low, mud splashing on polished leather. Ludendorff picked up his pace, stepped into water again, a hole in the boards, the odor of death rising up from the muddy ground. He kept his eyes to the front, would not think of what lay in the ground around him.

The signs of the most recent fight were increasing now, the planks beneath him broken and splintered, many small cave-ins, what had once been the walls of the trench. He saw pieces of every kind of hardware, broken rifles and shredded backpacks, canteens and gas masks. The smells had meaning now, remnants of gas and spent powder, strong enough to overpower the stink of death. He had avoided looking into the dark holes that lined the trench, many of them collapsed, small openings in the earthen walls that only partially hid what remained of their occupants.

The officers began to slow, gathering, looking back at him. Their hesitation was more pronounced now, their nervous glances and jumpiness annoying him. There were no other sounds, no thunder from distant artillery, no pinging of rifle fire, nothing to cause anyone here any alarm. He moved up closer behind them, put his hands on a young captain's shoulders, moved him aside, pushed past the rest of them, thought, Is there one man among these clerks who is not afraid? He was the guide now, snaked his way past more riflemen, the trench winding in a sharp turn to the left. In front of him, the narrow lane opened up into a wide circular pit, the edges lined high with sandbags. He saw men with binoculars, lining the parapet in a wide semicircle, one man staring into a periscope, all of them looking west. He pointed to the periscope, said, "You . . . Lieutenant. I should like to see."

The young man turned toward him with an impatient glare, realized with a shock that he was confronted by a gathering of immaculately dressed officers. He backed up a step, made a short bow, said, "My apologies, sir. Please."

Ludendorff leaned close to the periscope, ignored the commotion as Major Baum hissed a sharp command that brought the other observers scrambling down from the parapet. They fell into line now, the instinct of some long-forgotten drill, stood at hard attention. Ludendorff blinked into dirty lenses, could make out shapes, low mounds of dirt, nothing else. He stepped back, said, "What are we seeing, Lieutenant?"

The young man stood at attention, stared past him, said, "At present, sir, nothing."

"I assume, Lieutenant, that this is a positive thing?"

The young man looked at Baum, seemed unsure of answering the question.

Ludendorff said, "You will respond with frankness, Lieutenant. Do you know who I am?"

The man seemed to stiffen again. "No, sir. My apologies, sir."

Baum seemed to quiver beside him, and Ludendorff silenced him with a sharp glance. "It's all right, Major. This is not a problem. Lieutenant, I am General Ludendorff."

He saw the young man's eyes widen, but no other reaction. Very good, he thought. A man with composure. Baum moved out in front of Ludendorff, said, "General, if I may . . . only yesterday this battalion advanced to this ground, and swept the enemy out of his defenses. Once we had occupied these works, the French chose to run away rather than fight." He laughed now. "They might be running still! I would imagine the enemy has tasted enough of our steel for quite a while."

There was a smugness to the man's words that made Ludendorff clench his fists. He did not look at Baum, said, "So, at this moment, Lieutenant, your observers are content to stare out across empty ground? Do we not know the position of the enemy?"

He could see the young man glancing at the major with a slight frown. Baum took the cue, said to Ludendorff, "There has been some regrettable confusion at battalion headquarters, General. It is likely that much has happened during the night. I had hoped to discover the enemy's intentions, but I do not expect anything to happen. The enemy has been beaten here, sir, I can assure you of that! Since I am assuming them to be in full flight, I have considered preparing a letter, petitioning division headquarters to allow us to push on. These men have tasted victory. I should enjoy leading them into Paris myself!"

Ludendorff digested Baum's words, had heard this kind of empty talk before. This man has no idea what is happening in front of his own command. He *should* be a clerk. He commands nothing at all.

Ludendorff looked at the lieutenant, saw his own thoughts reflected in the young man's grim stare.

"Lieutenant, where is the enemy?"

"General, with all respects, they halted their retreat to a line of trenches beyond this field, sir. The position of their lines varies in relation to ours. Six to eight hundred meters distant. At that range, there is no immediate threat of surprise. I have deployed scouts to probe out in front of our position here. The condition of the ground provides cover, even in daylight. Since the French know that as well, my scouts are reporting back to this post every hour, using their advanced position to give us warning should the enemy attempt to move forward again. When you arrived, sir, my observers here were scanning the enemy's known position. It is the only means we have of protecting the scouts. We have already located one machine-gun post, and very soon I expect to know the precise location of more. Once I have verified the location of those machine guns, with Major Baum's permission, I will send the specifics to the artillery command."

Ludendorff was impressed, thought, Finally, an *officer*.

"Lieutenant, do you believe this battalion should advance on the enemy's position, whether or not he allows you to march into Paris?"

The young man looked again at the major, and Ludendorff said, "You will answer *me*, Lieutenant!"

The young man took a long breath, said, "With all respects to Major Baum, sir, I do not believe the enemy is beaten. Everything we have learned here indicates he is regrouping. I believe his position was resupplied last night, and possibly reinforced. The scouts reported hearing motor vehicles. I would respectfully suggest that we determine the enemy's strength before we advance farther."

"Then, do you expect him to attack?"

"It is likely, sir. This scenario has occurred before. There is more pride at stake here than tactical advantage. These are his trenches, and he will fight to regain them. It has been this way for some time now, sir. The attack could come as early as tomorrow morning. I cannot speak for any company other than what I command, sir. But the men in *this* company stand ready. Once the sun has gone down, the enemy will certainly send out scouts of their own. We are prepared to intercept them."

Ludendorff did not respond for a long moment, and the young man said, "My apologies, sir, but it is essential that my men maintain their watch. Major Baum, might I be allowed to man the parapet again?"

Baum seemed to shake with fury, said, "Lieutenant, your men shall remain in position until the general has completed his inspection!"

Ludendorff stared at the lieutenant for a long silent moment, the observers all standing straight. The officers gathered behind him seemed to hold their breath. The young man's words echoed inside of him, *we are prepared*. Yes, we have been prepared for ten months. And this one young lieutenant understands more than anyone here. This fight has become . . . routine.

"My inspection is complete, Major. Lieutenant, your men may resume their observation." Ludendorff looked at Baum now, said, "Major, you will accompany me back to division headquarters. As of this moment, Lieutenant . . . what is your name?"

"Krauss, sir."

"Lieutenant Krauss, I am placing you in command of this battalion." Ludendorff turned, saw wide-eyed stares on the faces of the other officers. "Surely, one of you has a paper and pencil."

One man stepped forward, a captain who had yet to say a word. "Yes, sir. Please . . . here . . ."

Ludendorff took the pad and pencil from the man's hand, wrote quickly, tore off a piece of paper. He looked at the captain, saw the face of a clerk.

"Take this to Major Baum's headquarters. Inform the staff that each one of them will report to this post for instructions. Before sundown, I want every officer in the battalion to come here, to see this place, to understand what is happening here. Then, they will establish the new battalion command center wherever Lieutenant Krauss determines." He looked at Krauss now, was pleased to see no change in the young man's stern expression. "Lieutenant, do you understand that I am placing you in command of this section of the line?"

"Yes, sir. I do, sir."

"Good. You will continue with your preparations, and inform division command of your location. You will encounter no resistance from any other officer. However, since this is not the appropriate responsibility for a lieutenant . . ." He took another piece of paper, another note. "When I return to your division headquarters, I will make the appropriate changes. You will receive new orders, and your promotion, within hours."

He looked at the other officers, focused now on Baum, who stared at him with stunned disbelief.

"There is one kind of officer who wins a war, Major. He is the man who knows what is happening around him. In the event you did not comprehend what has just occurred, I am relieving you of this command. I have no patience for uncertainty, and no tolerance for bluster. No officer anywhere on this ground should feel pride in what this army has accomplished here. We had a plan, a grand strategy that has failed. If this army ever marches into Paris, they will be led by officers who have earned their victory."

He spun around abruptly, startled the officers, did not wait for his escort to form, moved quickly past them. He stepped back into the muddy trench, the smells engulfing him again. He ignored the troops, the men who stood to the side, word of his presence known to them now. Behind him, the officers scrambled to keep up, boots thumping on sagging timbers. He glanced up to the parapet, to the men with rifles, most not looking at him, men staring out across the desolate landscape, waiting for the enemy to come forward yet again, waiting to endure more of their *routine*. He felt a heat rising in his brain, could not march quickly enough through the trench, thought only of headquarters now, the new job in front of him, all that must be done. He had always despised Falkenhayn, cared little that the man felt the same about him. But Falkenhayn was gone, and the stain of his failure must be erased as well. No, it is our time now. And the first thing we must do is rid ourselves of routine.

He had left orders at the division headquarters, no one arguing, even Baum accepting some vague new office assignment without comment. He had met briefly with his host, Crown Prince Wilhelm, the kaiser's oldest son, an unusually efficient commander for a man whose credentials came mainly from his birthright. Wilhelm had been put in command of most of the southern army group that faced the French, and despite the blunders of Falkenhayn's strategy, Wilhelm had become one of the few bright spots in the dismal tally of failures. But there would be no great feast, no useless celebration of Ludendorff's inspection. Von Hindenburg was on a train at Metz, waiting for him. And there was much to discuss.

As Ludendorff was led through the German defenses, he had

173

walked deep underground on concrete floors, electric lights over his head. The air had been musty, stirred by the hum of exhaust fans, but there were none of the smells of the French works. As his guides led him to the safety of the rear, he moved past a labyrinth of sleeping quarters and supply rooms, observation posts set high up on concrete platforms, protected by massive concrete walls. It was exactly as it had been up north, his first tour of the German defenses at Flanders, and he had taken it for granted that what the German troops and engineers had constructed was the only kind of defense that provided for both the protection and the health of the men who occupied them. But the journey out through the battlegrounds had shocked him, reminding him of the same conditions he had seen in Flanders, a tour of captured British trenches as well. He had been appalled at the condition in the enemy's works, was surprised to learn from intelligence that even in the enemy's rearmost shelters, conditions were rarely any better. He had tried to find the logic in the stark contrast, could only believe it was the perfect illustration of the difference between generals who chose the offensive rather than the defensive style of war. Even when faced with the misery of a stalemate, the French and British generals had never intended to stay put, had engineered structures for their men that might last a week. In 1914, no one could predict that their armies would be forced to hold this ground for years instead of days. The reality of war had changed. The methods of the enemy's generals had not.

From the beginning, when Germany had plotted the invasion through Belgium and northern France, the southern part of the front in Alsace-Lorraine was to be held in defense, manned by just enough German strength to discourage the French from making an assault of their own. The German trenches had been built as permanent structures, housing men who would maintain this part of the line for an indefinite period of time. But from what Ludendorff had just seen, the works now held by Krauss and his men, it was obvious that the French were still convinced their position was temporary. It was the first time Ludendorff felt some understanding of the way the French thought, the mind-set of their commanders, holding tightly to only one idea: *attack*. As he had made his way through the last stretch of captured trenches, the thoughts had rolled into his mind with perfect clarity. There can be only one explanation, that men like Joffre and Nivelle and Pétain consider themselves descendants of Napoleon. Perhaps it is no more than pride in that one glorious moment in their history, that somehow, France must always fight her wars as Napoleon would fight them, power on power, always moving forward. It was childlike in its simplicity, and he imagined generals saluting themselves under portraits of their great hero, pledging to carry on the traditions of their finest warrior. Never mind that Napoleon had eventually been beaten, by both the British and the Russians, the two armies who were now, ironically, French allies. But there was more stupidity. How could any army believe it could find success on the battlefield by using the tactics of such an antiquated era, the arms and methods of another century? No matter how carefully the French generals studied Napoleon's tactics, there was one inescapable truth they had apparently overlooked: Napoleon did not have the machine gun.

But if the French had been alone in their blunders, the war would have ended quickly. Ludendorff knew that in 1914, the German commander, von Moltke, had deviated from the great plan that should have made quick work of this war. Von Moltke had been afraid that the southern leg of the front was vulnerable, that France might concentrate too much power in Alsace-Lorraine, and if they attacked the German defenses there, they could open up a giant wound that would threaten all of Germany. Von Moltke's timidity had ripped the very heart out of the German strategy. What should have been the great unstoppable thrust through Belgium was weakened by the shifting of German troops down toward Verdun. Ludendorff had been stunned by the changes von Moltke had made, and outraged by the results they produced. The German invasion had been thwarted, the astonishing successes of August 1914 blunted by the lack of power necessary to drive the attacks directly into Paris. When the French obliged von Moltke by attacking through Alsace-Lorraine, von Moltke had felt justified in his decision. But Ludendorff knew that had the Germans continued their push from the north, Paris would have fallen, and no matter what feeble attacks the French thought they could make, the war would have been over. The mistakes of 1914 infuriated Ludendorff still, the weak-hearted generals who had cost Germany its greatest triumph. When Falkenhayn replaced von Moltke, there had been a renewed spirit throughout the army, hope that the early disasters of leadership would not be repeated. Now, as Ludendorff made his way through the impregnable German defenses, he felt the same fury toward Falkenhayn as he had always felt toward von Moltke. Verdun had been another catastrophic mistake, the Germans launching an attack right into the strength of the French defense. There had been no great breakthrough, no real advantage at all, not even the symbolic capture of the worthless fortress itself. Falkenhayn's gamble had cost the German army as much manpower as they had bled from the French. And they were virtually in the same strategic position ten months before. Ludendorff thought of the efficient young lieutenant, the honesty in the man's words. You are correct, young man, the enemy is not beaten. For all the planning, all the strategy, the loss of men and matériel, the ridiculous attempt to capture Verdun was simply another mistake. A bad decision by an incompetent commander. But this time there is a difference. This time, I can do something about it.

Near Metz, Germany—November 24, 1916

The train rolled northward, past brown fields and dense patches of forest. War had not come to this part of Lorraine, the fields cleared of their crops, the bounty that had fed the German troops who manned the great barrier to the west. Ludendorff knew little about this part of Europe, had been taught that Lorraine was simply another part of Germany, a notion that had produced wars with the French for generations. He gazed at the farmhouses, saw the architecture, the perfectly sculptured gardens, even the people, sturdy farmers preparing their land and homes for the new winter. It was all so clean, so . . .

German. With Germany's overwhelming victory in the Franco-Prussian War, this disputed land had become a part of Germany again, and Ludendorff had been taught that no one heard protest from the people here. Of course not, he thought. They know the French ways better than anyone, and they will fight to keep their borders. It is all they ask of us, to defend them from French invasion. Not . . . he shook his head. Not to capture French fortresses.

The train had a specially designed car, only two small windows, a row of chairs arranged around a long table. Against one wall were maps, a wireless station, and a small telegraph machine. The next car was the private quarters for the commanders and their staffs, but Ludendorff did not spend any more time in his room than what he required for sleep. The cars were attached to a train that carried no other passengers, was used more for supplies, or moving key personnel from one part of the war to another.

Ludendorff sat beside one of the windows, tempered his impatience by writing notes. They were for himself alone, an exercise to keep himself occupied while he waited for von Hindenburg to return. The old man was napping, his custom late in the afternoon. The strategy sessions often stretched late into the night, and Ludendorff understood an old man's needs.

A guard opened the door at the far end of the car, and a captain appeared now, said, "Sir, the field marshal will be here momentarily."

"Thank you. You may leave."

"Sir."

The door was pulled closed by the guard, the car quiet again. Ludendorff rose from the soft chair, a last glance outside, moved to the head of the table, sat. The door opened again, von Hindenburg moving past the guard, the old man pulling at his jacket.

"Thank you for your patience, General. I did not inquire, how much longer until we reach Kreuznach?"

"Three hours. We will be home well before midnight."

"Beautiful country out there. Did you notice?"

"Yes. I should like to see more of it someday."

Von Hindenburg nodded.

"I hope you can. I should like to show you some very scenic places. Someday, perhaps."

It was the closest the two men came to idle conversation, and Ludendorff knew that von Hindenburg would not push it. Von Hindenburg was always sociable, one reason he was now a favorite of the kaiser. It was not always that way, the kaiser keeping distance between them, as though von Hindenburg's popularity with the people was a potential threat. But Ludendorff saw nothing of a threat in the old man at all, knew that the gentle kindness opened doors and soothed tempers. Von Hindenburg could charm any audience, could disarm his rivals, the ambitious men of the German High Command who might hold dangerous jealousies. Whatever controversy had been stirred up by Ludendorff's quick accumulation of power had been tempered by von Hindenburg's unequivocal confidence in him. Ludendorff was not a man who made friends, and he appreciated the old man's attempts to reach out to him. Whether or not they would ever visit Lorraine together was not important. Ludendorff knew it was von Hindenburg's way of making Ludendorff comfortable, of encouraging the younger man to hold nothing back. Both men knew the importance of the other.

Von Hindenburg sat heavily at the far end of the table, said, "Do we require the presence of the aides?"

Ludendorff shook his head. "No, not yet."

"All right. Tell me of your visit to Douaumont. Conclusions?"

"It is time to bring that disaster to an end. I believe we should order the cessation of all offensive activity, and fortify our position."

Von Hindenburg nodded. "Yes. I cannot disagree. I am fairly certain the kaiser will have no objections."

Ludendorff could not help the frown, and von Hindenburg laughed, surprising him.

"Come now, General, we must not object to His Imperial Majesty providing his input."

"No, certainly not. I did not mean to suggest—"

Von Hindenburg held up his hand, stopped him.

"General, any decisions we make here are for the good of the army and the Fatherland. The kaiser is aware of that. He knows that our armies have been badly abused by the men he chose to manage his military affairs. By that experience alone, he must be made to feel comfortable with the decisions made by his generals. I depend on you to evaluate those decisions. The kaiser depends on me to tell him the decisions are the right ones."

Ludendorff's expression did not change, and von Hindenburg continued. "General, you must understand that royalty are like children. They awake each morning to birds singing and servants fluttering around them. Their milk is always cold, their bread is always warm, and their beefsteak is always tender. They do not live in a world of inconvenience, and since this war has become an inconvenience, someone must help them digest that. The kaiser wishes to believe that he controls fate, that his decisions are wise because he is born with the gift of wisdom. So many generals and politicians are men of clumsy ambition who believe they must impose their will on him, educate him, convince him of their wisdom. Such men do not survive under a monarchy for very long."

Ludendorff thought of the kaiser, the unhidden hostility directed at Ludendorff every time they met. He had seen it directed at von Hindenburg as well, said, "I recall that our Imperial Majesty did not always welcome you into his confidence."

Von Hindenburg laughed again. "Discretion and subtlety, General. I admit it was a lesson I had to learn. There were war games once, a mock battle created for the kaiser's entertainment. He had suggested we approach this like a great campaign, and he established himself in a grand headquarters with maps and an enormous staff. It was quite fun, actually, though not much of a challenge. But I made the mistake of defeating him. I assumed it was my duty to do so. On the contrary, it was my duty to do anything but. From that moment forward, he was said to speak ill of me at every opportunity. It was a situation that took years to correct."

179

"How . . . ?"

"Discretion and subtlety, General. You are not the master of either one. Please, this is not an insult to you. I have confidence in your abilities. You must be confident in mine. Draw up your plans, your strategies. Leave the kaiser to me."

Ludendorff could not help smiling at von Hindenburg's good humor. "Of course." He paused, moved a pad of paper in front of him, studied for a moment, said, "I believe that General Falkenhayn's original philosophy was correct, that the way to win this war now is to bleed the enemy until he is too weak to fight. His error was in choosing the aggressive attack as the means to achieve this. What worked for us against Russia will not necessarily work in France." Von Hindenburg leaned back in the chair, listening to every word. Ludendorff continued, "If we had been allowed to destroy the Russians altogether, this would not be a discussion. We could focus all our power against the West."

"General, you know very well that no one will ever destroy the Russians. No matter how poorly they are equipped or how inferior their training, there are too many of them and their country is too vast. You may defeat them on a dozen battle-fields, but even in defeat they can take the advantage. The strategy of retreat is most effective for them. No army can hope to follow them into the abyss of their country. They will always live to fight another day. The important thing is to accomplish exactly what you and I have already accomplished. Remove them from our land, and defend our border so they can never strike effectively."

"Someone should teach the Austrians that."

Von Hindenburg sniffed, and Ludendorff knew it was the one subject that could anger the old man. From the start of the war, the Germans had been forced to send a constant stream of assistance to their Austrian allies. Von Hindenburg was scowl-ing now, said, "There is no lesson for them to learn. It is not about their generals, but their soldiers. Germany is one land, one people. Austria is a great bowl of soup, filled with every manner of tribe and culture, whose very differences weaken their monarchy. The Russians have discovered this, certainly.

And so, the Russians will concentrate their attention away from Germany and strike where the weakness has presented itself."

It was a subject they had discussed many times, and Ludendorff said, "I have been recently asked why Germany has allowed herself to be allied with an Austrian corpse. I admit, I still have no good answer."

"Politics, General. Simple as that. Emperor Franz-Josef is a relic, a tired old man who bends to the will of anyone he fears. He fears the kaiser, and so, he obeys. Kaiser Wilhelm sees Austria-Hungary as a land of opportunity. He probably believes that one day he might unite the two empires, if not by a military alliance, then perhaps by marriage. It is, after all, what monarchs do."

"But Austria cannot fight!"

"Do not exaggerate, General. The Austrians can certainly fight. What they cannot do is *win*."

Ludendorff was always affected by von Hindenburg's rare dark moods. He scanned the papers, knew they had many things to discuss, did not want von Hindenburg to dwell on the problems of Austria. He searched for a way to conclude the topic, said, "Then we shall continue to assist them."

Von Hindenburg leaned forward, his thick arms resting on the table. "Quite right, General. It is all we can do, after all. This war has spread far beyond Germany's capacity to engage every enemy on every front. We require our allies, whether we respect them or not. Whether we have confidence in the Turks, the Bulgarians, or the Austrians is not important. It is not necessary for our allies to claim overwhelming victory in Arabia, or in Italy, or even in Russia. It is only necessary for them not to be defeated. The real war is right here, on the Western Front. If France falls, if Britain retires, make no mistake, General, this war is over. The Turks may claim Mesopotamia if they wish. Bulgaria and Austria may divide the spoils of the Balkans." He paused, ran a hand across the large expanse at his waist. "General, here on this train, in the privacy of this car, we can make our jokes and dismiss the kaiser for his failings. But let us be clear, General. The kaiser is superior to the king of England or the rulers of France for one very important reason. Britain and France worship their past. The kaiser has his eyes focused firmly on the future, one Europe, under one ruler, and in that, he is correct. In all of history, there is a constancy. Nations either progress or decay. Germany will either assert her place as a world power, or we will be swept under the carpet of history. There are so many examples of this: Turkey, Italy, Greece, Spain. So many empires reduced now to the role of minions, General. Only France and Britain are capable of denying us. If we dominate them, we dominate the world. We are at a crossroads, and it is in our hands, you and me. It is up to us whether Germany realizes her destiny, or collapses into stagnation. Humanity is governed by certain truths, and with all my soul I believe one of those truths to be that war is the natural state of mankind. We will conquer or we will die."

12

RICHTHOFEN

La Brayelle, France—January 10, 1917

He stood at rigid attention, watched as the driver stepped quickly around the car, opening the rear door. The older man emerged slowly, straightened, stood tall and rigid, a thin man, gaunt face. The man moved toward Richthofen now, said, "I assume you are my host, Lieutenant."

"Yes, General von Hoeppner. I am Lieutenant Manfred von Richthofen. I am at your service, sir."

The old man looked past him, seemed to search for something, said, "Is there no one else here, Lieutenant? I had not thought you would man this squadron by yourself."

"I have ordered the squadron to take one day of recreation." He glanced up. "The weather is unfortunate. The fog has prevailed. It is my intention to begin an intense period of instruction for the pilots in this command. I do not believe classrooms produce good pilots." He stopped, had said far more than any lieutenant should volunteer to a general. Von Hoeppner was wide-eyed, seemed to expect more, and Richthofen said, "Forgive me, sir. If you feel classrooms are essential to training, then of course we shall employ classrooms."

Behind him, there was a burst of barking, the huge dog suddenly pursuing a rabbit across the open field. Behind the dog, a young man scrambled to catch him, shouting vague obscenities Richthofen could not quite hear. He grimaced, closed his eyes for a brief moment, and von Hoeppner laughed, said, "One of your pilots, Lieutenant? Are we recruiting dogs to train our fighters now?"

Richthofen did not expect the smile on the old man's face.

"No, sir, that is my orderly, Corporal Menzke. Please forgive me, General. He is a free spirit. I have tried to deter him from the habit of chasing rabbits."

"Your orderly pursues rabbits?"

"Oh, no, sir. My dog. My orderly has been instructed to maintain control of my dog. It has been a difficult task." Richthofen felt his face reddening, felt a sudden urge to shoot his dog. He tried to put words together, some explanation, but von Hoeppner seemed not to notice. The general glanced back, said to his driver, "Remain here. I will meet with the lieutenant, and we will be on our way."

Richthofen had expected von Hoeppner to stay the night, was suddenly relieved the general's visit would be brief. He had no idea what the commander of an air squadron was supposed to do to entertain the senior commander of the entire German Air Service. Von Hoeppner was far higher up the German chain of command than any officer Richthofen had met, and though he had no idea exactly why the general had scheduled this visit, he was certain von Hoeppner would be testing him, making sure that this new position was not merely another ribbon Richthofen would hang on his wall. He stepped back, waiting for von Hoeppner to give him some sign that they could move inside, thought, If he is here to confirm that I am up to this task, the first impression has not gone well.

Richthofen was now the commander of Pursuit Squadron Eleven, which had been stationed in a small village near the French town of Douai. The squadron had been assembled in October 1916, and had distinguished itself for one very dubious achievement: in the three months of its existence, Squadron Eleven was one of the only fighter groups on the entire Western Front that had yet to shoot down a single enemy plane.

The opportunity to command his own squadron had no appeal to Richthofen. He respected what Stephan Walz had already done with the Boelcke Squadron, understood that every command needs an efficient administrator, someone who understands and has patience for all the minute aggravations of managing an aerodrome and its pilots. As he departed Boelcke's aerodrome for the last time, the wineglasses had been raised, the handshakes extended, and Richthofen did his best to share in their celebration for his new position. It was certainly an honor, and Richthofen already understood the challenge of teaching merely adequate pilots to become expert fighters. Boelcke's lessons were still within him, and now, Richthofen would be the teacher. It was a challenge that filled him with absolute dread, but at least, as commander of Squadron Eleven, they would learn *his* way, or they would leave.

"You may not feel this chill, Lieutenant, but I prefer to have this conversation indoors. Have you an office here?"

Richthofen made a short bow, said, "Forgive me, sir. Please, this way."

The general followed him to the wide open entrance of a hollow wood-frame building, what had once been a barn, the hard dirt floor barely hiding the pungent scent of its former occupants. In one corner were two hastily built walls that carved out a space that he now called his office. Richthofen moved quickly to the single wood door, held it open, grimaced as his dog suddenly bounded through the opening behind them, a cascade of barking.

"Fine animal, Lieutenant. Great Dane, yes?"

"Yes, sir. I call him Moritz, sir. I apologize for his . . . energy, sir."

Von Hoeppner glanced around the room, sat in the one small chair, said, "Nonsense. No better companion. Completely loyal, resolute in his efforts to please. The perfect characteristics of a soldier, wouldn't you say?"

Richthofen moved to the small desk, reached down, adjusted a gas heater, the orange glow now brighter, slid the heater forward, closer to the general. Von Hoeppner seemed to ignore the gesture, said, "A great many of us are growing old, Lieutenant. Headquarters is filled with generals who are held captive by their glorious pasts. I must admit, I envy the boundless energy of your companion out there. If we are to win this war, the challenge will fall to the young, to men such as you."

Richthofen caught the word: *if*. It was a surprise.

"We are doing our best, General."

"Some of you. I must tell you, Lieutenant, your name is

185

mentioned in every staff room in Berlin. For quite some time, the Air Service suffered a considerable amount of neglect. That is, until men like you gave us an identity. You are certainly aware that my own position was lightly regarded for some time. We are fortunate that Herr Ludendorff appreciates the value of aircraft. In some ways, we must be grateful to the French. Their ingenuity awoke the High Command to the fact that aeroplanes are essential to a modern war. If we had not responded as we did, the French would control the air from here to Switzerland. Have you engaged the French, Lieutenant?"

"Not yet, sir. I much prefer fighting the British. All I have heard of the French is that they prefer to lay traps, to fight by deceit and trickery. Their attack is like bottled lemonade. It lacks . . . tenacity. The British believe they can confront us and win. What their pilots believe to be pluck and bravery is all too often merely stupidity."

Von Hoeppner laughed, and Richthofen was embarrassed, realized he may have become too informal. Von Hoeppner said, "So, you would rather face an opponent who will confront you, eh? More dangerous that way, certainly."

"Forgive me, sir, but from what has been confirmed, my victories have all come against the Englishman. I prefer an opponent who believes he is brave, who believes he has the best aeroplane. None of that prepares him for combat against a foe who has the superior skill."

"I cannot argue with your logic or your accomplishments, Lieutenant. Be aware, however, that the British are a Germanic race. Though they may not match you in skill, they can be our equal in tenacity."

Richthofen was surprised at von Hoeppner's warmth, was feeling much more comfortable in the old man's presence. He had never expected any general to speak to him this way. He reached down, adjusted the heater, the air in the room growing oppressively warm.

"What do you think of your pilots, Lieutenant? Can you better the record of Squadron Boelcke?"

Richthofen sat upright again, realized that von Hoeppner was staring at him with cold eyes, the playfulness suddenly gone.

"I had not considered my former squadron's record to be . . . attainable."

Von Hoeppner frowned, said, "Of course it's attainable. That's why you're here. I'm surprised you don't appreciate that. You have one primary duty here, Lieutenant. You are to turn Squadron Eleven into a *fighting* squadron, not merely one that flies aeroplanes. You must give them something of yourself, whatever it is that has made you a hero to the German people. I want this squadron . . . I want *every* squadron in the Air Service to prove to me, to the High Command, to the kaiser himself, that they are the finest squadron in Germany. In other words, Lieutenant, I want competition. Squadron Boelcke has a formidable record of confirmed kills."

"Over a hundred, sir."

"Yes! Over a hundred! It is obvious what you must do, Lieutenant! You must put these men to work! And, one more thing." Von Hoeppner paused, seemed to search for words. "I have noticed that many of my pilots have been adding nonregulation adornments to their aeroplanes. I had considered disciplinary action as a means to end this reckless practice. However, I noticed that these adornments have become a source of pride, as well as recognition. Despite my earlier reservations, I have decided instead to encourage this sort of practice. What is your feeling about this?"

Richthofen was surprised von Hoeppner would ask such a question, thought carefully, said, "Captain Boelcke had painted the motor cover of his Albatros red, so that in a large engagement, we might know which plane was his. I had thought of doing the same here. I thought as well that it might be an appropriate tribute to the captain. I am aware, of course, that it is against regulations."

"Not any longer. Of course, his principle of recognition is entirely correct. By all means, you should do the same. Consider it a fine tribute, if you wish." He paused, thought a moment. "It occurs to me that there is another reason why a skilled pilot should be recognized. Do you imagine that the enemy came to recognize the band of red on the motor of Captain Boelcke's aeroplane? I would think so. I would assume that a British pilot who suddenly realized that his opponent was Boelcke . . . imagine, then, what he would experience, the fear that would spring into his mind in that moment of awareness. Surely, that provided some advantage."

"I had not considered that, sir."

Von Hoeppner stood now, seemed energized by his own words. "Regulations! A colossal mistake, Lieutenant." He looked at Richthofen, leaned close to him, the old man's hands on the small desk. "I told you that every staff room in Kreuznach echoes with your name, every bureaucrat's office in Berlin. Lieutenant, I want more. I want every staff officer in *London* to know your name. I want every enemy pilot who flies the Western Front to live in dread that his next opponent will be Richthofen!" He straightened, turned away, a wide smile. "Indeed. This is precisely what we need. The newspapers will put this on every front page." He moved toward the door, and before Richthofen could rise, von Hoeppner pulled it open, then turned toward him, said, "This meeting is concluded, Lieutenant. I will follow the progress of Squadron Eleven with great interest. And you will immediately order that your personal aeroplane be painted red. Do you understand me, Lieutenant? Not just the motor. The entire plane!"

January 17, 1917

The Order Pour le Mérite had finally been awarded to him, a brief ceremony the day before. It had been without fanfare, Richthofen avoiding the photographers, accepting the medal with somber silence. It occurred to him to offer his own tribute to Max Immelmann, something the newspapers didn't need to know. He would wear the medal under his flight suit, would always have it close to him every time he flew. It would become a habit, a part of his clothing. He did not want the ceremony of it, would wear the medal only as his private gesture. As much as he had wished for it, and as hard as he had worked, he was already looking ahead.

With the medal and the new command there had been something else new to Richthofen, a sense of pride he had never really known before. It was not merely the newspaper headlines, or the enthusiasm of von Hoeppner. All his life he had been the focus of his father's critical eye, had gone to military school to please the old man, had joined the cavalry to satisfy his family's dependence on honor, something that had stayed inside Richthofen from his first days in the military. But flying had been his choice alone, and it had humbled him. It was a new kind of aristocracy, with excellence the new bloodline. No one had inherited the right to be a good pilot. The rich man could make as many mistakes as the poor, and even a small error could kill you. Boelcke had taught him not just to be a good flyer, but to be the best fighter a man could be. Despite the newspapers, Richthofen understood that he was still learning, that each experience, each victory added to what Boelcke had given him. There had been significant changes in the air, and he thought of von Hoeppner's words, that the British were not so different from the Germans. Richthofen had seen it himself, could no longer depend on the enemy to make his usual mistakes. The British were learning themselves, the quality of their planes and the skills of the men who flew them increasing with every confrontation. Lanoe Hawker had been an exceptional pilot, and Richthofen would no longer deny himself the accomplishment, the pure skill it had required to bring Hawker down.

When Richthofen arrived at La Brayelle, his first task had been to study the records and reports of his pilots. Though the men made something of a motley appearance and seemed to lack pride in themselves and in their skills, there was nothing on the papers in front of him that condemned any man to mediocrity. He realized now something that Boelcke would certainly have told him. What they require is *leadership*.

He knew they were waiting for him, had observed them through the small window of his office as they gathered into formation. He had never tried to offer anyone a speech, had no intention of making one now. It is not my job to give them passion, he thought, to heighten their loyalty to the kaiser. Any one of them who does not understand why he is a pilot would never have volunteered in the first place. But still . . . I am here . . . I have this command . . . because I have *won*. If they are not inspired by that, then my job here will be more difficult than I imagine.

He looked at one paper on his desk, held it up, had studied it repeatedly, the mechanical specifics of the new aeroplanes. He still didn't understand what some of the numbers meant, but he knew enough to be excited. Von Hoeppner had sent Squadron Eleven a group of the new Albatros D-IIIs, a machine vastly superior to the plane Richthofen had already mastered. The D-III was only slightly faster than its predecessor, but it could climb more quickly, and could fly comfortably at more than seventeen thousand feet. It will take more than a new aeroplane to make them good pilots, he thought. But it will be a very good way to begin. He glanced again out the small window, saw a flurry of snow, thought, They have waited long enough. And I must get this over with.

He moved out through the door, the vast open building smelling more of gasoline now, several of the new planes lined up nose to tail. He enjoyed looking at them, had already singled out his own, stared at it for a long moment, then stepped out into the blast of cold air.

Each man was bundled up in the thick overcoat that would accompany him in the air. A few were talking, low voices, some watching him as he approached. He kicked his boots through the snowy grass, stopped in front of them, was pleased that most of them reacted by coming to attention. He was still putting names to faces, had been surprised to learn that some of them had as much experience in the Air Service as he had. He looked at the large man on the end of the line, his heavy coat giving him the appearance of a great brown bear, the name coming to him now: Konstantin Krefft. Krefft was a young lieutenant whose record surprised Richthofen, the man actually flying alongside Max Immelmann. Krefft was also a man who had demonstrated a strong aptitude for mechanics, something that impressed Richthofen even more. Beside Krefft were the two brothers, Karl and Wilhelm Allmenroder, who had learned as Richthofen had learned, by flying the two-seat bombers. He scanned the line of men, could see that they were appraising him as well, thought, Certainly. You are entitled to know something of your new leader, to wonder if I am anything more than what is in the newspapers. His eyes stopped at the far end of the line, and he focused on a tall, thin man, who seemed to bend with the wind. Kurt Wolff was something of a mystery to him, a frail man not quite twenty-two years old, who appeared much younger. Wolff had the unfortunate distinction of having killed his flight instructor by crashing during his very first flight. More crashes had followed, but despite a permanent injury to his shoulder, Wolff had persisted in the Air Service. Richthofen had already heard something about a nickname, some reference to Wolff as a *delicate flower*. We have no use for delicate flowers, he thought. But I cannot condemn a man for a history of recklessness. It is something I share with him. He is serious about flying, and as much as any man here, he seems eager to learn.

Richthofen pulled his heavy coat tightly around him, braced himself against an icy breeze, patches of loose snow blowing into small powdery clouds across the open ground. He had put it off long enough, the task was unavoidable, and he stepped closer to them, said, "Does the cold bother any of you? Would you prefer to be inside?"

No one spoke, and he nodded, thought, I dare them to show weakness; they dare me as well.

"Very soon, we will fly. I am as impatient with this weather as you must certainly be. I have not called you out here just to torture you. You have seen the new Albatroses. You know what they are capable of doing. We must use their climbing ability to our advantage, and that means you will fly higher than you have ever flown before. And, I am hoping you understand just how cold you will get." He paused for a moment, saw only nods of confirmation. "Very good. Now, does anyone here believe he knows how to kill the enemy? Your record would indicate that you do not."

They glanced at each other, no one responding, and he said, "Does anyone here believe he can survive when the enemy tries to kill him?"

One man stepped forward now, did not look at him, said, "We have mastered that, sir."

Richthofen was not amused, looked at the ground at his

feet, pushed the toe of his boot into a lump of snow, flattened it.

"I have examined your records, your reports. You have fought several engagements with the enemy that should have resulted in great success, and yet you have achieved nothing more than your own survival. Despite what your sweethearts may have told you, survival is not victory. Some of you have survived this war by merely keeping your distance from the enemy. If that describes *you*, then you have no place in this squadron. I do not intend to die because my wingman is distracted by dreams of his loved ones. Very quickly I will know if I can depend on you. Not too far west of here, your countrymen are dying in trenches, while you enjoy the privilege of gazing down upon them from the lofty perch of the eagle. There is many an infantry commander who would welcome a former pilot into his command." He looked up at them now, felt an unexpected anger, his words growing hotter as he spoke. "Germany has given this war some of her finest men. I have known some of them personally. A great man taught me how to fight. I do not pretend to be Boelcke. No matter what my orders are here, I am still Boelcke's student, his lessons are with me every time I fly. You will learn—" He stopped, the emotion choking off his words. No one was moving, no smiles, all eyes focused on him, and he was embarrassed now, could not talk about Boelcke without emotion, and he had no cause to scold them. Not yet. He found the control, took a long deep breath.

"It is my intention to instruct this squadron to pursue a single purpose: killing the enemy. I am not ashamed to admit to you that I have never before been in command. I could not have accepted this responsibility if I did not believe I could teach you how to be better pilots. It has been said in the newspapers that simply because I am here, Squadron Eleven will certainly become Germany's finest. Those are foolish words. Nothing written in Berlin will change anything you do here. I have accepted the challenge assigned to me. You will as well. I have set one goal for myself. If I am killed, I will die knowing that one of you has learned the lessons necessary to take my place. If we are successful here, one day, when you receive your

Order Pour le Mérite, each of you may say: I have learned the lessons of Boelcke. And I have learned them from Richthofen."

The lessons began as the weather improved, and Richthofen was pleased that among the young pilots of Squadron Eleven, a few began to surface as outstanding fighters. As the men increased their efficiency, Richthofen himself began a remarkable string of victories. On January 23, the first day of good flying weather in more than two weeks, Richthofen led them aloft in his newly painted red Albatros. The scene before them had unfolded like a perfect classroom display, and he took full advantage, keeping his pilots back as Boelcke had done, confronting by himself a small group of British fighters. Richthofen scored his seventeenth kill in plain sight of the entire squadron, the British fighter tumbling out of the sky in a streak of fire. Every member of the squadron got his first les-son in the tactics of Boelcke, and the skills of Richthofen. And Pursuit Squadron Eleven had recorded its first victory.

Within weeks his pilots had begun making kills of their own, Krefft and both Allmenroder brothers scoring victories. But it was their instructor who seemed inspired by the performance of his students. By the end of March, Richthofen had confirmed thirty-one kills, more than any living pilot in the war. General von Hoeppner's wish was soon fulfilled. Photographers flocked to the aerodrome, and posters and banners began to appear in Berlin and every city in Germany, glorifying Germany's "Red Battle Flyer." The people began to speak more of this new hero, and less of the desperation that had swept through their country. Even the British pilots who had not yet seen the red Albatros were speaking of it, and in London, the British press obliged von Hoeppner exactly as he had hoped. As Richthofen's successes mounted, so too did the aura around the man the British were now calling the "Red Baron."

13

LUFBERY

March 1917

The original founders of the squadron continued to drop away. On March 19, Jim McConnell flew his last mission, disappearing into the combat zone, with no word of his fate until French cavalry happened upon the wreckage of his plane. McConnell was close to thirty, nearly as old as Lufbery, a midwesterner, the son of a prominent judge and railroad magnate. From the beginning, he had been the hard-luck case of the squadron, had been injured the previous summer just badly enough that flying was painfully difficult. As McConnell's effectiveness decreased, Captain Thenault had ordered him to recuperate at the American hospital. But McConnell pushed his convalescence too hard, had made several attempts to return to active duty. Each time, his injuries proved too uncomfortable. With the long winter finally drawing to a close, he had come back again, had endured his discomfort long enough to retune his skills, to become proficient in the air. But if his physical condition had improved, his luck had not. He was the fourth escadrille founder to die.

The end of the year saw another founding member depart the escadrille, but it had little to do with combat. Though he had been officially credited with three confirmed victories, Bert Hall had built a reputation more for his mouth than his flying. From the squadron's first days, Hall was a man who made it clear that he intended to leave the war a hero, with all the trappings and fringe benefits that would guarantee back home. Throughout the escadrille's first year, Hall made continuous claims for victories that no one could confirm, and seemed to shine most when no one was around to observe. Lufbery had stayed clear

194

of Hall, respected that Kiffin Rockwell had despised the man. When Hall was caught cheating at cards, it was the final straw. Hall himself seemed to appreciate that he was unwanted, and to the enormous relief of everyone in the squadron, Thenault recommended him for a transfer. He was first assigned to another French squadron, but soon after, word came back to the escadrille that Hall had requested transfer again, had given up the French Air Service to serve instead in Romania, presumably seeking further adventures. Lufbery had no doubts that Bert Hall had chosen to find that adventure in a place where no one had yet learned of his reputation as a consummate liar.

With the coming of spring, and clearer skies, the Lafayette Escadrille had exactly one remaining founding member: Bill Thaw. Lufbery was now the second highest in seniority. To the new and inexperienced pilots, the two men carried all the prestige befitting the glory of the outfit. While Thaw seemed to enjoy the respect, Lufbery could not avoid the gnawing feeling that his longevity simply meant that every day he flew, he was pushing his luck.

With the battlefields along the Somme quiet once more, the squadron had been moved again, to an airfield somewhat closer to Paris. The town was called Saint-Just-en-Chaussée and was located near an airfield as primitive as it was miserable. There were no barracks at all, no facility yet provided for the comfort of the men. With the coming of spring, the speculation began as to which side would launch the first major offensive of the new year. All the pilots were told was that the purpose of the move was to position the Lafayette Escadrille closer to the center of the entire Western Front. The orders from the Aeronautique Militaire were no more specific than that: sooner or later, someone will launch an attack. Be ready to assist.

The winter had been horribly severe. Though it was suggested that all air squadrons make periodic patrols over the front lines, flying meant enduring temperatures so desperately frigid that a pilot might die from exposure. If the air on the ground was cold enough, the oil in the motors would simply freeze, making flying impossible. Well into February, the wind howled, and the air had been ripped by blinding snowstorms. It was a reprieve many had prayed for. Regardless of what expectations came down to them from command, every pilot understood that despite their orders, until the air grew warm again, no one had any business in the air.

March 28, 1917

With the frozen silence of the battlefields, and the tempting proximity of Paris, the pilots had sought leave at every opportunity. Thenault had been obliging, most of the men hitching a ride on whatever mode of transportation happened by. At first, Lufbery had made his usual rounds to the familiar bars, and both he and Thaw had made regular visits to Clyde Balsley. Balsley was still confined to the American hospital, and would be for a long time. The severe wound to his leg had yet to heal, and despite Balsley's amazingly positive spirit, Lufbery was certain the man would never fly again.

Lufbery had begun to tire of the constant partying in Paris. As much as he loved the city, the bouts of revelry seemed to appeal far more to the younger men, the new members of the squadron, some of whom seemed to think that wars were fought with champagne bottles. Lufbery had grown weary of starting each day suffering through the aftermath of an alcohol fog, usually with a blinding headache. Though Paris still beckoned, he had found another distraction. With the warmer air, the number of flights was increasing dramatically, and so the motors required stepped-up maintenance schedules. In addition, headquarters had responded to the increased activity in the air by providing several new aeroplanes. Despite the attraction of the nightlife, Lufbery had returned to his first love: digging his hands into the grease and oil of new pistons and valves and cylinders.

He sat under the rippling fabric of the canvas hangar, surrounded by the disassembled fragments of a motor, the newer Clerget that was replacing the standard LeRhone that had powered most of the Nieuports. The distinction meant little

196

to the other pilots, beyond the added power of the Clerget, which increased the speed of the Nieuports to nearly one hundred fifteen miles per hour. To the rest of the pilots, the Clerget was simply the tool that dragged the Nieuports into the air. To Lufbery, it was a marvel. The design was just different enough that many of the parts scattered around him were unfamiliar. It was an exploration he could not pass up.

He heard a strange rattling, a rumble of metal out beyond the hangar. It stopped, and he heard a voice.

"Eh, Mr. Lufbery! You are invited to come along!"

He looked out, saw DeLaage seated in the cab of a severely dented flatbed truck. Two of the mechanics were standing up in the back, and Lufbery said, "Thank you. I'll remain here. Where did you get that . . . um . . . vehicle?"

There was laughter from the mechanics, and DeLaage shrugged, said, "I know better than to ask. In the army, we encourage the men to improvise."

Lufbery waved, and the truck jumped forward, a burst of black smoke spewing out the rear. They were gone now, and Lufbery picked up one of the Clerget's valves, slid his fingers around the top, measured it with a calipers, heard a voice behind him.

"There is talk that you are insane." He saw LeBlanc walking up beside him now, staring down at him.

"That what you think?"

"Me? No. I would rather play with my motors than with my wife. But don't tell her I said that."

LeBlanc knelt down, and Lufbery said, "Have you seen the springs? Tighter, thicker steel. Should last longer."

LeBlanc picked up one of the newly designed valve springs, said, "Yes. Many improvements. So, you do not go to Paris with the others?"

"You didn't either."

LeBlanc stood again, pointed to the line of Nieuports in the open field.

"Too much work to do. I thought it better to catch up on maintenance." He paused, and Lufbery waited for more. "If you don't mind me asking, what do you think of the new men?"

197

Lufbery leaned back on his hands, looked up at LeBlanc, thought, Well, here's something new. They all had felt the dividing line between mechanics and pilots, made more pronounced by their different nationalities. Every pilot had his favorite mechanic, and it was no secret that the mechanics respected some pilots more than others. Lufbery knew that some of the mechanics spoke harshly behind their backs about those pilots who could not avoid abusing their aircraft. Lufbery ran the faces through his mind, said, "Anyone in particular?"

LeBlanc shook his head. "No. I just wonder about them when the fighting begins. They are very good with the bottle, yes?"

"Not much else to do. Have to keep the blood from freezing."

LeBlanc was silent for a moment, and Lufbery said, "They'll be ready when the time comes."

There was the sound of a motor now, and LeBlanc looked up toward the opening in the hangar, the sound coming from beyond the far rows of trees. The motor seemed to spit, uneven, was closer now, and LeBlanc said, "That's not one of ours."

Lufbery scrambled to his feet, scanned the trees out beyond the edge of the field, said, "Bombers? They just come at night."

LeBlanc shook his head, "No. Smaller. Only one."

The motor spit again, and they saw the plane now, drifting toward them over the treetops, dropping down toward the open field in front of them. Lufbery saw the wings dip and tilt, the prop suddenly motionless, the motor silent. LeBlanc said, "He's coming in! Good God, it's a Boche!"

Lufbery did not wait for the plane to land, ran into the makeshift hangar, scanned the wooden crates, boxes and cans, saw now, propped up in one corner, an old Lewis gun. He grabbed it, jerked the bolt, saw the drum was empty.

"Damn it!"

LeBlanc shouted, "He stopped. It's a two-seater. What do we do?"

"You have a gun? A pistol?"

LeBlanc ran past him now, shuffled through a cloth bag, pulled out a small revolver. "Here! I'll go get the guards!"

"You're not going anywhere! I can't fight them by myself! Come on!"

LeBlanc followed him into the field, and Lufbery struggled to run with the unwieldy Lewis gun. He scanned the plane, saw the rear machine gun hanging limp, and he moved out to the side, avoiding the aim of the plane's front machine guns. He hefted the Lewis gun, pointed it toward the men in the plane, moved closer, fat black crosses staring at him from the wings. The pilot raised his hands above his head, the observer now doing the same, and the observer said, "Please! We will not fight!"

Lufbery moved around the wingtips, the Lewis gun growing heavier in his arms. LeBlanc was still in front of the plane, seemed mesmerized, staring at the unfamiliar motor. The Germans pulled off their goggles, and Lufbery saw a cold glare from the pilot. The observer said, "You may put your weapon down. We did not come here to engage you."

"You speak English?"

"Yes, I am an American. German by birth, actually. My family lives in Florida."

Lufbery's arms were screaming from the weight of the Lewis gun, and he looked at LeBlanc, said, "Corporal! Come here, please!"

LeBlanc seemed to regain his wits, moved around beside Lufbery, the pistol dangling in his hand. Lufbery set the Lewis gun down, flexed his arms, plucked the pistol from LeBlanc's hands. The observer stood up in his cockpit, said, "Might I step down? I have a favor to ask. I assure you, I am not armed."

"All right. Step out. Let me see your hands."

The man jumped down, motioned to the pilot to stay put, the man complying, staring at the pistol in Lufbery's hand. The observer kept his hands high, and Lufbery looked him over, the thick leather flying suit, fat furry boots. The man said, "Sorry to trouble you, but, as you can see, we had some difficulty. We seem to have gotten off course, and before we could right ourselves, we ran out of fuel. Could you possibly spare some gasoline?"

The man smiled pleasantly, and Lufbery absorbed his request, heard a sputter from LeBlanc.

"You want us to give you . . . fuel?"

"Yes, if you don't mind. It was either land here, or go down in the trees. As we came down, I saw the Indians on your planes. Quite a relief. I assumed I could count on a more friendly reception, countrymen and all. Captain Rieger is my pilot. He was not so certain, but once the motor quit, well, there wasn't time for discussion."

LeBlanc said the word again. "Fuel?"

The observer nodded, and Lufbery could see him straining to keep his smile as friendly as any man could. Lufbery looked past the man to the pilot, who stirred uncomfortably in his cockpit.

"Tell him to keep his hands outside."

"Oh, certainly." The man turned, said something in German, and the pilot raised his hands, let them hang out.

Lufbery nodded to the pilot, said to the observer, "What's your name?"

"Otto Klein. You?"

"None of your damned business." The man's smile began to show strain, and Lufbery felt a hard burn expanding in his chest. "Mr. Klein, you are our prisoners. You will tell your pilot to rise from his seat slowly, with his hands visible."

"Oh, please, sir, I ask you, as one American to another. Have you no respect for the chivalry of the skies? Even a splash of fuel, and we will be on our way."

LeBlanc said in a low growling voice, "We are not in the skies."

The pilot said something, and the observer turned, replied to him, then said to Lufbery, "All right, if you must be strict about this, Captain Rieger has a proposition. Allow us to refuel, and then, one of your pilots can follow us into the air. If you wish to be so barbaric about this, we can fight a duel aloft. The winner goes home, the loser . . . well, the loser does not."

Lufbery could see the arrogance on the man's face, felt his hands beginning to shake. He raised the pistol, pointed it at the man's forehead. His voice was choked away by the tight fury in his throat, and he said, "Mr. Klein, if I was barbaric I would shoot you right now. I would execute you for spying on our airfield. You will tell your pilot to climb down now."

The man's smile had disappeared, and he glanced back, said a few words. The pilot shouted something, and Lufbery thought, Swearing at me won't help, you Boche son of a bitch. The man climbed out of his cockpit, was on the ground now, stood beside his plane at attention. Lufbery said to LeBlanc, "Search him. He might be armed."

LeBlanc moved quickly, unzipping the man's flying suit, Lufbery motioning with the pistol for Klein to open his coat.

"Please, sir, in all fairness . . ."

"If you speak again, I will kill you."

Lufbery wanted to say more, to scream at the man, felt the boiling outrage surging through him, right down to his finger that wrapped around the trigger of the pistol.

LeBlanc had the pilot by the arm, pulled him forward, said, "Uh . . . what do we do with them?"

Lufbery stepped back, motioned with the pistol, the two men falling into line in front of him.

"We turn them over to the army. They have appropriate places for prisoners of war."

LeBlanc picked up the Lewis gun, was beside him now, said, "What do we do with the aeroplane? It's a beauty. A new Albatros. God, I'd love to take it apart."

Lufbery held the pistol against the pilot's back, heard soft sobs coming from the observer. Out in front of them, soldiers appeared, and LeBlanc said, "They finally got word. Some farmer probably saw the aeroplane coming down."

The soldiers were scrambling toward them, rifles at the ready, an officer drawing a short thin sword. Lufbery looked down, stared at the observer's boots, saw soft brown leather, fat swirls and tufts of fur caressing the man's ankles. He made a mental measurement, could see the man's foot was about the size of his own, and the anger began to give way. The logic of it was calming his mind, the perfect restitution for the man's treachery. He pushed the pilot to one side, poked the pistol into the observer's back, said, "Tell you what, Klein. I'll tell them not to shoot you. You give me your damned boots."

* * *

"They wanted gasoline?"

"And got all ticked off when you refused?"

The laughter was contagious, and Lufbery responded, the memory of the strange afternoon clouded by a heavy dose of Lafayette Cocktails. Thaw was close beside him, said, "An empty Lewis gun? For chrissakes, Luf, what would you have done if they'd starting shooting?"

Lufbery shrugged, said, "Hell if I know. Thought never crossed my mind." He paused, pondered the question. "At least LeBlanc had the pistol."

There was a roar of laughter, and he saw LeBlanc now, the man sitting quietly in the corner, surrounded by a flock of his mechanics. LeBlanc held up a glass of champagne, toasted him silently, and one of the men said, "Sorry to tell you this, but Corporal LeBlanc doesn't even know how to load a pistol."

Lufbery realized he had no idea if the pistol was loaded or not. He laughed with the rest of the room, felt Thaw's heavy hand on his shoulder.

"Hell of a thing, Luf. What do we call that bastard? A Boche American? Or an American Boche?"

"Bastard's good enough."

"Hell, for all we know, he's been shooting at us for months. One of those tough sons of bitches who won't go down. One of Parsons' duels."

Thaw laughed now, and Lufbery looked at Parsons, who nodded with a pained twist on his face. Parsons said, "To hell with you, Thaw."

The laughter came again, and Lufbery could see that Parsons was not sharing the joke.

Ted Parsons had come to the squadron in January, a blue-blooded New Englander who had immediately established himself as the most successful man in the escadrille when it came to attracting the women of Paris. But Parsons' enviable conquests of the French female were the only victories he could claim. Lufbery had made several flights with Parsons, had seen Parsons engaged in combat more times than Lufbery could remember. But despite all variety of point-blank encounters, Parsons had not yet downed a single enemy plane. Unlike some, who seemed to suffer the misfortunes of jammed machine guns, or misfiring motors, Parsons had suffered a new kind of misfortune. More than once, his bullets had shredded enemy planes, broken struts, and even wounded the pilots. But every time, the enemy had made his escape. Parsons was convinced that the Germans were using armor on their planes, that his bullets were bouncing off. Anyone else who had witnessed his misadventures knew that Ted Parsons was simply unlucky.

There was commotion outside the room, and Thaw stood, said, "Our guests have arrived!"

The room grew quiet, Lufbery sharing the anticipation, and Thaw moved to the doorway, made a bow, said, "Welcome!"

He backed into the room, and Lufbery saw a line of khaki uniforms, wide brown belts, and stiff round hats, most of them young lieutenants. The men scanned the room, examined the Americans as the Americans examined them.

While the escadrille had been based at Luxeuil, the British pilots had been regular visitors, had been welcomed for their particular talent for energizing the drunken rowdiness. But this group was unfamiliar, had just arrived at a field a few miles away. It was natural that the Americans would extend an invitation to their new neighbors. Thaw broke the awkward moment, said, "I hear one of you is called Tommy. Damned common name for you chaps, eh?"

The men seemed to appraise Thaw's observation, and one man said, "Until we are certain of your respectability, you may refer to us all as . . . *Thomas*."

The man broke into a wide grin now, extended his hand to Thaw. The Americans came forward, hands out, Lufbery joining in the greeting. The wine bottles began to move forward as well and Thaw said, "I assure you, *Thomas*, we are a respectable lot. How, exactly, do we prove that to your satisfaction?"

Lufbery saw the Brit take a bottle of wine, examine it for a brief moment, then put it to his lips. The bottle was raised, a sloppy chugging sound, and Lufbery was amazed to see the contents disappear. The man held the empty bottle out, and Thaw said, "Now . . . that's respectable!"

Another man stepped farther into the room, a captain, and the man said, "Might I meet the man who scored that victory today? Damned decent of you to bring that Boche right into your parlor. Quite the trick!"

Thaw pointed to Lufbery, said, "That would be our crack ace, Mr. Lufbery. Never fired a shot. In fact, we've established that he couldn't have fired if he'd tried. He and his mechanic captured a whole aeroplane with an empty pistol."

The captain moved toward him, a huge brick of a man, held out his hand, said, "Lufbery? Yes, indeed. We've heard of you. Is that your secret then? Just snare the enemy in your trap? The spider and the fly, eh?"

Lufbery felt his hand swallowed by the captain's grasp, saw seriousness through the good humor, something intense in the man's eyes.

"I should hope your skill rubs off on us all, Mr. Lufbery. Might I inquire as to your tally?"

Lufbery felt the captain leaning over him, the man's gaze boring into him. He was feeling uncomfortable now, rarely mentioned his score of victories. Thaw moved up beside the big man, rescuing Lufbery.

"Ah, old Luf here doesn't like to brag. We do it for him. Not sure we can add his little adventure today. But otherwise, he's got eight confirmed kills. And at least that many more unconfirmed. Damned Boche pilots have the miserable habit of falling down behind their own lines."

The captain still stared down at Lufbery, said, "Honor to meet you. No offense to your compatriots, but we hear you're the best American pilot in the war."

Lufbery felt smothered by the man's graciousness, said, "There have been better. We have lost some good men. I have been more fortunate than some."

The captain nodded, seemed to appraise Lufbery still. "Modest of you. Of course, in war, truth is always a suspect quality. Regardless, I offer a toast to you. To . . . all of you." The captain turned toward the rest of them, said, "To the Americans of the Lafayette Escadrille! May your nation appreciate the stand you have taken! And may your president as well! God knows your newspapers have!"

The glasses were raised, but there was tension in the man's words. Lufbery drank from his glass, scanned the faces of the other British pilots. There were few smiles now, the only sounds the clinking of glasses, the bottles emptying. Even Thaw seemed unsure of what to say, the stench of politics rarely infecting the parties.

It had become an embarrassment to the squadron that in America, the newspaper stories had blossomed like flowers in a field, and none of them were accurate. The American people were being fed a steady diet of exaggeration about the Lafayette Escadrille, ridiculous accounts of their success, claims that no American pilot ever took to the air without destroying entire squadrons of German planes. To the Americans, it was a minor annoyance, the cascade of letters pouring onto them from well-wishers and admirers, none of whom had any idea what was actually happening in France. But to the French and British pilots who fought the same enemy, it was an offense, many of them assuming that the stories were originating at the airfield, that this small group of Americans was spending as much time promoting their own glory as they were engaging in actual combat.

The bottles continued to appear, and Lufbery felt a nagging sense of danger, that as more wine was consumed, the simmering antagonism of the Brits might erupt into something far more unpleasant. He heard the sound of the inevitable piano, raised himself up, was surprised to see DeLaage in his familiar seat. But the music was unsteady, DeLaage struggling slightly, no voices joining in. There were small conversations around the room, some of the Brits focusing on individuals, others keeping to themselves. Through it all, Lufbery was growing more uncomfortable, sought out Thaw, saw him mixing a drink for the huge British captain, imparting the secrets of the Lafayette Cocktail. At the piano, he saw DeLaage working the keys, and Lufbery eased his way through the crowd, could sense the young Frenchman's nervousness. DeLaage saw him coming, nodded to him, a tight smile on the Frenchman's face. He continued to play, the music having no effect on the growing hum of conversation. Lufbery set his glass down on the piano, watched one of the British pilots stagger slightly, the alcohol taking its toll. He looked for Thaw again, saw him dwarfed by the captain, the big man suddenly raising a glass, shouting, "A toast! To President Jellyfish Wilson! *Peace at any price!*"

The Brits raised their glasses, and Lufbery flinched, his shoulders curling up tightly. He looked at the Americans, scattered throughout the room, could see the surprised anger rising in all of them. The Brits began to repeat the toast now, a scattering of insults pouring out toward Wilson, toward America in general. DeLaage stopped playing, stood up beside Lufbery now, and Lufbery said quietly, "Lieutenant, it's about to blow. . . ."

The first fist was launched close to the bar, and Lufbery paid little attention to the participants, knew it was just the start. The response was immediate; another man punched, falling back, shattering a small table. DeLaage shouted something, and Lufbery ignored him, felt suddenly protective of the Frenchman, had never thought of DeLaage as fragile until now. The fists were swirling all around him, most of them hitting nothing but air, drunken staggers and lunges by men who could barely stand. But not all of them were ineffective, and he saw the British captain launch a thundering blow into the chest of a man, saw it was Parsons, crumpling to the floor. Lufbery felt the rage now, had seen too many bullies in his day, the big men who went first for the weak opponent. He put a hand on DeLaage's chest, said, "Get behind the piano!"

He didn't wait for DeLaage to respond, moved toward the captain, saw the big man scanning the room, seeking another target. Lufbery was close to him now, said, "There is no purpose to this!"

The captain turned to him, the hardness in the man's eyes focused, his hands curled into massive fists. "Well, the hero! I have something for your president. Give him this. . . ."

Lufbery saw the man's right hand begin to move, leaned instinctively to the left, the fist whistling past his jaw. Lufbery felt the hair rising on his neck, the tight animal instinct engulfing him. He waited for the big man to regain his balance, saw the dark fury in the man's eyes again. The captain pulled his fist back, words coming again, "You little . . ."

But Lufbery didn't wait, dropped his left shoulder slightly, his own right hand shooting out, a hard chopping blow squarely on the side of the big man's chin. He heard a crack, the dark eyes suddenly staring past him. The large man seemed to tilt forward, and Lufbery backed up, stepped to the side, the man falling facedown, the floor bouncing beneath Lufbery's feet. Lufbery was shaking, turned, bracing for another attack, expected the Brits to swarm over him. He saw their faces now, could feel the fights around him burning themselves out with alcoholic exhaustion. One of the Brits said, "You put out the captain. How the hell . . . ? Nobody's ever done that."

The man moved closer, and Lufbery cocked the shoulder again, but there was no menace in the man's eyes. He wobbled slightly in front of Lufbery, smiled, said, "I'll be damned! Hey, chaps! Will you look at this little bloke?"

The other Brits were gathering, and Lufbery looked for allies, saw most of the Americans trying to pick their way off the floor. He was still expecting a punch, but the man was suddenly down on his knees, bending over the captain, prodding the big man's shoulder.

"Jesus. He's out like a herring!" The man pulled himself upright, looked at Lufbery with bleary eyes, said, "Mr. Looberry, I should like to offer you a drink!"

Men were finding glasses now, sorting through the chaos on the floor for bottles that still contained wine. The Americans were finding their feet now, each as confused as Lufbery was. A full glass appeared, pushed at Lufbery, who took it. The man raised his own glass, spilling wine on the fallen captain, said, "To our comrades in arms!"

The others responded as well, the startled Americans joining in. The debris from the fight was pushed aside now, the talk beginning again, laughter erasing the tension. Lufbery saw DeLaage settle onto the piano seat, the music coming quickly, some men responding, gathering close to him, voices trying vainly to find the right key. Lufbery leaned down, saw the captain move slightly, the man rolling himself over, looking up at him with glazed eyes. Lufbery knelt, was ready with an apology. The big man put a hand to his own chin, probed the bruise that was already spreading across his jaw.

"You got a punch like a damned mule."

Lufbery held out a hand, said, "Help you up?"

The captain took his hand, struggled to his feet, towered over him again. The man steadied himself against the bar, and Lufbery saw Thaw rising up from behind, facing both of them, nursing a bruise of his own. The captain looked at Lufbery, smiled, said to Thaw, "Now . . . you can call us *Tommy*."

Saint-Just-en-Chaussée—March 30, 1917

Thaw walked with him, the two men probing the dark solitude of the forest. The ground was soft and muddy, the aftermath of a daylong soaking rain. Thaw had learned that Lufbery would time these expeditions, that the rains would inspire the mushrooms to sprout. He had brought his fishing pole, but there had been no fishable ponds, just shallow mud holes, and Thaw had given up the search, seemed content to follow Lufbery up into the trees.

The basket was nearly full, and Thaw had slipped his way down a muddy embankment, waited for him on a narrow trail, called out, "Getting dark soon."

Lufbery had said nothing for a very long time, something else Thaw had grown accustomed to. Lufbery looked up through the treetops, a light breeze stirring the thin branches. He glanced at the basket, satisfied, said, "Yep. That's enough. Let's go."

He joined Thaw on the trail, the two men retracing their steps. They walked in silence, as they had done most of the afternoon, and finally Thaw said, "You ever think about what those Brits said? All that stuff about the president?"

"I do now."

"Never occurred to me how pissed off they were. Makes sense, I guess. They're fighting their guts out, while we sit off to the side. Like we're waiting to see who wins, so we can throw in with the right folks."

Lufbery stopped, said, "I don't think it's like that at all. I don't think the president understands his own people. Look at us. Look at all the men who want to join us, all the Foreign Legion boys. I think the American people want to fight. But the government's afraid, for some damned reason. I can hear that Brit spouting off Wilson's words: Peace at any price. It's like a bad joke to them. The French too. What peace is Wilson talking about? It's like his head's in the sand."

Thaw laughed.

"You calling the president of the United States an ostrich? I thought that kind of thing's what started the fight with the Brits." He rubbed his chin. "Damn. This is gonna hurt for a while."

Lufbery started to walk again. "I shouldn't insult the president. Don't mean it like that."

"Well, on behalf of Woodrow Wilson, no offense taken."

They walked in silence for a few minutes, Thaw beginning to hum some unfamiliar tune. Lufbery said, "I just wonder what the government thinks is gonna happen over here. These countries are killing each other off. How's it gonna end? They fight to the last man? How about us? We supposed to keep shooting down Germans until there's none of them left? Or maybe they'll do the same to us. I hate that word . . . stalemate. All it means is nobody knows what to do next."

Thaw moved up beside him, put a hand on his shoulder, said, "Luf, if it was up to me, everybody could go home tomorrow."

"Bill, nobody's going home until this war ends. And the only way this war is gonna end is if somebody *makes* it end. I just wish the president would realize that."

14

RICHTHOFEN

The British were calling it "bloody April," the most catastrophic period in the brief history of the Royal Flying Corps. Despite innovations in British aircraft, the massive April offensives launched by both British and French forces along the Western Front had compelled the British to throw every available plane into service, many of them outmoded and decidedly inferior to the German Albatros. In a single month, while British and Canadian troops fought a valiant and costly struggle around the city of Arras, in the air above them German fighter squadrons took a horrifying toll on British planes and pilots. Nearly every day brought widespread engagements high over the front lines, and though the Germans lost more than sixty aircraft, more than one hundred fifty British planes went down.

His brother Lothar had joined Squadron Eleven. Richthofen had been enthusiastic about his brother's arrival, the younger man determined to follow in Richthofen's illustrious footsteps. There was never jealousy between them, no sense that Lothar resented the attention his older brother was receiving. If anything, Lothar was simply ambitious, would make a name for himself regardless of what his famous brother had already accomplished. Richthofen was careful about Lothar's training, and although the young man had gone through the same learning process as Richthofen, had been both an observer and a pilot in the two-seat bombers, flying the single-seat fighters was something Lothar would have to study. After two weeks of the same intensive training the other pilots of Squadron Eleven had experienced, Lothar had been ready for combat. Almost immediately, with Richthofen watching him nervously, Lothar had attacked and shot down his first victim.

Richthofen's pilots had claimed far more than their share of victories, and by the end of the month, Squadron Eleven had scored eighty-nine confirmed kills. Though few outside of Air Service Headquarters in Cologne were calling it a competition, Richthofen was quietly aware that during the same period, Squadron Boelcke had shot down only eighteen.

In mid-April, Richthofen was surprised to receive his second promotion in barely two weeks. Everyone in the squadron had expected him to be elevated to first lieutenant, entirely appropriate for a squadron commander. But then, another telegram had come from Cologne, and with it another cause for celebration. On April 17, he became Captain Richthofen. His men toasted him with typical enthusiasm, and Richthofen allowed himself to celebrate as well. He had achieved the same rank as Boelcke.

The good flying weather meant that each plane was in the air every possible minute of daylight, and since the Albatroses carried little more than ninety minutes of fuel, the pilots were making several flights every day. Though the routine was exhausting, the men were energized by their ex-traordinary success. But Richthofen had been performing this routine for far longer than most of his pilots, and von Hoeppner was keenly aware that his foremost flying ace was badly in need of a rest. As April drew to a close, Richthofen received a dismaying order. He was instructed to take six weeks of leave.

April 29, 1917

Richthofen was planning his formal protest, had already prepared a carefully worded letter to von Hoeppner. He could not imagine so much time with nothing to do, could not simply leave his men behind, only to wander off to some quiet sanctuary. But the order did not precisely take effect until the end of the month, and Richthofen had taken advantage, had put his protest aside to devote one more day to leading his squadron aloft. The morning had begun as so many had before, success not only for Richthofen, but for his brother as well. As he led the squadron back to the aerodrome, he was as enthusiastic as when he had taken off. He and Lothar had a visitor. Their father would be waiting for them.

Baron Albrecht von Richthofen had been the first in his family to choose life as a soldier, had risen to the rank of major in the cavalry. He had sustained a serious injury that resulted in near total deafness, and so had been forced to end his active military career prematurely. But with the start of the war, Albrecht had been vocal about returning to service, and the High Command had accepted gratefully. He now served as one of the many military mayors governing the occupied French towns, a purely administrative position, but one that allowed the man's pride to be preserved. He was still in uniform.

When Richthofen had requested transfer to the Air Service, it had been a shock to his father, the old man suspicious that anyone could achieve a soldier's honor or perform any good service to the Fatherland by dancing around the sky in these new aeroplanes. But with his oldest son now a national hero, Albrecht's blithe dismissal of the Air Service had grown silent.

Albrecht was still beaming, sat at the honored place at the head of the table, and Richthofen could not help smiling with him. The food was piled in great steaming mounds in front of them, the other pilots enjoying the company of this old cavalryman as much as his sons. The room was alive with chatter, Lothar loudest of all, and Richthofen knew his father was struggling to sort out the sounds. He could see his father growing frustrated, and Richthofen motioned to him, *eat*, mouthed the words slowly, *we will talk later*. His father seemed to appreciate the gesture, stared at a mound of beefsteak in front of him, the smile returning, said to no one in particular, "No cavalry ever ate like this."

Richthofen could feel himself relaxing, a tight coil unwinding inside of him. His mind was already drifting to thoughts of home, the great stretches of forest around Schweidnitz, and he had allowed himself to daydream about hunting, long quiet walks, and then, a visit with his mother. He had missed her most of all, wrote letters as often as he could. The letters were always positive, carefully worded to avoid upsetting her, filled with only the vaguest details of his successes, never a hint that there was any real danger to her son.

He would make the journey to Schweidnitz by plane of course, found it ridiculous that Germany's most celebrated flyer should ride home in a train. But he would not pilot himself, would be ferried by Krefft, who had been granted a leave of his own. Though Richthofen thought his younger brother was too reckless, no one in the squadron could deny that Lothar was indeed fit for a command of his own. Not one of the pilots objected when Richthofen named Lothar to serve in his absence, even though Karl Allmenroder, Wolff, and Karl Schafer outranked him. Richthofen had thought Wolff was the most qualified, the frail young man having led several flights on his own. Wolff also was building his own impressive reputation. By the end of April, Kurt Wolff had confirmed twenty-seven kills. But a message had come from von Hoeppner, the wording subtle, the meaning clear. The High Command had expressed their "comfort" with the decision that a Richthofen should remain in command of Squadron Eleven. Richthofen had been stoic about von Hoeppner's message. After all, Lothar had a reputation of his own. He had already downed eighteen enemy planes, and was already awaiting the final confirmation from Cologne for his own Order Pour le Mérite.

The table had been cleared, and Richthofen could see that his father was tiring. He glanced around the long table, thought of calling an end to the evening, that surely, with the old major at the head of the table, the men would retire with proper respect. He pushed back his chair, stood up slowly. The others knew the sign, the room growing quiet.

"Gentlemen, I should like to bid you a good evening. My brother and I are honored by your kindness toward Major Richthofen." There was low applause, the old man understanding what Richthofen was doing. He stood himself, said, "Thank you . . ." His words were broken by the harsh ringing of a telephone in a small room to one side. Albrecht seemed to hear, could tell he was being interrupted, turned toward the sound.

Richthofen saw his orderly now, the corporal moving quickly, answering the phone, speaking quietly. Richthofen could hear pieces of the conversation, and quickly, the call was over. His orderly stepped into the dining room, moved close to him, said in a low voice, "Sir, forgive me. It was Captain Hassler. Infantry. They have now confirmed all of your kills."

The others were silent, hanging on the orderly's words, heard as Richthofen heard, and now fists were pumped in the air, a loud cheer rising from the men. It had officially been his finest day as a flyer. During the day's engagements, Richthofen had sent four British planes out of the sky. He could not help smiling, looked at his father now, the man confused by the roar of noise, and Richthofen formed the word, said slowly, so the old man could understand.

"*Fifty.*"

His father sat on the end of the bed, focused on the vast stretching dog lying beside him. The old man seemed uncertain what to do, and Richthofen leaned close, said, "Like this." He scratched the dog's ears, Moritz responding by rolling over on his back, his belly in the air.

The old man understood now, laughed, said, "Yes, Moritz. Much as I prefer it." He rubbed the dog's belly, Moritz groaning softly, and Richthofen watched them for a long minute, surprised by the old man's gentle touch. In a minute, the dog had enough of the attention, rolled back onto his side, and Albrecht looked up at Richthofen, said, "When I am too old to care for myself, I want you to hire a nurse. A young one. She should do that to me at least once a day. It will add years to my life." His father's indiscreet words surprised him, and Richthofen wasn't sure it was a joke. Albrecht looked past Richthofen now, gazed at the trophies that covered his walls. "This is becoming a museum." He stood, moved close to the glass cabinet, every shelf now lined with the silver cups. The old man shook his head.

"I never could have dreamed . . ." He looked at Richthofen now. "When you were attending Wahlstatt, I had to use all my influence so they would not expel you. You simply wouldn't do what they told you to do. Not good practice for a soldier."

"I was not a soldier, sir. I was a boy."

"All soldiers begin as boys. The training must start early." He laughed again, looked at the cabinet. "Not one of your instructors believed you would have a career in the army. They were convinced you did not have the discipline to fight. Apparently, they were mistaken." He looked at Richthofen again, said, "What of Lothar?"

Richthofen was unsure what his father meant, and the old man could see the expression on his face.

"I mean, what kind of soldier is he?"

"He is a hero. Eighteen victories."

The old man thought a moment. "He is a shooter, not a hunter. Yes?"

Richthofen smiled, nodded his head. It was the old lesson, a very small boy following his father into the forest. It was the lessons that had made Richthofen successful, whether he pursued the wolf or the aeroplane. It was a lesson that his brother had never seemed to learn.

"Lothar does not have the patience to be a hunter."

His father nodded, his face showing a glimpse of sadness. "No. He is a shooter. Always will be. Karl, however . . ."

Richthofen had wanted to ask about his youngest brother, the boy only fourteen.

Albrecht paused for a moment, said, "He will be a soldier. Speaks of nothing else. Well, he speaks of you, of course. You are his inspiration." The old man smiled now. "Unlike you, he actually enjoys Wahlstatt. Appreciates the value of taking orders. He has his eye on you, will do everything in his power, and mine, to join you someday. He'll fly, that's for certain. You dreamed of the forest. He dreams of aeroplanes."

Richthofen stared at his father for a long moment, the old man peering again into the small cabinet.

"This war cannot last that long, Father. It will not take that many years for Germany to prevail."

The old man stood straight now, stared at the wall for a moment, said, "You have heard that the High Command has

215

withdrawn our forces back to the main defensive fortifications, what they now call the Hindenburg Line."

"Yes, of course. It was a wise strategic move. Our lines will be more compact now, easier to transfer men and supplies."

His father cocked one eyebrow at him, said, "You memorize that story word for word? We are told every day that our army is crushing our enemies. An army who is doing so has no reason to withdraw. If men and supplies are plenty, there is no need to contract your lines. When we withdrew, we laid waste to the countryside we abandoned, absolute destruction in our wake. I do not believe we would have done so if the High Command expected to occupy that ground again."

Richthofen absorbed the old man's words, felt a rising heat inside of him. "Father, I cannot allow such talk. Every day I see proof that we are winning this war. Every report says that the French are destroying themselves in the South, that Alsace will soon be liberated completely. Here, I have seen for myself. We . . . my own squadron is sweeping the air of British planes. When we are masters of the sky, then our forces on the ground will have every advantage."

"And what of the Americans?"

Richthofen laughed. "Surely you cannot suggest this war will continue so long into the future. The Americans are no threat to us now, and will not be for years. By the time they arrive here, it will be over. I have every confidence that the High Command has matters well under their control. You should share that confidence, Father."

There was a knock, and Richthofen moved quickly to the door, was surprised to see Lothar, a broad smile on the young man's face, oblivious to the tension in the room.

"Manfred! A magnificent surprise! Father, I am glad you are here to share this!"

He handed Richthofen a piece of paper, a telegram. Richthofen read, his eyes growing wider. He moved to the bed, sat down, read the words again. Lothar was in the room now, slapped Richthofen on the shoulder, "Incredible! Go on, tell him! Tell Father what it says!"

The anger was gone and Richthofen looked at his father, saw

the silent dignity, the man bent slightly from so many years of simply doing his duty.

"Father, it seems I will be delayed in reaching home. I have been ordered to make a stop in Kreuznach. It seems the High Command . . . both Field Marshal von Hindenburg and General Ludendorff are requesting my presence."

Lothar seemed to sway now, could not hide his pure glee. "There's more! I saved this one." He reached into his pocket, withdrew a notepad. "The call came in a few minutes ago. Allow me to read the message: '*His Imperial Majesty, Kaiser Wilhelm, requests the honor of a visit with Captain Manfred, Baron von Richthofen, for the purpose of making his acquaintance.*' Making his acquaintance! The kaiser himself!"

Richthofen took the notepad, saw the unmistakable handwriting of Corporal Menzke. He realized his own hand was shaking, looked now at his father, saw a smile in the old man's eyes.

May 1, 1917

Despite his orders to begin his leave promptly by the end of the month, Richthofen was not completely comfortable to remain on the ground while Lothar led the squadron himself. Against the nagging advice in his own head, he had climbed aboard his red Albatros, caught up to the squadron, and, before noon, had added two more enemy planes to his tally.

Krefft had flown him first to Cologne, to meet with von Hoeppner, and Richthofen was astounded at the reception that awaited him. He had expected a brief visit to the Air Service offices there, paying his respects not only to his commander, but to the officers of supply who kept his men so well provided for. When Krefft brought the plane down onto the wide flat field, Richthofen was amazed by the vast sea of people who had gathered around the aerodrome. As he jumped down from the plane, Richthofen found himself surrounded by men in formal suits, local officials who introduced themselves with their titles, and behind them a cluster of brightly dressed schoolgirls, each breathlessly holding a bouquet of flowers. To one side stood a formation of military school cadets, sharp gray uniforms, each boy staring at him with wide eyes. Beyond the formal gathering was a much larger crowd, the people of the city, straining against ropes and a line of surprised soldiers simply to get a glimpse of the great man.

The speeches began, each important man with something profound to say to him, and the words swept over the crowd in a meaningless tumble. He felt himself pressed back toward the plane, fought the urge to make a sudden dash for the cockpit. Krefft was still close to him, and he thought of some signal, something to let the young lieutenant know that he needed to escape. Krefft seemed to read his expression, held up his hand, said to one man who was just commencing his tribute to the greatness of the Fatherland, "Excuse me. It is imperative that Captain Richthofen meet with General von Hoeppner. Very important military matters. Your attention is most welcome. Thank you for your kindness!"

Richthofen heard small groans, the disappointment flowing out through the crowd. Krefft had him by the arm now, and they moved quickly through a narrow opening, the hulking frame of Krefft clearing the path. Richthofen moved as quickly as Krefft would lead him, saw soldiers pointing the way to the Officer's Club, guards manning the door. They were inside now, the crowd noises silent, and Krefft began to laugh.

"I do say, Captain, I was looking forward to your speech!"

Richthofen felt only relief, said, "I am in your debt, Lieutenant. Uh, what speech?"

"The speech they were expecting from you. That last fellow was all primed up to introduce you. All those fat men in their suits were politicians, you know. They can't do anything without either hearing a speech or making one themselves. Today, they expected to do both!"

Richthofen felt a cold shiver, had never been comfortable in front of any crowd, especially civilians. The thought of actually speaking to them . . . he shivered again.

There were staff officers gathering, waiting politely, and one man said, "Sir, if you wish, General von Hoeppner is available to see you now."

Krefft patted him on the back, said, "See? I did not have to lie. You have your port in the storm, Captain. Forgive me, I'll find some refreshment."

Richthofen felt the tiring monotony of the flight blossoming into a headache. He followed the aide, realized he was still wearing his flying suit. He brushed at the oily grime on his coat, pulled a handkerchief, wiped his face. The aide led him down a long hallway, then outside, the official buildings around the aerodrome blessedly quiet. He followed the man down a long straight walkway, a sudden right turn, a door held open, and he was inside again. There were desks now, men on telephones, great maps hanging on each wall. He could feel the energy, tried to see details of the maps, heard a voice, "Captain. If you please, this way."

He passed through another office, saw an open door, and the tall frail man waiting for him.

"Captain! Do come in! I have a surprise for you."

Richthofen followed the old man into a wide, brightly lit office, von Hoeppner easing himself down behind a massive wood desk. Richthofen watched as von Hoeppner retrieved a folder of papers from his desk, thought, *Another* surprise?

"First, Captain, allow me to congratulate you on the achievement of your fiftieth victory. Or should I say, fifty-second? I must admit, I am not altogether pleased."

"Sir?"

"It had been decided some time ago that your success should be kept at a moderate level. Various tallies were considered, and most believed that forty-one would suffice. That would place you ahead of Captain Boelcke, and certainly maintain your status as the Fatherland's most celebrated flyer."

Richthofen was confused, waited for more.

"You might imagine our surprise, and concern, when the number of your victims continued to rise. There is the general feeling here that you have gone far enough, that you have tempted the fates, so to speak. Of course, now that you have reached this new plateau, you have realized a level of success that has elevated you far beyond what the German people should require of you."

Richthofen was feeling a nervous twist in his gut, the headache starting to pound in his ears.

"Are you all right, Captain?"

"Sir. Forgive me, but I am not certain what you are telling me. Are you saying that my services are no longer required?"

Von Hoeppner laughed, picked up the folder again, said, "Oh, my, no! Certainly not, Captain! I have no doubt that you will always perform exemplary service to the Fatherland. It was something of a controversy here, I admit. There were some who suggested you be assigned to my staff, to do as Captain Boelcke had done, touring aerodromes, an effective tool of morale, or spending your time instructing fighter squadrons. Life is never so fragile as in wartime, Captain. A flyer endangers himself every time he leaves the earth, yes? Forgive me for saying so, but should something unfortunate occur, your loss would be catastrophic not only for the Air Service, but for all of Germany. After much discussion, the final decision was placed on my desk."

Richthofen felt the room beginning to spin, a swirl of heat rushing through his brain. He wanted to say something, the word rising inside of him. No. Please, no.

"Captain, I have your new orders right here. Despite the judgment of others, I have decided to reorganize the Pursuit Squadrons into larger groups, a Jagdgeschwader, a Hunting Wing, consisting of four squadrons. The first wing will be referred to as JG-1 and will consist of Squadrons Four, Six, Ten, and your Squadron Eleven. While you are enjoying your leave, you will consider who your successor should be for Squadron Eleven. I will accept your recommendation. When your leave concludes, you will assume the organization and command of the entire first wing, JG-1. Congratulations again, Captain."

Von Hoeppner handed Richthofen the folder, a list of pilots in each of the four squadrons, a roster of their aircraft. He felt himself deflating, a wave of cool relief rushing through him. Von Hoeppner watched him for a moment, said, "I am surprised by your reaction, Captain. I expected you to be more, um, pleased."

"Sir? Oh, my, yes, thank you. Pleased, indeed. I thought . . .

from what you said, I thought you were ordering me not to fly."

Von Hoeppner laughed. "Yes, well, there were some who suggested precisely that. But I promise you, Captain. You keep shooting down aeroplanes, and no one here will order you out of the air. There is, however, one concession I had to make to the High Command. There is a department that handles those matters of relations between the military and the people. They are designated the Information Section. It is their job to sift through the news that comes from the front lines, to ensure that the morale of the people is not injured."

Richthofen nodded, thought, *Censors*.

"They are quite good at their work, and I respect their suggestions." He sat back in his chair. "I will be frank with you, Captain. It was necessary to make an arrangement between the Air Service and the adjutant general's office. Call it a compromise. Your command of JG-1 was agreed to by everyone. That you would continue to fly was not. However, fly you will. There is only one condition. Commencing immediately, you will begin writing your memoirs. The Information Section feels that by putting your experiences down on paper, the people will have the opportunity to share in your triumphs and adventures. This will be far more useful than the newspapers. I have to admit, I think it a marvelous idea."

"Write . . . my memoirs? Sir, how do I do that? I have no idea how to write such a thing."

"That's the beauty of this arrangement, Captain. You will have all the help you need. The Information Section will provide you with an assistant, a stenographer. You need only relay your thoughts, the details of your life, each day's adventures, and someone else will write it down. Later, the ministry will provide a skilled professional to assemble those notes and organize them into a format suitable for publishing. Think of it, Captain. Your life, your accomplishments, your legacy, all on paper, an inspiration for generations to come. In fact, Captain, not only will this be of benefit to Germany, but you could profit as well. Considerably."

Richthofen sank down in the chair, thought a moment. "I'm not completely comfortable with this, sir. My life will become quite public. I would not wish to offend anyone by making some indiscreet observation."

Von Hoeppner laughed again. "Captain, leave those problems to the Information Section. As I said, they are skilled professionals at this sort of thing."

Richthofen saw the smile fading on von Hoeppner's face, the old man now showing signs of impatience. Of course, he thought. Skilled professionals. More censors.

"So, every day, I am to tell my thoughts to some . . . stenographer?"

Von Hoeppner leaned forward again, his arms on the desk, no smile now. "Yes, Captain. And, in return, you continue to fly."

Kreuznach, Germany—May 2, 1917

He had not expected the field marshal to be so elderly in appearance. Von Hindenburg seemed to expand into the great chair behind his desk, every part of him heavy and round, his face loose with age, masked only slightly by the bushy white moustache. Von Hindenburg watched him for a long moment, and Richthofen stood at rigid attention, was embarrassed by his lack of dress uniform. He had hoped to make his apologies immediately; if the field marshal allowed, it would be the first topic of conversation. Pilots did not normally travel with baggage. There was simply no room. It was understood and accepted easily at Air Service headquarters, but here, every officer he had seen had been adorned with perfect crispness. All Richthofen had packed was his toothbrush.

There had been only a few words spoken, all from von Hindenburg, casual conversation, pleasantries that surprised Richthofen. He had not even responded, felt completely dominated by von Hindenburg's presence. Richthofen could feel the weight of history in the room, the power of the man's influence, something that von Hindenburg's longevity had only enhanced. Despite the newspapers, despite everything von Hoeppner had ever said to him, at this moment, Richthofen felt nothing like a national hero. The man in front of him was not only a hero, but the very symbol of Germany.

"Would you care to sit down, Captain? Forgive me. I have been rattling on, and did not even offer you the basic comforts."

Von Hindenburg raised a heavy hand, pointed to a chair across the room. "Move it up close. My hearing is not what it once was. Most everything is not what it once was."

Richthofen obeyed, moved the chair close to the desk, sat, kept his back straight, had yet to say a word. "Thank you, Field Marshal."

"Is your aeroplane outside? I should like to see a red aeroplane. Wonderful notion. Let the enemy know who is killing him. May I see it?"

"My apologies, sir. I flew here in a two-seater. My red Albatros is still at the Squadron Eleven aerodrome. I'm sorry, sir."

Von Hindenburg waved his hand, "No matter. I will come to your aerodrome one day. I would love to fly, Captain. Soar above the clouds." He glanced down at the expanse of his uniform, a low chuckle. "Unlikely. I know that you would show proper etiquette, a kind offer to take me up and whisk me around the heavens. Your politeness is appreciated, but I do not require such patronizing. I am aware of my place in this war. The heavens will wait for . . . another time."

The offer to pilot von Hindenburg had already formed in Richthofen's mind, was drained away now by the old man's surprising frankness. Von Hindenburg seemed lost for a moment, searching for something to say.

"Certainly General von Hoeppner has briefed you on the reorganization of the Air Service."

"Yes, sir."

"Hmm, of course. Good man, von Hoeppner. Unusual for a man his age to see so clearly into the future. I was not always convinced of the value of aeroplanes. It was General Ludendorff who convinced me to see beyond the old ways. I am not a stubborn man, despite what anyone here may tell you. I am simply a soldier from another time. You, Captain, are the voice of the future, calling back to us. If we fail to heed that call, we will be swept aside." The old man retrieved a handkerchief, coughed

223

into it, looked at Richthofen for a long moment, as though for the first time. "You're very young."

"I am twenty-five today, sir."

"My word! Happy birthday, Captain. May you enjoy many more."

"Thank you, sir."

Richthofen began to feel affection for the man, had not expected the gentleness, von Hindenburg seeming more of a kind old grandfather than the military leader of a powerful nation.

"Are you aware, Captain, that the British have put out a bounty on your head?"

The change in topic caught Richthofen off guard. "No, sir, I was not aware."

Von Hindenburg was smiling, said, "Oh yes. I'm surprised you don't know. It was in the newspapers. The Royal Flying Corps has apparently grown frustrated with you. Cannot say I blame them. Our intelligence tells us that they have formed a squadron for just one purpose, to seek out this *Red Devil* in his damned Albatros. They intend to make quite a production of it, have required that a photographer accompany the squadron, to record the incident for posterity. They are offering a reward of five thousand pounds and a Victoria Cross, and all manner of gifts to the successful pilot." Von Hindenburg stopped smiling, seemed suddenly embarrassed, said, "I apologize, Captain. I do not mean to make light of this. Despite the reliability of our intelligence, I have my doubts as to the authenticity of this British scheme. This is your life we are talking about. You may not be so amused. It was indiscreet of me."

Richthofen absorbed the concept, wondered if it could be true. "I am not upset, sir, except on one account. If I were to shoot down this special squadron, could I make my own claim for the reward? I should rather enjoy receiving a Victoria Cross."

The smile returned to von Hindenburg, and he pointed at Richthofen, nodded, "Yes! Very good! I should insist on it!"

The old man's warmth had returned, and Richthofen was feeling genuinely comfortable.

"If nothing else, sir, perhaps I should simply shoot down the photographer."

He had waited for more than an hour, perched uncomfortably on a flat wooden bench, watching the activity flow in and out of Ludendorff's staff rooms. The contrast to the relaxed atmosphere of von Hindenburg's office was unmistakable, and for the first time, Richthofen understood where the decisions of the High Command originated. The officers moving quickly through the waiting area were men of importance, soldiers and civilians both, men speaking in hard serious tones, some with hushed voices. Though Richthofen felt awkward hearing the fragments of conversation that flowed past him, he passed the time by watching the secretaries, seated behind rows of desks, all of them occupied with some intense amount of work. There was the constant ringing of phones, the sound of typewriters, and behind them, he could see a doorway, a sign above: "Telegraph Room." Messengers stood in line along the wall, each one either delivering or receiving some piece of information, each man then hurrying away to some designated office.

Richthofen had been told to wait, a curt order from a colonel who showed no recognition of his name. The man appeared again, handed a folder to one of the secretaries, stepped quickly toward him, said, "You have five minutes. The general is quite busy. This way."

Richthofen followed the man, felt a painful stiffness in his back, the effects of an hour on the hard bench. The colonel moved quickly, and Richthofen matched his pace, was suddenly confronted by a massive wooden door, which the man opened. Richthofen peered in, saw a flutter of activity, a flock of aides hurrying past him. The colonel said, "Enter, Captain."

Richthofen stepped into the room, the door closing behind him with a hard thump. The room was silent, anchored by a great fat desk, larger even than the impressive furnishings that had surrounded von Hindenburg. Ludendorff sat behind the desk, a dark spark plug of a man, staring at him with hard eyes.

"Come in, Captain. Sit there. So tell me, can we win this war with aeroplanes?"

Richthofen moved obediently to the chair, felt the energy of the room, Ludendorff's question sounding more like a demand.

"Yes, sir. I believe so."

"I believe so as well. We require people like you, Captain. A great many people like you. And very soon. The strategic retrenchment of our defensive positions has caused the enemy considerable hardship. We are prepared for any offensive he dares to throw toward us. Ah, but infantry is not your concern. Perhaps you are aware that we have perfected the use of the long-range Gotha bombers. Even as we speak, Captain, London is being assaulted directly, the populace there suffering the direct effects of their insanity in continuing this war. The British have responded by reducing their air strength along the front, and pulling some of their air power back to the English Channel. There is added opportunity for you, Captain. Make good use of it."

The words came at him like a burst of machine-gun fire, and Richthofen felt buried by the man's raw energy.

"I will attempt to do so, sir—"

"Attempt, hell. We know what you can do out there. Every man in this army must perform if we are to win this war. There must be more to a fighter than what the newspapers print."

"Yes, sir. I agree, sir."

"The Americans are soon to arrive. They are no threat now, but we must address their potential. Some are comparing the Americans to the Russians, vast resources and the inability to use them properly. I do not agree. The Russians have been swept aside, but their army was empowered by the old and weak, unrest and turmoil is spreading through their country. America is young, a clumsy restless child who does not yet understand its own strength. We must not allow them the luxury of time. The Italians are no match for the Austrians. The French are already a beaten army, and the British have exhausted their manpower. Why am I telling you this? Because I want you to understand something, Captain. Victory is right here, right in our grasp! We can tolerate no failures. You will carry that message to your new command. Every pilot must perform. I am told you are on leave. How long?"

"Six weeks, sir. General von Hoeppner—"

"*Six* weeks? Very generous of General von Hoeppner. No matter. Time passes quickly, Captain. When you return, I expect a renewed effort on your part. How many planes have you shot down?"

"Fifty-two, sir."

"Fine work, Captain. I'd like to see a hundred."

He moved out through the headquarters in a daze, Ludendorff's words still boring into him. He had been lulled by his time with von Hindenburg, the soft comfort that the war was in the hands of wise old men. But a few minutes with Ludendorff had taught Richthofen an unexpected lesson. It is not wisdom that wins a war. It is power. Richthofen felt exhausted, Ludendorff using him up like some piece of notepaper, words cluttering every free space of his mind. He had been nervous about meeting men in such positions of authority, the ridiculous concern for his unkempt uniform, his clumsiness with words. Now he was terrified. As he stepped out into the open air and sunshine he realized he was one small piece of a vast world controlled from behind those very walls. He felt ridiculous thinking he was ever in command of anything. Even his new assignment, the name that still meant nothing to him, JG-1, was simply a speck on a map, a minuscule part of a vast show of power. And for a brief few minutes, he had been in the presence of the man who controlled it all. He had dared to believe that he was indeed a hero, and despite his grumbling to the others at the aerodrome, he had been growing accustomed to the photographers. It was a foolish exercise in self-indulgence, and he scolded himself for it now. You are merely a tool, a weapon, an extension of the machine guns on your plane. Your red plane. A good commander knows how to make the best use of his resources. So they have made the best use of you. You are not merely a pilot who kills the enemy, you are a weapon to inspire the people as well. Your memoirs will be a candle in the darkness, distracting the people from what is really happening in this war. He could not avoid his father's words, *a victorious army does not retreat*, thought now of Ludendorff's elaborate description of the withdrawal,

227

strategic retrenchment. Is Ludendorff right, is victory within our grasp? Or is he simply using the words as another tool, something to inspire me? He stopped, realized he was close to the airfield, could see a row of planes spread across the open ground. He thought of Krefft, the flight home, felt a small sting of irritation, how Ludendorff had shamed him for his leave. Six weeks. Am I not entitled, after all?

His visit with the kaiser had been pleasant and social and utterly meaningless, and Richthofen was ecstatic to be away from all the trappings of royalty, and on his way home. He had arrived with the same nervousness as before, the rumpled gray uniform standing out among the grandeur of the kaiser's entourage. He had always believed that Wilhelm was as close to God as any man could be, had been given the right to rule the German people by some mystical decree that no mere soldier could understand. But from his first minute in the presence of so much luxury he could not escape the vision of Ludendorff's office, the image held tightly inside of him. The kaiser had welcomed him like an old friend, the luncheon an elaborate and lazy affair, fluttering servants and great mounds of strange food. He had been surprised that Wilhelm knew it was his birthday, the kaiser making much show of the event. There had even been a gift, a bronze bust of Wilhelm that any soldier would treasure, and Richthofen had been appropriately grateful, could tell by the kaiser's own surprise that the presentation was a hastily arranged formality, prompted by the efficiency of some unnamed assistant, someone who had simply plucked the bust off some shelf in the vast palatial residence.

May 3, 1917

The visits and social obligations were complete, and the last leg of the journey home had finally begun. They flew east, the ground sliding below in a patchwork of peaceful farms and vast blankets of forest, no visible signs of the war that rolled on in all directions. Krefft motioned to him, pointed ahead, and Richthofen could see a dark mass of clouds forming out in front of them. Krefft seemed to ask a question, and Richthofen understood, should we go around or through? He could see the ground disappearing beneath the blackness, thought, Rain, and probably a good deal of wind. But he had flown into a storm before, and Krefft was an excellent pilot. They would pass through the storm quickly. And, he had delayed the start of his leave for long enough. He tapped Krefft on the shoulder, pointed straight ahead.

The plane began to bounce, tossed about by the turbulence of the storm, but Krefft kept the nose steady, held the compass heading. Richthofen tried to relax, turned his thoughts to home, his mother's gentle smile, woods and streams and the deer that waited there. Six weeks. He thought of Ludendorff's emphasis on the number. Yes, General, you are correct. I will return energized, I do understand my duty. I will assume command of JG-1, and I will write my memoirs. But right now, I'm going home.

Krefft moved them closer to the rain, and Richthofen looked down at the vast shadows covering the dark patches of forest, but his thoughts would not yet release him from the experiences of the last two days. There had been a considerable number of dignitaries at the kaiser's luncheon, including, of course, von Hindenburg. But Ludendorff was nowhere to be found, and Richthofen had paid special attention to that, realized that no one even acknowledged Ludendorff's existence. It was a clear message, and Richthofen knew now what none of them seemed comfortable admitting. Ludendorff was, of course, tending to more important matters. Regardless of what elaborate feasts were created for the kaiser and his guests, no matter how many fat politicians gave speeches for every national hero at every aerodrome, it is this war that will decide our future. And, in the end, what happens with this war will be decided inside the mind of one intensely frightening man.

For nearly two years since the sinking of the *Lusitania*, Germany had grown confident that Woodrow Wilson's passion for neutrality would keep the United States from entering the war. Wilson's diplomatic outrage had been received in Germany for what it was: words. No matter how much the American president objected to German policy, no one in the German High Command believed that Wilson could be pushed to violate his campaign promises to the American people. Wilson's reelection had been energized by his steadfast declaration that America was "*too proud to fight,*" and Wilson himself believed that the American people respected him because, as his campaign banners had boldly proclaimed, "*He kept us out of war.*" With the effectiveness of the British stranglehold on German shipping, drastic measures were required to relieve the pressure on the German people, and reluctantly, the kaiser had finally agreed to resume Germany's policy of unrestricted submarine warfare. The decision was made public in January 1917, and President Wilson had received word that any shipping bound for ports in England or France would be subject to the wrath of German U-boats. Wilson realized that the consequences of Germany's decision were inevitable. The threat to American shipping would once again put civilians at risk, and the chances had greatly increased that another catastrophe like the *Lusitania* could occur at any time. Though Wilson still insisted there could be a diplomatic solution, privately he recognized that the American public had become increasingly skeptical of his stance. Wilson's continuing reliance on diplomacy delighted the German High Command. Confident now that the American government could be relied on to avoid entering the war at any cost, the kaiser's ministers had continued to push their own aggressive agenda. On March 1, Germany's Foreign Minister Arthur Zimmerman sent a telegram to German ambassador Bernstorff in Washington, informing Bernstorff of the specific details of the kaiser's decision to resume the torpedoing of neutral supply ships. But Zimmerman's note also included details of a proposal that Germany intended to offer the government of Mexico. Should Mexico agree to an alliance with the kaiser, that nation would reap the spoils of the inevitable German victory, including the annexation of significant amounts of American territory, the lands that Mexico had lost in the Mexican War seventy years earlier. Zimmerman's telegram was intercepted, and the details were revealed to the American public. Though Zimmerman was given the opportunity to defuse the situation, to deny that the telegram was legitimate, to calm any fears that his government would so antagonize the United States with such a flagrantly ridiculous threat, the Germans instead trumpeted the telegram's accuracy. Wilson's hopes for a peaceful resolution to the Great War were swept away by public outrage over Germany's clumsy maneuvering. In Washington, even the most fervent advocates of diplomacy understood what the Zimmerman note represented to the American people: it was the final straw.

On April 2, the gathering clouds of war finally extinguished the hopes of the pacifist influences in Washington. Woodrow Wilson submitted his declaration of war to Congress, and four days later, Congress overwhelmingly approved. To the surprise of the kaiser's ministers, and to the desperate relief of Britain and France, the United States had finally entered the war.

PART II

THE KILLING MATCH

War is the only place where a man truly lives.

—George Patton

15

PERSHING

Fort Sam Houston,
Near San Antonio, Texas—May 1917

The last Americans had been withdrawn from the frustrating
morass that had become the expedition to Mexico. Throughout
the furious pursuit of Pancho Villa, Pershing had answered to
his immediate superior, General Frederick Funston. But Funston
had suddenly died, and the War Department ordered Pershing
to leave his command post at Fort Bliss and transfer himself and
his staff to San Antonio to take Funston's place. To his officers,
the move was logical, a reward for Pershing's capable service in
Mexico, and certainly, the men in Washington knew that
Funston had relied completely on Pershing south of the
Mexican border. Pershing himself was not so sure. He had never
expected to leave his troops behind, to find himself promoted to
the position of commanding general of the entire Southern
Department, overseeing the army's operations throughout all of
the southwestern United States.

He had been shocked by Funston's death, had considered the
man a friend, a commander capable of handling the storm of
politics that swirled around the excursions into Mexico. From
the first days below the Rio Grande, the mission to capture
Pancho Villa had been a futile exercise, a three-legged dog pursuing a rabbit through the vast underbrush of northern Mexico.
The pursuit itself had made good press in Washington, all manner of headlines trumpeting how the powerful hand of
American justice would strike swiftly into the chaos of this
uncivilized land. The War Department had cooperated fully in
furnishing all the manpower Pershing felt was needed. But the
reality had driven his officers and men to utter frustration, had

propelled some of his more undisciplined units to take matters into their own hands, something that would not make good press at all. In the more remote outposts south of the border, reports began to filter back to Fort Bliss, sketchy details of assaults against innocent villagers, whose only crime might have been to allow Pancho Villa and his men a night's rest. The failures to corral Villa's slippery forces had taught Pershing several lessons. No matter how superior your troop strength, no matter your firepower and technology, in the enemy's land, the enemy has the advantage. No matter how you pursue him, he is either everywhere or nowhere at all.

Despite the good press that Washington poured over the Mexican campaign, Pershing had never expected to be congratulated for the futility of his efforts. He had been given a mission, and the mission had failed. No matter what the newspapers said, no matter the pats on the back that came from the War Department, Pershing could not escape his own judgment. With the final withdrawal of troops from Mexico, there was no way now to correct the errors, no opportunity to launch some new offensive campaign that might benefit from the mistakes of the past. Pancho Villa would remain free, while in Washington, President Wilson would tiptoe along the fragile line of diplomacy with Mexico's President Carranza. Since the start of Pershing's pursuit of Villa, the Mexican government had been a reluctant partner, would never fully cooperate with the American forces, despite Carranza's hatred of Pancho Villa. It was another lesson for Pershing. Though Villa had been a huge thorn in Carranza's side, the two enemies had more in common than either would admit. When the Americans stepped in, the enemies seemed suddenly to find common ground, had shown a tolerance for each other just long enough to focus a shared hostility toward Pershing and his troops. It was the one piece of the Mexican puzzle Pershing was grateful to avoid. The problems of maintaining the delicate relationship with Carranza's government no longer belonged to the army, but to Woodrow Wilson.

The one benefit to Pershing's new responsibility was that, finally, he could look beyond the dismal countryside below the

236

Rio Grande and focus on the deepening turmoil that the Great War was causing the American government. Most of his officers felt as he did, that despite the president's claims of neutrality, it was essential that the American army begin its own preparations for war. In no other part of the country was there a significant presence of trained soldiers, no kind of organization to prepare the troops for what they might encounter should they be called upon to go to France. With the Mexican campaign now concluded, Pershing realized that his command might become the foundation upon which the American army would have to rely. Mexico had brought out both the best and worst of his officers. The worst were either gone, or would be kept to harmless responsibilities. The best were finding new orders, new duties, had already begun to sort through the thousands of soldiers under their various commands, selecting those men whose discipline and spirit could be the cornerstone of a new army.

"Under plans under consideration is one which will require among other troops, four infantry regiments and one artillery regiment from your department for service in France. If plans are carried out, you will be in command of the entire force. . . ."

The telegram had come from the chief of staff, General Hugh Scott, had been labeled "For Your Eye Alone," a designation Pershing had rarely seen. The cloak of security had caused a hum of excitement among his staff, all as curious as he was why Washington would suddenly reach out to him with such an obvious show of dramatics. Pershing had found it unlikely that San Antonio would be crawling with spies, German or otherwise.

The telegram from General Scott was not the first hint that something significant was brewing in Washington. Before Scott's order had come another brief note that was far more casual, with the return address of his father-in-law, Wyoming senator Francis Warren. Pershing had distinctly mixed emotions about any note he received from his in-laws. Despite their respect and continuing kindness toward him, any communication carried a hard reminder that his relationship existed with them only because of Pershing's marriage. He knew that his wife's death had certainly devastated her family as much as her loss tore into him even now. Pershing knew his relationship with her family could never be comfortable, no matter how often they tried to reach out to him. But their connection through the tragedy of their shared loss had been intruded upon by events that enveloped the entire nation. Warren's brief telegram had surprised him far more than General Scott's official statement about military planning. Though Pershing had put the machinery in place to prepare his men for some eventual use overseas, his father-in-law had brought the stark reality home. The note had simply read: "*Wire me today whether and how much you speak, read, and write French.*"

Near Washington, D.C.—May 9, 1917

The train was close to the city now, and he stared out the window, had given up trying to concentrate on his notes, all the details of the new combat unit the War Department expected him to command. In the short time since General Scott's instructions had arrived, Pershing had spent as much time as his waking mind would allow going over the details, organizing what would become a fully staffed division. He had no orders yet, no specific assignment that called for so much preparation, but it was simply his way. He would focus first on the numbers, what would be required to supply a force of twenty-five thousand men, nearly double what he had commanded at Fort Bliss. He had assaulted the task with a burst of enthusiasm, something he had never experienced in Mexico. He found pleasure in immersing himself in the creation of an efficient fighting machine, one division of what might become a massive buildup of American force. Pershing's energy was fueled by the reports that flowed out of Washington. Congress had responded to Wilson's declaration of war with unbridled support, and vast sums of money had already been allocated to fund the military expansion. It was gratifying to Pershing that the politicians seemed to be aware that sending American troops to France would require an enormous mobilization of men and equipment that the country had not seen since the Civil War.

As the train rolled through the last remnants of a long day, his mind began to let go, to focus more on the lush greenery of the Virginia countryside, and finally, the lights of the city, the train rumbling onto the bridge across the Potomac. There would be nothing else for him to do today. Tomorrow was another story.

Washington, D.C.—May 10, 1917

He had gone first to see his father-in-law, the unavoidable responsibility, an obligation that was so much more than simple courtesy. The visit had been cordial and blessedly brief, neither man wanting to explore the one topic they shared deeply in common. Pershing had been surprised that Senator Warren had no real idea why Pershing had been called to the capital, beyond the obvious. The details would have to come from the men who had their hands on the real power. By midmorning, he was at the War Department.

He waited now in a quiet office, manned by a single sergeant at a reception desk. The room was strangely quiet, and Pershing watched the sergeant, who seemed to perform his particular function with an emphasis on absolute silence. He had seen officers in the hallways, men moving about with casual politeness, acknowledging each other with a friendly nod. A few had offered the same gesture toward him, nameless men in identical uniforms. Pershing had moved through them at his usual pace, brisk short steps, did not speak to anyone, had been energized by the surroundings, as he was by his expectations. On the train, he had imagined his arrival there, marching through the hallways that would bring him to the office of the army chief of staff. He had expected a steady flow of activity and energy, an atmosphere he had tried to inject into his own command in Texas. It had always been a challenge, the combination of the duty and the climate oppressive enough to drain the fire from any man, except perhaps Pershing himself. But this was *Washington*, the very origin of power for everything he served. He could not help feeling the odd lethargy that seemed to surround the officers he encountered now, men moving with a leisurely stroll, seemingly unaffected by the monumental events of the past few weeks, virtually ignoring this new man in their midst, who marched sprightly past them, his boots echoing down the vast hallways.

He had imagined General Scott's office to be a chaotic hub of activity, had anticipated working his way into the rhythm of an enormous vortex of policy and decision making carrying his country toward their first engagement of the war. But the fantasy had slipped away. As he stared at the quiet sergeant, he began to fidget, a nervous habit, had nothing to keep his hands occupied. He tried to see details of anything on the man's desk, some bit of work, wondered now if the man was actually doing anything at all.

"Ah, General Pershing! Welcome! Excellent, do come in!"

Pershing stood, saw the familiar rigid pose of Hugh Scott. Scott was older than Pershing by a dozen years, but he still maintained the posture of a commander. He held out a hand, which Pershing accepted.

Pershing followed Scott into the brightly lit office, tall windows on two walls, the sunshine adding heat to a room that was already stiflingly hot.

"Quite a job in front of us, right?"

"Yes, sir."

Scott nodded, as if speaking to himself, ran a finger across the thick gray brush of his moustache. "Not like Mexico, I suspect."

Pershing waited for more, then said, "No, sir."

"It's an honor, you know. Quite a responsibility for you. You will command a full division. Some people around here think that's a new idea, that all we've ever had in this army is an organization of regiments. Disgraceful ignorance of our own history. People don't realize that what we're putting into place has been done before. It's the legacy of men like Sherman and Hancock, men who understood that a division must be the foundation of the modern army. Are you prepared, General?"

"Quite so, sir. I've been working on the details. Going through the process of selecting those regiments I feel are most appropriate—"

240

Scott held up his hand, "Yes, yes. Certainly. You may discuss that with General Bliss. I have every confidence that you will assemble the kind of fighting unit our allies are expecting from us." He paused. "I wish it was me, you know. I'd give anything to lead men into this war. It's what every old soldier here hopes for. I spent the best part of my career chasing Indians. Something to be proud of, I suppose. But, not like this, John. Nothing like this."

"Yes, sir. I'll do my best, sir."

"I don't imagine you've heard much of the talk that's rattling around these buildings."

"I just arrived last night, sir."

"Hmm. Well, ignore it. Jealous old fools. That damned Wood. You know Leonard Wood?"

"Yes, sir. I served with General Wood in the Philippines."

"Yes, of course. We all served under him at some point. Used to sit right here, in this chair. Well, hell, you know that. If it wasn't for me, he'd be sitting here now, and you wouldn't be enjoying this pleasant conversation. He thinks the job should be his, you know. Your job, leading the first division of our troops to France. He thinks the army owes him that, that a man should be entitled to go out in a blaze of stupid glory, like George Custer."

Pershing said nothing, could see that Scott was watching for a response.

Scott laughed now. "Very good. Keep your damned mouth shut. It's all right, John, you'll make a good many more enemies before this war is over."

Pershing was surprised, absorbed Scott's words. *Making enemies* was something that had not occurred to him at all.

"General Scott, if I may ask . . . who will be in overall command of the European effort? If not General Wood, then will General Bliss . . . ?"

"Hasn't been decided yet. The president will choose. You should see all the jockeying going on here, every man with a star on his shoulder putting his face in front of Wilson's parlor window. The Capitol hasn't had so many military visitors since the British occupied it in the War of 1812. Just sit tight. Keep

241

working on the details of your own command. Things will sort themselves out soon enough."

"Sir, how many men do you expect we can mobilize? How many divisions?"

"The quartermaster general guesses that he can feed a half million in a few months or so. What do you think?"

It was not a question Pershing expected. "I . . . don't know, sir."

"Don't worry about it. We'll get this ball rolling soon enough. Now, I believe we're expected at the secretary's office. Mr. Baker can become rather testy if he's kept waiting. Shall we go?"

Scott was up, and past him, and Pershing followed. They moved out through the same hallways, and Pershing saw the same uniforms, the friendly nods, some of them noticing him now, walking in the shadow of the chief of staff. Pershing matched Scott's pace, felt a dull throb in his head, the energy in his steps growing sluggish. Scott's words were plowing through his brain . . . *things will sort themselves out.* . . .

He realized now what was missing, what had drained the fantasy he had so nurtured on the long train trip. Hugh Scott was chief of staff, would be responsible for managing all the tools of this war, everything required to recruit and equip and train the enormous gaping emptiness that was all that existed of the United States Army. He realized now, it had been a month since the president had declared war. A full month. And the army chief of staff still had no idea how many men were to be assembled, or who would lead them.

The secretary of war was Newton P. Baker, and Pershing had been leery of his first meeting with the man. Since 1914, Baker had been a supporter of Woodrow Wilson's obstinate grip on American neutrality, and Pershing had long heard from many of the old career commanders that a tendency toward pacifism was hardly the proper qualification for the man who sat at the head of the War Department. But the meeting with Baker had surprised Pershing. The secretary was a much younger man than Pershing had expected, junior to Pershing by ten years. There was another characteristic about Baker that Pershing found oddly unnerving. The man was quite small in stature; were it not for the position the man occupied, presiding over a meeting of such magnitude, Baker could have been mistaken for a moustachioed schoolboy.

The meeting had included nearly every senior commander stationed in the capital, some whom Pershing knew well, others known by name and seniority only. Baker had seemed pleasant and likable, and despite his unlikely physical stature in the face of so many old-school military veterans, he impressed Pershing by holding tight control over the meeting. Ultimately, the meeting was as much about vagaries as anything of substance, a social opportunity for Pershing to be introduced to the men who still held seniority to him, any one of whom might become his immediate superior in Europe. The meeting had not been lengthy, but Pershing had left the War Department engulfed by the same aura of lethargy he had experienced with the chief of staff.

Washington, D.C.—May 12, 1917

The hotel was small, the compact rooms overlooking the Potomac. He had tried keeping to his room, occupying his mind with reading, but the boredom was stifling, his mind rolling in all directions with thoughts of duty, and the amazing lack of urgency he found in every official function he had been invited to attend. He had finally escaped the confines of his small prison, paced slowly now in the hotel lobby, his mood darkening with each turn. He was surprised to learn that he was the only general officer assigned to the specific duty as division commander, and Scott's prediction had proven to be correct. Already he had begun to feel the oppressive stench of politics from officers who regarded Pershing as a usurper, this commander of a backwoods outpost who had somehow cajoled and manipulated his way past them to secure this new path to certain glory.

"Sir!"

He turned, saw the young man moving toward him, the sun

243

at the man's back, hiding his face. But the man's crisp gait was familiar, the stiff posture much like Pershing's own.

"Lieutenant Patton. Didn't expect to see you. How is Mr. Ayer?"

Patton saluted him, and Pershing responded, Patton still keeping himself stiffly at attention.

"We are hopeful, sir. Thank you for asking. The family sends you their respects."

Pershing motioned to a small table in the corner, said, "Let's sit, Lieutenant. Please tell me of Mr. Ayer's condition. I know that he is quite elderly."

"Yes, sir. Nearly ninety. The family is prepared for the worst. Mrs. Ayer is somewhat fragile as well. My wife feels her mother will not outlive Mr. Ayer by very long."

Pershing nodded, began to feel trapped by the conversation.

"Beatrice . . . Mrs. Patton . . . is well then?"

"Oh, yes, sir. She offers her regards."

"Thank you. Very kind."

George Patton had served with Pershing in El Paso, had an extraordinary reputation for rashness that some described as a foolish tendency to place himself in harm's way. Throughout the misery of the quest to capture Pancho Villa, Patton had led patrols that had come into more violent contact with Villa's deputies than anyone else in the army. In one of the rare opportunities for an actual fight, Patton had shot and killed one of Pancho Villa's senior deputies, Julio Cardenas. The confrontation had been one bright spot for Pershing in an otherwise dismal experience, but to Patton, the hard brush with violence had been nothing short of inspirational. He would do anything he could to relive the feeling. It had always been true for young officers, those men who graduated from West Point just at the right time to be thrown into a war. It had happened in the 1840s, the late 1850s, and Pershing knew that it would happen again. Young lieutenants became men facing the guns of the enemy, and when their war ended, the young officers could not tolerate the silent emptiness of peace. In the past such men turned their fiery ambition into legend, the names every soldier knew well: Grant, Longstreet, Jackson, Hancock, Lee. Pershing had seen that same fire in Patton, knew of the young man's worst fear, a letter Patton had writ-ten to his father, confiding to the old man the fear that followed him every day: *I wake up at night in a cold sweat imagining that I have lived and done nothing*.

Though Patton seemed suited for a command of infantry, Pershing knew that the young man's own dream was life in the cavalry. In Mexico, cavalry had become motorized, the automobile often carrying men rapidly across vast stretches of wilderness that would have taken far too long on horseback. It was a change Patton had adapted to readily. Despite Patton's desire to move up through the ranks of the cavalry, Pershing wanted him close, believed that Patton's quest for adventure might best be served if he was under the watchful eye of a tough superior, a lesson once learned by Pershing himself. In early 1916, he had given the thirty-one-year-old lieutenant a new position on his headquarters staff. When Pershing was called to Washington, there had never been any doubt in his mind that Patton would be among those who would follow.

During their shared duty in Texas, Pershing had become well acquainted with Patton's family, had developed a friendly correspondence with Patton's father-in-law, Frederick Ayer, a wealthy New England industrialist. But Pershing's acquaintance with the young lieutenant had opened the way to another relationship that had caught Pershing completely off guard. It had been less than two years since the death of his wife, and he had poured so much of himself into his work as the only salve that could hold the awful pain away. Pershing had rarely been a sociable man in the first place, and no one would ever have suggested that the recently widowed man should make any attempt to fill that emotional gap in his life. But then, he had met Patton's sister, Nita.

It could easily have become the stuff of scandal, and both Pershing and Nita knew enough about social chatter to maintain discretion. When they met, Nita was only twenty-nine, not much more than half his age. Neither of them had expectations of romance, and as their relationship continued to grow more serious, he could not help wondering why a charming and pretty young woman would be drawn to a crusty old soldier. No

245

one had been more surprised at their connection than the young Lieutenant Patton, and if Pershing had any fears about the dangers of idle gossip, he soon discovered that George Patton was the perfect weapon against anyone's indiscreet talk. Patton could exude a fierce athleticism that would intimidate any man in Pershing's command. To Pershing's immense gratification, the young man had made it very clear to everyone in the headquarters that the general's private life was precisely that.

Pershing led the young man to a small table in the corner of the lobby, and they sat, Patton keeping himself stiffly upright, something Pershing encouraged in all his officers. Both men sat quietly for a moment, and Pershing knew that Patton would never speak until Pershing resumed the conversation. He glanced up, saw a couple descending the staircase, waited for them to pass by, saw Patton staring ahead. Pershing smiled slightly, thought, Neither one of us does this sort of chitchat very well.

He had always felt a strange kinship to the young man, saw so much of himself in every habit Patton had, felt above all else that he could trust him. Pershing was beginning to understand that in Washington, trust might be a rare commodity. He glanced around the lobby again, saw no one who might overhear, said, "Have you prepared Beatrice for the probability that you will be leaving soon for France?"

Patton seemed to snap awake. "Absolutely, sir. She knows well my responsibilities."

Pershing grunted, saw Patton looking at him, a question in the young man's eyes.

"Lieutenant, permit me to be blunt. I'm not certain I know *my* responsibilities, much less yours. I have detected a reluctance in this place for anyone to actually . . . *do* anything. It is puzzling. I don't pretend to know everything that must take place to create a force of arms sufficient to our needs. But I believe I know how to begin the process. The word is mobilization. Simply put, Lieutenant, we require motion, organization, the appointment of men in the proper position who have the authority and the ability to get things done. Everything from artillery to boots, from rifles to rations, every detail must be addressed."

"Yes, sir. Most definitely, sir."

Pershing glanced around the lobby again, saw a desk clerk now, the man tending to his paperwork. Pershing leaned forward, his arm on the table, his voice in a whisper.

"Nothing is happening, Lieutenant. Meetings. Talk. I've been invited to a dozen parties. I've been told to organize the division I will command, and I find that I have satisfied the chief of staff's requirements by merely listing the regiments I feel are best suited. I don't even know who I answer to, except for General Scott. There are five generals here senior to my rank: Scott, Tasker Bliss, Leonard Wood, Franklin Bell, Thomas Barry . . . any one of whom could become my commanding officer. But I dare not speak candidly to any of them. There is a distressing amount of intrigue swirling around this place. Frankly, Lieutenant, I don't know what to do next."

"May I speak freely, sir?"

"I have opened the door, George. You may step through."

"You have not once mentioned Mr. Wilson, sir. Is it not the responsibility of the president to begin the process? Should not the policy and the energy come from him?"

Pershing knew that, like so many of the officers who had been in Mexico, Patton had little respect for Woodrow Wilson.

"Correct. But the president must delegate."

"Has he? You have said yourself that no one is designated to command the effort. How does this nation build an army that for a generation has been allowed to dissolve itself? Except for the Southern Department, of course. But sir, someone must make the important decisions, and that has to begin with the president. The man lacks iron, General. He always has. You know how I feel. It was the same with William Jennings Bryan. A suitable secretary of state for a country that intends on becoming the world's punching bag. At least Mr. Bryan had the decency to resign. But Woodrow Wilson . . . any man who claims he is too *proud* to fight . . . forgive me, sir, but that is a coward's boast."

"Enough, George. I am aware of your feelings about the president."

"You gave me permission to speak freely, sir."

"Freedom is reliant on wisdom, Lieutenant. Regardless of what we believe to be his errors, President Wilson is still our commander in chief. I cannot allow such talk in my presence."

"Of course, sir. My apologies."

"Apologies are not necessary. What I would prefer is to find some breath of fresh air in this city that would allow me to prove you wrong."

He looked toward the door, saw a man in uniform moving quickly toward the reception desk. Patton watched as well, and Pershing stood, said, "Appears to be a courier. Perhaps he is looking for me."

He saw the clerk point in his direction, and the soldier saw him now, stepped crisply in his direction, saluted, said, "Forgive me, sir. Are you General Pershing?"

"Yes."

The man handed him a piece of paper, said, "This is for you, sir. Secretary Baker requests your presence, at your earliest convenience."

Pershing unfolded the paper, saw the same request in writing. He looked at Patton, said, "Excuse me, Lieutenant. Another meeting to attend."

The marine held the door open, waited for Pershing to step through, then closed it firmly behind him. He expected another gathering of army brass and gray suits, was surprised to see Baker by himself, dwarfed by the man's wide desk.

"Please take a seat, General."

"Thank you, sir."

Baker was looking at a stack of papers on his desk, slid them into a drawer now, said, "You need to know something about me, General. Despite what you may have heard, this office is firmly committed to waging war on the enemy."

"Yes, sir."

Baker tilted his head forward, smiled. "Don't believe me, right?"

Pershing wasn't sure what to say, and Baker still smiled, leaned back in his chair.

"I'm not just talking about the Germans. There are enemies to our commitment right here, in Washington, and I'm not talking about spies and such. Perhaps you've already encountered some of the problems we face."

Pershing felt a screaming need for caution, said nothing. Baker seemed to appraise him for a moment, said, "Despite the insults and criticism so many of your colleagues are spewing about with such vigor, the president is genuinely committed to providing the means to win this war."

Pershing had heard the word too many times, *commitment*. He looked down for a moment, said, "Excuse me, Mr. Secretary, and I mean no disrespect. But I was called to Washington because I was to be given command of a combat division to be designated for assignment to France. Those are the only specific instructions I have received."

"The *first* combat division, General. Be clear. No one was selected before you."

"All right, sir. The first. Thus far I have spent considerable thought appraising those regiments which I believe should compose that division. I believe the men under my command can be made ready in a short time." He paused, could see Baker staring at him with full attention, something he was not used to. "Mr. Secretary, I have not yet seen anyone else doing what I have been asked to do. No one, from the chief of staff on down, has provided me with any tangible orders. I have tried to find out if my division is to be a part of a larger force, and if so, how much larger. No one seems to know. I have tried to learn how exactly my division is to be equipped, if, for example, we are to put into the field a number of machine-gun units similar to what the British employ. Not only can I not find the answer, but no one in the Ordnance Department seems clear on what kind of machine guns we are to use in the first place. I have inquired of the quartermaster general how long it will require his department to furnish sufficient uniforms, boots, rations, backpacks, canteens, gas masks, and whatnot, before my men are fully prepared to sail for France. He has told me in plain language . . . he doesn't know." He felt his anger rising, tried to hold it tightly in his clenched fists. "Mr. Secretary, I appreciate your pledge of

249

commitment to our efforts. I would be much more confident of our success if I heard less about commitment and more about activity." He stopped, clamped his jaw tightly shut, closed his eyes for a brief second, thought, Too far, dammit. Too far. This is not the place—

"General Pershing, I believe I can address several of your concerns. First of all, you are quite correct that there is lethargy in Washington. It's a disease that infects the comfortable. When I was appointed to this position, I discovered quickly that the offices around me were staffed primarily by men who spent long hours contemplating their eventual retirement, men who would do very little to disturb the calm waters of government."

Baker retrieved a piece of paper from the drawer, held it up, said, "General Pershing, I have here the preliminary draft of an order the president and I have been constructing. It is not yet complete in its details, but it will be soon. Every observation you have offered me is essentially the same as I have experienced. Like you, General, I am not pleased. And the president is not pleased either. However, I assure you, wheels are beginning to turn. The machinery is coming to life. The president is, even now, summoning some of the most influential corporate and industrial leaders in this nation. Congress has appropriated the necessary funds. The American people are firmly behind the president's declaration of war. What I find most distressing is that the lack of activity for which you have so little patience is found right here, in my own department. The men whose job it is to organize the army into a viable force are the very men who seem unwilling or uncertain how to begin the process." Baker paused, thought a moment. "Do you know what *embarrassment* is, General?"

"Certainly, sir."

"I'm not so certain. Let me define it for you. When the president confided in his closest advisers his determination to respond to the increasingly dangerous moves by the Germans, he pointed a finger in my direction and inquired if the military minds in this department had considered any kind of specific plan for mobilizing the armed forces of this country. I was forced to respond that the only plan anyone had brought to my attention was a carefully crafted strategy for our potential invasion of Canada."

Pershing felt his mouth opening, clamped it shut.

"*Canada*, General. Some military genius here decided that since our neighbor to the north was the most *convenient* place for us to engage in combat, we should look to drawing up a plan. So, there is a plan. It is the only plan. And I had the president staring at me with the same look of utter disbelief which I now see from you."

Baker raised the piece of paper again. "General, the president and I are in agreement that what this nation requires is leadership that comes from outside of Washington. What the army requires is a man who understands what leadership means in the field. Hence, we have begun to prepare this order. Allow me to read the first part."

Baker held up the paper, read: "*To: Major General John J. Pershing. The president directs me to communicate to you that effective immediately, you are to assume command of all the land forces of the United States operating in continental Europe and in the United Kingdom.*" He lowered the paper. "The complete order will be in your hands in a few days. Do you understand what I am telling you, General? You are no longer to command merely a single division. The president and I are assigning you to command the entire military operation."

Pershing stared at Baker for a moment. "Sir, you cannot . . . I am not the ranking officer."

Baker laughed now, surprising him. "Chain of command, eh, General? Yes, I know. You are the sixth-ranking major general in the army. But I would argue one point with you. Not only can the president advance you to overall command, but he has. You want action, General? Then take action. You want a fire lit under the chairs of all those cogs in the army's machine? Then light them."

"Sir, what of General Scott . . . and General Wood?"

Baker laughed again. "General Scott shall accept your appointment like a good old soldier. I'm certain General Wood will not. It's just part of the burden of command. Some people won't like you. If the president had allowed his naysayers to

251

influence his actions, he wouldn't still be president. You have been in the army long enough to know how often an officer advances because of who he knows, or who his relatives are. That system suffices in peacetime, but, as you have already observed, it won't work now. I told you that President Wilson is committed to winning this war. It is the president's decision that you are the most qualified man for the job. I agree with his decision."

Pershing felt himself straightening in the chair. "Thank you, sir."

"Since you have such respect for chain of command, there's something I want to make clear to you." He turned away, and Pershing saw him pull a book off the shelf behind his desk.

"General, are you well acquainted with the writings of Ulysses Grant?"

Pershing saw the book now, Grant's own memoirs. "Yes, sir. I have read that several times. General Grant has always been an inspiration to me."

"Excellent. He should be. Do you recall President Lincoln's promise to Grant, when he promoted Grant to overall command?"

"Yes, sir."

"I won't insist you recite it. Instead, I offer you my own pledge, from me and from the president. It is my intention to give you two orders. This paper, when it is completed in detail, will be the first. The second will come when your job in Europe is finished. It will be the order for you to gather your army and return home."

16

LUFBERY

May 1917

There was a distinctly mixed response among the pilots to the declaration of war by President Wilson. No one protested the decision itself, which had certainly been welcome news to the French and British pilots who flew from the same airfield. But with the news had come all manner of rumors, and the pilots of the Lafayette Escadrille had no idea what might become of their own squadron.

The letters poured in along with the newspaper clippings, a massive flood of news and information from across the Atlantic. Much of it was from family, the hope that their sons would find their place now with the American Air Service, flying American planes under the flag of their own country. The difficulty for the pilots was not their mixed loyalties. With all the well-wishing and optimism that came their way, they were all aware that there was no existing American Air Service at all. The question was not whether they would serve. The question was *what* they would serve.

"Here's another one."

The faces turned, waiting for Parsons to read.

"In only weeks, the valiant struggle against the oppressive Hun shall be given renewed energy by the overwhelming wave of American youth. A thousand aeroplanes, flown by a thousand young pilots, shall soon embark on their nation's greatest adventure. The Hun shall be vanquished from France, nay, from all the world, never again to plague civilized humanity with the scourge of their

253

bloodlust. From the most blessed skies of their homeland, to the troubled skies of Europe, this unstoppable tide of American flying machines shall obliterate the Hun, and cast him into the dusty memory of the past."

Parsons looked up from the newspaper, waited for the response.

Thaw was mixing a drink, said, "Impressive. A thousand aeroplanes. In only a few weeks."

Lufbery was feeling a hard weight in his chest, felt the gloom spreading around the room. DeLaage moved to the piano, a particularly shabby-looking instrument. He sat, said, "Shall we salute the spirit of America?"

Thaw had completed his task, took a drink, sampling his work, made a twisted face. He said to Lufbery, "I don't have your knack for this." He looked at DeLaage now, said, "Lieutenant, you may salute America. You may salute President Wilson, France, and anyone else you choose. But I would hold off saluting the *unstoppable wave* of American aeroplanes. That is, until they exist."

DeLaage played, the notes grinding through Lufbery's despair. He watched the lieutenant's delicate fingers, coaxing the melody from an instrument that had lost most of its dignity. The piano was missing its outsides, and when the word had come that this strange rattrap of a bar had suddenly opened for business, DeLaage had been as excited about finding the piano as the men were for a source of drink. The bar was owned by a withered old man who seemed to despise everyone who came to do business with him. No one knew how the old man had procured the piano, or how it had come to rest in this ramshackle structure. The old man seemed not to care what DeLaage did to it, as long as he didn't steal it, and the lieutenant had spent several evenings hovering over the wounded instrument like a mother caring for a crippled child. He had repaired and tuned it as well as anyone could, using instruments from LeBlanc's tool chest. But despite the occasional sour note, DeLaage and the grease-covered wrenches had given music back to both the piano and the men who gathered nearly every night to listen.

254

The music that filled the drafty building was something Lufbery had heard DeLaage play before, some kind of waltz, slow and soothing. Lufbery could see the effects on the faces of the others, the same look he had seen on faces that were no longer there. The music stirred something of home, or peace, or whatever particular dream each man held inside. Lufbery tried to let his mind drift away, but he was pulled back by the sound of a brief argument, watched as Thaw gave money to the old man, satisfying some complaint about wasting his good brandy.

Thaw caught Lufbery's look, did not smile, unusual, and Lufbery moved closer, said, "He giving you trouble tonight?"

"No more than usual. I'm still wondering how he survived the Germans. I suppose he's just a good businessman."

Lufbery laughed. "An entrepreneur."

Thaw pointed to Parsons, the piece of newspaper still folded in Parsons' hand. "You hear that crap? It's bad enough we get trumpeted about as God's gift to the war. Now, those damned papers are filling people's heads with nonsense about . . . hell, about all of it."

"You sure it's not true?"

"What do you think, Luf? You know of a single aircraft factory anywhere in the States? Hell, I don't. You got people like Parsons' buddy, Curtiss. Probably can build a new aeroplane once a month, using parts he's making himself out of some horse wagon. Where're they getting the motors? And what kind of motors? They intending to start from scratch, create a brand-new design? Or they gonna use what the French and English are using? How the hell are these people here going to spare a thousand aeroplanes? And who's gonna train a thousand American pilots? In weeks? Unstoppable wave. It's all crap, Luf. Our country's going to war with rainbows in its eyes."

He had never seen Thaw so angry, saw Parsons listening as well. Parsons tossed the newspaper aside, raised himself out of the chair, moved close to them, said, "It's just *good news*, Bill. You know the president didn't want to fight. He's probably scared that now he's made some giant awful mistake, so he makes sure the newspapers say nothing but good stuff, get the whole country to agree with him. Shows our allies that we're all primed for a big fight. Makes everybody happy."

Thaw made a grunting sound, stared into his glass, said, "How happy are they gonna be six months from now when the whole world realizes it's all bull. The only ones who are gonna be happy are the Boche."

With the consolidation of the German northern defenses, the Aeronautique Militaire decided that the position of the escadrille at Saint-Just-en-Chaussée was now too far from the front lines to be effective. On April 7, the orders had come, and the squadron was moved again. Their new airfield lay close to the village of Ham, a place like nothing the pilots had ever seen. Ham had been behind German lines for nearly three years, but as the Germans withdrew, they left a wide swath of utter devastation, and Ham was not spared. What the artillery had not destroyed, the Germans had. What had once been a quaint farming village was blasted into ruin.

In mid-April, the inevitable spring campaign had begun, but the outcome was nothing like anyone in the escadrille had expected. The plan had come from the French commanding general, Robert Nivelle, the man who had replaced Joseph Joffre. Joffre's failure to end the stalemate had drained him of power, and his enemies in the French government had taken advantage. Nivelle wasted no time in asserting his own power over the French military. He organized a massive surprise attack in the region along the Aisne River, midway between the Verdun sector and the British lines to the north. But as had happened too often in the past, the attack was plagued by delays and difficulties, so that, when Nivelle finally ordered the plan into motion, the Germans were completely prepared. Despite serious reservations from the British, and many of Nivelle's own commanders, in mid-April, a million Frenchmen had surged into the German defenses between Soissons and Reims. Signs of disaster were immediate. On the first day of the assault, the French suffered forty thousand casualties. But Nivelle stubbornly persisted, launching a continuing series of fruitless and costly attacks, until finally, by early May, Nivelle was forced to concede total defeat. The disaster cost Nivelle his job, but to an enormous number of weary French troops, it was the final straw. All along the Aisne front, thousands of French soldiers just quit, many laying down their rifles, refusing to fight, many more simply marching away, large groups of *poilus* clogging the roadways, an uprising that threatened to dissolve the French army from the inside out. The panic that resulted in Paris brought immediate change to the French High Command. Command was given to General Henri Pétain, an immensely popular commander, who quickly addressed the despair of his troops. Within a few short weeks, most of the mutiny had collapsed, and the *poilus* had begun to filter back to their positions in the line. Amazingly, word of the mutiny had been contained within the French army itself, and even the British were unaware what had happened. More important for the French, for several agonizing days a wide section of the French defenses had been almost completely unmanned. Before the Germans were even aware of the crisis, Pétain had contained the mutiny, and the gap had been filled. The German High Command had lost an extraordinary opportunity.

With the escadrille now some twenty miles closer to the front lines than they had been before, they had once again become prime targets for nighttime bombing raids. Within their first week, the pilots had been forced into underground shelters, while above them, the flimsy canvas hangars had suffered the fiery effects of the German assaults. It had become as dangerous to be a ground mechanic as it was to be airborne.

The Lafayette Escadrille had seen another change as well. The technology of the French air machines continued to improve, and the Nieuport 17 was rapidly becoming obsolete. All the flying squadrons had begun to receive a new aeroplane, sturdier and more powerful. Though it didn't have the dancing flexibility of the Nieuports, it more than made up for the deficiencies by its ability to absorb punishment and remain in the air. It was called the SPAD.

Ham Airfield, France—May 15, 1917

The narrow creek wound out across a wide stretch of open ground, and as he climbed a small rise, his eyes followed the snaking line to the horizon. Lufbery had hoped to find at least a small patch of trees, some bit of woodlands, some place where he might find success in his search for mushrooms. But the woods had been stripped from the land, and the only sign of any trees at all were ragged clusters of burned and broken timbers. He tried to imagine what this land had looked like before the war, wide pastureland, this one lone creek marking the property lines perhaps, centuries of cultivation carving permanent furrows in land that had been used by generations of family farmers. Now the furrows were gone, the ground rolling and broken by a new kind of machinery. As far out as he could see, the dirt was black and muddy, water-filled shell holes, punctured by ragged disfigured hulks, the crushed remnants of the tools of war. He stood for a long moment, his eye following the line of the creek. He could hear the sound of the water, a soft trickle, the creek undisturbed by the decay and desolation, flowing steadily forward, carrying the human stain, cleansing and renewing the soil as it made its way finally to the Somme River.

He looked down at the basket in his hands, felt suddenly ridiculous. For so much of his life he had enjoyed the forests, had sought out the peace and isolation of the dense sanctuaries in every part of the world. But this land offered no sanctuary, had not known peace now for three years. He could not help feeling that out there, in the upheaval of the tortured ground, bodies were scattered, most never to be identified, death covered over by more death. It will change one day, he thought. Eventually, this land will be green again, the trees will come back, the farmers will return. But the death will remain, the bodies feeding the soil, until one by one they are disturbed by the innocent work of some yet unborn farmer. It will be the plow, probably, exposing the bones, revealing the history of this place, a shocking reminder to every man who ever works this land that no matter how much you bury the past, what happened here can never truly be forgotten.

He glanced back at the setting sun, the western sky washed by a red haze, the smoke from distant fires, so common now. There was always a fire, sometimes hundreds of fires, darkening the sky, masking the sun in a bloody curtain. In the field behind him, he saw Parsons, the man poking about some wrecked cannon, peering down into a barrel. Parsons had asked to accompany him, laughingly curious about Lufbery's odd quest for mushrooms. Lufbery had never minded anyone tagging along, would still go about his search in silence, responding only to the questions they might ask, how and where do you find them, and, of course, the inevitable: is that one edible? Parsons had kept beside him at first, but when the creek led them out into the open ground, he had fallen back, had begun a quest of his own. Lufbery didn't collect souvenirs, had never thought of carrying home any lifeless piece of this war. But Parsons had been as curious as most of them, began to scamper off toward the various ruins, examining the wrecks of guns and trucks and wagons, while Lufbery kept moving out near the winding creek.

As he took in the panorama of the desolate landscape, Lufbery knew the search for mushrooms was futile. He moved off the low rise toward Parsons, saw the man with a handful of metal, small bits of destruction.

Parsons moved to meet him, said, "Amazing. Incredible. I never imagined. They just left this stuff here. God, Luf, I saw bones, a helmet with a damned hole in it." He looked at the empty basket in Lufbery's hand. "You done? I don't think I wanna be out here when the sun goes down."

"Yep. Let's head back."

"No luck, huh?"

Lufbery shook his head, thought of the word. "Hasn't been any luck around any of us for a while now."

They moved in silence, Parsons slipping out toward a shattered cannon, staring down into the barrel, something Lufbery had seen him do before, something they all seemed to do. What does he expect to find in there?

Parsons was beside him again, walked for a few moments, then said, "I have to say, Luf, when I signed up, I never thought that part of the job was going to funerals. I'm damned tired of it."

Lufbery nodded, stepped up and over another low rise, down toward the trail that would lead them back to the airfield. Parsons was looking at him, seemed to wait for an answer, said, "Sorry. Didn't mean to stir up something. You've been to a damned sight more funerals than I have."

"It's okay. You're right. We're all tired of it."

The latest had been a few days before, the second member of the escadrille to die in as many weeks. Both Edmond Genet and Ronald Hoskier had come to the squadron at the first of the year. Genet was barely twenty, Hoskier only a few months older, and the teasing was relentless, all the usual comments about children doing a man's job. Both had taken it well, had seemed energized by the need to prove something to the "older" men around them. They had flown several missions with Lufbery, and Genet in particular seemed to have the knack for aerobatics, for evading the enemy and turning the tide of a confrontation. Lufbery had been with Genet on patrol when the young man had skillfully maneuvered away from a fight and had broken for home. Lufbery had seen it all, the German pressing the attack, filling the air around Genet's Nieuport with bullets, the young man appearing to dodge the best the German had to give. When Genet had sought escape, Lufbery assumed his machine gun had jammed, but the German did not pursue, seemed content to let him go. Lufbery could not follow Genet, had been involved in a duel of his own with a German two-seater that ended with the enemy making good his own escape. But when Lufbery returned to the airfield, the awful familiar scenario had played out once more. The pilots had gathered; the telephone calls had been received from the ground observers. Genet had crashed near the French line, his Nieuport ramming straight into the ground with his motor at full power, the wings stripped away. The impact of the crash was so devastating, the plane and Genet himself were buried in a crater of their own making, the young man's body unrecognizable.

Genet in particular had a knack for friendships, and, like many of the newer pilots, had formed bonds that made the sudden death of any one of them particularly painful. Lufbery had seen too much of that, and though he was never unfriendly, the others had learned that their most celebrated veteran was not a man you could warm up to.

Lufbery felt differently about Parsons, who was a bit older, and though Parsons had come from blue-blood roots, the man himself showed no signs of being an aristocrat. Parsons had been attracted to aeroplanes even as an adolescent, had escaped the rigidity of New England prep schools to flee to the adventurous unknown of California. There he had become friends with aviation pioneer Glenn Curtiss, who, besides teaching Parsons how to fly, had given the young man the inspiration that would shape his future. Parsons loved everything about aeroplanes, something that Lufbery could easily appreciate.

They moved away from the stream, followed the path as it grew wider. Parsons took the lead, confident in the route home, and Lufbery glanced out toward the stumps of fat trees, his automatic habit, still searching the ground. Parsons stopped, waited for him to catch up, said, "You mind if I ask you something?"

"Nope."

"You ever afraid to get into your aeroplane?"

Lufbery didn't hesitate.

"Not anymore."

Parsons seemed surprised by the answer. "I wish I could feel that way. Just go up with the mission in my head. Maybe that's why I haven't done any good. You think it's bad to be afraid?" Lufbery shrugged, said nothing. Parsons said, "The early morning patrols are the worst. I don't sleep worth a damn."

"You get used to it. Wine helps."

"God, I've drunk more wine here than I thought there was in the world." He paused. "You mind me asking you something else?"

Lufbery could see fear in Parsons' eyes, something he had never noticed before. "What?"

"You've shot down, what, ten?"

"I guess so. Confirmed. A few more they didn't count."

"I've heard that. That ever bother you? If I ever get my first

261

Boche, I damned sure better get a confirmation. Hell, I've shot ten thousand rounds of ammunition at those bastards. That oughta be worth something."

"You'll get him sooner or later. Every time you go up, you get better at it. I can see it."

Parsons seemed to brighten at the compliment. "Thanks. I'd really like to see that, the whole thing, shoot some Albatros up so bad that he just falls out of the sky. That has to be damned exciting. When you nail one, do you watch them all the way down? Dive after them? I would. Make damned sure I got the bastard."

"Used to. But after a while, you just *know*. You shoot a few pilots, you know when he's not going to make it. Sometimes there's fire. Makes it pretty obvious."

"God, I'd love to see that! Watch some big two-seater just explode right in front of me! I thought about aiming for the gas tank, but it's tough. I'm happy just to hit the bastard."

Lufbery thought a moment, said, "Don't care for it myself."

"What?"

He looked at Parsons, saw clear-eyed respect, the man absorbing every word. "I don't care for the fire." He thought a moment. "You asked me about being afraid. Sometimes, that's the one thing I think about." He felt embarrassed admitting a weakness. Parsons was wide-eyed, watching him, and Lufbery tapped the basket against his leg, said, "We best be getting back."

"Wait. Tell me. I want to be prepared."

Lufbery shook his head. "There's no such thing. Nothing I can tell you will prepare you for the sight of a man burning to death. I don't know why, but it's different. Shooting a man, or watching someone fly hard into the ground. Sometimes they dive so fast, they lose their wings, the plane comes apart. Like Genet. Full throttle, straight in. You figure he was dead already, or out cold. But even if he saw it coming, he hit so hard he never would have felt it. Fire . . . you feel every second of it. I would rather die from a bullet or a crash, anything else. Burning alive . . . you have nightmares? That's mine."

Lufbery felt himself shiver, was still embarrassed. He looked at Parsons, expected to see a smile, the prelude to the usual teasing of any man's exposed frailties. But Parsons was just staring at him, dark, serious eyes, said nothing.

Lufbery said, "Look, I'd appreciate it if you kept quiet about this."

"Certainly. Whatever you say, Luf."

"Let's go."

They moved along the path, the flat ground of the airfield opening out before them, walked toward the row of distant hangars. Parsons said in a low voice, "Burning alive. Wonderful. Something else to keep me awake."

May 23, 1917

Thenault waited for the last of them to sit, looked out into the open hangar, satisfying himself that no one was missing. Lufbery was surprised to see the mechanics present as well, LeBlanc's men seated to one side of the pilots. Thenault waited for a long moment, then said, "I am pleased to inform you that the Lafayette Escadrille will very soon be receiving a greater number of the new SPADs. The Aeronautique Militaire has informed me that by July, we will turn over the last of our Nieuports, and will be equipped only with the SPADs. I know that several of you have already made flights in the new aircraft. If you have any useful information to share, please assist whenever you can. Lieutenant DeLaage is currently aloft in his new machine, making some test maneuvers. Upon his return, we will begin final flight preparations so that our patrols may commence as quickly as possible. According to everything I've heard about the new aeroplane, the Boches are in for a surprise. The SPAD is a formidable weapon. I do not expect your transition to the new craft to be difficult, but, as you are aware, there are always differences in aircraft, especially ones that have come by a different manufacturer. Are there any questions?"

Lufbery glanced around, saw a hand rising. It was Thaw.

"Captain, what the hell is a SPAD?"

There were a few laughs, and Thenault seemed confused by the question.

"If you mean, the name . . . well, yes, the aeroplane is manufactured by the Société Anonyme Pour L'Aviation et ses Dérivés. If you prefer, we can refer to the new aeroplane in that manner."

Thaw nodded, seemed to ponder the decision. "Nope. SPAD will do."

They gathered at the opening of the hangar, watched as DeLaage brought the SPAD down, the wheels settling into the low grass with only a slight bounce. Lufbery smiled, had always been impressed by DeLaage's talent for a smooth landing. The SPAD circled slowly toward them, the motor clucking unevenly, and Thenault trotted over to the plane, said something to DeLaage. Thenault was back now, said, "He will take it up again. I wish you to observe the SPAD's angle of ascent, the added power that will help you gain altitude more rapidly than the Nieuport."

DeLaage waved to them, revved the motor, spun the plane in a tight half circle, rolled out toward the long field. The SPAD was in full throttle now, and Lufbery could hear the low whine of the motor, deep and throaty, different from the Clerget, different from anything he had heard before. The plane left the ground, and Lufbery could tell that DeLaage was pulling the stick back at a steep incline, much steeper than they were accustomed to. But the SPAD rose steadily, its nose up, gaining altitude, a hundred feet, then quickly, two hundred. The plane banked now, turned sharply to the right, DeLaage keeping the nose angle high, and Lufbery focused on the sound of the motor, was surprised to hear a choppy break in the low steady groan. The plane was still in its steep banking turn, the nose still high, and the motor spit again, then suddenly was silent. Lufbery felt an icy burst in his chest, heard voices, the men shouting, "Straighten out . . . put the nose down . . . !"

The SPAD seemed to cling to the air for one silent moment, then slipped sideways, falling. The men were screaming in an awful chorus around him, and Lufbery felt the cold race through him, could only watch the plane fall, helpless, the slow horrible tumble, the plane impacting the ground in a sickening explosion of shattered wood. The men responded with a mad rush, scrambled across the field toward the wreckage. Lufbery did not move, watched them running, the shouts growing quiet as they moved farther away. The sickness rose in him now, and he dropped to one knee, felt a hand on his back, heard the voice of LeBlanc.

"He could have survived. It might be all right."

There was no feeling in LeBlanc's words, and Lufbery stared down, could only shake his head.

It had been two dreary days since DeLaage's funeral, and the rains had come. No one could fly today. When the rains soaked the creek beds and dry streams, the others had come to expect Lufbery's long walks, his customary search across the muddy ground. He had not asked for company, was relieved that no one volunteered; no one seemed interested in looking for mushrooms in the rain, and so he was alone. He had not brought the basket, something none of them had even noticed, had walked out along the road instead, hoping that someone would happen by. It did not take long. The truck was an ambulance, and he stood in the center of the road until it stopped, a cursing driver grudgingly making room for him. Lufbery offered no explanation, and the driver was too weary to press the issue. But Lufbery's journey would not be long, and the driver was surprised at the request to stop. He escaped the ambulance at the familiar intersection, by the ramshackle bar that perched beside the muddy road.

He moved inside, was relieved to see no one there, saw a door opening, the old man emerging from his small room in the back. The curses came first, but the old man recognized him now, one of the Americans, the men with big thirst and deep pockets. He saw something in the man's withered face, a look that acknowledged something about Lufbery. The old man had made some observation of his own, that this one American was different from the others, older certainly, a serious man who does not suffer from the noisy foolishness of youth.

A bottle appeared, and Lufbery shook his head, pointed only to the old man's room, a silent command. Leave. The old man did not argue, surprising Lufbery, and he saw something new on

265

the old face, a slow nod, understanding. The man disappeared behind a rickety door, and Lufbery stared at the door for a long moment, had never thought of the old man as anything but a nuisance, a foul-tempered barkeep. But Lufbery was curious now, thought, Of course, he *knows*. And in this place, no one grows old without seeing death and misery, without feeling loss. Lufbery suddenly wanted to talk to him, ask him about his life, a woman perhaps, a wife now dead. Had there been cruelty from the Germans or compassion? How many friends . . . no, how many of his *sons* were gone, buried in the mud of no-man's-land?

But he didn't have the energy for questions, and the old man had shown him rare kindness by leaving him alone. He stood for a moment, staring at nothing, and all his reasons for being there flooded over him. He felt a shuddering fear, thought, This is a mistake. I should not have come. He clenched his fists, scolded himself for his fear. He had come with a purpose, like every day he flew the planes, a purpose, and the fear could not stop him, had never stopped him. He took a long deep breath, looked toward the piano, and he moved that way, leaned down, pulled out the lone chair, sat slowly. He thought of the bar-rooms and hotels, all the loud parties, the amazing volume of alcohol, fights and jokes, shouts and laughter. So many times they had not given DeLaage a second thought, the man settling in at the always-present piano, playing the same songs, guiding their moods, calming tempers, inspiring their joy and their melancholy. The image was hard in his mind, and he heard the words now, some song that had become commonplace, some-thing they had sung only the night before. He thought of the gathering crowd of pilots, the drunken revelry of men too blinded to learn anything. He tried to recall, thought, Who started this one? Parsons? Someone else, perhaps. No, it doesn't matter. Lufbery was bad with lyrics, could never remember the songs, but he had picked up the one verse, and the words were there now.

> *So, stand to your glasses steady,*
> *The world is a web of lies;*

Then here's to the dead already;
And hurrah to the next man who dies.

The night before, like every night before, the glasses had been raised, the men who could still stand making their final toast of the evening. He looked down at the piano keys, thought, *The next man.* The thought flowed through his brain every time he flew, or more often now, with every dawn, whether he flew or not. One day they'll sing to you as well. There's nothing else to do, after all. It had become so terribly routine to him, the men who went down, some of them now barely known to him before they were gone. They were growing used to funerals, sharing their respect, some small show of grief, but there were rarely tears anymore, just a grim acceptance that men were dying. The grief was a luxury for the pilots, and he thought often of the infantry, men who watched entire companies disintegrate, entire squadrons dead in an instant. Do they resent us for our vanity, for the grand spectacle we make of death? In the end, the result will be the same, a dead squadron of pilots instead of foot soldiers. The only difference is that we go one man at a time. He thought of Bill Thaw, the only man in the escadrille who was there before him. At the start of every patrol, Lufbery had come to fear for Thaw's life more than his own. There was a depth to Thaw that Lufbery had tried to avoid, but try as he might, he couldn't deny his affection for the playful man who could make anyone smile. Me and Thaw. We are the veterans. Another word for . . . *survivors.*

He put both hands softly, silently on the keyboard. He did not play the piano, had no idea how to make the music, something that came so naturally to DeLaage. The keys were chipped and yellowed, and he studied them for a long moment, felt something cold and silent open up inside of him, something that had been shut down for a very long time. As the men of the escadrille had fallen away, death had become more than commonplace, it had become expected. But he remembered that one awful day, nearly three years before, when death had been a crushing devastating shock. In 1914, the war still seemed unreal to him, some kind of screaming match between braying jackasses, posturing fools who shouted down from the heights of palace walls. And then, Marc Pourpe had died. Lufbery had known grief then, the kind of paralyzing sadness that he had never known before. It had changed him, as it had changed every infantryman in this war. The mind took control, showed you how to ignore the pain, gather the grief, and put it all away. That's the real survival, he thought. You lock it all away in that dark place, and if you are fortunate, you do not return. He pressed a key on the piano, the silence of the room shattered by the sound. The single note echoed in his mind, faded slowly, jarring the dark place, stirring the pain. I never thought we would lose you, Lieutenant. You were a kind soul. He couldn't see the keys now, lowered his face gently down on his hands, and began to cry.

17

PERSHING

Washington, D.C.—May 24, 1917

He had laid the letter on top of the pile, stared at it for a long moment, picked it up again. He could not just toss it aside, treating it as just another piece of paper from yet another earnest old soldier, hoping to find his last bit of glory by sailing to France. He scanned the letter again, looked now to the bottom, read the postscript.

> *P.S. If I were physically fit, instead of old and heavy and stiff, I should myself ask to go under you in any capacity down to and including a sergeant; but at my age, and condition, I suppose that I could not do work you would consider worthwhile in the fighting line (my only line) in a lower grade than brigade commander.*

The letters were finding him now every day, requests for assignment, some from officers who had been retired for years. To so many, the request was more of a demand, that Pershing would somehow owe it to those who had given their service once before, some in the Spanish-American War, others simply by their longevity in the army. The requests shared one characteristic, beyond each man's desire to serve. Not one of them seemed willing to accept any position that did not involve command, usually at a general's level, and, of course, every one of them expected to lead troops in the field of combat. He read the postscript again, the writer acknowledging he was too old for field work, and so would naturally expect command. He had begun to lose patience with this type of request, as though each man believed that command was simply a reward, that it carried no expectation of any real work, nothing physically demanding. It was exactly the sort of applicant Pershing had no use for. His responses to these kinds of requests had become routine, respectful and polite, with the door left open should the emergency arise. It was the only kind of offering he could make to these old soldiers, a small gift of hope, that if the emergency was so great, they might be called upon after all. But the letter in his hand was different, and he stared at the words now without reading, knew that he could not answer this one by the template he was using for the others. The letter was from Teddy Roosevelt.

The former president was the most popular public figure of his day, and had been the loudest voice criticizing Woodrow Wilson for his policy of American neutrality. Pershing had served under Roosevelt in Cuba, and like every officer in Roosevelt's command, Pershing shared the respect and affection for the man who had become an iconic hero to the American people. But Roosevelt was past his time, the words in his letter reflecting what Roosevelt himself knew to be true. Pershing was surprised by the man's hope for a senior command, as though by his status alone he could once again lead an army. It gnawed at Pershing that it might be his task to deny Roosevelt's request by offering a carefully worded lesson that Roosevelt himself must surely know. Longevity is not a qualification for ability. But there was more to Roosevelt's request than some search for a final day in the sun, and it brought home to Pershing how the army had changed. Roosevelt had been vocal in promoting his own efforts to raise a division of volunteer soldiers, with himself in command. The news was trumpeted loudly by the popular press, and Pershing had little doubt that a sizable number of men would rally to the great man's call. It was reminiscent of the problems that had plagued the army during the Civil War, and before, popular public figures placing themselves at the head of their own troops. From George Washington to Robert E. Lee, military leaders had found themselves dealing with personalities instead of leadership, and in nearly every case, personality had not been enough. Eventually, even the most popular political figure had been swept aside,

270

defeated by his inability to do the job. As much as Pershing loved Teddy Roosevelt, the old man's request had to be rejected.

Roosevelt's letter, and his public campaign on his own behalf had taught Pershing a hard lesson. From his first hours of receiving his new responsibility, he had found himself thinking of the men who had filled this role before him: Washington, Winfield Scott, Ulysses Grant, each man in his own time confronted by a job that required the one ingredient most of the old guard in their armies would not understand. Each one of them must surely have made the same observation, Washington at Trenton, Scott at Mexico City, Grant at Petersburg. Each had been successful because each one understood that he faced a war that was different from any that had been fought before. He stared at Roosevelt's letter, thought, The nature of war has changed yet again, and the men who gained their experience twenty years ago might not be the men who can adapt. There is always technology to contend with, new weaponry, communication, new ways of moving troops. But nothing in our training has prepared us for what is happening in France. In the Civil War, generals committed their men to slaughter because they did not understand the power of the rifled musket. Now, there is the machine gun, poison gas, the grenade, the flamethrower, even the aeroplane, so much deadly genius, so many new and efficient ways of killing. For all the death and horror of this war, the only adaptation those generals have made is to dig deeper holes in the ground, protect the foot soldier by hiding him. Both sides have accepted that the best response to the new technology is defense. And so, three years later, no one has any idea how to make it end.

He set Roosevelt's letter aside, stood, moved to the window, stared out into sunlight. There was a gathering of small boats on the Potomac, men in white suits, a group from some local college. He watched them for a moment, the young men paddling their rowboats into some kind of formation. Before this war is over, he thought, we may need all of you to go to France. There must be a better reason, a deeper inspiration than the simple call to arms, the great rallying around the flag. Teddy Roosevelt would inspire you by his energy, by the wonderful

271

fantasy that if you joined him, he would lead you every step of the way, the great man out in front, sword held high, crushing his enemies, invincible, making you invincible as well. He is a symbol, and no one understands that more than he does. But symbols are not enough, not anymore. If we are to have any kind of impact on this war, we must change the very flow, the very nature of what is happening there. I cannot tell any man that he can serve us best by crawling into a hole and waiting for the enemy to find him. If I am to lead an army, I must be able to look those men in the eye, and convince them that they can rise up and charge the machine guns. I must convince those college boys to put all their dreams aside, their bright futures, and join us in our efforts. And the only way I can ever expect them to follow me is if I can show them that we can *win*.

The White House, Washington, D.C.—May 24, 1917

He scanned each one of the portraits that lined the walls, could not help feeling intimidated by the history around him. There was activity in every direction, very different from what he had seen at the War Department. Now, the men were civilians, smartly dressed, moving with the crisp efficiency of responsibility. He watched them, thought, What must it be like to be here every day, to work closely to the center of so much importance? He looked back toward the entrance doors, saw two Marines in dress uniforms, the only other military men he had seen. They seemed to be watching him, stoic and unsmiling, and he nodded to them, reflex, shared the soldier's inherent respect for the elite class of fighting man. Yes, if I lived in the White House, I would want those men watching my door as well.

For several days he had wondered if Wilson would summon him, would require a face-to-face meeting to bolster his confidence in this man who was to lead his army. Pershing had no idea what Wilson was like, or whether he might have some trait that Wilson would suddenly find objectionable. The president might still reconsider, he thought, might still regard me as one candidate among several.

He could not avoid the nagging doubts, had felt himself

sucked into the vortex of intrigue that swirled through the capital, thought, How much pressure is Wilson under, how many of the old soldiers in this place have voiced their displeasure at my selection? He was still not comfortable with the thought of so many ruffled feathers huffing around the War Department, all the senior commanders who had been passed over for this ex-traordinary command. The talk had been muted, at least in Pershing's presence. But they might be unleashing their rage right here, right into the face of Woodrow Wilson.

The door was pulled open, and Pershing glanced out to see more Marines, the men who had saluted him as he entered. They stood back, holding the door, and Pershing saw Baker, the small man stepping quickly, moving right past him.

"Let's go, General. The president abhors tardiness even more than I do."

Pershing obeyed, allowed Baker to lead him through the hallways the secretary had walked many times before. They stopped at a large office, and Baker moved toward a reception desk, said something to an unsmiling young man, who stood, disappeared quickly through a doorway that was flanked by another pair of Marines. Pershing began to feel more nervous now, fidgeted with his jacket, adjusting what was already perfect. The man emerged from the doorway, said, "Mr. Secretary, the president will see you now."

The young man returned to his desk, had not even looked at Pershing. Baker was already moving through the door, and Pershing followed, glanced at the Marines, caught one looking back at him, saw sharp cold eyes. He gave the man a short tight nod, straightened his jacket again, took a deep breath, and stepped through the door.

Baker seemed to wait for him, and Pershing was surprised at the magnitude of the office, wide, oval-shaped, a broad expanse of windows, and behind the desk, Woodrow Wilson.

Pershing drew to a stiff halt, stood at attention, waited for instructions, saw Wilson pointing to a chair without looking up. Baker sat, looked at Pershing, smiled, pointed to another chair, said, "General, um, at ease. There is no need for you to remain standing."

Pershing continued to watch Wilson, who was still focused on the papers on his desk. Wilson picked up a pen, scratched his signature, looked at Baker now, said, "Railroads. They insist that I personalize every contract. Annoying men and their petty demands."

Baker laughed, said, "I'm certain that one of them has a room entirely decorated with your letters, sir. You're merely supplying his hobby."

Wilson didn't acknowledge Baker's humor, looked to one side, pointed to a stack of papers, said, "We have a serious problem with the tonnage available for transport. The British are being dog stubborn about it. I've been urging the shipping people to jump into this with a bit more enthusiasm. Like trying to start a fire with a bucket of water. Ridiculous. Only way I can get any activity out of them is to sweeten their piece of the pie. I'm discovering that when you toss these industrialists the notion of a war, they begin to drool like so many children at a candy shop."

Baker said, "They'll come around, sir. The entire country is behind this."

Wilson seemed to squint at Baker, nodded, said, "More or less. But I've learned already that we need the proper men in the proper position if we expect any real action. Forgive me, Newton, but most of us government fellows have been far too isolated from the actual workings of commerce. It has been brought to my attention that if we want to mobilize this nation, we must approach it as a business. If you want industry to cooperate, you must show them that they are going to turn a profit. We require ships. The shipbuilders require incentive to comply. Whoever believes patriotism is fuel enough is sadly misled."

Pershing hung on Wilson's words, was surprised by the man's pale skin, his words coming in short labored bursts, breathless, a man who seemed totally exhausted. Wilson looked at him now, said, "Sorry to bore you with all this complaining, General. I suppose we should be formally introduced."

Pershing stood abruptly, and Baker said, "Mr. President, may I present Major General John Pershing."

Wilson leaned back in the chair, and Pershing held himself

274

stiffly upright, didn't know what to do. Wilson said, "Oh, please sit down, General. There are no photographers here. You're making my back hurt."

Pershing saw a smile on Baker's face, eased into the chair again.

Wilson said, "General, we are giving you some very difficult tasks these days."

Pershing glanced at Baker again, said, "Perhaps so, Mr. President. But that is what we are trained to expect."

"You performed admirably in Mexico, General. Difficult tasks there as well. Or impossible. You caused this nation, and me, no embarrassment, which, in that situation, was perhaps the most important responsibility you had. Quite a different situation now. I imagine the French and the British have embarrassment enough to contend with. That shall not be our concern. I'm not especially cautious about what the newspapers have to say anymore. It's the one advantage to serving out a second term. Though my enemies may continue to molest me in the public press, I can now ignore them. In this office, there is too much priority given to reelection, so much time spent by a first-term president watching his every step. The draft, for example. Some would say that was political suicide. You see the photograph in the newspapers, General? Embarrassing, to say the least. They put a blindfold on me like I was a ten-year-old playing some party game, had me choose the first lottery numbers out of a bowl. But despite all the predictions of doom, the public has begun to respond positively. Letters are arriving here daily, people whose birth date places them at the top of the list. People are eager to join your army, General. You approve of the draft?"

"Yes, sir. Under the circumstances, it is an efficient means of bringing a large number of men into immediate training." Wilson seemed to weigh his response, nodded, looked at Baker. Pershing felt words rising up inside him, said, "Mr. President, if I may . . . I would suggest that the draftees be kept separate from the regular army units. It would make their training more efficient. Otherwise, there could be unhealthy competition within units, a display of elitism from the regulars that would only cause problems of discipline."

Wilson looked at him, thought a moment, said, "Whatever you think is best, General. It's your command."

There was a quiet pause, and Wilson glanced over to the pile of papers. Baker said, "Thank you for your time, Mr. President. Your schedule is certainly busy these days."

Baker stood, and Pershing followed his lead, was surprised by the abruptness of the meeting. Wilson leaned forward now, and Pershing saw tired sadness in the man's eyes. Wilson nodded, said, "I'll see you tomorrow night, Newton. A considerable gathering of African diplomats will be joining us for dinner. They are mightily pleased we are intending to rid their continent of the German menace. Not for you to worry, General. I don't intend to send you to Africa. It's simply another exercise in diplomacy."

Baker made a short bow, moved away, and Pershing saw Wilson returning to his papers. He was uncomfortable now, felt something missing, had expected much more. He glanced at Baker, who waited for him at the entranceway, looked again at Wilson.

"Mr. President, please allow me to say . . . I appreciate the honor you have conferred upon me . . . the assignment you have given me. I realize the responsibility it entails. You may count on the best that is in me, sir."

Wilson looked up, nodded slowly, said, "General, you were chosen for this task entirely on the basis of your record, and I have every confidence you will succeed. You have my full support." He paused. "Oh, General, when you complete your journey, should the occasion arise, please offer my personal respects to both King George and President Poincaré."

"Certainly, sir. Thank you."

He spun around, followed Baker out of the office, and Baker kept moving, led him out toward the main entrance, the Marines obliging by opening the doors. They were outside now, the afternoon sun hovering over the Potomac.

Baker stopped, turned to him, held the same smile. "Nicely done, General. You've impressed him."

Pershing was confused, said, "How? We didn't discuss . . . I was anticipating some orders from him, details of what he expected me to do."

276

Baker looked back toward the grand façade, the rows of tall columns that lined the entranceway of the White House.

"Tomorrow, General. I'll have your orders in my office. Allow me to send a compliment your way. It is quite likely that the president appreciates that in all the myriad details he must contend with, between all the various industries that must supply our efforts, all the politicians who must be caressed, our allies, who are already thrusting their self-interests into his administration . . . General, it may be that the president feels as I do. Neither one of us expects that we will have to peer over your shoulder at every instance. You are the one man we can depend on to simply do his job."

The roster of officers who would make up his staff was nearly complete, the result of long days examining the records of dozens of capable young men. But they were not all young. For the critical position as his chief of staff, Pershing had chosen an old friend from his long service in the Philippines, Major James Harbord. Harbord had been in the army for more than twenty-five years, had served with Pershing in the Tenth Cavalry. Of all the applicants Pershing had considered, Harbord's name kept rising to the top. He was a midwesterner, only a few years younger than Pershing, was now in the capital attending the army's War College as an unlikely student. But Pershing recalled a man with a quick mind, and a man not afraid of his own opinion. If Pershing was going to begin an effective command, he required a chief of staff who had both the intellect and the experience, and a man who would not hesitate to tell his commanding officer if he thought there were mistakes being made. The square-jawed Harbord was the perfect choice.

With Harbord's assistance, Pershing worked his way through the process of assembling his full staff. To Pershing's surprise, the tasks laid before him required the services of nearly one hundred sixty officers and enlisted men, as well as a number of civilian assistants. To build an army, he first had to build a headquarters.

Washington, D.C.—May 27, 1917

In the military operations against the Imperial German Government, you are directed to cooperate with the forces of the other countries employed against that enemy; but in doing so the underlying idea must be kept in view that the forces of the United States are a separate and distinct component of the combined forces, the identity of which must be preserved.

The official orders had finally come, and Pershing read each paragraph with increasing delight. Baker had been true to his word. The command was Pershing's alone, and according to every clause in the lengthy document, once he was in France, it would be the civilian government's job to support his decisions.

Baker had summoned him again, the visits becoming routine now, discussions that Pershing was relieved to find had been as much for Baker's benefit as his own. If there had been dissent at the War Department over Pershing's authority, the voices continued to be muted, and Pershing could already see the wheels of change taking place there as well. Hugh Scott had scheduled his retirement for September, and already, Scott's duties as chief of staff were being handled by his immediate subordinate, Major General Tasker Bliss. Pershing had no quarrel with Bliss, knew that Baker was far more comfortable with Bliss than he had been with Hugh Scott. The only disadvantage Pershing could see was that Bliss was elderly, nearly as old as Scott, and speculation was already filtering around the War Department that Bliss might soon retire as well. Ultimately, the man occupying the office was not as important to Pershing as long as the chief of staff understood that, in Europe, Pershing was in charge.

Pershing stepped briskly toward Baker's office, passed by officers and civilians who moved at the same pace as he did. It was a subtle change in the atmosphere of the place, and Pershing had no idea if the sudden flood of energy was inspired by him or something Baker had imparted to his staff. He

278

rounded a corner, saw a small crowd of men in Baker's outer office. There were civilians and uniforms as well, different, a distinctive blue: French. They noticed him as well now, and Pershing made a short bow, backed away, made room in the entranceway, said, "Excuse me. I did not intend to interrupt."

He heard Baker's voice now, the small man hidden by the entourage. "Ah! General! The perfect moment."

Baker emerged from the crowd, and Pershing saw an older man behind him, large and round, his thick face dressed by a bushy white moustache. The man stepped up beside Baker, dwarfing him, and Baker said, "Marshal Joseph Joffre, please allow me to introduce Major General John Pershing."

Pershing felt a shock, had not expected to meet a man with the stature of Joffre. The large man extended a thick heavy hand. "Oh, yes. General Pershing. I am delighted."

Pershing took the hand, studied the old man's face, saw deep tired eyes, a fragile smile.

"Marshal Joffre, it is my honor, sir."

Joffre turned to Baker, said, "This is quite fortunate. May I have a word with the general? Is it . . . appropriate?"

Baker nodded, said, "Certainly. We can return to my office."

Joffre said something in French to his staff, the men obeying, moving away, settling into chairs that lined one side of the office. Baker backed away, allowed Joffre to move in front of him, the old man moving slowly into Baker's office. Baker closed the door behind them, said, "The marshal is preparing to depart for France. He has been here for nearly a month now."

Pershing said nothing, waited for Joffre to speak. The old man seemed uncomfortable in his chair, shifted his large frame to one side, said, "I am supposed to be pleased that my government has found a place for me. My official title is chairman of the French Mission to America. It is a kind description for a man who has been put up on a shelf." Pershing sorted through the man's syrupy accent, didn't know how to respond. Joffre shifted in the chair again, said, "Forgive me for getting to the point, General. If you are not offended, may I offer you some advice?"

"Certainly, sir."

"I am told you are a man who does not enjoy the sound of his own voice. In France, that will make you the exception. I believe it will also serve you well." Joffre chuckled now, put a hand on his round stomach. "Forgive an old man his memories, General. When I was in school, very young, and not so . . . large, there was a group of older boys, a nasty lot, who enjoyed taking advantage, what you would call a bully. I had been abused by these boys for some time, several of my friends as well. I grew tired of explaining to my father why I had bruises on my face. It does a boy no good to have his father accuse him of cowardice. So I devised a plan. I found a weapon, a short piece of stout wood. I hid it in the brush, where I had been assaulted many times. I imagined the event over and over in my mind that I would launch into my enemies with screaming fury, bashing them to bloody submission. I believed it to be a perfect plan. One day, they were waiting for me, and instead of submitting to their beating, I quickly retrieved my weapon from its hiding place. I ran at them like some madman, swinging the stick wildly, shouting all manner of threats, fully intending to gain my revenge. One of the boys jumped at me and pulled the stick from my hands, and just like that, I was defenseless again. They found my exhibition so amusing that after that, they left me alone. But I will never forget the boy's words. He said, 'Next time, get a bigger stick.' " Joffre paused, cocked one eye at Pershing. "Forgive me, General. Old men talk too much. You do not understand my meaning."

Pershing glanced at Baker, who was watching Joffre with silent respect. Pershing said, "On the contrary, sir. You are telling me that if I am to achieve any respect in France, I must have the weapons."

"Very good, General. That is exactly what I am telling you. There is much speculation what America can bring to this war. There are hopes and there are doubts. It will be up to you, and your people, to show all of us what kind of ally America can be. I must warn you as well. All the loud men, civilians and generals, they will try to seduce you. You are the young maiden, descending into a labyrinth of power, jealousy, and mistrust. Forgive the description, General, but I know of no other that describes what you are yet to experience. My country and the English are both desperate for the weapons you can bring to this war. Both sides will claim that their needs are the greatest, that their sacrifice has been the most painful. Both will call on you to offer up your men to their army first. And they will test you. They will want to see how big is the stick you wield, and they will seek out your weakness. I see you have a stiff back, General. Your resolve must be stiff as well. Already, my government is making its demands. I am certain the English are as well."

Baker said, "I was prepared to discuss that with the general today, Marshal Joffre."

"Of course. That is not my affair. Forgive me, Mr. Secretary. I have talked for too long. I am now trespassing."

"Not at all, sir."

Joffre pulled himself up from the chair, and Pershing stood as well. Joffre looked at him again, said, "I will leave you to your duties, General. I understand you will be departing very soon. We should perhaps meet again in France."

"By all means, sir. I would look forward to that."

Joffre moved slowly toward the door, stopped, looked again at Pershing. "I hesitate to say this. No. You must know all that is happening. Do you know of General Nivelle?"

"Of course, sir. He commands—"

"He took my place, General. There is no need to be delicate. But if you are not yet aware, you should know that General Nivelle is no longer in command. I am certain the secretary has heard some rumors of this, yes?"

Baker seemed unsure how to respond, said, "Some rumors, perhaps."

"The rumors are true. Nivelle is a fool, a man who insisted on repeating the same mistakes that every commander in this war has already made. This war has been a continuous flood of disasters. Nivelle has now made his foolish contribution, yet one more disaster."

He paused, and Pershing could see that Joffre was debating the wisdom of saying anything more.

The old man closed his eyes for a brief moment, then said,

"Because of Nivelle's stupidity, the French army has nearly collapsed. He has been replaced by Henri Pétain. Pétain is not so much a fool, and may be the only man who can inspire our troops to continue the fight. I am violating my government's orders by revealing this. But you deserve to know the truth about what you are to confront, General. You must understand that no matter how much talk you hear, no matter how many demands are placed on you to comply with French demands or English demands, no matter how your authority is disregarded, there is one inescapable fact. The Germans are firmly entrenched on French and Belgian soil. If this war continues for much longer, I believe they will remain there, possibly forever. Boundaries will be changed, French land will no longer belong to French people. And thus far, no Englishman, no Frenchman has found the means to change that. Without your help, General, without America in this war, we cannot win."

He turned, moved to the door, pulled it open, looked back again. "Au revoir, gentlemen."

The commotion in the outer office was immediate, Joffre's staff rising to meet him. Joffre did not stop, disappeared into the wide hall, the staff following. Baker moved to the door, closed it, and said, "He is a powerful presence."

Baker moved back behind the desk, and Pershing waited for him to sit, both men in their chairs again. Pershing stared down for a moment, could feel a hollow silence in the room, the old man's sudden absence leaving an open hole inside of him. Pershing said, "I never expected . . . such sadness. He is a defeated man."

"Take that seriously, General. Marshal Joffre knows more of what is happening in his country than any man alive."

"Had you heard about Nivelle's replacement?"

"Until now, only rumors. The French are keeping very quiet about the whole affair. We're just so damned far away. Which is why you must leave quickly. Is your staff assembled?"

"Yes, sir. I received your office's approval of all my selections. However, I am prepared to go over each name if you wish."

Baker seemed not to hear him, opened a drawer in the desk, pulled out a folder of papers. "What? Oh, no, quite all right,

General. I do not pretend to know what kind of men you should engage on your own staff." He held up the folder. "I didn't want Marshal Joffre to see this. That seems rather ridiculous now. I don't think we are hiding anything from him. This letter was passed to the chief of staff's office from Major General Bridges, of the British High Command. It's rather lengthy. No need for you to read it now. You can take it with you. But the message is simple. The British are requesting that we not bother to give training to our draftees and new recruits, that we simply ship them to England for training, so that they may be best suited for service in the British army."

"*What?*" Pershing felt a shock from the volume of his own voice, stiffened, said, "Forgive me, sir."

"Quite all right. That was my reaction as well. That's only half of it. Here we go, another letter, this one rather lengthy as well. It was presented to me by Monsieur Viviani, of the French Mission. You can have this one too. I made a notation . . . here. This part might give you a general idea of the French approach to this situation. They request that we ship our troops directly to France, to be trained by French officers. It is further requested that other than yourself, we send no officer of a higher rank than captain, so that no American would outrank any French officer they would assign to us."

"They cannot be serious."

Baker tossed the letters toward him, the pages spreading across his desk.

"Oh, but they are, General. And I have a feeling that this is just the beginning, the first volley, if you will."

"I cannot believe Marshal Joffre would know of this."

"Of course he does. He offered us a prediction of this very thing. Rules of diplomacy, General. He cannot simply tell us everything he knows. You had better get used to that. You must learn to sift through the talk to understand the meaning of what is being said. Forgive me, General, I do not mean to lecture you. But you will discover that men in positions of power often have a well-developed skill at saying one thing and intending another. Marshal Joffre is well aware of the orders you have been given. I can't be certain, but I felt as though he was measuring you.

Likely, they will all do that, each man pushing against your backbone, to see how much you will bend. I don't mean to embarrass you, General, but I believe you passed Joffre's test. I think he was pleased with what he saw." Baker pushed the folders toward him, gathered the papers together. "From the contents of these letters, it seems apparent that our allies intend to push you harder than I predicted. Make no mistake that regardless of what kind of absurd expectations our allies place upon you, your command is the army of the United States of America. You will facilitate the final training of your troops by the means you deem most effective, and you will place your men in the field under your own terms. Neither the president nor I will ever suggest that you be dictated to by our allies."

Pershing could hear anger in Baker's voice, matching his own.

"Sir, I have no intention of allowing my command to become a recruiting agency for either the British or the French."

Baker seemed to cool, said, "No, of course not. I am simply astounded by the presumption of their demands. I fear that once you establish your headquarters, you will be bombarded by this sort of pressure. Joffre is right. They will attempt mightily to seduce you."

Pershing reached out, pulled the papers together, straightened the pile. "Sir, I assure you. They will not succeed."

New York Harbor—May 28, 1917

They moved with as much discretion as the operation would allow, Pershing's entire staff and support personnel making the trip to New York dressed in civilian clothes. The War Department had been warned of German spy activity all around New York, and the possibility of someone having a line of communication to a German submarine carried the potential for disaster.

Pershing gathered the men on the wharf, prepared them to board the tender that would carry them out to the pier at Governors Island. He followed their anxious looks, every man scanning the rooftops along the waterfront, aware that army sharpshooters were discreetly in place, prepared to intercept any threat to the general and his staff. Pershing felt the same churning excitement as his men, waited as each man stepped aboard the tender. He would go over on the first boat, Major Harbord leading the second. Pershing watched as the seats were filled, one last space reserved for him, and he nodded silently to Harbord, moved quickly down the short plank.

The tender began to move, belching a thick cloud of black smoke, swirling the water behind them, the boat moving away from the dock. He did not try to hide his excitement, could not stay seated, pulled himself up, braced himself against the bulkhead. He could see the ship now, a British merchant vessel, the *Baltic*, watched as the tender brought them closer, could see cranes lowering great bundles of supplies into the ship's cargo hold.

In minutes, the journey was complete. He boarded at the waterline, moved quickly through the bowels of the ship, caught the stale odor, the odd smells that filled the lower decks of every ship, carrying him back to his days in the Philippines, the memories of long tedious hours on the Pacific. He climbed the stairway, reached the open deck, welcomed the fresh air. He moved to the rail, looked down at the wharf, where the supplies had been piled. The longshoremen moved with rapid efficiency, and Pershing recognized some of the crates and boxes, all the equipment and matériel his men would need to establish his first headquarters. The crates had been brought to New York as inconspicuously as the men themselves, but he saw writing now, large bold letters, realized that every pallet on the wharf had been marked, clearly identified with the words: *General Pershing's Headquarters—France*.

He felt a cold turn in his gut, looked out toward the open waters of the Atlantic. How long had those crates been just . . . sitting there, for anyone to observe? He turned away, his back against the rail, looked across the deck of the ship, saw the black wisp of smoke from the second tender, Harbord and the rest of the staff now on board as well. Men in civilian dress were coming up on deck, seeking the fresh air, and Pershing looked down at his own gray suit, his clever disguise for this oh-so-secret of departures.

"Sir!" He saw Harbord now, the man puffing from the climb, and Harbord rushed to the rail, pointed, "There. I didn't see them until the tender had docked."

The music began now, and Pershing could see the band, a dozen bright gleaming instruments, a formation of guards holding a large billowing American flag. His men were lining the rails now, all staring down at the unexpected salute. The notes echoed up and over the ship, drifting across the open water, carried by the breeze, to any audience who might happen to hear. They were playing "The Star-Spangled Banner."

"Good God. Who ordered that?"

"I don't know, sir. But it appears they had plenty of preparation. They may have been here for hours waiting for us."

Pershing looked back toward the city, thought of the newspapermen, so wonderfully cooperative, agreeing to print nothing of Pershing's schedule, no mention of his departure, what would certainly be the most monumental piece of news a New York paper could print this day. He endured the final notes of the music, heard cheering from the wharf, could not look at it, wondered who else was hearing it as well. Now there was a sharp thundering roar, and he spun around, heard Harbord saying something, pointing again. Pershing saw the smoke, the battery on Governors Island unleashing the full fury of their guns, their own salute to the general's voyage. Pershing lowered his head, closed his eyes, felt the vibration beneath his feet, the cannon continuing their thunderous ovation. After a long minute, it was over, and Pershing looked at Harbord, was surprised to see the man chuckling.

Harbord said, "Excuse me, sir. May we have permission to change into our uniforms again? I believe our secret is out."

At Sea—May 30, 1917

They sailed by way of Halifax, the ship delayed by the thickest bank of fog Pershing had ever seen. He had already begun the assemblies and meetings, the schedules posted for the department heads and their smaller staffs, the men becoming more familiar with their specific duties, the training that had begun first in Washington. They were not the only passengers on the *Baltic*, and Pershing was delighted to meet a number of British and Canadian officers, veterans, men who were generous enough to relate their various experiences to the Americans. The ship had become one great floating office building, conference rooms and classrooms, the staff adapting quickly to Pershing's expectations of their roles. Even in their off hours, many of the men were studying French, reading whatever materials were available on life in both England and France. But there was one stark reminder that their brief stint on the *Baltic* was not quite like the routine they had left in Washington. Every day there were lifeboat drills, the men reminded that a small boat filled with men in uniform was a ripe target for an enemy gunner. They had all expected to lose sleep thinking of the possibility of the submarines that might lurk close by. Now, they were reminded all day long. They went back to wearing their civilian clothes.

He had planned small gaps of time in his carefully structured schedule, just enough to allow a short stroll on the deck of the gently rolling ship. He had stepped gingerly across the slick wetness of the deck, but his boots did not have grip, and he moved to the rail, one hand gripping the freshly painted steel cable that lined the bow. He stared out through the fog, tried to find some hint of a horizon. The fog was washing along the sides of the ship, rising up and over the deck, more chilling wetness, and he looked out over the rail, saw the spreading wake as the ship cut slowly through smooth black water. He stared straight down, thought, How deep? Not feet. Fathoms. A great many fathoms, probably. I should take a look at the chart. Well, perhaps not. Some things are best unknown.

He had already seen men who would not sleep in the confinement of their small quarters, who would suffer the discomfort of a thin hard blanket, just to be near the stairways. Many of the men had never been at sea, knew only what they read, the horrific tales of U-boat attacks, mass drownings, the names of those ships that inspired the fear: *Lusitania*, *Arabic*, *Hesperian*. Some of the men were more afraid of the fragility of

287

the ship itself than they were of enemy U-boats, speaking to themselves in soft whispers of names like *Titanic*. Pershing tolerated their uneasiness, would never order a man to confront his most irrational fears. Pershing understood himself that U-boats were as real as any menace these men might ever encounter. To deny that was foolishness.

He kept his own mind focused on the job at hand, all the challenges of assembling the headquarters. The First Division would be embarking only a few weeks behind them, would arrive in France through seaports that Pershing had never seen, twenty-seven thousand men making their way finally to facilities provided by the French, where they would complete their combat training. Pershing's first responsibility would be to those men, to guaranteeing that what the French offered was genuine, that the housing and supply depots even existed at all. The First was mostly regular army, consisting of the regiments that Pershing himself had selected, some of them veterans of Mexico, the units that he had once believed would be his only command. Now, their designation carried more significance than Pershing could ever have predicted. The First Division would be the first American army unit ever to set foot in Europe, would most likely be the first Americans in the combat zone of the Western Front.

He kept his gaze downward, tried to measure the ship's speed, guessed, ten knots, maybe less. The lack of progress was frustrating.

"Ah, General. I thought that was you. Saw you from the bridge."

Pershing saw the figure of the man moving toward him through the fog, knew the voice before he saw the face.

"Captain Finch. No need for you to come down. I took a stroll. Had a few minutes to spare."

"No problem, a'tall, General. Love the fog, truly do. No U-boats about, for certain. Jerry can't see for damned in this stuff any better than we can. Makes for a slow but carefree voyage, if you know what I mean. Won't last though. We get close to Iceland, we'll start the old zigzag. Should pick up a destroyer escort thereabouts."

Finch always brought a smile to Pershing that he tried to hide. The man was near Pershing's age, had been at sea all his life, knew his ship like most men know their own beds. Finch spoke with a salty growl, a voice that reminded Pershing of all those stories of pirates. Pershing could not help thinking of *Treasure Island*, Finch sounding much like some peg-legged old man with a knife in his scurvy-stained teeth. Finch looked nothing like a pirate, wore the sharp captain's uniform of a British merchant seaman, but every word from his mouth conjured up the image of a skull and crossbones. Pershing had liked him immediately.

Finch moved up to the rail beside him, said, "Some of your chaps are a bit uneasy. Nothing to worry about. I've brought quite a few blokes across this stretch of soup. Ha'nt lost a soul yet. Good crew. It's gettin' harder to replace 'em though. Damned army keeps haulin' 'em off to get blown to hell."

"I'm keeping them occupied. We have far too much work to do. The more we can get accomplished on board ship, the further along we'll be when we get to France."

Finch slapped the rail, turned, looked across the deck.

"If you want, I can give 'em my usual lecture. They should know that there's little to be worried about from Jerry. Most men who die out here don't drown. They freeze to death first."

Pershing wasn't sure if Finch was teasing him or not. "Thank you, Captain. We'll manage."

"You been to sea, have you, General?"

"Yes. The Far East."

"Ah, o' course. Your tidy little war with the Spaniards. How 'bout Europe? You oughta take a trip to the Mediterranean sometimes. After this war's past, though. Not such a fine idea these days."

Pershing had kept the thought sealed tightly away, could not avoid it now.

"I've been across the Atlantic. With my family."

"Ah, now, that's nice. Holiday, then?"

Pershing did not answer, did not want to have this conversation. After a long moment he said, "When I left the Philippines, we came the long route. Had a lengthy holiday before we left Europe. A few years ago."

Finch studied him, said, "Not a pleasant memory?"

Pershing stood up straight, his hands releasing the rail. "Sorry, Captain. I don't mean to be rude. Might we change the subject?"

"My apologies, General. I had best be gettin' back to the bridge anyhow. It'll be dark soon. Change of shift."

Finch backed away, and Pershing stared into the fog again, said in a low voice, "Thank you, Captain."

It had been nine years since he had made the journey back to America by way of Europe. It was a much-needed vacation, an extraordinary opportunity for his wife and their two young daughters to see a part of the world so different from anything he had experienced, or anything they could ever imagine. Once they had returned to the States, Frances had given birth to two more children: a third daughter, and their son, Warren. Finch's innocent question had stirred that awful place inside of him, the memories he did so much to erase. Warren was with Pershing's sister, the eight-year-old held purposely out of the public eye. It was the unfortunate necessity now, the horrifying possibility of some enemy, German or otherwise, assaulting the general by assaulting his only remaining child.

Pershing stared again into the darkening fog, held tightly to the rail, closed his eyes for a brief moment. He glanced up toward the bridge, thought of Finch, of the man's kindness. I should apologize. He has no idea. No reason for me to be rude.

He glanced at his watch, thought of the schedule, the next meeting with Harbord. He let go of the rail now, turned, moved carefully across the wetness on the deck, made his way to the stairs.

As the *Baltic* plied her way slowly eastward, in Washington, the streets and offices were coming alive with activity, a flood of citizenry who responded to Wilson's entreaties, calls that appealed to both patriotism and pragmatism. All across the nation, the government began to rally all those who could perform the services that would ultimately prepare the country for the sacrifices and costs of the war. From food to fuel, textiles to hardware, to the creation of training facilities to house the vastly increasing number of young recruits, the entire country had begun to accept the challenge, and in every state, the wheels had begun to turn. The machine was far from efficient, and successes were tempered by the frustrations of poor planning and uncoordinated efforts. The mistakes would magnify. The men who arrived at the army's designated training centers found that there were no weapons, inadequate housing, miserable sanitary conditions. But still they arrived, and slowly, the camps came to life, the buildings went up, the numbers and effectiveness of the instructors increasing as well. If they had no rifles, they drilled with broomsticks. Prospective artillerymen built cannon out of bales of hay with clay pipes for barrels. They endured both the comical and the exasperating, a process that often seemed beyond repair, hopelessly tangled in bureaucracy and inefficiency. But still the recruits continued to arrive. And despite what some believed to be the insurmountable task of creating an army from the ground up, the troops and their fledgling officers kept their focus on the challenges before them.

Though the German government continued to insist to its war-weary civilians that the United States was a toothless infant, flailing uselessly from its own clumsiness, the government and the American people held to their belief, inspired by the stiff resolve of their commanding general, that the vast resources of the country and its people could be brought into focus toward accomplishing a single goal.

In London and Paris, the Allies had doubts of a different kind, fears that the obstacles were too great, that the United States could not possibly field an effective army in time to prevent the utter catastrophe of a German victory. Already, feverish plans were in the works to parcel out the Americans as they arrived, to feed Pershing's army piecemeal into the vicious meat grinder of the Western Front. To the Allied commanders, the Americans who would cross the Atlantic had only one purpose: to plug the gaping holes, to rebuild the manpower of the battered units of the British and French armies. Whether the Americans ever fought as a single force, whether the United States could ever put a distinctly American army into the field mattered not at all. Except to Pershing.

18

PERSHING

Liverpool, England—June 8, 1917

The British welcoming committee had boarded the *Baltic*
immediately after the ship had docked, and Pershing could see
that the preparations for his arrival had obviously been well
planned. The introductions had been made all around, the
most-senior members of Per-shing's staff reacting with polite
smiles to the cordial greetings they received from the British
dignitaries.

He followed his hosts down the gangplank, stood close
behind British admiral Stileman, the only official representative
from the British military. There were other men in uniform, officers from the British Home Guard, but Pershing had received
their introductions from the admiral with the unmistakable tone
in the man's voice, a surprisingly indiscreet shrug that the Home
Guard held no particular importance for a senior commander of
the British navy.

On the wharf, a band stood ready, flanked by a formation of
perfectly dressed soldiers, two men supporting the flagstaffs of
both the Union Jack and the Stars and Stripes. The two flags
moved slowly, overlapping each other with the soft breeze of the
harbor. The symbolism was obvious, something he had
expected, the British going out of their way to demonstrate the
unity between the two nations. As he reached the concrete pier,
the band started up, a flawless rendition of "The Star-Spangled
Banner." Pershing stopped, removed his hat, glanced back to see
his senior staff doing the same. They stood motionless for a long
moment, waited for the piece to be completed, and Admiral
Stileman turned to him, said, "General Per-shing, your honor
guard is from the Third Battalion, the Royal Welch Fusiliers. In

292

the event you are not aware, these men are part of the very same unit that made their valiant charge up Breed's Hill in June of 1775. Each man wears a slip of ribbon from the original uniforms of those gallant fellows, a tradition that is of special importance to these chaps. They know their history, General. Would you care to inspect the ranks?"

"Certainly, Admiral."

He followed Stileman along the first row of troops, each man standing stiffly at attention. As he walked slowly beside the admiral, he saw that some of the Fusiliers wore the chevrons that signified a wound, some men displaying more than one of the insignia that carried such grim meaning. Of course, he thought, a unit of this much stature in the British army would have been among the first to go to the front. These men are veterans, as were those who climbed that hill in Boston. History indeed. Stileman leaned close to one of the soldiers, said something, a low sharp critique of the man's collar. Pershing noticed nothing wrong with the man's uniform, suspected that Stileman was putting on something of a show for him. He moved behind the first row, could see the backs of the uniforms now, the strip of antique cloth Stileman had referred to. Of course, he thought, the British pride themselves on their history as much as anyone. He held tightly to the words rolling through his mind, his response to the admiral's show of polite arrogance. He could never say the words aloud, would not begin his introduction to the British military by insulting their pride. But Pershing knew his history as well, thought of Breed's Hill, spoke to the admiral silently in his mind. In the event you may not be aware, those men in 1775 left a sizable percentage of their comrades on that hill. I assume if they know their history, they know that on that day, the British army received a serious bloodying at the hands of a band of ragtag rebels. Pride goes both ways, Admiral.

Buckingham Palace—June 9, 1917

"It has always been my dream that the two English-speaking nations should some day be united in a great cause, and today my dream is realized. Together we are fighting for the greatest

293

cause for which peoples could fight. The Anglo-Saxon race must save civilization."

The glasses were raised, and Pershing made a short bow. "Thank you, Your Majesty. On behalf of my president, I assure Your Majesty that the United States will make every effort."

King George V wore the uniform of a British field marshal, the prerogative of royalty, another observation Pershing would never comment on publicly. The king was a short thin man, carried himself with perfect gracefulness, the officials surrounding him exhibiting their decorum, applauding or laughing at precisely the right moment, in precisely the right volume, so characteristic of the unquestioned respect the British aristocracy had for their monarch. Pershing had been interested to learn that the king had made changes to his monarchy in response to the effects the war was having on his countrymen. The changes were more symbolic than substantive, seemed to be a self-conscious attempt by the king to remove any traces of the combined British-German heritage of his line of succession. George's family name had been Hanover, a direct link to German royalty, changed now to Windsor. Pershing had assumed the British people appreciated such a gesture, especially since no one, not even the king himself, could hide from the fact that Kaiser Wilhelm was his first cousin, and was as close to the British chain of succession as George was himself. Both men were grandsons of Queen Victoria, and in another century, Wilhelm might well have claimed his place on the British throne. Like so many Americans, Pershing was amazed by this strange quirk of European royalty, nearly every monarchy connected to their counterparts by a system of marriage and breeding that seemed nearly incestuous.

King George had made gestures that even his subjects knew were gestures of empathy. Again, the king sought to inspire the newspapers and the citizenry to feel that he shared their sacrifice. The glass in Pershing's hand contained apple juice. George had ordered that no alcohol was to be served in the palace until the war was over. Even the typical grand feasts had been curtailed, eliminating the usual excess so common at the royal luncheons and parties. It was a gesture to the belt-tightening that was increasing throughout England.

The invitation to the palace had been a surprise to Pershing, the monarch providing transportation for Pershing and his senior staff right at portside, a special royal railcar attached to a train that had carried them directly to London. Pershing expected a stiff and formal ceremony, grand propaganda for the newspapers, all manner of bluster and pronouncement for America's unity with her mother country. But the king was personable, even informal with Pershing, something that seemed to surprise some of the British dignitaries. Pershing watched George carefully, keenly aware that any clumsy mistake an American might make in this extraordinary surrounding could be magnified enormously in the press, and even in Washington. The king seemed to ignore his audience, spoke to Pershing as if they were alone.

"I should look forward to meeting your President Wilson someday, General. I admire a man of conviction. It is no simple task to unite a great nation such as America."

"Thank you, Your Majesty. President Wilson has instructed me to offer his sincerest respects, to Your Majesty and the English people."

It was the one remark Pershing had rehearsed, but George seemed to appreciate the sentiment. "Your president is far more intimately involved in the policies of his government than the monarchy here, you know. It is a marvel to me that he has such powers, particularly in times of war. In England, the monarch must entrust the leadership of his government to stay the proper course. Have you made the acquaintance of the prime minister, Mr. Lloyd George?"

"No, Your Majesty, not yet."

"Ah, you shall, certainly. Exceptional man, the prime minister. All business. Takes this war quite seriously, as of course we all must. This nation has made extreme sacrifices, General. The losses have been unbearable. It outrages me that the kaiser allows his aeroplanes to bomb our cities, with no regard to the damage he inflicts on those who have no say in this war. And what is worse, he has unleashed his submarines to prowl our waters without conscience. Their destruction of our vessels has cost uncountable civilian lives. Even the innocent suffer, General. I am hopeful that your navy will make a significant contribution to stopping this menace. We should expect a considerable quantity of destroyers, so I've been told. Please convey my deepest hopes to your president in these regards."

"I shall do that, Your Majesty. The affairs of our navy do not fall under my direct command. I can only advise."

"Ah, certainly. Your Admiral Sims is presently in London. I expect that you have much to discuss with him. But you do control your aviation forces, yes?"

It was one of the questions Pershing had expected, though perhaps not from the king of England.

"Yes, Your Majesty. Any American aviation which will be deployed in Europe is under my authority."

"Splendid, General. I find that truly wondrous, the modern era, soaring high above the earth. I can only imagine the terror struck in the hearts of the foe in his underground shelter as these beasts of the air swoop low, guns ablaze! It inspires me, as it must certainly inspire our men in their trenches. I am told that in a very short time, your country might be providing us with fifty thousand aircraft. It is a magnificent gesture, to be sure. The enemy cannot withstand such an onslaught."

Pershing hesitated, felt the hum of expectation in the room, all eyes boring into him, the anticipation of his encouraging response.

"Your Majesty, I regret that someone would offer such a claim. My command has no such plans, and I know of no aeroplanes that are awaiting shipment. It is an unfortunate fact that hope often breeds exaggeration. My country has every intention of fulfilling its goals. However, I have learned that my own expectations must be tempered by the reality of our situation."

It was as diplomatic as Pershing had ever tried to be, and he sipped the apple juice, avoided the silent gaze of the monarch. He felt the roomful of eyes still on him, thought, What else am I to say?

"I understand, General. Britain has endured a great deal of suffering. No one believes that it will simply cease because the

Americans have joined us. You are correct. Exaggeration is optimism, but we must have optimism. We must be allowed our hopeful expectations, General. It is what keeps us going."

He left the palace feeling an odd mix of dread and relief. George V had been nothing like he had expected, no pomposity in the man, no obnoxious boastfulness. Pershing was impressed that the monarch seemed to have his finger squarely on the pulse of his nation's people, and involved himself in the details of their military campaigns, if only as a bystander. It was far different than what Pershing knew of countries such as Belgium, where the king was in fact the active commander of the military, leading his men into the field against their enemies. The comparison between George and the kaiser was inevitable, and though Pershing had no real notion of what life was like for those who fluttered about Wilhelm, he had to believe that the German monarchy was surely a different world from the calm and cordial pleasantries of Buckingham Palace.

The long day's appointments had filled pages in his calendar, and already, Pershing was feeling an itch to get on with it. He was driven now to the American Embassy, felt another mix of dread and relief, facing the American diplomats who had already been the target of so much pressure from their British counterparts, so much energy directed by official En-gland toward convincing America to enter the war. There was probably no one more relieved by Wilson's decision than the men who occupied the offices of the American Embassy.

The meetings were brief and formal, lengthy introductions, allowing Pershing to put faces on the lists of names he carried in his files, all those American personnel who would serve as a conduit to the British civilian government. The ambassador added more to Pershing's calendar, requests for visits to Parliament, luncheons and dinners with all manner of the British hierarchy. But Pershing had been told that one man in particular expected to meet with him immediately, to discuss the unpleasant reality of America's naval situation.

Admiral William Sims of the United States Navy had been recently assigned to his post in London as a liaison with the

Royal Navy, and he was the man responsible for American efforts to combat the German U-boat threat. Pershing had known of Sims from the controversy the man had caused as early as 1910, when he began to insist publicly that America and Britain should be formally aligned to confront any conflict that might threaten the seagoing trade between Europe and America. It was a prescient point of view, but one that flew into the face of Washington's official stance of neutrality. Though Sims' promises to the British had once been maddeningly inappropriate, Washington could only concede that, now, the admiral had earned his position, and Sims had been appointed to what he felt to be his rightful place of authority.

Sims had been among the many who had welcomed Pershing and his staff the evening before, a friendly handshake in a room filled with the stiffness of formality. The reception had been at the Savoy Hotel, where Per-shing and his staff were to reside during their stay in London. Sims was older than Pershing by a few years, a ruggedly handsome man who had grown more outgoing with age, obviously unafraid to pour out his opinions in a profession where most men learned to keep their thoughts to themselves. Pershing was still unsure about Sims, whether the man had any intention of cooperating with the army's efforts, or, like Hugh Scott and Tasker Bliss, might have all his energy focused on his eventual retirement.

"General Pershing, how was your meeting with royalty? Serve you apple juice, did he?"

"Apple juice. Yes. Quite a pleasant affair, actually."

Sims led him into his office, closed the door, said, "Not surprised. Pleasant is the word I hear most often. I didn't have the opportunity to ask you yesterday, how was the trip? No problems, I understand. Should have been fine, once the destroyers gathered you up. U-boat captains are smarter than the average German. Won't often tangle head-on with a destroyer."

Sims had answered his own question, and Pershing waited for Sims to sit, then moved to his own chair. Sims was still talking, suddenly pointed a finger at Pershing's face, said, "Without those destroyers, we might easily have lost you. The U-boats patrol that stretch of ocean on a regular basis. Can you imagine the stupidity of that? Send our army's top man over here with-out a hint of protection. They would have done it too. Damned fools."

"Who—"

"Bill Benson. That whole department. How the hell can the navy's chief of operations make any decisions about what we need out here when he sits in his cozy office in Washington? I have been insisting for weeks that they put more antisubmarine forces out here, but Benson and his timid little cadre of secre-taries claim that the coast of the United States cannot be left vulnerable. Vulnerable to what? Does anybody truly believe the Germans are suddenly going to begin shelling Charleston? Or that Kaiser Bill is going to send his troops ashore in Massachusetts? The greatest threat to us is right out there, General. Ask anyone who has cruised anywhere close to Ireland lately. That's where the Germans are; that's where the ships are being sunk. And that's where we need the damned destroyers. Not in some backwater yacht basin in Virginia. Washington has a lot to learn. Have you seen the figures? The shipping losses for last month alone are staggering. You won't read about it in the papers here. The Royal Navy gives out about a quarter of the real figures. They're worried that the British people might find out how bad off they really are. All the civilians know is that it's getting tougher to buy sugar and gasoline. In a few months, even bread could be a luxury. I don't know what you've heard in Washington, General, but these people are in serious trouble. Our allies are crumbling, and if we don't get some real man-power and hardware over here soon, this war will end."

Pershing felt punched by Sims' words. He thought of King George, the exaggerated expectations.

"I had not heard the situation expressed in quite that way, Admiral. I admit that I was caught off guard by the king's somewhat overstated hopes."

"You didn't make him any promises, did you?"

"Certainly not. The only promises I can make are what I believe myself. The First Division should arrive in France in a few weeks. Beyond that, I can only offer what Washington pro-vides, at the speed they provide it."

"Take my advice, General. Don't promise anyone anything. Until you see the First Division marching down the gangplanks of their ships, even you can't be sure when they'll arrive. Right now, not just their arrival, but their very existence, is just one more rumor. And, if I may ask, General, why are they going to France? The British have been expecting our troops to arrive *here*. I had thought we would be turning our infantry over to the British army."

Pershing was growing annoyed now, would not begin a debate with the one man in England who should not have those kinds of expectations.

"Admiral, my orders are to maintain the American army in Europe as a distinctly American force. I thought you would have been informed of that. Perhaps it was an oversight."

Sims grunted. "Fine little hole they've dug for you, General. You been to see Robertson yet?"

"No. My appointment with General Robertson is day after tomorrow."

"Well, you'll find out for yourself what the British expect. I get a great deal of information from General Robertson's office. He's nothing like Tasker Bliss. You might assume that the Chief of the Imperial General Staff would simply be another puppet officer, dancing to the tune of his prime minister. Not so. Wully Robertson has guts, General. Just like Douglas Haig. The British have some good people in the right places. You'll see that for yourself before long. I just wish Washington would recognize that. The only way to end this war is to stick close to the British. The French are finished, worthless in the field. I'm surprised as hell the Germans haven't marched into Paris by now. But they will. Count on it."

Pershing stood, had heard enough. "Admiral, if you will excuse me. I should return to the Savoy Hotel. My staff is quite busy with our arrangements. I don't expect to be in England for very long."

Sims stayed in his chair, looked at Pershing with mild disgust. "I suppose you have your orders. Certainly you must obey them, if you can. But Washington has a lot to learn about its allies."

Pershing made a short bow, pulled open the door to Sims' office, moved out quickly. He did not stop, aimed for the front door of the embassy, passed between the Marine guards, moved out onto the walkway that led through a tall green garden. He stopped, took in a long breath, the thick fragrance of flowers and wet grass. He realized his fists were clenched, and he tried to calm himself, could hear voices behind him, Harbord, some of his other aides, catching up to him. He thought of Sims' words, *Washington has a lot to learn*. Perhaps, Admiral. Perhaps we all have a lot to learn. But I do know that if we are to make any difference in this war, it cannot be by turning over our priorities to the British. And we probably don't need American admirals saluting a British flag.

London—June 11, 1917

William Robertson had risen up from the lowest rank in the British army, had competed with Douglas Haig for overall command of the British Expeditionary Force in Europe. That job was made available after the removal of Sir John French, who had first led the British into the war in 1914. As the stalemate spread along the Western Front, Field Marshal French pressed hard for Britain's withdrawal from the war. Though Sir John insisted his concern lay with protecting the British homeland from German invasion, his stance caused his commanders serious problems in their relationships with their allies in France and Belgium. London had no choice but to replace French, and Robertson, who had served as French's chief of staff, assumed himself to be in line for the man's job. But Robertson underestimated Douglas Haig's political connections, including a warm friendship Haig maintained with King George V. When Haig was chosen to command the BEF, Robertson accepted the only position that allowed him to save face, that of Chief of the Imperial General Staff. As such, he was the link between Haig and the civilian power in London, specifically Prime Minister David Lloyd George. It was a difficult post at best, since Lloyd George despised Douglas Haig, and anyone who supported Haig's strategies.

301

Robertson was a short pugnacious man, who made no effort to hide the social differences between himself and the rest of the British High Command. He spoke with a distinct cockney accent, dropping his "aitches," the telltale British trait that labeled a man as a product of the lower classes. But Robertson spoke with no self-consciousness, was so completely different from the chilly tightness of good breeding, the elite who spoke with the perfect lilt of the king's English. Robertson seemed to enjoy emphasizing his lack of breeding. There was something appealing about that to Pershing, a man who made no show of hiding his humble roots. It was a trait that seemed almost American.

"Call me Wully. They all do."

Pershing released the man's hand, tried to unlimber the crushed bones that Robertson's sturdy handshake had inflicted on him.

"Thank you, General, er, Wully. Not sure I can get used to that."

Robertson retrieved a bottle of something dark, held it up. "No matter. Care for a bite of the tiger, General?"

"No, thank you. I must admit, things seem to be rather celebratory here this morning."

"You mean the staff? Yes, I encouraged it. Pass around the old tart, as it were. Liven up the place. Hell, General, even Parliament's raising their trousers over this one. We finally gave them something to cheer about!"

Pershing had seen the morning newspapers, broad bold headlines, reports of a major British success in Flanders. He knew better than to accept the newspaper's word as gospel, waited for Robertson to expand on his joviality.

"You could hear the blasts right here, right in this office. The whole damned place shook to bits. Blew the damned Jerries sky high, they did! We had our eye on Messines Ridge for months. Damned nuisance, that. Gave the Jerries the high ground from Armentières all the way to Ypres. We lost so damned many fine men trying to take the damned thing, so Doug agrees to a new idea. If we can't knock the Jerries off the damned ridge, we'll knock the damned ridge out from under them. Took the engineers months to finish the job, but we dug mines all under the Jerry trenches. Nineteen of the damned things were rigged to blow at the same time. Rattled my damned teeth when they went up too, right here in this office! Punched out gaping holes all along the Jerry position. General Plumer led the attack, and the Jerries were so stunned, Plumer just waltzed right over and scooped 'em up! We're still pushing, got the Jerries backing up all along the line. I expect to hear the word any time now that Messines is completely in our hands. Glad you could be here for this one, General. Give you a taste what's to come."

Robertson moved to a map on the wall, pointed, and Pershing moved close, saw a long arc, red pins marking the position of the mines. He could not help thinking of Ulysses Grant, commanding the engineering marvel of its time, a mine that Union engineers tunneled under Lee's troops, near Petersburg, Virginia. That was 1864, and it was only one mine, but the result had been a catastrophic blast that killed scores of rebel soldiers, opening a gaping hole in the Confederate defenses. He scanned Robertson's map, thought, Nineteen mines. How many tons of explosives must they have used, better explosives too, nothing like the simple gunpowder Grant had to rely on. Robertson moved away, and Pershing studied the map for a few moments. Robertson said, "Some of our best troops took part in that, General. Not just the English, either. You know about the Anzacs?"

Pershing returned to the chair, said, "Certainly. Australians and New Zealanders. From what I've heard, they've equipped themselves well since the start of the war."

"As I said, General, some of our best troops. They'd have taken Gallipoli if they'd been allowed to fight. Damned shame, that. Failure of leadership. But that's history, and it won't happen again. Douglas Haig is righting the ship, General. These are critical days for us. Since the Nivelle disaster, it's up to us to turn the tide. Let me paint a picture for you, General. This war has moved forward into something no one could ever predict. Our command's moved along with it. The British army in the field right now consists not just of British soldiers. Besides the Anzacs there are Canadians, territorial troops from India. Imagine, General, what Jerry will say when he sees Americans as well. The symbolism alone brings a tear. All parts of the British Empire united in one cause, all of civilization rallying to defeat the kaiser and his evil scourge. Once your troops arrive in sufficient force to reach their intended place on the line, this war will come to a rapid conclusion. The triumph at Messines, and your arrival here. No coincidence, I think, General. We speak the same language, come from the same roots. It must be inspiring to you, eh?"

Pershing felt crushed into his chair. Our intended place in the line? Intended by whom? "Congratulations on your apparent success at Messines, General. From everything you say, it seems as though Marshal Haig has opened up a much-needed breakthrough. I'm sure this will be gratifying to the French as well."

Robertson seemed to deflate. "The *French*? General Pershing, with all respects, the French had nothing to do with this. The French have shown us that they cannot face any more adversity without the possibility of complete collapse. What we've accomplished at Messines could well have saved France from being overrun. They have no defense, General. They can barely put an army in the field. If Jerry is to be sent packing to Berlin, it'll be the English who make the chase."

They are your allies, General. Pershing held the words inside. He shared none of Robertson's enthusiasm, said, "I appreciate your desire to see a unified front against our common enemy. But I cannot commit to placing American troops anywhere in line until we have assembled numbers sufficient for them to become an effective fighting force."

Robertson paused. "How much time do you expect you will need, General?"

The cheer had evaporated from Robertson's voice, and Pershing felt himself relaxing, no longer swallowed up by Robertson's waterfall of energy. "We are bringing forth a division of primarily regular troops first, men whose training has come mostly from experience. These are being supplemented quickly by National Guard units, who require only a moderate amount of training. Beyond that, as you may know, the president has instituted a draft system, which along with a great number of volunteers, will supply the vast bulk of our armed forces in the months to come."

"How many months?"

"I have no way of answering that, General. My country is committed to making a difference in this war. But I'm certain that you understand that sending inadequately trained soldiers into the line is . . . unwise."

"Then by all means, General, you should adopt our suggestion, and bring your troops here. Nowhere in America can they receive the training that will equip them for trench warfare. In a short few weeks, the basics of survival on the front can be imparted without difficulty."

Trench warfare. The words stabbed into Pershing's brain. "Perhaps we should discuss this further. Please accept my apologies, General Robertson, but I have a number of meetings today, including one I am especially looking forward to. I am expected at Ten Downing Street within the hour, to meet with the prime minister."

Robertson sniffed, said, "Well, certainly, General. Even Mr. Lloyd George should be in a positive frame of mind today. Our success at Messines should brighten up even those dreary hallways."

Pershing stood, thought a moment. "Oh, one more point I must address. I have been concerned about the availability of transport tonnage. Though we are prepared to use every available transport ship, the floating tonnage available in America is minuscule compared to Britain's merchant fleet. I'm sure you have received our official requests through the navy. I cannot seem to find anyone who can offer me some exact figures on how many ships and of what capacity can be provided to assist in the transport of our troops and supplies."

Robertson had lost all of his bluster now, said calmly, "Not much I can offer you on that point. If you don't know now, you will find out soon enough. We lost some three million tons of shipping in April alone, another million and a half in May. If the German U-boats continue to destroy merchant shipping with this rate of success, in a short time England will face starvation. You want shipping, General? Come up with a plan to stop the damned U-boats."

He sat in the rear of the large automobile, the grand limousine provided by his hosts. He had exhausted his calendar and his patience, thought now of the Savoy Hotel, the place where his staff had made the most of their temporary quarters.

The auto stopped at an intersection, and Pershing looked out, saw slow-moving crowds, people finding their way home after the routine of their workday. He studied the faces, saw an occasional smile, some spark of energy in a conversation. But most of the people moved in silence, a slow plodding gait, expressionless faces, no outward sign that anything in their lives was amiss. He had heard the talk at the various receptions, how many families had lost at least one soldier, how many more were caring for young men who came home with the awful debilitating wounds. But the people in the street seemed to go about their routines with mindless purpose, and Pershing thought of Sims, the man's insight into the British way. The government would not dare tell the people how severe their challenge might still become, no one wanting to risk a panic over the impending food shortages. Instead, the people would hear of Messines, of Marshal Haig's abrupt change of fortune, inspiring stories of the soldiers of the commonwealth, coming home to fight for their motherland. This time it was the Anzacs, a story so similar to what had happened two months before. Then it had been the Canadians, four divisions of gallant men who charged out of their trenches alongside Nivelle's Frenchmen, and, after a vicious fight, captured crucial German high ground along a stretch of land called Vimy Ridge. It was one of the few bright spots in Nivelle's grand disaster, and the outpouring of celebration for the Canadians had given the English people a much-needed cause for cheer. Of course, there is no disputing the need, he thought. In every war, it is the people who give so much, whose morale is so tested. But these people have already given far more than even their own government will tell them. And what of Messines, the

306

magnificent triumph? He had learned more about the British breakthrough at Messines. The fighting is still going on, and no one, not Robertson, not any civilian official, knows what might yet occur. He thought of Ulysses Grant, the mine explosion at Petersburg. Another history lesson. The mine had worked, accomplished all that Grant's people had told him it would. But then, there had been breakdown, poor execution, and Lee's troops had rallied, closing the gap. The enormous opportunity had clamped shut, and in the end, even Grant himself accepted that the great success had turned to defeat. If that happens at Messines, what will the newspapers say then?

His meeting with Robertson was a heavy stone in his mind, and Pershing was beginning to have a new appreciation for diplomats, those men who must hold so tightly to their true feelings. After three years of war, the British High Command was still training their men on the tactics of trench warfare, and, of course, they would insist the Americans should do the same. Pershing felt a twisting frustration in his mind. *It is simply all they know how to do.* And yet no one believes it is the right way to win a war. No, we will not teach Americans anything of the sort. The only way to remove your enemy from in front of you is to *remove* him. A man with a rifle and a bayonet is far more useful than ten men sitting in a hole, hoarding their supply of hand grenades. He thought of George Patton, the young man who had his own saying about how to fight. You advance until you bump your nose. No matter what the British believe, Americans will learn to move forward.

He sat back in the seat, stared to the front, could see a man in uniform hobbling past the front of the limousine. The driver waited patiently for the man to pass, the car beginning to move again. Pershing could see the man clearly now, one pants leg rolled up, supporting himself on a wooden crutch. Pershing closed his eyes for a brief moment, his weariness complete. In two days, I will be in France, he thought. More parties, more celebrations, more heads of state and generals and men who will tell me what they expect me to do. He thought of the telegram from his father-in-law, so far in the past now: *How much do you speak French?* Pershing's response had been absolute in the affirmative, the only logical response to what was obviously a question from the senator that carried a great deal of hidden meaning. Once Pershing was in Washington, the question of his fluency in French had not been raised again. Obviously, he thought, in the next few days, the issue might indeed come up. There was only one problem. It was his one great failure from his years at West Point. He spoke very little French at all.

19

PERSHING

Paris, France—June 13, 1917

They docked at Boulogne, the French port closest to the English coast, the journey brief and quiet. At the wharf there had been another reception, another band welcoming him with the playing of "The Star-Spangled Banner," more military guards and civilian dignitaries. The ceremonies had been blessedly short, and Pershing and his staff had boarded a train, were told it would offer them a scenic journey through some of the most beautiful land in France. Pershing was appreciative of the hospitality, welcomed the train ride, but not for the reasons his hosts had suggested. His visit to England had been grueling, an unending flow of appointments, five days of meetings and receptions, a continuous display of social pleasantries, pledges of respect and mutual admiration which had too often been combined with patronizing lectures and discreet browbeating from his British hosts. He had learned a great deal in London, did not begrudge his British counterparts their opportunity to have their say. But for the first time since his arrival, he could admit to himself, and to his staff, that he was utterly exhausted. As the train rolled and bounced through the region called Picardie, Pershing did not gaze at scenery. With the ceremonies on the French wharf behind him, he took full advantage of a quiet few hours on board the train. While many of the staff officers passed their time by gazing at the lushness of the French countryside, Pershing made his way to a private berth and slept all the way to Paris.

They rode now in a procession of grand automobiles, Pershing in the lead car. He sat beside Paul Painlevé, the French minister of war. It was a singular honor, of course, carefully planned so that Pershing's entire senior staff would feel included in the formality of the official welcoming. The hosts had been insistent, and Pershing had agreed that his staff should be spread among the procession of limousines, each accompanied by a French official of some considerable rank and importance. It was a symbolic gesture so that none of the Americans would feel slighted, something that seemed to matter a great deal more to the French than to anyone on Pershing's staff.

Painlevé was as pleasant a host as Pershing had met so far, reminded Pershing of Newton Baker. Neither man had been formally trained in the military: Baker was a lawyer first, Painlevé rising to prominence as the French education minister. But both men had stepped into their roles with the backbone to confront their generals. It was typical of any military, that the men in uniform believed themselves to be the only ones who understood strategy and tactics. That kind of arrogance had cost Marshal Joffre his job, and Nivelle as well. To Painlevé's credit, he had campaigned vigorously against Nivelle's bombastic claims about his great plan, insisting that France's beleaguered army should settle into a defensive posture. When Nivelle's attacks collapsed, Painlevé's star had risen further, and he had moved quickly, pushing Nivelle aside, and elevating Henri Pétain to the position of commander in chief. Painlevé and Pétain had already shown that the civilian ministry and the field commanders could work together, something that had not yet happened in France. Pershing could not help wondering if Pétain and Painlevé had cemented their relationship at the expense of the former commander of the French forces, Marshal Joffre. Since his arrival Pershing had already learned to read significance into seemingly insignificant arrangements. In the procession of limousines, Joffre was somewhere far behind the lead car.

As the procession moved out in line from the train station, Pershing was surprised that the limousine had its top removed, that he would ride beside Painlevé in the open air. He had removed his hat, would not suffer the embarrassment of suddenly losing it should the driver not see fit to drive slowly.

But the car moved at a leisurely pace, and Pershing had another surprise. Along the streets outside the railway station, an enormous crowd of people had gathered. He had expected that Paris would be busy, that even with the war, the daily lives of its citizens would carry on, much as he had seen in London. But now, with the autos making their way down tightly packed streets, he began to see something different. Pershing began to understand why he was perched high in the open backseat of the auto. The people were focused on *him*.

The sounds were reaching him now, people calling out, the voices growing louder, one continuous chorus. He glanced at Painlevé, saw the man raise his hand, a casual wave to the crowds, the gesture inspiring the peo-ple to a new burst of cheering. The crowds were closing in on the street now, the limousine slowing to a crawl. The people continued to press forward, hands touching the car, some reaching out, voices calling directly to him. He pulled himself tightly together, felt an odd fear, had seen something like this in the Philippines. There the crowds were menacing, the hands reaching out from faces that wore the sickness of desperation, hunger, and disease, the soldiers working hard to push them away, each soldier knowing that the begging hand might also hold a pistol, a bomb. But there was no menace in these people, and Pershing saw the faces, old and young, men with children perched on their shoulders, young women clutching fat bouquets of brightly colored flowers. The chorus was more distinct now, the people recognizing Painlevé, some shouting his name, others focusing only on Pershing, this stranger in a strange uniform. He heard a thump, something impacting the car, flinched in response, but saw a bunch of flowers sprayed across the hood. Now more flowers came, a large soft bouquet landing in his lap, more, floating down from above. He looked up, saw hands waving from windows, higher up, rooftops, more flowers raining down. He turned, saw the same thing on the cars behind them, a vast shower of color filling the air. He moved the bouquet aside, and immediately another took its place, flowers filling the space all around him. A woman suddenly surged forward, leaned up against the car, reached out, touched his arm, and he could see tears, saw she was very young, heard her voice above the others, close to him, "*Vive l'Amérique! Vive l'Amérique!*"

He smiled at her, took her hand, didn't know what else to do, and she began to sob, held her grip tightly on his hand, pulled along by the slow movement of the car. Behind her, more people were surging forward, more hands, and she released her hold, seemed to fall away, disappearing into the mass of people. But the words still came, rising in the chorus of voices, finding a rhythm, one voice now, "*Vive l'Amérique!*"

The car was still moving, the people in front giving way grudgingly. He could see the street opening up into a wide circle, a fountain in the center, a garden of colorful flowers all around the base. But the crowds were still there, a vast ring of faces and raised hands, a small flutter of French flags, one old man holding a tattered Stars and Stripes. The limousine moved into the circle, and a new round of cheering began, more flowers launched at the parade of limousines. Pershing was relaxing now, allowed himself to smile, waved to them as Painlevé waved, realized the limousine was nearly full of flowers, covering his legs. He allowed their cheering to flow through him, felt foolish now for his concern. He felt foolish as well for assuming that his reception in France would be the same as it was in England. He was not sure why these people had come out into the street this way, why so many flowers. He leaned toward Painlevé, said, "This was unexpected. I don't understand."

Painlevé continued to wave, said, "It is simple, General. You are American. And you are *here*."

The crowds had surrounded his hotel, and he could not simply ignore them. His room had a narrow veranda, overlooking the street, and he stepped outside yet again, knew by now what to expect. The cheering began again, his appearance inspiring them to push closer. He waved for a few moments, both hands above his head, thought, All right, that is enough. It is not necessary that you treat me this way. But no one seemed interested in leaving, not just yet, and he backed again into his room.

Harbord closed the doors, and Pershing saw a wide smile on the face of William Sharp, the American ambassador.

"They won't leave, you know. They have heard about this day for too long."

Pershing shook his head. "I never expected this. So much emotion in these people."

"Exactly, General. They have endured the worst part of this war. Not one of them is unaffected by some sadness. So much despair. You cannot imagine what I hear every day. Did you see how many women there are? It used to be that a woman alone in some parts of Paris had, well, a meaning. Now, she is more certainly a widow than a prostitute. The city is so very different than when I first arrived here."

Pershing moved to a chair, sat, an aide filling a cup of coffee for him. "How so, Mr. Ambassador?"

"It was appropriate once to describe Paris as a paradise of sorts, unique in the world. But these people have been crushed by this war. Every day they wake up wondering if today is the day the Germans will arrive. Every leader has tried to give them hope, has given them the same promise, that soon their army will be victorious, that their land will be rid of the Germans. There have been too many promises, and none have been kept. These people have lost hope, have lost confidence in their government, in their generals. The only promise that seemed to make any difference was that, one day soon, the Americans were coming. I was truly apprehensive that if that promise was not fulfilled very soon, the French would simply give up fighting the war. It almost happened, you know."

"Yes, I was informed. I met with Marshal Joffre in Washington."

"Ah, yes, he informed me. The savior of that particular crisis was General Pétain. You will meet him very soon. He is a man beloved by his people. But he is giving them promises as well. I just hope that you have not arrived here too late."

Pershing sipped from his coffee cup, said, "I'm not sure what benefit my arrival will have. It will require considerable time to bring sufficient troop strength here, train and equip them, and put them into the field where they can be of good use. Surely General Pétain understands that."

Sharp laughed. "General, look outside. Your arrival has already changed these people, renewed their hope. I know very little of equipping troops, and all that you must still accomplish. But the despair of every official of the French government will be brightened by what happened today. In every office, at every reception, you will be appreciated for all that you have brought to their people."

"But for how long, Mr. Ambassador? America is still a long way from fighting this war."

Paris—June 16, 1917

Pershing had already gone through much of the same routine he had experienced in London, meetings and luncheons, putting faces on the familiar names. But the differences between London and Paris continued to multiply. No dignitary, from the president, Raymond Poincaré, to the various ministers, to Joffre himself, had sought to impress him with their advice, their appraisal of just how the Americans should fit in to the war. It was clear that France had suffered badly from the breakdown in relations between the civilian government and the military command. Joffre's heavy-handedness, his insistence that the civilians simply stay out of his way, was replaced now by a spirit of compromise that made Pershing uneasy. It was one thing for a military commander to respect the authority of the civilian leadership. But the generals still had to command, had to focus their energy on the enemies in front of their army, could not seek out the approval of the various ministers for every major decision. Though Henri Pétain was revered by his troops, morale alone could not change the obvious. Neither the French nor the British had found a way to push the Germans away. The French had been so badly bled and so frightened by the mutiny in their army that Pershing began to wonder if what Wully Robertson insisted was in fact true. They might have little spirit left for the effort and the sacrifice that was needed if there was any hope of winning the war.

Pershing had already absorbed a heavy dose of the dark

314

despair that draped over every part of the French government, and the shatteringly desperate hope that poured out from the French people. He still had to learn if the French army would allow the Americans the time and the resources that Pershing required, and what the French would expect them to do. The one man who had the answers was Henri Pétain.

Pétain was sixty, only four years older than Pershing, but there was age in the man's face that told Pershing a great deal about the pressures of the war. Like Joffre, Pétain was a large man, with a thick white moustache, but unlike Joffre, Pétain was now in the epicenter of everything the war was doing to France.

They had met at Pétain's headquarters, and there had been lunch, a modest affair, nothing like the grand spectacles that Pershing was becoming used to. Harbord had come with him, the rest of the staff far too busy now to enjoy any kind of lengthy luncheon. Most of Pétain's senior staff had been present, as well as several front-line commanders, all of them cordial. Pershing had been surprised by how many of them had a reasonable skill for speaking English, something he deeply appreciated. But the dishes were gone now, the wine bottles whisked away by a stiffly efficient swarm of orderlies. Pétain led several of them to a large sitting room, and Pershing saw one wall covered by a large map, hanging over a long narrow table. The table was covered with smaller maps, thick pads of paper, and Pétain moved toward the table, stopped, and Pershing saw a self-conscious hesitation, thought, Well, of course, a roomful of military secrets.

Pétain seemed to think to himself for a brief moment, then turned, said, "Gentlemen, I wish to spend a few moments alone with our guest. General Pershing, if you wish, my chief of staff could provide Colonel Harbord with a tour of my headquarters. Is that acceptable to you?"

Pershing glanced at Harbord, who had stayed just behind him, and Harbord made a quick nod. Pershing said, "By all means, General. Colonel Harbord, please report to me when your tour is complete."

"Yes, sir." Harbord made a short bow toward Pétain, said, "Thank you, sir."

The others filed out, and the room was empty now except for Pershing and Pétain. Pétain moved toward the map, said, "I do not make good the, um, small talk."

Pershing laughed, caught himself. "Neither do I, I'm afraid. I enjoyed the company of your staff. General d'Espérey is most impressive."

Pétain turned, faced him, said, "He is one of the best we have. It is the one good fortune that can result from disaster. Good men rise to the top. One great service Marshal Joffre performed for this army was that he would not be patient with stupidity. In peacetime, it can be forgiven. In war, a bad general is even worse than a traitor. He is a murderer."

A dozen responses ran through Pershing's mind, but he said nothing. Pétain turned away again, moved toward a lone window at the end of the room, pushed a dark curtain aside, glanced out through piercing sunlight. He pulled it shut again, darkening the room, said, "My apologies for the thickness of the air. We keep the window covered. I trust my security, but one pair of eyes in the wrong place . . . well, I do not have to tell you. You have been busy, I understand."

"Quite busy. The French people have been most gracious. Our hosts have offered every convenience."

"A polite way for you to say that you wish they would leave you alone."

Pershing started to protest, let it go. Pétain was smiling now, and Per-shing saw kindness in the man's face.

Pétain said, "I would prefer that you not be regarded as some sort of special guest while you are here. Does that suit you?"

"Whatever you prefer. This is *your* headquarters."

Pétain was looking at him, studied his uniform, scanned down to Pershing's boots. "You are not a man who enjoys relaxation, eh, General? I can tell by your stance, your posture. Are you as hard on your staff as you are on yourself?"

Pershing didn't know what to say. "I believe my staff understands what is expected of them."

Pétain made a soft laugh, pointed to a chair. "Would it be

316

satisfactory to you if we sat? These boots are new, and my feet are not yet happy."

Pershing moved to a chair, timed himself to sit as Pétain reached his own chair.

"I am wondering, General Pershing, if you require such rigidity from your soldiers as well?"

Feeling Pétain leading him in a particular direction, Pershing said, "I am happy to discuss with you any detail of our army, General Pétain."

Pétain put up his hands, shook his head, laughed again. "I have had quite enough of this. My name is Henri. Am I correct that your name is John?"

Pershing smiled. "Indeed."

"Then, John, while you are in my headquarters, and no one else is around, I will not refer to you by your rank. I intend that you and I shall work together, not as rivals, not as enemies. I admit that this has not often been the way. I do not place blame for that. I merely seek to eliminate one small obstacle between us. I fear that before long, we will experience a great deal more obstacles. Despite our best intentions."

Pershing looked now at Pétain's boots, saw they were not new at all. "Henri, you do not require an excuse to sit in my presence."

Pétain looked at his boots, laughed. "As you wish. You were standing so straight, I thought perhaps you had some difficulty with your back. I did not want to make you uncomfortable, by making you . . . comfortable."

Pershing was feeling more comfortable by the minute, glanced around the room, so many details he had seen before, the familiar signs of any headquarters, stacks of orders, dispatches, blank pads of paper, pencils scattered across every surface.

Pétain said, "So, what did the English tell you? Are you planning to join their army?"

"Not at all."

"But they did expect that, eh?"

"There was some suggestion that the Americans would be well served by completing their training in England. I disagreed."

"That is a positive sign, John. I do not always understand the English way. They are not the most convenient of allies. I am quite certain they say the same about us. It has been this way since the beginning."

Pershing did not respond.

Pétain pointed to the map, said, "Should you wish any details explained to you, please inquire. Presently, there is little offensive activity. You have no doubt been told of the British success at Messines."

"Yes."

"Fine effort. I applaud them. For now, the Germans seem content to allow the English to keep their gains. It has not always been thus. I suspect the Germans understand that their loss was not as significant as the casualties they inflicted on the English. We have too often measured success in kilometers. As this war has lasted for so long, the greatest victory is now in the death of your enemy. Kill more of him than he kills of you. All sides in this war are running out of men. Field Marshal Haig does not seem to agree with this. He is entitled to claim victory at Messines. But the Germans are not so likely to allow it to happen again."

"I have not yet made Marshal Haig's acquaintance."

"No? In time. He has a great many difficulties before him. There is a great difference between London and Paris. Paris has been properly frightened by the possibility of German boots marching down the avenues. London has no such fear. The civilian government there still believes it knows what is best for its army. I assume you were introduced to the prime minister?"

"Yes. We met at some length."

"What do you think of him?"

Pétain had a smile, and Pershing felt a stab of caution. "He has ideas that . . . I found him not to be so flexible."

Pétain laughed. "Nicely stated, John. Practicing your diplomacy. Mr. Lloyd George despises his commanding general, and Marshal Haig feels the same way about his prime minister. It is not a good means of managing a war. I believe that London is allowing Marshal Haig only the freedom to carry his army . . . no . . . there is a phrase you use. Mr. Lloyd George has granted Marshal Haig just enough rope to hang himself."

"I have no reason to believe that. Messines was—"

"Yes, yes, Messines. Douglas Haig's great triumph. Now what? Are the Germans in a mad retreat toward Berlin? No. Marshal Haig captured a hill. The English newspapers have something positive to write about. So what happens now? I am concerned that Marshal Haig is, as you Americans say, drunk with victory. Is that unfair? Perhaps. Time will tell. Already he is talking of a new plan, pushing his army forward across Flanders."

Pershing had heard nothing of a new strategy, could not hide a frown.

Pétain said, "Surprised? Ah, that is not a good thing. You spent a week in London and no one thought to inform you what was happening?"

"It seems not." Pershing was impressed and made a little uncomfortable by Pétain's insights, felt as though the man was reading him a little too clearly.

Pétain stood, moved to a small desk, pulled a piece of paper from a drawer. He returned to the chair, said, "I wonder if the same can be said for your government, John?"

"I'm not sure what you mean."

"In a moment. First can you tell me your expectations, when you hope to have troops on the ground?"

"The First Division will arrive in weeks. Twenty-seven thousand men, approximately. As you know, we have organized our divisions to be roughly twice the size of a typical French or British division. Monsieur Painlevé has already put my staff in contact with your people, who will guide us to our training facilities. We must still send several thousand support personnel before the First can be put into the line. I do not have to explain to you, of course, the logistics required in housing, feeding, and equipping these men."

"What of your Second Division. The Third? How many more?"

Pershing took a deep breath.

"I don't know precisely. So much is up to Washington. We are intending to lay considerable groundwork for transporting an enormous force across the Atlantic. We are already facing challenges of shipping, of armament. The training facilities in America are only now being constructed. My best estimate is that the American Expeditionary Force will not be combat-effective until next spring. If you wonder if I am embarrassed by our lack of preparation, then, yes, I am considerably embarrassed. My country did not adequately prepare for the possibility of war. I have always believed that was a mistake. But it was not in my power to change that. It is now." His voice had risen, and Pershing gripped the arms of the chair, calmed himself. "Forgive me."

Pétain glanced at the letter in his hand. "But you do expect an army, yes?"

Pershing was puzzled by the question. "Of course. That's why I'm here."

Pétain handed him the letter now, said nothing. Pershing saw it was from the chief of staff, Tasker Bliss. Pétain said, "This was passed to me from . . . well, from someone in my government. You understand that sometimes discretion is required. It was anticipated that you might be interested in its contents."

Pershing read, felt himself sinking into the chair.

General Pershing's expedition is being sent abroad on the urgent insistence of Marshal Joffre . . . we have yielded to this view and a force is being sent solely to produce a moral effect. If all necessary arrangements are not made on the other side, it is the fault of the French General Staff and not of ourselves, since their officers . . . are fully cognizant of our unprepared state for sending a serious expedition for serious business. Our General Staff had made no plan for prompt dispatch of reinforcements to General Pershing, nor the prompt dispatch of considerable forces to France. . . . Thus far we have no plans for this.

Major General Tasker Bliss—Acting Chief of Staff

Pershing felt his brain beginning to boil, the two words burying into him. Moral effect. Pétain said, "According to General

Bliss, your mission has been a success. The French people have already given you your . . . moral victory."

Pershing handed him the paper, could not look at Pétain. He expected to hear more from him, some show of French outrage, thought, He must believe me to be a thorough liar. But Pétain said nothing, folded the letter, slipped it slowly into his pocket. Pershing saw Bliss in his mind, an old man who was sliding along on his way to retirement. What could he have thought, writing this? What would he accomplish by telling the French, or anyone else, that officially, Washington still had no plans to produce an army? Is he jealous after all? This is not his command, and so, in his mind, no command exists. Pershing felt the heat in his brain, sorted his words, "General Bliss is incorrect on one very important point."

"Which point, John?"

"Please, let me be clear. I did not assemble a staff of nearly two hundred people so that I could sit in limousines and enjoy showers of bouquets. I am pleased the French people have responded with such emotion to our arrival, but you have my word, General Pétain, that an American army is coming to France. We are faced with enormous challenges, and we will overcome them."

"I have a suggestion, John. Do what you must to assemble your regiments, then ship them to France. Their training can be completed here, under the expert hand of French instructors. The art of trench warfare is second nature to our officers, and this will save us both considerable time. Unlike what the English have proposed to you, I accept that your regiments will wish to remain together, and so it shall be. They can be placed into line beside French regiments, as part of French divisions, and still they will maintain their integrity as a fighting unit. But, most important, they can be placed into line. We can begin immediately, with your First Division. So many men could be of immeasurable benefit to our defenses around Verdun, for example. We must assume that General Bliss speaks for your president. If a moral benefit is of such importance, then we shall take full advantage. The French *poilu* will welcome his American comrade in the trench beside him. It may be the spark we must have to secure victory."

Pershing stared at Pétain, saw hard eyes peering through the man's soft grin. Of course, it will always come down to this. The French want the same thing the English want. They just phrase it differently.

"General Pétain, please forgive me. I did not make myself clear. General Bliss is incorrect that the American Expeditionary Force is being assembled solely to produce a moral effect. I have every intention of producing a *military* effect. But I am realistic, and I must ask the same of you. No division, regiment, no single American soldier will willingly fight under the flag of another country. I do not believe that, in this instance, General Bliss is speaking for President Wilson. The president has placed his confidence in my command, and has issued orders to me that are extremely clear. There will be an American army, and it will fight as a single force. You and I and Marshal Haig may discuss where the AEF may be the most effective, and we will make preparations accordingly. We will consult on strategy, and we will work alongside our allies to secure a victory. General Bliss is correct that we have been caught unprepared for the challenges of creating an army where none presently exists. The fact that General Bliss has put his thoughts on this matter on paper, and has made those thoughts available to you and your government, is simply one more challenge among many I must confront."

Pétain stood, put out his hand. "John, this has been an enlightening meeting. I hope you understand that it was required that I make my request in that manner. I respect your answer. I will do everything in my power to assist you and your troops. Of all the talk you will hear, and all the demands that will be made of you, you must not be led astray from the most important fact. My country is suffering. If America cannot bring her army here, we may not survive."

July 1, 1917

On June 26, the First Division had landed at the port of St. Nazaire, southwest of Paris. It was becoming apparent that this one port would become the single most important hub for the debarkation of American men and equipment. It was woefully disorganized, stevedores going about their routine with the lackadaisical attitude of men who seemed unaware of the war. With the men of the First flowing ashore, marching inland to the cantonment that would house them for their final training on French soil, the most immediate concern was the port itself. Pershing understood that American engineers and others who had expertise in matters of transport and tonnage were an immediate priority. Yet another challenge had been added to his list, convincing Washington to send those men across the ocean, and, if they did arrive, convincing the French officials to stand aside and let them do their jobs.

"Captain Patton requests to see you, sir."

Pershing looked up from a mound of papers, blinked hard, focused on the young lieutenant at his door. "Yes, I'm expecting him."

Patton was there now, all energy and motion, stood in front of his desk, waited for Pershing to acknowledge him.

"Sit down, George. Be with you in a minute. Damn it all." He took a deep breath, slapped his hand down gently on the papers, said, "All right, enough of this for now. This is an amazing country, George. For every colonel who commands a military installation, there's a civilian official who gets in his way. It's a game to them. Who has the most influence, who is better at having his own way. It's not the top people. They've been wonderful, totally cooperative. It's the local despots, little men who control their little corner of France. They have an uncanny talent for keeping their heads down, so that no one in Paris knows what they're truly up to out there. Once I mention a problem to Monsieur Painlevé or General Pétain, it gets handled immediately. But I can't go running off to the highest authority every time some idiot gets in our way." He paused, saw a frown on Patton's face, matching his own. "What do you want, Captain?"

Patton's eyes widened, and he said, "You asked me here to discuss . . . personal matters, sir."

Pershing nodded now, said, "Sorry, yes of course. I need to

make a decision about Nita. She has written me about coming here. I assume you've heard something of this?"

Patton frowned again, thought a moment. "Sir, I don't have so much influence over my sister. As you know, sir, she possesses a formidable will."

"You and I must be united in our efforts, George. I cannot have her here, not now. There are many reasons. I am concerned that our engagement was a mistake. It seemed like the right thing to do at the time. I didn't want to leave her behind without some feeling that I would return to her. Damn these women."

Patton seemed surprised at Pershing's frankness. "Sir, my sister was as happy as I have ever seen her. I thought your engagement was a wonderful thing."

"Yes, yes. I agree. I don't mean to suggest I did it as a favor." Pershing stopped, felt a wave of frustration. "You see? This is just one reason I do not need her in France. I cannot be distracted from my work, and she is . . . quite the distraction. Besides that, her presence will inspire *talk*, George. There is enough talk around this place already, without adding a juicy slice of gossip. These Frenchwomen are a curious lot. All the wives I have met seem so completely wrapped up in the lives of their husbands, basking beside him in his importance. But then, when you meet the single ones, they seem only to be wrapped up in you. A more flirtatious lot I have never imagined. It is not an environment Nita would find . . . amusing."

"Sir, I will write her immediately, and instruct her to put aside any thoughts of travel. Perhaps, sir, you should do the same."

"I have a better idea, Captain. You write both letters. Make mine . . . softer. You can be the bull. Prepare both of them by this evening. I cannot be distracted from all of . . . this."

"As you wish, sir."

Patton seemed to hesitate, and Pershing said, "What is it?"

"Sir, I was wondering. You know that I deeply appreciate the post you have granted me here. I am grateful that you consider me worthy of commanding your headquarters personnel. But with the arrival of the infantry, I am wondering if you might consider . . . um . . ."

"You want to fight, George?"

Patton seemed to jump in his chair. "Just the opportunity, sir. Please, I do not dislike my current assignment. I just hoped that perhaps at a later date—"

"Not yet. Too much to do here. I need people who know how to put discipline into the air. You've done a fine job managing the support personnel. I have thought you might do as well running the motor pool. We're receiving a number of vehicles very soon. I want them kept in perfect condition, maintenance, and appearance."

Patton seemed to sink. "The motor pool, sir?"

"They need discipline too, George. We're still a long way from doing any fighting. Show me you can handle a squadron of trucks, and we'll see what else might develop."

"As you wish, sir." There was no energy in Patton's voice, and Pershing felt himself pulled back to the papers on his desk.

The young lieutenant was at the door, said, "Sir! Excuse me, sir, but you should see this!"

"What is it?"

The young man moved into the office, stood stiffly at attention, clutched a newspaper in one hand. "Sir, this was just brought in by one of the men. It is the newspaper from Nantes." He held it out.

Pershing unrolled it, saw the headline, stood up, slammed the paper down on the desk, shouted, "What the hell is this? Who authorized this?"

Patton leaned forward, read the headline, and the young lieutenant held his pose, said, "No one here, sir."

Pershing shouted again, "Out! Both of you! Get me the press liaison, Major Palmer. Now!"

The office was empty now, and Pershing paced behind his desk, sat heavily in his chair. He held up the paper, said aloud, "Dammit. What the hell are they thinking?"

He sorted through the words, could see numbers, details of regiments and brigades, the names of commanders, Sibert, Bullard, Bundy, his commanders. It was a full account of the arrival of the First Division, details of the strength of each regiment, the names of the ships they had debarked, where they were stationed. He could hear the telephone ringing in the outer office, heard a flood of conversation, and in a short minute he saw the lieutenant again, the man standing in the doorway, stiff and formal.

"Sir. Major Palmer has just telephoned. Also, Ambassador Sharp. They have seen the newspaper accounts as well. It's in all the papers, sir. French and British."

"Have Major Palmer in my office as quickly as he can get here."

"Yes, sir."

Pershing was alone again, tossed the newspaper aside. Palmer will deal with this, he thought. I won't have to tell him twice. Frederick Palmer was the military overseer of the American press contingent, but Pershing had no one who dealt directly with the reporters from the Allied papers. Well, he thought, we will now. Whether it's Palmer himself, or someone he recommends, we will find someone who knows what a damned secret is. Is this the way it happens here? Some gentlemen's agreement between the French, English, and Germans? You tell us where your people are; we'll oblige you in return. No, of course, it's not like that. This is just more of the same, more of what I've seen everywhere I've gone. They are desperate for good news. So here you have it, in the tiniest detail. Tasker Bliss and his damned moral victory. Well, General, here's another one for you. The French have been informed that our First Division has landed. Of course, this victory can be shared all around. The Germans will know as well.

Paris—July 4, 1917

The request had come from President Poincaré himself that Pershing allow the French people to express their gratitude for the arrival of the first wave of American combat troops, by offering a celebration in honor of Independence Day. Despite all the logistical problems that Pershing still had to confront, the increasing workload for him and his staff, this was an invitation that he could not refuse.

It had been suggested that the parade include a contingent of

326

American troops, to demonstrate to the people of Paris that, indeed, the American soldiers were prepared to march beside their countrymen. Pershing ordered a battalion of the Sixteenth Infantry Regiment to make the journey from their base at St. Nazaire, regular troops who had been among the first to arrive at the port. It was all about symbolism, the Americans to parade directly beside their French counterparts, a show to appeal to the hopefulness of the French people.

They assembled first in the lush courtyard at Les Invalides, the enormous art and military museum that had been constructed originally by Louis XIV as a hospital for his wounded veterans. Les Invalides was also the burial place of Napoleon, and to the French people, there was perhaps no more sacred piece of ground. The elite of French society had been assembled, and Pershing stood beside President Poincaré, studied the crowd, so many of Paris' most familiar faces. He saw Joffre now, the old man leading his wife by the arm, stopping to greet friends, making his way through the crowd with no show of self-consciousness. Pershing had met with Joffre several times, had found the man's wife completely charming, had begun to feel a genuine affection for the man who still allowed himself to be seen at such events. It would have been easy for Joffre to sink into bitter hostility with the government, his removal from power seen by some as a shameful disgrace. But Joffre had a new role now, was still sought after for counsel by some of the most powerful men in France. Joffre was an asset to his country for another reason as well. He was greatly revered by his veterans, old soldiers who joined him in the procession even now, survivors of the Franco-Prussian War, men with canes and wheelchairs, whose loyalty to Joffre would never waver. It was the same affection the young soldiers felt for Pétain, that intangible dedication that the foot soldier feels for a select few at the top. It often had nothing to do with a commander's skills or genius at tactics. It was respect in the mind of the private that the general was *one of us*. Too many generals tried to capture the love of their troops by big talk and bluster, a strategy that had never worked. Pershing had never tried to do anything like that himself, had sought only to lead his men with his eyes focused firmly on accomplishing their task. He had never expected to be loved, never thought that he would ever have the mystique of men like George Washington or Robert E. Lee, men who inspired their troops as much as they led them. Now, it was Pétain, the man who some said had single-handedly put down the French mutiny.

The French troops had been put into formation, all the while, a band playing soft music, welcoming the crowds as they assembled. Pershing knew the Americans were waiting out beyond the grounds, and he caught a brief nod from Poincaré, the signal for the Americans to join the assembled mass. Pershing glanced to the side, saw his staff watching him, and Pershing made a nod of his own, the prearranged order, a signal passed out beyond the crowd. Pershing gazed over the French battalion, perfect and precise, the men in their sky blue uniforms, each face staring ahead, no distraction from the audience that surrounded them. He looked now at the gate, saw the first glimpse of movement, the Americans marching in, moving to their designated space. Pershing could not hide a slight smile. The crowd began to hum, audible over the music, and Pershing saw now that the Americans were not as precise, were having difficulty keeping the lines together, finding their place. The uniforms were not as neat, wrinkled shirts, men in tired khaki and dull leather boots. Pershing felt a low burn in his neck, the smile long gone, had never thought the men in his command looked like anything other than soldiers. But now, with the perfection of the French formation and the perfect neatness of their uniforms, he was suddenly embarrassed.

The Americans were all in formation now, their entry complete, and the band began to play something louder, more upbeat, a well-rehearsed selection that seemed to excite the crowd. He saw Poincaré moving away from him, the president stepping down from the platform, taking a flag-staff from a French officer, marching himself in precise cadence to the front of the American formation. Poincaré handed the flag to the officer, a major whose name Pershing couldn't remember, made a short bow to the man, then turned, climbed the steps again, returned to his place beside Pershing without looking at him.

* * *

The ceremony at Les Invalides was complete, and now, the second phase of the day's events would begin. Pershing was escorted down from the platform, guided to a waiting limousine, while back in the open ground, the American troops were filing out into the street, preparing to resume their march. Pershing had already made arrangements to move ahead of the parade, to take a parallel course that would put him in front of his men, reaching their destination first. The car began to move, and he saw Poincaré climbing into another limousine, the various French dignitaries making their way out, most not following, satisfied with their participation in the event. Pershing felt a gnawing sense of depression. He did not expect anything spectacular from the men of the Sixteenth, would scold no one for their appearance. They were regulars, but many of them were new recruits, so typical of nearly every unit in the new army. They had come to Paris only after enduring the misery of a dangerous sea voyage, terrified by constant rumors of submarine attacks. Once they had docked at St. Nazaire, they had disembarked into an alien land, were still finding their way to camps and training facilities where each man knew that for a long while yet he would continue to drill and march and learn. Pershing could find no fault with the men or their officers, and yet, there was something wrong, something he struggled to explain to himself. Nothing had been said, the French officials perfectly polite, but Pershing had seen the looks, glances among the officials, the hum from the audience. The word came to him now: doubt. What did they expect? I have told everyone who would listen, every meeting, every social gathering, *we need time*. Do these people require a better explanation than what they saw today? These men are soldiers, and they might be the best we have. But they are not ready to fight, and they are not veterans of this war. They are not prepared to stand up beside your battle-weary regiments. If you wish us to fight, then we must first create an army, and it cannot happen overnight just because you need it to happen. If that makes you uncomfortable, if the appearance of my men causes you to whisper and mock, then perhaps that will be of benefit to both of us. Perhaps now you will believe me.

His limousine left the main avenue, moved along a side street.

The driver had his instructions, stopped at an intersection, the car now perched on a hill, overlooking the parade route. Pershing could see down to the main avenue again, was surprised at the thick mass of onlookers who had lined the way. The American soldiers had left their French counterparts behind, were marching under their own flag along the route that would take them to their final destination of the day. Pershing left the car, walked down the side street, moved up behind the massive audience who stared out, already waving their banners, a surprising number of flags from both countries, nothing like the politely restrained audience of aristocrats at Les Invalides. People were calling out, glimpsing the American soldiers, and Pershing found his smile again, could see the vanguard of his column, their colors flying briskly, the men glimpsing out to the sides at the mass of onlookers shouting to them. The flowers began now, the crowds responding as every French crowd had responded, noisy and happy, flowers raining down, this time directly on the soldiers themselves. Women began to step out of the crowd, some curling their arms into the arms of the delighted soldiers, marching alongside them, some draping wreaths around the necks of startled privates. But the march continued, and Pershing slipped back to the parallel avenue, climbed into the car, moved forward again.

The march would take the Americans to the Picpus Cemetery, another piece of sacred ground. This was a place Pershing had especially wanted to see, the one place in Paris that held more meaning to the Americans than it would for the French. It had been nearly a century and a half since one French officer had sailed to America, a man who disobeyed his king so that he could fight for George Washington and the rebels who were desperately trying to wage war against the British. The man had indeed served the colonists, had become one of Washington's most respected generals, had made a contribution to American independence that had endeared him to America and put his name in the schoolbooks, familiar now to every American child. The man had died in 1834, and a tomb had been erected in his honor. Pershing would finally see it. The tomb was at the Picpus Cemetery, and the man was the marquis de Lafayette.

* * *

The men marched into formation, and Pershing was waiting for them, smiled at the sight of a massive moving garden. The women began to fall away, finding their own place in a wide gallery of spectators, the soldiers self-consciously removing the flowers from their uniforms, many of them staring up in his direction.

There were speakers again, most of them brief, and Pershing could not help but notice that the highest-ranking French official was now the Minister of War, Painlevé. He wasn't sure if he should feel slighted by the absence of so many of those from the first ceremony, Poincaré, even Joffre not finding the time to attend. No, this is not about them, this ceremony is ours alone. Perhaps they know that. Perhaps it was appropriate to allow us to come to this one very special place.

The speakers had come and gone, the words of the American ambassador to Belgium now drifting out over the crowd. Pershing could see his soldiers still fumbling with the flowers, some of them discreetly slipping a blossom into their shirt, something to carry to a place . . . not nearly so pleasant. The thought shocked him, and he focused on the men, could see faces now, men in glasses, some with moustaches, some with freckles, most of them very young. He felt embarrassed at himself, so much concern about their appearance, thought, What does it matter? If anyone doubts our resolve, and dares to judge us by our martial appearance, to hell with them. I have had enough of parades and luncheons, and petty arguments about which of our allies we prefer. In a little while, these men must be prepared for anything that awaits them. It has been so in every war we have fought, and it will be no different now. They will learn discipline and they will learn the mechanics, they will shoot and march and become proficient with the bayonet. But more, each man will know in his own heart why he is here, and what he must do. He had thought of it often, what it was that made a man fight, what propelled a man to step into the line of fire. We have had it in us since the beginning, he thought, since Boston and Chapultepec and Gettysburg. It is something in being an American, perhaps, an anger bred into us, defiance,

331

rebelliousness, a kind of strength we draw upon when the cause is just, when the challenge is set before us. Some would say it is the worst part of man, and anyone who lived through our Civil War would understand. We don't always require an enemy beyond our borders to call out the fire. The inspiration comes from the heart, and the cause might divide us, or even destroy us. In the Civil War, we suffered a cost that was beyond any horror we could imagine, because we poured that fire into each other. That fire is still in us, in every one of these men. If I did not believe that, I could not lead these men into this fight. *Out there* we will face an enemy who knows what it is to win. We will stand up to soldiers who have become accustomed to the face of death. And when this army marches out onto that ground, there will not be a man among us who is not prepared. If the French doubt us, if the English doubt us, it will not matter. The enemy will discover what these men can bring to this war. Every one of these men, and every man still to come, will come here to fight.

On the platform, another speaker emerged, and Pershing watched him, nodded to the man, a quick grateful smile. It was Colonel Stanton, of his staff, a man good with words, who had volunteered to speak to the French audience with the eloquence Pershing did not have. As the men waited dutifully, Pershing scanned their faces again, imagined a vast sea of men just like this, an army a million strong, with a job yet to do. Beside him, Stanton began his speech, said, "*Lafayette . . . we are here!*"

PART III

A WORLD AFIRE

It was not a question of would *you die, it was just* when.

—SERGEANT CARL DOLAN
The Lafayette Escadrille

20

RICHTHOFEN

Marcke, Belgium—June 1917

All four of the pursuit squadrons of JG-1 had been relocated farther northwest of Douai, the German Air Service matching the concentration of British air patrols in that area. The British success at Messines had allowed several British squadrons to relocate, closing the gap between their bases and their German targets. Their bombing runs were increasing as well, the British pilots growing more adept at night flying, daring to drop their bombs farther behind German lines without fear of antiaircraft fire, or any interruption from German fighters.

Richthofen had made his headquarters at the field where Squadron Eleven would be housed, and established his residence at a nearby home, a magnificent mansion called Château de Bethune. The home was chosen much more for its proximity to the aerodrome than for any pretensions Richthofen had about living in splendor, and the mansion's owner made every effort to keep it that way. The man still maintained his own residence there, and he did everything he could within Richthofen's tolerance to make his German guests feel unwelcome, including sealing off the majority of the house for his own exclusive use. Despite the grandeur of the home's exterior, inside, Richthofen had to be content with sparse surroundings, his host removing all but the most basic furnishings from Richthofen's part of the house. Richthofen paid little attention, avoided his host as much as the host avoided him. Nothing could prevent Richthofen from providing his own decor: his ever-increasing volume of trophies and souvenirs.

When Richthofen arrived at the new base for JG-1, he was delighted to discover he would actually have a staff. His first command decision had been to name Kurt Wolff to command Squadron Eleven, a choice that satisfied not only von Hoeppner, but the pilots Wolff would lead. Despite Wolff's nearly childlike appearance and damaged body, the young lieutenant had already received his own Order Pour le Mérite, and was shooting down enemy aircraft at a rate that nearly exceeded that of Richthofen.

He named Konstantin Krefft to be the technical supervisor to the JG-1, in charge of the mechanical health of the fighter wing's fifty-odd aircraft. Krefft had already demonstrated a knowledge of the inner workings of the planes that impressed even the most senior mechanics in Squadron Eleven. But Krefft brought something more, the large man's physical presence masking a smooth persuasiveness that made him a natural choice to deal with the constant wrangling over supply and equipment with his counterparts in Cologne.

Richthofen had an adjutant now as well, Karl Bodenschatz, a familiar face from the old Boelcke Squadron. Bodenschatz seemed to be everywhere at once, a man with a distinct talent for handling the paperwork required by the High Command.

As promised, the Information Section had assigned him a stenographer, and he was amazed that it was in fact a young woman. Women had never been a presence at the aerodromes, and every man there had made an admiring glance in her direction. Richthofen had been relieved to see that she did not return the attentions. It was a distraction none of them needed.

Richthofen's six weeks of leave had not been all peace and quiet. He had been home barely a week when news had come that Lothar had been shot down and was recovering from his wounds in a hospital nearby. That particular engagement had been a wild free-for-all in the fading daylight of a dark misty day, and though Lothar had taken a severe wound in his hip, his adversary had not been so fortunate. Captain Albert Ball had been England's most illustrious flying ace, had shot down forty German planes, and had been considered by the Royal Flying Corps to be their answer to the nearly mythical domination of the Red Baron. News of Lothar's victory had spread throughout all of Europe, the younger Richthofen suddenly as celebrated as his famous older brother.

June 27, 1917

He looked around the office, realized that for the moment he had nothing to do. He glanced out the window, bright sunshine, the damp mist of the early morning now burning away. He cursed silently, thought, You should have gone out with them. Perhaps this afternoon. Bodenschatz was out of the office, some matter that required his attention at Squadron Ten, and he looked over at Bodenschatz's desk, neat stacks of papers, thought, Perhaps I should go through them, examine the details. The task held no appeal, and the thought abandoned him as quickly as it had arrived.

Across from Richthofen, Krefft was talking on the phone, some discussion of motors and oil consumption. The stenographer sat at a desk behind Krefft, and was sorting through papers. He watched her for a long moment, soft blond hair, the perfect neatness in her appearance, her collar buttoned up tightly, discreetly. He had tried to guess her age, was too shy to ask, scolded himself for his awkwardness around her. She looked up, caught his gaze, smiled. He turned away, embarrassed, felt he had been caught at some inappropriate mischief. He knew that talk had already begun of some romantic connection between them, and it had infuriated him, a needless waste of energy from men whose focus on their job had to be absolute. He had finally succumbed to the questioning looks, informing his entire command that he had no interest in the woman at all beyond the job she was assigned to do. The pilots accepted his word, but the newspapers wanted more. The reporters would not accept the simple truth, and finally, Richthofen had ordered them out of the aerodrome, would allow them to attend briefings only at his discretion. If they wanted to know more about her, they could ask the Information Section.

He looked at the floor, pretended to adjust his boots, felt completely foolish. It annoyed him intensely that he was as uncomfortable around her as he had been around girls all his life; even as a youth he had confronted his shyness by simply avoiding the problem altogether. But she was there every day, sitting quietly at her desk, notepad ready. He was rarely in the mood for anything of the sort, but then the inspiration would come, prompted usually by the thought of von Hoeppner's veiled threat to pull him out of the sky.

From her first day, he had tried to become comfortable speaking of himself, had thought it logical to begin by relating his family's history. She had been diligent, recorded every word he said, preparing the text into neatly arranged pads, something that some *professional* would sort out later. But there were days when he just didn't want to talk about any of it, and he felt guilty avoiding her. She had begun the process with professional detachment, but his story seemed to affect her, and he quickly realized she had a talent for casual flirtation. But it never went beyond the smile, the soft glance, and no matter how much intimate detail he would share with her, he did not believe she had any ambitions beyond doing her job.

He stopped fiddling with his boots, sat up, glanced at his own desk, looked for something that might require his immediate attention. Krefft was off the telephone now, said, "Captain, the new Albatros D-V appears to be no better than what it is supposed to replace. There is still a design problem with the lower wing. It has the nasty habit of coming apart in a steep dive, and not even the chief mechanic has a hint of how to address the problem."

Grateful for the interruption, Richthofen moved to Krefft's desk, pretended to scan the paperwork Krefft had been studying. He fought the urge but couldn't help it, glanced up to catch the young woman peeking up at him over a piece of notepaper. "Yes, Lieutenant, keep at them. I will not have my pilots falling out of the sky because of inferior engineering."

Krefft seemed surprised by Richthofen's interest, something he rarely saw. "Oh, yes. There is some news from England, sir. We have of course seen their new Sopwith triplanes, but they are apparently introducing a new model of biplane as well. According to a report from the Air Service office, it is called the Camel, and is claimed to be superior to any model of Albatros."

Richthofen was genuinely interested now, ignored the girl's glances. "Camel? Do we know if it is faster?"

"Possibly. Claims to be more maneuverable by far. I will inform you if I learn any further details."

Richthofen thought a moment, said, "The quality of the box matters little. What matters is the man who flies it."

"Of course, sir."

The words had come from Boelcke, and Richthofen had voiced the phrase often. He had even considered putting a sign up on the wall, a motto for every man to remember before he climbed into his own box. He moved back to his desk, sat down, felt an odd coldness, Boelcke's philosophy clouded now, the words spoken so many times they seemed to lose meaning. He thought of his brother, the wound, and another name came to him: Albert Ball. The finest pilot those people had, and he is dead. What would Boelcke say about that? Ball was superior to forty opponents, until he confronted Lothar. More names came to him, men he had known from Squadron Boelcke, and before, very good pilots who are gone. He had lost men in his own command as well, his good friend Karl Schaefer, another Order Pour le Mérite, thirty victims to his credit, killed only three weeks prior. And of course, Boelcke and Immelmann. Does it matter *now* what kind of pilots they were? Their achievements are frozen in time, the clock stopping the moment of their deaths. No, if this Camel is a better aircraft, then we must do better ourselves.

He could hear the drone of motors, saw motion outside, mechanics emerging from the aerodrome. The squadron was returning from the morning's first patrol. He stood, watched the planes, a ritual now on those days when he was not with them. The planes had all manner of odd markings now, some with red cowlings, some with red tails, various symbols, unique to each pilot. Squadron Eleven had adapted red as their particular color. The other squadrons had followed suit, each one unique. In the other squadrons, how the paint was used was up to each pilot himself, and the designs on the planes had been as varied as the personalities of the men themselves. Very soon, von Hoeppner had sent him a wire, mention of a London newspaper report, the British pilots returning home speaking of these new brightly dressed aircraft, referring to JG-1 as Richthofen's Flying Circus.

He saw Wolff's plane rolling to a stop, let out a breath, had grown to depend on the frail young man. Wolff had led Squadron Eleven by example as Richthofen himself had done, aggressive without being foolish.

He watched as Wolff jumped down gingerly from his plane, the thin man always seeming to crumble when he hit the ground. His injuries would have kept him out of any other branch in the military, but Wolff had defied those who insisted he was too crippled to fly. Richthofen was surprised to see him walking quickly toward the office, saw the look on Wolff's face, and the cold opened up inside of him again. He sat down, stared at the door, Krefft now silent as well. The door opened, and Wolff stepped inside, still engulfed by his thick flying suit.

"Captain."

"You have something to report, Lieutenant?"

Wolff looked down, then put a hand on his face, pressed at his eyes. "I must report, sir, the loss of Lieutenant Allmenroder. There was nothing anyone could do to help him. I am terribly sorry, sir."

Richthofen stared straight ahead, heard a faint cry from the young woman across the room. He leaned back in the chair, said nothing for a long moment, allowed Wolff time to collect himself.

Karl Allmenroder had become reckless, a sharp streak of revenge in him that affected the way he approached the enemy. It had begun when his brother Wilhelm shot down a British pilot, the plane crash-landing in plain sight. When Wilhelm flew low to see the condition of his opponent, the pilot had detached his machine gun from the wing of his crumpled plane, and fired at Wilhelm as he passed by, wounding him so severely he had been forced to leave the squadron. The entire squadron had been outraged that the British pilot had refused to accept his defeat with the grace that men on both sides had come to expect. Karl had insisted on adding his brother's flying time to his own, would revenge the dishonor by killing every Englishman he could find. Though Karl Allmenroder had shot down thirty enemy planes and received his Order Pour le Mérite, Richthofen knew that it was a matter of time before his hatred caused him to make a mistake.

"Thank you, Lieutenant. I will notify his brother. You must tend to your aircraft."

Wolff composed himself, nodded, stood straight, said, "Yes, sir. Of course."

Wolff was out the door now, the office silent, Krefft staring down at his desk. Richthofen saw the face of Allmenroder in his mind, the others as well, so many, *too* many. He motioned to the young woman, said, "We will walk outside. You may bring your notepad."

21

LUFBERY

Chaudun, France—July 1917

The desolation at Ham had been left behind, the Aeronautique Militaire ordering the Lafayette Escadrille to make another move. The airfield at Chaudun was farther south, close to the town of Soissons, an oasis of civilization the pilots had thought they might never see again. Chaudun was as sophisticated as any airfield in France, housed six complete escadrilles. The field itself was groomed and maintained, had none of the hidden pot-holes and tufts of thick grass that so often plagued the pilots and their landing gear.

The missions would be as so many had been before, escorting the observers and bombers, but there was no urgency, no major push along this part of the front lines, and the schedule had set-tled into a routine that Lufbery found maddening. Thenault had agreed that the pilots could make their own impromptu patrols, usually in pairs. But Lufbery often chose to fly alone, something Thenault rarely allowed the others to do. It was an understand-ing between them, Thenault's confidence in Lufbery's abilities. It was something of a mystery to the others, but no one took offense. They seemed to understand that there was nothing in Lufbery of loud bravado, no selfish quest for personal glory that sent him aloft on his solitary patrols. And as long as he was suc-cessful, not even Thenault could object.

Lufbery coaxed the plane forward, eased the rudder to the side, the early-morning breeze catching the tail, the plane swinging around slowly, the nose centering now on the long straight field. He switched the ignition to full throttle, felt the power, the familiar roar, the plane surging forward through the gray

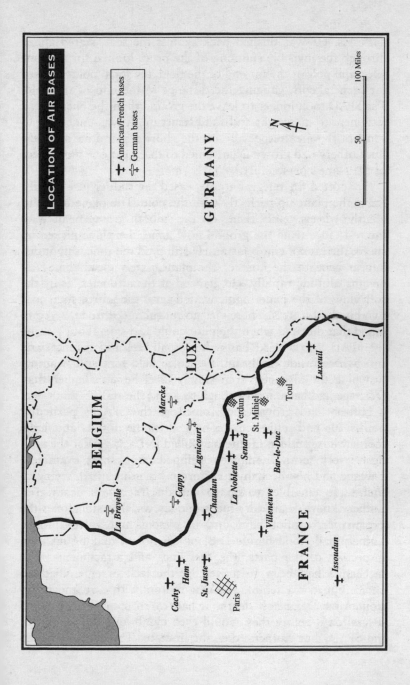

LOCATION OF AIR BASES

✝ American/French bases
⊕ German bases

GERMANY

BELGIUM

LUX.

FRANCE

Marcke ⊕

Lagnicourt ⊕

Cappy ⊕

La Brayelle ✝

Chaudun ✝

La Noblette ✝

Senard ✝

Verdun ⊕

St. Mihiel ⊕

Bar-le-Duc ✝

Toul ⊕

Laxeuil ✝

Villeneuve ✝

Issoudun ✝

Cachy ✝

Ham ✝

St. Juste ✝

Paris ⊕

N

0   50   100 Miles

darkness. He was pushed back against the seat, stared ahead through the invisible spinning of the prop, looked for the lone telegraph pole at the far end of the field, the focal point he used for each takeoff, gauging the distance to the end of the field. The SPAD took longer to leave the ground than the Nieuport, a testament to its weight and solid structure. It was unnerving to some of the men, especially on the shorter, primitive airfields. But Lufbery had grown accustomed to that, just one more piece of the plane's personality.

He spotted the telegraph pole, eased the rudder just slightly, lining the plane up perfectly with the pole. The plane began to lift, the wheels gently rising off the smooth grassy field. With the resistance from the ground now gone, the plane picked up speed, the rate of climb faster. He still eyed the pole, saw it disappear beneath the nose of the plane, safely clear, the SPAD gaining altitude rapidly. He glanced at the altimeter, lit by the soft glow of the panel light, waited until the gauge spun past two hundred meters. There was no rule about altitude, no command that dictated when the pilot could feel safe about putting the SPAD into a hard bank. It was all feel and instinct, and somewhere inside his brain, the voice held him still, waiting, watching the altimeter spin slowly until he was higher than DeLaage had been, high enough to avoid the stall.

Lufbery had grown accustomed to the SPAD's particular quirks. He had refused to be nagged by the doubts about the motor whose sudden failure had killed DeLaage. After the accident, every motor had been stripped, every part examined, LeBlanc and his mechanics performing a grim ritual, trying to find some tangible reason to explain DeLaage's death. But Lufbery knew what every mechanic knows, that sometimes the explanation cannot be found in pistons and valve springs. Lufbery had stood beside LeBlanc for hours, making his own inspection of the parts, the fuel lines and attachments. The mechanics had been frustrated by the lack of clues, had no choice but to reassemble the new motors with care and precision. After DeLaage's death, it had taken some of the pilots several days before they would even climb into the cockpit of the SPAD, but Lufbery did not hesitate. There could be no superstition, no fear of the unusual accident. He flew as he had always flown, with his mind wrapping itself around the sound of the motor, all the mechanical movements becoming a part of his thoughts. He had his own theories about DeLaage's accident, something as simple as an air bubble forming in the gas line, or some impurity in the gasoline itself. It had become one more part of his personal inspection, straining the gasoline through a wire mesh filter, one more precaution that the other pilots had copied.

He could see the red glow of the dawn, turned the SPAD eastward, aimed for the rising sun. The Aisne River snaked below him, and he could begin to see the spires that marked Soissons, the town that offered them many of the same temptations they had sought from Paris. Though they didn't make the journeys to Paris as often now, the city had provided them with one more unique gift, something that even now made Lufbery smile. Bill Thaw had found another lion cub, a female, who seemed to be the perfect companion to Whiskey. There had been doubts at first, a careful watch as the two cubs confronted each other, all the usual sniffs and inspections. But then, the playfulness had begun, and the doubts had vanished. Whiskey did indeed have a new friend. With perfect logic, they named her Soda.

He scanned the horizon to the south, still too dark to see, focused again on the reddening sky to the east. The ground below him was becoming more visible, a dark smear in the earth that spread all the way to Verdun. He banked the plane to the left, knew the German lines were closer to the northeast, ignored the altimeter, could tell by the sharp chill in the air that he was passing ten thousand feet.

The Aisne River was behind him now, and he could see the desolation of the front lines, the rows of barbed wire twisting through the center of no-man's-land. He continued to climb, looked down toward the German lines, thought, You hear the motor, eh, Boche? Get those antiaircraft guns tuned up. But, sorry, I'm too high for you. Maybe later, I'll come in low, give you a look. He had no fear of the gunners on the ground, had seen too much of the manic spray of shrapnel the guns threw in the air, the random scattering of lead that some artillery commander must believe was an effective way to down an aeroplane. When he was low enough to be in their range, Lufbery had seen the predictable pattern of the gunners, every one of them setting their shells to ignite at the same altitude, trying to anticipate the direction the plane would fly. It required very little genius for a pilot simply to change his altitude, or alter his course, so that the gunners would have to start their calculations all over again. By that time, any capable pilot was long past them.

He began to search the skies, focused mainly on the German side of the lines. He knew of their airfields, some close behind what they were calling the Hindenburg line, the German defensive position that no commander seemed to know how to break. He scanned the French side of the lines below him, wondered how many men were there, how many French soldiers were still staring out at their barbed wire.

He had been as skeptical as anyone when rumors of the French mutiny reached the airfield. Thenault had been furious, suspected the reports were fabricated by spies and malcontents, someone's vicious assault on French pride. But then, the columns had passed by on the road, ragged soldiers in their filthy blue uniforms, some unarmed, all marching away from the front. Thenault could not simply let them march past, had gone out to confront them, to try rally them. But the captain had found himself staring at dozens of angry men who had no interest in listening to officers. Their response was the bayonet, backing the surprised captain off the road, out of their way.

They had all expected word of a sudden German push, that surely the German High Command would take advantage of the weakness in the French defenses, but amazingly, it did not come. The pilots could only guess that, for once, the Germans had no idea what was happening in front of them.

Lufbery didn't think much about tactics and strategy, had rarely met a senior officer he cared for. He had heard too many stories from those pilots who had come first through the French Foreign Legion, the men like Kiffin Rockwell and Bill Thaw, who had known the war from the trenches. Too often it was about breeding and class, so many of the officers believing in

346

their inherent superiority to the nameless troops who obeyed them. But good breeding had no impact on good leadership, and the results were known to every army in every war the Europeans had ever fought: it was the soldier who died, while, too often, the man who sent them across the bloody field was safely in the rear. Lufbery had seen class distinction all over the world, touring with Marc Pourpe's air exhibitions. In Europe or Asia or Arabia, rich men gave the orders and the poor obeyed. To Lufbery, it was the one reason why America had to fight this war. In the escadrille, the rich men flew beside men like him, and respect came from ability, not class. If the war was lost, if the kaiser's arrogance prevailed, Europe might never again see that kind of equality.

He scanned the ground beneath him, caught a flash of light, then another, bursts of fire from an artillery battery. He looked across to the far side of the lines, waited for the result, the impact of the shells, saw more flashes there, a battery responding to their enemy. He looked out ahead of him, searched the sky, tried not to think of what was happening beneath him. It was the luxury of flying, of being so far removed from all of *that*. He tried to flex his toes, numb and stiff even in the captured German's plush boots. At least I have boots, he thought. Some of those fellows down there are knee-deep in mud.

He was well over German territory now, dipped the wings to one side, looked out toward the lines of trenches, searching for aeroplanes, observers perhaps, someone flying low. The sun was behind him, the perfect position, and he scanned for reflections, some speck of light, any sign that someone else was up here with him. His heart jumped: he saw them, an open V formation below him slightly, moving parallel to the trenches, as he was. He ignored the misery of his frozen feet, focused on the planes, thought, I'm in the sunlight. How perfectly damned convenient. He watched for a few seconds, could see the sun reflecting off the top wings, black crosses yawning up at him, five planes. In a few more seconds they would be past him, and he measured the distance, a half mile, closing quickly. They had not responded to him at all, and he knew they were looking away, scanning the French side of the line, trying the same tactic he was, keeping the sun behind them to blind the enemy. He flexed his fingers around the stick, thought, You should get up earlier, Boche. Or is your bed too comfortable?

The formation was moving past him, and he continued to flex his fingers, trying to bring the feeling back, the precision he would need. They were behind him now, and he banked the SPAD in a hard turn, the nose dropping, could feel the speed, the heavy plane slipping rapidly down, curling around, bringing the German formation straight in front of him. He was breathing heavily, dropped the nose again, the planes seeming to rise up slightly in front of him. He had seen their markings clearly, all manner of swirls and odd patterns, starbursts and geometric shapes. They were Albatroses, and he had seen this before, each squadron's coloring, each pilot's own design. Some said it was camouflage, and Lufbery had laughed at that, had seen too many of these Boche machines to believe they could hide from anyone. No, he thought, it is just vanity, your arrogant pretense that somehow each of you is unique, worthy of attention. Well, I shall give you my attention now.

The SPAD had closed the gap between them and was nearly underneath the last plane in the formation. He looked out toward the second Albatros, across the wide mouth of their V formation. He doesn't see me either. Too bad for you, Boche. He pulled back gently on the stick, the tail of the first Albatros just above him, the gun sight squarely on the plane's body. He pressed the trigger, the gun firing a long burst, ripping the belly, blasting pieces off the tail. The tail section of the plane suddenly disintegrated, large pieces breaking free, coming apart, and the Albatros spun away violently, the pilot losing all control. Lufbery looked across at the second plane, saw the pilot banking toward him. Lufbery was surprised by the move, the Albatros crossing right in front of him, right into his gun sights. He fired again, could see the face of the pilot staring at him, the man's head now jerking away, the impact of the bullets, the cockpit splintering to pieces. The second Albatros began to spin, falling away as well, and Lufbery looked at the next two in the formation, could see wings tilting, the pilots searching for him, one plane banking away, trying to move around behind him. He pulled the stick hard to the side, pushed the nose straight down, dropping into a steep dive. He was pressed hard against the seat, stared ahead, glanced at the wings, stiff and solid, the SPAD showing no strain. He held the nose down, did not look for the Germans behind him, knew that with the head start, they could not catch him now. He continued the dive, faster than he had gone before, the SPAD still showing no sign of stress. He looked through the prop, could see details on the ground, rows of cannon, movement, a truck on a road, thought, All right, that's low enough. He pulled back slowly on the stick, the SPAD responding, coming out of the dive. He glanced quickly at the altimeter, barely five hundred meters, and he made a quick turn, a tight circle, scanned the sky above him, saw nothing at all, the Albatroses not pursuing. He focused on the artillery below, turned the SPAD in the direction of the cannon barrels, the old lesson. If you're lost, aim the same direction as the enemy's cannon. He did not look for the two planes he had destroyed, thought instead of the pilot he had shot. What was he thinking? Perhaps he didn't see me at all, was just following his friend. It was his final mistake. With the tail shot to hell like that, no chance his friend could gain control. Bastard probably went in at full throttle.

He could see no-man's-land still out in front of him, the boundary that was so crucial to so many of the pilots. Lufbery thought of the Albatroses, both going straight down. They hit the ground back here, the wrong side of the line. There won't be any confirmation. He glanced back behind him, looked again for pursuers, saw nothing, the sky empty. But *they* will know.

"Dammit, Luf, there's gotta be a better way!"

Lufbery had heard it before, shrugged. "Doesn't bother me."

"Well, hell, it bothers me!" Thaw wore a hard frown, was pacing in short quick steps. The parlor was narrow, and Thaw was forced to move in tight circles, glaring frequently at Lufbery, who sat in a plush velvet-covered chair.

Parsons sat across from him, frowning as well, and he said, "I agree. Maybe we can convince Thenault to fly over there with a truce flag. Make some sort of deal. Hey, Boche, we'll be honest with you if you do the same. No secrets. Try to be gentlemen about this."

Lufbery had seen Thaw go through this exercise before, knew what was coming.

Thaw stopped pacing, stared at him, pointed a thick finger. "It's your own damned fault. If you'd stay on this side of the lines, those bastards would fall where we can find 'em. Luf, sometimes you can be one seriously dumb son of a bitch."

Lufbery knew to let Thaw have his say, saw the man's energy wavering. Lufbery said, "Bill, I fly on the German side because that's where the Germans fly. I have to keep the sun to my back. The only way I can fly on *this* side of the line is if the Boche decide to change places with us. Don't think they'll agree to that."

Thaw stared at him, put his hands up on either side of his face, seemed to hold his head in place, leaned over close to Lufbery. "Then, why don't you wait until the afternoon? The *sun* will change position for you!"

Lufbery shrugged again. "I'd rather fly in the morning."

Thaw let his hands drop to his side, turned away, said to Parsons, "I quit. The dumb bastard won't play by the rules. He doesn't understand that there's no point in going out and being a hero if nobody finds out about it. How we gonna win this war if nobody *knows* we're winning? This brick head has shot down more damned Boche than the rest of us combined, and headquarters just throws up its hands, and says, Well, hell, if the Boche don't fall over here, they don't count."

He glared at Lufbery again, and Lufbery said, "Just let it go, Bill."

Thaw shook his head, and Lufbery knew the routine, that Thaw's explosion would exhaust itself, and the only conclusion would be a round of drinks. Lufbery sat back, absorbed the humor of the playful argument, knew it could go on all night long.

July 5, 1917

Thenault waited for the men to quiet, and Lufbery looked at the other officer, a thick bulldog of a man, in a uniform

350

he had not seen for a long time. It was American.

"Gentlemen, if you please. I should introduce to you Major Mitchell. He requested to speak to you."

The man stepped forward, scanned the faces, said, "Billy Mitchell. I am honored to make your acquaintance. I am here under the authority of General John J. Pershing, commander, the American Expeditionary Force. I have been given the responsibility by the general for organizing and training an American Air Service, under the direct command of Brigadier General William Kenly. We hope to have this vital part of the AEF fully operational six months from today. I am here because I have been able to convince General Kenly and General Pershing that you men represent the finest spirit of American aviation. Allow me to state plainly that the American people feel you to be heroes, in every positive sense of that word. I believe you and other Americans like you, who have distinguished themselves in service to the French and English air services, can assist me by becoming the core of our training program. We require both seasoned flyers and competent instructors. I know your records. You have given a great deal to the defeat of our common enemy. I am hoping you men will agree that your first duty is to your own flag."

Mitchell seemed to satisfy himself, stopped, looked around the room. Thenault said, "I have nothing to add, gentlemen. This decision is yours alone."

Thaw stood up, said, "Major, how many American aeroplanes do you expect to have in service in six months?"

Mitchell stared at Thaw for a brief moment, the hard stone of his expression beginning to break. He smiled now, said, "You're Bill Thaw?"

"Yep."

"You read newspapers, Mr. Thaw?"

"Yep."

"You ever work in a stable?"

There were low laughs and Thaw said, "Yes, sir. With a shovel, sir."

"Then you understand newspapers. I've seen the same bull you've seen. There are some people in Washington who insist you men aren't needed, that we can build a home-grown air force from the ground up. I happen to believe that kind of thinking comes straight out of Mr. Thaw's stable. The men who have been appointed to oversee the formation of the Air Service know as much about aeroplanes as a hog knows about skating. All I can do is shovel my way through as much of that nonsense as General Pershing permits. I have confidence in the general, and you should as well. But I'll be honest with you, Mr. Thaw. The entire American Air Service presently consists of one Nieuport, which is flown exclusively by me. I'm here because your country doesn't require any more dreamers. We need men who know how to fly."

22

RICHTHOFEN

July 6, 1917

The sky was warm and cloudless, and he had waited impatiently in his office for Wolff to lead them back home after the early-morning patrol. As the planes began to land, the call had come from an infantry observation post, a flight of British planes heading east, passing over the German positions near the small village of Menin, not far from Marcke. Within minutes, Squadron Eleven had been refueled, and minutes later, Richthofen led them aloft in the red Albatros.

It didn't take him long to locate the enemy planes, bombers, large two-seaters, protected by an escort of Sopwith triplanes. Richthofen led the squadron down into their usual dives, the British responding by maneuvering into a large circle, nose to tail, a tactic that Richthofen had not yet seen. His pilots stayed just out of range, skirted around the British in wide sweeping circles of their own. The British machine guns chattered in short bursts, too far away to inflict any real damage. No, it is just their warning, he thought. He climbed the Albatros above the swirling activity, looked down at the ring of British planes, began to enjoy himself, not just the hunt, but more, the entertainment the British were offering. Do they truly believe this will save them? He imagined a British officer in some aerodrome, chalk on blackboard, imparting this new bit of ingenuity to his pilots. The British are like that, he thought, full of arrogance, the man probably congratulating himself on this defense that will counter our success. Did any of them believe we would see this impenetrable ring of planes and simply run away? Did it never occur to them that they cannot maintain this formation for more than a few minutes? They are far beyond their own lines, and the bombers did not have time to complete their mission. They are still carrying their heavy eggs. Very soon their fuel gauges will show them the folly of this grand defense, and then they will have to run for home. Those who survive this day can return to the officer and his blackboard, and offer him the lesson *we* shall teach them.

He kept the Albatros banked at a steep angle, studied the targets circling below him, knew some of them would be watching him, this lone red hawk, circling the prey, while the other Albatroses flitted in and out of range, seeking to separate or break up the formation. One of you will be the first to jump, he thought, like the partridge, nervous, bolting out of your protective cover. I will just wait.

After several minutes, the ring of British planes seemed to collapse, someone giving the order to break formation, and Richthofen smiled. Yes, you know you have no fuel. It is a long way home. The other Albatroses began the pursuit, some trying to get in close to the slower bombers, others already dancing around the triplanes. He eased down on the stick, nosed into a dive, could see one bomber trying to keep close to their formation, shook his head. No, little bird. Not this time.

He was closing the gap, could see the British observer, the man suddenly standing, the machine gun swinging up toward the Albatros. The gun began to spark, and Richthofen could hear the small zips and hisses in the air, smiled again. You are too nervous, sir. I am still out of range. Just wait a moment, and you will have a better target. He dipped down, began to slip the Albatros under the tail of the British plane, but the bomber dropped down quickly, the pilot banking hard, the observer still holding to his gun. He was still out of range, but the gunner was spraying the air around him, and Richthofen saw sparks, bullets suddenly glancing off the barrels of his Maxims. Suddenly he felt a hard punch to his head, throwing him back, his hands knocked free of the stick. He reached out, jerked the stick to one side, his head suddenly swirling, sky, sun, then nothing at all. He was blind.

He felt himself spinning, his arms whipped numbly to one side. He pulled his elbows in tight, tried to keep his hands inside the cockpit. The numbness had spread through his body, and he groped for the stick, could feel nothing in his fingers. He tried to see, ripped at the goggles, his face now blasted by the wind, swiped a gloved hand across his eyes, felt a wet smear. The roar of his motor engulfed him, the wind tossing him side to side, a hot knife slicing into his brain. He tried to stab at the rudders beneath his feet, could feel nothing in his legs, his whole body paralyzed by a tingling numbness. The fear began to rise up in him, the pain in his head screaming at him, louder now, deafening. He fought to feel his hands, jerked himself sideways, one arm finding the stick, stiff dead fingers trying to close around it. He had it now, tingling in his fingers, tried to pull it straight, the blasting wind and the spin of the plane still pressing him back. He could see flashes of light, wiped at his face again, more wetness, but his eyes were clearing, glimpses of light and darkness. His brain was shouting at him: Stop this! Get control! He could see the dull shadows of the wings, blinked hard, felt a wave of relief. Thank God, the wings are still there, the plane is holding together. He held tightly to the stick, struggled to see the instruments, the altimeter, how far . . . how much time do I have left? The hard roar in his ears had grown quiet, his brain now swirling with a soft hiss. He fought to see, could tell the prop had stopped, realized he had switched off the motor, pure instinct, the sounds all coming now from the spin of the plane. He felt sickness, could not focus, the dizziness and the wetness masking his vision. He wiped hard at his eyes again, a glimpse of the altimeter, five *hundred meters*, the needle moving, the plane falling still, a new wave of searing pain rolling through his head. The numbness in his feet gave way to small bits of movement and he could feel the rudders, had the stick in both hands, pulled hard to one side, his foot punching the rudder. The plane shook and vibrated, fought against him, the whining groan of the twisting wings, the stick unyielding. But he would not give in, the plane growing calmer, the Albatros now in his hands, the control returning, his mind working through the pain. The plane began to ease out of its spin, the swirling ground beneath him slowing, the wave of sickness passing. The ground was drifting beneath him now, and he could hear new sounds, motors, stared up through the thick crust in his eyes, saw a plane, then another, circling above him, bits of red, a glimpse of black crosses on the wings, the small voice in his head again, Thank God.

There were open fields below him, dull and brown, a wide uneven cluster of circles, and he thought, Shell holes. He could see troops emerging from dark slices in the ground, some waving to him, and he was relaxed now, the plane a part of him again, the pain in his head growing numb as well, his eyes closing, soft sounds, soothing him. He could hear the cheers of the soldiers, softer sounds, his mind taking him to some other place, cheering crowds, wide grateful smiles, women and children, like some holiday parade. The plane was dropping quickly, and he fought with his own mind, blinked through the thick hot wetness, tried to look beyond the prop, saw the bare ground flattening out. He held tightly to the stick, pulled back, raised the nose, the pain in his head carrying him back into blindness. He had no idea how far he still had to drop, every part of him numb again, the stick pulling out of his grip, the plane falling, uncontrollable, like Boelcke. . . .

The room was white, small windows, sunlight blinding him. He felt soft comfort beneath him, blinked his eyes, turned to the side, felt a sharp stab of pain in his head. He clamped his eyes shut, made a sound, lay still again, felt with his hands, a bed, soft sheets. He wanted to see, but the pain held him still, and the smells began to find him, alcohol and sickness. He wanted to call out, felt pressure on his shoulder, a voice, a woman's voice, "You are awake. Very good."

He opened his eyes again, saw a white shadow hovering over him, the voice again, "You have had enough sleep for now. The doctor insists you should eat."

A hand slid under his back, slowly lifted him, the pain in his head torturing him, and he said, "Stop! What are you doing? Who are you?"

He was sitting upright now, his back cushioned by thick pillows. His eyes opened and he could see her, the voice again, "You are at St. Nicholas Hospital. Don't you remember? You insisted they bring you here. Quite a stir. There were more doctors tending to your one scratch than I usually see in a month."

"St. Nicholas. In Courtrai."

"Ah, so you do remember. Your dinner will be brought soon. I am told they have prepared something special. One would think you are a general." She laughed, a soft giggle that only annoyed him. He realized he was hungry, fought through the pain to see her face.

"A general. No, I'm a captain. You're a nurse."

"To be correct, I am *your* nurse. I have been removed from my other duties and placed at your disposal. I was not allowed to protest the decision. You are very important, so I'm told. How is it possible for a captain to be so important? Just because you fly aeroplanes?"

She stood at the foot of the bed now, shaded him from the sunlight. He realized she was young, a thin, short woman, dark, and . . . very pretty. He tried to recall her question, but the pain was pushing at him from inside.

"My head. It hurts."

"I am certain of that. Quite a little bump. You are heavily bandaged, but don't go feeling around. I will change the dressing soon. I am told you are a hero."

"I am a flyer."

She seemed to appraise him with a soft frown. "Yes, I said that. That's how you got here. They said your aeroplane fell out of the sky."

The images were coming back to him, small flickers in his brain, the circling British planes, sparks on his machine guns, fighting to control the Albatros. He remembered the ambulance now, soldiers, a lieutenant, the man crying over him. They had taken him to a field hospital, awful stench, a heavy cloth on his head, many hands holding him. He tried to look to the side, the pain holding him again, yes, a hospital. I told them . . . take me here. Courtrai. Close to Marcke.

"Do they know? Have my pilots been informed?"

She laughed, a small giggle. "Captain, they descended on this hospital like a swarm of bees. My job was to keep you quiet, allow you to sleep. They did everything they could to see you, but I had my instructions. I'm afraid I upset them. One fellow, a very big man, was not so very pleasant about it."

Richthofen thought, That would be Krefft. No, he would not be pleasant at all.

"They certainly know where you are. When the doctor allows it, you may have visitors." She glanced down, a small plaque hanging at the foot of the bed. "Mr. Richthofen." She moved around the side of the bed, soft hands on his shoulders, straightened the pillow behind him. "Better?"

The pain had eased, and he nodded slowly, testing, turned slightly to the side. There were beds in a long row, most of them occupied, other nurses moving about. She was leaning low across him, one hand gently probing the bandage on the side of his head, and he could smell her now, the scent of lilacs. She stood up straight, said, "Would you like to see?"

"See what?"

She giggled again, and it was not annoying after all. "Your bandage. They did a wonderful job."

"Yes, thank you."

She moved away quickly, and he watched the flow of her dress, soft and graceful. He closed his eyes, eased his head back into the softness of the pillows, but she returned quickly, said, "Here you are."

He looked into a mirror, was shocked to see a thick white dome on his head, his face etched with small red cuts. He stared for a long moment, and the image fell away, the mirror down by her side.

"So, what do you think? The doctor did a fine job, I believe."

The sight of his bandage had turned his hunger to sickness, his stomach cold and twisting. "What happened to me?"

"You were shot in the head, Captain!" It was a man's voice, startling him, and he saw the dark suit now, moving close to him, the nurse standing back. "Dr. Kraske, at your service, Captain. It was my honor to have assisted with your repair." The man sat heavily on the edge of the bed, and Richthofen was engulfed by a new smell, stale cigars.

"Thank you, Doctor. What happened to me?"

"A bullet impacted along your scalp. Made quite a nice incision actually, nearly ten centimeters long. You were extremely fortunate, Captain. The bullet parted your scalp as cleanly as any wound I've seen, but did not enter your skull. The bone itself was exposed perfectly. You still have some bone splinters embedded. But we shall tend to that later. Congratulations to the enemy on this one. Nice and clean." The man laughed at his own joke. "You will have one substantial headache for a few days. Considering the possibilities, it's a small price to pay, wouldn't you say?"

"My face . . ."

"A few bruises, and a good many small cuts. The soldiers who accompanied you here said you jumped out of your plane, and landed in a rather nasty thicket of briars. I pulled quite a few thorns out of you."

More memories flooded through him, the plane landing in a tangle of wire, still upright, struggling to climb out, falling . . . yes, thorns. He put a hand up to his head, felt the thick cotton cloth, said, "How long . . . must I wear this bandage? Will I be allowed to fly?"

"I can answer the first question, Captain. A few weeks at least, until the wound has closed completely. As to the second, that is not my area of authority. But I see no reason to recommend that you be kept from your duty. In any event, I would not want to be the one to make that decision."

Kraske stood, motioned to the nurse, "Miss Otersdorf, I insist he eat something. Change his dressing afterward."

"Yes, sir."

Kraske leaned close to him again, said, "I'll look in on you later, Captain. Anything you require, anything at all, just ask Miss Otersdorf. I assure you, sir, you are in quite capable hands. You are an honored guest here. Please take advantage."

The man moved away, and Richthofen put a hand on the thick bandage again, the nurse moving closer.

"No you don't, Mr. Richthofen. That's for me to do. An honored guest. Dr. Kraske isn't often so generous. I should like to hear more about our honored guest. Forgive my ignorance,

Mr. Richthofen. Perhaps it is your, um, father who is the general?"

The hunger had returned, and he said, "Is there food? You said—"

"Right away, Mr. Richthofen. The orderly is bringing your tray now."

He saw another woman, older, a silver tray covered with a white cloth. The nurse removed the linen covering, the smells rolling up to him.

"Well now, Mr. Richthofen, we have quite the feast here. Not every patient here receives fresh vegetables."

He was ravenously hungry now, and she sat on the edge of the bed, picked up the fork, stabbed at something green on the plate, put it into his mouth. He swallowed quickly, ready for more, said, "It is not necessary that you feed me, Miss . . ."

"Otersdorf." She made the giggle again, put another bite in his mouth. "Nonsense, Mr. Richthofen. I have my orders."

He surrendered, felt ridiculous, like some small child, but she was smiling as she worked, and he noticed her light brown hair, pulled neatly up under her nurse's cap. He studied her eyes now, the same color as her hair, waited for her to put the fork on the plate, tried to form words, his shyness fighting him more than the ache in his head. He heard a soft sound, realized she was humming, another bite, meat this time, and she caught his stare, smiled at him, sweeping his shyness away.

"Is it proper to inquire of Miss Otersdorf if she has a first name?"

She sat back, seemed embarrassed at the question. "Why, no, I have no objection at all. My name is Kate, Mr. Richthofen."

"Please," he said. "It is Manfred."

St. Nicholas Hospital, Courtrai, France—July 10, 1917

The headache was with him most of the time, but had become less severe. Despite the caution of the doctors, Richthofen was growing impatient, felt there was no reason at all why he could not leave this place and return to his command. He had received visitors, but nothing like he expected, no great throng of reporters, no photographers. The reason was made clear to him in a note from General von Hoeppner. Dr. Kraske showed him the orders, that Richthofen was not allowed to leave until he was completely healed. But the orders also included instructions for the staff of the entire hospital. Very few people outside of the High Command knew he had been shot down, and even the soldiers who had come to his aid were ordered into absolute silence. On July 6, the official daily report from the Air Service claimed merely that an aeroplane had gone down over the front lines, the pilot surviving, though wounded. The British press made nothing of the incident, and von Hoeppner concluded that, amazingly, even the British gunner whose lucky shot had sent Richthofen's plane to the ground had no idea who his target had been. Richthofen grudgingly accepted the need for secrecy, that if the British knew he was out of action, the Royal Flying Corps might redouble their efforts in that part of the front. Von Hoeppner reassured him that once he had returned to duty, and could again lead JG-1 into combat, there would be no further need for secrecy. For the time being, the German people were to be kept as uninformed as the British.

She walked with him in the garden, a beautiful expanse of luxury behind the hospital, protected by a stout stone wall and one tall iron gate. The gate was manned by soldiers, the only reminder of the war. He had walked through the narrow pathways, prodded by her playful insistence on exercise. He chose the moment precisely, waiting until they were close to a small narrow bench, shaded by a single wide tree. It was then that he complained of being tired, and she had insisted that they sit, but it was not just rest he was seeking. His excuse had worked exactly as he had hoped. Despite the attention he was ordered to receive, she had no real idea of his fame, and he told her only that he flew aeroplanes. He had amazed himself that his shyness had not paralyzed him, even allowed himself one indulgence, a bit of pride. He had shown her his medal, the Order Pour le Mérite. It had been around his neck when he had crashed, had been returned to him by Dr. Kraske, and Richthofen had been surprised to see a brand-new ribbon. The explanation had been obvious: there was too much blood on the old one.

Richthofen saw no need to fill her head with any of the horror of the war, would not speak of the enemy or give her any details of his successes. He knew that she had seen her own horror, saw it every day, the young men who flowed through this hospital, an unending stream of blood and suffering and death. She spoke of it without emotion, surprising him at first, but of course, he thought, she cannot have emotion. None of them can. None of . . . us.

They had passed half the day under the canopy of the great tree, shaded from the piercing summer sun, engulfed by the soft fragrance of the garden around them. He had worn himself out with his words, something that he had rarely ever done, and he looked at her now with tired eyes.

She said, "It is time for you to rest. I should not have kept you out here for so long."

He held up his hand, said, "Nonsense. It was my wish." He made a small laugh. "Remember what Dr. Kraske said. I am to be indulged. Besides, you have given me a wonderful gift. You have listened patiently while I bored you with endless talk of flying."

"I assure you, Captain, I am not bored. I enjoy your enthusiasm. Your love for flying is, I admit, somewhat contagious."

"I do love it . . . perhaps more than anything in my life." He saw her wide smile, caught the hint now. "Would you . . . perhaps you would one day like to fly with me? I could show you so much that you would never imagine."

She put her hands on his, was still smiling, said, "I would enjoy that very much. But there are matters that must be tended to first. You must recuperate. And, the war."

Her smile was gone, and he could feel the dark weight settling on both of them.

"Yes, I know. But it cannot last much longer."

She shook her head. "I pray for that. But so many men come through here still. I read in the papers how the German soldier is the superior to every enemy, how we will triumph over the crimes committed against us. We receive notices here, to be posted on the walls, to raise the morale of the staff, that the kaiser is leading our armies in the destruction of the enemy." She stopped, turned her head away. "I should say nothing further."

He put a finger on her cheek, pulled her gently back to him. "Say what you think. I already know of such pronouncements. There are so many ridiculous claims. I am not even embarrassed anymore."

"So many officers have come here, many have survived terrible wounds. Many have not. But I hear so much talk of fighting, but there is . . . there is never news of *victories*. I suppose I do not understand much about war, but if we are winning, should we not be hearing of great battles?"

He had no answer for her, thought a moment, said, "I can only do my duty. If I win victories, then I am helping end the war in the only way I can."

She leaned close to him, surprised him with a quick kiss on his cheek. "Then perhaps one day, you can carry me above the clouds."

The sun was going down, and he felt the headache returning. He stood up slowly, and she responded, her hand moving quickly under his arm, helping him.

"I'm sorry. I'm feeling tired. Hurting a little. We should go back."

She held him by the arm, and they moved out onto the walkway. The air was warm and rich with the perfume of the flowers around them, and he looked at her, saw both the nurse and the young woman, felt her arm wrapped around his, supporting him, but more, holding him close to her. They walked slowly, Richthofen setting the pace, using the cane she had given him. It was black wood, etched the entire length with delicate carvings. He gripped the silver handle, helped himself along, wondered if she knew that he really didn't need it. She called it a crutch, something merely to assist him, but he knew it was far too ornate for a hospital issue, had to have been purchased by her. He thought of the silversmith in Berlin, the man who engraved the small cups for him. I should have him do something on the handle, perhaps, something about this place. Or her name. The thought embarrassed him, and for a moment, he could not look at her, wanted to draw his arm away. He fought the urge, thought, She wants nothing from you, asks nothing of you. How different from everyone else. All she knows of this war is what she sees of the men who come to this place. Her question settled into him. Where are the *victories*? It is a question a soldier cannot ask. I can only do what I am told.

They reached the entranceway, and she stopped, said, "I must leave you for a while. My mother has been ill. I must look in on her."

His hand gripped her arm, and he wanted to protest, no, stay here. She was looking into his eyes, and for a brief second he did not turn away, did not want to release her arm, did not want to be away from her at all. He looked down now, forced himself to draw back.

"Yes, of course. I hope she will be well."

She slipped her arm away from him, made the giggle again, that soft lovely sound. She seemed to know what he was thinking, said, "I will return tomorrow, in the afternoon. I am certain you will have visitors. You will not even miss me."

She began to move away from him, walking back out through the garden, turned, looked at him one more time, kissed the air, aiming it toward him. He felt suddenly awkward, childlike, didn't know what to do, smiled, watched as she moved past the guards at the gatehouse, then out, down the street, the last glimpse of her white dress. No, you are wrong. I already miss you.

He saw the guards, two men looking back at him, smiles of their own. He ignored them, felt his face flush red, a surge of pain in his head, moved through the entranceway. He met the familiar smells, walked through the rows of beds, felt the need for the cane. He helped himself along past wounded men, tried to ignore them, remembered now why he hated hospitals. He passed one man who made a sudden sound, deep and liquid, the smell suddenly worse. He kept moving, saw nurses coming quickly toward him, then past, a doctor emerging from a side room, hurrying past him as well. Richthofen did not look behind him, had seen this before, thought, Tomorrow, another empty bed. He moved down the row of men, some motioning to him, friendly gestures, men with lesser wounds, healing, who knew by now who their famous companion was.

He made his way closer to his bed, was surprised to see a uniform, the man sitting on the bed, then standing, moving toward him, the tall, clumsy enthusiasm of his brother.

"My God, Manfred. I didn't know what to think. Your bed was empty, and no one would tell me anything. I thought . . ."

He saw the teary warmth in Lothar's eyes, his brother gripping him by both shoulders.

"No, I'm fine. Out for a walk, that's all. They should have told you."

Lothar gripped his shoulders hard, smiled now, the fear in his eyes wiped away by the sight of his brother. The playfulness returned, as it always returned, and Lothar lowered his voice, glanced around, a part of the conspiracy now.

"They say nothing to anyone. We're all under orders, you know that. At the aerodrome, the reporters have been trying to get an interview with you for days. Bodenschatz is a positive terror, keeps them cowering in a corner, tells them you're far too busy killing the enemy. He told one man that if you didn't knock the enemy down today, you might go mad, could roll your Albatros right into the aerodrome and start shooting anyone that moved, starting with them!" He laughed, his voice growing louder with each word of his story. "How much longer, Manfred? When are you coming home?"

Richthofen motioned with his hand, *quieter*, said softly, "It's not my decision, you know that. General von Hoeppner has these people falling over themselves to keep me in good spirits. You should see all the food I'm eating."

"Not just von Hoeppner, Manfred. I hear Ludendorff himself is threatening to shoot anyone who even speaks your name!" Lothar laughed again, tapped him on the shoulder. "So, tell me about the girl."

Richthofen was surprised, had not spoken to anyone about Kate. "What do you mean?"

"The girl, Manfred! We're all dying to hear about her. Word

is, she's your own personal healer. A cure for every ailment, eh?"

He felt a fury burst inside of him, magnified by the pain now throbbing in his head. He stared hard at Lothar, said in a quiet hiss, "There is no girl. I have a nurse. Tell the men they will concentrate more on their duties, and less on what goes on here!"

Lothar seemed surprised by his anger, pulled himself back, his hands out in front of him. "Certainly, Manfred. My apologies. It's just . . . there are rumors."

"There are always rumors! Rumors will not help you shoot down the enemy!"

He saw the wounded look on his brother's face, felt guilty now for his anger. He knew his brother too well, nothing in Lothar's inquiries that went beyond playful curiosity. Lothar stayed back for a moment, seemed to drift into his own thoughts.

"Manfred, I need to speak to you. Is there a private space?"

Richthofen felt his own curiosity now, said, "We can go to the garden, back here. What is it? Is Mother all right?"

Lothar's mood had changed, the smiles gone, said, "Mother? Oh, yes, she is well. They are both well. I need to speak to you about another matter."

Richthofen had rarely seen such seriousness from his brother, moved toward the rear doorway, Lothar following, still limping from the aftereffects of his own wound. He led Lothar into the garden, but the daylight was gone, the only light a small glow from the guardhouse. Richthofen looked toward the one bench, under the wide tree, but stopped, could not take his brother to that special place.

"We are alone. What is it?"

Lothar shook his head, said, "I don't know what I should do. It has gone too far already." Richthofen waited, knew Lothar's energy would push his words out soon enough. "You know, Manfred, that the entire country believes I killed Albert Ball. The High Command, von Hoeppner, you should see the letters, all the congratulations! They are comparing me to you, saying I am the second Red Flyer, a great hero!"

"Praise can be difficult, Lothar. I have struggled to accept—"

"No, Manfred! You don't understand!" He glanced around, lowered his voice again. "We had a British flyer brought to the aerodrome, a prisoner. Surprisingly nice fellow. Captain . . . Poole, I think. He told me that Ball flew a biplane, usually an SE-5. He never flew anything else. Manfred, I was thirty yards away. The plane I shot down that day was a triplane, one of the Sopwiths. I have tried to get confirmation of the plane I sent down, something about the identity of the pilot, but the Air Service won't hear any more of it. What do I do? I don't feel right taking credit, especially not for someone like Ball. He was certainly brought down by one of our men who doesn't even know it."

Richthofen put a hand on Lothar's arm, said in a low voice, "Let me tell you about the *official word*. The official word is that I am flying today. The official word is that every German soldier is a better man than every other soldier in this war. The official word is that we do not retreat." He paused. "What you and I believe to be the truth matters to no one. If you want truth, just look in the newspapers. If it says in the headlines that you killed Captain Ball, then you will add Captain Ball to your list of victories. And if General Ludendorff offers you his congratulations, and the Air Service celebrates your heroism, then you say 'thank you,' and you drink their champagne."

July 11, 1917

He woke to the sounds of nurses, voices, a man moving close. He could hear the commotion around the bed beside him, and the voice was familiar now. He jerked awake, sat up, ignored the sudden headache, saw the man sitting on the edge of the next bed, a weak smile on the boyish face.

"Good morning, Captain. If you don't mind, I shall be your companion for a couple of days."

It was Kurt Wolff.

Richthofen saw the bandage on Wolff's hand and arm, a thick wad of white cloth, said, "What happened? An accident?"

Wolff shook his head, raised the left arm. "Perhaps that is a good word for it. Early this morning, I led the patrol up this

367

way, a little farther north. We had a call from the infantry, some British photographers were making a pest of themselves to the artillery. We got there pretty quickly, ran into a dozen DH-2s, hiding in the clouds above. They thought they had laid us a tight little trap, but I had suspected the observers weren't alone, and we were ready for them. It was a pretty mess for a while. I was signaling to my wingman, and apparently I held my hand precisely where an Englishman was shooting. It was not a fair fight, the bullet being somewhat harder. Two bullets actually. I have a nice clean hole through my hand, and a broken bone in my wrist. Since I'm fairly certain the Englishman was not aiming precisely for my hand, I would call it an accident."

Richthofen sat back, leaned against the pillow behind him. "Are you in pain? I can have the nurse . . ."

"It's all right. More blood than I was prepared to see. Made quite a mess of the Albatros. I offered my apologies to the orderlies, but they seemed more concerned about . . . this." Wolff looked at his hand, then at Richthofen, and he studied the bandage on Richthofen's head.

"A pretty sight yourself. Better than when I first saw you. You didn't know your own name. They were pulling bushes out of your face." He made a small laugh, but Richthofen saw more, something beyond the show of good humor. Wolff studied his own bed, pushed at a pillow with his uninjured hand. "Comfortable place. Don't expect to be here long. Should take advantage. I hear you've done all right on that account."

"What do you mean?" The words came out with more force than he had intended.

Wolff looked at him, said, "Sorry. Lothar said you didn't want to talk about it. It's none of my business."

He always felt affection for Wolff, had regarded him like some kind of hurt puppy that needs attention. That description would infuriate Wolff himself, the man earning every bit of the attention he was receiving for his flying skills, putting to rest any of the indiscreet comments about his injuries, or supposed frailty. At Squadron Eleven, Wolff's record of thirty-three kills had put a stop to the unflattering nicknames, and it had nothing to do with any order from Richthofen.

"I'm sorry, Kurt. It's a sensitive matter. I don't discuss my personal involvements."

Wolff managed a smile, nodded. "Personal. Very good, Captain. I am happy for you. It is a difficult thing, having such a situation. I must send a letter to Maria immediately, telling her of my injuries. She will cry for days." Richthofen knew that Wolff had a fiancée, the young man looking toward the end of the war as much as anyone in the squadron. "If I may ask, Captain, is it true she is a nurse here?"

Richthofen glanced around, was still nervous about revealing anything to prying ears. But he trusted Wolff, a young man who seemed much older than his years. Richthofen knew that anything he said would go no further.

"Her name is Kate. She should be here very soon. You will meet her."

Wolff sat back against the pillow, said nothing, watched two nurses walk by, seemed to wait for privacy. He cradled the injured arm in his right hand, rubbed one finger along the rough bandage.

Richthofen was growing uncomfortable now, something strange in Wolff's mood, something beyond the injury. "You have something to say, Kurt?"

Wolff stared straight ahead, said in a low voice, "I never thought you would be shot down."

Richthofen smiled, said, "Is that it? Thank you, Lieutenant, but I am fine. This thing on my head looks much worse than it should, I promise you. I will be back at Marcke soon. Once your hand has healed, we will make the British pay for their momentary good luck."

Wolff turned toward him, then looked down, stared at the floor between them. He shook his head. "Forgive me, Captain, but I am not so confident that it is luck. What is happening? In the spring, we were told we had destroyed most of the enemy's air strength, and now, the sky is black with their new fighters. Every day I see more enemy planes than I have ever seen before. The Air Service says the new Camel should be in the air very soon. We are seeing more and more of the SPADs, and the Nieuports are improving as well. And what of the Americans?

How long before we see new aeroplanes whose design we can only imagine?"

Richthofen looked around, saw no one close enough to hear, said quietly, "Kurt, we are still better flyers."

Wolff looked up at him now, a hard frown. " 'It is not the quality of the box, it is the man who sits in it.' Yes, I know, Captain, we have all memorized that. I believed it once. Before you were shot down."

"You will feel better when your hand has healed." Richthofen didn't know what else to say, had never seen Wolff so discouraged.

Wolff ignored his words, said, "Do you believe God watches over us?"

Richthofen had rarely discussed his religion with anyone, thought a moment. "I don't know. I would like to believe so."

"I believed so. I truly believed that all of Germany was in His favor. I have been taught all my life that His Imperial Majesty is anointed by God Himself, that God's wisdom governs this nation and all who serve her. Manfred, did we truly believe the Albatros was invincible? How many good pilots are gone? *You* were nearly gone. There is no end to this. You and I will both return to duty, we will both fly again, and face the enemy again. What will happen next time? How many more times can we ask for God's protection?"

Richthofen tried to summon anger, to put an end to Wolff's destructive mood. But Wolff was looking at him, the man's sad eyes searching him for answers.

"Manfred, if you marry this girl . . . are you prepared for her to be a widow?"

Richthofen felt punched by the words, the anger coming more easily now. "Enough! First my brother, now you!" He stood up, tried to ignore the sudden dizziness, moved to the end of the bed, could see faces turning toward him. He fought to calm himself, to hold his temper. He paced a few steps, sat down again. He kept his words low, saw the dark despair in Wolff's eyes.

"Kurt, we cannot ask such questions. We can only do what we are told. We are flyers. We have one duty, and we will

370

continue to serve the High Command as best we can." He put a hand on Wolff's shoulder. "What else can we do?"

Wolff nodded, looked down again, said, "I just never thought . . . so many of us would have to die."

There was commotion at the far end of the room, voices at the door, and he heard her calling out: "I am sorry to be so late!"

Richthofen felt her words slicing him like cold steel. She was there now, in perfectly pressed white, a smile that brought the sun inside. He stood, felt weakness in his legs, and she was closer now, lowered her voice, "You have a new friend! I am jealous!" He did not respond, and her smile vanished. She took his arm, said, "Are you all right?"

He eased away from her, said, "Fine, yes. Sorry, I stood up too quickly." He looked at her again, saw the dark concern, tried to laugh, to bring her smile back. "Yes, this is my friend, Lieutenant Kurt Wolff. He had a rather unlucky time of it this morning."

"So I see. I am pleased to meet you, Mr. Wolff."

Wolff stood as well, made a short bow, motioned with his bandaged arm. "I did not have my captain there to protect me."

"Lieutenant, this is my nurse, Miss Otersdorf."

Wolff made another bow. "The pleasure is mine, Miss Otersdorf."

They all stood for a silent awkward moment, and Wolff said, "I'm sorry, but may I have something to drink? Water?"

Kate moved closer to him, the softness in her face now focused only on her job. "Certainly. Are you in pain? Can I get you anything else?"

"No, thank you. Just water."

She moved quickly away, gave a sharp command to an orderly, a soft flurry of white disappearing through a far doorway. Wolff sat again, looked up at Richthofen, said, "She is very special."

He nodded a reply, had no words. Across the room, she reappeared, marching toward them with prim efficiency, followed by an orderly with a tray of water glasses, and one large pitcher. He watched her come closer, saw her smiling at him again, and he felt a sharp stab of pain. He could not

371

look at her, turned slowly away, Wolff's words digging into him, twisting and burning, and the answer now clear, the words echoing in his mind. Am I prepared to make her a widow? He sat down, stared ahead through the wetness in his eyes. No.

23

RICHTHOFEN

It began as so many of the grand battles had begun, a massive display of artillery, the British guns in a ten-mile front across the Ypres salient launching more than four million shells against the German defensive positions. It was the third time in three years a great assault had taken place on this same muddy landscape, the third time a massive wave of foot soldiers would rise up and out of their trenches to throw themselves at the enemy's strength. This time the plan had come from British field marshal Douglas Haig, who had loudly proclaimed that the British success at Messines was only the first volley of his great campaign to end the war on British terms. Haig's strategy had been bitterly opposed by his own government, especially Prime Minister David Lloyd George, who insisted that Haig had squandered his advantage, had allowed the best weather of the year to pass by. But Haig's unbridled enthusiasm had quieted his critics, and on July 31, twelve British divisions, nearly one hundred fifty thousand men, pushed their way across the muddy no-man's-land of Flanders. Whether or not the British soldiers shared their commander's optimism, they were soon faced with a stunning dose of reality. The artillery barrage that had preceded their assault was designed to demoralize the spirit of the German defenders, or eliminate them altogether. Instead, the shelling had so churned and blasted the water-logged landscape that a swift attack by men on foot had become impossible. But there was another problem as well. Haig's plan to blast a breakthrough in the German fortifications did not allow for the one obstacle that neither side could control. Within hours after the British push had begun, the rains came. The prime minister's predictions about the weather proved to be tragically accurate. From the shelter of their concrete bunkers, the German defenders faced an enemy whose attack simply drove itself deeper into the softening ground, Haig's grand assault drowning itself in a great ocean of mud. Those British troops who could move at all finally confronted their objectives, but the numbers were too few, and the machine guns of the German defenders were waiting for them. In a matter of days, Haig's great attack was at a standstill.

Whether driven by desperation, or the urgent need to give his country another victory, Haig ordered his soldiers not to retreat. The Tommies could only gather themselves into any shelter they could manage and wait for more orders. After two miserable weeks the skies began to clear, but instead of allowing his men to retreat, to refit and resupply, Haig ordered the assault to resume. With the new British tanks wallowing uselessly in the mud, the British supported their desperate troops with the only other offensive weapon they could muster. The new Sopwith Camel was finally reaching the front lines, and alongside the new plane, the British threw every available aircraft into the fight, the only means available to hold back what every British soldier but Haig presumed to be a certain German counterattack.

Richthofen had returned to command of JG-1 on July 25, finally winning his ongoing fight with von Hoeppner to allow him to return to duty. He still wore the bandage, would still have to make visits to St. Nicholas Hospital, the doctors still needing to examine and probe and redress the wound.

The relief at leaving the hospital had been tempered by his good-bye to his nurse. For the last few days he spent at St. Nicholas, his thoughts had turned to flying again. It was the excuse he gave himself, the explanation in his own mind why he had detached himself from her. But he could not escape the gnawing guilt, made worse when she did not respond. She seemed to accept his change of heart without any emotion at all. Their walks ceased, her attention to him confined to the duty of changing his bandage. The nurse had replaced the woman, and Kate had resumed her duties without ever asking him why he had suddenly pulled away. Despite the guilt, it was a relief to him, but a curiosity as well. When the day came for his farewells, he was surrounded by a friendly gathering of patients and doctors, and those soldiers who could leave their beds. She was there as well, simply a part of the crowd. He had hoped for the chance to talk to her, not sure what kind of good-bye he should offer her. He had thought of his invitation to take her flying, the scene too unreal in his mind now. But if he survived this war, there could still be time, his mind telling him that it was the right thing to do, that she might still accept. It was a fantasy he kept buried deep inside, that there might still be something for them to explore, some way to restart what had begun so unwisely in the hospital. But there was to be no private good-bye, the crowd capturing him, officers and pilots, and the car waiting to take him back to Marcke. At the final moment, he had searched the crowd for her, but she was gone, and so the invitation would not be made. As he rode back to JG-1, he scolded himself for his foolishness, a schoolboy's infatuation. He carried the doctor's instructions, knew he would return within days for another examination. But he wondered if Kate would even be there, and if she was, if she would even remember his name.

Marcke, Belgium—August 16, 1917

Richthofen had suffered through the rain with the rest of the squadron, most of them passing each miserable day poring over the tidbits of news from the front at Ypres. The High Command sent regular reports to each aerodrome, but Richthofen had only glanced at them, had become too accustomed to the grandiose claims of certain German victory. After two weeks, the skies were finally clearing, and the reports had changed, a steady flow that came not from headquarters, but from the infantry observers, urgent requests for JG-1 to confront the great squadrons of British planes pouring up into the sky. The other pilots had looked to him, had wondered when

Richthofen would finally return to his Albatros. As the day had dawned, the clouds had seemed to break apart, and Richthofen had felt the old energy, decided that, finally, it was time for him to fly.

He still wore the bandage, caressed gently by the leather helmet, had climbed into the red plane with an odd twinge of fear he had not felt since his first flight. He taxied the Albatros into the open field, four other planes following him, the routine so familiar to all of them. He knew they were all watching him, waiting for the final hand signal that would tell each man to pour the fuel into each motor, pulling them through the short grass until each plane lifted itself slowly into the warm morning breeze. But he sat for a long moment, feeling the wind from the prop against his face, stared across the open ground aware of a small tremble in his hand. He fought it by clenching both fists, furious voices shouting in his head: What is wrong with you? It angered him, the show of hesitation, something the rest of them could not see. But finally the instinct took over, the hand signal given, and now, they were following him up past the thick patches of gray and white, the last remnants of the great storms.

He had seen the concern in their faces, the words none of them would say to him, that a pilot must fly often to keep his skills from rusting. It had bothered him every day in the hospital, and then every day since. But the fear was gone now, swept out of him with the stiff blast of air that held him tightly in his seat. The rush of wind was invigorating, and he glanced out toward the others, saw all faces watching him. He shot his fist into the air, shook it, the sign all of them would understand. He was back in the sky.

The ground beneath them was a swarm of activity, great lines of troops in motion, trucks and trains, all the energy to support the massive fight that was beginning again in front of them. He glanced downward, the patterns and movement meaningless to him. He had not read the latest reports, knew nothing of what was happening on the ground. He stared ahead through gaps in the clouds, thought of Wolff, returning from the hospital only days before, his wounds healing as well. Wolff's dark mood had tempered, the young man pushing Richthofen hard for

376

permission to lead Squadron Eleven again. Wolff still joked of vengeance against British luck, the other pilots sharing a good-natured toast to avenging their leader's misfortune. But Richthofen did not share the good humor, had spent long hours reliving his own experience, trying to recall every moment that could have gone differently. He did not dwell on the crash or his wounds, that he could easily have died. What ripped into his mind was that his death could have come at the hands of an inexperienced gunner who had simply gotten lucky. His mind had taken him back to his pursuit of the two-seater, the image of the observer who had stupidly fired at him from too far away. Richthofen had wondered about the man's name, thought, He would have been an undeserving hero, and I would have died for no other reason than bad luck. There is no worse fate.

The clouds began to slide behind them, and he could see the terrain more clearly now, a vast sea of brown, flecked by plumes of smoke, small fires. But there was more, and he focused to the front, a formation of planes moving parallel to the fighting below, artillery observers perhaps. He could see another formation just behind them, thought, Yes, that would be their escorts. The men on either side of him were watching him, had seen what he had seen, and he gave the signal, *dive*, knew that each man would find his target. He nosed the Albatros down, the British planes beginning to twist and maneuver, their observers already aware of what was to come. As he closed the distance between them, he could see that the enemy fighters were French Nieuports, single-seaters, the entire formation now turning away. They clearly did not want a confrontation, were instead seeking an escape. He saw one plane dropping lower, offering protection to the slower observers, and Richthofen moved in behind the Nieuport's tail, the fast dive of the Albatros bringing him nearly within range. The Nieuport suddenly banked hard, trying to maneuver away from him, and Richthofen matched the move, smiled, felt the calm resolve, the familiar touch of the trigger, the Nieuport now squarely in front of him. The Maxims came alive, the Nieuport splintering, a direct hit, the plane suddenly spinning downward. He pushed the Albatros into a dive, followed, would make sure, knew the British trick of feigning a spin. But the Nieuport was tumbling now, more pieces breaking off, and he eased back on the stick, circled, watched as the Nieuport dove hard into the ground.

He pulled the Albatros back into a climb, looked for the others, could see the enemy planes far to the east, making good their escape. He saw flecks of red, all four of the Albatroses, felt a wave of relief. We have survived. They began to gather, moving toward him, regrouping for the trip home. There were fists in the air, those who had seen his success, and he smiled. Yes, it seems all is well. They were close now, and he made the signal, turning them toward Marcke, suddenly felt a cold stirring in his stomach. His eyes began to blur, and he put a hand on the goggles, blinked hard, his head now swimming with dizziness. He gripped the stick, closed his eyes for a moment, the dizziness passing, but the nausea was growing stronger. He took a long deep breath, stared out past the prop, thought, This should not be. Take control!

He clamped his anger tightly around his sickness, passed the long minutes in a cascade of distracting thoughts, none of them effective. At last he could see the aerodrome, nosed the Albatros straight in, did not make the usual slow circle. The plane bounced hard, and he cut the motor. He held the nose up, slowed to a stop. The other planes were landing behind him, and he ignored them, saw the mechanics swarming out, the usual routine. He pulled himself up, swung his legs over the side of the plane, heard a voice, "Captain! The call just came in! A confirmation from the infantry! Your kill . . . number fifty-eight!"

Richthofen stared at the ground, a spinning blur, felt a cold fury, anger at his own weakness. He held tightly to the side of the plane, waited for his eyes to focus, the nausea twisting him inside. The mechanics were there now, asking the usual questions, but he ignored them, dropped to the ground, fought to hold himself upright. The nausea began to pass, replaced by a heavy throbbing in his head. Men were talking all around him, and he still said nothing, began to walk slowly back to the hangar, the wound burning into his brain. He thought of the hospital, the soft bed. Was it too soon? The altitude? How much time will it take, after all?

Wolff was there now, dressed in his flight suit, preparing to lead the second squad.

"Good shooting! What did I say about British luck?" Richthofen stopped, saw Wolff's foolish grin disappear. "Are you all right?"

Richthofen put a hand on Wolff's shoulder, felt weakness in his legs, Wolff holding him up now. They were moving again, toward his office, and Richthofen said, "If I am to survive, Kurt, I must become healthy again. It will not have anything to do with luck."

24

LUFBERY

Senard, France—September 1917

They were as close to Verdun now as they had ever been, ordered to the airfield to support a massive new French assault around the fortress city. The mission for the pilots was routine, escorting the increasing numbers of bombers, targeting German defensive lines and supply dumps, opening the door for General Pétain's all-out surge to remove the enemy from the Verdun sector.

In the North, around Ypres, the British were still struggling against both the stout German resistance and the soaking misery of the autumn rains. At Verdun there had been rain as well, but it was not as pervasive, and when the clouds parted, the pilots found they could fly at least three full missions per day. It was the most exhausted any of them had been.

The replacements had continued to fill the ranks of the escadrille, and none had been more anticipated than the man who would replace DeLaage. His name was Antoine Arnoux de Maison-Rouge, and from his first day's service as Captain Thenault's second in command, Lufbery despised him. Maison-Rouge was a tall, angular man, whose every movement betrayed the nervous twitching energy of a frightened spider. While his appearance alone stood him in stark contrast to the pleasant congeniality of DeLaage, it was Maison-Rouge's attitude that alienated him from the entire squadron. He regarded Americans in general, and these pilots in particular, as barbaric savages. But the Aeronautique Militaire had based their decision on Maison-Rouge's capabilities as a pilot, and Thenault had no choice but to accept the lieutenant as his executive officer. Whether the Americans would accept him was another matter entirely.

The squadron roster had grown to twenty-two active pilots, and their continuing success over their German rivals ensured that the Aeronautique Militaire would keep them supplied with a sufficient number of aircraft. Though Thaw and Lufbery continued to be respected as the squadron's old veterans, Lufbery was no longer the oldest member of the group. That honor now fell to Walter Lovell, another New Englander, a Harvard man who had come to the escadrille by the familiar route of Dr. Gros' American Ambulance Service. But Lovell, and the others who had added their names to the squadron's roster, understood that in the Lafayette Escadrille, if you wanted to know how to combat the enemy, you spent time in the air with Raoul Lufbery.

Billy Mitchell had an ally in his efforts to bring the escadrille's pilots into the American air arm. The squadron's founder, Dr. Gros, had championed the move, using his influence with the men to ease their uncertainty about what could certainly become a dramatic change in their routine. Gros had made himself an example, had signed up in the new American Air Service, was commissioned a major, surprising everyone who had thought an experienced doctor would fit more ably into the medical corps. Like Mitchell, Gros had made his own speeches to the pilots, encouraging them to make the change. The pilots had met the proposal with enthusiasm, bolstered not only by Gros' optimism, but their shared sense of patriotism as well. But as the weeks dragged on, the frustrations mounted. Despite the energy put forward by Mitchell, and despite General Pershing's constant pleas to Washington, no one across the Atlantic seemed to understand how to create an air force. Worse, to the pilots of the Lafayette Escadrille, it seemed that no one in Washington considered their experience and abilities to have any value at all.

He wiped his hands on a soft rag, moved out toward the mouth of the hangar, was surprised to see Parsons, supervising some work on the wing of his SPAD. Lufbery moved that way, said, "A problem?"

Parsons leaned close to the wing, seemed not to hear him, was focused on the work of the mechanic.

381

"Tighten it good. Don't need the damned thing blowing away."

The mechanic stepped back, said, "It's tight. The wire will hold, Mr. Parsons. Anything else?"

Parsons seemed genuinely excited, said, "Thank you, Henriot. No, that's very good."

Lufbery was curious now, moved around the end of the wing, saw a black mass attached to one of the SPAD's wing struts. "What the hell is that?"

"That, my dear Luf, is . . . um . . . well, he doesn't have a name. I'll think of one. It's my talisman."

"Looks like a stuffed cat."

"Precisely. Vicious little monster. Look at the claws. He's facing forward, hissing his venom in the direction of the enemy."

Lufbery leaned close, saw the cat was made of black velvet, its back arched upward, the mouth open in a snarling growl. "A toy?"

Parsons seemed to puff up. "Hardly! I told you: my talisman. Renée is quite certain this will change my luck."

"Renée?"

"Oh, you haven't met her. My new friend in Paris. She is quite a talisman herself. Something mystical about her. She claims to be the expert in this sort of thing, and she guarantees this will work. I have no reason to doubt her. She's already shown to be an expert in quite a few . . . other things."

Lufbery held tight to his smile, said, "Is this the same woman who insisted you wear her stockings?"

Parsons looked at him with a frown, seemed annoyed by Lufbery's lack of clarity. "Of course not. That was Marie. And just to be clear, I wear her stocking on my *head*, under my helmet. I'd rather avoid any confusion on that point. Actually keeps my ears warm. You should try it."

"Right. I forgot. And the medals? How many good-luck charms do you require?"

"Now you know damned well I'm not the only one who does that. I didn't originate the custom, I just take advantage of it. Every girl I've ever met here gives me some sort of little medallion. Hell, I've run out of room on my neck chain. Put a bunch on my ID bracelet now. There seems to be a common theme. Look here." He held up his arm, and Lufbery saw a half dozen small silver and bronze discs dangling from Parsons' wrist. "Nearly all of these are Saint Elijah, the Patron Saint of Aviators, so I'm told. Rode triumphantly into heaven in a chariot of fire. Seems rather appropriate."

Lufbery didn't respond, saw the smile fade from Parsons' face.

"Sorry, Luf. That's not funny."

Lufbery moved toward the wing again, examined the cat.

Parsons seemed pleased to change the subject. "So, Renée tells me as long as I have him with me, I can't be hurt."

"How do you know it's a *him*?"

Parsons thought a moment. "I figured it has to be. If the Boche thought it was a female, they'd probably just laugh."

September 4, 1917

Lufbery heard the motor, wiped the grease from his hands, stepped out into the cool dusk. The single SPAD dropped rapidly down, a hot landing, bounced once, then again, and Lufbery said aloud, "Slow down. Easy, now."

The plane made a slow circle in the grass, rolled toward him, the motor quieting, the prop jerking to a stop. The plane was still rolling slightly, and the pilot was up already, jumped to the ground, tore at his goggles, ran at Lufbery, one hand in the air. It was Parsons.

"I got him! Big bastard! Blew him to hell!"

He stopped in front of Lufbery, breathing heavily, put both hands on Lufbery's shoulders.

"Big two-seater. Right in front of me. Not even thirty yards. Just fell apart, busted to pieces right in front of me!"

Lufbery smiled, felt Parsons' hands gripping him hard. Lufbery said, "I guess it worked."

Parsons was nodding, still holding the wide smile, then seemed confused, said, "What worked?"

Lufbery pointed out toward the SPAD, the small black mass wired to the wing. "Your talisman."

Parsons turned, let out a yell, jumped, both fists high. "Yessir! It worked! Hee-hee!"

Lufbery saw others coming out, responding to Parsons' infectious joy. There was another sound, the ringing of the telephone, and Lufbery heard a new shout, one of the mechanics running out, the words that Parsons still needed to hear. Lufbery already knew what the message would be, knew that when a man's time came, all the signs would be with him. Talisman or not, Parsons had his first confirmation.

Lufbery heard voices, saw Thenault moving into the hangar, was surprised to see Dr. Gros as well. The two men were talking, and Lufbery could tell the conversation was not pleasant. He moved that way, and Thenault looked past him, said, "How many pilots are here? Five in the air, right?"

Lufbery nodded.

"Plus two. Lieutenant Maison-Rouge is out with Campbell, Peterson, Bridgman, and Marr. Been gone about two hours. Lovell and Thaw just went up a half hour ago." He nodded a silent greeting toward Gros.

Gros said, "How are you, Luf? Got your twelfth confirmation, eh?"

"So they tell me."

Gros looked down, had run out of small talk, and Lufbery could feel the awkwardness, said, "I didn't mean to interrupt. I have some work to do over here—"

Thenault held up a hand, said, "No. Does not matter. I will tell them all as they come in. We have gotten word from your Air Service. There is still no decision on the issue of rank."

Gros put his hands on his hips, seemed to stare down at Lufbery's feet. He was nearly fifty, a tight-faced man, with sharp dark eyes. After a long silent moment, Gros said, "Clerks and secretaries. The whole damned army." He looked at Lufbery now. "The War Department asked Mitchell for his recommendations. Pershing told him to be aggressive, so Mitchell tells them that we should commit twenty thousand aeroplanes to this war, that we should deliver five thousand here by next spring. They just stroked their chins and said, Oh, well, that sounds very good indeed. All the while he knows that if we can produce three hundred, we'll exceed our most optimistic expectations. I give him credit for audacity. Apparently, he's learning the way this game is played. Ask for too much, then take what you can get." He paused, and Lufbery felt Parsons standing beside him. Gros continued, "We've been talking to the French about using their motor designs. The British as well. We propose to supply the raw materials, they supply the specifics, allow us to use the existing manufacturing plants. Sounds perfectly reasonable, eh? We have the Rolls-Royce, Clerget, Bentley, LeRhone, the Hispano-Suizas in these SPADs, plenty to adapt to our purposes. Any one is proven reliable enough. But no. Someone in Washington is convinced that Americans should fly only American motors. Mind you, we don't actually have one yet, beyond what some dreamer in the War Department has sketched on paper. They've even given it a name, the Liberty, someone in Washington telling Mitchell that we'll have no less than thirty-five thousand of them in no time at all. All we need is for Woodrow Wilson to wave his magic staff, and we'll have enough aeroplanes to darken the skies over Germany. Poor Mitchell. I'm surprised he hasn't shot someone by now." Gros caught himself. "I apologize. I didn't come here to spew out my frustration. The real reason for my visit concerns you pilots. Captain Thenault will pass this along to everyone. I am sorry to say that the Air Service is still not convinced that the Americans presently flying in France should receive any kind of automatic rank in the United States Army. So, of course, that means we don't know if you're going to be paid or not."

Lufbery said, "It also means we don't know who's going to be telling us what to do."

Gros nodded, stared at the ground. "I don't know what else to say. The way things stand now, if any of you transfer to the Air Service, you might very well be under the command of some desk sergeant who's never seen an aeroplane." He looked at Lufbery again. "I'm doing my best. Mitchell, General Kenly too. I never thought this would be such a battle. Logic and intelligence matters so little to those people in Washington. I can't even imagine all the other stupidity General Pershing is faced with."

The sound echoed into the hangar, and Lufbery heard a voice, one of the mechanics.

"They're coming in. All five."

Lufbery let out a breath, saw the same relief on Thenault's face, the same emotion they felt every time a full patrol returned.

They began to move outside and Parsons said, "What the hell?"

Lufbery moved out quickly, looked up as the planes passed over the hangar, beginning their landing formation.

Thenault was beside him, pointed up, said, "What the hell's he doing?"

As the planes circled toward the open end of the field, Lufbery could see something unusual in the formation. Two of the SPADs were nearly stacked together, one on top of the other. The top plane seemed to tilt and bounce above the other, and Thenault said, "The one below . . . is Maison-Rouge. What the hell?"

The mechanics had come out now, more men gathering, and Lufbery stared up at the odd spectacle, thought, Whoever that jackass is, he's playing with Maison-Rouge. He's playing with him.

Thenault had binoculars now, seemed to share Lufbery's thoughts, said, "It's Campbell. That insane bastard. He's going to kill them both."

Parsons was close to Lufbery again, said, "It has to be Campbell. That stupid son of a bitch. He nearly chopped my tail off last week, flew right up my ass, put his prop inches away, just to get a laugh. He gives me the creeping jitters."

Andrew Courtney Campbell had been with the squadron since the spring, had established himself firmly as the court jester of the escadrille. But he was far more than a source of amusement. He had already destroyed several aircraft, some by surviving near-certain catastrophe at the hands of the Germans, a wave of good fortune that had only bolstered Campbell's recklessness. Lufbery had tried to stay clear of him, had seen enough of those men who believed themselves invincible. While Campbell had shown he could be a capable fighter, he fancied himself a daredevil, would often take ridiculous chances just to impress the others with a reckless show of bravado. Some of the younger pilots spoke of him with reverential awe. But the veterans were in agreement with Lufbery. The escadrille had no room for what Parsons called a *wild man*.

Lufbery stared at the two planes, could see the lower one locked in place, no effort to break away. Of course, he thought, Maison-Rouge is terrified. If he moves in any direction, they'll probably collide. That's right. Keep calm. Let Campbell do whatever stupid thing he's going to do. Then when he lands, kick his ass.

The other three planes were still circling, the pilots watching the spectacle just like the men on the ground. The top plane was bouncing up and down, each time closer to Maison-Rouge's top wing, flirting with the collision.

Suddenly Thenault let out a shout. "He hit him! His wheels are into the wing! Oh, God, they're tangled!"

Lufbery could see the planes making a slow turn, locked together, the men around him shouting out. The futility settled over them now, painful memories of DeLaage, the men helpless to do anything but watch the awful spectacle. The shouts became muted now, small prayers, men cursing at Campbell, urging him to pull himself free.

The planes were slipping lower, not more than a couple hundred feet above the field, and Thenault shouted, "Call the ambulance! Get water! They could come down anywhere!"

No one responded, the men frozen, all eyes fixed on the two planes. Lufbery could see Maison-Rouge waving at Campbell, gesturing for him to pull up. After another turn toward the hangar, Lufbery heard the hard revving of a motor, and suddenly Campbell's plane jerked up, the landing gear ripping out of the wing of the plane beneath him. The two planes were apart now, Maison-Rouge turning, dropping quickly, the fabric on the plane's wing flapping wildly. He brought the SPAD down with a hard bounce, and the men cheered, began to move forward, but stopped, held back by the approach of the rest of the patrol. They came in one by one, each one revving up close to the hangar, then abruptly shutting down their motors. Now

Campbell came in, seemed to hover over the length of the field, then revved again, was up, another circle around the landing area, one low swoop above the hangar, the final act of his show. The men were gathering around Maison-Rouge, and Lufbery saw him climbing out of the SPAD, screaming something in French, his goggles off, his face ghostly white. Campbell was coming in low again, brought the SPAD down this time, taxied farther out from the hangar, shut down his motor. He seemed to take his time and Thenault shouted out, "Everyone. Stand back!"

He moved in a slow deliberate march toward Campbell's plane, and Lufbery felt his own pulsing anger, looked again at the lieutenant, Maison-Rouge, sitting on the ground, his hands shaking in a pathetic quiver. Thenault reached Campbell's plane and was speaking to him, but Lufbery could hear nothing; there was no volume to Thenault's words. Campbell climbed down from his plane, responding to Thenault with a wide beaming smile. As he hit the ground, Thenault had Campbell by the arm, seemed to escort him away, the two men moving together out past the hangar. Campbell turned, waved back toward all of them, gleefully ignoring Thenault's lecture. They were past the hangar now, out of sight, and Lufbery felt his insides twisting up, half expected to hear a gunshot from beyond the hangar, thought, If it was me, I'd break his bones first. Then I'd shoot him.

If there had been one faint glow of a silver lining to Courtney Campbell's terrifying harassment of Lieutenant Maison-Rouge, it came quickly. Within a few days, Maison-Rouge's nervous tics and short-tempered disagreements with the Americans gave way to a complete inability to face the stress of flying into combat. Thenault ordered the man to begin a recuperative leave, and until a replacement was named, the escadrille would again be without a second in command.

It infuriated Lufbery that Campbell was allowed to continue flying, and the word had passed through the squadron that Thenault's hands had been tied; the captain was powerless to discipline the man beyond the usual stern lecture. To the dismay of Lufbery and everyone in the squadron, Campbell's exploits and near-death adventures had made him something of a celebrated hero in America, the man putting a smiling boyish face on the growing legend of the Lafayette Escadrille. Though his family was wealthy, Lufbery realized that there was more than financial influence at work here. In the battle that was raging through the War Department, men with the high visibility of Courtney Campbell could be an asset to the efforts being made to gain legitimacy for the American pilots. Lufbery swallowed the reality like a lump of hard clay, and could respond only by refusing to fly with the man. But Lufbery's impatience was not tested for long. Not long after Campbell had terrorized Maison-Rouge, the jester's luck finally ran out.

The word had come back to the squadron from Henry Jones, a young Pennsylvanian who had gone out with Campbell on a two-man patrol. Jones' SPAD had already taken a beating, his plane badly damaged by their confrontation with a formation of two-seaters. As Jones limped away from the fight, Campbell chose instead to lunge into the fray. Within seconds, Jones had seen Campbell's SPAD swirling downward in a hail of bullets from the German guns. There was no word yet of the exact whereabouts of Campbell's plane, the only certainty was that he had gone down far into German territory. Unless the Germans were cooperative, there would be no recovery of the *wild man*'s remains. Lufbery had taken word of Campbell's death with the same stoicism he had shown so many of the others. It was the common experience of the veterans now, another name erased from the roll, another replacement certain to fill his place. But Campbell's death had been a lesson that Lufbery already carried inside of him: that arrogant confidence did not mean victories, that no matter the man's bravado or his disregard for fate, none of them could stare at death for very long without reaping the ultimate reward.

Word had come from Dr. Gros. The fledgling American Air Service had finally, reluctantly, agreed that any American pilot with combat experience could transfer from the French Escadrilles and receive a commission as a lieutenant in the

United States Army. The one condition was that every man who applied had to undergo, and pass, a rigorous physical examination.

The doctors arrived in a bulky black limousine, a hulking quartet of black wool suits, descending on the airfield like a flock of gloomy crows. They were Americans, stern-faced men who had been forced to accept that their service to the army might actually include some duty outside the pleasantries of the brightly lit headquarters of Paris. The one bit of hopefulness for the pilots was that Dr. Gros was among them, trying desperately to force a lighthearted mood on the other three, men whose involvement in the war thus far had been as vacationers who kept as far away from actual duty as their special skills would allow.

The pilots had been examined singly, each man poked and prodded and bled, offering up all variety of fluid and specimen, ordered to demonstrate physical dexterity as well as acuity of sight, sound, and smell. As each pilot exited the examination, the humiliation of his body and spirit could be made well again only by a lengthy visit to the bar. It was an opportunity no one passed by.

Lufbery waited for Thaw, expected some sort of joke, something to cut through the grumbling that filled the darkened room. The bottles had been drained, and replaced, something that had once been commonplace, but now had become a gesture of rebelliousness, especially to the veterans. There had been an urgent plea from their beloved and invaluable matriarch Madame Vanderbilt, whose husband was responsible for much of the escadrille's financial support. The good Mrs. Vanderbilt had been appalled that some newspapers in America were making note of the particular talent the American pilots had shown for absorbing alcohol, some suggesting that the men were more often confronting the enemy with a trigger in one hand and a flask of brandy in the other. To address this obvious slander, Mrs. Vanderbilt had asked them to abstain from the numbing necessities of drink. The pilots had done the proper thing. They removed all liquor from their residences at the airfield, and made a loan to a French squadron stationed nearby, with the express understanding that the French facilities were to be available to all. The French had agreed, made more willing by the bribe of several cases of Scotch that Thaw had secured in Paris. The arrangement had satisfied everyone. But with the indignities suffered by the men during the examinations, all concerns for the fragile feelings of Mrs. Vanderbilt had been temporarily set aside.

The talk was quiet, each man more focused on the glass in his hand. Lufbery heard a door close, the same sound that preceded each man's arrival at the bar. The doctors had invaded the kitchen of the large house, and when Lufbery's turn had come, he understood why. With a kitchen came a sink, and glasses, and the torturously hard surface of a table, blessedly shielded with a cotton sheet. The latest man to be released was Lovell, and Lufbery watched him move purposefully to the bar, retrieving a full glass, already set out by the diligence of the bartender.

Lovell turned, saw Lufbery, said, "Well, did they tell you too?"

He shook his head. "They didn't tell me anything. Said just wait for the results."

"Well, they sure as hell told me. I'm too old. Thirty-two is too old to be a pilot. I shouldn't even have bothered, they said. Just like that. Jackasses."

Lufbery had liked Lovell from his first days in the squadron, and it had nothing to do with the man's age. Like Parsons, Lovell had the instincts to be a good pilot; he was a man who would not panic under pressure.

Lovell drained the glass, handed it to the bartender, said, "Think there's any difference between thirty-one and thirty-two? If they haven't told you yet, they will."

The others had listened to Lovell in silence, faces turning to Lufbery now.

He didn't know what to say, had no encouraging words, thought a moment, said, "I had trouble walking backward. That line on the floor. I kept turning to look at it."

He had thought it funny at first, the doctors asking him to perform the ridiculous act as some sort of joke to relax him. But their expressions had not changed, and even Gros had seemed concerned. He looked around the dimly lit room, saw no one smiling. From a chair in the corner, he heard the low voice of Henry Jones.

"They said I have flat feet. Thought the examination was going to end right then. Dr. Gros convinced them to keep going."

Carl Dolan spoke now, another of the younger men, and the only one among them who didn't seem to enjoy alcohol. "They say I have a bad throat. Dr. Gros said my tonsils need to come out. I didn't know what tonsils were until they explained it."

Lufbery could feel the blanket of misery in the room, said, "It can't be as bad as they're trying to make it. Hell, everybody's got something wrong with 'em."

Thaw was there now, filled the doorway, said, "You're right, Luf. Like me, for instance. I'm blind. Well, almost. Can't see for crap out of one eye. Hell, it never bothered me, but sweet Mother Mary, you shoulda seen their faces. Even Gros was upset. I thought he was gonna cry." Thaw looked around the room. "Who's left? Anybody they haven't humiliated yet?"

Lufbery shook his head. "You were the last."

Thenault had given each man a letter, sealed inside an envelope that carried the insignia of the American Medical Service. Some of the men had gathered, would share the experience, easing the suspense by comparing their own results with everyone else.

Thaw examined his, said, "Anybody open theirs yet?" Heads were shaking, and Thaw laughed, said, "Well, hell, it's not as bad as a farewell letter from your sweetheart."

He ripped open his envelope, slid the paper out, glanced at Lufbery, made a slow ceremony out of unfolding it. He read, made a grunt, said, "Well, gentlemen, it's your war now. Seems I'm not fit to fly."

The others began to examine their own letters, voices rising around the room. Lufbery opened his, saw the words he had expected: ". . . *deemed unfit for duty in the American Air Service*."

He looked around the room, saw men staring at the words on

the paper, said, "Anybody here make it?" He saw the faces of the younger men, expected happy nods, saw tears instead, low curses.

Thaw said, "*Anybody?*"

Thenault was in the doorway now, said, "I thought I would allow you time to read for yourselves, but I could have told you. Every letter is the same. Your medical service has determined that none of you meets the standards they have established for American pilots. I do not understand this. I assure you, Dr. Gros is most unhappy with this conclusion."

Lufbery moved to the door, moved past Thenault, stepped into the hallway. He looked toward the front door, saw fading sunlight, heard the voice of Thaw behind him.

"Where you going, Luf?"

"There's still daylight. Thought I'd make a flight."

Thaw moved up close to him, put a hand on his shoulder.

"You okay?"

Lufbery shrugged.

"Yep. Doesn't really matter, does it? Even if the Americans don't want us, we still got a job to do right here."

"Whatever you say, Luf."

Thaw took his hand away, and Lufbery moved toward the door, pulled it open, looked up, soft gray clouds hovering low, the deep blue spreading out beyond. He could see the hangars in the distance, the rows of SPADs perched outside. He stepped down through the low bushes, moved into the road. He realized the letter was still in his hand, didn't look at it, just folded it and stuffed it in his pocket.

25

RICHTHOFEN

September 1917

"Captain Manfred von Richthofen is hereby instructed to commence a four-week recuperative leave of absence, to begin immediately."

Bodenschatz finished reading, waited for his response.

Richthofen sat back in his chair, said, "No room for maneuver, is there?"

"No, sir, apparently not. General von Hoeppner must have reason to believe that your wound is still troublesome."

"The only thing troublesome about my wound is this ridiculous bandage. There is more to this order than what it says on that piece of paper. There is pressure from above. This is coming from Kreuznach, from General Ludendorff's office." He paused, stared at the desk, sniffed. "Or the Information Section. Some ink spiller feels I'm more valuable to the Fatherland as the subject of a simple photograph, so they can say, 'Observe, all of you who fear for your future. Take inspiration from the *great man* standing beside his *great aeroplane*.' "

Richthofen looked up at him, wondered how Bodenschatz felt about his indiscreet comment, saw nothing on the man's face, no hint of judgment. Of course, Bodenschatz had heard it before. He looked over to the corner of the office, the space entirely filled with the great mass of his sleeping dog. Richthofen shrugged his shoulders, said, "An order is to be obeyed. I suppose I can persuade you to tend to Moritz."

"Certainly, sir."

"Then I can offer the Air Service no further excuses. It seems I shall go home for a while."

Bodenschatz seemed to be relieved now, set the order down in front of Richthofen, moved away toward his own desk. Richthofen ignored the paper, looked out the window. The sky was clear, unusual for September, a perfect day for flying. Two squadrons had already completed their patrols, and he had planned to lead another just after lunch. He looked at the order now, the official seal of Air Service headquarters, thought, All right, General. If you want me on the ground, I will remain on the ground. He looked toward the red triplane, could see mechanics at work, one man up on a ladder, doing something to the top wing. Richthofen watched them working for a moment, thought, Perhaps it is just as well.

As much as Richthofen loved the new models of the Albatros, another aircraft manufacturer had secured the full attention of the Air Service commanders. His name was Anthony Fokker. Though Fokker's earlier fighters had been nearly as successful as the Albatros, Fokker had been innovative, had responded to the success of the Sopwith engineers with some engineering of his own. Finally, Germany would have a new plane to counter the Camel. It was the Fokker DR-1, Germany's first triplane. And JG-1 would have the honor of receiving the first one to reach the front.

After several weeks of use, it had become apparent that the Fokker DR-1 had not been the salvation the Air Service had expected. As more of the triple-winged aircraft were delivered to the pursuit squadrons, there were accidents, signs of a serious design problem that caused the plane's top wing to be unstable. In some cases, the damage had been catastrophic, the wing tearing free completely. Though Richthofen enjoyed the maneuverability of the triplane, and had used the new aircraft to shoot down his sixty-first victim, he had begun to look again to the faithful Albatros.

Richthofen picked up the order, folded it, put it in a desk drawer. He stood now, Bodenschatz responding, "Sir? Can I get you anything?"

Richthofen waved him away, said, "There is little for me to do here. Since I have been ordered to a month of peace and quiet, I might as well go home."

He moved toward the door, glanced at the empty desks, knew

that Krefft was outside supervising the mechanics. The small desk in the back of the room had not been occupied for several days now, the stenographer no longer required. Richthofen had completed work on his memoirs, the manuscript now in the hands of someone in Berlin. He had been told to expect it first in serial form, individual chapters released as articles in various official publications. The complete book would come soon after, once the final editing work had been completed. When Richthofen sent the young woman away, he had not even read the manuscript himself, knew that whatever she had written would be changed anyway, would be converted by the *experts* into something they would find useful. In the days since she had gone, it surprised him that he actually missed the work, all the explanations of his missions, pausing to watch as the young woman wrote furiously on the pads of paper. He had even enjoyed talking to her about his family, some of the history he had to research himself. His father had been helpful, providing information about his ancestry that Richthofen had never learned as a child. It was nothing like the adventure of flying, and he appreciated that the stenographer had seemed as interested in his family's background as she was about his conquests in the air. But despite the occasional flirting glance, Richthofen had been relieved that her behavior had remained professional. He was especially cautious now. The painful experiences of his stay at St. Nicholas, of Kate, were still with him.

He had taken a train to Berlin, felt no urgency about arriving anywhere official. But even in the huge city, he could not escape his celebrity, and his presence was regarded as more than just another special event. He endured the obligatory receptions in his honor, countless photographs with high-ranking officers who sought their own memento of the Red Battle Flyer. But Richthofen found nothing pleasant about the social turmoil of the city, and after performing his social duties for a few days, he was grateful to accept an invitation to go hunting on one of the nearby royal estates.

His host was the duke of Saxe-Coburg-Gotha, a genial man

whom Richthofen had met by chance on the train to Berlin. Richthofen's visit had of course thrown the man's entire estate into a frenzy of social planning, a bevy of servants scrambling to make ready for the sudden arrival of Germany's most famous soldier. Richthofen accepted the duke's hospitality with smiling graciousness, but he knew that with the parties would come the crowds, and especially the women. His week in Berlin had engulfed him in too much of that already, hordes of fluttery eyes, soft arms curling through his without invitation, indiscreet proposals that many of the other officers seemed to accept as a matter of course. He had never been brusque, did not have the oily skills of some who knew how to escape the grasping tentacles of the ambitious. But he did have one very convenient excuse: his wound. Though he rarely suffered anymore from the aftereffects, the dramatic white cap on his head proved to be the perfect means to escape overbearing officers as well as their mistresses.

Richthofen was grateful that the duke understood his guest's priorities, and their days were spent roaming the vast woodlands of the man's estate. The hunt had been wonderfully successful, the duke offering his enthusiastic surprise at Richthofen's marksmanship and his skills in the wild, the kind of praise Richthofen had grown accustomed to. Despite his success in the forest, the hunt itself had soon become a distraction. As each day passed, he could not escape thoughts of Schweidnitz, of seeing his mother. Now, after more than a week of recreation, he really wanted to go home.

September 15, 1917

The duke had summoned his chauffeur, and Richthofen was surprised the duke had accompanied him to the aerodrome, a small cramped airfield outside of his estate at Reinhardsbrunn. Richthofen realized his impatience was showing, but the duke took no offense, instead had arranged for a pilot to fly Richthofen to Schweidnitz. It was a gracious favor from an accommodating host, and Richthofen would certainly not object; he was feeling more anxious to be home as each day passed. The thought of taking the slower train had no appeal to him now, a part of him already imagining the quiet reception from his family, the short walk through the tall iron gates of the Richthofen estate.

The chauffeur brought the automobile to a gentle stop, and Richthofen waited dutifully as the man scampered around to open his door. He stepped out of the auto, could see the plane parked at the far end of the field, surrounded by what seemed to be the entire staff of the aerodrome, four men standing in some sort of formation. Richthofen focused now on the plane, a large ragged-looking two-seater, empty bomb racks beneath the wings. Of course, he thought, it would require someone with royal prestige to have a bomber pulled away from the front just to be used as a personal carriage. Or, perhaps he told them it was for . . . me. He shook his head, knew there could be no protest for this ridiculous show of the duke's high-handed influence. He felt a heavy hand on his shoulder, and the duke said, "Captain, it was a privilege to have you as my guest. You are always welcome. Always!"

The duke was beaming at him, stood back now, seemed to stand at attention. Richthofen suddenly realized he was expected to say something formal.

"Thank you, Your Excellency. Please convey my respects to the duchess and your family. Um . . . your hospitality is unequaled."

There was a silent moment, the duke expecting more, and now another auto appeared, drove up rapidly, stopped abruptly. A man emerged, another of the duke's aides, held up a piece of paper, said, "Captain! A telephone call . . . just now, sir. A message for you, sir!"

The duke intercepted the aide, proper protocol, took the paper, the aide now backing away. He glanced at the paper, handed it to Richthofen, said, "I do hope, Captain, it is nothing unfortunate. I have a rather sincere dislike of the telephone. It has been my experience that the sole purpose of that instrument is to impart bad news."

Richthofen unfolded the paper, a sprawl of blue ink. The duke was still talking, but Richthofen heard nothing, the words on the paper shooting through him. He felt his knees grow weak, leaned back against the side of the car. He read the message again, the same words, no mistake, nothing misunderstood.

The duke leaned closer, said, "Forgive me. I fear the worst. May I inquire . . . ?"

Richthofen held out the paper, his words choked away.

The Duke read for a moment, said, "Oh, my. How awful. Yes, I have heard of this fellow. He is one of yours, yes?"

Richthofen nodded, straightened himself, said, "Yes. Kurt Wolff was indeed one of mine."

Wolff had been shot down while leading Squadron Eleven. Richthofen had to know more, had to know it all. He found a telephone in the aerodrome, contacted his office at JG-1. The voice on the other end of the line belonged to Krefft, the man's words pouring into Richthofen like some awful sickness, his mind absorbing every detail of Wolff's last flight.

Wolff had flown Richthofen's own triplane, had led the squadron as he had so many times before. But the fight had been one-sided, a large formation of Sopwith Camels laying the perfect ambush, and even the Fokker's extraordinary maneuverability could not save the young man from the odds against him. When the plane impacted the ground, it had erupted into a massive ball of flame. It was the one blessing—that Wolff had been killed instantly.

Krefft had run out of words, and Richthofen had heard enough, caught some polite comment from Krefft about his visit home as he hung up the phone. He left the tiny office in the small hangar, walked outside, moved across the field alone. The duke and his aides were waiting for him with the others, out by the two-seater. Richthofen said nothing, and even if he had wanted to tell them anything, he could see from the tightly fixed smile on the duke's face that this was a man who did not want to hear about death. There were more words, a final farewell from the duke, the man still avoiding Richthofen's subdued silence. The pilot had difficulty climbing into the plane, had to be assisted by the mechanic, and Richthofen could see now that one of the man's legs was mostly gone, replaced by a stout wooden staff that emerged from his trousers. Richthofen was not concerned with the man's injuries, had known too many good pilots whose bodies were used up, but who still had the talent to fly. Richthofen climbed aboard, could not avoid the disappointment on the faces of the men who had gathered around him. There would be no parting speech, no bombastic call to victory from this magnificent hero. The plane jerked, and the motor roared to life, a smoky blast of power. Richthofen silently thanked the pilot for not delaying. The battered bomber rolled slowly forward, and Richthofen adjusted his goggles, blew the smoke out of his lungs, glanced out across the short field, felt a hard bounce. The plane rumbled into the air, the pilot making a long shallow climb, the field and the men who waved to him now falling away.

Richthofen sat silently in the rear seat, behind the pilot whose name he could not remember. He could not recall now if he had said anything more to his host, or to anyone else. I will write a letter, he thought, the proper thing to do, send some sort of apology for my behavior. They were only gracious, after all, and it was not appropriate to show them rudeness. I should have complimented the duke again. He is a man who enjoys compliments.

He stared down at his knees, jerked as the plane jerked, breathed the thinning air through a hard knot in his chest. The only image in his mind now was the painfully boyish face of Kurt Wolff. A new memory burst into his thoughts, Wolff's fiancée. He tried to recall her name . . . Maria. They were not yet married. So she is not a widow. Does that matter, after all?

He thought now of another awful day, Wolff crying when he brought the news of Allmenroder's death. I should have scolded him for such a display, should have told him to take control of himself. We cannot respond with so much sadness. So many have gone, so many more . . . will yet be gone. We cannot shed tears for any one man. Had I been there today, I would have made them face me with the news with their heads held high, tell me exactly what occurred so they would learn from the mistakes. He thought of the names, the pilots of Squadron Eleven. He did not think to ask Krefft who else had been in the

400

squadron. Who saw him go down? Did they cry for him? No, it cannot be like that. We cannot allow it.

He saw the awkward sadness of Wolff's smile, a man too young for his wisdom, the keen mind, the good fighter. But the image would not stay, the young man's face fading to a soft blur. He blinked through the wetness, could not stop the tears, squeezed his hands into tight fists, his sobs blending now with the low quiet song of the plane.

Schweidnitz, Germany—September 23, 1917

He was surprised that his father had come home as well, the atmosphere of the household always a little different when the major was there. Richthofen had always felt it as a child, a bit more formality, a hint of martial airs as though his father should command some sort of military respect even in his own home. But there was a softer air in the house as well, the quiet relief of his mother. Both of her sons had endured their scrapes with death, and both had survived. It was the answer to her prayers.

Richthofen awoke surprisingly late, stared at the small clock beside his bed: nine-thirty. As each day passed, he had become more relaxed, amazed at himself, enjoying every night's sleep more than any he could remember. He yawned, rolled over, felt the softness beneath him, looked toward the drawn curtains of his room. It was the same every morning, the daylight screened by the thoughtfulness of his mother. He smiled, sat up slowly, thought, Of course, I would not have considered closing curtains. There is no need when you must awake before the dawn.

He pushed himself out of the bed, probed the bandage on his head, still secure. It was his routine now and quite necessary. If the bandage came apart, it meant a trip to the doctor, and Richthofen had grown too weary of hospitals.

He moved toward the window, glanced at the walls of the room, covered with so many of his souvenirs. It had become a necessity, rumors from the Air Service that JG-1 might be relocated, that the front lines could always change on short notice. It was an embarrassing inconvenience to order his staff to pack up his mementos. It was far more practical to have most of them shipped home.

He drew back the curtain, looked across the garden, up at the gray sky, thought of his pilots. They can fly today, I would think. It will rain a great deal though, now until the winter. We must take advantage of every good day. The enemy will do the same.

There was a quiet knock on the door, and he reached for his robe, wrapped himself, said, "You may enter."

She held a tray, a teapot, a single cup, said, "Good morning. I must tell you that you have caused concern to the major. He has grumbled all morning that you are sleeping too much." She could not hide her smile. He took the tray from her, set it on the bed, said, "Perhaps I should tell him I have been ordered to rest. Even he cannot overrule General Ludendorff." He expected her to laugh, but she turned away, moved toward the door, closed it.

"Before we join your father, may I speak to you?"

"What is it? He cannot hear you, you know."

She shook her head, said, "It's habit. I always assume he knows everything I'm thinking." She moved toward the bed, straightened the linens, another old habit, and he saw sadness on her face, noticed now how much older she seemed to be.

"Mother, what's wrong?"

She sat on the bed, looked down for a moment, said, "Do you read the newspapers?"

He started to protest, said, "Mother, you can't pay attention to all that *glory* nonsense—"

"Oh, no, I don't mean that." She paused, seemed unsure of her words. "You know, when your father is here, he pores through every word of every paper he can find, scribbles furiously in the margins, yells at the stories." She laughed now. "You should hear the language he uses. He thinks because he is nearly deaf, that I can't hear him either." She paused, the smile fading. "Manfred, all I read is the obituaries. So many local boys are gone, so many families I have known for so many years. Some of them, barely a few words, a name, his age

402

perhaps. I have seen the ones you have written for the pilots who have died. I admire you for doing that."

"Thank you. It has become customary. The Air Service approved the suggestion, that I should write a few words about each man who has fallen. It is thought that if my name accompanies the tribute, the families would be appreciative." He saw her still searching for words, said, "Mother, what is this about?"

"Manfred, a man came to the gate this morning, a soldier. He had a message for you, a wire. It came to the army post in town. The man was very kind, wondered if you knew already, but I don't see how. I feel foolish making such a drama about it."

Her words were too familiar, another *message*, another piece of news that he would have to swallow. "Who is it this time?" The words came out in a hard burst.

She looked up at him, said, "Manfred, I'm sorry. Your Mr. Voss was killed this morning. I don't know any more than that. The soldier apologized for not having any more information."

Richthofen sat down beside her, closed his eyes for a moment. "It doesn't matter. I will find out later." He felt a laugh rising up inside of him, couldn't help it, the sound surprising her. He put an arm around her shoulders, said, "He was quite a talker. Came to us not even twenty years old, so full of arrogance, prepared to give us the proper lessons on how to fight the enemy. I have never heard a man so confident of his place in the world. Voss had one goal above any other. He would become the hero of all heroes. The newspapers loved him for it, put him into some kind of competition with me, kept score of our victories as though we were in some kind of sporting match." He paused, the humor exhausted, unable to hold back the anger he felt now. "I suppose he would be pleased on one count. He won the contest that matters most. He died first." He regretted the words instantly, felt her stiffen beside him. "I'm sorry. That was not kind."

"No, Manfred, it was not, either to Mr. Voss or to me. Do you not understand what news like this means to me? I know all about Mr. Voss and his accomplishments. He is another *hero*, Manfred. Just like my sons!" She fought tears, put a hand

403

to her face, and he held her tighter, didn't know what else to do. She wiped at her eyes with a small handkerchief, said, "I pray for you every day. All I ask is that you be allowed to do your duty and then come home. Your father scolds me, says I must not show such weakness. An officer's wife must accept her fate. But my sons. There is no solace for a soldier's *mother*. Unlike your father, I draw no inspiration from your victories. I do not boast of your kills. I do not worship the glory that comes from the destruction of your enemies."

"*Our* enemies, Mother."

"Really? I suppose I am to accept that without question. My men are soldiers, and so I am to feel protected. And yet every day there is one more item missing from the market. Today, it is meat. For a week now there has been no coal. We have not seen green vegetables in many weeks. I do not complain, because I know that in this house we have more than most. The army provides for us because my sons are heroes. I hear talk in the town of some kind of meeting, angry men gathering, threatening violence against the soldiers here. Your father says they are called Bolsheviks, that they want to fight the kaiser. I've never heard of such a thing. Manfred, it is frightening. What do they want?"

He had heard only the official reports, mostly from the seaports in the North, small mobs of laborers threatening to incite riots. He had paid little attention to it, had known for a long time that the shipping blockade had put many men out of work. But the official word was that these men were signing up instead for the army, were training to join the fight on the Western Front. If there was unrest at all, it came from those who simply refused to work, drunkards and troublemakers, who would take to the streets shouting politics as their excuse to loot the markets.

"There is no danger, Mother. The army has complete control. Any such talk will not be tolerated. I admit, I have not heard of such a thing happening around here."

She did not answer, seemed lost in her own thoughts.

He stood up now, tried to put on a smile, said, "Am I allowed to inquire about breakfast?"

She looked up at him, said, "What of your Mr. Voss? You will have to prepare another obituary. You can go into town and telephone your headquarters."

He did not want to think about Voss, but her words took away the energy for his smile. "Yes. I will go later. There is little I can do about any of this now."

"You are wrong, Manfred." He saw anger in her eyes, the tears again, and she said, "You can stop flying. You have done your part. No one would ever find fault."

He turned away from her, moved slowly around the room, stopped at the window, stared out at the garden. "Father would not agree with you."

"I do not speak for your father. If it is selfishness to want my sons alive, then I am selfish. I want you to have a wife. I want you to know what it is to see the face of your own babies, to watch your own children grow up." Her voice was rising now, and she stood, faced him. "You have done enough for your country!"

He had not seen her angry in a very long time, felt suddenly helpless. "Mother, you cannot understand. If everyone felt this way, no one would fight!" His words lay hanging in the air, and she stared at him for a long moment.

"Then, my son, no one would die."

There was a knock at the door, and she ignored it, still looked at him, rubbed her hand on her face.

"Manfred?"

It was his father, and Richthofen moved quickly to the door, opened it, saw the old man in his uniform. His father seemed surprised, said, "Oh, I didn't realize . . . sorry to interrupt. My dear, I was hoping we could commence breakfast, now that our hero is awake."

There was sarcasm in his voice, and Richthofen said, "My apologies, sir. I blame the comforts of this bed. We shall retire to the dining room."

The old man was watching his wife, and Richthofen saw concern, curiosity.

"Yes, well, we should make some haste, before breakfast is replaced by dinner. I've not had even a good cup of tea! The entire house waits for my son! One would assume me to be a corporal. Shall I shine your boots?" He knew there was no anger in the old man's words, the familiar smile cracking through his father's stern demeanor. The old man moved into the hallway, glanced back at his wife. "You coming, my dear?"

She moved past her son, out into the hallway, said, "Patience, Major. Your tea will keep."

Richthofen smiled, said, "Allow me one moment to dress. I will be there quickly."

He opened the doors to the dressing closet, pulled out a shirt, heard a sound, turned, was surprised to see his father in the doorway. "Go on, get dressed. Can't have you lounging about in your bedclothes all the damned day."

Richthofen obeyed, his father glancing back out into the hallway, and the old man said, "What did she want?"

He was surprised at the question, continued to dress, said, "She brought me the message about Lieutenant Voss."

The old man nodded. "Hmm. Yes, I know. She insisted on it. Wouldn't let me come up. Damned strange of her. That all she wanted?"

Richthofen saw more than idle curiosity on his father's face, said, "She is concerned about me."

His father moved into the room now, reached down, handed Richthofen his boots. "Supposed to be. It's her duty. She wants you to stop flying, you know."

"She shouldn't ask me that."

"No, suppose not. Wouldn't do any good, anyway. I hear even Ludendorff can't get you to change your mind. Not too many people defy the High Command. Maybe no one but you."

Richthofen sat, pulled on the boots.

His father stood back, stared at him with his arms folded on his chest. "If you won't come down out of the air for Ludendorff, what about for your father?"

Richthofen was annoyed now, said, "You as well? You want me to stop doing my duty? You think I should become an ink spiller in von Hoeppner's office, wear my uniform just so I can lead parades?"

He saw no change on the old man's face; his father just shook his head.

"I would never tell you that." He paused, rubbed a hand through the rough beard on his chin. "It was not prudent of me to ask you such a thing. Forgive me. Sometimes I allow her emotions to overrule good sense. Despite what the clerks in the High Command suggest, Ludendorff knows how valuable you are *up there*. Whatever hope there is of winning this war depends on men like you doing their job. There are too few of you left."

"Fewer every day, so it would seem." He absorbed the rest of his father's words, one word rising in his brain. "*Hope*? Is that what we are depending on now? What happened to the *inevitable defeat* of our enemies?"

The question had no answer, and his father backed away, stood in the doorway again. "The High Command does not consult me with their strategies."

Richthofen stood, was dressed now, caught the rich smell of warm bread coming from downstairs. He waited for his father to step out into the hall, but the old man hesitated, put a hand on his arm, said, "Only one thing I would ask of you. If you cannot stop flying, then at least you can be a little more careful up there." The old man walked away down the hallway, his boots thumping heavily on the stairs.

Richthofen moved to the doorway, stopped, thought, You cannot be angry with them, certainly not with her. He thought of her suggestion, the telephone at the army post. His mind was swirling now with images, the aerodrome, the men mourning Voss as they had mourned Wolff and Allmenroder and Schaefer . . . and how many more? He snapped his mind shut, said aloud, "Enough of this!"

He looked back into the room, all the small trophies and mementos that spread across the walls. This is what everyone wants, is it not? If not for all of this, for the *victories*, then what good am I to my country, to Ludendorff or von Hoeppner or the kaiser himself? He thought of his father's word, *careful*. A careful flyer is a defensive flyer, and a defensive flyer will shoot down no one. No, Father, you do not kill your enemy by being *careful*.

26

PERSHING

November 1917

Despite the unbridled optimism that poured out through the communication lines of British headquarters, the news from every European front of the war had done nothing but devastate the morale of soldier and civilian alike.

In 1915, the Italians had joined the war on the side of France and England, causing an immediate response from the Austrians to their north. But after two years of stalemate along the newly opened front in northern Italy, the German High Command had grown weary of the Austrian army's inability to force a breakthrough. Ludendorff had sent German units southward to boost the fighting strength of the Austrians, and in October 1917 the results had been decisive. The battle was called Caporetto, a massive surge by the German and Austrian forces that had finally broken the back of the Italian defensive lines. The breakthrough was so complete that the Italian army simply collapsed, a massive chaotic retreat that handed the entire Italian front to their enemy, and effectively eliminated the Italians as an effective ally who could help divert pressure away from the French and English along the Western Front.

The Italian collapse followed another blow to the Allies. The Romanians had joined the war in mid-1916, spurred on by the opportunity to satisfy old ethnic conflicts against their neighbor Bulgaria, who had sided with the Germans. But the Romanian army was ill prepared, underequipped and poorly led, and when they launched an attack against their hated neighbor, the German-led Bulgarians not only crushed the Romanian forces, they pushed the Romanians back so far into their own territory that within a period of less than four months, Germany was able to capture the invaluable Ploesti oil fields and drive the Romanians completely out of the war.

While the Italian and Romanian catastrophes had been distinct and definite, for over a year the reports emerging from the Russian front had been wildly inconsistent, a mix of success and failure, hope and pessimism for both sides. In 1916, the Russian army had launched a massive attack, named for its commander, Alexei Brusilov. The Brusilov Offensive had successfully pushed the Austrian army back nearly fifty miles. But the Austrians were soon reinforced by far more effective German troops, who stopped the retreats and inflicted a horrifying toll on the Russian forces. Though the offensive cleared their enemy from a large swath of territory, that success cost the Russians nearly a million men. The propaganda value of the offensive could not offset the devastating blow to the Russian people, already suffering from deprivations and shortages. Increasingly disillusioned with their leadership, particularly the autocratic and aloof Czar Nicholas II, the despair of the Russian people gave considerable fuel to the cause of the Marxist revolutionaries. By the spring of 1917, the hapless czar had been swept from power. Though the moderate Russian government tried to maintain some control, the Marxists, led by Vladimir Lenin and Leon Trotsky, had secured the loyalty of much of the Russian army, which had virtually ceased to exist as an effective fighting force. The German High Command had taken full advantage of Russia's internal crisis, quietly supporting the revolutionaries, especially Lenin. Once the revolutionaries took control, Russia would certainly be out of the war. With a cessation of fighting along the Eastern Front, the Germans would then be free to transfer a massive number of troops to their lines in the West, seriously altering the balance of the three-year-old stalemate. The Allies could only predict that very soon after, Ludendorff would launch some massive new offensive, which neither the British nor the French could contain. As each day passed, the war of attrition had drained too much life from the Allied armies. The only realistic hope lay with the American soldiers, whom Pershing could not yet send into the field.

After months of holding off the Allies' insistent demands, Pershing finally secured a commitment from General Pétain that the Americans should be assigned their own distinct position in the line, their own theater of operation. Pershing and Pétain had considered the most logical location to be in Lorraine, just south of the ragged battlefields of Verdun. That part of the front contained a fat bulge in the German position known as the Mihiel Salient, which extended deep into the French defenses between Verdun and the city of Nancy. The salient had brought the Germans dangerously close to critical rail hubs and transportation lines that connected the entire southern section of the Western Front to their bases of supply and communication. On the German side of the salient lay important coal- and iron-producing areas, the Saar Basin and the Moselle Valley, and the key rail and communications centers at Metz and Thionville, ripe targets should the Americans spearhead any new attack. Pershing had studied all sections of the front, knew what Pétain knew, that without the strength of the fresh American forces, the French weakness at the salient was severe, and worse, should the Germans open a breakthrough and expand the salient westward, they would have a short march to Paris. It was not a situation that gave any comfort to the French people. Pershing had followed the First Division's training closely, knowing full well that the earliest opportunity for those troops to man some part of the front lines would provide a surge of morale to the Allies. On October 21, the men of the First marched forward, guided by French officers who chose their particular location because of its relative quiet. All over France the word spread that the Americans had finally joined the fight. Though the sector they were assigned was chosen primarily to allow the soldiers to gain a feel for the ground, and discover the realities of life in a community of trenches, the Germans had no intention of allowing the Americans to become comfortable. In the predawn darkness of November 3, a German raiding party burst into the American lines, startling the inexperienced guards. Three American soldiers were killed. The AEF had experienced its first bloody taste of the war.

* * *

Pershing's headquarters had been established at Chaumont, southeast of Paris, a convenient rail and communications point that lay between the capital and the southernmost section of what would become the American sector. Throughout the summer and into the fall, Pershing continued to call upon his staff for the mammoth task of organizing the army. Though the rate at which new troops were arriving was a continuing disappointment, Pershing knew that a sudden flood of American soldiers could create more havoc than benefit. Assuming the ships could be found to bring the men across the Atlantic, they still had to be transported inland from the ports, fed, supplied, and housed. Until the infrastructure for all of this was established, soldiers would be of little use to anyone.

Gradually, the right personnel were put into place, including a number of prominent civilians who had been brought over from the States. The challenges of working within French systems had proven frustrating at best, and though the French leadership proved willing to assist the American efforts, often the expertise at the local level was inadequate. Immediately there had been problems with the chaotic French telephone system, and Pershing had ordered the construction of an entire network of cables and communication stations that would bypass the French system altogether. The railway system was not as haphazard, but the French were hard-pressed to furnish supplies and transportation even for their own army. While the American Corps of Engineers had been hard at work constructing and rehabilitating the overused French track system that would serve the American ports of entry, Pershing brought in a team of civilian experts to manage the railways themselves, including William Atterbury, the manager of the Pennsylvania Railroad. Atterbury had assessed the problems immediately, and he worked willingly with Pershing's staff to bring over more civilians, including men who held high positions with the Long Island and New York Central Railroads.

From the construction of barracks for the troops, to the installation of telegraph poles, the Americans had need of

411

enormous supplies of lumber, which the French reluctantly agreed to supply. Pershing recruited Henry Graves, the chief of the United States Forestry Service, to assemble a massive team of loggers and sawmill operators. As the civilian workers came ashore, the organization came together, and within a few short months, the American specialists had put into operation a system designed to transport and house as many troops as Pershing could eventually put into the field. Despite the occasional roadblock put before them by various French bureaucrats, the French government and Pétain's headquarters began to understand why the presence of the Americans was so critical. The French had exhausted their labor force as well as their army, and could never have expanded their decaying efforts that barely provided for the basic needs of their own troops. Pershing's rapidly expanding organization was affecting the morale of the French people in ways that even their government did not expect. From the port at Nazaire, to the training facilities that spread inland through Paris, to Pershing's headquarters at Chaumont, the people began to see past the celebrations and parades and began to realize what the presence of the Americans might truly mean.

Paris—November 7, 1917

"The enemy is tottering! Have you seen the latest reports? Magnificent!"

The room was mostly silent, small voices in one corner. Haig seemed frustrated that his announcement had not brought a cheer. "Gentlemen, we have but one direction in which to advance: to the Rhine. Every indication is that the Hun is beaten, that his army has suffered far more than we have. I had hoped to find you in a mood of cooperation."

Pershing glanced at the others, saw Pétain nodding politely, the other French commanders staring down silently.

Pétain said, "Very well, Marshal Haig. You should be congratulated on your success. May your soldiers have every piece of good fortune."

Haig sniffed, said, "Thank you. However, I assure you, we

make our own good fortune." He looked at Pershing, said, "General, as this meeting seems concluded, I wonder if I might have a word. We so rarely have time for personal conversation."

Pershing looked toward Pétain, saw no expression, watched as Pétain assisted his staff in gathering their notepads and books, the obvious sign that the French had nothing left to say. "Certainly, Marshal Haig."

"Excellent. I'd fancy a cup of tea. Some lunch perhaps. You as well?"

Haig was already moving toward the door, and Pershing saw the two staffs pulling apart, nothing sociable between them, no parting words. The meeting had lasted for barely an hour, the American officers with Pershing playing little role.

Pershing said to Harbord, "Colonel, if you wish, you may return to the hotel. We should prepare to leave for Chaumont within the hour."

Harbord seemed as weary as Pershing felt, had pulled his own notes together, the other officers gathering close. Harbord said, "Yes, sir. We shall wait for you at the hotel."

The room was empty now except for the Americans, the French departing from a different entrance than the British. It was so completely normal for the meetings to conclude this way, that when the two high commands made the effort to discuss strategy, very little pleasantness flowed through the talk.

Harbord moved to the doorway Pétain had used, held it open, allowing the others to leave, then stopped, said, "General, what is the purpose of this?"

Pershing was surprised by Harbord's question, was used to the man's stoic silence, most of Harbord's energy directed inward, the man commanding a brutal efficiency for the details of his job. Pershing looked toward the door Haig's men had closed behind them, said in a low voice, "They are *communicating*, Jim. To them, to both of them, this is something they must do whether they want to or not. We are fortunate; we don't have civilians leaning over our shoulder. Marshal Haig has his hands full of problems with London, and Pétain feels the pressure of Paris, as well as his own citizens. And they are allies, after all."

"Doesn't feel that way, most of the time, sir. Seems more like a competition."

Harbord's words had gone through Pershing's mind often, and he shook his head, said, "Napoleon said it best, Jim. His favorite enemy was a coalition. Two diverse nations, fighting side by side, two cultures, two personalities, two goals. They are so focused on what the world might be like after this war, who will dominate, who will gain, that they lose sight of the effort they must make to defeat the common enemy. The French and the English are oil and water. They have been enemies for centuries and suddenly they must cooperate. It may not work. The Germans must certainly understand that. Ludendorff has no doubt read Napoleon as well. Oil and water. It can be . . . seriously distressing."

The door opened, and Haig's aide was there, said, "Oh, General. The field marshal was concerned you had perhaps taken the wrong route."

"A minute, Major. Just conferring with my chief of staff."

"Of course, sir. Might I inform the field marshal you will be along shortly?"

"Please do, Major."

The door closed again, and Harbord said, "The wrong route. That's bull, sir. He's concerned you were speaking with General Pétain."

Pershing smiled. "Keep that to yourself, Jim. I don't need you sharing my cynicism. I have a hard enough time being so very polite all the damned time."

"Yes, sir. Sorry."

"Go on. I'll see you back at the hotel."

Harbord moved out the door, and Pershing went the opposite way, pulled the door open, saw Haig standing with his aides, waiting for him.

"Marshal Haig, sorry to keep you. Had a few last-second instructions for Colonel Harbord."

Haig seemed to accept Pershing's explanation, tugged at his jacket, straightening the already perfect uniform, was all smiles now. Haig waited for Pershing to move up beside him, then began to walk, Pershing alongside, and Haig said, "I admire

414

your restraint, General. You kept quite to yourself today. Must be difficult. Every man has his point of view. I should like to know yours."

Haig's aides seemed to hang back, giving the two men privacy, and Pershing heard the familiar voice in his head: Be *careful*.

"I hope your advance continues to be successful. We all require victories." Pershing felt awkward, the words an empty formality.

Haig seemed not to notice, said, "Ah, yes. Quite. No worry. Every intelligence shows the Hun to be demoralized all along our front. We are taking enormous sums of prisoners. The beginning of the end, as I see it. If it wasn't for this bloody weather, we'd have gained every objective."

Haig's optimism seemed forced, something Pershing had grown accustomed to. It had been the same in every meeting, the British commander putting the best face on his army's progress, always the advantage, always the short road to certain victory. Haig was roughly Pershing's age, a stocky stump of a man, his boots adorned with spurs, the man always with a walking cane or riding crop. Pershing could sense Haig's aristocratic breeding, the distinctly British stiffness that made him the complete opposite of Wully Robertson. It was all the more amazing that Robertson and Haig should be such close allies. Though Prime Minister Lloyd George was clearly Haig's political enemy, openly criticizing Haig's decisions and strategies, Robertson had been successful at holding the prime minister at bay. For the moment, Haig's command seemed secure, no obvious candidate waiting in the wings to replace him. But Pershing had seen intelligence reports as well, knew what so many in the French High Command seemed to know, that the great battle raging across Flanders was little more than a war of attrition. Despite Haig's rosy predictions, every report Pershing had seen hinted that the British were losing as many men as the Germans, a terribly high cost to pay for what seemed to be modest gains of territory. But Haig still held tightly to his optimism, and as long as he commanded the British sector, it was apparent that the British attacks would continue.

Pershing followed Haig into a small building, could smell food now, the warm aroma of fresh bread. A tray of teacups was offered to them, Haig's aides snapping to their duty. Pershing took a cup of steaming water, followed Haig's lead, submerged a metal ball into the cup, the tea leaves spreading a light brown stain through the water.

Haig said, "I see that your troops are arriving at a somewhat slower pace than predicted. Difficult situation, no doubt. If I may inquire, what kind of strength do you have on the ground now?"

"Approximately eighty-five thousand, including the officers. I have maintained for some time that expectations must be realistic. I cannot produce soldiers out of the air."

Haig rubbed his chin, nodded. "Ah, quite so. But this truly does bring home the point. Your recruits are undergoing a great deal of training in the States, which consumes considerable time. I should think you would acknowledge our invitation as an appropriate one, General. However, knowing your objections, I have modified it a bit. General Robertson and I have conferred, and have devised a plan where your battalions should be introduced and incorporated into British brigades, their percentage of the whole increasing on some fixed schedule we may yet determine. As their numbers increase to the majority in the brigade, your officers would assume command. This will eventually free up the British lads to go on their way, where they will be used elsewhere, likely to be transferred into other British divisions, which, as you know, are dreadfully undermanned. Eventually, these brigades will be wholly American, completely under your command, having received their training, I might say, by the finest officers in the world."

Pershing sipped his tea, absorbed Haig's words, a different proposal than he had heard before. "I fear, sir, that the French would have objections. We have agreed that the Mihiel Salient is an appropriate sector for our concentration. If I accepted your plan, where would we position these brigades?"

Haig set his cup down, and Pershing was suddenly uncomfortable, as though Haig was sensing a weakness, some crack in Pershing's unwavering resolve.

416

"Your agreement with General Pétain places you in the midst of French forces, which I have always found to be . . . inconvenient. I believe that any American army should more appropriately be placed at the intersection of our lines and the French. I would insist that we begin incorporating your battalions at that point. I believe General Pétain could be convinced of the wisdom of this plan."

I am not sure of that at all, Pershing thought.

Haig continued, "You realize, General, that this would allow us to make available additional shipping that might otherwise be engaged in different pursuits. I believe the navy could be convinced that your agreement with this plan could constitute a priority in the allocation of our transport tonnage."

Haig had laid his cards on the table, and Pershing understood, it was the same game the British had always played: Do it our way, and we'll provide you the ships.

"I should take this under advisement, sir. It is not a decision I would make without discussion with Washington."

"Of course! I would expect nothing else!"

Haig was beaming again; Pershing kept his polite smile and finished his tea.

Headquarters, AEF, Chaumont, France— November 9, 1917

He paced behind his desk, stared down at the dispatch, thought, It's not their fault, not Baker's, perhaps not even Bliss's. It cannot be anyone's fault. That's always the defense for this sort of stupidity. If no one is truly in charge, then no one can be held accountable. Damn them all to hell!

"*Colonel!*"

Harbord appeared at the door, seemed to anticipate the outburst. "Sir?"

"Who's here? Anyone else?"

Harbord stepped into his office, said, "Yes, sir. Major Drum, Colonel Connor, Colonel Rockenbach, and Captain Patton. We were just going over—"

"Bring them in. Everybody. I want every one of them to know

417

what kind of support we're getting from Washington. Every man on my staff has been questioned by somebody, some damned reporter, some French officer, all asking the same question. What the hell is wrong with your army? Why are you so damned slow bringing your men to France? Well, I want my people to know the answer. Damn it all!"

The others had gathered behind Harbord, and Pershing shouted again, "Well, come in!"

They filed in, each man standing straight, waiting for what would come next. Pershing looked at each one of them, thought, All good men. I am so damned fortunate. Why does no one in Washington perform like this? He sat down, pushed the letter toward the front of his desk, said, "More talk of delay from the chief of staff's office. Hand-wringing and apologies for our lack of preparation. No ability to see beyond the moment at hand. No ability to create a plan, and even if I furnish the plan, they have no ability to put it into motion. No assigning of responsibility. No action!"

They stared at him in silence, and Pershing shook his head, looked down for a moment. "As you may know, the French have supplied us with instructors at most of the training facilities in the States. These instructors are assisting our recruits by indoctrinating them in the only role the French expect them to play. They are teaching our soldiers every specific nuance required to defend oneself in a trench. I have written the secretary, I have written the chief of staff, and it has done no good at all. Our own instructors are so new, and so poorly trained, that they defer to French expertise. The French were sent over to assist us, and instead, we have given them complete control, because our officers are too incompetent to know what else to do. The results have become obvious. Did you hear about the mess at Valbonne? I was asked to attend an exhibition—some sort of mock battle staged for the benefit of the newspapers, and of course, the French. General Bullard was all puffed up with pride, claimed I would be impressed by the skills of the most recently arriving officers. I stood on the damned reviewing stand surrounded by French officials, proudly observing as a regiment of our newest recruits stumbled all over themselves. Instead of showing our allies how well we were prepared, we showed them how poorly we have been training our recruits. I thought the best way to deflect my own embarrassment was to offer some boast to our horrified allies by assuring them that we would do better in a show of marksmanship. I thought Bullard was going to faint right in front of me. There is no show of marksmanship, he says, because there is no marksmanship at all. *These men have had no training with a rifle!* No one in the War Department has thought it necessary to teach our new recruits how to aim! Why? The French instructors insisted they not waste their time. It isn't necessary! The rifle is obsolete! It seems all of our West Point training is out of date, out of step with the new era of *defensive* warfare. Victory by inactivity. Our men are being instructed that they can best defeat our enemy by dying more slowly than he does."

He stopped, pulled back on his temper, looked at them one by one.

"Regardless of how often our allies insist, I will not commit our soldiers to anyone's war of attrition. I was trained . . . hell, you were all trained to believe that success on the battlefield comes only from aggression and movement. I have repeatedly expressed my views to Secretary Baker, and I believe he shares my frustration. But it is apparent to me that he is considerably outnumbered by *old soldiers* in the War Department who are doing everything they can to impede our progress. I cannot understand why this is so, why there is such hesitation. You know that we hope to field a million trained men by spring. But the secretary has informed me that unless our shipping capacity is increased dramatically, we will be fortunate to receive half that many."

He paused, reached into a drawer beside him, his fingers probing a file. He retrieved a piece of paper, said, "Here. One of the first calculations we made was a conservative estimate of the artillery we would require. The immediate necessity was twenty-five hundred guns, of varying calibers. I have received word that we can expect precisely *one hundred and twenty* cannon by the end of the year, with no further deliveries from our foundries until *next June*. We currently have no production

419

of tanks, no factories that are producing aircraft. And the chief of staff has given me no indication that this is of concern . . . to *anyone!*" He paused, rubbed a hand across his forehead. "We are desperate for transport ships. I have been screaming at the top of my lungs to anyone in authority: British, French, and American. I received a stack of manifests, the cargo that was reluctantly unloaded by the French stevedores at Nazaire. Of course, I cannot completely fault them for their complacency. You should see just what our valuable tonnage is being used to transport: to date, we have received an excessive supply of bookcases, bathtubs, office desks, floor wax, stepladders, lawn mowers, window shades, and cuspidors. *Cuspidors!* Feel free to spit to your heart's delight, gentlemen. We shall never run out of cuspidors." He stared up at them, saw no one smiling. "I appreciate that someone one day will find humor in this. Perhaps I might even find humor in this. We received one ship designated to carry a significant number of long wooden pilings, timber that was not available to us here. The timber companies from the Pacific Northwest obliged our needs admirably. But the gentlemen at the New York pier who were charged with loading these long timbers onto the ship found their length to be inconvenient, and so, to make their job easier, they sawed the timbers into shorter lengths! Imagine the joy of the engineers at Nazaire when they anxiously unloaded their much-needed pilings, and found that they had been transformed into firewood!"

He paused again, his words choking away. He took a breath, said, "Forgive me for unburdening myself, gentlemen. We have an exceptionally good staff here, all of you included. Our progress on this side of the Atlantic has met my expectations, and has sincerely impressed our allies, regardless of what their politicians may say. But the past few months have provided me several lessons in command, for which I may not have been prepared. As you know, I have been assured by both the secretary and the president that there would be no interference in my judgment as to how the AEF is to be trained, equipped, and deployed. In *France.* I understand where my authority ends, that I can only *request and suggest* to the chief of staff. What I am learning is that my expectations, and yours, conflict with the views of many in the War Department. The secretary has hinted to me that there is a general attitude brewing in Washington that we have exceeded our responsibilities to our allies. There is talk that this war can be decided in our favor without the involvement of so many American soldiers. Can you imagine the reaction of our allies to such a concept? We completely support your cause, but heaven forbid we should actually risk American lives to secure peace in Europe. It has been suggested that President Wilson has had second thoughts about his own commitment, his own reasons for declaring war, that perhaps now he is reluctant to grant so much power to the essential industries that are such an important part of this process. I don't know if that is accurate." He paused, saw Harbord fidgeting.

"What, Colonel?"

"Sir, this might be the appropriate time to inform you. . . . I believe I know one reason why Washington seems unwilling to respond to our needs. If you will permit, I should show you something."

Pershing nodded, and Harbord moved quickly out of the office. The others seemed content to wait, and Pershing felt his temper cooling, thought, I should not have done this. They should not be expected to listen to my bellyaching.

Harbord returned, held out a newspaper, said, "This arrived this morning, sir. I was about to bring it to you."

Harbord held up the paper, and Pershing saw it was *The New York Times*, with the headline:

British and French Smash Through Wide German Front North of Ypres: All Haig's Objectives Gained

He sat back in his chair, felt a hard lump in his chest, stared at the paper. He read the details, saw one inaccuracy after another, the reporter perfectly mimicking Haig's public pronouncements, what Pershing knew now to be an obscene disregard for what was really happening to the British forces at Ypres.

"You're quite correct, Colonel. The press is telling the

American people that everything is just rosy over here. How can I expect the War Department to listen to me, when The New York Times tells them the war is nearly won? All they hear from me are demands, something that would require the clerks and bureaucrats to actually go to *work*!"

He had run out of energy, realized there was nothing for any of them to say. "You gentlemen have things to do. Might as well get to it."

"Sir."

"Yes, sir."

They began to file out, and Pershing said, "Colonel Rockenbach. A moment. Captain Patton as well." The two men returned, and Pershing pointed to the chairs against one wall. "Sit down." The men obeyed, and Pershing saw the usual impatient curiosity on Patton's face. "Colonel, the French have given us assurances that they will eventually provide a sufficient number of their Renault light tanks so that we may proceed with the formal training of our own tank corps. As you know, I should like you to command that department, and work to coordinate the efforts of that training with the organization of the rest of the AEF. Your most valuable skills are administrative, and that is no insult. I hope you do not take it as such."

Rockenbach said, "Certainly not, sir. I am flattered."

"There are considerable responsibilities involved in coordinating with the French on this, and there is no reason to believe you will be spared the usual bumps in the road. You will continue to serve as a mem-ber of my staff, though your responsibility will include what I expect to become a fully operational schooling program for tank operators and personnel."

"Of course, sir."

Pershing looked at Patton, saw the young man staring at him with wide, expectant eyes. "Captain, you know how much I value your per-formance as chief of the trucking and auto pool. I am also aware that you hope to transfer from that duty to something more, um . . . adventurous?"

Patton straightened his back, said, "Oh, certainly not, sir. I would never suggest that I was not pleased with my assignment."

422

"You command a squad of mechanics and a fleet of trucks, Captain. There is no shame in hoping for something with a little more . . . flare. I am well aware that you are hoping to move a bit closer to the action. I believe I've found a suitable position. Colonel Rockenbach, I am assigning Captain Patton to you as second in command of the Tank Corps, with the specific duty as chief of the Tank School. Colonel, you will run the overall program. Captain, you will teach our people how to run the damned tanks."

November 20, 1917

The British army had gone as far through the mud of Flanders as even the optimistic Haig could claim, and to the desperate relief of the British, Canadian, and Anzac troops, the third Battle of Ypres was brought to a close. But Haig was not content to allow his army to settle into the inevitability of winter. The energy for yet one more attack had come from General Julian Byng, the man who had commanded the rescue of the Anzacs after their harrowing disaster at Gallipoli in 1915. Since his return to the Western Front, Byng had become an outspoken advocate for the use of tanks, as the one effective means of ending the strategic stalemate. Haig's failure to make good on his claims for a breakthrough in Flanders opened the door for Byng's plan to be approved. The criticism from London, particularly from the prime minister, gave Haig all the incentive he needed to allow Byng an opportunity to end the year with a legitimate British victory.

The objective was the town of Cambrai, which lay behind the German lines that extended south of the churned-up battle zone of Ypres. Byng insisted that a massive force of armor on a narrow front could sweep away the usual obstacles of barbed wire, could be sent across the tops of trenches, and since armor was invulnerable to the machine gun, the tanks could target the machine-gun nests as they advanced and eliminate the German army's most effective defensive weapon.

On November 20, they rolled out through a dense mist that masked the awesomeness of the attack. Three hundred twenty-four heavy tanks lumbered forward, crawling along in front of a quarter million British infantrymen. The attack was a complete surprise to the Germans, and though the tanks could only advance at a top speed of four miles per hour, the German defense crumbled before them; the shocked and often terrified infantrymen were helpless to stop the massive machines. But Byng's optimism had led him to commit all his forces in the first wave without making allowances for reserves. The British pressed forward, a seemingly unstoppable force, and with Byng's initial success, word had gone back to Haig, and then on to England, joyous reports of a stunning breakthrough. For a week, Byng's attack seemed to rout every pocket of resistance, opening a wide hole in the German lines. But Byng's lack of reserves meant that his grand assault began to exhaust itself. Though German infantry and machine guns alone could not stop the tanks, many of the huge machines began to stop themselves, many with mechanical problems, some failing to negotiate the wider trenches, tumbling into holes that left them completely useless. The lumbering slowness of the machines provided little protection for the British soldiers who followed them, and as the German resistance began to stiffen, the Tommies began to suffer the same horror that every infantry advance had experienced, the open ground swept by German machine guns, well hidden in long-established shelters. With the British infantry melting away into whatever shelter they could find, the tanks had to advance alone, relying only on the protection of their armor and their own guns. As they continued their push, the tanks began to roll into narrow streets of small villages, costing them their mobility, their gunners suddenly without a field of fire. The Germans began to take advantage, began to realize that this frightening new weapon could in fact be disabled. As the tanks rolled closer to the German artillery positions, they became perfect targets. The German foot soldiers had overcome their terror of the huge mechanical beasts, and men began to seek out the blind spots, began to learn that the tanks were vulnerable after all. As the tanks continued their advance, German troops scrambled out of hidden bunkers, tossing bundles of hand grenades into the tracks, or detonating explosives beneath the tanks themselves. With no reserves to assist the helpless tank crews, Byng's assault was stopped before it could even reach the town of Cambrai. As had happened so many times before, the glorious attack was ordered to halt. While Byng continued to insist that the tank would yet be the dominant weapon on the battlefield, even Haig could not ignore the numbers. The British had lost just under fifty thousand men, nearly equal to the losses they had inflicted on the Germans. But the battle had not yet ended. The Germans were not content to simply allow the British to hold tight to the ground they had gained, nor were the tanks allowed to simply limp away. On November 30, ten days after the attack had begun, the Germans counterattacked and drove most of Byng's forces back to their original lines. The stalemate would go on.

November 30, 1917

Pershing had endured several days of continual meetings, military and civilian. He appreciated the growing number of opportunities to speak with Pétain, both men understanding the challenges and logistics they had to grapple with. The civilians were another matter, and Pershing had been called upon by various ministers who held tightly to their own importance. It had become his routine, nearly every day a visit from some local official, a low-level minister of some department, the typical annoying protest that the man's authority was being ignored. The wounded official would almost always be accompanied by Pershing's own staff officer, or some other American who was the target of the complaint, whose duty had somehow trespassed into the Frenchman's perceived realm of total authority.

The requests for his time came from higher-ups as well, from Lloyd George to Painlevé to ministers from other Allied governments, includ-ing both Italy and Portugal. More often the meetings came about because someone in authority felt the urgent need to impart their advice or criticism to the American commander, or make some attempt at lobbying their own view-points as to how the Americans should perform, advice that

Pershing could now predict before the meetings even began. Not even Ambassador Sharp could serve as a buffer between Pershing and the affairs of state he was called upon to address, Sharp himself having no expertise at all when it came to military matters. But occasionally, the requests for his time came from someone Pershing actually enjoyed talking to, Pétain in particular, as well as the generals under his immediate command, men like Fox Conner and Hugh Drum, or the First Division's efficient and likable operations officer, George Marshall. Included in that select group was Billy Mitchell.

"Sir, Colonel Mitchell is here."

Pershing pushed his papers aside, stifled a yawn. "Send him in."

"Hello, General. Nice day for a plague of locusts, wouldn't you say?"

Pershing knew to expect some strange greeting from Mitchell, usually laced with humor. But Mitchell was not smiling, and Pershing said, "If you say so, Colonel."

Mitchell sat down without permission, was the one man Pershing would allow to make himself so completely comfortable without the proper show of protocol. It was the one concession Pershing made to the man's extraordinary tenacity for confronting anyone's incompetence, no matter the offender's rank or status. Pershing glanced at his papers again, his mind drifting over the blur of words.

"What's on your mind, Colonel?"

"Mind. Now there's something. We all have one, you know. Problem is, there's so few men around who actually know how to use the one they've been given."

Pershing looked at the man, had gone through this routine before, knew that Mitchell had a serious point behind this show of curmudgeonly grouchiness. But there was still no humor in the man's words. He was surprised by the anger in Mitchell's scowl, said, "Whose mind might you be referring to, Colonel?"

"Well, for one, there's the pea-brained genius who set the physical standards for our pilots. That wouldn't be . . . you, sir?"

"No. I consented to allowing General Foulois to implement the policies that the War Department sent with him."

"Ah, yes. Ben Foulois. I haven't checked my French dictionary, but I'm guessing the translation of his name. *Fool-wah*. Now there's a man whose name fits him like a well-oiled boot."

Foulois' arrival continued to be a sore point to Pershing. His original selection of William Kenly to head the AEF's Air Service had been suddenly preempted by Tasker Bliss, Bliss deciding to appoint Benjamin Foulois to replace Kenly, without even discussing the matter with Pershing at all. Foulois had simply arrived in France, with orders from Bliss to assume command of the Air Service. Pershing had known Foulois in Texas, a woefully inept commander of the army's futile attempt to bring aircraft into the pursuit of Pancho Villa. The project had been abandoned almost immediately, but to Pershing's dismay, Foulois had gained considerable influence at the War Department. When he arrived in France, Foulois had been accompanied by an entire staff of officers, none with any experience at all in dealing with either aircraft or pilots. Though Bliss' orders recalled Kenly to Washington, Mitchell had simply been overlooked, to Pershing's enormous relief, and Pershing had made it clear to Foulois that Billy Mitchell would maintain his position and his authority. In a short time, Foulois had established his command over the nonexistent air force, and wisely kept his distance from Pershing, relying on Mitchell to act as go-between. Pershing had to hope that Foulois might yet grow into his role, and Pershing had assigned the man's entire staff to focus on one priority: training pilots. If Pershing needed to know something about aeroplanes, he spoke to Mitchell. But Pershing was not in the mood for Mitchell's carping, did not need to be reminded of this most blatant interference by Tasker Bliss.

"Get to it, Colonel."

"Now, General, it makes sense to me that if you are building an air service from the ground up, the most valuable commodity would be experience. Put the right men in the right place. I realize that Washington is as yet unaware of that piece of wisdom." He winked at Pershing through his hard frown. "Yourself excluded, sir." Pershing's weariness was shortening his patience, and Mitchell seemed to sense it, said, "General, I know of no more capable and useful addition to our efforts at creating an air service than the pilots of the Lafayette Escadrille."

"Agreed."

"Well, that's good to hear, sir. Because, you see, General Foulois insisted that every prospective pilot be given a physical examination. Sounds logical, certainly. But I regret to inform you, sir, that every damned member of the Lafayette Escadrille was found to be below the standards required by our esteemed General Foulois. In other words, sir, the best American pilots on God's green earth have been found to be unworthy to fly for us."

Pershing felt his mouth opening, stared at Mitchell, expected a smile, instead saw quivering anger in the man's face. "You're serious."

Mitchell reached into his coat, retrieved a paper. "It's all right here, sir. The entire list. Every damned one of them."

Pershing scanned the names, many of them familiar. "Lufbery? Thaw?"

"Especially Thaw. Blind as a bat. Of course, that hasn't kept him from knocking a few Fokkers out of the air. Lufbery's got rheumatism, or some damned thing. One of the few men in France who I'd back in a fight against the Red Baron. But, he's no good for us, no sir. We need men who are *physically fit*."

Pershing focused on the list, said, "Have you brought this to General Foulois' attention?"

"What do you think, sir? Of course I did. The stupid . . . sorry, sir. The regrettably inflexible man said, Well, rules are rules."

It was one more annoyance, one more lead weight settling down into Pershing's brain. He shouted, "Lieutenant!"

A young man appeared at the door. "Yes, sir?"

"Bring yourself and a pad of paper. I have an order I need to communicate to General Foulois. We're going to make a few changes."

Mitchell finally smiled.

27

LUFBERY

La Noblette, France—December 1917

They were farther west of Verdun now, another strategic re-location to place the squadron toward the center of the front-line activity. With the winter would again come the quiet time, and already some of the pilots had been granted leave by the Aeronautique Militaire. Ted Parsons had made the danger-ous sea voyage to America, was visiting his family in Massachusetts for the first time in two years. Others were gone as well, but for some it was not time for a vacation.

With the increasing organization of the American Air Service, the French had complied with the request of the American command to release the American pilots from their official attachment to the French army. The Americans had to face the reality that unless they took steps to transfer their services, by December 1, their French commissions would simply expire. If they didn't pursue other assignments with the AEF, they might still fly their SPADs for the French. But they would do it as civilians.

December 14, 1917

Thenault was waiting for him, had already filled a wineglass, motioned to it as Lufbery came into the room. "Please, join me."

Lufbery moved toward the desk, picked up the glass, took a small sip, was not in the mood for alcohol. He pulled a chair toward Thenault's desk, sat, said, "What are we supposed to toast?"

Thenault did not respond, drank from his own half-empty

429

glass. Lufbery heard him let out a long breath, and Thenault said, "Have you made your decision?"

"Does it matter?"

"Of course it matters! I do not understand you. Are you not will-ing . . . do you not share the enthusiasm of the others? What did you discover in Paris?"

Lufbery saw the flash of frustration on Thenault's face, had not heard him raise his voice in a long time. "Captain, is it your intention to take me out of the air?"

The question seemed to surprise Thenault. "No, of course not."

"Well, that is the intention of the American Air Service. Paris? What I *discovered* is that they have an office waiting for me. My own desk, just like this one. They even offered me a secretary, some eighteen-year-old cadaver who's too consumptive to carry a rifle. Do you understand, Captain? An *office*."

Thenault rubbed his chin, looked down, stared at the desk. "I do not understand, Mr. Lufbery. It is all very curious."

"I don't find it curious, Captain. I find it infuriating. And I'm not alone. How many of the others feel the same way?"

Thenault looked up at him now. "A few. Most of them are expecting to fly; some will serve in different ways. I understand Mr. Johnson has accepted an instructor's position at the American center at Tours. Mr. Parsons is still on leave, so I do not know his decision. Some intend to remain here until a final decision is reached about the escadrille's status." He paused. "Perhaps your command feels you are more useful for what you have already accomplished. I do not wish to embarrass you, Mr. Lufbery, but more than any man here, you are a hero. You represent something the young pilots can look up to. I don't know why else they would assign you to . . . an office."

Lufbery could see the doubts on Thenault's face, thought, He doesn't even believe that himself.

"Captain, I know of no good reason why I should give up flying just to become . . . what? A symbol?"

Thenault thought a moment, poured another glass of wine, saw that Lufbery's glass was still full.

"Mr. Lufbery, I do not claim to understand Americans. Even

430

though you were a child of France, you know what it is to be American, you have experienced the differences between us. All that I know of America comes from all of you. This escadrille was created by men who left their homes and families and traveled to France possibly to lose their lives. Why? To protect my country. Every day I watched you take your aeroplanes into the sky, wondering if you would return. I do not have to tell you how often your friends did not return. But still you fly. All of you. Not one of you quit; not one of you chose to return home because of what you saw here. I understand fear, Mr. Lufbery. There are few soldiers in France who have not witnessed the death of a friend. I know what you feel when you climb into your aeroplane, what it does to your insides when you see a Boche in the air. How many of you were wounded, how many aeroplanes were shot to splinters, how many times have you felt the Boche on your tail, knowing that he has only one thought, one purpose: to kill you." Thenault took a drink, and Lufbery saw a quiver in the man's hand. "And still . . . you fly. I don't know what to call that, Mr. Lufbery. What is your word? Guts? No, that is not sufficient. When I took command here, I was encouraged by the optimism of Dr. Gros, by Mr. Prince and Mr. Thaw. Their enthusiasm was entertaining to me, such men who dream of changing the world. But, to be honest, no one in the Aeronautique Militaire was confident this escadrille would endure for very long. Please understand. The gesture was always appreciated, and many people in this country feel great affection for America because of what you came here to do. But there was doubt as well. No officer I knew expected any more of the Escadrille Américaine than some very nice newspaper stories. No longer. No one has doubts now. Forgive me, Mr. Lufbery, but I believe I know you quite well. In your mind, the credit belongs to the entire escadrille. That is simply your way. But you are wrong. More than any man here, you, Mr. Lufbery, are the reason why the Lafayette Escadrille has gained such respect. *You*." Lufbery heard Thenault's words choke away, could feel the weight of the man's emotions. Thenault drank from the wineglass, looked down again, and there was a long silent pause. He smiled now, said, "Mr. Lufbery, I have thought of your little friends outside. Well, no, they are not so little anymore."

"Who . . . the lions?"

Thenault nodded, still smiling. "When you go out to the hangar, look at your lions. Especially the male, Whiskey. He is growing quickly, is very strong now, maybe too strong. He has no idea how badly he can hurt you. He is still a child, full of energy, full of . . . adventure. But to others, the visitors who come here, he is terrifying, a mighty beast."

Lufbery smiled himself now, thought, This isn't about a lion cub at all. He said, "Are you trying to tell me that this is what America is to you? I have heard that before, that America is some large clumsy beast who is just now coming out of her slumber. I'm sorry, Captain, but all I've seen is delay and incompetence. Most of the officers who are taking charge of the Air Service have never flown an aeroplane. They are no more than clerks with too much power."

"Very young clerks, Mr. Lufbery. A very young army. Like your lion cub, you do not yet know how much power you have, or the proper way to use it. But you will learn. General Pershing seems to be a man who is determined to succeed. He has already shown us he will not tolerate . . . how would you describe it? Idiocy? Men like that know that they must first find the right people who perform as they do. He has already promoted Mr. Mitchell, for example. Mr. Lufbery, I believe that men of excellence deserve a special place in history. But they are not born to it. It comes slowly, often with a great deal of frustration. History will record that General Pétain saved the French army, ended the mutiny that could have lost this war. But in 1914, he was only a colonel." He paused. "In 1914, Mr. Lufbery, you were a mechanic. Now . . . well, I will not embarrass you. You are not a man who values medals. I would always welcome you in my squadron. When I fly to meet the Boche, there is no one I would prefer beside me. But I believe America must have help from men like you. If they give you a desk . . . so you will sit at a desk." He laughed, patted the wooden desktop with his hand. "It is not always so unpleasant." He paused, leaned forward, the smile gone. "America is making an enormous leap, a dangerous leap, on very young legs. It will require time. And as much as I would like to see you up there in a SPAD, I believe that you have other duties to perform. Take the desk, for now. The American Air Service is an infant who needs guidance, just like your lion cub. I remember that he did not always listen to you, and your patience was tested. But no matter how large or how frightening he becomes, you are a part of him now, he will always listen to you. I believe, Mr. Lufbery, that you will one day lead your own escadrille, that your Air Service will learn quickly to listen to what you can teach them. That is the opportunity that awaits you."

Issoudun, France—January 25, 1918

The desk was large and dark, deep empty drawers, a hulking monument to the silence that surrounded him. He felt dwarfed by the massive unpadded chair, felt the hard seat pushing a dull pain up through his backside. He ran his hand across the desktop, a thick slab of oak and varnish that bore the cuts and carvings of long years of misuse. There was all manner of etchings, names, various figures, a heart, someone's idea of a lightning bolt. For three days he had gone through the same exercise, finding some entertainment in the myriad assortment of vandalism on his desk. Since his arrival at Issoudun, there had simply been nothing else for him to do, no duty, no official awareness of his presence.

Issoudun was south of Paris, and the new home of the primary training center for the supposedly massive influx of new American pilots. The facilities themselves covered an enormous piece of ground, a thousand acres of open fields and hangars, low buildings honeycombed with classrooms and windowless offices, none more oppressing than the one he occupied now.

He had accepted Thenault's challenge, but he could still not muster any enthusiasm for his future. There was no home for him any more comfortable than the cockpit of his SPAD, and at Issoudun, he was dismayed to learn that the Americans had yet to secure any aircraft at all. Even if the men now in charge of

433

building the Air Service were aware of the experience he was offering them, they had no way to carry that into the air.

There had been another dramatic change for him as well, something unexpected that had nearly caused him to change his mind about leaving Thenault and the escadrille's base at La Noblette. When Lufbery was ordered to Issoudun, he had been told that there would be no place for the lion cubs. Those pilots who still remained at La Noblette had tearfully accepted that the only option was to turn Whiskey and Soda over to the Paris zoo. It was one of the most difficult farewells Lufbery had ever endured.

He began his reconnaissance of the desktop yet again, found a small glimmer of inspiration by noticing a bit of carving he had not yet seen. He focused on the variety of gouges for a moment, tried to picture the various artists, some minor officials, made so desperate by the insufferable boredom of their particular position as to assault this piece of furniture. He looked by his right elbow, saw the familiar name, small block letters: maurice. He had spent long minutes in speculation, wondered now, was it some tribute to the man's supervisor, the name of the demon responsible for sentencing some free spirit to a life of despair behind this wooden prison? Of course, it could be the man's own name, a brief display of vanity. No, that would make no sense. Lufbery ran his finger over the dull edges of the carving, thought, No sane man whose years were spent behind this oaken monstrosity would have any vanity left in his soul. His mind brightened at another possibility. Perhaps it is the name of a brandy, or even better, some obscure cognac, a symbol of the man's longing, the only sanctuary the poor soul could find after a long day sitting *here*.

He had squeezed the last remnant of humor from his day-dreaming, sat back, felt the square ribs of the chair cutting into him. He twisted slightly, tried to use the chair back to scratch the unreachable places, felt more pain than relief. He abandoned the effort, leaned forward again, his arms resting on the desktop. He looked up now, scanned the bare drab stains on the walls. On the first day, he had tried to pass the time finding shapes in the oily stains, like a child staring at white puffs

434

of clouds, seeing the faces of animals. But that too was exhausted, and he focused now on the only other distraction in the room. Beside the closed door was a small painting, hanging crookedly, a girl holding a basket of faded flowers. He realized it wasn't the flowers that were faded, it was the entire painting, matching the muted color of the walls. The painting had been hung just beside the doorframe, and he saw now, if the door was opened, the painting would be hidden. Of course, the painting must have been someone's private piece of heaven, hidden from the rest of the office, from those people *out there*. It had to mean that whoever hung it there kept his door closed. Of course. What's a prison without a gate?

The door opened suddenly, jarring his thoughts, and he saw the starched uniform, the familiar pimply face of the young sergeant.

"Good morning, sir! You'll be pleased about this! I wasn't sure anyone remembered we were here, and then, look here! Major Gray sent word he will be arriving at nine o'clock. Just a few minutes now."

Lufbery looked at the man without expression, said, "Why will I be pleased about that?"

"Well, sir, it means they found something for you to do! Besides, sir, there's something about officers that brightens up the place. They bring so much authority. Makes me feel part of something important. Surely, sir, you know what I mean."

There was the sound of a door out beyond the office, and the sergeant vanished in a rush, voices now filling the outer room. Lufbery stared at the vacant doorway, said aloud, "I have no idea what you mean."

The major was there now, a man not much older than the sergeant, a skinny runt of a man with his hat pulled firmly down on his forehead. He marched into the office, and Lufbery waited for the inevitable, the whining voice that cut a deep slice into Lufbery's brain.

"Mr. Loverbee, the thought occurred to me this morning that your experience could be put to good use. You have some paper, yes?"

"No."

435

"Sergeant! Bring a stack of writing paper."

The sergeant appeared at the door, said, "Excuse me, sir, but should I also bring a writing instrument?"

Gray scanned Lufbery's desktop, seemed disappointed at the barren landscape. "Certainly, Sergeant."

"Should I bring a pencil or a pen, sir?"

"Which do we have in greater supply?"

The sergeant hesitated, said, "I best go see, sir."

The major stared at the blank wall above Lufbery's head, seemed lost in thought for a moment. He nodded, said, "That was very good, you know. The man's using his head." He looked at Lufbery now, as though seeing him for the first time. "You're not used to this, I'm betting. There's more to being in the army than just flying around the countryside. I don't cherish the thought, mind you."

Lufbery stared at the man through a growing tightness in his brain. *Have you ever cherished a thought?* He imagined the man suddenly exploding into nothingness in front of him, fought the temptation to make it happen.

"What thought do you cherish, Major Gray?"

"Training you! Scraping away all this . . . Frenchness. From what I've seen of you former pilots, there's a remarkable lack of discipline. Not sure how that sort of thing was ever allowed. It won't happen again, I can assure you. Not here! Every day that passes new pilots are arriving, men who are here because America *wants* them here! In a few weeks, these men will darken the skies over Germany!"

Lufbery felt his brain curl into a ball. *That phrase again.*

Gray pointed at him. "Some advice for you, Mr. Loverbee. Just because the army has commissioned you a major does not make you an officer in my book! I checked. Your commission is dated January tenth. Mine dates from the first. According to regulations I am your superior officer. Under my command, if you expect to share any of the privileges of rank, you must earn it! At this facility, we will teach men who have never seen an aeroplane not only how to fly their machine, but how to turn themselves and their craft into a single instrument of deadly force. At Issoudun, the Air Service must first mold the weapons

436

that will make us successful. I want to see some cooperation, and some evidence that you have come here to do things the correct way! Put aside all that you have learned from these Frenchmen, and in time, you'll do quite well here."

The sergeant appeared, held a thick stack of yellow paper, a handful of writing instruments. "Sir! I thought it best you should decide, sir!"

Gray wagged his finger at Lufbery, a knowing smile on his face. "You see? Discipline!" He turned to the sergeant, examined the various pens and pencils, and after a long moment, he held one up, then pointed to Lufbery's desk.

"Take this one. Put the paper down there, Sergeant. Well, Mr. Loverbee, there you have it. Your tools of the trade, so to speak."

Lufbery was all knots inside, his hands curled into tight fists, his brain screaming at him to kill this man.

"What do you want me to do, Major?"

"Didn't I say? I should like you to prepare some sort of instruction booklet, something that draws on whatever form of experience you had in the air. I am told that you actually engaged the enemy with some success. Since the Air Service has seen fit to grant you the rank of major, you will have the opportunity to perform a task befitting that level of responsibility. If indeed you have bested the deadly Hun, then surely you can assist our efforts in training the new pilots by authoring a training manual detailing the proper technique."

Lufbery's eyes were closed, his chin pulled down to his chest. "The proper technique for what?"

"Why, for killing Germans, of course!"

February 18, 1918

He moved past the low buildings, glanced at his watch, annoyed that Major Gray held so much power over him, the little man who so enjoyed keeping this *former pilot* in a cage. He climbed the short steps, heard low voices in distant offices, saw no one in the main office. He let out a breath of relief, slipped quickly toward his own dismal space, pushed the door open, was surprised to smell the hard stench of a cigar. The door swung wide, and he saw a man seated behind his desk, feet up, his hat low on his face. The man peered up at him, raised the hat, said, "About time you got here. How in hell have you survived this godforsaken place?"

It was Bill Thaw.

Lufbery smiled, felt a bright beam of sunlight flowing through his mind, watched as Thaw straightened himself in the chair, the cigar clamped tightly between his teeth.

"Bill . . . what are you doing here? When did you get here?"

"Whoa there, soldier. That's *Major* Thaw to you. Oh, well, hell, you're a major too. Looks like everybody around this place is a major. Found any mushrooms around here? I could use a good French meal."

Lufbery was still smiling, said, "No mushrooms. No good ground here."

"And I bet you searched your ass off, too."

Lufbery laughed, moved around the side of the desk, and Thaw stood, put a hand on his shoulder, said, "Good to see you, Luf. You making out okay?"

Voices flowed into the office, and Lufbery turned, saw Major Gray.

"Oh, you're back. Good. I've been working on some new ideas for incorporating the infantry's marching drills into our pilot training. Thought it would be . . . oh." Gray noticed Thaw now, said, "Who are you? Haven't seen you here before. Did Colonel Mitchell send you down here? I told them we would get the supply forms completed by the end of the day."

Lufbery made no attempt to hide the smile, said, "Major Gray, this is Bill Thaw. He's from the Lafayette Escadrille."

Gray seemed to wince, said, "Pilot, eh? Just what I need. Look, Thaw, I only have a limited amount of office space. You can share this one for now. Since you and Loverbee are acquainted, shouldn't be a problem. You should know that I don't have much patience for junior officers who think they're still in France."

Thaw looked at Lufbery, said, "We're not in France? Who is this jackass?"

Gray puffed up, said, "Watch your mouth, Thaw. My commission dates from January first. In case you aren't aware of protocol and rank in this army, that places me in command of this department."

Thaw laughed, said, "Really? Hadn't thought of that. Well then, I suggest you watch *your* mouth, Major. I got my commission on December tenth. I guess that means I outrank your scrawny little ass. And one more thing . . ." He reached into his jacket pocket, pulled out a piece of paper. "Here's some more protocol for you. I have orders here relieving Major Lufbery of his responsibilities to your department. He has been assigned to the Ninety-fourth Aero Squadron, effective right now."

Lufbery felt numbed by the words, realized that Thaw was serious. He felt Thaw tugging at his arm.

"Let's go, Luf. This place is giving me a bellyache." He pulled Lufbery toward the door, and Gray sputtered a protest, held up a hand, seemed to melt back against the wall. Thaw handed him the order, said, "Go on, read it. Now, as your superior officer, I order you to get the hell out of our way."

On February 18, 1918, the Lafayette Escadrille officially ceased to exist. Those pilots who had chosen to remain with the unit were transferred into the American Air Service as the 103rd Pursuit Squadron, commanded by Major Bill Thaw. Lufbery's orders were to report to the airfield at Villeneuve, closer to Paris, to serve as senior flying officer for the Ninety-fourth Aero Squadron, as well as assuming the role of primary combat instructor for the newly trained American pilots, the first men who would fly for the American Air Service. There was nothing in his orders about writing pamphlets.

28

PERSHING

January 1918

The chaos in France had finally reached a hard claw into the civilian government. For several months Paul Painlevé had assumed the role of prime minister, holding together a weak coalition of opposing ministers. Painlevé's government had no more positive effect on the suffering of the French people than his predecessors, and by November, his fragile coalition had collapsed. Though Raymond Poincaré still held office as president, the title was mostly ceremonial. Poincaré was confined to recommending the men who would serve in the cabinet, where the real power of the civilian government was found. The unrest that had spread through the country called for a prime minister who could inspire the affection of the people. Poincaré sought out the only man who seemed capable of confronting the ongoing despair that had settled over France.

Like Paul von Hindenburg in Germany, Georges Clemenceau was the aging symbol of his country, the grandfatherly leader who brought with him memories of better times. Unlike von Hindenburg, Clemenceau was not a soldier; he had climbed to power through the civilian government. He had been semi-retired for several years, accepting a post in the French senate that provided him a public forum. Throughout the war, the feisty seventy-six-year-old had become an aggressive critic of the mistakes that had plagued the Allies since 1914. Clemenceau was not a man who feared making enemies, and as the army's mistakes multiplied, Clemenceau's unbridled criticism had alienated him from both Joffre and Pétain. But the people of France were hungry for someone who could offer them hope. Despite his crusty demeanor and lack of diplomatic gracefulness, Clemenceau, whose nickname was "the tiger," seemed to be the only man for the job.

Pershing was learning quickly that powerful civilians made for powerful intrusions into the affairs of the military. In November, the civilian leaders of France, Great Britain, and Italy had met to discuss the immediate crisis of the Italian army's collapse at Caporetto. But the leaders, especially David Lloyd George, saw the summit as an opportunity for the civilian officials to organize what they labeled a Supreme War Council, each man to play a greater role in the affairs of his army's frustratingly ineffective strategies. To the military commanders—Haig, Pétain, and Pershing—it simply meant that the civilian leaders had every intention of interfering in military planning far more than they had before.

The interference began almost immediately. Pershing learned that Clemenceau had contacted Washington directly, indiscreetly suggesting that Pershing be ordered to assign American regiments to French front-line divisions as a means of hastening the Americans' training. Pershing had continued to fend off the same pressure from Pétain, rejecting the proposal for one obvious reason. If American units were made a part of French divisions, they would be used to fill the gaps that the war of attrition had caused. Though a limit might be placed on how much time the Americans would be "loaned" to the French divisions, when that time period elapsed, it would be nearly impossible to recall the Americans into their own divisions without effectively disabling the French units they left behind. Pétain seemed to understand the problem. Apparently, to Pershing's intense annoyance, Clemenceau did not.

Pershing was careful, phrased his words with precision. "Monsieur Prime Minister, is it not convenient for you to pass your requests through the channels that my government has established? I had thought General Pétain and I had reached an agreement on this matter. I apologize if you were given a different impression."

Clemenceau showed no emotion, seemed to stare past him. Pershing had expected him to be a larger man, someone with the commanding presence of Joffre or even Pétain. But Clemenceau showed the effects of age, a worn, round face, a thick, bushy white moustache with eyebrows to match. Clemenceau ran a wrinkled hand over his bald scalp, seemed bored with Pershing's protest.

"It is entirely proper of me to send a cable to the French ambassador on any topic that my duty calls me to address. Forgive me, General, but there are conversations taking place in Washington as well as Paris that have direct bearing on the future of my country. If the ambassador chose to reveal my inquiry to Secretary Baker, that is not my responsibility."

The man's words rolled over him like a syrupy blanket. Despite Clemenceau's display of disinterest, Pershing could see the steel in the man's eyes. Even old age had not dimmed Clemenceau's fire.

"I shall continue my discussions with General Pétain, sir—"

"General, forgive me if I display loyalty to my country."

Pershing wasn't sure what he meant, saw Clemenceau staring away, as though recalling some pleasant memory. Pershing waited, and after a long moment Clemenceau said, "There is much to preserve here, General. Our enemies would drive us into oblivion, erase France from the pages of history. We fight the desperate battle, and as you know, General, the battle does not go well. I am not so concerned that your army achieves your standards of preparedness. I am more concerned that we receive your assistance, to defend France against the scourge that seeks to destroy us. Is that too much to ask of you? Have you no sense of history, of compassion for your ally?"

Pershing wanted to respond, but Clemenceau seemed to drift away again. The man's words hung in the air, pushing away reason. So, it matters not if our men are prepared, just so they fill your trenches. The arguments rolled through him, but Pershing could feel the futility of trying to convince this man of anything he didn't want to hear. Pershing stood, made a short bow, said, "We shall do our best, Prime Minister."

He walked out into the street, saw his car waiting up the block. The wind was sharp, a blade of ice cutting through his clothes.

He felt frustrated, empty, had accomplished nothing in his meeting with Clemenceau. The door was held open for him, and he dove into the car, sheltered from the wind, said, "The hotel, Lieutenant."

"Yes, sir."

He felt himself growing angrier, realized he had been completely mastered by Clemenceau. He had been surprised by the man's appearance, had seen nothing of a *tiger*. But no, he thought, this tiger does not have to bite you to win the fight. All the absent stares, the carefully chosen words, all designed by a craftsman, someone who knows how to make his point without having to listen to yours. He thought of Joffre, a man used to making his own point, accustomed to stifling any disagreement. No wonder they despise each other. They both understand that power does not come to the man who shouts the loudest. It is certainly something that Douglas Haig does not understand. I expected bluster, grand pronouncements, and Clemenceau knew that, and so he kept it soft, sentimental. How can anyone argue with an old man who simply loves his country? But Clemenceau believes that President Wilson can be pressured, and so the cables and letters will continue to go to Washington. He recalled Baker's letter, the first hint that Clemenceau was going above his head. Baker had been blunt to the French, had deferred the entire matter to Pershing's authority. Pershing understood now that Baker's confidence in him was a luxury that his colleagues did not share. He was beginning to realize how delicate the hold on command was for men like Pétain and Haig, and how much pressure they had to tolerate, thought, It's a part of their everyday experience. From the beginning of the war, the lesson has been learned: Generals come and go, easily replaced by the next man in the chain. But a desperate country will cling to leaders who know how to exercise power, men like Clemenceau and Lloyd George. A general is judged by the battles he wins. It is no wonder that Haig insists his every attack is a victory. Any military commander who believes himself to be the final authority is either a dictator or a fool. I don't believe I'm either one. But if the British or French are persuasive enough, President Wilson might indeed change his mind, might give in to our allies' judgment. And where will that leave me?

He stared out the window of the car, saw people shuffling along wrapped in thick bundles of clothing, the brutality of winter pressing down on the city. He fought the reminder, what the winter meant to the soldiers, the men flowing into the lines along the American sector without sufficient protection against the brutal cold. It was the worst winter anyone could remember, and Pershing had begged the quartermaster's office in Washington for suitable clothing, coats and leggings, yet another urgent request seemingly tossed into some basket, to be ignored by someone with better things to do. If the cold was not enough of a challenge, the troops were marching mostly on foot, since very little motor transportation had been made available. It was another source of Pershing's fury; no one in Washington taking seriously his requests for trucks. We are the world's largest producer of motor vehicles, he thought, and they insist that the trucks should be kept at the training centers. Those people can use horse-drawn carriages, for God's sake. Here, we have men marching in a war zone with frozen feet along icy roads, because some damned colonel in Louisiana can't be inconvenienced.

It had become almost routine now, so many of his army's needs going unmet, ignored by the various offices in Washington, a theater of the comically absurd. But through his frustration, the effects of his staff's ex-traordinary efforts in France were bringing results. Slowly, the ports were becoming more efficient, and the pipeline of supply was beginning to flow with more regularity. Much of it was due to a radical change that had swept across the waters of the Atlantic. The horrific effects of the U-boat war had been blunted by the increasing use of convoys, large groups of transport ships traveling together, swarmed about by antisubmarine destroyers and gunships. For the first time since Wilson had declared war, the rate of sinkings inflicted by the German submarines had actually dropped, and dropped significantly. Though the flow of troops was far slower than he and the Allies had hoped, the men were coming, and as the training camps in the States continued to turn out soldiers who had at least rudimentary training, those numbers would only rise. Clemenceau's lack of concern that the Americans be given any real preparation was an annoyance, but it would not affect the system Pershing had put in place. He knew that regardless of what the British and the French demanded or expected, as each American division was sent into line, they would be prepared for whatever they would face. And every day, there were more of them.

Tasker Bliss had finally stepped down as chief of staff, but instead of settling quietly into retirement, he had requested assignment to Europe, and now he was serving as a delegate, a nonvoting member of the Supreme War Council, to represent the interests of the American government. Pershing respected the man, but had received so little cooperation from Bliss' offices in Washington that he had few expectations Bliss would accomplish anything of substance. His new role carried no authority, and Bliss' sole responsibility was to report back to Baker and Wilson those points which the council wished the Americans to address. Pershing still had little confidence that such a council of government leaders could make any decisions that would radically alter the success or failure of their armies. But Bliss had his assignment, and for Pershing, it was a relief. It meant that Pershing himself did not have to spend his own valuable time attending the council meetings.

In Washington, the position of chief of staff had gone to General Peyton March, who had served Pershing well as a forceful and no-nonsense chief of artillery instruction. Secretary Baker had asked Pershing for his recommendations, and though March had not been Pershing's first choice, Baker had decided on March based on the man's straight-ahead aggressive style. It was the one ingredient that both the War Department and the General Staff had been lacking. Pershing could only agree.

While the Supreme War Council had yet to intrude directly into military decision making, the quiet winter provided time for both the civilian and military leaders to feel their way through a process that was designed to improve cooperation among the armies, something that had rarely worked. Pétain, Haig, and Pershing each had absolute control over his own domain, and each man answered only to his civilian government. With Russia now completely out of the war, Germany was free to reinforce its strength all along the Western Front. Unless the allies found an efficient means to coordinate their three distinct armies, the German advantage could be overwhelming.

The French military representative to the Supreme War Council was General Ferdinand Foch, who had served both as a field commander and as Pétain's chief of staff. At Foch's insistence, the allies began to discuss the formation of a large general reserve, to be composed of divisions taken from both the British and French armies. The general reserve would act independently of Haig or Pétain, could be used to strengthen any part of the front that was under immediate threat. Though debate swirled around who might actually command this reserve, Clemenceau had pressed hard for the authority to go to the man who had done the most to design the concept in the first place: Ferdinand Foch. Though the new position would carry no real authority over the three commanding generals, to the civilian leaders, Foch's plan was a monumentally positive step toward securing coordination along the entire front. Whether or not the generals would accept Foch's efforts remained to be seen.

French General Headquarters, Compiègne, France—January 24, 1918

Pershing had sat quietly as each of the others stated his own position, so many of the speeches offering nothing more than what they had all heard before. Pétain had begun the meeting with a grim assessment of the condition and preparedness of his army, something he had frequently shared with Pershing. Pétain's mood seemed to set the tone, and the entire group was subdued, even Haig and Wully Robertson forgoing their usual claims that great victories were just ahead. Haig in particular seemed to accept Pétain's pessimistic appraisal, that neither army could withstand what would certainly be a major thrust by Ludendorff's strengthening forces sometime in the spring.

Pershing had met Foch only briefly, but now he found himself hanging on the man's words, an unusual experience. Foch was a diminutive man, slim and frail, showing every one of his sixty-six years. Pershing had heard speculation around Pétain's headquarters that Foch was simply a man past his time, like so many of the aging generals. As Foch spoke, Pershing glanced at Pétain, could see that divisiveness plagued the French camp as well. Pétain had yet to agree with anything Foch had said.

Foch continued, "We must be prepared to launch an immediate counteroffensive, a rapid, powerful response to whatever assault the Germans send forth. It has been the only tactic that has yet been successful. We did not stop the enemy at Verdun by our defense. We stopped them by launching an attack elsewhere, along the Somme. We cannot hope to repeat that success without sufficient planning. We must anticipate what the enemy is going to do, and be prepared not only with a stout defense, but the ability to strike back. We must consider the entire front to be one theater. We cannot continue this absurd distinction of a British front and a French front, with the Americans somewhere in between. Our enemy does not suffer from such difficulty. It is a disadvantage that we have not been able to overcome."

Pétain shook his head, said, "Verdun was different, a different time, a different enemy. The Germans now possess far superior numbers, and can strike at any point along the entire front with a force such as we have not faced before. To subtract a large percentage of our front-line strength merely to assemble a large general reserve does not answer the question: How is this reserve to be employed? If the enemy causes a significant breakthrough in our lines, there may be no time to gather this reserve and organize them for an entirely separate attack. We require a defensive reserve that can be called upon locally, to stop a breakthrough when and where it occurs. General Foch, with all respect, if you can demonstrate the ability to accurately predict where the enemy will strike, then I will support your plan for a general reserve. I have seen no such ability in any of us."

Haig stood up, said, "If we were to receive troops from other theaters of the war, from Salonika, from Arabia, then we could commence our own offenses. It would not matter what Herr Ludendorff had in mind. I for one am not disturbed by the reports of greatly increased enemy numbers. The greater their numbers, the greater will be their destruction."

Pershing saw a slight wince on Robertson's face. Of course, he has been hearing this sort of thing for a long time now. And all they have to show for Haig's bluster are casualty lists.

Foch responded, "Marshal Haig, I am not referring to any offensive strategies on our part. I am focusing on a plan for counteroffensives."

Robertson said, "You're talking about whisking reinforcements from one end of the front to the other, depending on where the enemy attacks. Is that the best we can hope for? I do not believe that putting our troops in a defensive stance will prove successful. Surely we can accomplish more than this."

"Not without the Americans." The words came from Pétain, and all faces now turned to Pershing.

Robertson said, "I am tending to agree. So, General Pershing, perhaps you can enlighten us. What sort of timetable do you predict before your army will be an effective force?"

"By late this spring, we shall have sufficient strength to effectively man our designated sector. If you wish, I shall provide you with a lengthy list of challenges we have had to confront and overcome."

Robertson said, "Certainly, General. But tell us, given the severity of the crisis before us, can we not persuade you that perhaps you should make the best use of the limited shipping to transport only those men who can immediately fill the lines? I have often thought it best if the Americans send infantry and machine gunners first, and save the rest of your personnel for later." Robertson's words hung in the room like smoke from a sour cigar.

"General, we have addressed these concerns repeatedly in the past."

Pershing was surprised to feel a hand on his arm, saw Tasker Bliss rising beside him.

"I am certain, General Robertson, that General Pershing is

open to any discussion that proves helpful to the cause of our allies. I believe it could be a positive boost for morale in both armies if American units were assigned to support their British brothers. Only good could come from such a plan."

Pershing felt an explosion building in his brain, stared at Bliss, who seemed oblivious to what he had just said. Pershing caught a look of shock on Pétain's face, said, "Excuse me, General Robertson, but General Bliss has apparently not been informed of the AEF's official position on this matter. There has been no change in my view that the American army is to fight as a cohesive and distinct unit. I do not believe any American soldier will readily accept a place in a British or French unit, fighting and marching under a foreign flag, and accepting orders from an officer foreign to him. With all respect to our allies in this room, I have made this position known with as much clarity as I can muster. By late spring, I anticipate that between ten and fifteen AEF divisions will be prepared to join the fight. And our strength will continue to grow as more shipping is made available to us. Our president has pledged support for our allies in such strength to materially affect the outcome of this war. I have been given the authority to fulfill the president's commitment in the manner I consider appropriate. If you will allow me, I should like to explain to you the challenges that have been set before us, some by our own lack of preparation, some by the inept or unwilling among our allies."

He spoke for another thirty minutes, his anger focused and precise, detailing the lengthy list of difficulties, shortages, and roadblocks that his staff had finally worked to overcome. He was pleased that his words had the desired effect, so many men with so much authority, listening with wide-eyed surprise at the difficulties of equipment and supply Pershing and his men had confronted. From Foch to Pétain, from Robertson to Haig, came surprising pledges of support, assurances that each man would look hard into the failings of the various bureaus and ministries that should have been monitored more closely, promises that the minor officials and bureaucrats who had done so much to delay the Americans' progress would be dealt with. He stopped short of detailing so many of the problems across the ocean, the delays in providing adequate training facilities, the continuing challenges of mobilizing the industrial might of the United States toward the priorities Pershing had begged for. The fault lay with many, mostly in the offices of the General Staff in Washington, the men who languished in the lackadaisical atmosphere inspired by their leadership, men like Tasker Bliss, who stood beside him now wearing an expression of profound shock and embarrassment. Pershing would say nothing to him in such a forum, would wait until later, a private moment, when Tasker Bliss would be reminded who carried the full authority of President Wilson, and who commanded the AEF.

Paris—January 26, 1918

His calendar was a mass of scribbled appointments, his staff scrambling to sort out the incessant calls for his attention. But through the noisy clamor for his time had come one invitation to a simple lunch. It was to be an informal affair, and Pershing had received the assurance that there would be no official presence, no need for proper diplomatic protocol. Pershing accepted gratefully, felt instinctively that for one brief moment he was being offered a quiet port in the storm.

"Marshal Joffre, this was delightful, thank you."

Joffre pushed himself back from the table, rubbed the round mass of his stomach. "Small delights can be made large in times such as these. I thought you might enjoy a diversion from your routine. And, perhaps some conversation. Not all of the old men who hover around you have evil in their hearts." Joffre laughed, and Pershing smiled, felt himself loosening up, relaxing for the first time in weeks.

Throughout the pleasant lunch, Joffre had been true to his word, no talk of strategy or the business of the army, none of the pressures Pershing had become used to weathering from so many of the men of influence. Joffre's wife had dined with them, a pleasant surprise. Pershing had met her several times before, at many of the various functions that her husband was called upon to attend. She spoke with a quiet sweetness, but there was strength behind the softness; Pershing sensed that she was not at all hesitant about speaking her mind. Even Joffre had acknowledged that though he once held an iron grip on France's military, he was not quite so powerful in his own home.

They sat in silence for a moment, Pershing taking the cue from Joffre, who waited while the maid whisked the plates away from the table. The table was cleared now, the maid gone, and Joffre said to his wife, "My dear, would you permit us to take leave of you? If the general will allow me a few moments longer, I should enjoy a word or two more."

The old woman rose from her chair, and Pershing saw a brief grimace on her soft face, betraying her frailty, some ailment she kept to herself.

She smiled at Pershing, said, "My apologies, General. It must be obvious to you that my husband's invitation was not entirely without motives. I, however, always enjoy your company, regardless of the occasion."

"The pleasure is mine, madam."

Joffre led him now into a sitting room, closed the door, said, "Forgive me, John. I do not usually feel the need for such privacy."

Pershing felt the man's mood changing, waited for Joffre to lower himself into a wide soft chair. Pershing sat as well, said, "As you prefer, sir. It is your home." He was still not completely at ease referring to the old man by his first name, despite Joffre's frequent requests.

Joffre seemed to catch the formality, shook his head, smiled, and said, "I should hope you would consider me your friend, John. I have nothing further to gain it seems. It has been made clear to me that my country is done with me."

The words carried a heavy sadness, and Pershing said, "Nonsense. You have far too much to offer."

Joffre shook his head again, no smile now. "You are aware that General Foch is being considered to command the combined armies on this front?"

"Combined armies? No . . . I am not aware of any such thing. We have met to discuss his plans for a general reserve—"

"Yes, yes. I know all of that. Endless debate. Clemenceau

451

insists it be so; Pétain insists it will not happen. The British are divided as well. The generals know how insecure their positions are, and so they do all they can to protect themselves. To Haig and Pétain, Foch is a threat. Perhaps even to you. It is why I had hoped they would choose someone else for the position. Foch is a good man, but he is fragile. There were other options open to Monsieur Clemenceau."

Pershing understood now. "Options, such as you?"

Joffre nodded slowly. "It was not to be. For such an old man, I am regrettably naïve. I had thought that my experience would reopen the door, that the Supreme War Council would consider that, if they desired one man to lead the Allied armies, it should be a man who knows how to lead. It seems, however, that I have made too many enemies."

"I'm still not certain. . . . I have heard nothing about choosing anyone to lead the armies. Foch is merely proposing—"

"The general reserve, yes. Do not think me a fool, John. I often find a way to hear what is being said behind closed doors. The talk has been more energized in recent weeks. The Supreme War Council may not have the wisdom of military strategy, but they understand what so many of the generals do not. This war cannot continue to be fought as it has before. If we are to avoid catastrophe, we must fight as one army, with one supreme commander. Mr. Clemenceau has, I believe, convinced Mr. Lloyd George that the man should be Ferdinand Foch. Foch is not yet stained by defeat, and, despite his age and his infirmities, they believe he is capable of doing the job. He is certainly a man capable of holding a tight rein on Douglas Haig, which must be pleasing to Lloyd George."

"But how can they bring that about? Pétain and Haig won't even consider allowing Foch to command the reserve. I admit, I have agreed with their position. You are suggesting that one man, a Frenchman, will be accepted by the British as a supreme commander? I agree that the concept is a good one, perhaps essential. But how can it happen?"

Joffre shrugged. "They will find the right moment. War causes change, whether we wish it or not. Men rise and fall, heroes become fools, the anonymous become icons. Henri

Pétain rose at the right moment to save the French army from its mutiny. President Wilson found . . . you."

"Thank you for the compliment, but I am not yet certain—"

"I am only trying to help you understand that you are in the midst of a storm that is far more complicated than you might realize."

"Why? Why is it important that you tell me these things? I cannot just accept what you say as truth. How do I regard Foch now? Am I not to say anything of this to Pétain? I feel as though you have made me part of some conspiracy."

Joffre looked down, cradled his round face in his hands, thought for a moment. "You must look beyond such small concerns, John. There is something much greater in motion here. You have heard this before, but I will repeat it. We cannot prevail in this war without the assistance of the Americans. Regardless of what kind of impression the Supreme War Council is trying to make on the world, on your government and mine, Mr. Clemenceau and Mr. Lloyd George are in control of the council, and they are men who know how to use their power. All the rest are like so many birds, perched high on the limbs above, watching the two great cats prowling below. Mr. Lloyd George is not a man who cares for generals, whether they be French or English . . . or American. He is a bit too public in his views, I'm afraid. It is not helpful to morale. It is certainly not helpful to Marshal Haig. Mr. Clemenceau is more practiced in the art of subtlety."

"Yes, I've had some experience with that."

"The French people are very aware how difficult is the condition of our army. The British have hidden instead behind the strong words of their prime minister. But along the front lines, the British army is in no better condition than ours. Very quietly, they have reduced the strength of their battalions. They simply do not have the reserve of manpower to call upon anymore. The newspapers in London have not been informed of this—the prime minister's attempt to keep his people's morale high. Here, we are already bringing into our army boys who normally would not serve until next year. But we cannot afford to wait for them to age. Look at any division in our army, and you will see officers with young faces. Company commanders above the age of thirty are practically nonexistent. They are simply gone. I would suspect that the ranks of British officers have been affected in the same way. The wells have run dry. Except, of course, for the Americans. This is why they fight over you. It is not about good strategy and convenience, it has nothing to do with proper training for your soldiers. It is desperation. Survival. When Lloyd George ridicules Marshal Haig, he points to British success in other theaters of the war, such as Arabia. But that is deception. He knows, as does everyone here, if the Western Front collapses, if the British are backed into the sea, if German troops march into Paris, nothing else will matter, not the defeat of Turkey, not the liberation of Syria. This war will end right here."

"Do you believe I am wrong to insist that we keep the American army together?"

"Oh my, no, John. Quite the opposite. Your president and Mr. Baker are wise to have chosen you for the storm that swirls around you. A weak man in your position would succumb to the pressure, and the result would be that your army would simply dissolve. The British could temporarily rebuild their battalions. *Temporarily*. But nothing else would be gained. The Germans are afraid of you, John. That fear could be of great benefit to them, and a very great problem for us."

"I don't understand."

"Ludendorff knows he has only a short time before you put a serious obstacle in his path. He will act accordingly. He must make his move before your army tips the balance in our favor. If he can crush the British, or take Paris, nothing you can do will alter the outcome."

"We are doing all we can to fill the American sector. I am confident that before the summer, we will be strong enough to make the fight."

"I hope you are correct, John." Joffre glanced back at a clock on a mantel behind him. "You have been more generous than I could have expected. I will allow you to return to your duty. There is no doubt an enormous clamoring for your attention."

Pershing felt himself weighed down by the words. "Yes, I am

quite certain my staff is eyeing the road for some glimpse of my vehicle. My desk is most certainly buried in correspondence. I should return to Chaumont."

He stood, and Joffre stayed in his chair, said, "Allow me to offer you one more bit of advice, John. Despite the desperate fight in front of you, there is another war being waged that you cannot win. If Germany is defeated, there will be a feeding frenzy among the civilian leaders, each one desperate for their proper share of the glory. Germany will become irrelevant. What will matter is which one of our ambitious leaders can cement his place in history as the man who engineered the great victory. To these men who place so much value on power, that will be all that matters. It is one of the obscenities of history. It may be that the Americans are the perfect foil. If we lose the war, you can be blamed, all your failures will be magnified. But if we win, you will receive none of the spoils, none of the glory. I hope you are immune to that. But I also hope you are prepared for it."

The meetings continued, incessant debates among the supreme War Council and their generals that frustrated everyone involved. Foch's plan continued to be endorsed by Lloyd George and Clemenceau, and rejected by Pétain and Haig. While the Allies debated and grappled with each other's pride and priorities, to the north and west, fresh German divisions continued to march into an ever-strengthening line, troops flush with their success in putting Russia out of the war. The winter was passing, the mud and the chalky swamplands drying, the ground growing firmer.

On March 3, Germany and her allies and the new Bolshevik leaders in Russia signed the Treaty of Brest-Litovsk, which officially ended the war in the East. To the German High Command, the advantage had swung completely their way. Inspired by an increase in troop strength along the Western Front, Ludendorff put into motion the plan that the Germans had every reason to believe would end the war.

It began on March 21, on a forty-mile front, from Arras to La Fère. Nearly three quarters of a million German troops surged

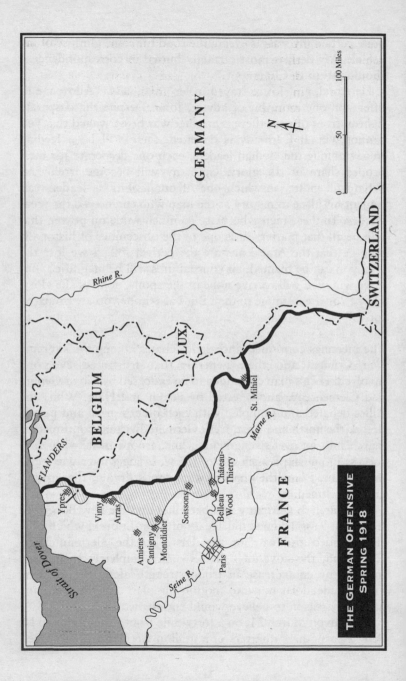

THE GERMAN OFFENSIVE
SPRING 1918

GERMANY

SWITZERLAND

Rhine R.

LUX.

BELGIUM

St. Mihiel

Marne R.

FLANDERS

Ypres

Vimy

Arras

Château-
Thierry

Soissons

Belleau
Wood

Amiens

Cantigny

Montdidier

Paris

FRANCE

Strait of Dover

Seine R.

100 Miles

50

0

N

forward toward the British lines, outnumbering the British defenders by three to one. The shock of the assault was complete and devastating, and opened a massive hole that no one could fill. In two days, the Germans had advanced to Mont-didier, thirty-five miles from their starting point, and had yet to confront any British force formidable enough to slow their advance. Though Ludendorff continued the push, the German troops had gone as far as their supplies and their physical stamina would allow, and the advance slowed from the exhaustion of its troops. As the Allies struggled to contain the breach, Joffre's predictions of change were realized. Desperation had turned to catastrophe, and the civilian and military leaders in France and Britain accepted that if Germany was to be stopped, the Allied forces must be coordinated and commanded by one man. On April 3, Ferdinand Foch was named generalissimo of the Allied armies.

Pershing could only respond to the disaster by stepping up the intensity of his own efforts, and American troops continued to fill the lines of the sector that lay just beyond the southern limits of the German breakthrough. It seemed that Ludendorff had focused his assault so as to ignore the Americans. Pershing had to wonder if the Germans had put into motion some grand design that might yet engulf the raw troops in their new positions. But he could not dwell on what had not yet happened. Throughout the American sector, the troops continued to prepare themselves, every part of the AEF, from the fledgling tank corps to the inexperienced Air Service, bracing for what might yet come. Through it all, as the reports flowed into his headquarters, detailing every moment of the disaster to the north, Pershing had to wonder if perhaps Ludendorff had made a gross miscalculation. If the assault had come in the American sector, the German breakthrough might have been equally as successful, and quite possibly could have destroyed the American army within its own defenses. Instead, the Americans were growing stronger every day.

29

LUFBERY

Near Villeneuve, France—March 1918

He scanned the horizon, glanced above and below, his eyes tuned to any movement, any sign that the enemy was close. They were flying east, into the sun, were passing over the German lines now. Far below, the flashes of fire began, and he held tight to the stick, waited for the antiaircraft shells to reach them. The first bursts erupted down to his right, puffs of black smoke, but the aim was too low, and he looked out toward the other two planes, raised his hand, waved slowly: *this way*.

Lufbery banked the Nieuport, and they followed, and immediately another series of black bursts filled the sky, closer, the gunners on the ground making the adjustments. But Lufbery knew the routine too well to give them the time, waved another hand signal, banked the plane again. The ground fire was increasing, and he felt the Nieuport rock, the shock from a blast only a few yards below him. He held the stick steady, looked out to both of his companions, saw them staring at him, steady as well, keeping their planes in the formation. He nodded so they could see, yes, that's right. It's just a little bumpy. Use your head and they won't hurt you.

There was another cluster of black puffs far below, off to the south, a formation of two-seaters paralleling his course. The Germans gunners had turned their attention to a more immediate threat, French bombers, and Lufbery felt himself relaxing, hoped the pilots on either side of him would do the same. The lessons he had taught them were rolling through his mind, stay focused, scan the skies, keep close in formation, no daydreaming. But they had absorbed those lessons for weeks now, and if they had learned, those same words would be rolling through their minds as well.

He turned again, a sweeping circle, did not want to move too far past the German lines. He could see another trio, a mile or more to the north, higher, heading toward the morning sun. Below them, he saw another formation, a wide V, as low as the two-seaters, coming westward. He stared hard, yes, those are Boche. All right, this is far enough. He motioned to the other two, another prearranged signal. *Home.*

They kept the formation together with surprising precision, the other two Nieuports staying just behind him, on opposite sides of his tail. They were soon on the French side of the lines, and still he scanned the horizon, knew that they could run into a returning Boche patrol, but at least, the sun was behind them now, and they would have the advantage, could make the first move. That move had been well rehearsed, the instructions given to the other two pilots with absolute authority. There would be no confrontation with the enemy. None. No close-up inspections, no flirtations. The pilots were not hard to convince. Their Nieuports didn't have machine guns.

It had taken the American Air Service nearly a month to secure any usable aircraft, and despite the frustration and anger of his new pilots, Lufbery had made good use of the idle time to instruct them on the ground. He expected them to be overconfident and full of bluster, the same idiotic boastfulness that infected so many of the administrators, the men whose jobs would never require them to fly. But the pilots seemed to understand that if they were going to succeed, they could make good use of the experience of the men who had done this before. Lufbery had been amazed at their attentiveness, not one of them trying to tell him how it *should* be done. It was such a pleasant contrast to Lufbery's experience at Issoudun, enduring the men like Major Gray who considered the seasoned veterans to be obstacles to the glorious future of American aviation.

Despite Bill Thaw's enthusiasm for Lufbery's new assignment, Lufbery went to Villeneuve carrying the same dread that he had felt for his duties at Issoudun. But his low expectations were pleasantly erased. The Ninety-fourth Aero Squadron was commanded by Major John Huffer, an experienced pilot who had shared both respect and friendship with Bill Thaw from their days in the French Foreign Legion. The contrast between Huffer and Gray was immediate and obvious. Huffer welcomed Lufbery with open arms, and he immediately turned over to Lufbery all responsibility for teaching the fledgling pilots the skills he thought necessary. Though Huffer might still fly the occasional patrol, he was fully immersed in the administrative duties of the squadron. To Lufbery's enormous relief, Huffer made it clear that, in the air, Lufbery was the authority.

Without aircraft to fly, Lufbery could spend time on discussions of tactics and strategy, from the most basic rules of combat to all the nuances of formations and communication in the air. For the first two weeks at Ville-neuve, he suspected that the lessons had been learned because the pilots were not distracted by a fleet of aircraft waiting for them in the hangars. Though Lufbery had never thought of himself as a teacher, the lessons had been helpful to him as well, had given him time to know the personalities and quirks of these young men, to find the bright lights among them. He had seen enough from his days with the escadrille to know that lessons alone did not make flyers, that a man who talks too much on the ground is probably the man who forgets to cover your tail. The long wait for aircraft had raised his frustrations as well, but he kept it hidden from them. On that glorious day when the planes arrived, he could hide it no longer, had led them with a mad rush onto the field as the formation of Nieuports had finally dropped down. The men had gathered around the aircraft like children circling the tree on Christmas morning. Every man was eager to take the first flight, no one more eager than Lufbery himself. But the excitement of the men had blinded them to two disturbing things Lufbery had noticed immediately. First, the planes were Nieuport 28s, a craft the French had considered obsolete on the front lines. Since the Americans had yet to produce any aircraft of their own, the AAS had negotiated with the French to provide any suitable combat fighter, and the French had obliged by offering the one aircraft they could spare in

460

abundance, the Nieuport 28s. The 28 was a long slender craft, with a large motor that gave the plane the advantage of a cruising speed of more than one hundred twenty miles per hour. But the plane's speed was offset by one enormous problem. In a dive, the fabric on the top wing tended to rip; when the pilot would most require the plane's high speed, to either pursue or escape the enemy, the top wing might suddenly strip itself of fabric, making the plane fatally unflyable.

The second problem was more obvious to the men who knew little about aircraft specifications. The Nieuports arrived without machine guns. Despite the immediate outcry from Huffer, the AAS could only offer the disheartening news that the French had committed to furnish guns only as they could be spared. So although Lufbery could finally give his students precious time in the air, should they ever stray carelessly into an enemy ambush, the Americans would be defenseless.

He brought them down in a shallow descent, wanted them to get the feel for the 28, to know every nuance of the plane's handling. His wheels touched down, and he cut the throttle, heard the other two behind him repeating the pattern. The hangar was in front of him now, and he revved the motor, a short burst of power, saw the gathering crowd of pilots and mechanics, realized that they were greeting him the same way he had met so many flights before, the nervous expectation of a problem, each man making his silent count, making sure all three planes had returned. The two pilots moved their Nieuports up on either side of him, maintaining their formation even on the ground. Lufbery could not help smiling, removed his goggles, sat for a moment listening to the uneven rumble of the idling motor. He had no idea what day it was, paid little attention to calendars, thought, Someone will notice. Someone should. The Americans have made their first flight across the lines.

He realized the other pilots were still following his example, their motors idling as well, and he cut the power, the silence now giving way to the enthusiastic greetings from the men on the ground. Lufbery climbed slowly from the plane, saw the

461

attention flowing around the two young pilots, saw their expressions, the pure excitement, every moment of the experience fresh in their minds. It had been the same for him, so long ago, climbing out to greet the knowing smile on the face of Marc Pourpe, a moment Lufbery would remember for the rest of his life. But these men would have a different memory, had flown right over the war itself, had seen the awful destruction of no-man's-land, had even come under fire, the hapless inaccuracy of the antiaircraft guns. He watched them telling the tales, pouring out the adventure to their audiences. He felt an unexpected pride in his students. There was nothing significant about the mission itself, nothing more than an opportunity to gain valuable experience. But they had done everything right, no foolish maneuvering, none of the bullheaded disobedience of Victor Chapman.

Now would come another lesson, and Lufbery waited for the furor around the two men to quiet, said, "Mr. Campbell, Mr. Rickenbacker, we should discuss what you observed. This will be good for all of you."

Lufbery removed his flying suit, and the two men did the same, each man eyeing the fur boots that Lufbery still treasured, his reward for capturing the German pilots. The men had gathered in a tight half-circle, were quiet now, and Lufbery said, "Comments?"

Rickenbacker spoke first, said, "I was . . . um . . . nervous about the archie. Didn't expect it to toss the plane about so. Lucky thing we weren't hit."

Lufbery smiled at the word, archie, the term the British used for antiaircraft fire. It was the telltale sign that Eddie Rickenbacker had spent time at the training facilities in England.

"Lieutenant Rickenbacker, are you quite certain the Boche missed you?"

Rickenbacker seemed unsure, said, "Well, I suppose, sir. I didn't feel like I got hit."

Lufbery moved toward Rickenbacker's Nieuport, looked along the wings, moved around to the fuselage. He bent low, put a finger out, poked it into a ragged hole just behind the cockpit.

"What do you suppose did this?"

Rickenbacker was close beside him now, and Lufbery heard a low groan. He moved back along the fuselage, saw another, larger hole, several more small ones near the tail.

The men were making their own low sounds now, and Lufbery said, "Every one of those antiaircraft shells is like a bucket of nails. They toss 'em up and let 'em blow all to hell. They don't do much damage usually." He looked at Rickenbacker, who was probing the holes, his face a soft shade of white. "But they usually hit something. That's why you change direction often. Don't give them time to do any more than sting you. Right, Lieutenant?"

Rickenbacker nodded furiously, and Lufbery said, "Other comments?"

Douglas Campbell had stayed back, quietly inspecting his own plane, said, "Um, sir, I was surprised we didn't see anyone else up there."

Rickenbacker seemed relieved for the change of subject, said, "Yes, I was thinking the same thing. Forgive me for saying so, Major, but I was disappointed we didn't get to see a Boche."

It was a theme Lufbery had heard so many times before, from nearly every new pilot he had flown with. "I see. Yes, the Boche stayed away from us for the most part. That formation of Albatroses ignored us completely, probably had better things to do. Good thing, since even if we'd been armed, they had us outnumbered five to three. Of course, the SPADs that flew below us would have helped us out. I suspect the Boche were looking for that patrol of observers we passed over no-man's-land. At least three French two-seaters, which seem to be their favorite prey. Not much we could have done to help them."

He hid the smile, waited for the reaction, saw both young men stepping forward, eyes wide. They glanced at each other, sharing the same dismay. "It's all right, gentlemen. You must train your eyes. The Boche won't come up and tap you on the shoulder. You must see him before he sees you. Otherwise, when you do see him, he'll be filling your ass with lead."

He saw the gloom on the faces of both men.

"Next time, don't assume the skies are empty. *Assume* he is there. When you're not actually in a fight, that's all you have to think about. *Where* is he? You'll get better at it. You'll begin to see those little black spots up there for what they are, you'll learn to pick up movement below you, to tell what's on the ground and what's above it." He let the words sink in, saw a flash of fear on Rickenbacker's face. Good, he thought. If they don't have the fear, they will never learn. He looked toward his own Nieuport, saw a small rip in the fabric of the fuselage, the effects of the archie on his own plane. His eyes moved forward, over the cockpit, stopped at the bare cowling that shrouded the motor. Of course, if we don't get machine guns, none of these lessons will matter.

His choice of Eddie Rickenbacker and Douglas Campbell to make the first flight was not random. Though there was considerable contrast between the two men, both had shown Lufbery the same intangible ingredient he had occasionally seen in men like Kiffin Rockwell. It was more than intelligence, or a keen mind for learning lessons. It came from the eyes, the determination that seemed to touch Lufbery in a personal way. There was always talk, too much talk; some men were desperately impatient to begin killing the enemy. Lufbery had learned that the talk was a substitute for fear, that a man who boasts of plunging the bayonet into the enemy's heart is deathly afraid of having the same done to him. Both young men seemed to respond to the job that lay ahead of them the way Lufbery had. There was one goal. It was never about glory and medals and impressing your buddies. Neither Campbell nor Rickenbacker made speeches about their passion for war. Like Lufbery, both men carried an intensity that some found unnerving. They all just wanted to kill Germans.

Douglas Campbell was the younger man, barely twenty-one, something that concerned Lufbery. Too often, with youth came stupidity, a stubborn inexperience about life that let the boy believe he was invincible. But Campbell was surprisingly old for his years, had come to the Ninety-fourth Aero Squadron by way of his experience flying the Curtiss "Jenny" biplane, the only aircraft produced in America that was any use at all for training

464

the new pilots. Campbell had come east from his home in San Francisco, had then dropped out of Harvard University when Woodrow Wilson brought the United States into the war.

Edward Rickenbacker was entirely different. He was older, twenty-seven, a midwesterner, had first come to the army not as a pilot but as an engineer. Rickenbacker brought the skills of a trained mechanic, something Lufbery could immediately appreciate. But Rickenbacker had not studied aeroplane motors. Lufbery was surprised to learn that in the States, Rickenbacker was famous, especially among the other young pilots of the Ninety-fourth. Before the war, he had been a race-car driver, one of the most successful of his time, had made his name racing at an increasing number of public spectacles, such as the Indianapolis 500. Lufbery knew little about automobile racing, but he learned that Rickenbacker had already witnessed violent death, had experienced the loss of friends on the racetrack, had even flirted with death himself. There was a seriousness to the man that separated him from the younger pilots. If Rickenbacker continued to be the good student, Lufbery knew the man had all the ingredients to be an outstanding flyer.

Épiez, France—April 1918

With the massive German wave rolling through the British defenses, the American squadrons were moved from Villeneuve to a position closer to the newly changing front. The pilots rose each dawn to a rolling thunder from the North, the continuous artillery barrages that were destroying the land and the armies who clung tightly to whatever shelter they could find. The rising sun brought up the observation balloons, great fat cigars that spread out behind the defenses of both sides, carrying their crews aloft in small hanging baskets, courageous men with telescopes and wireless radios who fed a steady stream of reports to the infantry and artillery commanders beneath them. From their new position, the American pilots could see the long row of balloons hovering on the horizon, and Lufbery's immediate lesson had been to ignore the temptation to go after what they all supposed to be easy targets.

465

The balloons had always been tempting targets for the flying squadrons, but the temptation could be a deadly trap. The balloons were protected by batteries of antiaircraft guns, whose accuracy was considerably better when focusing on aircraft who were assaulting their target from only a few hundred feet above the ground. Each balloon was held to its mooring by a series of wire cables, which could be another deadly hazard for the careless pilot. As many overeager pilots had learned, emptying your guns into this ridiculously easy target was no guarantee of success. The flammable gas in the balloons did not always ignite, and by the time the frustrated pilot realized his attempt had failed, he might find a squadron of enemy fighters on his tail, waiting for precisely the right moment for their ambush.

April 6, 1918

Lufbery had been out on patrol alone, still learning the feel of the Nieuport 28, testing and pressing the plane into short steep dives, maneuvering all manner of twists and loops. The Nieuport was not nearly as solid as the SPAD, and Lufbery knew he had been spoiled by the SPAD's willingness to take any aerobatic abuse a pilot could give her.

The daylight was fading rapidly, the sky darkened by thick clouds. It had been his one advantage, that if he had suddenly been ambushed by a flight of Germans, the unarmed Nieuport could seek easy refuge in the cloud layer. The promises continued to come from the French, but every day the pilots waited for the trucks to arrive, hauling the heavy wooden crates that would carry the machine guns. For two full weeks since the Nieuports had come, there were still no guns.

He brought the Nieuport down gently, testing the stall speed, let the plane settle in a short, quick drop to the ground. He was pleased with the plane's ability to prolong its glide, a trait distinctly missing from the SPAD, which, according to Bill Thaw, had all the gliding characteristics of a brick. If a motor failed over German territory, whether by mechanical failure, or by taking fire from the enemy, it was comforting to know that the Nieuport might still allow you to reach the safety of your own lines. The SPAD would simply fall.

He turned the Nieuport toward the hangar, was surprised to see two large trucks, surrounded by the entire squadron, including the mechanics. They were waving at him now, and he cut the motor, saw Huffer moving toward him, a wide smile on the man's face.

Huffer said, "Nice surprise this afternoon, Major. Give our kudos to Colonel Mitchell. He kept pushing until the French finally caved in."

Lufbery looked toward the trucks, could see men unloading the long boxes.

"I assume—"

"Yep. We got our damned machine guns."

Toul, France—April 14, 1918

They were surprised to be moved again, far to the south, below Verdun, and just west of the city of Nancy. Toul was a critical railway center, and it lay close enough to the front lines that, when the weather allowed, the Germans had made a routine out of bombing the area. Lufbery had experienced this before, and very quickly, after several bleak nights dodging a storm of German firebombs, the pilots understood that the safest place they could be was in the air.

Lufbery had continued to lead the patrols, but the men were gaining confidence and skills, and Huffer had authorized him to turn the men loose. They were sent out in small groups, two or three planes, Lufbery assuming they would be less likely to attract attention, less likely to find themselves swallowed up by some enormous chaotic confrontation. It was becoming more common now that, as the fights on the ground intensified, so too did the combat in the air. Squadrons on both sides were combining their numbers, and an engagement could easily draw the attention of dozens of fighters, swirling around each other in a firestorm of confusion. Though Lufbery had confidence in his pilots, until they had more direct experience facing the enemy, it would be senseless to throw them into that kind of brawl.

"Anybody here know how to draw?"

The pilots glanced at each other, and Lufbery saw one man raise his hand, a slow feeble gesture. It was Wentworth, the young midwesterner.

"Uh, yes, sir, I used to paint signs for my father. Livestock and such."

Huffer pointed to the fuselage of the Nieuport, said, "It's about time we had our own insignia. Major Lufbery and I have discussed a few ideas. I know some of you rather like the Indian design used by the Lafayette boys. Sorry, but the One hundred third staked their claim to that pretty quick. If I know Bill Thaw, he had those war bonnets sketched on his aircraft the minute he took command. You recall the medical examinations last week? Dr. Walters, Captain Paul Walters, tossed out an idea that seems to rise above anything Mr. Lufbery and I have come up with. Luf?"

Lufbery shrugged, said, "You tell 'em."

"Well, all right. Every one of you has heard something of the griping we've gotten from our allies, about how long it took President Wilson to let us join in on all the fun over here. Captain Walters says we should let our allies, and certainly the enemy, know that, at long last, Uncle Sam has finally tossed his hat into the ring." He paused, seemed to wait for the pilots to absorb the image.

They glanced at each other, and Lufbery could see nods of approval, and little else, said, "Major, perhaps you should show them what you have in mind."

Huffer grunted, pulled a folded paper from his pocket. "Well, yes, I have it right here. Lieutenant Wentworth, since you claim some talent as an artist, you may have the honor of applying paint to this Nieuport." Wentworth came forward, and Huffer handed him the paper. "Here . . . just like that. Something I believe the Ninety-fourth will soon be known for all over Europe. The symbol . . . the hat in the ring."

Lufbery watched them leaving the ground, the two Nieuports nearly side by side. He scanned the skies out beyond the field, the ceiling low and thick, waves of fog drifting over the open ground. The call had come in from the French infantry, a pair of German scout planes moving in low over the lines, and Lufbery had ordered Doug Campbell and Alan Winslow to intercept them. The two planes leveled out now, only a few hundred feet above the ground, held down by the blanket of fog above them, and Lufbery watched them banking toward the east, felt a hard twist in his stomach.

They had been flying combat patrols for days now, but the action had been sporadic. The young pilots released their frustration by boisterous claims that the Germans were purposely avoiding them, did not want to suffer the consequences of this new American power. Lufbery let them have their big talk, knew it was a release for the steam building up inside them. He knew it was nothing more than chance, that if they kept flying, their time would come, and all the talk would stop.

There were others out on the field near him, watching the thick gray skies as he was, and he let out a long breath, shook his head, felt foolish, a nervous father watching his boys go out to play. There was a shout and he turned, saw men pointing out, could see it for himself now, a trail of black smoke, a flaming aircraft tumbling out of the thick clouds. He felt ice in his chest, saw the bright ball of fire bursting on impact, the plane crashing into a thicket just beyond the field. Men began to move in a rush, but the sight of the fireball held him in paralyzed silence. The voices rose around him, the words he wanted to scream, the awful question.

"Did anyone see . . . who it was?"

He forced himself to follow them, saw one man running toward them, hands waving. "It was a Boche! A Boche!"

He kept moving, automatic steps, the ice in his chest giving way. Now the cheering began, a flood of men emerging from the hangars all down the field. He heard another shout, a man in front of him suddenly stopping.

"My God! There's another one!"

Lufbery looked up, saw the black crosses on the crumpling wing, no fire this time, something inside of him opening up, thank God.

The German plane made a short weak spin, straightened out slightly, the pilot fighting to hold it up, the plane dropping just over the tree line. The gathering crowd parted, some moving toward the closer plane, others plunging into the thicket, toward the column of black smoke. He stopped, heard the sound of motors, saw two Nieuports emerging from the foggy skies, circling low around the field. The men were gathering at the fallen planes, and Lufbery waited for his pilots to land, pushed the image of the fiery crash out of his mind. He began to walk out into the field, watched the planes coming in, could see one pilot raising a hand in the air already, thought, No, get her on the ground first. There will be time for celebrating later. The Nieuports rolled in side by side, and Lufbery felt a smile, the nervous father now gleefully proud of his boys, sharing the perfect moment they would always carry with them. There would be no controversy, no haggling with the French over confirmation. Campbell and Winslow had scored the Ninety-fourth Aero Squadron's first kills. And they had done it right on their own doorstep.

30

RICHTHOFEN

Lechelle, France—April 1918

He had relocated JG-1 to the new aerodrome selected by von
Hoeppner, keeping the fighters close behind the advance of the
German infantry. They had stopped first at Lechelle, a field that
had belonged to the British, the airfield abandoned quickly by
soldiers and flyers alike in front of the unstoppable wave of
Ludendorff's spring offensive. The pilots of JG-1 slept now
where their enemy had slept. But there was no luxury, no grand
château. The villages were charred ruins, few houses left
standing, and Richthofen ordered his men to occupy the
simple accommodations that the British had abandoned.
The men slept in large round tents pitched over makeshift
wooden floors. Their planes were housed in great flimsy tent
hangars, enormous flaps of thin cloth suspended by cables and
tall poles. It was a surprise to him that the British bases had
been so temporary, so lacking in any kind of comforts for the
men who flew the Camels. But now, with his own pilots
moving westward, everything was temporary. If the German
offensive continued to push the British toward the sea, JG-1
would move again.

He had spent a quiet winter enduring the consistently dismal
weather, passing much of the time performing duties at the
request of the High Command. He made visits to various aircraft manufacturers, often little more than ceremonial
appearances for the benefit of the ever-present photographers.
But his visit to the Fokker plant was kept mostly private, conferring with officers of the Air Service and frantic Fokker
engineers, who were making every effort to cure the structural
problems with their triplanes. Richthofen could offer nothing

constructive, and he was soon bored with the rest of the ceremonial routines. In early January, he was surprised to receive an invitation to go to Brest-Litovsk, a fortress city east of Warsaw, where German negotiators were hammering out the terms of the peace treaty with the new Russian government. His host was Prince Leopold of Bavaria, who had commanded the German forces that now controlled what remained of the Russian front. Richthofen had no good reason for being there, but the invitation was a strangely appealing diversion. Upon Richthofen's arrival, he joined an audience of expectant onlookers, an assortment of important dignitaries. To Richthofen, the appeal wore off quickly. It was obviously intended as a showplace for the prince, the man strutting about like some grand conquering peacock, lording his triumphs over the submissive Russians. But the Bolsheviks who now controlled the Russian government had been anything but submissive. The prince was embarrassed to learn that the defeated Russians would not simply roll over at his command. The negotiations were difficult and noisy, and after several excruciating days, Richthofen had all he could tolerate of political wrangling and, with gracious apologies to Prince Leopold, he made his escape.

With his planes still sitting quietly in their hangars, Richthofen continued to bow to the wishes of the High Command, traveling to Berlin once again, and once again, the crowds had followed him. But the city had changed, and even a hero's welcome could not hide the turmoil that was brewing. The conditions for the German people continued to worsen, a hard stranglehold on all manner of food and supplies, enforced by the British naval blockade. But those who held tightly to their faith in the kaiser received a hard shock with the collapse of the czarist government in Russia. In the streets of the larger German cities, where the suffering of the people was most severe, the success of the Russian Revolution gave a new burst of energy and inspiration to those who saw the war as a cause celebrated only by Kaiser Wilhelm and his cronies. To many, the kaiser was not so different from Czar Nicholas, just another symbol of the arrogance and excess of old Europe, another despotic ruler whose folly had accomplished nothing but the starvation of his own people. The German Bolsheviks were bolder now, workers defying orders not to march, shouting their protests into the faces of frightened soldiers, some of whom were beginning to show sympathy for the workers they were supposed to be arresting. In Berlin, Richthofen had been kept clear of any kind of public unpleasantness, the High Command still taking advantage of his presence as the symbol of the inevitable German victory. The smiles from the crowd were as they had always been, and the photographers continued to annoy him as they always had. But Richthofen soon escaped Berlin as he had escaped Prince Leopold, wanting only to slip free of the clinging tentacles of politics and return to his planes.

In March, with the beginning of the German offensive, there was only one place for Richthofen to be, and with a great battle exploding across the ground below him, he had again led JG-1 in a string of dominating successes. But the celebrating was marred by the crash of his brother, whose triplane had lost a wing while engaged in a difficult fight with a squadron of British scouts. Lothar had survived, but his injuries were severe, and he was confined to a hospital in Dusseldorf for a lengthy stay. JG-1 had lost one of its best pilots, a gap that Richthofen had taken great pains to fill. But the loss was received differently at Schweidnitz. Richthofen knew that his mother would enjoy the peace of mind that at least one of her sons would not be flying again for some time.

With the stunning success of the German offensive, official Berlin could begin to ignore the turmoil erupting outside the government buildings. The loud Bolshevik voices of dissent were drowned out now by cheers, the civilian government rallying around the military commanders who were finally bringing them tangible victory on the battlefield. For the first time since Richthofen had taken command, the civilian officials began to appear at the aerodrome, each one overflowing with the enthusiasm that only success can bring. The orders had come from von Hoeppner's office, and Richthofen would obey, would offer an open door to the aerodrome and a gracious

473

reception to the civilian officials who had suddenly been allowed to see themselves as a part of Germany's great military effort. The civilian government was an important part of the kaiser's regime. As the cost of the war had affected the German people, the civilian members of the Reichstag had grown restless, some of them speaking out more openly, echoing the dangerous words that came from the streets. Ludendorff had long ignored most of what came out of the Reichstag, but their brazen protest of the kaiser's policies, and their increasing criticism of the war, had forced the kaiser to offer some appeasement; thus, Ludendorff had been pressured to cooperate. The success of the March offensive had given Ludendorff what he needed most: a victory. If officers like Richthofen were inconvenienced by the snooping of the occasional politician, it was a small price to pay to quiet their harping. The High Command had found another use for their most celebrated flyer.

They had come to the aerodrome mostly in clusters, large staff cars driven by civilian chauffeurs, each polished auto bearing wide-eyed men in smartly tailored suits. Today, Richthofen was alone, would suffer the duty himself, Bodenschatz off on some administrative duty that was not quite significant enough for Richthofen to claim as his own. He was relieved to see only one automobile, had forced himself yet again not to be annoyed. He stood now with his well-rehearsed smile fixed tightly on his face, watched as a huge round man struggled to rise up out of his limousine, pouring out in a cloud of cigar smoke. Another man followed him out of the car, a pad of paper in his hand. Richthofen winced, forced the smile again, recognized the unmistakable sign of a newspaperman, a man who would preserve every detail of this visit for someone's notion of posterity.

The fat man looked at Richthofen for a long moment, seemed to jump suddenly, pointed his finger at him, nodded vigorously. "Ah, yes! You are Captain Richthofen! I recognize you! This is an honor, sir, an honor! I am the third assistant minister of domestic commerce, Jurgen Schmidt. "

The man rolled toward him, and Richthofen accepted the

flabby mass of the man's hand, could feel the sweet stench of the cigar flowing over him. Schmidt backed away, appraising the field around him, and the man with the paper moved up closer, said, "Fleckmann, sir. I have been assigned to accompany Minister Schmidt, to record his impressions of our heroes of the skies."

Richthofen caught a glint of sarcasm in the man's cliché, thought, Of course, an ink spiller who must pretend to enjoy the company of *men of importance.* Fleckmann held out his hand, and Richthofen responded with a brief firm handshake, could see Fleckmann studying him, questions already billowing up in a writer's mind. Richthofen still had the smile, said, "Welcome to you as well, Mr. Fleckmann. I hope that Minister Schmidt's impressions are favorable ones."

Fleckmann ignored the platitude, said, "I hope to speak to you later, Captain. There is much you can tell us. The Air Service has always been somewhat stingy with information, but that seems to be changing. It has taken me some time to secure official permission to visit an aerodrome." He glanced behind him, lowered his voice. "It required me to accompany the minister on his tour of the field. Opportunity is where you find it, I suppose." There was no enthusiasm in Fleckmann's voice, and Richthofen looked at the larger man, saw him scowling, gazing now at the small village of dirty white tents.

"I say, Captain, not quite what I expected. Hmph. I understand, however, that you took this from the enemy! Fine work! Our boys should have better conditions than this though." Schmidt caught sight of the hangars now, four Fokkers perched inside. He pointed, said to Fleckmann, "You see there? The Fatherland's finest, right there! Poised in all their glory, to drive the enemy away!"

Fleckmann made a note on his pad, and Richthofen forced himself to move up closer to him, said, "Actually, the British abandoned this base. It wouldn't be accurate to say that we took it. . . ."

Fleckmann ignored him, continued to write, and Richthofen felt himself draining of energy. He pumped up the smile again, said, "Minister, I would be pleased to offer you a tour of our

475

facilities, such as they are. Certainly you would enjoy a closer inspection of the aeroplanes?"

Schmidt was all smiles now, rubbed his hands together.

"Quite so, Captain! I must ask you . . . where are your pilots? I expected something more . . . um . . ."

Fleckmann said, "Captain, we had been told to expect a formal reception from your command."

Richthofen lost all strength for the smile, thought, Of course, a *formal reception*: an empty promise from some overly gracious officer in Cologne. He pulled at himself from the inside, heard a voice in his head: *calm*.

"Sir, this particular field is the operating base of Squadron Eleven. Most of the pilots are presently on a mission. It was my intention to have them assembled for you; however, the enemy was not aware of your visit, and some of their pilots inconvenienced us by attacking our troop positions. I thought it important that we respond."

Richthofen instantly regretted his sarcasm, but Schmidt seemed not to notice, nodded his agreement. "Excellent, Captain. Then I am fortunate indeed. I shall have the opportunity to hear of their mission firsthand, just as you will!" He looked at Fleckmann now, nodded toward the man's pad of paper. "This will do nicely, yes."

Cappy, France—April 18, 1918

They had moved again, the entire fighter wing swarming over the charred ruins of another village, assembling and organizing at another abandoned aerodrome. Richthofen paid little attention to maps, knew only that Cappy was west of Lechelle, farther west than he had ever been. Again they occupied a field that had once been British.

The reports flowed through his headquarters of the vicious fight on the ground in front of them, the great German thrust widening a gap many miles into the strength of the British defenses. But the success of the German advance was exhausting itself, the select shock troops of the infantry moving too far too quickly, outdistancing their own supplies. It had been the same since the beginning of the war, every major offensive stalled by the inability of the support behind them to keep up. It was not always the fault of men, but of equipment, the railway lines inadequate to the task, many of the tracks having to be rebuilt by the same men who had destroyed them. The roads were desolate wastelands, obliterated by the artillery, and so the engineers had to be sent forward, to rebuild the pathways for the supply trucks. Far out in front, the German foot soldiers who had so completely shattered the British defenses found themselves without food and shoes and even ammunition. And so the generals had to slow them down, infuriating Ludendorff as well as the infantry. Every man on the German front lines knew that if they could only push the fight another week, widen the gap a few more miles, the British might collapse completely, might seek the sanctuary of the French coastline, scramble onto the ships that would carry the Tommies back to England, and right out of the war. But there was no more energy for the push, and along the front lines, exhausted German soldiers watched helplessly as shattered remnants of British units regrouped and dug in and faced them now with a renewed defiance.

Dusseldorf, Germany—April 19, 1918

The weather had been bad for several days, heavy spring rains keeping the air fighters on the ground. As winter passed, Richthofen had continued his string of victories, had stunned the High Command on April 2, when word of his seventy-fifth kill had been confirmed. He had given the number little thought, but there was something of a milestone in the figure, another opportunity for the photographers of the Information Section to offer the German people a new outpouring of Richthofen publicity. Richthofen ignored the attention to this one arbitrary number, and within another week had shot three more British planes out of the sky.

He had not been able to fly now for nearly ten days, but would not endure the idleness by sitting quietly at the aerodrome. The poor weather had given him the excuse to visit his

477

brother, and he left Cappy carrying a list of greetings for Lothar, kind wishes from every pilot in JG-1.

Richthofen had taken the train, unavoidable with the weather, was surprised that he had not been recognized. The passengers had been a subdued lot, a few men in uniform sitting quietly, most just staring out the windows into gray mist. There had been women as well, both young and old, some sitting in small groups, some traveling alone. But there was no cheer in these people, none of the bright chatter he had heard so many times before. Many of them were draped in black, some with faces covered. When he finally arrived at Dusseldorf, his mood was as black as the mourning dresses.

The hospital was enormous, and nothing like the pleasant airy surroundings of Courtrai. The open grounds around the oppressive buildings were packed with ambulances, both horse and motor, and he understood now that this place was one of those final stops for the long trains of wounded.

He did not talk to anyone, moved quickly through the front entrance, received a polite salute from a guard. He scanned the corridor in front of him, a bustling mob of white gowns, wheeled carts, and walking wounded. To one side there was an office, and he moved that way, saw a man in a dark suit seated behind a desk, said, "Excuse me. Are you a doctor?"

The man ignored him, was writing on a pad of paper, and Richthofen felt his anger boiling up, had no patience for bureaucrats.

"I asked you, sir, are you a doctor?"

His voice had a hard edge that the man could not avoid. He looked up at Richthofen, unsmiling, seemed to appraise Richthofen's uniform, said, "No. I am the assistant administrator. Do you require a doctor?"

Richthofen forced himself to calm, thought, Just an ink spiller. "What I require is the location of my brother. Lieutenant Lothar von Richthofen. He is a patient here."

The man stood abruptly, said, "Oh, yes! You are Captain Richthofen! I am honored, sir! If you will allow me, I should inform the administrator you are here. He will be most excited to meet you!"

The man moved past him in a rush, left Richthofen alone in the small office. Out in the corridor, the assistant's voice rose over the din, and Richthofen winced as he heard his name, the man enthusiastically spreading word of the Great Hero's presence. Richthofen saw faces turning his way, the bustle giving way to silent stares. The assistant was coming back now, another man following, both of them halting in a stiff formality, crowding the doorway. The assistant said, "You see? I told you, sir. It is him!"

The other man seemed unable to speak, reached into his pocket, retrieved a small card, looked at it now. "Yes. It is him." He held the card up, one of the thousands of postal cards that had filled pockets all over Germany. Richthofen recognized the particular card, the image of himself standing in front of a wrecked British fighter plane. The photo was a fabrication, his actual image clipped from a far more mundane setting, pieced together with a generic photograph of a crash scene. But to the civilians who cherished the memento, whether or not the photo was authentic made no difference. Richthofen forced a smile, and the man said, "If you would put your signature to this, it would honor me, sir."

The man seemed to tremble, and Richthofen took the card, had no pen of his own, saw an inkstand on the desk. He signed his name, handed the card back to the man, whose hands were shaking.

"Oh! Thank you, sir! My wife will not believe me!"

The men continued to block the door, both of them staring at him like schoolboys. After a long moment, Richthofen said, "Please? May I see my brother?"

Lothar was lying flat on his back, a thin pillow beneath his head. His jaw was wired shut, a thin brace around his face extending up into the white cloth bandage that wrapped the top of his head. Richthofen moved close to him, was surprised to see Lothar's eyes open.

"Oh, you are awake. I thought I might be disturbing you."

Lothar raised his arms, took Richthofen's hands in his. He

479

spoke with a soft hiss, his teeth clamped tightly together by the taut wire.

"Manfred. Thank you. I am so happy to see you!"

Richthofen could not take his eyes from the metal hardware attached to Lothar's face, said, "Are you in pain?"

Lothar shook Richthofen's hands with his own. "No. Not so much anymore. Morphine. Not needed often. Hurts when I try to move. So I do not move."

Richthofen glanced around the ward, familiar rows of beds, none of them empty, the room reeking with the same smell he had grown used to at Courtrai. There were men lying on the floor, filling many of the spaces between the beds, something very different from the relaxed atmosphere of St. Nicholas. Lothar still held his hands, pulled at them, and Richthofen looked down at him.

Lothar said, "Worst nurses I have ever seen."

Richthofen was concerned, said, "Are they mistreating you? I shall have a word with the administrator!" He caught the slight smile on Lothar's lips.

"No. Not mistreating. Look at them. Fat and old. Not one pretty one in the place. Takes all the enjoyment out of bathing. The young ones must all be in France. You were fortunate."

He was surprised at Lothar's good humor, sat down now on the edge of the bed.

"I am fortunate that my brother is alive. Twice now." The words rolled up in his brain: *You should stop flying*. But he caught himself.

Lothar said, "I should paint the figure of a cat on my aeroplane. Let the enemy know I still have seven more lives." He smiled again, made a grunting sound, a hard grip on Richthofen's hands, shock in Lothar's eyes. His eyes closed for a brief moment, opened again, and Lothar said slowly, "I cannot laugh. It causes a problem. Enough problems already." Lothar hooked a finger into the side of his mouth, pulled at his cheek, and Richthofen saw a gap, two missing teeth. "Only way I can eat. My insides are floating in soup."

Richthofen took his brother's hands again, said, "Do not talk. It cannot be good for you."

480

"All right, Manfred. You talk. I have been here for a month. I have many questions. I was wondering. How many Camels have you sent down?"

Richthofen absorbed the question, had been asked the same thing by von Hoeppner. "I believe it has been seven. There is always chance for error."

Lothar closed his eyes, patted his hand. "Very good."

Richthofen knew how the boredom of the hospital could put questions in your mind, trivial ideas that served only to fill the time. The Camels had been a curious subject since they first confronted the German flyers, and the Air Service had been particularly interested how the German aircraft had measured up. There was no real answer—both sides claiming superiority of their equipment, both sides finding some success in shooting their enemy's finest planes out of the sky. But Richthofen had paid little attention to the claims of either side, knew that, ultimately, Boelcke's principles still applied. It was not the plane, but the man who flew it. Though he would never admit it to anyone, Richthofen had indeed kept count, not just the Camels, but every other plane he had shot down. Lothar was watching him, waiting for more. Richthofen already knew the next question that his brother would ask, said, "Seventy-eight."

Lothar squeezed his hands again, said, "You order the cups too?"

He had never been sure what his brother thought of his trophy collection. No one in the fighter wing ever questioned his rigid dedication toward securing the scraps of cloth, or the pieces of hardware from his victims. Many pilots on both sides collected their mementos. But to Richthofen's knowledge, the silver trophy cups had been his idea alone.

"The jeweler tells me silver is very hard to get now. He made a few of them in pewter. But I have not given much thought to that for a while now."

Lothar looked up at him for a long moment, then said, "I miss the fight. I truly miss it. I don't know how much longer I must stay here."

Richthofen had spoken to the doctors weeks before, had heard talk that Lothar might require several months of recovery.

He must know that, he thought. And surely he knows that when he leaves here, von Hoeppner will insist on sending him home.

"You are supposed to be talking, Manfred. Tell me about the squadrons."

Richthofen sorted through the words, the names, said, "So many new faces. Only a few have good experience. I am not happy with their recklessness." He saw the look in Lothar's eyes. "Just as I have never been happy with yours." He made a small laugh, saw the smile on his brother's face. "I fear the instructors are teaching them the wrong lessons. They come to the aerodrome eager to show off what they believe is skill." He paused, had given this same lecture many times before, scolding the young fresh pilots. "Flying upside down makes you an acrobat. It does not make you a fighter pilot. The new aeroplanes are very forgiving of such stunts, but it can only give these young men false confidence. And that will get them killed."

It was a sore subject with him, and his voice had risen. He realized now that faces were watching him, a small crowd of white-coated men was gathering behind him. He turned, said, "I apologize. I do not wish to make a disturbance."

Lothar pulled his hand again, and he looked down at his brother, saw something new, sadness. Lothar said quietly, "Why are you angry? This is not like you."

Richthofen looked down, saw fragility in his brother's hands. *You should not fly again.* But he had heard the same words, would not inflict that kind of selfishness on Lothar. He shook his head, said, "I apologize to you as well. You do not need such a sour visitor."

"What is wrong with you, Manfred?"

Richthofen glanced behind him, the white-coated men moving away. "I do not enjoy hospitals. Not when my brother lies here." He paused. "I have told no one this. My seventy-fifth victim was a two-seater, a bomber. We fought for a long while. The observer was very skilled with his gun, the pilot was an exceptional flyer. We pursued each other for some time before I gained the advantage. I nearly collided with them. We were not more than five meters apart when I shot them."

He paused, and Lothar said, "Very good. Not much chance of missing."

"I did not miss. The gasoline tank exploded. The plane was immediately engulfed in flames right in front of me. As it fell, I followed. I could see the men trying to free themselves. I watched them burn to death in their seats. The sight made me ill. In all the fights, with all the deaths I have inflicted, none has ever affected me like that. Because it was my seventy-fifth, everyone insisted on a celebration. Von Hoeppner sent a wire, the High Command as well, all cheers for the great victory. That night I sat down at the dining table and enjoyed the feast in my honor, while the ashes of two men lay scattered out on some ground." He stopped, could see questions in his brother's eyes. "It has never bothered me before."

"Then why does it bother you now? You should be accustomed to such things. We all are."

"What if the ashes were mine? Or . . . yours?"

Lothar squeezed his hands hard, said, "They were not. They were the enemy! I do not understand you. You cannot tell me that you have lost your heart for the fight. I cannot accept that. No one . . . no one in this country will accept that." Lothar's words were choked away by a grunt, and Richthofen could see pain on his face, the emotion in Lothar's words stirring his injury.

Richthofen leaned close, said, "No, of course not. I am sorry. I would never say that. Do not worry. Please, calm yourself." He put as much softness in the words as he could muster.

Lothar squeezed his hands again, gently this time. "It's all right, Manfred. It passes."

Richthofen was overwhelmed now by the gloom of his day, the women on the train, the mindless reverence he received from the hospital officials. He could not help staring at the wire that clamped around his brother's face and head, the bandage, so similar to what Richthofen himself had worn for so many weeks. He stood, and Lothar released his hands.

"I should leave now. Allow you some rest. It is not appropriate for me to upset you." He could see a protest forming on his brother's face, held up his hand. "Say nothing. Consider this an order from your commanding officer. If you wish to fly again, you must allow your wounds to heal. I will return as soon as I can."

Richthofen could hear the wail of the train, looked at his watch, thought, Ten minutes. The station was close, and he moved that way, felt a hard chill in the dampness of the air. He glanced up, saw a blanket of solid gray, no chance that anyone could fly today. He moved at a steady pace, did not look at the people who passed by, was relieved that no one recognized him. He felt guilty about upsetting his brother, scolded himself now, Do not tell so much. There is no need for you to cry on anyone's shoulder. There is no need for you to cry at all.

The image of Lothar's face would not leave his mind, the awful wires holding his jaw together. He knew that von Hoeppner would order Lothar not to fly again, and that Lothar would fight the order. It is what we must do, after all. It is what they expect of us. He knew that once Lothar's wounds had healed, his mother would expect him to come home. But Richthofen had heard none of that from her in a long while. She had grown strangely silent about her fears for her sons, her letters speaking only of family now, the idle gossip of Schweidnitz. He wondered if his father was responsible for that, stern lectures to her about meddling in her two sons' perfectly heroic lives.

It had been months since von Hoeppner or anyone else had suggested that Richthofen stop flying, the energy for such a foolish effort drained away by the necessities of war. He knew that in Cologne, they spoke now of the Americans, whispers from dark corners of the Air Service of a vast wave of new pilots, like so many big-hatted cowboys riding in from the West, rumors of thousands of new aeroplanes no one had yet seen, new motors, better guns. As the rumors grew more fantastic, Richthofen forced himself to ignore them, instructed his men to do the same. The real enemy was still right in front of them, the same British pilots flying the familiar planes. If the Americans arrive at all, they will bring loud talk and no experience, nothing to prepare them for what we can do to them. He winced, the image of the two burning men digging into him again. Why? You have seen death before. A great many deaths. Is that it? Too many? How much longer, how many more will die in front of my guns? *Seventy-eight*. He knew the number was on everyone's mind at the Air Service, that every newspaper was keeping a close watch on the tally. He thought of Ludendorff now, the casual expectations, *one hundred*, the general tossing out the number to him as a foregone conclusion. Perhaps it is. Richthofen did not believe in fate, could not accept that some unseen hand was guiding him. And if there is no angel protecting me, then what? Destiny? Luck?

He glanced up at the column of smoke that rose above the train station, the train firing its engine. He quickened his steps, heard his name now, a man's voice, calling out to the Great Hero. He ignored the man, kept his head down, focused on the uneven cobblestones, the rhythm of his boots. *Seventy-eight*. If Boelcke had lived, he would have more, certainly . . . the thought jarred him, as it always jarred him. Boelcke had not lived. None of the good ones . . . he froze his mind. *You are alive, and tomorrow, if the clouds permit, you will fly again. And if someone over there finds your weakness, outflies you or outshoots you, then perhaps destiny will ride with* him.

Cappy, France—April 21, 1918

The skies had cleared the day before, and Richthofen had led them aloft at first light. He took six Fokkers of Squadron Eleven into a confrontation with what soon became a much larger number of British Camels. The fight began as a melee of pursuit and maneuver, but what could have become a disastrously one-sided fight for Squadron Eleven was suddenly transformed by Richthofen himself. In just under five minutes, he shot down two of the Camels. The impact was immediate, the rest of the British pilots breaking off the fight. When Richthofen returned to the aerodrome, he was celebrated again. His total had reached eighty.

* * *

He moved out into dense gray fog, stared up into thick mist. He could feel the wetness in the air, said aloud, "Damn!"

In the hangars, the pilots were gathering, expecting him to lead them again, the mechanics already servicing the planes by dull lamplight. He stepped out of the dampness, a black fury growing in his mind, moved toward the red Fokker, saw pilots watching him, expectant faces, waiting for orders.

"The weather is fickle. We had our one good day. But now, the fog has returned. We must wait for the sun to rise higher. Perhaps the sky will clear."

No one responded, even the newer pilots knowing the hard tone in his voice.

"Mechanics, continue your work. We will be prepared to fly at the first sign of improvement."

He moved toward the makeshift office, the cloth walls of the hangar billowing out now with a soft chilling wind. He rounded a corner, a ragged wall built of wooden crates, moved through an opening, saw a light, Bodenschatz sitting at his small desk. The man stood abruptly, and Richthofen held up his hand, moved to his own chair, sat heavily.

"Sit, Karl. The weather has turned bad again. We must wait."

"Yes, sir, I heard. France in the spring. No place for a war." Bodenschatz laughed at his own joke, defying the hard scowl on Richthofen's face. After a silent moment, he said, "Captain, the weather will clear soon enough. You have always said, if we cannot fly, neither can they."

The young man's words cut through Richthofen's gloom, Bodenschatz's good humor always infectious. Richthofen felt his dark mood lighten, said, "Yes, of course."

He could see out through the opening in the hangar, dawn already spreading through the fog. He stood again, said, "Where is Moritz? I have not seen him this morning."

Bodenschatz seemed suddenly nervous, hesitated a moment, said, "Um, sir. He is fine. I did not authorize . . . I wish to say that I had no part in this. The men thought it might lift your spirits."

"What might lift my spirits?"

"I'm not certain I can answer that, sir. The men have

observed that Moritz has been somewhat lonely, sir. They feel you have been neglecting him. Forgive me, but there is a conspiracy afoot. All in good humor, I assure you, sir."

Richthofen was concerned now, said, "What have they done to my dog?" He didn't wait for an answer, left the small office, stepped out into the cool mist, saw a gathering of men at the far end of the hangar. He looked around, called out, "Moritz!"

He focused on the men now, saw stifled laughter, heard a sudden clattering of wood, saw the dog, a mad scamper into the hangar, coming straight toward him. The dog was trailed by a wooden wheel chock, and Richthofen could see now that the block of wood had been tied to the dog's tail. The dog came to an abrupt halt in front of him, spun around, the wood rattling after him.

"Stop! Moritz!"

Richthofen waited for an opening, leapt forward, grabbed the dog by the collar, held tightly. "Be still!"

The dog obeyed, settled down in a whining heap, and Richthofen knelt down, fumbled with the coarse rope, untied the knot. He stood again, looked toward the far end of the hangar, saw pilots scurrying away, disappearing rapidly out of the hangar, the mechanics staring intently into their motors.

"*What is the meaning of this?*" He tried to feel anger, but there was no cruelty in the men, Moritz as much a part of this squadron as he was a pet to his master. Richthofen looked down at the dog's woeful expression, could not help rubbing the clipped ears, the dog responding by rising up, standing upright against him, his forepaws on Richthofen's chest.

The mechanics began to look at him with sheepish grins, and he saw Krefft now, the big man emerging from under the red triplane. "Your dog has been lonely, sir. His master has been occupied. We felt he required your attention. No harm was intended, sir."

Moritz was licking his face now, and Richthofen could not avoid the sloppy wetness, began to laugh as the dog wrestled him. He held the dog's head away, let him drop to the ground, said, "All right! So everyone thinks I have neglected you, eh? Well, we have some time now. Come!" He left the hangar, stepped out into the wet grass, the dog bounding along beside him. He glanced up, saw a small patch of blue, a brief opening in the thick gray. Yes, good, he thought. The fog will not last.

He walked out across the open field, the hangars now behind him. The dog stayed close, unusual, keeping pace with him. They walked for several minutes, and then Richthofen stopped, could see the edge of the wide drainage ditch that bordered the airfield. He looked at the dog, was prepared to give a cautionary shout, knew that Moritz would typically launch himself into the deep muck in the bottom of the ditch. But the dog stayed beside him, seemed to wait for his master to make the next move.

"You surprise me. You are a fine fellow this morning." He scratched the dog's ears, thought, They are right. I have been neglecting you. He pointed toward the ditch, said, "I suppose, if you wish to swim in the mud, I will allow it. Just keep the mud to yourself."

The dog sat, simply watched him.

"No taste for mud today?" Richthofen saw a short stub of wood lying in the grass, said, "Ah, it is pursuit, then? All right." He picked up the stick, tossed it out into the short grass, the dog responding in one great leap of motion. It was a simple familiar game, the dog making a bounding scramble to retrieve the stick, dropping it dutifully at Richthofen's feet. He picked it up again, another throw, the dog again playing the game. He made several throws, and the dog was panting heavily now, Richthofen flexing his arm, stiffness in his shoulder.

"It has been too long since I threw anything. We both need the work." The stick was at his feet, the dog waiting for the next throw. But the game was over, and Richthofen stared at the exhausted joy on the dog's face.

"Is this all you require of me? Very well. It seems your day is now made perfect." He looked out across the field, the fog beginning to thin. He moved toward the hangars, and he realized the anger had drained out of him, the gloom that seemed to follow him every day. Is this all I need, after all? Walk out into a field and throw a stick to my dog? He stopped, the dog halting beside him, and he looked down, said, "You ask nothing more of me than this. I am fortunate to have such a friend."

He could see more patches of blue above him, the sun burning through the gray mist. He started to walk again, could see the men gathering outside the hangars, pilots who knew another game, who would wait for their master to give the order. The dog was trotting beside him again, the stick forgotten, and they crossed the flat ground, moved closer to the hangars. He waved his arm, pointed upward, the signal they all understood, the men stepping into motion, planes rolling out of the hangars. He noticed a cluster of automobiles now, some just arriving, the inevitable visitors, but there would be no time for them, no tour, no interview. He moved toward the red triplane, the mechanics standing back, their work complete. Corporal Menzke appeared now, hurrying toward him, holding the heavy flying suit, the helmet and goggles. The orderly was out of breath, said something about the visitors, photographers, but Richthofen focused on the clothing, began the routine, pulled the heavy fur up over his legs, then higher, sliding his arms through the thick sleeves of the suit. He looked at the dog again, Moritz sitting, tongue dangling, simply staring up at him. The orderly held out the helmet, but Richthofen waved him back, put one hand on the dog's head, smiled, the dog rising up, leaning against his master's chest with the big paws. Richthofen laughed, thought of the dog flying with him, a puppy, days long gone now. So many things have changed, he thought. But there must always be time for this. Moritz still wrestled with him, the dog's tongue spreading wet goo on Richthofen's face. He laughed again, thought, Yes, every day, there must be time.

He heard a voice calling out to him, turned, saw a man aiming a camera at him. The man lowered the camera, waved to him, "Thank you, Captain! Very nice!"

Richthofen froze, and the dog sensed the change, dropped away from him. "Who are you? How dare you photograph me!"

The man was already moving away, oblivious to Richthofen's sudden anger.

The orderly moved up close now, some of the others as well,

and Menzke said, "Sorry, sir. I should have stopped him. He did not ask permission."

Richthofen wanted to pursue the man, wanted the camera shattered, felt an uncontrollable rage at the violation of his private moment. But the man was gone, swallowed up by the swarm of visitors. He saw guards appearing, the belated effort to herd the civilians back beyond the hangars. They will complain, he thought, but so be it. We do not fly so that important civilians can gawk at our aeroplanes. Must they always bring photographers? He looked at Menzke, the man still holding his helmet, saw concern on the orderly's face.

Menzke said, "He had no right to take your photograph, sir. All of them know about the jinx."

Richthofen took the helmet, said, "Foolish talk, Corporal."

"If you insist, sir."

It had begun with Boelcke, though some believed it was a curse on every pilot who flew. To many it had become a rigidly accepted custom, that no pilot should be photographed before taking flight. Boelcke had died the same day his photograph was taken. But Richthofen had endured the intrusion from photographers for so long now that it had not occurred to him if his picture had ever been taken before a combat flight.

He took the goggles from the orderly now, said, "There is no jinx, Corporal. The captain of the guard was remiss this morning. That's all."

"Yes, sir."

Richthofen stepped toward the triplane, adjusted his flying suit, put one foot up on the step, lifted himself into the cockpit. He slid his legs down, settled in, adjusted the suit again. He looked to the side, saw the rest of the squadron following his silent command, all climbing up into their planes. He glanced up, the fog completely gone, looked now at his watch: ten-thirty. Good. The sun will be behind us still. In front of the plane, his mechanic, Holtzopfel, stood with one hand resting on the prop, waiting for his signal. Richthofen raised his hand, then paused, was surprised to see the dog, still sitting upright, watching him. He smiled, waved his hand, said, "Don't worry, Moritz. I will return soon."

He pointed to the prop now, the mechanic giving one hard pull, the motor roaring to life.

Richthofen saw them first, a squadron of Camels, swirling around two German observation planes. The others knew to wait for his signal, followed him as he turned the triplane toward the outnumbered Germans. He had counted eight Camels, had glimpsed another cluster of planes farther off, probably British as well, but the five Fokkers had the momentum, were closing fast on the first group of Camels. In seconds, the fight was on, a swirl of confusion as each pilot sought out his own target. He roared right through the formation of Camels, could see his men spinning off, each one trying to find the advantage, the Camels answering with spins and loops of their own. He turned the Fokker hard to one side, banked around in a tight turn, saw a Camel dropping down, escaping the fight. He smiled, thought, No, you will not go home today. There is no escape.

He felt the heat rising in his chest, his eyes coming into sharp focus on his prey. The Camel did not evade him, and he thought, So, you do not think anyone will follow you. It will be your final mistake. He nosed the Fokker down, gaining speed, closing the distance on the Camel. He stared hard at the brown mound in the center of the plane, the pilot's head, moved the stick slightly, the Fokker dancing at his commands. The triplane slipped sideways, the Camel now coming into his sights. He felt the button that would fire the Maxims, caressed it gently, waited, measured the space between them. He pressed the trigger, saw the Camel dip down at the same moment, the pilot suddenly aware of the danger. The spray of bullets flew harmlessly over the Camel's wings, and Richthofen shouted a curse, dropped the Fokker down again. The Camel was all frantic motion, the pilot tilting and weaving his plane in a desperate maneuver to avoid Richthofen's guns. The Maxims fired again, but the Camel was moving too quickly, darting and jerking from side to side, dropping down farther. Richthofen held the stick steady in his hands, eased the nose of the Fokker down, held the grim smile, the Camel's pilot making yet another mistake. Every dip, every turn slows you down, he thought. You cannot escape me.

The Camel continued to drop, and Richthofen forced himself to be patient, glanced toward the ground, very close, trees winding along the banks of a river. The Camel went lower still, and Richthofen followed, could see the ground undulating now, was low enough to see the rise and dip of shallow hills. He caught movement on the ground, glanced to one side, men in earthworks along the river, unfamiliar colors, the uniforms nothing like the solid gray of the Germans. The plane shook suddenly, a burst of white smoke engulfing him, behind him now, and he cursed again. *Antiaircraft guns*. He stared to the front, to the wobbling tail of the Camel, thought, Well, you have succeeded, my friend. You have reached your own lines. But I'm too low for your foolish gunners. The Fokker lurched again, more smoke, and he fought to see through it, saw the Camel rise up, then turn hard, slipping over a rise along the river. The Camel was gone for a brief second, and Richthofen fought the urge to follow, no, stay straight. He will come back. This is the only way home. He stared toward the river, saw it bending across in front of him, a valley opening up. He held his breath, held tightly to his patience. Come on. I know you are there. Your time is just about up. The Camel was there suddenly, nearly broadside to him, the pilot twisting to avoid him, the Maxims' gun sights squarely on the motor. Richthofen pressed the trigger, but the Fokker lurched again, more gunfire from the ground, smoke blinding him again.

"Damn you!"

He guided the nose toward the Camel again, could see he was barely a hundred meters above the ground, the trees racing past beneath him. He fired the Maxims again, another miss, thought, You are very lucky today, Camel. Suddenly the air ripped around him, streaks of fire. He turned, could hear a machine gun, caught a glimpse of a plane behind him.

He jerked the stick, still focused on the Camel in front of him, thought, You will not yet get away, my friend! The plane behind him fired again, bullets ripping the fabric on his top wing. He moved the nose, tried to put the Camel in his sights again, heard

492

more bullets punching the triplane, saw flashes of fire from the ground, heard a chattering of rifle fire, machine guns. The plane behind him fired again, shredding fabric, the sickening crack of wood behind him, bullets smashing into the tail. He twisted the Fokker to one side, still searched his gun sights for the Camel. He was very close again, twenty meters, the Camel gyrating up and down, and he waited, anticipated, could see it settling right into the path of his guns, slowly, the perfect place, the head of the pilot in his sights. . . .

The hard shock punched a burst of fire through his chest, sucked his breath away. He still held tightly to the stick, could not help the reflex, pulled the plane up, tried now to hold it steady. He fought to breathe, still tried to see the Camel, the voice in his brain, no, not yet! I must find him! He tried to calm the triplane, felt the fire spreading inside him, put one hand on his side, where the shock had come, his suit ripped, saw his glove wet with blood. There was no breath at all now, the hot wetness rising in his throat, the fire spreading up into his face, his eyes, blinding him, the sound of the motor and the guns around him one great roar. He put his hand against his side, felt the wetness surging out of him, but there was no strength now, no control, and he let his hands go free. The plane danced and spun around him, and he felt the wind against his face, the voice in his head silent now, the rush of sounds growing quiet, the wet darkness swallowing him, the image flickering in his brain, the Camel, just one more shot . . . the face of Boelcke. . . .

The triplane tumbled and rolled into a shattered mass, was surrounded quickly by the soldiers who had poured so much lead into the sky. They were Australians, men who knew little of Fokkers and Camels. But they knew this one, word quickly spreading that a solid red triplane had been brought down behind their lines. In the air above them, two Camels circled, one man breathlessly grateful to be alive, the other convinced he had sent the Red Baron to his death.

At Cappy, the men of JG-1 could only wait, pilots and mechanics taking turns staring into the empty sky, not knowing if their leader was still alive, the most optimistic of them praying

493

that he had been captured. The German Air Service broadcast repeated messages to the Royal Flying Corps, while German infantrymen under white banners crossed no-man's-land, carrying dispatches to the British trenches, asking for some definite word. A full day later that word came, a single message dropped into German lines by a solitary Camel.

Captain von Richthofen was fatally wounded in aerial combat and was buried with full military honors.

31

LUFBERY

Toul, France—April 30, 1918

The first patrol had completed their mission, and Lufbery watched as they circled, made the instinctive head count, his mind registering the number . . . *three*, confirming that everyone had come home safely. He turned, saw the mechanics coming together, their usual routine, saw a hand go up, pointing.

He looked again at the circling Nieuports, was surprised to see a fourth plane, falling in behind them, mimicking their landing pattern. The Nieuports were coming down now, and Lufbery moved out into the open field, could see that the fourth plane wasn't a Nieuport at all. It was a SPAD. The questions were coming from the men behind him, and he responded, said, "Seems we have a visitor."

The three Nieuports taxied up close, the SPAD following, and Lufbery saw the Indian head on the plane's fuselage, smiled. The pilot was looking at him, and Lufbery could see that beneath the man's thick goggles spread the familiar bushy thatch of moustache. Lufbery walked out, waited for the SPAD's motor to stop, said, "You get lost, Major Thaw?"

During the past month, the Ninety-fourth Aero Squadron had received two new pilots, transfers from Thaw's 103rd. David Peterson and James Norman Hall had been sent over to assist Lufbery in the ongoing training of the new flyers. A growing number of men were arriving from the States, taking their turn at the beginner courses at Issoudun before receiving assignment to the combat air squadrons. As the commanders of the AAS saw the numbers of pilots increasing, they wisely called upon the experienced veterans to make their contribution to the proper training of the fledgling pilots. Peterson and Hall fit the description perfectly. Both men had been members of the Lafayette Escadrille.

Peterson was the younger, a stoic twenty-three-year-old from Pennsylvania, a bright young man whose education had seemed to open the way to a lucrative career as a chemical engineer. To the other pilots, he was the picture of the college boy, and he accepted the ribbing without protest. In the air, he seemed to transform into something altogether different, an overeager pilot who sought out the disadvantage, who recklessly charged into fights most often when he was outnumbered. His time with the escadrille was marked by constant repairs to his bullet-ridden plane. There was little teasing about Peterson's apparent need to kill himself in combat, and each time he returned to the airfield with a wounded aeroplane, the others had wondered if perhaps his final flight would come next time. But despite his strange need to put himself in harm's way, Peterson had in fact survived. The AAS recognized that Peterson's experience was an asset. Lufbery wondered if the man would stop trying to destroy himself long enough to give his students some skills they could actually use to survive themselves.

Jimmy Hall was the antithesis of Peterson, a man not much younger than Lufbery, a midwesterner who had sought adventure instead of academics. Hall had journeyed to England in mid-1914, intending to study creative writing, but when the war broke out, he decided that war could be the greatest inspiration of all. Hall joined the British army, allowed only because he claimed to be Canadian, and served in front-line combat in France as a machine-gunner. Later, after a visit to the States, Hall had learned of the formation of the American Escadrille. Encouraged by a publishing house to write articles based on his own experiences, he traveled to France, where, instead of merely researching, he decided to fly. It was Hall's particular distinction that, on New Year's Day, 1918, he was the victor in the Lafayette Escadrille's final confirmed kill. If Peterson sought out the most dangerous combat, Hall could not avoid it. When Hall was transferred to the Ninety-fourth, he made his first introduction to the squadron by rolling his

Nieuport over on its back right in front of the hangar. To the rapidly gathering crowd, the first assumption was that this newly arriving pilot was surely a recruit, utterly unskilled. As Hall climbed unceremoniously from his wrecked plane, it was Lufbery who realized the opposite. Even a veteran could make idiotic mistakes.

Lufbery had sent word of Thaw's surprise appearance to both Hall and Peterson, and they had brought the appropriate greeting: a bottle of wine. Thaw sat heavily in a soft chair, behaved like the honored guest, and waited while his glass was filled.

The others raised their glasses, and Hall said, "A toast to the Club of Should Be Dead."

The phrase had been Parsons', and Thaw drank, said, "What happened to Ted, anyway? He should be here."

Lufbery shrugged, and Peterson said, "I heard he stayed with the French. Didn't want to put up with all the aggravation."

Thaw laughed. "Parsons might use a different word than *aggravation*, College Boy. They not teach you how to swear at Harvard?"

Peterson seemed to blush, and Lufbery shook his head, said, "All right, Major, what the hell are you doing here? They toss you out of the One hundred third? You cause a mutiny?"

Thaw drank again, said, "Nope. They tossed the whole One hundred third out. We're off tomorrow to Dunkirk. The Ass decided we're needed up along the Channel, do something to help out the British. They're getting pounded pretty bad, you know."

Hall raised a glass, laughed at Thaw's use of the word, the slang many of them were using to describe the American Air Service. "To the Ass."

Lufbery ignored the toast, said, "You happy about that, Bill?"

Thaw shrugged. "Sure. What the hell, if I feel like it, I can take a jaunt over to England. Flying is flying. The Boche are everywhere. Doesn't much matter if we shoot them up there or down here. What you think about Richthofen?"

There was a silent moment, Hall pouring another glass of wine. Lufbery stared at his half-empty glass, said, "About damned time."

Peterson cleared his throat, seemed to struggle for words. "Never thought . . . I mean, he was the best there was, right?"

Lufbery thought a moment. "Nobody's the best. No such thing. Makes no difference how good you are, all it takes is dumb luck, one half-blind moron who squeezes his trigger at the right moment, some antiaircraft clown who happens to guess right."

Thaw sat forward, said, "Jeez, Luf. You going to a funeral?"

Lufbery drained his glass, set it down on the small table beside him, stared at the floor. "We all are. Just a matter of time. Richthofen proved it. Nobody's immune." He watched the others as they drank in silence, caught Thaw looking up at him.

Thaw said, "Not sure when I'll get to see you chaps again."

Hall seemed to fidget, and Lufbery could tell he was uncomfortable with the somber mood.

"Well, hell, Bill, they move us all over the place. We'll bump into you sooner or later."

Thaw nodded, still looked at Lufbery. "All right, I need to get out of here. We're loading up all our equipment on the train, have to get the hangars cleared out before I send the pilots up. At least the pilots get to fly there. Long damned trip otherwise. You been on a train lately? The French are patching their tracks with scrap metal. I feel bad for the ground crews."

He stood, the others putting down their glasses. Thaw held out a hand to the other two, said, "Keep 'em flying. You got a good group here. The Boche have their hands full."

He turned to Lufbery now, who looked down again, felt a dark hole opening up inside of him. He had done all he could to keep the word out of his mind, *friend*, the great mistake, growing close to the men around you, the men who so often didn't come back. He saw Thaw's hand extended toward him, let out a long breath, took the hand, held it tightly for a moment. Thaw said, "Dammit, Luf. This was supposed to be a celebration."

"For what?"

"Well, hell, did we ever need a reason? I don't know. Richthofen's dead. That's worth a drink, right?"

Lufbery released Thaw's hand, nodded slowly, looked up, saw the familiar smile on the man's thick round face. He tried to fight through his gloom, said, "Yep. One more Boche in the ground."

Thaw patted him on the shoulder now, said, "Okay, I gotta take off. You guys keep an eye on each other, right? You screw up, and Luf here will kick your ass. I've seen him do it too. Throws a right hand with a kick like a damned mule."

Lufbery forced a smile, felt angry at himself now, something holding him back from their playfulness. Hall and Peterson followed Thaw out of the room, and Lufbery waited, heard their voices, some rude comment about Peterson's college days. He picked up the wine bottle, saw it was empty, set it aside, had no more excuses for staying there alone. The voices were gone now, and he knew Thaw would be in his SPAD quickly, that if he had a mission there would be no delay. He moved toward the door, could see the hangar, the rows of Nieuports, the activity, thought of Thaw's words, *a good group*. It's true. I never thought it would happen, so much confusion, so much incompetence. And yet, here we are. It's working. There's more of us every day. Yep. A good group.

May 7, 1918

He watched them coming in, felt the cold hole opening in his chest. Three had gone out. Two were returning. He waited for them to taxi close, saw one man put his face down in his hands, the other snatch away his goggles. It was Rickenbacker. Lufbery moved up to the Nieuport, waited for the news. Rickenbacker looked over at the other plane, then looked at him, said, "I don't know what happened. I'm sorry, sir. Ask Green."

Lufbery moved slowly around to the other plane, heard soft sobs. The ice grew in his chest. The missing man was Jimmy Hall. He suddenly had no patience for the show of emotion, said, "Lieutenant Green. Get hold of yourself. What happened?"

He saw the young man stiffening, fighting with himself, and Green said, "All I saw . . . Jimmy went in first. I thought there were too many of them . . . but he attacked, so I followed him. They must have gotten on his tail. I saw him going down . . . the top wing was gone. I didn't see him crash."

Rickenbacker was beside him now, and Lufbery said, "*Where*, Lieutenant? Where were you?"

Green said, "Just west of the woods at Montsec."

Lufbery let out a breath, thought, Behind German lines. No way to find him.

He moved away from the plane, carried the familiar weight inside of him. He looked toward the hangar, saw his own Nieuport, began to walk that way. The mechanics responded, the men gathering at the plane, and he motioned to the wheels, said, "Remove the chocks. I'm going up."

They obeyed, pushed the Nieuport out of the hangar. He retrieved his flight suit, went through the tedious routine, heard his name, ignored it. He pulled the boots on, heard his name again, turned, saw Rickenbacker.

"You going after them, sir?"

Lufbery nodded, said nothing.

"Let me go with you. I can show you where—"

Lufbery cut him off with a sharp stare, shook his head slowly. Rickenbacker backed away, said, "Good luck, sir."

Lufbery moved past him, was up and into his cockpit in a single mo-tion. He pointed to the prop, the mechanics obeying, the motor coming to life. The Nieuport rolled forward, and he turned out toward the open ground, revved the motor, and within seconds he was in the air.

He had exhausted most of his fuel, knew he was far behind the German lines. He could see Metz in the distance, the great fortress city surrounded by several German airfields. For a long two hours there had been only one squadron of Albatroses, but he had completely surprised them, none of the Germans expecting to see a lone Nieuport suddenly falling on them out of the sun. The fight had been brief and automatic, almost too simple, pouring his fire into one of the German planes, which spun

500

down in a streak of black smoke. The others had disappeared before he could relocate them. He had seen nothing else in the air, frustrating, had hoped for more of a response to his presence, but not even the antiaircraft batteries had spotted him.

He wrapped his memory around Jimmy Hall, had stopped holding it away. If he didn't do this now, it would haunt him, pulling him awake in the middle of the night, just like the memory of all the others. It was the lesson of a veteran, something he had seen in Bill Thaw. You could not pretend you didn't care about them, that you wouldn't miss them. You couldn't forget all the quirks and pieces of their lives that made each of them part of the group. He thought of Rickenbacker, wanting to come with him. He thinks . . . they will all think that this is just revenge. They don't understand. An hour ago I killed a Boche, probably. And it doesn't change anything. There is no eye for an eye in war. The killing is random and mindless, and you do it because it's your job, or you do it to survive, not because there is justice in it.

He felt his shoulders slumping down, stared ahead at nothing, his mind growing numb. No, this cannot ever be about revenge. He remembered DeLaage, their first meeting, the Frenchman making the obvious assumption that Lufbery flew to avenge the death of Marc Pourpe. I believed that too, in the beginning. Of course, it's powerful inspiration. But I have not felt that for a while. Pourpe is gone, after all, and no matter how many Boche I have killed, he is still gone. He tried to recall how many German planes had gone down in front of him, too many to remember. And Jimmy Hall . . . he thought of Rickenbacker, of course, he wanted revenge of his own. He does not yet know, there is no such thing. Just because a friend is killed, it does not make us better fighters. We can be angry, angry at the war, angry for caring about the ones who are gone. But the enemy . . . is just the enemy. It is our job, after all, to kill him. Lufbery thought of the young pilots. What do they know of loss and death? Yet they must perform just as the rest of us do. To kill a man they must draw inspiration from something else. Patriotism? Perhaps. I will never know the answer to that

501

now. He thought of Richthofen. Eighty confirmations. Remarkable. Richthofen had to know how many, certainly, someone over there kept score. Even if that never mattered to him, Richthofen was never allowed to forget. Like some damned contest, a sporting event, a baseball team, winning eighty games in a row. But Richthofen had to know that every winning streak has an end. And so, he is dead.

Lufbery focused again, looked at his watch, knew he had gone as far as his fuel would allow. He was tired now, felt the end of the day settling around him. The sadness was filling him, the great weight of the loss: Jimmy Hall is gone. Dead . . . well, we don't know. The Boche will tell us, probably. Both sides are good about that, one piece of chivalry we still care about. He thought of Rickenbacker again, and Eddie Green, the young man's grief. You will learn, you cannot have so much emotion. And if you cannot avoid it, sometimes it is best to do *this*, to just come up here and get away. And tomorrow, we will climb into our Nieuports, and do it all again.

He looked at the compass, banked the plane, headed for home.

May 19, 1918

He sat in his room, drinking a cup of coffee. The morning patrol had been quiet, unusual, the Germans seeming to focus their attention to another part of the line.

He scanned a sheet of paper, the pilot roster, a growing list of figures, flight statistics, hours in the air. Lufbery had begun to separate the pilots in his mind, had instinctively gravitated toward the ones who were improving, several of them, like Rickenbacker and Douglas Campbell, already scoring impressive victories over the Boche fighters. He had tried to be impartial, still allowed some of the other men to accompany him on patrols, but the gap was widening among them, the men who simply wouldn't learn, or worse, who thought they already had what it took to charge into the fight on their own. It had been the same with the Lafayette pilots, some of them missing what Lufbery believed to be the intangible ingredient, the difference between the steady hand and the sharp eye, and those who found a way simply to stay alive. He thought of Parsons' own description, the Club of Should Be Dead. Not all of the pilots were members, and the more Lufbery led the young men aloft, the more he realized that many of them would only perform their service. When the war was over, they would return to their homes, claiming some heroism. But even they would know, somewhere in that hidden place, that death had never really been close, and that too often, when the opportunity had come to them, the chance to kill a man, they had backed away.

He tried not to show any kind of favoritism, felt like the father who must treat his sons with the same affection, no matter their differences. In the Lafayette Escadrille, there were some pilots who never flew alongside him, mostly by the luck of the draw, or the decision made by Thenault, for reasons the Frenchman never explained. But now, with the Ninety-fourth, it was Lufbery the instructor's job to be in the air with all of them. And so he had begun to avoid the men who could not be taught, who would take to the air with all the show and pride of their squadron, and never make a contribution that anyone would remember. It wasn't always fair of him to pass judgment. Every man who passed the training at Issoudun had qualified himself to fly. Yet Lufbery could not help feeling respect for the good ones, the men you could depend on to cover your tail, who would pursue the enemy for as long as their guns would fire or their planes would fly. These were the men who would gain entry into Parsons' morbid club.

He raised the coffee cup, saw the muddy grounds in the bottom, set it down again. He had considered going back up, but his Nieuport was in the hands of the mechanics now. The plane had joined the long row of Nieuports that were undergoing a general maintenance. It had angered him, too many of the planes going out of action at one time, a mistake by the chief mechanic. No, I suppose I will just stay here. Or, perhaps, go to the hangar. Get my hands greasy, speed things along a bit.

He heard a low rumbling, moved to the window, thought, It can't be bombers, not in daytime. Must be . . . antiaircraft batteries. He heard voices in the hallway.

Huffer was shouting, "Infantry reports a Boche observer, heading this way. By himself. Some damned idiot. Who's available?"

Lufbery went to the door, saw Huffer speaking into the telephone, knew he was talking to someone in the hangar. Huffer looked at him, made a frown, said, "Who's that? Gude? No one else?" He paused, seemed to ponder the decision. "All right, send him up." Huffer put the telephone down, said, "They spotted a single Boche coming this way, straight for us. Photographer, most likely. I guess we should line up and smile, make for a good portrait. The only pilot who was ready to go is—"

"Gude, yes, I heard. Not a good idea. He's never been in a fight."

Huffer nodded slowly. "I know. But infantry says it's only a single Boche. Maybe it's meant to be. The man's gotta face it sometime."

Lufbery said nothing, turned away, moved quickly toward the door, and Huffer said, "You going out there?"

Lufbery didn't look back, pushed through the doorway, said, "Yep."

He stopped, heard the rumbling closer now, more antiaircraft fire, could see the puffs of smoke, closer than he expected. He heard the whine of a single Nieuport, the motor revving, the familiar sound of takeoff. He cursed to himself, saw a motorcycle parked beside the barracks, jumped on, cranked the starter hard with his foot, the motor spitting to life. He pushed the bike forward, began to roll, saw men at the door, more of the pilots emerging from their rooms, some following him on foot.

The ride to the airfield was short, and he roared around the opening of the hangar, stepped hard on the brake, slid the motorcycle to a stop. The mechanics were already gathering, a few with binoculars, staring up, and Lufbery joined them, said, "Where the hell is he?"

Hands pointed, and Lufbery saw them now, a German two-seater, the untested Gude working his way closer. The German plane seemed to be crippled, and Lufbery listened hard to the uneven rhythm of the motor, thought, Maybe the antiaircraft boys actually hit something. Gude was still climbing, too far away for a fight, but Lufbery heard a new sound now, the faint rattle of machine-gun fire, the Nieuport pouring out its bullets. Lufbery said, "Someone, I need binoculars!"

He felt the glasses pressed into his hand, raised them, found the Nieuport, saw the flashes of fire from Gude's machine guns. "No, dammit. Too far away! Wait! The bastard's not going anywhere. You'll catch him quick enough." The Nieuport continued to fire its guns, the German plane rolling and bouncing, and Lufbery felt raw frustration spinning into anger at Gude's inexperience. He turned, said, "Enough of this."

He looked for his Nieuport, saw it now, the cowling removed, the motor already in pieces. "Damn! Whose bus is ready to fly?"

"One there, sir. Lieutenant Davis."

Lufbery was already moving, ran to the row of lockers, threw open the door, pulled out his flight suit. He hesitated, listened, heard only the whine of the two motors, thought, Of course, he's out of ammunition!

He jerked on the boots, and the mechanics were already pushing the Nieuport into position, the men outside the hangar clearing the way. He jumped up, climbed into the cockpit, and the man at the prop said, "The magazine is full, sir. Should we check the guns?"

"No time. Start her up!"

He spotted Gude's Nieuport, the man circling helplessly, and Lufbery ignored him, pushed his plane into a hard climb. He glanced at the altimeter, four thousand feet, thought, Good, not much room for him to escape. He focused on the horizon, saw puffs of white smoke, the French antiaircraft batteries still taking their shots at the wounded German. He could see the plane now, thought, Albatros . . . two-seater. Yep. Photographer. Well, Boche, here's a portrait you'll enjoy.

He was moving up quickly on the German plane, could see it was flying unevenly, the pilot working furiously to keep it straight. There were fragments of wood hanging from one wing, and he nodded. Good, he's hit. This won't take long at all.

The Albatros began to roll to one side, trying to escape him, and he followed, measured the distance, the Nieuport gaining rapidly. He could see the observer, the man's machine gun up, pointing back at him, the German waiting for the right moment, just as Lufbery was. He was within range now, and he saw flashes from the German's gun, dipped the nose of the Nieuport, dropped quickly beneath the tail of the Albatros, out of the line of fire. The gap was closing, and he waited, felt his own breathing, the hard heaving in his chest, the raw pure excitement, the kill so close. He pulled up on the stick, his finger on the trigger, watched as the Albatros drifted into his sights. He pressed the button, the gun firing a sharp burst, then it suddenly stopped. He saw a piece of the tail of the Albatros fall away, but the German was still moving forward, and Lufbery shouted, "What the hell . . . ?"

He pressed the trigger again, nothing happening, and he looked at the gun in front of him, could see now, the bolt partially open, a shell stuck halfway. The gunner in the Albatros was firing at him again, and Lufbery jerked the stick, pulled the Nieuport in a sharp bank, looked back, the Albatros not following him. No, he thought, he's in no condition to fight. He's trying to get home. And unless I can fix this damned gun, he'll make it.

He unbuckled the belt across his waist, stood slightly, leaned out over the windscreen. He kept his head down, fighting the hard wash of air from the prop, trying to keep his goggles from blowing off. He felt for the gun, wrapped his gloved fingers around the bolt, and he jerked hard.

"Come on, dammit!"

The bolt gave way, the spent cartridge tumbling out, the breech clear, and he pulled the bolt again, smooth, the gun ready once more. He eased back, sat again, adjusted the goggles, scanned the sky, said aloud, "Now, you son of a bitch. Where are you?"

He circled, saw more of the white puffs, could see the Albatros snaking its way westward. He straightened the Nieuport, followed again, let out a long slow breath, flexed his fingers. All right, he thought. I'm ready for you. Let's try this again.

The Albatros was swerving, the pilot struggling, trying to avoid the shells bursting around him. Lufbery felt a small jolt, shrapnel scattered in the air around him. It was typical, the ground gunners not caring whom they shot at, and Lufbery cursed, kept the Nieuport in a straight course, aimed for the tail of the Albatros.

He was close again, saw the gunner standing, the machine gun coming up once more. He held the nose in a tight line, measured again, saw flashes from the German gun, streaks of fire ripping past him. He leaned forward slightly, stared at the man, the gap closing, his finger on the trigger. It's time now, Boche. . . .

He pressed the trigger, the gun chattering, throwing a stream of lead into the Albatros, but the German plane was rolling, dipping again, and Lufbery held steady to the stick, thought, All right, one more time. The German gunner raised his head, seemed to look up at him, the two men only yards apart, and the man lowered his head again, staring through his gun sights, finding his own aim. Lufbery pressing the trigger again, felt a sudden sharp jolt, his hand punched free from the stick, a sharp stinging burn. Blood was coming from his glove, and he fought to grip the stick, but his hand was still burning, and he saw the thumb of his glove gone, blood spilling out onto his flight suit. The pain came now, and he tried to grip the stick again, but there was no control, no grip. He looked up, saw the Albatros still in front of him, grabbed the stick with his left hand, fumbled for the trigger, heard a sharp ping, more bullets striking the motor. He pulled his right hand up to his chest, tried to bank with his left, and suddenly the motor exploded in fire, great sheets of flame sweeping back around him. He released the stick, his left hand fumbling for the ignition switch, and he stabbed at it, his hands quivering, the flames now on him, burning his face. He pulled the stick to the left, the flames sweeping out to the right for a brief second. Yes, that's it. Slip dive, slide back and forth. The motor was silent now, and he could smell the sharp odor of burned cloth, the flames engulfing the motor, the slip not working. The cowling was consumed by the fire now, the flames starting to roll over him, the fire spreading out on the wing above him. The plane began to tumble, and he tried to see out, his flight suit burning, his arms carrying the flames. The screams came now, carried off by the rush of wind, and he beat his arms against his chest, fought the fire, but the flames were circling him, his suit igniting, and he stood, saw a snaking line on the ground, a river, the terror in his mind giving way to a single thought, water. . . .

They were watching from the ground, deathly silence, saw the small figure fall from the burning plane, dropping away, the only escape a man had from the horror of the fire. Rickenbacker held the binoculars, watched as the figure trailed a faint stream of black smoke, continuing to fall, disappearing to the ground, and he heard the soft words, prayers, a faint whisper coming from the men around him.

"No. Oh God. No."

He had fallen near a stream, coming to earth in a garden, close beside a small house owned by an old woman. The people of her village had seen it as well, the fight in the air above them, the horror of the fire, the last desperate seconds of a man's life. In a few long minutes, the men of the Ninety-fourth Aero Squadron would reach the place, only to find that the villagers had taken up the body, had carried him to the small square in their village, had already covered him with flowers.

PART IV

OUT OF MANY, ONE

*Come on you sons of bitches! Do you want to
live forever?*

—Sergeant Daniel Daly, USMC
Belleau Wood—June 6, 1918

32

TEMPLE

Northeast of Paris—May 30, 1918

Their boots had been lined up against one wall, and now the uniforms were coming off, the large room humming with the soft growls of mostly naked men. They followed the instructions of the lieutenant, tossed their clothes into designated bins, which filled slowly with heaps of dull green shirts and pants. With their uniforms now gone, the men gathered toward the tables at the far end of the room, began to form a line. Temple stood beside Parker, the big man from Virginia.

Parker said, "This had better be for a good reason."

Across the table, the lieutenant stood behind three seated orderlies, the men presiding over neat stacks of khaki, pants and shirts.

"You have a problem, Marine?"

"No problem, sir."

Temple moved into line behind Parker, watched as each man before them received a new pair of pants, a new shirt, each piece of clothing selected from a different stack according to the orderly's quick appraisal of the man's size. The men moved away from the table, began to pull on the new uniforms, and Temple saw one of the orderlies eyeing Parker, then reaching into one of the piles, repeating the process.

"Above average. These'll fit you."

Parker moved away, and the orderly gave Temple a quick glance.

"Average. Here you go."

Temple took the new uniform, walked over to where Parker was fastening his shirt.

"Not bad. Sleeves too short."

Temple pulled his own pants on, pulled the trousers up, the waist too small. He inhaled, pulled his stomach in, hooked the button.

Parker said, "Too small, huh? Don't worry about it. A few weeks in this place, and we'll all be shrinkin'. Don't expect any biscuits and gravy."

Temple smiled, always enjoyed Parker's soft drawl, the big man from the mountains whose voice reminded Temple of Sunday afternoon.

Roscoe Temple was barely twenty, had come to the Marine Corps from the picture-book town of Monticello, Florida. It was lush green farm country, spread out over the hills east of Tallahassee, where cotton fields and cornfields rolled and dipped above the muddy lowlands of cypress swamps. He spoke with a southern accent as well, simple words that hid nothing, a soft lilt that he inherited from his mother, a woman whose hands carried the stains of farmland, who knew of birthing calves and birthing her own children.

To the others, the two young men sounded alike, and both were teased for their slow drawls the same way the others were teased for whatever peculiar accent they had brought from places so foreign to a boy from north Florida, places like Jersey City and Missoula and Pittsburgh. But throughout their training, the teasing of nervous young men had been replaced by something few of them had expected, a bond that began to draw them together in a way no civilian could understand. It was taught to them by the instructors, a lesson as important as anything they had learned in the field, as important as the drill and marching and building their bodies. It was about history and legacy, of sacrifice and valor in places many of them still couldn't find on a map. It was what it took, and what it meant to be a Marine.

When Roscoe was eight, his grandfather had taken him hunting, a reward for growing up in a land where turkeys swarmed every open field. His grandfather seemed as old as the trees, a quiet soft-spoken man who taught him to shoot, taught him patience, the pure skill of silence and stillness, the only way to outduel the instinctive genius of the game they pursued. It was not easy for an eight-year-old, and success did not come, not for several years. The old man did not scold him, was always the teacher, and if Temple was not a good hunter, he had soon become skilled with the long guns. The shotgun had come first, the old man tossing flat rocks high over the muddy pond, the boy peppering them with a spray of pellets, delighting the old man. The rifle had come next, an old Winchester, hard brass the boy would polish with his fingers. There were more targets, old cans on fence posts, close up at first, then farther back, and farther still, until the boy could outshoot even the old man. His grandfather began to talk of the army, that the boy had a talent for shooting that the old man had seen in only a few, and not for a long time now. The boy began to ask questions, and the old man obliged him with the stories, what it was like to be a soldier, a glorious surprise to the boy. The old man did not brag, had never been one to captivate an audience around the dinner table, gather a crowd at a picnic. He told the stories only when they were alone, stories of adventure that ignited the boy's imagination, the camps, the guns, great glorious battles. Then, when the old man thought Roscoe was old enough, the stories began to change. His grandfather began to dig deep into well-hidden memories, and the adventures became honest and sad. The boy learned of misery and death, of places called Spotsylvania and Petersburg, stories that would shock him, not just for the horror, but because the old man could not tell them without crying.

His grandfather had never pushed him to join the army, and his mother would howl in furious protest at the very suggestion that her only boy should be a soldier. But Temple had seen the look in the old man's eye, and the advice had come in quiet moments. The words had found a home deep inside the boy, his grandfather's gravelly voice with him still, that every man had one purpose, should serve God or his country or his neighbors in one way or another, but at the end of a man's life, the only judge would be the man himself. Temple had been shocked by the old man's lack of respect for the preacher, all the Sunday school lessons, but the old man had insisted that if a man could look into a mirror and respect what he saw, then he would never fear to stand tall in front of God, and God would feel just fine about that. But there was one more lesson the old man would teach him. It came on a fall day, when the leaves drifted away from the trees, and the family spoke of harvest and Thanksgiving. They would go hunting again, deer this time, the pursuit of one old buck that had made a home in the swamp beyond the old man's cornfield. Temple had risen early, had made his way in familiar darkness, but for the first time, the old man was not waiting for him, no soft voice greeting him at their private meeting place. When the sun pushed away the darkness, the boy made the long walk to the old man's cabin near the muddy pond, and learned his first lesson about death.

Temple finished high school, something of an accomplishment in the small towns of north Florida, but the young man would not listen to all the advice about work and career. He already knew the career he would pursue. Instead of the army, he would do the old man one better. He would become a Marine.

"Let's go! Fall in outside!"

The men were dressed now, and the platoon filed out into the yard. He saw buses, more men stepping down, a lengthening column of green, lining up at the far entrance to the building, more uniforms to be exchanged. He followed Parker again, stepped up into the empty bus, realized the lieutenant was behind him. He stopped, said, "Sir, these uniforms . . . they're just army. There's no Marine insignia."

The lieutenant was a tall, thin man, older, hard dark eyes. He stared past Temple, said, "I'm aware of that, Private. Nothing we can do about it for now. If General Bundy says we're to wear army khaki, then we'll wear army khaki."

"Yes, sir."

He boarded the bus, saw an open seat, sat, and the man beside him said, "You know what all this is about?"

"No. Don't think I'll ask."

"I figured out they're gonna disband the Corps. I bet the British told Pershing they won't let Marines fight over here. They're still pissed about how we kicked their ass in the Revolution."

514

There was laughter behind him, and a hand slapped Temple's shoulder.

"Don't listen to this dumb Italian. Hey, Guido—"

"It's Gino."

"Yeah, Gino. We're changing uniforms so the army boys won't be intimidated by us. The Second Division's got a lot more army boys than Marines, and General Bundy doesn't want the rest of them to feel inferior. I figure the general don't want the infantry whining all the damned day. Those boys might do better to follow us anyways."

"Some of you are dumb as tree trunks." The words came from the lieutenant, who stood in the front of the bus. "Ballou, where'd you get your little gem of intelligence?"

The man behind Temple said, "Um, sir, I just heard—"

"All right, shut the hell up. Ballou, Scarabelli, all of you. General Bundy doesn't feel the need to confide in every one of you, but I will. If nothing else, I won't have to listen to all these rumors, and find out just how dumb you are. We have been ordered out of our Marine uniforms because they bear a very close resemblance to what the Germans wear. Their gray looks a lot like our green from a distance. Now, unless some of you think it's a good idea to confuse our allies any more than they're already confused, why don't we just obey General Bundy's orders?"

Temple weighed the officer's words, heard Scarabelli muttering beside him.

"Better not disband the Corps. I'll make a stink. General Bundy will hear from me, dammit. My uncle knows a senator."

The lieutenant was up again, looked at Scarabelli with disbelief. Temple could not help smiling. The lieutenant said, "How did you make it into my Corps, Private? We need to find something for you to do that doesn't require you to think."

They had been in France since January, reinforcements for the Fifth Marine Regiment, men who had come across the Atlantic with the first wave that followed Pershing. Temple and his squad had come not to fill holes in the ranks, but to add strength to the regiments, the Fifth and Sixth now making up the Fourth Marine Brigade, which had been assigned to the AEF's

Second Division, commanded by Major General Omar Bundy. The veterans had never expected they would be on the ground in France. Most had assumed that if the Marines were to fight, they would be sent to those places Marines were accustomed to going, naval engagements, or assaults against shore targets. But the war in Europe offered no opportunities for deployments like Cuba, the Philippines, or Panama, where most of the veterans among them had gained their first real experience.

The suggestion to combine the Marines with the army troops had come from their commandant, General George Barnett, and Pershing had agreed. With the Americans scrambling to put trained men into the field as quickly as possible, it made perfect sense to incorporate the seasoned Marine veterans into one of the earliest front-line units to be deployed. With the Second Division now prepared to enter the line, the Marine Brigade received another surprise. On May 5, they had a new commander, James Harbord, the rugged no-nonsense officer who had been Pershing's chief of staff.

The men were to be bivouacked around the village of Chaumont-en-Vexin, word filtering through the ranks that they might move north, rumors flying through the entire division that they were to relieve the exhausted First Division at Cantigny.

It had been the AEF's first offensive assault, a strike engineered by Pershing against a bulge in the German line. The apex of the bulge had engulfed the French town of Cantigny, and Pershing had insisted to the Allied commanders that the First Division be allowed to recapture the town. Though the town itself held no major strategic significance, the value lay with the test that the Americans would face confronting the Germans for the first time. The attack began on May 28, and after two days of bloody combat, the men of the First Division succeeded in capturing and holding the town. Though the Americans suffered heavy losses, the cost was measured more by the extraordinary boost in morale that spread through Allied soldiers all along the Western Front. To every commander on both sides of the barbed wire, the First Division's accomplishment was enormous. The Americans had shown they were ready to fight.

To the men of the Fifth Marine Regiment, many of whom had been in France since the preceding June, it was about time. To Private Temple, and the others who had barely completed their training, it meant their first real opportunity to find out if all they had been taught about the pride and legacy of the Marine Corps had actually made them soldiers.

The trains had been in motion all morning, a continuous stream of bouncing cars and coughing locomotives. The Marines were to follow close behind the Ninth Infantry Regiment, mostly recruits who had barely completed their training. The Ninth had already spent time in front-line positions, gaining valuable experience in what the French had said was a quiet sector. But the Germans had not ignored this new presence along their front, and the trench raids had begun almost immediately. The Ninth had suffered from German artillery as well, a carefully targeted barrage that cost the division its first significant casualties, dead and wounded who were swept out of the war before the rest of the division could even reach the front. In every regiment, every company, the Marines and infantrymen of the Second Division accepted the news with silent tributes, knowing that the time for training had passed.

The next train in the long procession belched its way forward, and Temple heard the voice of the sergeant, the sharp growl that brought the platoon to stiff attention. There was no hesitation, the entire company falling into double file, climbing up into the first of the empty railcars.

Temple had been fascinated by the odd cars from the first time they had been herded onto the trains, only hours after they had disembarked the great ships. They were a strange sort of cattle car, a single axle in the center, so the car rocked slightly like a child's teeter-totter. There were no seats, no hint of anything that suggested comfort. The men would stand, pressed tightly together, their gear piled high in cargo boxes that trailed behind the cars. Beside the wide sliding door of each car had been a sign, bold and distinct, the same sign that Temple saw now:

Hommes 40
Chevaux 8

Temple imagined it had something to do with weight, like the bridges back home, a warning in case the train was too full. But every man had his own theory on the meaning, the men gathering their nervousness to focus on this one odd bit of French lore. None was more vocal than Scarabelli. The short man was close behind Temple, making his way forward with the rest of them, said in a low voice, "I still think it's a ball game. Some French team everybody's proud of. Must have been some kind of national championship, and the Homs boys kicked the hell of the Cheevax. Wonder how they'd do against the Giants?"

Beside Temple, Parker said, "You are one dumb—"

"*Quiet in ranks!*"

The sergeant was glaring at them, and Temple stifled a grin, had heard Parker's own theory, knew that Scarabelli wouldn't leave it alone.

"So, Mountain Man, you still think it's a road sign?"

"Has to be. This is a strange country. They probably have it figured out that wherever we're heading, we'll be forty miles from Homs and eight miles from Cheevax."

Behind him, Ballou said, "You're both idiots. Chevaux means horse."

Scarabelli glanced back. "How the hell do you know that, Cowboy? You can't even read."

"I can read just fine. There's lots of horse shows in Montana. Chevaux means horse."

"All right, Cowboy. What the hell is a homs? A cow?"

"Hell if I know."

They reached the car now, and Temple stepped up inside, knew to push in as far as he could, the men pressed tightly together, no empty space. Behind him, he heard the lieutenant. "Thirty-nine, forty. That's it. The rest . . . to the next car."

He tried to turn, felt the huge mass of Parker's body pressing against him.

"I figured it out. Homs is men. The car fits forty men or eight horses."

Scarabelli was on his other side, the small man turning, low curses.

"Forty Frenchmen, maybe. They don't have anybody as big as you damned farm boys. I can't breathe."

The car lurched, the mass of men suddenly crushed toward the back of the car. Scarabelli cursed again, and Temple knew to wait, that the car would tilt the other way, bringing them back upright. He could hear the engine now, a thick cloud of black smoke swirling around them, the train rolling, the men finding their balance.

Above the sounds of misery, the sergeant called out, "Next stop boys, the Gates of Hell."

Chaumont-en-Vexin, France—May 30, 1918

The company was spread out over a cluster of small farmhouses, and the fifty-eight men of Temple's platoon occupied a farm that could not have covered an acre of ground. In the house itself, there were at least six men to each of the small rooms, more than a dozen in the compact barn that had once housed a small herd of livestock. Temple had accepted that the veterans should occupy the houses, none of his squad making much of an argument that the new men should of course sleep in the barn. It was their second night gathered around a mound of hay, a makeshift mattress on which they could spread their blankets. To the vast relief of the men, there were no other occupants of the barn. Whatever livestock had survived the war had certainly been led away by their owners, or done in by whatever troops had occupied the place before. The barn was a simple box of four slatted walls supporting a roof of wood planks and a patchwork of woven tree branches. There was nothing watertight about the structure at all; the men grateful there was no rain. The floor beneath them was a blend of dirt and years of hard-packed manure, and despite the absence of animals, the smells remained. To Temple, it was not so different from any barn he had played in as a boy. To some of the others, it was hell on earth.

He unrolled his blanket, saw a faint shadow, glanced up, caught a glimpse of the moon through a wide split in the roof.

Scarabelli was closest to him, the small man sitting up, wrapped inside his own blanket.

Scarabelli said, "Savages. These damned people have no sense of clean."

A low voice responded, the slow drawl of Parker. "Where you expect us to sleep, Gino? They can't build us houses every time we set up camp."

"I don't care about that. It's the stink. Everything stinks here. Not just normal stink. I used to go to the Hoboken docks, watch my uncle unloading all kinds of crates from ships. Some amazing stinks there. Dead things, stuff rotting inside those damned ships. They found a dead man once, some poor bastard fell into a bunch of cargo, didn't find him until the ship docked. I never went back to the dock after that. But even that didn't compare to this place."

Parker moved closer, sat beside Temple.

"I figured every city smells pretty bad. I heard about all them rats and narrow streets. Don't the horses leave a pretty bad mess?"

"Hell, Mountain Man, they wash the streets. Jersey City is the cleanest place in America. I heard people in Virginia don't take a bath unless it rains. You oughta feel mighty comfortable in a barn."

"*Oh, dammit! Dammit! Dammit!*"

The voice came from outside, and Temple heard laughter, the other greeting a shadowy form as he stumbled into the barn. The man's face caught the moonlight now, and Temple saw it was Ballou.

"Son of a bitch! I did it again, stepped right into that manure pile!"

The odor drifted over all of them, and Scarabelli pulled his blanket over his head, said, "Aaaagh. I told you. Damned savages. Every house I seen, a big damned shit pile by the door. Get the hell away from me, you damned stinking cowboy!"

Ballou kicked at the ground, then scuffed his feet against the side of the barn.

"For once I agree with Jersey. What the hell these people saving their manure for? They use it for money? Seems the bigger manure pile a man's got, the more important he is to his neighbors. This ain't horse manure either. I been kickin' that off my boots since I was a kid. I don't know what the hell this stuff is. This is one damned weird place."

The voice came from under the blanket again. "I don't want to know what it is, Cowboy. Damned savages. Go throw your boots in a river somewhere."

Temple watched as Ballou continued his strange dance in the moonlight, rubbing and scuffing his boots against any surface he could find. Temple began to laugh now, said, "Won't do much good, Henry. It won't come off. It's like back home. Cow butter. Soaks right in."

Ballou exhausted his efforts, sat down in the hay, causing another groan from Scarabelli, who said, "Cow butter? You are all sick bastards."

Ballou rubbed hay on his boots, one last attempt to clean them, said, "I hope it's just cow butter. Not so sure."

Ballou was Temple's age, but he looked older, dark, with sun-burned skin. He had come to the Corps from Montana, inspiring all manner of questions from the rest of them. Temple wasn't even sure where Montana was, had thought it was some fictional place, the stuff of dime novels about Indians and myth-ical heroes, the land of Buffalo Bill and Sitting Bull. Henry Ballou was proof that someone actually lived there.

Ballou did not talk much of home, had joined the Marines for reasons he seemed reluctant to explain, a young man escap-ing from something he kept to himself. Temple had liked him immediately, appreciated Scarabelli's nickname, *Cowboy*. It perfectly suited the young man with the angular walk, Temple imagining Ballou to be as comfortable on a horse as he was in uniform. But for the long weeks they had been together in training, Temple had learned that Ballou had never been on a horse at all, knew very little about Indians. Despite Temple's hopes for stories of the Wild West, Ballou was just another young man from a strangely foreign place who, like Temple, had joined the Corps because it was the right thing to do.

Scarabelli was the talker, the most nervous man Temple had

ever met. He spoke long and often about Jersey City and Bayonne and Hoboken, and especially New York, places as foreign to Temple as the mysteries of Montana. When their squad was preparing to sail from New York, Scarabelli had been met by a vast crowd of smiling and teary-eyed relatives, a cluster of small round women in plain dresses, dark-haired men in ill-fitting suits, children who stared in wide-eyed respect at the young man's uniform. For days afterward, Scarabelli had told anyone who would listen how proud his family was, that he was the first of this immense flock of Italian immigrants to serve their newly adopted country. Days before they had embarked, Scarabelli had bragged about the grand tour he would give his new friends, and Temple had felt a fire of curiosity for New York, nervous reluctance to glimpse the temptations that so terrified the people back home in Florida, especially his mother. But the Marines had been hustled quickly from train to ship, and the tour could not happen. The only taste of that very different place was the sweet sadness from Scarabelli's family, one very vocal part of a large crowd of onlookers, held back by a line of guards as the young men boarded the ship.

"All right, enough talk! Breakfast at four, we're marching at five. Get some sleep!"

The voice silenced them all, and Temple tried to see the man's face, saw only the hulking shadow of the sergeant. Men were moving to their blankets all through the barn.

Ballou said quietly, "Marching where? Anybody heard?"

Scarabelli emerged from his blanket, said, "I don't give a damn. Anywhere that don't stink."

Ballou moved up closer, ignored the protest from Scarabelli.

"Since nobody asked me where the hell I been, I'll tell you. I found a place in the village that had some ving blonk. They took a wad of their money for it, but if they're going to pay us in franks, we might as well get some good use out of it."

The others gathered closer, sharp whispers, and Ballou pulled two bottles from his shirt.

"One with ink. The other's clean."

Scarabelli laughed, and Temple flinched from the volume,

other men hissing him quiet. Scarabelli ignored them, said, "You dumb cowboy. You mean red? There's two kind of wine, red and white."

There was silence, and Scarabelli made a short grunt. "It's not ink. It's the grapes. It's just . . . red."

Temple was curious now, had long suspected that Scarabelli knew much more about the world than any of the rest of them.

Ballou handed the small man the bottles, said, "All right, Jersey, since you're the damned expert, tell me how they make it red. If it's all wine, how come it's different colors? I've been told they do it with ink."

"Who the hell told you that?"

Parker sat up now, the big man leaning close to Scarabelli.

"I told him, Jersey. I figured it out myself. According to the sergeant, *ving* is French for wine. *Blonk* means white. You just gotta use your head."

Scarabelli began to examine the bottles, said, "Never mind. You bring a cork puller, Cowboy?"

There was silence again.

"How you expect to open the bottles?"

"*Shut the hell up!*"

The sergeant was hovering over them now, and Temple lay back on his blanket.

Scarabelli said, "Sorry, Sarge. I was just trying to educate these dumb bastards about wine."

"What wine?"

"Um, right here, Sarge."

Ballou said, "I bought 'em in town, Sarge. Figured it was a good way to get rid of this damned funny money."

The sergeant squatted down, said in a low voice, "I could use a gulp. God knows I'll never get any sleep with the lieutenant jumping my ass every half hour. What you got?"

Scarabelli held out a bottle, said, "We just need something to get the cork out."

The sergeant pulled a long thin knife from his boot, said, "The right tool for the right job. Remember that. Now, which one we got here? With ink or without?"

May 31, 1918

Breakfast had been cold and quick, and at five o'clock, they were packed into the trucks. The sergeant sat in the rear, stared down at his boots, never looked up at any of them. Temple was used to it by now, that so many of them always traveled in grim silence. He passed the time by watching them, wondering about their thoughts, trying to read through the silent habits of so many. He respected the men who stayed so tightly inside themselves, knew that some were praying, others probably composing letters they may not have the chance to write. Some of the veterans seemed to think about nothing at all, rode with their eyes closed, heads bobbing, men with the amazing talent for sleeping anywhere, saving themselves for whatever effort might be in front of them. Others chatted quietly, meaningless conversation whether anyone was listening or not. Temple simply watched, if not the men, then the land they passed, the houses and farms, small villages, glimpses of old bent men, working the fields alongside their women. He glanced at Scarabelli, who sat across from him, couldn't help smiling at the small man who seemed so annoyed at everything around him. Scarabelli still grumbled about the great mounds of manure that adorned each farmhouse, and Temple thought, This is not a place many of us will visit again.

They had ridden for nearly an hour, a long caravan of trucks. Temple imagined that far up the line, the senior officers were probably riding in autos, the men who actually knew where they were going. Temple had never been tempted to ask the questions, knew that it was not his place to know anything that the sergeant, or maybe the lieutenant, did not want him to. He had tried to sort through the rumors, had an instinct for sorting the truth from the ridiculous, knew that men like Scarabelli thrived on creating the most outrageous kind of stories, conspiracies and plots that Temple had once believed. Even the lieutenant listened to the Italian now, as much for entertainment as any notion that Scarabelli might actually know anything. The lieutenant seemed to go out of his way to set straight the misinformation, as though it actually mattered to him what his men believed about the war they had not yet seen. Temple had no reason not to like the lieutenant, a plainspoken, humorless man named Ashley. But it was a judgment he kept to himself, everyone around him seeming to hold some automatic prejudice against officers. Temple wasn't as sure of his feelings about the sergeant, Angus Dugan, the wildly profane veteran whose power over the squad was absolute. Sergeant Dugan was another secretive man, deflected every question about his hometown with a curt "It'll be on my tombstone." Temple had wanted to argue the point, thought, If we don't know where you're buried, how can we read your tombstone? But Dugan left nothing open to discussion, would cut off any man with a sharp command. He was far older than any of them, and a larger man than anyone in the company except Parker. Temple had hoped Dugan might one day offer them his own stories, satisfying their curiosity about the older man's service, what he knew of fighting, what places he had seen. The talk was that Dugan had been in the Philippines with General Pershing, and Temple was certain he would have marvelous tales to tell. But Dugan was not a man who answered questions, seemed not to notice the lore that swirled around him, the legend he had left behind him at Quantico.

Temple had been witness to the legendary confrontation in the barracks, Dugan tangling with a loudmouthed recruit named Brewster. Brewster arrived at the training camp the same time as Temple, had immediately isolated himself with his attitude. Temple never expected Brewster to complete his training, the man far too concerned with telling the others what he simply couldn't do, every excuse imaginable to avoid the unpleasant. No one really knew what started the fight, but Temple always assumed that Brewster's mouth made Sergeant Dugan's blood boil. Dugan had cemented himself into legend by picking Brewster up over his head and launching him out the window of the barracks, then retrieving him, carrying him back inside, and launching him out again. Dugan then tossed the man's cot out after him, along with all his gear. The officers had come of course, hard questions for the sergeant who ranked them all by years and experience. But no one spoke out, and no charges were filed. And no one ever saw Brewster again. As far as Temple knew, the man was still listed as AWOL. Scarabelli still maintained that no one would ever find him, since he wouldn't be recognizable after what Dugan had done to his face.

The truck bounced high, lifting them up, then dropping them onto their hard seats, inspiring a rumble of curses. Temple sat beside Parker, could hear faint murmurs from the big man, but it was nothing like the sharp words coming from the others. He knew by now that Parker was praying. The Virginian was as devout as anyone Temple had known back in Florida, always carried a small Bible in his pocket. All through training and since, Dan Parker had kept a quiet grip on his sobriety and had avoided the profane talk that flowed freely in every barracks and camp. He kept a diary, and Temple had watched over his shoulder as the big man filled the pages, some of it prayers he had composed himself. They had become friends quickly, the two southerners sharing the heritage that some of the others didn't understand. Like Temple, Parker's grandfather had fought for the Confederacy, the Virginian so familiar with the same kinds of stories passed along by Temple's grandfather. If there were differences between them, it came from Parker's upbringing, a family too poor to own a farm, to own anything at all, surviving from whatever bounty they could scour from the Allegheny Mountains. Like every big man, Parker had attracted challenges to his strength, to his skills as a fighter, made worse by the teasing he endured because of his slow, deep drawl. In the early days at Quantico, Temple had wondered if Parker would simply defer the verbal attacks, all the old Sunday school lessons about turning the other cheek. But Parker had surprised him, and everyone else as well. The big man had a temper, and when the teasing had gone beyond the man's quiet patience, he would seem to uncoil, his fists becoming deadly weapons. Temple had not been surprised by Parker's raw strength, knew that any man who grows up poor in rough country is made strong by all he must do to survive. In a few short weeks, the entire company had seen enough of Parker to know that in a fight, this quiet and devout man from the rugged

526

mountains of western Virginia, was a man you wanted on your side.

The truck stopped abruptly, the men pushed forward by their momentum. The sergeant stood now, shouted to no one in particular, "What the hell? All right, stay put." Dugan peered out around the rear of the truck, looked back to the convoy behind them, the trucks all lurching close together, avoiding the collisions. Dugan jumped down now, said, "We're being held up for some damned reason. Nobody move." He disappeared toward the front of the truck. Temple looked across at Scarabelli, who said, "Somebody's lost up there. We're gonna end up in Switzerland."

Dugan was back now, slapped the side of the truck. "Out! This is the end of the ride. We march now."

They all stood, and Temple waited his turn, then dropped to the ground. He could see back along the road behind them, orders shouting out, the snaking line of trucks disgorging the rest of the regiment. The column formed quickly, the familiar routine, and in minutes, the Marines began to step along past the trucks. The officers were in motion as well, some moving back along the column, others gathering near the trucks at the lead of the convoy. Temple pulled at the strap on his rifle, straightened his helmet, kept one eye on the man in front of him, the old habits from so many weeks of drill. He had always been intrigued by officers, the men who *knew*, imagined himself in that uniform, carrying his stiff formality even in the field. Like the enlisted men, the uniforms of the officers were different than what they wore at Quantico. They resembled the British, with the wide "Sam Brown" belt, and Temple had rarely seen boots that weren't perfectly polished, each man with the billed hat pulled low over eyes that saw beyond what the enlisted men could ever see. He watched them as he marched past, heard one lieutenant say something about the *old man*. The words intrigued him, casual reference to the man with the *power*. Who? he thought. General Bundy? General Harbord? He stared again to the front, thought, Everyone's an old man compared to us, except maybe the sergeant. He glanced up to a cloudy sky, could feel the sun on his back, dropping low behind the column. We're moving east, he thought. All those rumors about going north . . . no one's saying anything about that now. I guess the First Division doesn't need our help after all. He saw the column wavering in front of him, men moving off the side of the road. Now he saw why they had to walk.

Far out in front of the column, the road was choked with traffic, clouds of dust rising above wheeled carts, small wagons, livestock, and, for as far as he could see, a massive throng of people. They began to pass by him now, and the column was moving to one side, clearing the way. The man in front of him stopped, and Temple did the same, could see that the entire column was coming to a halt. There was an intersection up ahead, and the wave of people and vehicles was flowing in from two directions, all of it moving opposite from the way the Marines were marching. He stared wide-eyed, looked first at the vehicles, small carts and wagons, mostly with two squeaking wheels, some pulled by a mule or a cow. The sounds filled him, the squealing and groaning of the animals and their cargo, every kind of artifact, from clothing to plows, wooden crates stuffed with every piece of the lives these people were trying to preserve. Behind the carts were more animals, a small herd of goats, and then a dozen sheep, strung together in a slow sad parade, pushed along by a little girl who sang as she walked. Temple looked more at the people now, saw many children, dirty faces, some with bare feet, most of them looking back at him, at the Marines and their rifles, the different uniforms that these people had never seen. There were no young men at all, and Temple scolded himself for the thought. No, these people gave up their sons a long time ago. The men he saw were mostly old, the bodies fragile, the eyes filled with desperation. The women were all ages, some as old and frail as their men, some much younger, raw beauty in ragged dresses. But there were no smiles, none of the flirtation that the Marines had become accustomed to. Temple saw no joy on their faces, only hollow eyes that had seen too much of this war, soulless stares of loss and sadness. Some of the old men called out, words the Marines could not understand, but still they responded, trying to offer some kind of comfort. He heard Scarabelli, "Don't go far! We'll have you back soon!"

But the talk faded quickly, the Marines becoming numb to it now, overwhelmed by the sheer volume of misery that passed them by. Temple heard a shout from the sergeant, and the march began again, the men keeping to one side of the dusty road, single file now. Temple walked through the intersection, following the man in front of him, saw a sign, long and complicated names and numbers, arrows in all directions, distances measured in that strange "km." The column still moved to the east, and he tried to pronounce the name on the road sign, the place with the arrow that pointed straight ahead: Château-Thierry.

They had marched well into the night, with only brief stops for rations and rest. As they moved in the darkness, Temple could feel the urgency growing around him, the officers more hushed, the meetings brief. The road was still crowded, more of the civilians, but there were uniforms now, dimly glowing lanterns showing glimpses of the distinctive blue of the French *poilus*. There were camps as well, small clusters of men, wagons and horses, shadows dancing in the road from half-covered lights. He could see some of the *poilus* emerging from the shelters, coming out to the road just to watch the Marines moving past, many of them showing freshly dressed wounds. Temple had caught the smell of the aid stations, could glimpse the men in filthy white coats, moving through rows of men spread out on blankets. He had been shocked to see a nurse, and around him, low voices in the column reacted as he did, the sudden awareness that a woman was there, in the midst of this dimly lit horror. But no one had called to her, no crude remarks, the Marines watching instead with hushed reverence as she cared for the suffering *poilus* who lay scattered around her.

The column stopped again, and the order was passed, another few minutes' rest. Temple followed the wave of men away from the roadway, kicked at the soft dirt, a place to sit. There had been little sign of refugees for a long while now. The traffic on the road was mostly soldiers, shuffling past them in grim silence, all moving the opposite direction. Even in the dark, Temple could see the staggering rhythm of the walking wounded, and pairs of stretcher bearers grunting as they passed, enduring the weight of the man suspended between them. There had been ambulances, trucks too big for the narrow road, bumping and jostling the men inside, small cries that had cut into Temple's brain. With the trucks came the smells, the lumbering vehicles ripe with a stink that silenced even Scarabelli.

Close beside him, he heard the sergeant, a low hard grumble. "Rations. Dig out whatever you got. Lieutenant says we still have a ways to go. Might be nasty when we get there. No kitchens up here, boys."

Dugan moved past, repeated his words down the line, and Temple felt a sharp stab of cold, drilled into him by the tone of Dugan's voice. He looked to the side, tried to see Parker, saw only dull shapes, the rustle of backpacks, the men following Dugan's advice. He slid his pack off his shoulders, reached inside, put his hand on the ration tin, heard the others opening the cans, the sounds of men eating. His hands were shaking, and he gripped the tin, was grateful for the dark, that no one could see he was nervous.

Dugan's voice was there again, low and calm. "Five minutes. Then into the road."

The sun was rising in front of them, a hard orange glow. The *poilus* still came by them, and Temple could see the faces now, a flow of men that seemed unending. The French were as curious of the Marines as the Marines were of them, but Temple had seen too much of these people by now, too many of the ragged uniforms and bloody bandages. Many of them seemed to be uninjured, marching aimlessly, without purpose, seeking only to go anywhere there was no fight. They stared at him as they passed, filthy faces and black empty eyes, expressions of pain and loss and defeat. There was no talk, no one on either side offering to converse. The Marines were exhausted from their all-night march, many of them ignoring the *poilus* completely, just staring into the back of the man in front of them. Temple was doing the same now, could not ignore the pains in his back, the weight of his rifle and backpack, straps cutting into his shoulders, the gnawing agony of the blisters growing more painful on his feet.

With the dawn, he had eagerly scanned the land they passed, was surprised that there seemed to be no signs of war at all. He had heard the talk of no-man's-land, blasted desolation, the earth stripped bare of life. But the hills and woods along the road were green, patches of red flowers draped across the open fields. They had gone through more intersections, and Temple had lost track of how many turns and changes of direction there had been. The road they were on now was wide with broken pavement, but pavement nonetheless, more signs at more intersections. They were on something called the Paris-Metz Road, names that for the first time had meaning to him, and one significance in particular. Metz was . . . over there, on the German side. The men who marched might be told nothing of maps, but it was obvious to Temple that they were marching right toward the enemy.

Near Château-Thierry—June 3, 1918

They had spent the night in bivouac around several small villages, and for the first time, Temple had seen signs of the war. Most of the villages had been shelled, most of the houses and buildings damaged, great mounds of rubble spilling out into every street. For a full day the men had been allowed to rest, food finally reaching them, makeshift kitchens that served cold meat, cheese, and hard bread. They did not complain, could see that the officers were eating the same rations, heard the simple explanation: there could be no fires. Smoke would only offer the enemy artillery a target. And the enemy was very close.

Temple's squad had found another barn, another haystack, whose owner had long gone. The land was still surprisingly green and tranquil, rolling fields of wheat, clusters of fruit trees, so many of the small farms perched so near the war, but somehow spared by the destruction. But throughout the long night, the thunder of artillery took their sleep away. Temple found himself huddling deeper into the haystack, sharing the same thoughts as the rest of the men around him. The fire from the big guns seemed to erupt in long bursts, first one side, then the other, as though there were rules to the game, so many shots to be fired before the enemy could respond. In the silent moments, Temple could not avoid anticipating the next sounds, quickly learned to distinguish the impact of the incoming shells from the hard blasts of the guns. None had come down close to them, but that had been no comfort to Temple. Through a long and sleepless night, he had tried to measure the distance, his heart matching the thunder of the guns as one shell after another came down close enough to rattle the ground beneath him.

With the dawn, the officers had come, orders flowing all through the regiment. After one more brief breakfast, they began to move again, but there were no roads now. They marched through dense patches of timber, deep ravines that cut into green hillsides. All the while, the artillery duels continued, the air above them thickening to a stifling cloud of gray. Temple followed the man in front of him again, the only routine that mattered, passed by sergeants and men with maps, the occasional officer making sure they were on the right trail. The shelling continued for most of the day, but the Marines were not the target, the activity staying out to one side, or in front of them. They moved out of a patch of trees and began to climb a long grassy rise. Temple could see out into wide fields, distant patches of trees, the land cut by fat stone fences and dirt lanes. The farms seemed to be larger here, wide gardens bordered by more of the stone walls, farmhouses of stone and mortar, some rising two stories, huge barns that squatted in great open pastures, hillsides that fell away into the dense brush that hid small streams.

He saw a long ridge in the distance, draped by the spreading cloud of black smoke, saw flashes of fire, his heart jumping. He guessed the distance, a half mile perhaps, artillery shells bursting in great clusters, the smoke now obliterating the ridge. He strained to see, but the march led them down again, a well-trodden path, the men now stepping over a low wall, moving into one of the narrow dirt lanes.

"Keep close! Quickly!"

The voice came from an officer, a lieutenant, the man pointing the way. Temple glimpsed the man's face, saw he was young, his voice breaking, the man seeming to flinch with the sounds of the shelling. Temple was past him now, felt infected by the man's fear, stared at the back of the man in front of him, pushed the image of the officer away. They began to slow in front of him, and Temple saw a hand go up, halting the march. He saw Ashley now, the tall man showing none of the other man's fear.

Ashley pointed to a patch of trees, said, "Sergeants, move the company into the trees. Spread 'em out, lie low."

The sergeants were moving all along the line now, and Dugan pointed, said in a hiss, "Right here! Move down the hill. Squad keep in sight of me."

The men flowed down into the tree line, and Temple followed Parker, the big man dropping down beside a fat stump. Temple moved beside him, felt a hand on his arm. He turned, saw Dugan, who said, "Keep apart! Space out a few steps."

The sergeant's words stung him, some old lesson from training. *Keep apart.* Of course. He saw the men of the company flowing down the hill, another company behind them, hundreds of men spreading all through the woods. He scanned the trees and stumps around him, men in every gap, and he heard Parker, who pointed, said, "Roscoe. Sit there. Good spot in those tree roots."

Temple saw a V of two thick roots as they spread away from the base of a fat tree, sat down quickly. Most of the platoon was down low now, and he saw Ashley, more officers, one older man, a colonel, hushed voices, arms pointing out to the east.

Dugan moved toward him now, said, "Good spot, Temple. You can fire around the tree. Keep low, though."

Temple glanced down at his rifle, thought, Yes, fire around the tree. Good. Fire at what? "Sarge? How close . . . where are the front lines?"

Dugan looked at him for a brief moment, no expression on his face. Then he smiled, something Temple had never seen. "Private, we *are* the front line."

*   *   *

533

They had stayed in the trees for several hours, the sergeant prowling among them, advice to stay put and stay low, something no one needed to be told. Temple lay with his back to the tree trunk, the others in their own particular resting place around him. The only man among them who had a watch was Scarabelli, and Temple peered up from his sanctuary, said, "Hey, Gino. What time is it?"

"Three. A little after."

Temple lay back, stared at the small wisps of clouds in the treetops above him. Throughout the day, the artillery had continued their thundering duels, one battery in particular located not far behind them, beyond the protection of the trees. The battery seemed to launch its shells in some kind of regular interval, predictable now, Temple instinctively bracing himself when the moment was close. The guns would fire four times each, sharp shattering blasts that shook the ground and rattled the limbs of the trees.

The men stayed mostly quiet, coached by Dugan to keep ready, a warning that the order to move again could come at any moment. He watched the clouds, felt a strange calm, long silent minutes. He might as well have been home, the woods near his mother's house, imagined the massive live oak trees, old and crooked limbs draped in Spanish moss. But the daydream didn't last, was swept away by the sounds, a sudden screech of a small artillery shell, poorly aimed, falling out in front of the trees, throwing plumes of dirt and rock up in a cloud that would hang for a long second, the debris falling, the dust carried away by the breeze.

He tried to make himself comfortable, did as the others did, using his blanket for a pillow, his rifle resting on one side of his leg, his backpack close by the other. He felt protected, nestled by his two thick tree roots, but still he flinched from the sudden burst of machine-gun fire, then more, but different, a slower rhythm to the chatter. He had drilled with artillery and machine guns at Quantico, but the sounds were very different now, so much of the thunder coming from farther away, a vast drumming wave, many more guns than he ever expected to hear. There were the single pops as well, scattered and indistinct, snipers perhaps, or men who were just too nervous, firing at nothing. His right hand wrapped around the Springfield, and he felt the oily film on the steel, had passed the first few minutes in the trees doing what so many of the Marines always did first: clean the rifle. It was so much of the training and the pride of being a Marine. Even on the march, there would be that moment set aside to clean the rifle, to be sure every part was perfect, the words that Dugan always used, the right tool for the right job. He glanced at the end of the barrel, the old habit, made certain it was clear of any obstruction, no leaves or dirt. That lesson came from his grandfather, the story repeated so often, some long forgotten friend of the old man's whose musket had ruptured in the man's face, blinding him.

Temple looked over toward Dugan, saw the sergeant sleeping against his tree. Yep, Sarge, don't worry. We know how to take care of the tools.

He heard a droning hum again, had heard them all day long. He could see some of the men rising up slightly, staring skyward, through the treetops. The aeroplanes were mostly observers, and were mostly German. But the fighters had come as well, and the drone would suddenly become higher pitched, louder, the plane diving low to pour machine-gun fire on any target that unwisely appeared on the main roadway.

Dugan shouted, "Get down! This ain't a damned country fair!"

Temple looked at the sergeant, thought, No, I guess he wasn't asleep after all. Or maybe he just knows what we're doing whether he's sleeping or not. He obeyed Dugan's command, dropped his head back down on the blanket, stared up through the treetops. The droning was growing faint now, and he felt the familiar disappointment. Temple had yet to see any of the planes, the clouds growing thicker as the day passed. He knew the others were as disappointed as he was, just wanting to catch a glimpse of the wondrous flying machine, swooping in fast and low, close enough to see the black crosses. It had been the same with the submarines, all the nervous talk throughout the long sea voyage, so much speculation about the unseen beasts that could suddenly kill them all. Nobody saw one, of course, and when they reached the French port, Temple had heard the talk of regret, that some opportunity for adventure had been missed. Despite the talk of so much danger, the Marines seemed to be more curious than afraid, had been taught so much about these new and wonderful weapons of war, the massive tanks and German flamethrowers . . . and yet, all they had seen was the armament they had handled at Quantico. And in Virginia, there were no submarines, no tanks, and no aeroplanes at all.

He heard voices down in the woods below him, rose up, saw a cluster of men standing. He realized they were officers, but the Sam Brown belts were gone, and they wore the same tin plate helmets, their uniforms as plain as what Temple wore himself. He felt excited by that, thought, Of course, they don't just sit back here. They'll go out with us, when the time comes. He heard Parker, off to one side, soft words.

"Must be gettin' time. There's the lieutenant."

Temple realized he was right, Lieutenant Ashley speaking to other men Temple didn't know. Temple said, "What you think they're talking about?"

Scarabelli popped up now out of a pile of leaves. "It's not about our rations, I can bet you that."

Temple watched the conversation, saw another man come close, a runner, handing out papers pulled from a satchel. Scarabelli said, "Oh, hell. That's not a lunch menu."

There was a sudden roar in the trees to one side, a thunderous crash, the ground punching him from below. They all sat up, stared at a billowing cloud of smoke that spread out through the treetops. He saw trees falling, shattered trunks, cracking timbers, men shouting. Temple strained to see, heard Dugan, "Stay put! Nothing you can do!"

Voices rolled up toward them now, one man screaming, "First aid! Medic!"

He could see movement in the clouds of dirt, men scrambling over the broken trees. He looked at Dugan, who was staring at him with a hard scowl.

"Let it go, Private. There'll be more of those. That was a big

536

one, a one fifty. Just a lucky shot. If Fritz knew we were here, we'd be blown to hell by now."

Ashley moved up through the trees, said, "Sergeant Dugan."

"Sir?"

"Rations in two hours. The major doesn't expect anything to happen for the rest of today. We're staying right here, though. You boys make yourselves as comfortable as you can. This is home for tonight."

The officers were gathering again, and Temple heard loud voices, a line of soldiers moving down below them, through the trees.

Dugan said, "*Poilus*. What the hell are they doing?"

Temple could see more soldiers now, blue uniforms, men without helmets, a dozen, then more, a column of men, moving quickly.

"Hey, Sarge. The *poilus* are moving out."

Dugan stood up, his expression unchanged. "That they are. Some of 'em seem to be in a pretty hot lather. Officers too."

Temple could hear shouting, more French troops, swarming past the curious Americans in the woods. He saw a French officer now, the man waving his arms, urging his men to move more quickly. The American officers moved toward the flow of French troops, and the French officer began to shout at them, no one seeming to understand him.

Dugan said, "That chap's got the shakes. The whole bunch of 'em. We may have to help stop them. Temple, come with me. We'll see if the lieutenant needs us to do something."

Temple pulled himself out of his shelter, followed Dugan toward the commotion. More officers from both sides were gathering, and Temple saw one older man, a captain. The senior French officer was focusing on him now, obviously the senior American there. Temple could hear their words clearly, the older captain asking, "Dammit, what's he say?"

"He's telling us we best retreat, sir."

The French officer seemed to acknowledge the interpretation, nodded furiously at the American captain, pointed back toward the east. More French officers were gathering, and Temple stayed back, felt suddenly very out of place. The

French officer repeated the word, "Retreat! Oui. Retreat!"

The captain scanned the tree line to the west, stared for a moment at the flow of *poilus* coming toward them through the trees. He looked now at the French officer, said, "Retreat? Hell, we just got here!"

For nearly a week, the German advance southward had obliterated any attempts the French had made to hold them back. East of the Second Division's position, the Germans had pushed their advance to the banks of the Marne River, their engineers confident that solid bridgeheads could provide the avenues that would carry the German infantry straight down the Paris-Metz Road. But along the banks of the river, the surprised Germans were confronted by the American Third Division, who positioned themselves on the southern banks of the Marne. Though outnumbered and greatly outgunned, the Third Division plugged the gaps in the weakened French defenses and prevented the Germans from crossing the river. Faced with the unexpected blockade, the German commanders then focused their attentions toward the rolling farmlands west of Château-Thierry, where the small villages seemed virtually indefensible by the weakened French forces. The Germans hurriedly occupied several areas of high ground, and with reports from both aircraft and observation balloons, the German commanders knew that the French were melting away from large portions of the line that guarded the main road. But the observers had seen more than a desperate collapse of the French defense. German commanders read their intelligence reports with the same stunned surprise that had met them at the Marne. All along a five-mile front, the patches of woods and lowlands that bordered the vast open wheat fields showed movement they had not expected to see. By June 4, the Second Division had completed its march and had closed the wide vacancy the French could not hold. The French troops who remained along the lines on either flank of the Second had joyously welcomed the sudden influx of American strength. With the gaps closing, the French could regroup, pull themselves together into a stronger position.

The artillery on both sides had continued their relentless thunder, the French responding to the arrival of the Americans by the only show they could make, launching a meager counterattack against the Germans to their front. There had been no real success, the *poilus* charging into strongly held German positions, then retreating back to their lines again, reenacting the same assaults they had launched now for three years. The Germans had been halted, as they had been all along the Western Front, by the speed and depth of their own success. The German infantry had once again outstripped their own supply lines. Both sides knew that if the Germans were allowed the luxury of time, reinforcements and fresh supplies would reach them, and the massive wave could push forward again. If the Americans could not contain them, the Germans would have a main highway open to them that would lead straight to Paris.

Though the Second Division was faced with a rapidly entrenching enemy who occupied far superior ground, both French and American commanders realized that the only way to stop the German tide from advancing was to drive it back. Across from the area occupied by the Marine brigade, north of a small village called Lucy-le-Bocage, the French maps showed a patch of forest, said to be lightly manned by German defenders. The French believed the Germans had halted north of the woodlands, and that if the Marines could make a quick thrust, the woods could be cleared of any resistance. The Marines would then have a well-protected jumping-off point to launch a vital counterattack at the German positions to their north. The American commanders had no reason to doubt the assessment of their French counterparts. It would simply be up to the Marines to get the job done, to move quickly across the open fields to occupy this one-mile-square patch of forest the maps called Belleau Wood.

33

TEMPLE

Near Lucy-le-Bocage—June 6, 1918

The orders had come the night before, and by three in the morning, they were up and moving. Temple stayed close to Parker, who marched in front of him, the big man easy to follow in the darkness. Temple didn't know the time, but gradually the darkness had given way to dull gray, the early glow of the dawn masked by a heavy mist. The ground beneath him was wet and silent, the only sounds coming from the thick moisture dripping from the trees, dull pops of dew and rain-water. The Marines stayed mostly inside the tree line, a narrow trail that snaked through the thickets. But then, the trees were gone, and the ground in front of them had opened up to a large rolling field. The guides led them along a narrow lane, and Temple heard only the sound of their boots splashing in the soft mud. There was no talking, the guides who manned each turn, each narrow intersection, simply pointing the way.

Temple knew that the sergeant was in line just ahead, separated from him by the massive shadow of Parker. In the narrow road, the gray light began to show the outlines, more detail to the shapes. The line of men extended far out to the front and rear, an entire battalion moving into position, what the officers had called the jumping-off point. Temple felt a chill from the damp air slicing through him, his heart racing, the dampness from his own cold sweat blanketing his skin. His feet were still sore from the great long march, but he ignored the discomfort now, focused on the rifle clasped tightly in his hands. They had left their backpacks behind, carried instead two extra belts of ammunition, and no one objected to the added weight. As he marched, the heavy belts bounced against him, hanging just above the only other equipment he carried: the mess tin, canteen, gas mask, and, of course, the bayonet.

He glanced out to the side, could see only the field close by, too little light to see what lay beyond. He stared into Parker's back again, thought of the night before, the calmness of the sergeant, the final instructions before the order came for silence. Dugan had been clear and matter-of-fact, that they would reach the jumping-off point, then lie down and wait for the artillery to soften up what little opposition was waiting for them in the woods. There would not be much artillery fire, no long, drawn-out barrage that would tell the enemy too much about the assault that was coming their way. It was a lesson passed along from the French commanders, who had learned from the old mistakes, the lengthy bombardments that told the enemy exactly where you were going to hit him. Far better, Dugan said, to surprise him, to pump a short barrage into the first line, shock and confuse the front-line defenders, then mop them up quickly before anyone behind them could react. It seemed logical to Temple, especially if the woods were lightly defended. There might not even be any reinforcements to worry about. The confidence had come down to them from the senior officers, the word passing to each platoon that no grenades would be issued, no trench mortars. They simply wouldn't be needed, and the extra weight would be more of an encumbrance than an asset. The men who had gathered around Dugan had absorbed his confidence, as the old sergeant seemed to have absorbed it from the men above him. Temple could feel the excitement in all of them, that the Marines would have the honor of making the Second Division's first real attack, and by day's end, they would capture a valuable piece of ground, a spear point driven right into the German position. Dugan had listened to it all without comment, the nervous chattering from the men like Scarabelli. But the words that had mattered most to Temple were the final instructions from Dugan himself, the old sergeant's deep growling voice just soft enough that they had to strain to hear.

"When the artillery ceases fire, listen for the sound of a whistle. They'll only blow it once. That's when you stand up, take one good look at the woods out there, and then start walking. If things get gummed up, just follow me."

Temple felt the familiar comfort from the big man's words: *follow me.* You're damned right.

The gray mist was lighter still, and there were whispers up ahead, Parker stopping in front of him. Temple halted as well, saw men moving up alongside the column. As they passed by him, he tried to see in the dull light, thought, Officers, probably. With the march halted, he felt himself shivering, pulled his rifle close to his chest, clenched his arms in tight, fighting it. He saw men raising their arms, a silent signal, and the column began to move up out of the narrow roadway. He moved with the flow, stepped into tall soft grass, taller than his knees. The first section of the column was out in the grass now, and he saw a man out in front, facing him, the man holding his arms straight out to the side, silently marking the place they would halt, spreading out into a precise line. Behind him, another line was formed, and Temple turned, watched as the officers moved the men into the attack formation, the old drill straight from the training grounds. In a few short minutes, there were four lines of men, nearly three hundred men in each line, every man silent, staring hard into the mist in front of him.

Dugan was there now, another hard whisper: "Fix bayonets!"

The order had been repeated all through the formation, and Temple reacted with automatic movements, so many weeks of training. On both sides of him, the men began to kneel down, another silent hand signal from the men out front. He did the same, felt the wet grass beneath him, brushing his face. Dugan moved out in front of them, said something to the other man, then came toward Temple, stood a few feet in front of him, held his hands out low, the silent order, *lie down.* Temple lay flat on his belly, adjusted his helmet to cover the back of his head, put one hand between his face and the wet grass that was soaking through his already damp uniform. His breathing came in hard short gasps, his mouth open, desperately dry. He clenched his jaw shut, forced himself to breathe slowly, felt angry at himself: Stop this! Something touched his shoulder, and he jumped at the shock, heard a hard whisper.

"Quiet! Easy, Private. Just a few minutes."

The man was gone, and Temple knew it had been Dugan. He was embarrassed now, thought, He must have heard me breathing. He thinks I'm afraid, that I can't do this. Temple raised his head, wanted to find the man, tell him, No, dammit, I'm all right. Just . . . excited. He peered up over the top of the tall grass, felt a sharp cold stab, turned, frantic, looked the other way. There was no one there, no sign of anyone. Where did they go? What the hell? They left me here? He heard another whisper now, the same voice. "Get your damned head down, Private."

Temple dropped down again, realized, They're hidden in the grass. Just like me. He felt like laughing, thought of Scarabelli's teasing: Roscoe, you are one dumb farmer. He adjusted his helmet again, the cotton in his mouth drawing him to the canteen. No, better wait. His breathing was slower now, his mind taking charge, calming him. He let go of the rifle, flexed his stiff fingers, reached out into the grass, felt the wetness, thought, It must be wheat. It's a wheat field. Of course, makes sense. Good cover. Someone thought of that, I guess. There was a sudden sharp clap of thunder, the ground beneath him jumping as he jumped, the air above him ripped by a short high scream. Across the wide field, the shell impacted, the ground bouncing under him again. The guns began to fire in rhythm now, and he could tell that they came from behind him, *our* guns. The screams of the shells were erased now by the sounds of their impact, the shells coming down much closer to him than the distant guns that fired them. The thunder grew to a continuous pounding roar, and he felt himself flattening down against the dirt, hugging tightly to the earth as it rolled and tossed him. And then, just as quickly as it had begun, it stopped. He blew dirt out of his nose, felt a hard dull ringing in his ears, then a high piercing whine. He tried to shake it from his head, then realized: it was a whistle.

He lay frozen for a single moment, his brain taking over again, all the training, the orders, the words of the sergeant: *follow me*. He stood up, saw the wheat field coming alive with men, the entire battalion, twelve hundred men rising up in their neatly formed rows. He was up with them now, a part of them, gripped the rifle with shaking hands, his whole body wrapped in a cold chill. He glanced out to each side, his heart racing, his hands shaking, pure raw excitement. Dugan stepped out in front again, and to one side, another sergeant, and more men, some holding pistols, the officers. He focused on Dugan, the old sergeant staring straight at him, a slow scan now to the rest of the squad, his words rolling through Temple's brain: *just follow m*e. Dugan turned, faced forward, and across the field, the entire formation began to move, a rippling surge of motion, the men stepping through the wheat, a gloriously powerful parade.

The first line crested a low hill, the wheat stretching beyond for another two hundred yards. Temple could see the trees now, their objective, the woods that they would capture. There was a curtain of smoke hanging above the tree line, the aftermath of the shelling, and he stared into the dark recesses of the woods, thought now of the enemy, invisible eyes watching them, or perhaps they were gone, brushed away by the artillery, or ordered to pull back from . . . this. From *us*. He felt stronger with each step, impatient energy, wanted to run, to get to the woods quickly, to see the enemy melting away. Now, we might not see him at all. He wanted to say something to Parker, share the excitement of this moment, but his eyes were fixed on the trees, and on the back of Dugan, who stepped forward just a few yards in front of him.

His mind filled with the only sound he could hear, the soft brushing of boots through the wheat, a steady wave of men, rolling forward. He glanced to the side, Parker holding the Springfield out in front of him, the oily bayonet glistening, the perfect portrait of a Marine.

There was a quick shout down the line, and Temple saw streaks of light coming from the trees, then the sounds, dull pops. It was rifle fire. His heart jumped, the cold stabbing him, and he stared at the tree line, more of the streaks. From every dark space, there were flickers of light, small flashes, the air above him now buzzing, a tight high *zip* whistling past his head. Men were shouting all along the line now, one short scream, and Temple glanced at Parker, the big man moving steadily forward, Dugan in front of him, slow even steps. *Follow me.*

He heard a sharp ping, saw Dugan's helmet jerk, the big man turning slightly, his head cocked to one side, as if trying to speak. Then his legs gave way, the big man tumbling down into the wheat. Temple stopped, and behind him, there were shouts, "Stay in line!"

He jumped forward, stood over Dugan, saw the sergeant's hand upright, hanging in the air, reaching out, and Temple leaned down, said, "It's all right, Sarge. Here . . ."

He saw Dugan's eyes now, wide, a vacant stare, a small stream of blood flowing down the man's face. Temple felt a cold hole opening up inside of him, stared down at the empty eyes, "No! Come on, Sarge. Get up."

The air was alive around him, the wheat around his legs suddenly cut down. He heard the chatter of machine guns, muffled by the trees, and more men were shouting, some crying out. Temple looked out toward the trees, all the dark recesses alive with the guns of the enemy. All around him the neat lines of men were coming apart, punched and staggered by the sharp streaks of fire. There was a hand on his arm now, a voice, "Keep moving, Marine! Nothing you can do for him now!"

Temple wanted to protest, No, help him, but the hand pulled him away, another hand, a hard push now into his back. He looked down the line, no line at all now, men falling, their voices blending with the growing roar of fire in the trees. Officers were pushing into the men from behind, sergeants still out front, calling out to them, "Move! Advance!"

He began to step again through the wheat, his brain holding tightly to the dull shock, Dugan's eyes, the single hand upright. *Follow me.* He looked to the front, men advancing, still falling away, the dull crack of lead on steel, lead on bone, the air around him alive with whistles and shrieks, the cries and grunts from men all around him. Some of the men were dropping down to fire their rifles now, shooting at unseen targets. He saw another sergeant shouting at a man in the wheat, grabbing him, pulling the man up, and just as quickly, the sergeant was struck down, the rifleman falling with him into the wheat. More men were dropping down into the blessed protection of the wheat, lying flat, frozen in the only cover they could find, but others kept moving forward, what remained of the advance pushing past the men who had seen enough, who clung desperately to the earth beneath them. Temple quickened his pace, kicked through the wheat, saw another man tumbling right in front of him, curling into a heap. Temple did not slow, stepped quickly over the man, stared ahead, would not see the man's face. The trees were close now, the dark spaces opening up, the light finding its way into the trees, revealing the rocks, stumps, broken limbs, small cuts and ravines that hid the enemy.

What remained of the first line had reached the edge of the woods now, some of them stopping to fire, the targets still back in the darkness, flashes of light. Temple reached a tall thin tree, saw a splattering of bark, another, lowered his head, felt the spray of wood on his helmet. The voices were around him now, "Move forward! Take cover in the trees!"

One of the voices was his own, automatic, no one left in front of him, and he was running, moved into the dark shadows, shouted again, "This way! *Follow me!*"

The second line was moving into the trees behind him, the rattling of fire constant in front of him, and he saw a gap between two fat rocks, jumped that way, heard sharp clicks and smacks on the stone around him. He glanced back, saw a line of men pushing him from behind, seeking the cover of the rocks, and he drove ahead, dropped into a narrow crevice, heard voices behind him, "That way! Into the rocks!"

He glanced back again, saw a man pointing toward him, men streaming down into the crevice, bunching up, wide eyes staring at him. He turned to the front again, moved farther into the gorge between the rocks, saw the ground rising again, broken trees now hanging out over the rocks. He pushed forward, was suddenly in the open again, climbed a short dirt bank, saw a fat stump, a tree beside it, small rocks piled into a low wall. Behind the wall came blinding flashes of light, the hard rattle of the machine gun. The men were coming up the bank behind him, and Temple crouched, lowered the rifle, moved forward quickly, was at the wall now, only feet from the gun, saw four men, *Germans*, a hard shock, unreal, one man firing the gun out to

546

the left, the others crouched low around the gun. The Germans had not yet seen him, and Temple stared at them for a long second, saw one man turning slowly, could see the man's face, dirty, the man's eyes suddenly aware, wide, staring at him. The German tried to swing toward him, and Temple saw the rifle, but the Springfield burst to life, Temple firing into the mass of men, the machine gun suddenly silent. He stared at the Germans, one man moving slowly, new sounds, a soft groan, and a Marine rushed by Temple now, jumped down into the gun pit, rammed his bayonet into the wounded man. The Marine looked back at Temple, said, "Good work! Let's go. Keep moving!"

It was Scarabelli.

They climbed through the debris of the woods, small valleys cut between more of the fat rocks, tall thin trees, some broken and bent across the trails that cut all through the woods. The machine-gun fire was continuous, a sharp roar that engulfed him, the flashes of fire coming from all directions. He continued to move forward, crawling now, moving from stump to rock to fallen tree. Some men moved with him, a slow wave, surging forward. The rifle fire was in both directions now, many of the Marines finding the low places, seeking any target. Temple stopped behind a fat dead log, dropped his face into the dirt, tried to breathe, to find strength. He was soaked with sweat; a thick sheen of mud covered his uniform. Men were falling beside him, finding cover behind the same log. He heard voices, words, some men talking to themselves, some cursing the enemy, meaningless chatter. Others were silent, breathing in hard gasps. He turned to one side, saw a sergeant, said, "What do we do? Do we keep going?"

The man was reloading his rifle, looked at him, then past him, seemed to count the men close to them, then said, "It's hot, boys. The enemy's right up ahead. They've shot hell out of us."

The man was young, seemed to be shaking, and Temple felt a hot fury boiling up inside of him, saw nothing of Dugan in this man, none of the hard experience. He reached out, grabbed the man's shirt, the sergeant's eyes showing his fear.

"The enemy's out *there*, Sergeant! There's no reason to stay here!"

Temple rose up, saw the others looking at him, made a quick count, thought, Ten of us, at least. He looked at the young sergeant, saw no sense of command on the man's face. There is no time for this, for this kind of weakness. He raised up slightly, said in a low voice, "Three men stay here, keep aim on the trees in front of us. The rest follow me forward. If you see a target, take him. We can slip along until we find more of them. If we start firing, then the other three come up with us."

The men stared at him, some with wild eyes, others absorbing his words, grim determination. The young sergeant said, "There are too many of them. They're in every direction!"

"Sergeant, if you think you oughta stay here, then you stay here. If there's too many of them, then we have to change that."

The man stared at Temple for a long moment, seemed to gather himself, rolled over, looked at the others, said, "All right. You three . . . cover us. The rest, let's move out together. Follow the lieutenant. . . ."

Temple was surprised by the word, said, "I'm not an officer."

The sergeant rolled back toward him, said, "I thought . . . you seem . . ."

"Sergeant, I'm just a Marine."

The young man looked at him again, nodded. "All right then, Marine. Let's go to work. Move out!"

The sergeant rose up, launched himself out over the log, and Temple followed him, the others as well, each man spreading into some low place, crawling through whatever cover he could find. The sound of the guns rolled over them, the deadly zings and *zips* slicing branches, cutting leaves, splattering rocks around them. Temple moved up to another log, too small, heard a shout from out in front of him, voices, *German* voices, the brush bursting into fire. He rolled to one side, saw a fat thick bush, kept rolling, the fire from the German gun following him. He rolled behind the bush, dropped off a short ledge, fell a few inches, felt a sharp stab in his ribs. The Germans had changed their aim, were ignoring him now, and he lay still for a long moment, probed the pain in his side, felt a rip in his shirt, but no wound. No, they didn't get you. He rolled over on his back, jerked his helmet down over his face, held his rifle across his chest. He turned his head to the side, saw a narrow gully below him, sand in the bottom, like a dry streambed. He slid his legs that way, eased down the short hill, his boots landing in the soft sand. His breaths came in short painful bursts, and he probed the pain in his side, looked back along the sandy ground, saw dark shapes, felt a cold shock. The gully widened as it flowed away from him, and in the sand, a dozen bodies were scattered, torn and bloody, uniforms ripped. *Grenades*. He fought through the sickness, looked back up in the direction of the German gun. They thought they had cover, but the Germans knew they were here. They had nowhere to go. And . . . neither do I. He scrambled back up the side of the gully, looked to one side, saw bloody khaki, a man sprawled out against the bank, great bloody holes punched in the man's body, his face staring into silent death. It was Lieutenant Ashley.

The sickness overwhelmed him, and he turned his face to the dirt. A voice in his brain cried out, No, God, no. Are they all gone? The face of Dugan filled his mind, and Temple could not hide from the other horrors now, the images of so many twisted and broken men, the agony of the wounded, and worse, the men who were simply gone, so many right in front of him, right beside him. Parker . . . he hadn't seen the big man since he entered the woods, had no idea where he might be, if he was alive. Scarabelli he had seen, but where is he now? Ballou, Simmons, Baker, Gregory . . . how many never made it out of the wheat field? I have to find them, find out how many of us are left. There is still a fight here. Does anyone know what's happening? Are more men coming up? He grabbed at the thoughts rolling through his brain: *Stop this*. One image remained, the old sergeant, Dugan's hand reaching up to him, the empty eyes. Dugan might never have felt it, might never have known, might have been dead even before he fell. The best way to go.

He looked up the short hill, the fire continuing to roll all through the woods. The German machine gun opened up again, and he judged the distance, not more than thirty yards. I can't stay here. But they're ignoring me. One man's not worth a grenade, I guess. Or they think they got me.

He climbed up slowly, kicking his boots into the soft dirt, pulled himself up by a short stout root. He peered up over the edge of the gully, saw no movement in the woods out in front of him, heard one sharp explosion, then another, thought, More grenades. *German* grenades. We don't have any. He saw a brief glimpse of movement, then another, Marines making their way through the brush across the way, one man jumping into the open, tumbling down behind a fat stump. The machine gun fired, the stump coming apart, a spray of splinters, and Temple did not wait, slid close to the one thick bush, scanned the ground to the right, beyond the end of the gully, saw a large flat rock. He began to crawl that way, slow and deliberate, kept one eye on the German gun position, could see it was a pile of short logs, stumps, and tree limbs. The gun paused, then fired again, spraying the woods out behind him. He lay still, glanced back toward the one stump, saw the Marine lying flat, his face turned toward him, the man's eyes clear, staring at him. It was the young sergeant. Temple made a brief nod, began to crawl again. The German gunner still ignored him, continued to fire at the men Temple couldn't see. The gun stopped firing, and Temple froze, knew the gun crew was scanning the woods, would fire at any movement, or . . . they were reloading. In a few seconds the gun began to fire again, short bursts, still aimed out behind him. Temple slid forward, was safely behind the flat rock now. The gun paused again, and he lay flat on his stomach, his mind racing. What do I do? If I had a grenade! One damned grenade! Son of a bitch! The gun fired again, and he pushed himself forward, his rifle just in front of him, the bayonet pointing the way. He reached the far edge of the rock, took a breath, his heart pounding, eased forward again, tried to see the pile of stumps, peered out around the rock, was shocked to see a German helmet. The man's head jerked up, the eyes suddenly looking at him. Both men made a shout, and the German lunged forward, fell on him, punching at him. Temple rolled to one side, throwing the man off him, grabbed for the rifle, but there was a single shot, the German collapsing, and Temple looked back toward the blasted stump, saw the young sergeant's rifle pointing toward him, a thin stream of smoke rising from the muzzle.

Temple moved his fingers, the only salute he could manage. *Thank you.* He lay still for a moment, his face in the dirt, choking him. He slid forward again, peered again around the edge of the rock. The machine gun began to fire, another target, and Temple pushed himself forward with his foot, was just beyond the edge of the rock. He rolled over on his side, put the rifle against his shoulder, put the sight on the flashing muzzle of the machine gun. He eased the sight to one side, measured the length of the gun, saw a glimpse of movement through the branches, and fired. The gun was silent now, and he saw more movement, the gun crew scrambling, and Temple did not wait, was up on his knees, the rifle aimed again, firing, the Germans dropping, collapsing around the gun. He ran forward, jumped into the gun pit, bayonet ready, saw no movement, began to shout, "I got them! I got a machine gun! Here!"

He looked back toward the stump, saw the sergeant scrambling forward, more Marines emerging from the low places, men moving toward him. They were around the gun pit now, the sergeant crawling inside, two other men as well, and the young sergeant said, "We should use the gun right here. Good cover. Swing it around that way. Cover our flank. There's probably more of these bastards in those big trees ahead. How much ammo did they have left?"

Another man rolled a German over, reached for a large metal box, said, "This one's full, Sarge—"

There was a sharp crack, and the man fell straight down on the German. Temple saw the pistol now, the German soldier trying to free his arm. Temple shouted, raised his rifle, shoved his bayonet hard into the man's chest. The sergeant was yelling now, "Bayonet the bastards! All of them!"

The others obeyed, completed the gruesome task. Temple put his foot on the German's shoulder, pulled his own bayonet away. He stared at the man, the pistol still in the German's hand. The man's eyes were clenched shut, then opened slowly, dull and empty, the same vacant stare as he had seen on Dugan's face. The sergeant knelt down, probed the Marine's wound, cursed loudly, leaned down close to the man's face, searching for a breath.

551

Another man said, "He okay, Sarge?"

The sergeant rolled the Marine back over, shook his head, said, "Shot him in the heart. Dirty sons of bitches! Bayonet every one of them! Don't leave any wounded!"

Temple sat down, ignored the others as they began to work the machine gun, the sergeant directing their fire. The dead Marine was beside him, the Germans at his feet, and Temple cradled the rifle, felt the instinct taking over, cleared the bolt, reloaded, wiped the blood from the bayonet. The sergeant shouted something to him, and Temple understood. Behind him, the Germans had piled their ammo boxes, and he reached back, dragged one forward, slid it in the soft dirt toward the man who fed the belt into the German gun. The gun was firing again, and Temple tried to see, but the smoke and mist had filled the open spaces. He wanted to do something to help, but the sergeant was in control now, the makeshift gun crew doing their job.

He leaned close to the sergeant, said, "We should keep moving. Use this gun to cover us."

The sergeant looked at him, said, "You sure you're not an officer? All right, I'll stay here, at least for now. You push forward. Fritz must have a main firing line somewhere up ahead, his main defense. We need to find it."

Temple crawled up out of the gun pit, the others gathering close, and the sergeant said, "No prisoners, Private. You boys . . . follow him."

For the rest of the long day the fight continued, an unending hell of rifle fire, grenades, and machine guns blending with the fury and screams of men. As the night began to fall, Temple and the Marines around him settled into blessed cover, every man seeking the safe place, out of the line of fire, where they would endure the darkness so close to the guns of their enemy.

As they scraped and dug their way into some kind of sanctuary, none could escape the perfect horror of what they had tried and failed to do. Like the men around him, Temple could not escape the harsh judgment of his own arrogance, his casual expectation that their unstoppable wave would simply push

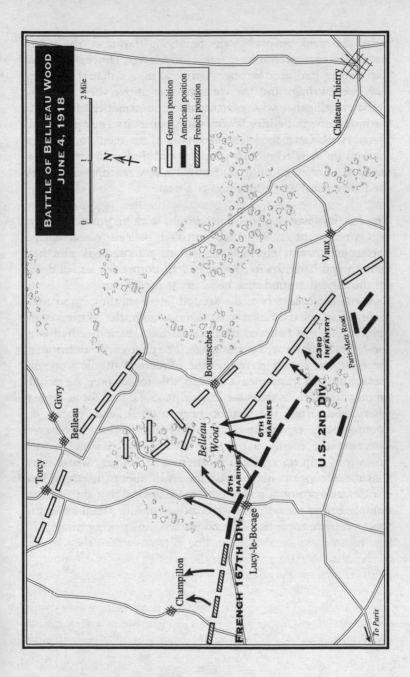

BATTLE OF BELLEAU WOOD
JUNE 4, 1918

German position
American position
French position

N

0   1   2 Mile

Château-Thierry

Vaux

Givry

Belleau

Torcy

Boursches

Belleau Wood

6TH MARINES

23RD INFANTRY

Paris-Metz Road

U.S. 2ND DIV.

5TH MARINES

Champillon

FRENCH 167TH DIV.

Lucy-le-Bocage

To Paris

away the weak enemy. In the terrifying darkness, the words were a mocking testament: *lightly defended*. He realized now that Dugan had been wrong. And so it meant that the officers had been wrong, and the commanders above them, and the French intelligence who gave them the information. Instead of pushing through Belleau Wood, the Marines had advanced only as far as the German defenders would allow them to, trapping them in the tangled morass of rocks and timber. Temple understood now: they had not confronted a few machine-gun nests; the entire place was a machine-gun nest.

The Marines had marched into a fight with an entire regiment of German troops, who had fortified Belleau Wood with a perfect network of interlocking machine guns and rifle pits, field cannon and barbed wire. As night fell, both sides settled down on the rugged ground they had fought for all day.

At the headquarters of the Second Division, the commanders were still in the dark as to what kind of fight the Marines were involved in, still believed that the German resistance had been too light to offer any real challenge. The chaos and confusion of the fight was so complete that the officers in the field weren't certain how far their men had been able to advance, or exactly where their various units were positioned. Gradually, as reports filtered out from the chaotic horror of Belleau Wood, the commanders, especially Harbord, realized that instead of sweeping the enemy out of the woods, the Marines held a precarious grip only on the southernmost fringes. Worse, now that the Americans understood the truth about the strength of the German position, it was even more critical that the Marines complete their mission. Despite the loss of more than a third of their strength, there could be no retreat, no backing away.

34

TEMPLE

Belleau Wood—June 7, 1918

He used his helmet to dig, scooping the soft ground, creating his own trench in front of a mass of rock. Beside him, other men dug as well, tried to silence the metal as they worked their tin cups and mess plates, anything that would cut into the ground beneath them. The Germans had seemed to back away, but not so far that their machine guns could not still find the careless. As Temple worked the ground, he realized what they all knew now; in the darkness, in the confusing tumble of the wood, there would be no relief. Regardless of what might be happening out beyond the trees, around the one small village of Bouresches, where other Marine battalions were making their own fights, in Belleau Wood, the confusion was absolute. Even if reinforcements or relief troops could be sent in, there were no front lines, no convenient stretches of defensive positions. The confusion lay not just with the Americans. In the tangle of the forest, some of the German machine-gun nests were still operating forward of their own primary line, isolated pockets of men who held out with what ammunition they had left, some still dug in to the dense brush and rocky crevices. Like the Americans, the Germans could only wait for the dawn, and begin the fight again.

Temple lay flat in his small trench, stared up at empty darkness, no stars, the night sky as thick and cloudy as it had been all day. He tried to ignore the clench in his gut, the hollow emptiness of hunger. When the order had come to leave the backpacks, he had grabbed a tin of rations, stuffed it in his pocket, another of the veteran's lessons taught to him by Dugan. But with all the crawling and tumbling along the ground, the tin had somehow slipped away, the empty pocket now a gaping cavern in his thoughts. His canteen was empty, a last splash drained in the darkness, barely cutting the dust in his throat. He knew there were more canteens scattered in the woods around him, and it was another lesson as well. Every man had been taught by the veterans to scavenge the dead, water and rations and ammunition. He had not thought of that until after dark, and now, he wasn't sure where any of the bodies might be, close by or . . . *out there*, where any sound would bring the German response. Despite his hunger, some part of him was thankful that there were no bodies close to him. Throughout the day, he had seen horrors that no one could have prepared him for, had done all he could to keep himself apart from the shock of that. But the idea of digging into a dead man's pockets, or drinking the dead man's water, was a horror of another kind, born of some childish fear of disturbing the dead, the defiling of the sacred. He argued with himself, thought of Dugan, knew the old sergeant would have dismissed his hesitation with a profane laugh. If you're starving, and the man has food . . . well, perhaps tomorrow. By then, whether or not you defile anything may not matter. In this place, it's hard to find the presence of God anywhere. He thought of Parker. No, he would disagree. He would see God's hand in all of this, the punishment of the sinful. My mother would feel the same way. Who in these damned woods is not a sinner? How many men did I kill today? His mind froze at the question. Stop that, Roscoe. If you didn't kill them, then *you* would be dead now, someone would be going through *your* pockets, a German perhaps, and he wouldn't be waging this stupid argument with himself.

He could hear muffled sounds, movement in the darkness. There were faint whispers, men finding each other, exhausted and nervous, rifles and bayonets pointing forward. There had been brief bursts of fire, single pops down through the woods, places where no Germans should have been. It was yet another horror, men whose minds had surrendered to the fear, who would shoot at any kind of target, the first hint of a whisper, a rustling in the brush. But the men still gathered, the Marines seeking out their own, strangers mostly, companies and their platoons tossed into each other in a confused mishmash of commands. Temple focused on the sounds, clung to the hope that someone from his own squad would find him. He had thought of shouting, calling out, a ridiculous fantasy. Any sound brought a burst of fire from some German gunner. The voices he heard now came mostly from the wounded, helpless, immobile, desperate pleas for water, some of the soft screams in German. Temple could not shut them out, knew what some had already learned, that the Germans were listening as well. Every few minutes a hidden machine gun would send a chattering burst of fire toward the voices, streaks of light whistling through the rocks and trees, or there would be a single sharp blast, a German grenade, sometimes finding the wounded man, a blessed end to the cries.

He heard movement in the brush, a few yards away, freezing his thoughts. The man was moving closer to him, and Temple lay flat, imagined the muzzle of the man's rifle pointed right at him. He took a deep breath, eased his rifle across his body, the bayonet ready, his arms cocked. The man crawled forward, and Temple raised his head up slowly, could see the dull shadow, caught the shape of the man's helmet . . . American. Thank God.

He whispered, "Here!"

The motion stopped, and Temple closed his eyes, oh God, please make him understand.

The whisper came back to him, "*Where?*"

"Here. By the rock."

The man was a few feet from his makeshift trench, and Temple tapped his hand flat on the ground. The man was there now, reached out, and Temple felt the man's hand, crusty fingers gripping his.

"Is this a good place?"

"Big rock right in front here. Soft ground. You can dig okay."

The man began to scrape the ground with his mess tin, and Temple slid up out of his shallow trench, put his hand on the man's shoulder.

"Helmet works better."

"No. Not taking it off."

The man kept digging, and Temple removed his helmet, began to dig as well, widening his own trench. They worked the ground for several minutes, Temple using his helmet to toss the dirt up onto the rock, adding height to their shelter. The man stopped, sat, and Temple heard a clink of metal, could tell that the man was holding his canteen. Temple felt the dusty cotton in his mouth, said, "Can you spare any?"

The man handed him the canteen, and Temple could feel it was almost empty. He returned it to the man's hand. "No. You don't have enough."

The man squirmed around, and suddenly Temple felt another canteen pressed into his hand, could tell by the weight it was full. "I have two more."

Temple unscrewed the top, hesitated, could hear the man gulping water. He raised the canteen, began to drink, warm and wonderful, washing the thickness from his throat. He handed the canteen back to the man, who pushed it toward him.

"We can get more. You hungry?"

The man held his hand out to him, and Temple felt something hard and square. It was hardtack.

Temple took a bite, the old stale biscuit breaking into thick dust, choking him, turning to glue in his mouth. It was delicious.

The man waited for him to finish the meal, said, "They say it's left over from the Civil War."

"I don't care. Thank you. What's your name?"

"Private Henry Ballou."

Temple wanted to laugh, grabbed Ballou's shoulder.

"Henry, it's Roscoe."

"Oh God! Thank God! I thought the whole platoon was dead!"

Temple said nothing for a long moment. "I think . . . most of 'em are."

Ballou sat for a moment, then said, "We best lie down."

The two men were side by side now, and after a long silent moment, Ballou said, "I saw the sarge go down."

"Yeah."

They lay in silence for another minute and Temple said, "They got the lieutenant."

"I figured that. They got most of the lieutenants. I saw a lot of officers go down. Poor bastards."

Temple tried to push the image of Ashley's body out of his mind.

Ballou said, "Only officers worth a damn are the lieutenants. Everybody else just sits back there and keeps score. I always figured the lieutenants were just killing time until they got promoted higher up. Never realized they'd be out here, that they had to do . . . *this*."

"Ashley was okay."

Temple waited for some response, and after a moment, Ballou said, "Doesn't matter now."

He jumped, realized he had been asleep. He raised the rim of his helmet, could see a faint gray haze in the sky, the distinct shape of tree limbs, broken and shattered treetops. He felt a cold chill, his uniform wet, the mist dampening his face. He lay still for a long minute, could hear Ballou breathing beside him, and now he heard low sounds, and a sudden sharp clang of metal. He sat up slightly, realized the woods were a mass of activity, low voices in every direction, unmistakable, metal tools, sharp chops and dull thuds as men worked the ground. There was a burst of machine-gun fire, the Germans seeking a target, and the work stopped, silence for a long moment. Temple raised his head, tried to see up over the rock, thought, The gun . . . not too far away. If they fire again, might see where it is. All around him, the work began again, the tools working, the sharp sounds of an axe.

Beside him, Ballou said, "What? What the hell?"

"Wait! Listen!"

The machine gun opened up again, streaks of fire spraying out through the woods. He focused on the direction where it had begun, marked the spot with the edge of the rock in front of him. All right, now we'll wait for some daylight. I'll find that son of a bitch.

The tools began their work again, and Temple began to see it in his mind, realized that all the new commotion could have only one explanation. If the Germans were shooting at them, the sounds came from Americans. Someone must have sent engineers into the woods, the men who carried the entrenching tools. As the sounds of shovels and picks and axes pierced the silence, Temple felt a wave of relief, that someone back there knew what was happening after all. When the dawn came, their first priority would be accomplished: cover.

The Germans began to fire again, some farther away, the distance impossible to gauge. He heard a twig snap in the brush behind his head, out past the end of the trench, and Ballou put a hand on his arm, a tight grip. Temple tapped his hand, then turned slowly, silently, eased his head up, tried to see. A man was pulling himself with his elbows, sliding on his stomach, and Temple waited for him to get close, saw the man's helmet, a glimpse of the uniform, and the man spotted them now, said in a whisper, "I'm Lieutenant Hovey. How many men around you?"

Temple raised the brim of his helmet, propped himself up on his elbows. The man's question was answered by soft grunts nearby, most coming from men Temple didn't know were there. Hovey crawled up close to the mound of dirt by Temple's trench, sat up, said, "Any officers?"

No one responded, and Hovey said, "How close is the enemy?"

One man emerged from a dark hole a few yards below Temple's feet, slid forward, said, "Not more than a hundred yards, some probably less, if they're moving around. Sound carries. They shoot at anything that makes a noise."

Temple said, "One machine-gun nest, maybe seventy-five yards out that way."

"You men have to hold this ground. Keep this position as secure as you can. Watch for infiltrators. The enemy might try to get closer before full daylight. The engineers are digging a good defensive line in those tall trees back there. If you need to fall back, it's a strong position. I'm going back to gather as many men as I can find, send 'em up this way. Be ready. We can bet that the enemy will try to push us out of here." He stopped, seemed to catch his breath, then slid back away from Temple's trench, crawled away, the other men disappearing back into their own holes. Temple lay flat again, the helmet down over his eyes. The memories of the day before were clouds in his brain, the march across the wheat field, pushing the Ger-mans out of the woods. Now, he thought, we're just to . . . stay here. Hold this ground *if we can*. He felt angry now, thought of Dugan. He died so we could . . . hold this ground? Ballou's words rolled through his mind, officers just *keeping score*. Is that what generals do? Is that what they're doing now? Measuring how big a failure our attack was? He was furious, sat up, surprising Ballou.

"What? See something?"

Temple felt himself breathing heavily, said, "We can't just hold this ground. We still have a job to do."

The day passed with no major fight, both sides pulling themselves together, sorting through their strength, measuring their weakness. The Marines had probed and scouted as best as any one could in the jumbled mess of the wood, and the commanders began to understand that the Germans had entrenched themselves into three lines, each at slightly different angles. Out on the eastern side of Belleau Wood, other Marine battalions had captured the village of Bouresches, but with the wood itself still firmly in German control, Bouresches was difficult to defend, the Marines there absorbing a continuous bombardment from German artillery. The next day, June 8, the Marines in Belleau Wood began to press forward again. The Germans had added reinforcements to an already strong position, fresh units moving southward into the wood from the main German lines to the north.

The fight was as it had been before, a chaotic nightmare, men fighting alone or in small groups, hand-to-hand confrontations, the enemy hidden in every crevice, machine guns nestled into every invisible hole. After two more days, the word was sent forward from headquarters. In the predawn darkness of June 11, the Marines were pulled back to the southern extreme of the wood, putting a safe distance between themselves and the German positions. Then, the massed strength of the French and

American artillery began the crushing obliteration of the woods, the assault that the commanders had first dismissed. With the bombardment from dozens of cannon, the woods were changed completely, the barrage shattering the trees into a tangle of broken limbs, uprooted stumps tossed around blasted fragments of rock.

For the Marines, who endured the shelling from the relative safety of the trenches constructed by the engineers, there had been little time to reorganize the companies, and by now, many of the officers were gone, or if they survived, had lost contact with their commands. There was no time to sort through the devastating losses to companies and platoons, and once the artillery had done its job, the Marines were sent forward, to seek out the enemy again. Though the artillery had devastated great expanses of the German lines, the Germans who had survived were simply dug in deeper, protected by a greater jumble of branches and broken trees than they had beenbefore. Despite the destruction of the wood itself, the fight would go on.

They climbed and crawled, pushed slowly through the short crevices, moved from fresh shell hole to blasted stump. Temple was one of a dozen men, a makeshift squad commanded more by each man's instincts for survival than by anyone's rank. Temple knew that at least two of the men inching their way through the brush near him were sergeants, but now, with the enemy poised in every hidden hole, orders and organization were useless. No one among them had to be instructed that if you could find the man shooting at you, or could locate the machine guns that continued to rip the air above them, simply pass the word. Then everyone would know their mission.

The sun had finally come out, a thick steam rising from the churned and blasted dirt. With the added warmth came something no one had taught Temple to expect, something no one could explain until a man found it out for himself. After four days of fighting, the woods had become a tomb for hundreds of men from both sides, and now, with the heat and the steam, came the smells. Temple had already experienced the grotesque shock of stumbling across bodies, and like any veteran of close-fought combat, had forced himself to ignore the dead who were scattered in every open space, blocking every trail. But the artillery had tossed and mangled the corpses, and had created a far greater horror for the men who now had to press forward again.

He glanced out to his left, saw Ballou peering up over a log, then ducking back down, looking at him. Ballou nodded, the silent *all clear*, and Temple crawled up and over a mound of fresh dirt, pulled himself quickly down into the shallow depression of a shell hole. The smells filled him, familiar now, the sharp odor of spent explosive, stronger even than the stench of the death that infested the blasted soil, the dirt itself holding the smoky stench. He crawled down through the depression, then up the other side, pulled his way through broken branches. He looked back, saw several faces watching him, Ballou sliding up close to the edge of the shell hole. Temple motioned with his hand, side to side, *spread out*, thought, We should move up on either side of this. . . .

He caught motion above him, saw the fat stick drop into the shell hole, bounce once, then lodge upright in the dirt, one end fat and round, like a small tin can. He made a sharp sound, pushed hard with his feet, drove himself up and out of the shell hole, kept pushing, flipped backward, fell hard on his back. The grenade exploded, the blast throwing the dirt up in a thick cloud. He tried to see, blinked through the dirt in his eyes, heard shouts, rifle fire, a sharp slap on the log beside him. He rolled over on his stomach, flattened himself, heard rifles all around him, deafening, felt a hard jolt in his head, his helmet punched to one side. He rolled sideways, up and over a small limb, branches stabbing his back. He searched frantically for cover, the rifle fire filling the air around him, different sounds, the Springfields, fire from the men behind him. There were sharp cries now, close to him, voices, loud and German, the leaves and branches beside him sliced and ripped. The rifle fire began to slow, and he heard more voices, behind the shell hole, a single shot, the sound of men scrambling forward, another shot. He gripped the rifle tightly to his chest, slid it forward, scanned the brush in front of him for a target. The brush was breaking, men running, another shot splitting the air from behind him. Men were moving low beside him, and he felt a hand on his back. "He's here!" He rolled to the side, saw one of the Marines staring at him.

"You hit?"

Temple tried to sit, felt a sharp pain in his back, rubbed with his hand, no blood. "Don't think so."

He realized he was bareheaded, saw his helmet a few feet away, and another man was there, knelt down, grabbed the helmet, examined it. Temple saw now, a neat hole through the flat rim, the leather strap cut.

"You sure you're okay? There's blood on your face."

Temple realized his face was stinging, and he touched it, saw blood on his fingers.

"I'm okay. I need a new helmet."

"Plenty to be found."

Temple thought of the man's name now, Murphy, a red-faced Irishman. Temple looked back toward the shell hole, said, "What happened? I saw the grenade."

"The Huns were waiting for us. Looked like eight or ten of 'em. They hightailed it, but we dropped a few."

More of the men were up around him, some moving forward. A low voice, one of the sergeants, called back, "We got four of 'em. Let's keep moving. They know where we are now."

Temple scanned the faces, said, "Where's Ballou?"

Murphy looked down for a second, shook his head. "In the shell hole. The grenade got him." Temple stared at the mound of dirt, crawled back that way, heard Murphy say, "No good. Come on, we gotta move. The sarge is right. They'll be dropping mortars on us pretty quick."

Temple ignored him, was at the hole now, a low wisp of smoke hanging low in the depression. He saw the uniform, half buried in the dirt, a wide black gash in Ballou's chest. He couldn't hold the tears, lowered his head, felt a hand on his back, Murphy beside him.

"Your buddy?"

"Yeah."

564

"I saw him go into the hole. I think he went after the grenade. Not enough time."

Temple wiped his eyes with one hard finger.

"Yeah, he would do that. Dumb cowboy."

"C'mon. We gotta get moving."

Temple turned away, bareheaded, naked. He glanced toward Ballou's broken body. "I'm coming. Just a minute." He slid down into the shell hole, pulled Ballou's helmet free, glanced at it, undamaged, put it tightly on his head, slipped the strap under his chin. He started to move away, stopped, turned again, saw the canteen on Ballou's belt. He unhooked it, unscrewed the top, and took a long drink.

Belleau Wood—Dawn, June 13, 1918

The American lines had begun to solidify, the Marine brigade now spread across the wood, connecting to their positions that extended to Bouresches. For another long day, the fighting had been as confused and piecemeal as it had been for a week, small pockets of men pursuing each other, attacks launched as much by instinct as anyone's strategy. As the Marines pulled themselves together, the Germans seemed to do the same, the two sides separating just enough so the men with the shovels and axes could go to work. Like the Marines, the Germans had pulled back into their strongest positions.

Along their strengthening lines, the Marine runners were working without rest, carrying messages from one part of their position to another, the only communication that anyone had. Gradually the cohesion returned, men responding to the efforts of the scattering of officers, companies defining themselves, the men and their commanders beginning to understand how severe the losses had been, how many men from their squads were dead or still missing somewhere in the confusion of the woods.

The Second Division headquarters had relied on disastrous intelligence provided by the French. But now the division sent its own scouts forward, probing and mapping the German positions. For the first time, the generals had a reasonably accurate picture of what the Marines were facing. With maps of the wood that were finally reliable, the artillery had been active, the gunners able to drop their shells onto what would certainly be enemy targets.

On both flanks of the wood itself, the fighting had continued, pushing toward the village of Torcy, northwest of the wood, with the Germans continuing their efforts toward pushing the Americans away from Bouresches, to the northeast. But the Germans were reinforced, and unless they could be swept out of Belleau Wood itself, the American position west of Château-Thierry would be dangerously unstable.

For nearly a full day, the two sides had seemed content to engage in a sporadic artillery duel that, during long pauses, had allowed the men to search for someone who might tell them where they should be. Temple had begun to find familiar faces, or they were finding him. As the platoon drifted together, the men met each other with hard handshakes, firm grips on sagging shoulders. Others sat alone, absorbing the names of the missing, quiet tears for best friends, for men who had known each other since training, or long before. The tears came even from the old veterans, the men who had so inspired Temple, the men with so much grit from experiences in bizarre corners of the world, the men who Temple had come to believe were invincible. After a week in Belleau Wood, the arrogance, the overconfidence, was gone. Now, they were *all* veterans.

Rations had been delivered, were distributed by a lanky corporal named Appleby. As the food tins were passed through the shelters in the dense thickets of underbrush, Temple had stayed close to the corporal, a few others doing the same, a silent creeping vigil, searching the faces, who searched them as well.

Appleby didn't seem to mind the others tailing behind him, dropped down into a wide trench, looked back at Temple, said, "You boys could save me some time. A couple of you go back to the wagon, grab another case of tins. Tell the mess sergeant I sent you."

There was hesitation, quiet protest, and Temple looked past Appleby, could see a dozen men spread out along the floor of the trench, one big man hunched over, sharpening his bayonet on a flat stone.

"Dan!"

Temple jumped down, moved quickly past the corporal, saw the big man look up slowly.

"Hello, Roscoe."

Temple knelt down, saw Parker focus again on the stone, grabbed the big man's shoulder, said, "Dan! You okay? Damn, I'm glad to see you!"

Parker nodded, stared down at his work. "You too, Roscoe. Worried about you."

Temple felt a strange creeping fear, scanned Parker's dirty uniform, said, "What's the matter, Dan? You hurt?"

Parker shook his head, ran his finger along the glistening blade of the bayonet, slid it into his belt. He looked at Temple now, dark, sad eyes, said, "I'm glad you're okay, Roscoe. We lost a mess of good people. Some say half the company. You seen anyone else in the squad? I figured I was the only one left."

Temple reached out, put a hand on Parker's shoulder again. "I thought the same thing. They got Ballou. I was there. The sarge, Lieutenant Ashley."

Parker shook his head, looked down again. "I knew that cowboy would get himself killed. I prayed for him. Just . . . had a feeling. Never thought the sarge, though. Saw you trying to pull him back up."

It was a memory that Temple had put far away, and he fought it now.

"What about Scarabelli? You hear anything?"

Parker shook his head, and down the trench, a man turned, said, "Scarabelli? You mean that big-mouth Italian?"

Temple stood, said, "That's him. You see him? Did he make it?"

The man smiled. "You could say that. He's back here in the hole, sound asleep. You wake him up, he's your problem. Never saw so much mouth on such a small man. He talks while he fights. Talks to every German he shoots. Gotta hand it to him. He shot a hell of a lot of them."

Temple leaned down, looked back into the brush, saw the bottom of a pair of filthy boots. He crawled into the hole, grabbed a boot, shook it, gave a short shout. "Hey!"

Scarabelli raised his head slightly, peered from under the rim of his helmet. "What the hell . . . Farmer Roscoe! I'll be damned!"

Temple backed away, and Scarabelli slid out of the makeshift cage, took Temple's hand, said, "I knew you'd make it, Farm Boy." Scarabelli was smiling, broad and toothy. Temple said, "Parker's right over there. Come on."

Scarabelli followed him, and Temple saw Parker watching them, the big man leaning back against the side of the trench. Scarabelli said, "Well, I'll be damned. I figured you were too big a target to miss, Mountain Man. It's good to see you."

Parker nodded, unsmiling. "Gino. God protected us. We're the blessed."

"If you say so." Scarabelli had Temple by the arm now, said, "So, what about Ballou? You hear anything?"

Temple shook his head. "He's dead."

The smile faded from Scarabelli's face. "Oh, hell. When?"

"Couple days ago. I was with him. He caught a grenade."

"Quick then. Damn. I'm gonna miss that cowboy." Scarabelli sat beside Parker, said, "Some kinda hell, wasn't it? Not over yet, either."

Parker said nothing, and Temple sat as well, said, "They say we lost half the company."

Scarabelli was looking at Parker, said, "At least. Bannister, Brown, Clark. Lost track. Most everybody I knew at Quantico . . . except you two. Even the officers. I heard Ashley's gone. Not sure what the hell we're supposed to do now. They'll bunch us in with a couple other platoons, most likely. Some new sergeant, probably. Hope like hell we don't get some ninety-day wonder for a lieutenant. If we do, he won't last long enough to be a problem."

Parker looked at Scarabelli now, said, "You sound like you're enjoying all this, Jersey."

Scarabelli thought a moment, the smile gone. "We're just doing what we're supposed to do. You got a better way, Mountain Man?" He looked at Temple. "What about you? You survived this with . . . what? That damned scratch on your face? What do you think about that?"

568

Temple heard a slight quiver in Scarabelli's voice, felt a tightness in his own throat. He fought it, said, "I don't know, Gino. I was never so scared in my life. I was afraid I'd freeze up. But when they started shooting at us . . . I just put my head down and kept moving. I didn't even think about what I was doing. Just shoot the bastards. Shoot every damned one of them!"

Scarabelli was staring at him, said, "More than that, Roscoe. For everything else that went on in these damned woods, nothing meant any more to me than putting my bayonet right into one of them son of a bitch's heart. All I had to do was think of Sergeant Dugan or Conway lying back there in the wheat. That's all it took. You oughta understand that, Mountain Man. The wrath of God. I enjoyed killing every one of them, and dammit, I'm ready to do it again!"

Parker looked at Scarabelli now, and Temple was surprised to see tears. Parker said in a slow drawl, "You're right, Jersey. As scared as I was, when I got close to 'em, when I could see that gray uniform in my sights . . . I enjoyed it. God help me. God help all of us."

Sleep had come, the long narrow trench lined with exhausted and filthy men, the warm air settling on them all. Out front the scouts and guards were spread in a thin line, fresh men, sent forward to watch the thickets, any sign that the enemy might begin to stir, each one of them holding tightly to the enthusiasm of the officers far behind the lines, rumors filtering forward that the Germans might well be pulling out altogether, giving up their position in the wood.

Temple turned over on his side, his arm bent beneath his head, his elbow aching. He was awake now, sat up, blinked through the dirt in his eyes, worked the kink out of his arm. The smells rolled over him, the trench ripe with the odor from the men and their uniforms. Temple scratched at an itch under his arm, scanned the trench in both directions, saw some men stirring, lumps of filthy khaki moving slowly, some now starting to sit upright, low curses. The itching continued, and he scratched his leg, massaged his back against the side of the trench. The sensation seemed to spread, and he rubbed one hand along his arm, down his side, along both thighs. His uniform was thick with grime, crusted mud. He realized that he had not removed any part of his uniform for nearly two weeks, and he understood something that Dugan had cautioned them about, long weeks ago. With the filth had come the cooties.

The men were coming awake all through the trench, and Temple continued to scratch his sides, felt as though his shirt was coming alive. He saw men undressing, ripping their shirts off, more curses, and one man close by said, "Bugs! Worms! What the hell?"

There was laughter now, and Temple started to unbutton his own shirt, the itching unbearable, heard a voice, "Well, now! We finally got our proper welcome to France!"

Temple looked up, saw the tall hulking form of a sergeant standing up on the edge of the trench.

The man was laughing, said, "Get used to it, boys! They'll scrub you off back at the delousing station, but while you're up here, you're gonna have lots of company! Do what you gotta do, but put your damned shirts back on. Nobody out of uniform, not up here."

There was a high scream, and Temple saw the sergeant looking up, the scream suddenly louder, a piercing whine, the shell suddenly impacting just behind the trench. The dirt blew high, and Temple covered his face, felt the shower of rocks and debris, looked up, saw no sign of the sergeant. The scream came again, then another, the shells coming in all along the trench line, falling mostly behind them. Temple felt the ground lurching beneath him, saw Parker rolling toward him, the big man shouting, "Stay up against the side! Stay low!" The screams were constant now, thunder rolling over them, and Temple curled up tightly, his helmet low on his face. Each shell shook the ground, the sides of the fresh trench crumbling, dirt falling on him. He could hear the different kinds of shells, the heavy tumbling roar of the big one-fifties, the higher whine of the seventy-sevens. There was a new sound now, and he heard a low whistle, the shell cracking into a tree out in front, landing with a hard thump on the ground.

There was a strange hissing sound, and now a loud frantic voice: "*Gas!*"

He looked up, heard the word again, repeated all down the line, could hear more of the odd whistling shells. The men seemed to freeze for a long moment, and now he saw it, a thin yellow mist, rolling into the trench, tumbling in a soft cloud around the shadows of men. He jerked at the gas mask on his belt, the lessons again, the drill repeated so many times, the mask pulled open, sliding quickly down over his face. He jerked, straightened it, could see through the dull glass eyepieces, the yellow wave filling the trench, drifting toward him. Men were scrambling up out of the trench, some without masks, and the screams began now, shirtless men running in the trench, one falling close to him, the man twisting in the dirt. Temple stared at the man, helpless, suddenly felt a hand on his arm, pulling him hard. He followed, was up and out of the trench, could see Parker following a wave of men back into the woods behind them. Men were falling, the air still screaming with the explosive shells, blasts of dirt sweeping men away. He ran past the bodies, some wounded, some burned by the gas, writhing agony, the barefaced men, no masks. He forced himself to look past them, followed the wave, saw men dropping down now, jumping and tumbling into another trench line. There were officers, men in gas masks shouting close to him.

"Keep the masks on! Don't take them off!"

Temple looked out toward the first trench, the yellow haze drifting across the ground, clouding the woods in front of them. Beside him, a man ripped off his mask, said, "I can't . . . I can't breathe!"

Temple shouted at the man, "Put it back on! Didn't you hear?"

The man stared at him with wide-eyed shock, then suddenly curled over, fell at Temple's feet. Temple dropped down, grabbed the man's mask, tried to slip it over the man's head, but the man fought him, was screaming, twisting away from him. Temple backed away, could do nothing, saw the man rolling in the dirt, the face bright red, hands covering his eyes. Temple turned away, stared down into the sweaty mist of his own mask, felt himself shaking, dropped to his knees. He realized the explosive shelling was falling far out in front of him, blanketing the first trench, and he peered out, saw rising clouds of fire and dirt blackening the air where he had just been. The officers were still moving by him, the flow of men from the trench slowing. Those who could make it were already in their new cover, those who could not escape the gas already choking in their own graves. The roaring screams of the shells continued to punch and obliterate the forward trench, the ground still rolling beneath him, men still dropping down beside him. There was nowhere else to go now, no place for the fear, no escape for the terror that filled his mind, the words rolling through his brain, Parker's words, God help us.

"Up! Keep your masks on! Move forward, find a place to shoot!"

The officers were driving the men from behind, the Marines climbing up and out of the safety of the trench. The shelling had stopped, and now, the scouts had come scrambling back from the woods in front of them, the word quickly passed to the officers. It was predictable, the intensity of the shelling not merely an accident, so much fire focused on one narrow section of the line. The enemy was coming.

When the shelling stopped, there was a long silence, and Temple waited as they all waited, slowly peered up out of the fresh trench, a strange smoky calm. In front of him, the yellow mist had begun to drift away, but there was still a sharp burn in the air, enough gas lingering to choke a man, or blister the skin, and so the masks stayed on. Temple climbed up with the men beside him, checked his rifle, felt the weight of the belt at his waist. The day before, each man had been given another hundred rounds of ammunition, the one commodity the division seemed to have in ample supply. Some had griped, protesting that the fight was done, others, like Temple, expecting that the Marines were not yet through with Belleau Wood. Now, they were advancing again over ground they already held, pushing their way out beyond the first trench, where the misty yellow cloud still drifted among the bodies of the men who had not escaped.

He struggled to see through the mask, his breathing fogging the glass, stumbled, nearly fell, used his rifle as a crutch. He felt nearly blind, the woods in front of him appearing impenetrable, a tangle of blasted trees. The panic began to rise, and he wanted to rip the mask free, heard an officer behind him.

"Far enough! Here! Form a firing line! Masks off! It's safe!"

He tugged at the mask, ripped it free, felt a rush of cool air on his face, rolled the mask into the pouch at his waist. Around him, some of the men were dropping their masks, and he thought, No, that's a mistake. There could be more gas. But the men were in motion all around him, dropping into holes, shoving aside limbs, stumps, some lying flat, others crouching, rifles pointing forward. He saw a lieutenant waving to him, to others behind him. "Here! Spread out through this area! Use the logs as cover!"

Temple obeyed, saw men scrambling up and over the logs, caught a glimpse of Scarabelli as the small man disappeared into a gap down be-tween two fat tree trunks. Temple looked around, saw Parker moving forward, and Temple pointed, said, "Dan! There! Gino's there! Good place! Come on!"

He slid down between the trees, saw Scarabelli resting his rifle up on the log in front, and Parker was down with him, did the same. Scarabelli looked at them both, said, "Well, this is just like Quantico. You two country boys can embarrass me again with your damned shooting."

Parker said nothing, and Temple adjusted his rifle, said, "You see anything? Where the hell are they?"

"Eyes to the front!" The voice came from behind him, the lieutenant again.

Parker said, "About a hundred fifty yards."

Scarabelli said, "How the hell you know that?"

"Look at the tops of the small trees. Out a ways. A man bumps the tree as he walks, the top moves. It's just like home, Jersey. Just like bear hunting."

Scarabelli aimed his rifle, said, "I thought you just hunted squirrels or something. Hell, anybody can hit a bear."

Parker seemed to ignore him, said, "Watch that gap about a hundred yards out, Roscoe, just to the right of that one fat stump. That'll be the first look you get."

Temple eased the rifle up, the sight now focused on the gap in the brush. He realized his hands were shaking, his chest pounding, felt a spark of fear. A hundred yards . . . too damned close. If they're coming . . . are they running? They'll be right on top of us. But nobody can run in this stuff. How many of them? He gripped the rifle hard, raised his head slightly, blinked, tried to clear his mind.

Beside him, Parker said, "Take a deep breath, Roscoe."

Scarabelli seemed to vibrate on the other side of him, said, "Dammit! Come on! These damned officers. They sure the Huns are moving up?"

Parker said, "Shut up, Jersey. *I'm* sure."

Far down to one side, a machine gun suddenly opened up, and Temple glanced that way, knew the familiar sound of the Hotchkiss gun, so different from the German Maxim. Yep, he thought. Somebody else is sure too. He watched the brush, saw a thin treetop suddenly quiver, felt his heart freeze. He stared at the opening just in front, his eye centered on the sight of the rifle, felt himself breathing, tried to slow it, calm himself, heard the voice in his mind: *Wait.* He saw the motion now, a splotch of gray, a man's belt, a rifle, tipped by a bayonet, and he held his breath, then let it out slowly, and squeezed the trigger.

The Marines began to fire, punching holes in the German wave that pressed forward through the thickets and tangled mass of forest. The Germans continued to come, closing the gaps, making their way through the desolation of the wood. Temple could see more of them now, the faces, grim and terrified men, cut down right in front of him. All along the line, the Springfields and the Hotchkiss guns rose to meet the attack in a perfect chattering chorus, and after a few agonizing minutes, the German advance began to melt away. As long as the Germans were within sight, Temple chose his targets, fired without thinking, centered his aim on the patches of gray. As the Springfield jumped in his hands, the targets fell. It was no different anywhere else, the Germans never really finding targets of their own. Once their main advance was blasted apart, they were unable to make any kind of stand. The German counterattack dissolved in the face of the marksmanship of the

574

Marines who waited for them in the blasted thickets, the men who had been trained with the rifle.

On June 15, most of the Marines were ordered back, replaced by infantry units from the division's other two regiments, the Ninth and the Twenty-third. For ten days, the Marine Brigade had fought over the worst ground anyone in the army had ever seen. And the fight was not yet done. After another long week of stalemate and struggle, the Marines were sent back into the wood for the final push. The unshakable tenacity of the Second Division had taken a devastating toll on their enemy, and on June 25, the German hold on Belleau Wood was finally broken. From Torcy to Bouresches, the Second Division had dammed up the German advance, and prevented them from capturing the vital roadway to Paris.

While the Marines were recuperating, the fight for Belleau Wood had received worldwide attention. Temple and his squad did not know that from the first day of their assault, they had been joined by Floyd Gibbons, a prominent correspondent from the American press corps. Within days, the fight at the Bois de Belleau was front-page news in every newspaper in America. The impact of the American victory was felt all through the camps on both sides of the Western Front. The most notable recognition was offered by French general Jean Dégoutte, who commanded the French Sixth Army, and the overall theater of the front occupied by the Second Division.

In view of the brilliant conduct of the Fourth Brigade of the Second Division . . . the general commanding the Sixth Army orders that henceforth, in all official papers, the Bois de Belleau shall be named "Bois de la Brigade de Marine."

35

PERSHING

Château-Thierry—June 30, 1918

They were standing when he entered, and he stopped at the door, scanned the faces, saw every man coming to sharp attention. They were mostly gray-haired, near his own age, each man flanked by senior members of his staff. He felt the energy in them, the pride, men who didn't need to be told what they had accomplished. But he would tell them anyway. He looked at Omar Bundy, the commander of the Second Division, the small thin man standing tall, staring past him, wearing a look of grim satisfaction, the awareness certainly of what his men had achieved. But there was no smugness to the man, there would be no boastfulness, no grabbing of newspaper headlines. In the agonizing fights around Belleau Wood, the Second Division had lost a quarter of its strength.

He scanned the face of Joe Dickman, the Third Division commander, a much larger man than Bundy, and saw satisfaction as well. Dickman was an emotional man, loud of voice, as prone to deep laughter as he was to tight-fisted anger. But there was no need for display now, Dickman as aware as anyone in the room that the Third Division had defied overwhelming odds, and by holding to a difficult line along the Marne River, had prevented the Germans from coming across. Though the Third had not suffered the ex-traordinary casualties of Bundy's division, Pershing knew that both men understood that if not for the heroics and resolve of the men who marched under their commands, the Germans would be in Paris.

He realized now that the only one looking directly at him was Harbord, and Pershing could not hide the smile, the tough square-jawed man offering him a silent nod. The others seemed

576

not to notice, would probably not understand what it meant. But Pershing knew. It was Harbord's thank-you.

Throughout the mountainous ordeal of organizing the AEF, Harbord had been the primary cog in so much of the machinery, the only man Pershing could easily send in his own place, the man who had even less tolerance than Pershing for the grotesque inefficiencies thrust upon them from both Washington and Paris. But as the AEF began to function more smoothly, Harbord had surprised Pershing by requesting that he eventually be assigned duty in the field. It was the sort of request Pershing had grown accustomed to. So many of the capable staff officers had become frustrated by the tedious misery of their jobs, none more so than the impetuous George Patton. Pershing understood the yearning, a need to fulfill some deeply personal mission that did not involve an office. Not all the officers pleaded for command in the field. Some were left over from the army's prewar custom of political reward, men who had no place anywhere other than behind a desk. Others were perfectly suited for the roles assigned to them, like the amazingly energetic George Marshall, men with a talent for organization. Though Harbord had been indispensable as Pershing's chief of staff, Pershing could not deny the passion and the abilities that lay behind the man's request. In early May, as the Second Division had completed its preparations for moving to the front, Pershing had finally granted Harbord his field command. Though Pershing had full confidence that Harbord could handle the task, he had to believe that not even Harbord himself expected to command anything like the firestorm that erupted around Belleau Wood. Though Pershing had felt the loss of Harbord on his staff, he had to concede that, at Belleau Wood, the right man may well have been put into the right job.

"Gentlemen, please sit. You've earned it."

The staff officers responded, and chairs were dragged forward, the senior commanders finding their seats. Pershing waited, the room growing silent again.

"You have no doubt seen the letters. I have ordered that the contents from every significant correspondence be communicated to your commands."

There were nods, low voices.

"Yes, sir."

"We received them, sir."

Pershing stared at the floor for a long moment, had rehearsed his speech, but it seemed ridiculous now. He had known most of these men for years, some for most of his career. They didn't need speeches. He thought a moment, looked up, said, "There is irony in this, of course. Those who are most vocal in their praise of our successes are the very leaders who have provided us the most formidable obstacles. I will not belabor the point. I have accepted their kind wishes exactly in the spirit offered to us. You should do the same." He paused. "I am meeting with Monsieur Clemenceau tomorrow. He will no doubt offer his own praise for our success. If so, I will communicate his words to you, though I doubt I can capture his particular talent for the perfect phrase."

He stared at the floor again, felt drained of words. He felt angry with himself, thought, So many meetings, so damned much talk. Now, it matters. And I don't know what to say. He looked at them, said, "We were given a task. Some suggested that the job was beyond us, that nothing we could bring to this war would have any impact, that we were too slow, too inexperienced, too incompetent. Too damned late. They were wrong. I have heard so much defeatism, gloomy talk that this war has grown too big for anyone to solve, that all of Europe is simply destroying itself, helpless to stop the inevitable. It is a peculiar trait of Europeans that they stare back at their own history, see the world as it used to be, and make their decisions based on what was." He paused, felt suddenly emotional, held it tightly. After a moment, he said, "Gentlemen, let no one hide the truth, let no patronizing words of praise from politicians disguise the honesty of what you have accomplished. Because of the sacrifice and the spirit of the men under your commands, right now, in Berlin, as well as in Paris, the maps are changing, the strategy is changing. You have accomplished what so many thought was impossible. You have changed the war."

With the stunning success by the Second and Third Divisions at halting the German offensive along the Marne, the voices of the Allies had grown louder still. The congratulatory letters came of course, all manner of gracious respect for the magnificence of the stand by the Americans, especially the work of the Marines. But with the hearty handshakes came raised expectations, and from London to Paris, the ministries and military command centers were already calculating new ways to put the Americans to good use in every front of the war.

The calls came from other quarters as well, from Rome, where Prime Minister Orlando began to insist that Americans be sent to northern Italy, to help contain the ongoing threat from the Austrian and German presence there. The British began to suggest other uses for the American troops, a mission to the Balkans perhaps, or Romania, freeing valuable British forces so they could be sent to bolster their ongoing drive through the rugged sands of the Middle East. The most prominent civilians, Lloyd George and Clemenceau, tempered their hopes with the smooth patronizing words of the skilled politician. It was the kind of pressure that infuriated Pershing, the carefully phrased kindness, the deference and respect, punctuated by word from Secretary Baker that all the while, entreaties were being made to Washington, the continuing clumsiness of the efforts to persuade President Wilson to bring General Pershing to the *correct* frame of mind. Though Pershing held tight to his anger, keeping his outbursts confined to his staff, the only man who could effectively defuse Pershing's fury was Baker. And no matter the pressure that flowed toward Washington, the secretary of war continued to assure Pershing that nothing had changed. Pershing was still in charge.

Chaumont, France—July 1, 1918

The crowd filled the plaza, old and young, flowers and flags, the tearful cheers for the man who brought out the emotions and inspired the wounded spirit of the French people. Pershing followed Clemenceau out of the hotel, watched as the people poured out their affections toward the old man, reaching out to him, some touching his hand as he passed. They cheered

Pershing as well, but Pershing knew by now: this audience belonged to Clemenceau.

He followed the old man into the limousine, waited for Clemenceau to get comfortable in the seat. Behind Pershing, the French officers moved to the second car. Pershing waited for them to be seated as well, saw an acknowledging wave from General Ragueneau, the liaison officer for General Pétain. The voices of the crowd poured over them still, Clemenceau waving, smiling to them, his kindness returned by more cheers. The car moved slowly at first, circled the plaza, Clemenceau's instructions, but it was not to be a parade, and when the limousine completed its slow turn, the driver drove the car out into the wide avenue, away from the crowds, out past the last few shops and small buildings.

They were motoring to Montigny, Clemenceau insisting on visiting a billet where Americans were still undergoing training, a concept that Pershing felt was still foreign to the old man. Pershing was still intimidated by him, knew that Clemenceau would control any conversation, and so, until the old man was ready to speak, they would ride in silence. After a long moment, Clemenceau said, "They salute you, General. It is no longer just for me."

"I am always impressed by the graciousness of the French people, sir."

He didn't know what else to say, had learned that any silence around Clemenceau would not last long.

"Permit me an observation, General. Mr. Lloyd George has his friends and his detractors, but I do admit that I admire his energy. When he pursues a goal, he is relentless. General, have you given further thought to the British demands?"

Which demands? The silent question rose in Pershing's mind, but he fought the urge to spit the words, said, "I'm sorry, Monsieur Prime Minister. Of what do you speak?"

"I am told that they expect one hundred American divisions on the ground by next spring. Is that a reasonable expectation?"

The subject had been wrestled with for weeks, Lloyd George and his ministers pounding the issue both in France and in Washington. Their urgency had been made even more intense by the American success at Château-Thierry. Pershing stared forward, measured the tone of his own voice.

"I appreciate the necessity of the British hopes, Monsieur Prime Minister. However, I must point out, as I have done to Mr. Lloyd George, and Marshal Haig, and several other British officials: Beyond the logistical problems of assembling, equipping, and training what would amount to nearly three million soldiers, plus another million support personnel, all of whom must be housed and fed and transported on your soil, there is another difficulty that I regret that my government and the American people would find difficult to accept. Given the size of our fighting units, one hundred American divisions would equal approximately two hundred French or British divisions."

Clemenceau said nothing, and Pershing paused, closed his eyes for a brief moment.

"Monsieur Prime Minister, right now, on the Western Front, the combined strength of the French, British, and Belgian forces totals one hundred sixty-two divisions. What the British are asking of us is that America furnish you an army that would be considerably larger than the total of what is now engaged. I have no doubt that this would have a positive effect on the outcome of the war. But in fact, sir, by a simple . . . by an exercise in mathematics, you can see that if we did what the British are asking, the Americans would outnumber the Germans on the Western Front all by ourselves. America is willing to make a sacrifice for our allies, but, as I have explained previously, there is a difference between what is possible and what is not."

Too far, he thought, you were too blunt. Dammit! He waited for some kind of explosion from Clemenceau, heard a small laugh instead.

"Mathematics is not a subject I enjoyed in school, General. I shall not mention the matter again."

Pershing let out a long breath, and after a pause Clemenceau said, "I am not surprised by the depths of British desperation. Great Britain has been defeated by this war. Her glory is past."

It was an oddly blunt statement, and Pershing was curious now, said, "Why do you say that, sir?"

"She has lost far too much of herself. Besides a generation of

581

her young men, her navy, her shipping interests have suffered to extreme. I do not believe they can ever recover. Her empire will suffer as well. Her colonial soldiers have fought extremely well. It will energize their own nationalism, their own identity as independent powers. As a result, Britain will lose control of her colonies."

Pershing absorbed Clemenceau's frankness, could not avoid the question. "Then, what of France, sir?"

"Ah, General! Yes! We will rise again to our proper place of leadership in Europe. It is the inevitability of history."

Pershing had no response, thought, Perhaps Germany would not agree.

Clemenceau continued, "Paris has been spared yet again, General. We owe much of that to you, of course."

The acknowledgment seemed to drop from Clemenceau like an afterthought, and Pershing clenched his jaw, said, "Thank you, Monsieur Prime Minister."

"But even if Paris was to fall, it would not matter. The French people understand that above Paris is France. And above France is all of civilization. Even the Germans know this. That is why they hate us so. They cannot escape the savagery of their race. We will always be above them."

Pershing did not respond, and Clemenceau leaned close to him, said, "I admire your country as well, General. It is a wonderful land, with unlimited possibilities."

There was no enthusiasm in Clemenceau's words, and Pershing stared out the window, said, "How very kind of you, sir."

French Army Headquarters—Bombon

"We will solidify our position. The enemy has been held in check. The surprise that gave them such success has now been erased." Foch looked at Pershing now, made a short bow. "We owe a debt to your army, General. You know my feelings on the matter. Paris has been saved. All of France is grateful."

Pershing returned the bow, Foch's reference not slipping past him. *Your* army.

"Thank you, General Foch. Have you given thought to my proposal for a counteroffensive?"

Foch turned to the map on the wall, said, "I have given instructions that a study be made, an examination of our available intelligence as to the enemy strength in each of these sectors. In time, as additional American divisions are made available, a counteroffensive could be practical."

Pershing glanced at Pétain, saw the same dead stare he had seen too often on the general's face. It was no secret that Pétain was not comfortable with Foch's authority, the former subordinate to Pétain now the senior. But Pershing was troubled by Pétain's apparent hopelessness, something the other commanders had observed as well. Pershing could feel the old familiar frustrations brewing, looked at the map now, said, "General Foch, I believed you and I were in agreement. Do you accept my plan to organize the various American divisions along the Marne?"

"Certainly, General. Those divisions are to constitute your First Corps, yes?"

"Yes, the First, Second, Twenty-sixth, Forty-second, and, as they become available, the Forty-first Divisions are now organized with command of the corps assigned to General Liggett. My point, sir, is that these divisions are either battle-tested or prepared as well as I could expect. The First Corps is in place, along a front that offers us an opportunity that may not present itself if we delay."

Foch stared at the map, said nothing. Pershing moved forward now, pointed at the map.

"Right here. The St. Mihiel salient. The enemy has provided us with a weakness in their lines, for which we should be grateful. But it is of no use to us if we do not act."

He struggled to keep some kind of calm in his voice, had learned already that Foch could not be pushed. "General Foch, your government has pressed my command for many months, urging us to provide assistance. In the past month, we have done so."

Foch looked at him, said, "Quite so. I have acknowledged your contribution. Do you require me to repeat what you have already heard? It is no source of pride to any of us, General, that the French divisions along the Marne were not capable of holding the enemy back. That must be extremely gratifying to you, and to your government. Must I continue to acknowledge that? We are grateful to you. We shall always be grateful to you."

Foch was close to him, leaning forward, and Pershing saw anger in the old man's eyes. He felt himself pulling away, had seen enough of the arguing and bickering. He looked to the map again, said, "General, the AEF's troops accomplished all that was asked of them. The enemy was prevented from crossing the Marne, and, for now, Paris is safe. *For now*. All I am suggesting is that we not allow our success to slip away. The troops in my command have been trained to fight in the open, on the move. They will not perform well if they are ordered to sit in their trenches and wait for the enemy. I have no doubt that Herr Ludendorff is planning his next attack. He knows the Second Division has been bloodied, and Paris is still a vital target. I respectfully suggest that we not allow him time to complete his plans. The St. Mihiel salient is a vulnerable point in his lines, and the AEF's First Corps is in position to do something about it. If we are successful at collapsing the salient, we might very well break through to threaten his rear. We could damage his supply and communications, and compel him to retreat from his gains of the past three months. I appreciate . . . my entire command appreciates your gratefulness. But the mission is not yet complete. I must suggest, sir, that if you measure success by the failure of the enemy to capture Paris, that Paris will not be safe until Germany has been defeated, and her troops driven from French soil."

Foch showed no emotion, seemed to study the map again.

"General Pershing, your commitment to the urgency of our cause has never been questioned. But this is not simply an American war to be fought as Americans would fight it. When this war is over, you will return to your home, to some position of authority in Washington, perhaps. We, on the other hand, must live directly under the consequences of our success or failure. If I am cautious in your eyes, it is because I fear for the future."

Pershing stared at him for a long moment, thought, Of course, that is exactly the problem. "General Foch, the families of the American soldiers who are dying in France will know the consequences of this war as well as any Frenchman. I have no choice but to offer you my judgment as commander of the AEF. If you want this war to end, we must win it. We cannot merely wait for Germany to lose."

"Then I have a suggestion, General. The Americans have given us something we have lacked for some time. Call it . . . energy. The morale of all France has been lifted by your success. Let us take advantage of that. You speak of a counteroffensive, an attack against one part of the front. There is a counter-offensive of another kind, an assault against the disease of despair that infects the French army. Consider the advantage if your spirit is infused into all of our forces. I have given thought to a plan that has already been approved by the prime minister. Consider the positive effect of placing one American regiment into each French division along the entire front. One regiment, still fresh from their glorious victories of June, can inspire, can change the fighting spirit of an entire division, and in doing so can bring renewed strength to the entire French army."

Pershing felt the wind leaving him. He stared at Foch with disbelief, thoughts tumbling through his mind: You would divide us, pull us apart . . . still? He had no energy for explanation, for debate, the subject so beaten and strangled now for more than a year. He kept his stare at Foch, saw the man's eyes glance away.

Pershing said, "No."

He walked with Pétain, his boot heels striking the hard ground with a sharp thump. They moved out through a wide garden, the air hot and thick, a faint buzzing from swarms of bees that hovered over the sea of flowers. Pershing felt the sweat on his back, would not remove his jacket, the heat coming as much from inside of him as from the July sun. He turned along a narrow trail, realized that Pétain was not beside him. He stopped, turned, saw the heavy man wiping his brow with a white handkerchief.

Pétain said, "Forgive me, John. I cannot keep up with you. If you wish, I will sit in the shade, and you can run around for a while. Several kilometers should calm you down."

Pershing saw the soft smile, felt the kindness in the man's words. "My apologies. I have no right to carry on like some angry schoolboy."

"Let us sit, then. That bench, there. Then I will tell you why you are wrong."

The meeting had concluded with a luncheon that Foch did not attend, and Pershing felt the rumbling in his stomach, the meal that seemed now to gather into one hard lump. He had said little throughout the meal, engulfed by his fury, the dull shock, the familiar frustration with Allied commanders who could not be swayed from their one unchanging chorus.

He had always enjoyed Pétain's hospitality, the privileges that a French general enjoyed, the chefs who provided the elegant table, the explanation why Pétain had difficulty fastening his belt. It only added to Pershing's anger, that a perfectly wonderful meal could not be enjoyed, had instead tied him up in knots.

Pershing followed him toward the shady place under the awning of an old shed, the two men sitting. Pétain continued to wipe his brow, and Pershing said, "We can return to your office. I did not anticipate the heat."

"No, it is fine. I should escape that place more often, summer or not. There is more that is stale than just the air." He paused, said, "You said exactly the right thing, John. General Foch shares an unfortunate trait with Monsieur Clemenceau. Neither of them enjoys hearing the truth. You cannot imagine how difficult it was for Foch to concede to you that our own troops could not have protected Paris."

"Forgive me, Henri, but do you agree—"

"I agree that our troops could not have protected Paris. We could not have prevented the enemy from crossing the Marne, and once across, the Germans would have had every advantage. There is no sector of our lines that can sustain a vigorous attack. It matters not what I believe. It is a fact. Since March, the Germans have extended their lines in three different sectors of the front. The only place where they did not stop themselves was at Château-Thierry, and that was only because you were there."

"Your prime minister believes that even if Paris falls, the French will go on fighting. I was surprised to hear that."

"I am not. Monsieur Clemenceau is the conscience of France, the master of all our hope. He does not see what you and I see, because he chooses not to. If Paris falls, Clemenceau, or someone else, will find himself at the reins of a government that must accept the price of defeat. All talk of war or support for the army will be replaced by talk of peace at any cost. Any cost, John. If Germany has her way, we will no longer agonize over such concerns as Alsace and Lorraine, as we have done for forty years. That will be like pennies to a banker. With the Germans in Paris . . . France might as well cease to be. It is my nightmare."

"The enemy will not cross the Marne as long as we are there. I don't believe he is anxious to test the Marines again. But Ludendorff will not sit still. He will push until he finds the weakest point."

Pétain leaned back on the bench, a hand on his stomach.

"Foch will agree with your plan. You may not see that now, but it will happen. First he must answer to Clemenceau, convince the prime minister that your plan is the final option. It is the dance that Clemenceau requires of him. It is a mystery, though."

"What?"

"Foch is a devout Catholic, as are many of the officers in this army. Clemenceau has a distinct dislike of Catholics. It is something in our culture that goes back to the revolution. Most officers are discreet in the manner of their religious practice; however, Foch practices his faith in full view. Some would call it defiance. And yet Clemenceau chose to put his full support behind him, out of all the possible candidates, Joffre, Guillaumat, d'Espérey, even me. It is a mystery."

Pershing thought a moment, said, "You said it yourself. Perhaps General Foch dances well."

Pétain laughed.

"Advice to you, my friend. When you retire, avoid politics.

You do not have the subtlety for it." Pétain stood now, put the handkerchief in his pocket. "I believe we should return to the maps. I should like to see more details of your plan. As I said, given time, General Foch will approve. I am greatly concerned that your predictions about Ludendorff will prove accurate. And when the Germans launch their next offensive, neither Foch nor the British will be in any position to argue with you."

Pershing stood, followed Pétain along the path, thought, It is one advantage Ludendorff will always have. There is no one to argue with *him*.

On July 15, Ludendorff acted again. From Soissons to Reims, the German gains of May and June had pushed a deep bulge toward their eventual goal of Paris. Despite the success of the Americans, Ludendorff would not simply walk away from his strategy. The spearhead of the German assault came near Reims, a quarter million German troops surging southward toward the Marne River. But this time the French had assembled reliable intelligence, and the French commanders had prepared for the assault by pulling their lines back into a flexible defense, designed to absorb the main German thrust. Though the Germans succeeded in crossing the Marne, the French fought back with surprising energy, and the German drive was halted.

Along the Marne itself, there was a different story. East of Château-Thierry, near the village of Varennes, the river formed a tight loop to the north, a finger of land that most strategists would ignore as nearly impossible to defend. This sharp bend of riverbank was manned by the American Thirty-eighth Regiment, part of the Third Division. In the predawn of July 15, two full regiments of German Grenadiers attempted to force a crossing of the narrow river, and discovered that the narrow finger of land was not indefensible after all. Commanded by Colonel Ulysses Grant McAlexander, the overwhelmingly outnumbered troops of the Thirty-eighth held their ground, and destroyed a significant percentage of the German force. Though abandoned by the early withdrawal of the French troops on their flank, McAlexander continued to hold his position for a full day, inflicting, and absorbing enormous casualties. McAlexander's efforts would not go unnoticed. Throughout the entire AEF, McAlexander would ever after be referred to as the "Rock of the Marne."

Elsewhere, the German drive was absorbing unaccustomed punishment at the hands of the rejuvenated French defense. The exhaustion of the German attack provided the Allied commanders with a sudden glimpse of the decay that was affecting the German army. Though the Allies were justified in their despair over the potential collapse of their own armies, the inability of the Germans to carry out Ludendorff's plan was a revelation that the Germans had serious problems of their own. After more than three years, the war of attrition was affecting both sides. For the moment, Pershing appreciated that his plans for the assault on the St. Mihiel salient could wait. From Soissons to Reims, the German forces lay exhausted and battered in a wide arc. It would be up to the Allies to do something about it.

36

TEMPLE

Near Montreuil-Aux-Lions—July 15, 1918

They had stood naked for long minutes, every man grateful to peel the awful filth of the uniform from his body. After a few minutes, the men were sent through a line of water hoses, gleeful orderlies dousing them from head to toe. Soaked and thoroughly embarrassed, they were given soft blobs of foul-smelling soap that carried away the last remnants of the creatures who had taken up residence on the skin and hair of each man, and then, more hoses. There were no towels, and as the men dried themselves in the hot sun, they were paraded to fresh piles of uniforms, socks, underwear, and, finally, boots. Some of the men still carried their old boots, had endured so much pain to break them in that they were reluctant to part with the leather that had been softened by the abuse of mud, rain, and a hundred miles of marching. But the resistance of the die-hards had broken down, and their old boots were tossed into a mound that soon became a stinking bonfire.

It had taken the division more time than expected to establish the delousing stations. But the filth was gone now, and as they rode back to their camps in the village, each man savored the feel of clean clothing. The veterans were laughing, warning the new men: enjoy every moment of it. It won't last long. As they reached the battered village, the men had been allowed some free time, precious moments to write letters, some, like Parker, wandering off to find some quiet place to add pages to his diary. Temple and many of the others had caught the astounding aroma of fresh coffee.

He stood in line, savored the smell, all the men straining to see the hands that held the coffeepots. The tables were set up just inside the wreck of an old house. The front of the house had been blown away, the rubble and stone piled along each side, someone's effort to clear the roadway. It had been a two-story house, the upstairs walls leaning inward, barely supporting the floor that curved down into a grotesque smile. But few of the men paid attention to the house or the destruction. As he inched closer to the wrecked house, Temple could see the painted sign, wedged upright into a neat pile of old brick: SALVATION ARMY

The name was vaguely familiar, but like most of the men, Temple had no idea what they did. Now he understood. These outposts had become a marvelous oasis, a small piece of luxury in the massive swamp of men and equipment. The soldiers had learned that these places could be found all throughout the American lines, some dangerously close to the front. They were usually set up in hastily constructed shelters, temporary locations that catered to the movement of the men they served. They were staffed by American civilians, and the smaller canteens in the villages offered little more than hot coffee and a doughnut. But far more than the simple offering, the Salvation Army and others—the YMCA and the Knights of Columbus—were a reminder that somewhere, far beyond this war, there was a nation that had not forgotten them. And they offered one more bit of sunshine as well. Nearly every one of the Salvation Army outposts was staffed by a small group of women.

Temple could see them now, was surprised to see uniforms, each one wearing a hat, her hair pulled tightly back. There were four of them, one much older, stout and matronly, clearly in command. But Temple focused on the others, sweating faces and young hands, working to fill the coffee cups, passing doughnuts out to the men from a massive tin tray. He was there now, held out the cup, heard the man in front of him say something crude and idiotic to the girl, her smile fading for a brief moment. But then she was looking at Temple, held the dark metal pot out toward him, said, "Here you go, Soldier."

Temple felt feathers in his throat, stared into soft blue eyes, a spray of freckles dancing across the girl's cheeks. She filled the cup slowly, a slight quiver in her hand from the weight of the pot. Temple could not take his eyes from her. She was the most beautiful girl he had ever seen. "Thank you, ma'am."

She glanced up at him, and he felt scalding pain, jerked his hand back, the cup tossing more of the steaming coffee on his arm.

She said, "Oh! I'm terribly sorry. Oh dear! Let me get a cloth."

He rubbed his arm, saw the painful concern in her face, felt suddenly guilty. "Oh, no, it's all right."

She shook her head, and he thought she was going to cry. "I can be so clumsy. Please forgive me. I heard your accent and . . . I'm so embarrassed."

He heard her accent as well, the soft lilt of magnolia blossoms. He was smiling at her now, and she seemed to blush.

"Please forgive me, Soldier." She returned the smile, and he was frozen in place, held motionless by the soft glow in her eyes.

Behind him, Scarabelli said, "Oh, for Chrissakes! Miss, he's a Marine. If he doesn't get hurt at least twice a day, he might as well stay in bed! Can I get some coffee?"

"Oh, yes, a Marine! We heard about you. You're heroes!"

Her smile lit every dark place in his soul, and he formed the protest, shook his head, suddenly felt a hand gripping his arm.

"Move along, Marine! Got a whole company back here."

Temple snapped awake, saw the growling frown on the sergeant's face. He backed away, watched as Scarabelli had his cup filled, saw her glancing up toward him, a sharp dart that clenched his gut.

Scarabelli was beside him now, said, "Jesus, Farm Boy. You got no girls at home?"

Temple let Scarabelli pull him away, turned with him now, balanced what was left of the coffee in the tin cup. He took a sip, hot and bitter, no sugar, and it curled his tongue.

"Oh . . . this is terrible."

Scarabelli cradled his cup in both hands, stared into the black liquid. "You're crazy. This is mother's milk. You don't want it, pour it in here."

"I like it sweet. Back home, we use a lot of cane sugar. My mother liked it like syrup."

Scarabelli laughed, drank from his cup. "Damn farm boys. I'm never going to the South. You people have some strange damned habits. Coffee has one purpose. It's the gasoline that starts the motor."

Temple looked back toward the wrecked house, the Marines still in a long line, the women working to keep it moving. He looked at the girl, saw her smiling at another man, nodding, talking. He felt bruised, a sharp punch to his thoughts. Of course. It wasn't just you. She's like that to everybody. He turned away again, his momentary love affair crushed.

Scarabelli was looking at him, said, "I bet you haven't ever been with a girl, huh, Farm Boy?"

Temple said nothing, pretended to drink the coffee. He was embarrassed now, the usual result of his encounter with girls. He thought of the night in Tallahassee, shortly before he left for Quantico. It had been his first long ride in an automobile, several of his friends daring to make the thirty-mile trip to some kind of social gathering in the capital city that few in Monticello would have approved of. There had been music, and girls who knew something besides life on a farm. His eyes had locked on a dark-haired beauty, and he had stared at her for hours, furious at the boys who danced with her, who dared actually to touch her. It had been a miserably painful night for him, made worse by her glances, curious, inviting, and terrifying. All he had to do was walk across the room and talk to her. But the fear had beaten him, and when the music ended, he had ridden home depressed by the laughter of the others, the good time they would speak of for days. To Temple, it had been a lesson in misery. Some people were meant for the city, so many of his friends had the courage it took to say the right things to the girls. He had convinced himself that when it came to women and marriage, he would simply grow old and die alone. It was far simpler. He glanced at Scarabelli, said, "Hell, yes, I've been with girls. Back home the farms are full of 'em."

Scarabelli finished his coffee, wiped the grounds out of the cup with his finger. "Right. The farms are full of something."

They moved across the wide roadway, and Temple eyed the company flag, a slow ripple in the distance. They moved out

593

into the open ground, could see the MPs flanking the path that led to the encampment. Scarabelli led the way, and Temple followed without talking, moved past the guards, crested the low hill, saw a wagon towed by a scrawny horse. A man stood up high in the wagon, tossed out bundles of white paper, and Scarabelli ran forward now, said, "Heeyoo! *Stars and Stripes!*"

Temple had not thought of the newspaper for weeks now. He enjoyed reading the news, the army's own version of events tending to be less ridiculous than what he read in the occasional glimpse from some American paper. *Stars and Stripes* had first been published a short time after Temple arrived in France, and many of the men, especially Scarabelli, treasured every page, scoured every word. Scarabelli had his own copy now, held it up toward Temple.

"Come on! Get you one! Let's get a bunch of 'em! We'll take 'em back to platoon."

The man on the wagon seemed not to care how many they took, and Temple grabbed a tall stack, followed Scarabelli toward their camp. A stream of men was coming toward them now, smiles and anticipation, the stack disappearing from Temple's hands in a few seconds. Most of the men dropped down right where they stood, sitting in the grass, scanningthe paper. Temple sat beside Scarabelli, who was turning the pages, searching.

"Here it is. 'Free Advice for the Lovelorn, by Miss Information.' This is my favorite part." Temple tried to find the page, and Scarabelli read aloud, "Dear Miss Information. My girl serves coffee with the Salvation Army, and damned if she isn't the most perfect angel on this whole wide earth. How many Marines do I have to whip up on before I can actually kiss her full on the lips?"

Temple found the column now, read, then crumpled the paper, looked at Scarabelli. "That's not what it says. Damn you."

"Well, it would if you'd sit down and write. The way you were staring at that girl back there, I figure you better do it soon. Your poor heart might flop right out of your chest."

"Go to hell."

Around them, the men were laughing, some reading aloud, talk spreading over the hillside. Temple looked up, saw Sergeant Briggs moving toward them in hard quick steps. Briggs was another of the veterans, not as old as Dugan had been, but every bit as grouchy, a hard square man with shoulders like rocks.

"All right! Party's over! You boys in my squad can get moving right now. Pack up your gear, clean your rifles. The rest of you, find your gear and your sergeants. Orders have come in. Lieutenant Colvin wants everybody prepared to march in one hour. Seems Black Jack wants us to go to work."

The backpack was tightly packed, the rifle oiled to a sheen, and he saw Scarabelli carrying a load of canteens.

"Here you go. All filled." He tossed them to the others, handed one to Temple, said, "Platoon's got lots of new faces. Still can't remember the names. Looks like we're close to full strength from what I can see."

They were gathering their equipment, rifles resting on backpacks, the men checking their gas masks, sharpening bayonets. He saw Parker now, the big man trudging over the hill, a large strange rifle dangling from one arm, several belts of ammunition crisscrossing his chest. Parker saw them, moved close.

Scarabelli said, "What the hell is that?"

Parker set the gun down, said, "*Chauchat*." He paused, seemed to recite from memory: "French-issue eight-millimeter light-field automatic rifle. The lieutenant said it's mine now. Heavy thing, so they figured a big fellow oughta carry it."

Temple leaned down, saw a long magazine, said, "Machine gun."

Parker raised the heavy ammunition belts up over his head, eased them down in a pile, began to pull long magazines out of his pockets.

"Yeah, sort of. Supposed to fire two hundred fifty rounds a minute, but the clips only hold twenty bullets. Goes through 'em pretty quick, when it don't jam."

Scarabelli lifted one of the belts, said, "A hundred rounds in each of these damned things? Glad they didn't give it to me."

Parker began to sift through his backpack, said, "Don't count on it, Jersey. The lieutenant told me to pick two buddies, to help carry these belts and clips. I figure you ain't much of a shot with that Springfield, so I picked you, for one. When the clips run empty, we need to load 'em quick. That means we gotta stick together."

Temple said, "Well, that's no problem. I kinda hoped we'd stick together anyway."

Parker looked at him, shook his head. "Not you, Roscoe. I figure we need your rifle. Don't want you weighed down. You're the best shot in the company." The others had gathered, several men fingering the *chauchat*. Parker looked around, said, "Okay. Jersey is one. Irish, how 'bout you?"

Brian Murphy had been with the company from the beginning, a quiet man who seemed perpetually relaxed. Murphy was from New York, but carried none of Scarabelli's nervous chatter. Four generations of Murphy's family had been Marines, something that Murphy communicated with soft-spoken pride. Temple had been reluctant to talk about his grandfather around the Irishman, knew from experience that the most excited Murphy seemed to get was when he spoke of his own grandfather, who had served aboard Admiral David Farragut's flagship. According to Murphy, his grandfather had actually been alongside the Union hero when New Orleans had been captured, a claim that carried no bluster. Temple was impressed by that, appreciated Murphy's pride in his heritage. The two young men had arrived at Quantico around the same time, and both men had worked to overcome their devout loyalty to their family legacies before they could even become cordial. It had been Temple's first real lesson in what it meant to leave home and venture into a world much larger than north Florida. No matter how many of the old folks around Monticello still seemed to cherish a fight with the Yankees, and despite how much Temple had loved his grandfather, the old man's war was long past.

Murphy lifted one of the belts, tested the weight, said, "Sure thing, Dan. About the same as a regular bandolier. How many you want us to carry?"

"Two each. Two clips too. I'll carry the rest. Keep the clips full. And from what the lieutenant says, when I start shooting this thing, stay behind me. He says the French gave us these things because they don't work so well. It's liable to blow up."

Parker was not smiling, and Temple saw Scarabelli's eyes grow wide.

"Stay behind you. You can count on it, Mountain Man."

In the distance the men began to move, the shouts of the sergeants cutting across the hillside. Temple saw Briggs now, pointing to the row of backpacks.

"Vacation's over. Up, you grunts. Those damned rifles had better be clean. We got no time for anything but marching." He moved close to the *chauchat* gun, looked up at Parker, then at the rest of the gathering squad. "Listen up. If the big man goes down, it'll be up to one of you to grab this chatchat. Only one we got in the platoon, and we're damned sure not leaving it behind. The trucks are over the hill here. Let's move."

The backpacks were all in place, the rifles slung on shoulders. Temple touched the gas mask at his waist, the bayonet, saw Parker hoisting the *chauchat* up onto his shoulder. *If the big man goes down*. What a hell of a thing to say. He was angry now, staring at Briggs as he moved away up the hill. You barely know him, and you just say that like it doesn't matter. You bastard. He glanced at Parker, saw no expression on his face. Murphy and Scarabelli were helping each other, the bandoliers across their chests now, the backpacks going up, their rifles on their shoulders. Temple felt sympathy for Scarabelli, thought Parker could have picked another man, someone who's bigger. He moved up beside Scarabelli, said, "You okay?"

He expected some profane griping, but Scarabelli said, "Worry about yourself, Farm Boy. I don't mind. This way, I can get a close look at what a machine gun can do to those sons of bitches."

Near Retheuil—July 17, 1918

They had suffered the ride in the French *camions* for hours, the procession of trucks trudging slowly through roads thick with soldiers and vehicles moving in both directions. The trucks had

597

finally been halted, the men pouring out in grateful agony, every man bruised and bounced to nausea, bones still rattling from their ride. The daylight had faded quickly, dark clouds rolling over the roads, the men knowing only that they were marching through some kind of forest, great fat trees and thickets of dense brush, a frightening reminder of Belleau Wood. As the darkness settled over them, the rains came, hard and blinding, boots and uniforms quickly soaked. In the darkness, the men were forced to march single file, had moved down into the ditch beside the narrow forest roads. The roadways themselves were nearly impassable, packed with a slow-moving train of ambulances, troop trucks, and foot soldiers, French mostly, moving in both directions. In the driving rain, the darkness was absolute, and Temple obeyed Briggs' command, walked with one hand extended out in front of him, hooked into Murphy's belt, the man behind him holding tightly to Temple the same way. It was ridiculously slow progress, each man plodding through the tracks of the man before him, slow steps in deep mud.

He had no idea how much ground they had covered, could only guess that it had been dark for more than an hour. He stared at black nothing, had grown used to the rhythm of the march, kept his face toward the ground, his helmet tilted back just enough to block the rain from running down the back of his neck. Up on the road, the only sound came from the French, what Temple could only imagine to be the most graphic profanity, officers and men trying to move past each other, some advancing with the Marines, the others moving to the rear, desperately exhausted men who endured the shouts and curses of the men sent to relieve them.

There had been no time for food, not even for the tins of beef they carried in their packs. Temple had seen nothing of officers, had no idea where they were marching, how long they would do this. Sergeant Briggs was in front of him somewhere, and Temple knew that Briggs didn't know anything either, was simply marching as they all marched, this chain of blind men joined together by the grip of their fingers.

The hours had flowed past him like the mud under his feet,

the sounds up on the road washed out of his mind. He realized now that the rain had stopped, his mind trying to focus, breaking the dull fog in his brain. His eyes were closed, and he blinked, felt the sting from the sweat that rolled down his face, his shirt still as wet as when the storm had soaked him. His arm extended out toward Murphy's belt in numbing stiffness, and he wanted to shift the rifle to the other shoulder, but he dared not break the rhythm, dared not release his aching fingers from Murphy's belt. Murphy suddenly stopped in front of him, and Temple ran into him, the man behind him doing the same. It had been like that all night long, sudden jolts that woke the men from their walking sleep. Temple waited for Murphy to move again, heard something up ahead, a voice in English.

"Up, into the road!"

The line surged forward, Murphy climbing out of the wide ditch, Temple following blindly along. The ground beneath him was hard now, the mud in his boots squeezing between his toes, his socks cold and rough. He saw a flicker of light, tried to focus his eyes, saw the hulking shadow of a house, a few yards from the road.

"Column halt!"

He stopped again, sagged under the weight of his gear, felt one knee give way, caught himself, his hand still hooked in Murphy's belt. Murphy grunted, and Temple pried his fingers out of the wet leather, was shocked by the stab of pain in his knuckles. He worked the stiffness out of his fingers, said in a whisper, "Sorry."

"Quiet!"

He jumped, startled that Briggs was beside him, the sergeant moving slowly along the line. The door to the house suddenly opened, a shaft of light blinding him, and Temple caught a glimpse of men, officers, moving through the door. There were muted shouts, coming from inside the house, and Temple tried to hear the words, heard one man above the rest, a violent tirade. The voices grew quiet again, and Temple was awake now, took a long deep breath. He focused on the direction of the doorway, his curiosity holding his exhausted brain on that one place, hoping for another glimpse of the men inside.

He heard a voice, Murphy turning toward him, a low whisper.

"The only ones who are allowed to yell like that are commanders. Must be headquarters."

"Which headquarters? Brigade? Ours?"

Murphy said nothing, and Temple thought, Of course, he has no idea.

The door opened again, four men emerging, low talk, heavy footsteps in the mud. They stepped out into the road, close beside the column, and one man left the group, hurried past Temple, moved toward the front of the column. Murphy said, "Gotta be an aide. Officers don't run."

They stood in silence for a long moment, and now the footsteps came again, the runner returning, followed by another man. They stopped close to the group of officers, and another man emerged through the lighted doorway, seemed to stomp his way out to the road.

Temple felt excited, leaned close to Murphy, whispered, "Something's happening."

"Shh. Listen."

Temple strained to hear one man's harsh breathless whispering.

"Major Turrill is up ahead, sir. These men are Marines. First of the Fifth."

Another man spoke now, seemed out of breath as well, and Temple thought, One of the runners.

"Sir, I'm Lieutenant Colvin."

"What are your orders, Lieutenant?"

"To march, sir."

"Son of a bitch! You think that's funny?"

The voice cracked through the darkness, and Temple felt a cold ripple on his skin.

Colvin said, "No, sir. General, Major Turrill was ordered by Colonel Feland to seek out the French guides along this road. Sir, we haven't seen anyone who appears to be a guide."

The word rocketed into Temple's brain. General. He strained to see in the dark, caught the glow from a cigarette, could see only shapes, heard the hard voice again.

"Colonel Feland is right here, Lieutenant. These are

apparently your men, Colonel. What the hell's going on?"

There was another voice now, higher.

"As I've been saying, sir, we were supposed to rendezvous with General Mangin's aides at the farm. I was surprised to find you here instead. All I know is that the Fourth Brigade is to advance along this road, and Major Turrill's battalion is to assume the front line. Do you have further orders, sir?"

"The Moroccans should be in position on our left, the First Division is north of the Moroccans. Mangin's people haven't bothered to give us anything but maps. We have almost no intelligence, no chance to reconnoiter the ground. All right, Colonel. Send word to Major Turrill. Send these men through the woods to the northeast, and assume position on the eastern edge of these woods. All I've been told is that there's a wide swath of open ground, farm country out to the north. Colonel, your objective is the Beaurepaire farm. You have the map. Get it into the hands of Major Turrill. His people will lead the way. He has to keep in touch with the Moroccans on his left. Once there, you will make a right wheel, and maintain contact with the rest of the division on your right."

"A right wheel, sir?"

"You heard me, Colonel. Damned complicated maneuver under fire. But we have no choice. If I had been given some reliable intelligence about the ground out there . . . but I suppose Mangin's people think they have better things to do. I've ordered an ammo dump to be placed up ahead. It's the one order tonight that I know has been obeyed. I'm making damned sure these men get some grenades this time."

"Understood, sir. Lieutenant Colvin, get your men moving. I'll go to the head of the column, find Major Turrill, and try to find out what happened to the damned guides."

One man emerged from the group, moved quickly toward the front of the column, and Temple thought, That's Colvin. He stared at the others, felt the excitement, so close to the power, to the men who gave the orders, Colonel Feland, and an actual general. Who? He realized that the Marines in the road had gathered silently, were listening as he was. He heard Scarabelli now.

601

"Moroccans? What the hell?"

Temple thought a moment, said, "What's a Moroccan?"

"From Morocco, you dumb—"

"Shut up! Column in line! Prepare to march!"

The voice came from Briggs, and Temple heard a quick shout in front, the line beginning to move. He glanced up, saw stars, a sliver of a moon, realized he could see enough of Murphy's shadow that he didn't need to hold the man's belt.

They marched for a few minutes, then turned off the road, stepped down through mud, a canopy of treetops above them. There was still a trail, and he followed close behind Murphy, matched the rhythm of his steps, heard low voices now, the column stopping again. He realized men were in the woods around them, saw several dots of light from cigarettes.

"Here. One per man!"

The voice came from up ahead, and the column moved forward slowly. He saw a glint of light, stacks of metal boxes, bandoliers hanging from the arms of a man beside the trail. He realized a truck was parked close by, saw movement, the sound of more metal, and the man said, "Take one each!"

He took the belt of bullets, slung it over his shoulder, heard another man farther along.

"Four per man, more if you can carry 'em."

He heard the rattle of steel, lids coming off heavy crates. Murphy reached out, and Temple did the same, felt the cold hard steel pressed into his hands.

"Four per man. More if you can carry 'em."

He hooked the grenades on his shirt, reached for two more, hooked them on as well, the weight pulling on him. Murphy began to move away, and Temple thought of Parker, the big man toting the heavy gun, and Scarabelli, all the extra weight.

"Give me two more."

"Here you go. Go get 'em, Grunt."

He caught up with Murphy, the grenades bouncing against his chest. The tension was familiar now, the way he had felt the morning of the advance into Belleau Wood. The ammunition meant they were close to something, and he tried to remember the words of the officers, realized, They probably wouldn't want me to hear, but it was dark, and it seemed aw-fully confused. And the general was angry. He felt a stab of fear. Generals shouldn't be angry.

He could hear his own breathing, realized the column was moving more quickly now, the trees around him more visible, the darkness slipping away. The memories of Belleau Wood flooded through him, and he thought of the wheat field, lying flat, the voice of Dugan . . . Dugan, his hand in the air. . . .

The air exploded around him, blinding flashes of light, the column seeming to collapse, Temple pushed down hard, the grenades punching his chest. He heard screams, shock and fear and the flashes continued, hard blasts deafening him. He felt a hand on his shirt, pulling him up, shouts in his ear, "Get moving! Keep moving!"

He staggered to his feet, off balance from the weight of the ammo, saw men rising, moving with him. The blasts were rolling all through the woods, great bursts of fire, white streaks of light slicing out away from him. He realized now, the fire was outgoing, a line of big guns anchored in the woods. He braced himself against the roar of sounds, hard ringing in his ears, the concussion jolting him, some men still falling from the thunder that blew through the column. He could see out on both sides, the fire of the artillery sending the streaks away, ripping the air with blinding light. The guns seemed to extend forever, far out into the woods, dozens, maybe hundreds of guns, all launching their terrible power toward the enemy. The fear was gone now, erased by the strength of the artillery, and he felt the pride, felt their power inside of him, driving him forward, driving all of them toward the enemy.

He saw more of the sky, the stars fading, realized the trees were thinning out. Along the trail, men were pointing the way, waving them on, the entire column moving forward at double time, exhausted, hungry men caught up by the pure energy of their momentum. Temple ran past the guide, followed Murphy, realized they were in the open now, a vast wide field that stretched far beyond the dim light. The streaks of fire from the artillery still rolled over them, painting the sky. He ran with the others through tall grass, glanced up, thought, We won't

603

need guides now. The artillery is all firing out . . . that way. And that's where the enemy is.

The column was stopped, and he felt his breathing in hard gasps, bent over for a moment, rested his hands on his knees. The grass was nearly waist-high, the tops just brushing against his face. He stared at it, his eyes opening wide. The exhaustion and hunger were suddenly swept out of his thoughts. He could see now. It was a wheat field.

37

TEMPLE

4:35 a.m., July 18, 1918

It was nothing like Belleau Wood, the field a flat plain that spread out toward the horizon. The forest they had marched through was still on their left, tall trees, some with bare tops, trunks broken and blasted, but the destruction wasn't fresh, the shattered wood dark, no leaves on the fallen branches. The men were moving slightly away from the trees, and he glanced at the glow on the horizon, thought, We're going north. Around him, the men stepped through the tall wheat, no one talking. The artillery was still firing, the air above them streaked with sharp ribbons of light. As they moved farther from the trees, he heard the sound of rifle fire coming from the left, machine guns now, a fight erupting in the woods itself. The faces around him began to turn that way, the voices behind him directing them forward.

"Keep moving. Watch for the stone walls."

It was the first real instructions he had heard, and he scanned the front, realized the artillery had stopped firing behind them. The fight in the woods was growing louder, and he glanced that way, saw nothing, the battle invisible, ghostly. Down the line to the left, the men closer to the woods seemed to bend slightly, bracing themselves for the enemy fire that had not yet come. Temple stared that way, then looked at Briggs, stepping through the wheat in front of them, the thick man staring ahead, ignoring the battle.

"Eyes front! That's the Moroccans! Keep moving!"

Temple obeyed the order, stared ahead, thought, The Moroccans. The word had no meaning to him, and he felt stupid, angry at his own ignorance. Far out in the field in front of him, the wheat was rippling, soft green waves, the first breeze

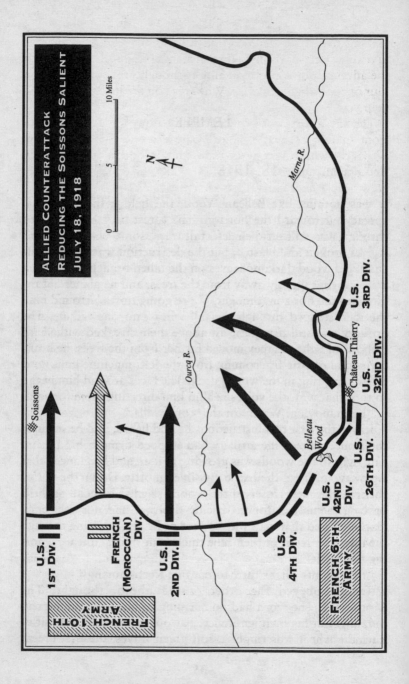

ALLIED COUNTERATTACK
REDUCING THE SOISSONS SALIENT
JULY 18, 1918

10 Miles

5

0

N

Marne R.

Ourcq R.

Soissons

Château-Thierry

Belleau Wood

U.S. 3RD DIV.

U.S. 32ND DIV.

U.S. 26TH DIV.

U.S. 42ND DIV.

U.S. 4TH DIV.

U.S. 2ND DIV.

FRENCH (MOROCCAN) DIV.

U.S. 1ST DIV.

FRENCH 10TH ARMY

FRENCH 6TH ARMY

drifting over them. He glanced toward the woods again, the invisible battle rolling forward, seeming to move with the advance of the Marines, and he thought of Belleau Wood, a blur of agonizing memories. Whoever you are, Moroccans, God help you.

The sky above was growing lighter now, the ground out in front of them clearly visible. He saw a sharp ravine cutting across the wheat field to the right, and beyond, a fat stone wall. The ravine cut across in front of them, narrow, then widened, grew deeper as it wound toward the woods.

"Straight ahead! Get across the cut. Get to the wall!"

Temple realized it was Lieutenant Colvin, behind him, off to the left. More officers were calling out, directing their men, and Colvin said, "Don't wait in the cut! Keep moving!"

Temple stared at the ravine, two hundred yards away, the wall beyond, and beyond that, more walls, jutting off in different directions, the boundaries of more wheat fields. The ravine was thick with short brush, only a few yards across, a gentle slope down and then up. The distance was closing, and he glanced again toward the woods, saw that the ground was falling away to the left now, the woods funneling down into broken ground, more ravines, brush, and rocks. He reached the edge of the ravine, stepped down into soft dirt, the men around him moving down with him. They were through the brush quickly, began to climb up again, and Temple punched the toes of his boots into the soft sand, reached up, one hand on the hard flat ground, pulled himself out. He saw Scarabelli, laboring with the ammunition belts, and he moved that way, but Parker was there, the big man reaching back, pulling Scarabelli up by the hand. Murphy was right behind him, and Temple reached down. "Take my hand!"

Murphy glanced up at him, unsmiling, his hand out, and Temple pulled him up, saw Parker looking at him, a slow nod, thank-you. Temple turned toward the front again, could see the network of stone walls, crisscrossing out to the right, in front of the right flank of the battalion. Down to the left, the woods were thinning, then no trees at all, the ravine spreading out into a wide patch of rough ground, the machine-gun and rifle fire rolling through the last stands of trees. He saw movement now, men emerging from the thinning woods, the distinct gray of the Germans, like so many ants, flowing back through their chopped-up ground. He stared that way, could see men stopping to fire, some of the Marines on that end of the line firing as well, picking targets in the low brush. Temple glanced around, tried to find Colvin, thought, The fight's over there! We should move that way! But Briggs was out in front of them again, waiting for the bulk of the men to rise up from the ravine, his voice cutting through the sounds of the battle.

"This way! Eyes front! Let's go!"

Temple obeyed, but couldn't ignore the Germans, gauged the distance, four hundred yards maybe. They're in the open! Dammit, I can shoot 'em from here!

"Easy, men! Keep moving!" Colvin was behind him, seemed to read his thoughts. "The enemy's in front of us. Straight ahead!"

Temple felt a sharp breath of air, his helmet tilting slightly, his heart jumping at the familiar sound. The air around him began to sing, cut by zips, a dull pop close by, one man suddenly tumbling forward. Briggs was still shouting, waving them forward, and Temple stared ahead, could see flickers of light, the enemy rising up from behind the spiderweb of stone walls. The sounds were growing in his head, familiar, the same as that one awful day, another field of wheat, but he could not hold the thought, heard the sharp thump of bullet and flesh, more men going down. He felt himself curling down, his head hunched low into his shoulders, his helmet tilted forward. He tried to ignore the hard grunts and sharp cries, blending now with the growing sounds of the guns in front of them.

Far off to the right, there was a new sound, but it wasn't guns. It was a low steady roar. He tried to ignore it as well, but the sound was strange, louder now, and he looked that way, saw low clouds of black smoke, and on that end of the line, men began to raise their rifles, pumping them up and down, seeming to ignore the death that filled the air around them. The roar was steady and growing louder still, the smoke drifting across the wheat field, the black fog sliding past him. He tried to see through the smoke, the rumble and cough of the engines louder still, and he saw movement, a fat gray hulk, rolling through the wheat field, the cheers of the men obliterated by the roar. His curiosity churned into excitement, the great iron beast rolling clearly into view. It was a tank.

They came in a line, and he counted at least a dozen, rolling slowly across the field in front of the advance of the Marines, belching their black smoke, rumbling and plowing their way over the uneven ground. Temple still moved forward, automatic steps, the men around him all staring in pure wonder at the mammoth machines, far bigger than Temple had ever imagined. The tanks were spreading into line in front of them, and the Marines moved up close behind, matching their advance. The tanks moved forward at a slow and steady pace, carving wide tracks through the dirt, their thick exhaust forming a smoke screen, drifting over the Marines in a stinking fog. Temple ignored the burning in his eyes, was only a few yards behind one of the great machines, tried to see the details on the tank itself. There were guns protruding from ports along each side, two fat cannon aimed toward the front. He wanted to run up and around the machine, thought, How many men inside? But Briggs was in front of him, the sergeants still in front all down the line, holding the men back, keeping them to the rear of the tanks, taking advantage of the obvious protection the powerful machines would give them. The roar of the engines was deafening, but he could see past them, small gaps opening in the black exhaust. The first stone wall was only a hundred yards in front of the tank, and Temple realized the bullets were still in the air, could see sparks on the tanks, the German gunners firing uselessly at the great fat targets. Suddenly the cannon on the tank erupted, a flash of smoke and dirt at the wall, the tank halting, firing again. The wall was blasted into rubble, and Temple could see bodies of men scattered around the opening, men jumping up, pouring back from the wall, from their protection. With a great belch of black smoke, the tank began to move again toward the gap. Temple heard the men around him cheering, and he raised his hand, shouted with them, glorious victory. He followed the tank toward the wall, could see past, the open ground beyond, German soldiers running through the wheat. The Marines began to line the wall now, some stopping to fire, propped up on the stone, taking careful aim. Temple moved out beside the tank, dropped down, laid his rifle up on a fat rock, realized there was a man down on the far side of the blasted wall. Temple looked at the man, saw the gray uniform, some kind of cross on the man's chest, realized now the man had no head. He felt the shock, closed his eyes for a brief second, my God. But Briggs was shouting again, "Up! Don't stop! Keep moving!"

Temple looked out to the open ground, German soldiers disappearing, dropping down into cover, some falling, shot down before they got that far. Colvin moved out close to the tank, waved the men forward, shouting toward them, his voice drowned out by the roar from the tank as it moved again.

The Marines followed, surging up and over the wall, and Temple was behind the tank again, could see the Germans beginning to fire from their cover, the unmistakable flecks and flashes from the machine guns, firing now from every low place, every clump of brush. The wheat field had ended, and there were more ravines, the ground in front of him turning uneven, the wheat fields and stone fences now spreading out to the right. The tank fired its cannon again, a deafening blast, Temple ducking in reflex. The fire from the Germans still flew past him, the sparks still striking the tank. Temple was only a few yards behind, realized the tank had stopped again, and he halted, braced himself for the cannon to fire. He saw Briggs, up beside the machine, confusion on the sergeant's face. A great mouth suddenly opened in the rear of the tank, and Temple stared in stunned surprise, saw a man emerge, his face blackened, no helmet. There were more men inside, some staring out at the Marines. The first man waved his arms, was shouting in French, Briggs now shouting back at him.

"What the hell? Get moving!"

The man suddenly disappeared back into the tank, the hatch closing again. Briggs moved around in front of the tank, began to shout again, the sergeant pointing his rifle into the gun port.

"Move, damn you!"

The tank was suddenly silent, the black smoke drifting away, the great powerful beast motionless, dead. Men were gathering, some crouching low, using the tank as cover, and Briggs looked at Temple, then the others.

"The son of a bitch is busted! Come on! We can't just sit here."

The air above them screamed, the blast impacting fifty yards behind the tank. Briggs shouted again, "Let's go! The artillery's getting the range. Gonna blow this thing to hell! Double time!"

Briggs waited for the men to move forward, was out in front again. Temple ran with the others, felt suddenly naked, helpless, glanced back at the tank, saw another artillery shell impacting close beside it. Now another shell hit, just behind, and Temple stopped, frozen, knew what was coming. The shell screamed past him, the perfect strike, the explosion buried deep into the tank itself. The machine was a ball of flame, seemed to collapse, one side falling away. Temple closed his eyes, thought of the Frenchman, Why did you go back inside? You could have escaped . . . a hand was pulling him now, and he turned, saw Parker.

"Let's move, Roscoe! Gotta get to that cut-up ground."

Temple followed, saw the ground falling away, clusters of brush, rock, open patches of bare white dirt. The Marines were moving on their own now, the line breaking up, men slipping through the brush. There was a burst of firing from somewhere ahead, and the men began to drop, some lying flat, answering, firing at glimpses of targets, or at nothing but the brush in front of them. He followed Parker, saw Murphy and Scarabelli crouching behind a fat rock, and Parker stopped beside them, raised the *chauchat* gun, said, "Find me a target! There's machine-gun nests all through this stuff!"

Temple crouched behind the rock, peered out under the rim of his helmet, the rock suddenly shattering in front of him.

Scarabelli shouted, "There! I saw the bastard. That brush . . . two hundred yards . . . just to the right!"

Parker had the gun up on the rock, said, "I got him."

The *chauchat* fired, a strange chattering sound, the magazine

611

quickly emptied. Scarabelli was staring forward, said, "You hit something! They're moving. Roscoe! You see 'em?"

Temple laid the rifle on the rock, sighted in on the clump of brush, waited, saw movement, a glimpse of gray, fired. In the brush, the German suddenly stood up, seemed to run, then fell out into the open ground. Parker shouted, "Again, Roscoe! There's more of 'em!"

Temple aimed, saw the flickers of light, the machine gun firing again, the rock in front of him splintering, sharp zips overhead. Temple lowered his head, waited for the machine gun to pause. Parker had reloaded, fired the *chauchat* again, and Temple fired as well, emptied his rifle.

Behind him, a loud voice, "Go! You got them. Advance!"

Temple was surprised by the sound, saw it was Colvin, the lieutenant suddenly up past them, moving through the low brush, his pistol in his hand. Temple stood, waited a brief second, saw Parker grab the *chauchat*, more men rising up from the rocks and brush, following the lieutenant. Temple began to run, staring hard at the brush, saw movement again, men with rifles suddenly appearing, most scampering away, using the rough ground for cover. No, we didn't get them all.

The machine gun opened up again, men tumbling down into cover. Temple dropped down behind a small bush, too small, and he clenched tightly from inside, tried to make himself a smaller target. The men were still trying to advance, the gun spraying the air, sweeping across the patches of sandy ground. He waited again, tried to slide the rifle forward, realized, You *didn't reload*. The machine gun continued to fire, and he saw men crawling past him. The bullets chopped the sand close beside him, freezing him, one hand on the ammo belt. Dammit! The machine gun was firing away from him now, and Temple glanced at the bayonet. No, you'll never get there. He peered up quickly, saw a wide patch of sandy ground in front of the brush, thought, Forty yards. A long damned way. Men were still crawling forward, the machine-gunner seeking targets all through the brush. The gun sprayed the air above him again, and Temple waited, heard a sharp cry, a man hit a few yards to one side.

A voice cut across the open ground, "Somebody kill that son of a bitch!"

Temple tried to roll over, eased his hand up to the magazine, put a bullet in, slid the bolt closed. He leaned out slightly, tried to see, but his cover was no cover at all, no room for him to aim the rifle. He felt a sweating rage, the gunner firing again, cutting the air, ripping the brush. One man seemed to wait as he did, was up suddenly, running forward, dropping down again. The gunner tore the ground around the man, and he waited for the man to move again, thought, If you draw his fire, I'll try to get a shot. But the man did not move at all, and Temple understood now. Dammit! Son of a bitch! He looked at the rifle in his hands, furious frustration. He tried to shift himself, the grenades on his shirt punching him from below. He froze again, put a hand on one of the grenades. Forty yards. The les-sons were there, all those days of training, screaming sergeants, men defy-ing their training by throwing grenades like baseballs. You couldn't ever hit that damned target, Roscoe. They passed you along anyway because no one could beat you with the rifle. Well, dammit, if there's a time . . . it's now.

He tugged at the grenade, the clip held by the loop on his shirt. He gripped it hard, his hand shaking, stared at it for a brief second. Please. Just once, let me hit something. Just one good throw. The gunner had paused, and Temple thought, He's looking for a target, or reloading again. All out through the low brush, men were calling out, the unmistakable voice of Briggs.

"Keep moving forward! Stay low. He can't get all of us!"

Another man rose, scrambled forward a few yards, the gun-ner finding him before he could drop down. The man tumbled forward, slid into the sand, the gunner now firing all across the stretch of ground. Briggs shouted again, "Goddammit, enough of this! Charge that bastard!"

Temple looked behind him, saw more men coming up from the brush, saw Briggs now, the glint of the man's bayonet.

"Charge him! Now!"

Briggs ran right past Temple, more men following, and Temple rose, saw the flashes from the gun, the men simply cut down, could see smoke rising from the brush, quick movement, forty yards. He heard the click of metal, the machine gun reloading, stood, jelly in his legs, took one step forward, threw the grenade. He watched it arcing high, turning slowly in the air, his hand already reaching for another. But the grenade disappeared down into the brush, and he heard a shout, the shock of the gunner, the man knowing what it was, knowing he had a second left, one second of his life. . . .

The brush erupted, the gun itself tossed up, pieces of metal tumbling out, a burst of smoke. Temple ran forward, held the rifle in both hands, the bayonet ready, reached the machine gun, searched frantically for movement in the smoke, for any sign of the gunner. But there was no motion at all, the gray smoke drifting, suspended in the brush, the bodies ripped, bloodied, one man faceless, an arm gone. Men were already moving up past him, shouting to him, "Good job!"

"You got the bastards!"

"Let's move!"

The sounds of the fight were out in front now, more cuts in the low ground hiding the Marines who still advanced, who sought out the machine-gun nests, grenades and bayonets and *chauchat* guns working alongside the rifles. He looked back across the brushy ground, saw a dozen bodies down, most lying in the open, bloody sand beneath them. The men were moving past him and he scanned their faces, saw most of them looking back at him, more words, sharp nods. The faces were familiar, so many of the men from his platoon, but he felt the fear now, began to move back, heard a man shout to him, "Let's go! This way, Private!"

Still he searched the faces, began to look down, stood among the men who would not get up, saw the one man who had made it closest to the machine gun, his face now staring up, the same look Temple had seen on so many, the empty peacefulness. It was Colvin. He moved past the body of the lieutenant, more men, familiar, saw the stripes on one man's sleeve, knew without seeing the man's face that it was Briggs, the powerful man now lifeless, lying facedown in the sand. He heard more voices, men still rising up, some tending to wounds, one man helping another to a shady place in the brush. Still he searched, and now, from behind a low flat rock, he saw Parker, the man

614

hoisting the *chauchat*, reaching down, helping Scarabelli to his feet. Temple felt a cold turn in his stomach, suddenly felt like crying. Thank God. Thank God.

He heard a shout, saw Murphy waving his arms. "I need a medic! Wounded men over here!"

A wave of Marines suddenly rolled down across the low hills behind them, flowing into the rough ground. It was the second battalion, the second line who had crossed the wheat field behind them. Officers were there now, ordering their first aid carriers to the wounded.

"Keep moving! The fight's ahead!"

An officer stopped close to him, said, "Good work! The Huns are running! Fall into this line. We'll handle the wounded."

Parker had the *chauchat*, said to Murphy, "Let's go!"

Murphy was there now, and Scarabelli said, "Who threw the grenade? Son of a bitch oughta get a medal."

Temple didn't respond, said, "They got the lieutenant. And Briggs."

Murphy moved past him, scanned the ground.

"They got a bunch of us. Whitbeck . . . Christ, known him for years." He paused, stared to the front. "There's machine-gun fire coming from over that ridge. We gotta go."

Temple looked that way, could see the men flowing up over a low rise, disappearing into more low brush. The fight was still rattling all through the rough ground, down to the left as well. The flow of men from the second battalion was all around them now, and Temple said, "We gotta go."

Parker put a hand on his shoulder. "Who threw the grenade?"

Scarabelli adjusted the ammunition belts across his chest, said, "It sure as hell wasn't you, Farm Boy. You couldn't hit your mama's barn from ten feet away."

Temple looked at Parker, said, "I'm glad you're okay. I guess we oughta get going."

The land was flat again, the stone fences converging on a distant farmhouse, a scattering of small buildings, steady fire cutting the air all across the open ground.

"Let's go! No stopping!"

615

Temple felt fire in his lungs, stopped, tried to breathe, saw men doing the same, more screaming from the sergeants, hands pushing him from behind.

"Let's go! To the wall!"

They had trudged through another wheat field, German riflemen firing from every direction, hidden in the wheat. But the Germans did not make a stand, and as the Marines moved forward the Germans pulled back, the Marines stopping to fire, some catching the men who ran before them, quick work of the bayonets.

They crested a low hill, a rolling undulation in the wheat, and Temple could see the wall clearly, a solid line of rifle fire rippling across the top of the stone. In front of him, a dozen men seemed to crumble, some curling up, grunts and short screams. Temple dropped flat into the wheat, stared ahead blindly, laid his rifle on his forearms, began to crawl, sliding forward, inching toward the rifle fire. Around him, they moved as he moved, slid-ing forward through the wheat. There had been no help from the tanks for a while now, the great hulks staying away from the rougher ground, the sharp drop-offs that sent one tank over on its side. Temple had been stunned by how many of them simply quit, grinding to a halt, silent tombs for the men who inexplicably stayed inside. He stopped, straightened his aching arms, lay flat in the wheat, his breathing coming in short hard gasps. He rolled over on his back, tried to find some way to aim the rifle. But there were no targets, the wheat thick in front of him, the sound of the German fire ripping through the air, slicing and zipping through the wheat close above him. The Germans were firing in a steady chatter, the staccato rifle fire popping through the steady chatter of machine guns. All through the wheat, men were calling out, sergeants trying to gather their squads, pulling their men forward. But every man stayed flat on the ground, every man realizing that any target, any movement above the wheat, would bring a solid wave of German fire. Around him, men were trying to return fire, but the stone wall was perfect cover, the Germans firing at will, invincible behind their stone barrier. Temple lay still, thought of the grenades, but the wall was too far, still a hundred yards, maybe more. He had seen enough of the wall to know it extended out in both directions, and that in the wheat field, a hundred men, maybe many more were lying flat, pinned down, helpless.

"Eyes to the front!"

The words meant nothing to him, some officer screaming in a panic, and now another voice close beside him, Parker.

"They might be coming, Roscoe. They know they got us."

He felt stupid now, the frantic order suddenly clear. Eyes to the front. If the Germans came out, charged the field, we wouldn't know it until they were on us. The rifle fire seemed to slow, and Parker was up on his elbows, working the *chauchat*, jerking hard on the bolt, fired a short burst toward the wall. The gun suddenly stopped, and Parker said, "Jammed! Keeps jamming! Jersey, where are you?"

There was movement in the wheat, a helmet creeping forward, the air cut by a new wave of firing from the wall. Temple said, "No! Gino! Stay down!"

Scarabelli lay flat, turned his head, and Temple saw his eyes, Scarabelli grunting, "I'm not going anywhere. What the hell you want, Mountain Man?"

"Chatchat's jammed. I need another magazine."

"What the hell are you shooting at?"

Parker continued to pound on the gun, pulled his bayonet from his belt, probed and poked the breech of the *chauchat*.

"Anything that moves. You better do the same. The Huns may charge us."

Scarabelli raised his head slightly, stared ahead into the wheat.

"Bastards." He rolled to one side, pulled a magazine from his pocket, tossed it forward. Parker grabbed it, kept the bayonet working at the chauchat. The big man jerked at the bolt again, the breech opening, said, "The lieutenant was right. This is a piece of junk."

He worked the bolt, slid the new magazine into place, and suddenly there was an explosion of rifle fire, and a new sound, loud voices, screams, coming from the wall. Temple felt his heart freeze, heard the high-pitched shouts of the officer.

"They're coming! Fire! Fire!"

Temple raised his head slightly, could see through narrow slits in the wheat, saw men behind the wall, some standing, one man tumbling, falling over into the wheat. He rose farther, heard another man shout, "They're not coming! What the hell . . . ?"

The men began to peer up through the wheat, and Temple raised the rifle, saw a German standing behind the wall, aiming his rifle out to the left, some target back behind the wall. Temple found the man in his sight, eased his finger on the trigger, but the German disappeared, seemed to fall straight down. The Marines began to rise up slowly, every man ready, some firing at targets behind the wall. Temple scanned the top of the rock, looked for targets, the patches of gray, saw something different, blue instead, and egg-shaped helmets.

"Wait! They're French!"

More men could see what Temple saw, the fight behind the wall growing, a surge of troops pouring in from behind the Germans. The Marines were up now, sergeants shouting, "Move! Charge!"

Temple climbed up out of the wheat, ran forward, stumbled over a body, bloody khaki, could see dead men scattered all through the wheat. He picked his way, kept his eyes on the fight rolling across the ground behind the wall, heard machine guns in the distance, the air still cut by German gunners. He was close to the wall now, crouched low, men coming up around him, heard Scarabelli.

"What the hell . . . ?"

There was a confused jumble of hand-to-hand fighting, the Germans trying to escape, some running back toward the farmhouses, pursued by the blue uniforms, bayonets cutting down the men who couldn't run. There was almost no gunfire now, the sounds human, metallic, cries and shouts. He saw another cluster of blue uniforms emerging from the left, close to the wall, men running up in front of the Marines, shouting into their faces, meaningless words, odd cries, waving them across. Temple stared in wide-eyed shock. The uniforms were French.

618

But the faces were black. He heard the word now, echoing all along the wall.

"Moroccans."

The German defenses could not withstand the hard push into the western flank of the salient, and by midafternoon, the Marines were firmly in control of the Verte Feuille farm, their first major objective of the attack. Far behind the fight, the chaos and confusion of troop and supply movements had continued, but by early afternoon, the division's artillery companies had begun to move forward, and the Marines were relieved to be joined by their own machine-gun companies, whose Hotchkiss guns were more effective against the German network of Maxim nests. Though the tanks continued to open the way for several advance movements, by dark, most of the tanks were out of action, either destroyed by German artillery or more often, rendered useless by mechanical failure. But the Marines could not simply rest at the farm. Under orders to wheel their battalions to the east, the attack was to resume, the exhausted infantry and Marines of the Second Division continuing their push. By nighttime, Temple and his squad had become part of a drive that included not only the Moroccans to their left, but beyond, the American First Division, who had accomplished as much as their comrades to their south. With darkness finally bringing the attack to a halt, the Germans had been pushed eastward, forced to retreat across an area several miles deep. In the twilight, the Second Division was scattered across a wide front, fights still erupting from stubborn pockets of the enemy. The Marines pressed forward, no one clear on exactly where they were to go. Several companies strayed into the Moroccan lines; others stumbled into the positions where the infantry regiments were supposed to be. With few officers to guide them, and the confusion of the landscape, the Marines were drifting too far north of where the headquarters maps had directed them. With the sun setting, Temple and the men around him found themselves at the outskirts of the village of Chaudon. The Germans decided not to make a fight, and the Marines, alongside several units of Moroccan soldiers, pressed straight through the town. Finally, with darkness quieting the fields, the battalion comman-ders were able to catch up to their men. As their advance was ordered to a halt, the Marines discovered a network of old German trench works, east of the town, blessed cover should the enemy begin shelling them in the darkness.

The trench was deep and narrow with several inches of mud lining the bottom. The smells were thick and musty, decay and filth and the stale odor of death. Overhead, old sandbags lay scattered, bits of smashed timbers tossed about, short coils of barbed wire lying in hidden clumps of brush. As the Marines filed into their bivouac for the night, Temple could see it was not a place that anyone had used in a long time.

He squatted, kept his backside above the mud, could see through the shadows as other men scooped at the mud trying to find a patch of dry ground. Scarabelli was across from him, the trench wide enough for two men to sit facing each other. The small man had been surprisingly quiet, and for once Temple was grateful that Scarabelli seemed to share the crushing exhaustion that kept them all quiet. When the men spoke at all, it was low and subdued, grunts and curses, the trench now filling as tightly as there was room for men to sit. Some began to call out names, trying to find their own, some attempt at bringing the units closer together. Temple felt the agony creeping through his knees, put one hand down into the mud, heard Scarabelli say, "Might as well sit, Farm Boy. Not so bad once you're down in it."

Temple surrendered to the inevitable, slid his feet out, easing the pain in his knees, lowered himself down, his pants sinking into the wetness. He had no energy to fight it, dropped down all the way now, the mud nearly covering his legs. He leaned back, felt soft dirt against the side of the trench, the brim of his helmet causing a small landslide down the back of his shirt. He was too tired to react.

"Simmons? Carrouthers?"

There was silence for a moment, no one responding. The voice came from down the trench, far too loud, hard whispers quieting the man. Temple could see the crouching shadow, the man stepping toward him, and he stopped, his voice still loud.

"Any officers? Lieutenant McClellan? Sarge?"

Silence again, and the man was a few yards away, moved closer still. There was a bright flicker of a match, someone lighting a cigarette, and Temple saw the man's face now, a brief glimpse of terror, no helmet on a bloody head.

"Sarge?"

"Put the match out!" The command came from Parker, close beside Temple. "Sit down, Marine. There's no officers here."

"There's gotta be. What are we supposed to do now?"

Parker reached up, grabbed the man's shirt, dragged him down, said in a hard whisper, "We're supposed to sit down and be quiet. You wounded?"

"I . . . I don't know. My helmet's gone. Dropped my rifle."

The voice was young, nearly childlike, and Parker leaned forward, a low call aimed down the trench.

"First aid? Any medics?"

Silence again, and Parker said, "Sit quiet, boy. Somebody'll be along soon."

They sat in silence for several minutes, and Temple felt the ground rumble beneath him, a roll of thunder drifting past the trench. The rumbling came again, closer now, the man beside Parker crying out.

"What's happening? Where's the lieutenant?"

Parker leaned toward him, said, "He'll be here soon. He said for you to . . . be quiet. There oughta be some rations up here soon."

"You an officer?"

Parker didn't respond, and after a moment said, "You'll be okay. Just sit quiet. You just need some rations."

The word drilled into Temple, *rations*, his brain focusing on the hollow chasm in his gut. They sat in dark silence again, the artillery barrage a constant rumble, aimed at some distant target.

After a long quiet moment, Scarabelli said, "Pretty amazing watching those Moroccans. Good damned fighters. Never seen Frenchmen fight like that."

Another voice came through the darkness, down to the left.

"I heard they enjoy it. They don't shoot much. Rifle's nothing

621

more than the butt end of a bayonet. Vicious sons of bitches. Cut a man to pieces for the fun of it."

"Glad they're on our side."

Temple heard a commotion down the trench, whispers flowing up toward them.

"Rations! Food carriers are here!"

Scarabelli said, "I'll be damned. You were right, Mountain Man. Maybe you *oughta* be an officer."

Parker said, "Jersey, they were either gonna get some food up here, or I was gonna send you back to get it. You just got lucky, that's all."

Temple leaned forward, stared down the trench, could see flickers of light, cigarettes, heard footsteps in the mud. There were low voices, men working along the trench, curses from trampled legs, the sound of bayonets and tin. The men were there now, three of them, standing upright, carrying boxes.

"Rations. Take two cans. There'll be more in the morning."

Temple reached up into the darkness, the cans pressed into his hands, the men past him now, the words repeated. He felt for the rifle beside him, pulled the bayonet off, wiped the blade against his shirt. He stabbed the first can, and a new smell filled him, meat and grease. He sliced through the lid, then poked with the bayonet, didn't hesitate, plunged the meat into his mouth. He felt his stomach turn over once, fought it, swallowed the lump of meat whole, stabbed at the can again.

Across from him, Scarabelli said, "Never thought I'd look forward to monkey meat. I'm betting they don't grow this stuff in Texas."

Murphy was beside Scarabelli, had been silent since they entered the trench. He seemed to grunt, made a choking sound, said, "You read the label?"

"What label?"

"I saw crates piled up, grunts unloading a truck back at the village. They have labels. It's from Argentina. It's supposed to be beef."

Temple had finished the first can, stared into the darkness at the second, debated saving it. He remembered the words of the food carrier now, more in the morning. The debate was settled, and he cut into the lid, and Scarabelli said, "Argentina? What kind of sick-assed cow they got there? Probably isn't a cow at all. They call this stuff monkey meat for a reason."

"Sir?" The voice came from the man beside Parker. "Sir? I can't open the rations."

Temple leaned forward, tried to see the man's face, Parker opening the cans.

"There you go. Eat it slow. You got water?"

"Not sure, sir. Can't find my canteen."

Parker leaned that way, dug into the mud, said, "Right here. You got plenty. Here. Drink."

The other men around them were silent, and Temple guessed that all eyes were on the wounded man. He leaned close to Parker, said, "Strike a match. Get a look at his face. See how bad he's hurt."

"I seen it already. I'll take care of him."

There was nothing Temple could say, knew the tone of the big man's words, that Parker would not argue.

The rations were gone now, the men tossing the cans up out of the trench. Temple took a long swig from his canteen, then shook it slowly, measuring. He leaned back against the dirt, thought, A long damned night. He felt an itch on his leg, scratched slowly, stared up at the night sky, stars, saw a stick poking out of the bank above his head. He scratched again, felt something move in his groin, a sudden sharp pinch. He jumped, splashing the mud, said, "Oh hell! Dammit!"

He was up on his knees now, scratched feverishly, heard curses down the trench. Scarabelli said, "What's wrong with you, Farm Boy? You got cooties again?"

"Guess so. Damn!"

Scarabelli laughed, but the curses grew louder. Parker suddenly said, "Oh . . . no . . . aagh." The big man began to slap at his pants legs, said, "Laugh, Jersey! They'll be on you too."

Within a few minutes, the trench was alive with dull splashes, men standing, hands digging into pants and shirts. Temple probed, reached his hands as far down into his pants leg as it could fit, scratched at the small squirming lice.

"Everybody! Sit down!"

There was silence for a moment, the men reacting instinctively to the command.

"Who said that?"

"Who was that?"

"An officer?"

"Lieutenant Wilkinson. Eighteenth Company. Any sergeants here? Any of my men?"

One man spoke, down to Temple's left. "Yes, sir. Private Jordan. Baker's here too."

There was silence now, and Temple could hear the officer's footsteps in the mud as he moved along the trench.

"Sit tight, Jordan. We're here all night. Cooties or no. Get used to it. The Huns are in the rough country a few hundred yards east of here, and we expect they'll either come after us in the morning, or we're going after them. Major Turrill is close up behind us, and Division knows where you boys are. Anybody not get rations?" He paused, no response. "Good. Now, we need to post guards, every ten yards or so. I've got no time to choose volunteers, so you do it yourselves. You could be the only thing that keeps us alive if the Huns move against us." He reached down, tapped a helmet a few yards from Temple. "Start with this man here. Count off, in either direction. Every tenth man is the guard for the first hour. Then switch to the man beside you. There's no parapet in this section, so you'll have to find some place you can see the ground out front."

The man waited, and Temple heard the counting, the voices rolling toward him, heard Murphy say, "Ten. Hell."

They continued to count down the line, and Parker said, "Sir, we have a wounded man here. Head injury, looks like."

"Where?"

"Beside me, sir."

Wilkinson knelt down, lit a match, the light blinding Temple. The lieutenant held it for a long second, then blew it out. "Nothing you can do. He's dead."

Temple blinked, tried to push the blindness from his eyes.

There was silence again, and Wilkinson stepped past Temple, said, "I'll try to find more officers. If anyone else in command comes through, tell them I'm down this way. Tell them of my instructions."

"Sir." The voice was Murphy's. "Are there any officers back up the other way? Any way we can sort out the platoons?"

Wilkinson stood silently for a moment, said, "I haven't found any officers. There's a sergeant back about fifty yards, Simpson, of the Sixtieth. As far as I'm concerned, he's in command of those boys up that way. As for platoons . . . Private, until we can see what we're doing, there is only one platoon, and it looks like it's mine. Now, guards up, find a place where you can see the ground out front. Anything moves, raise hell. The rest of you, get some rest if you can."

Murphy stood, and Temple said, "There's a tree limb sticking out right above me. Use it to climb up."

Murphy stepped close to him, and Temple leaned out of the way. Murphy kicked his boot into the trench wall, showering Temple with dirt, then reached up, grabbed the limb, suddenly let out a short scream. He fell now, landed hard across Temple's legs, splashing the mud over all of them.

"Oh, Christ! Roscoe! That's not a tree limb. It's an arm!"

Temple blinked through the mud, stared up, could see the bones now, a man's fingers. He stared at it for a few seconds, Murphy pulling himself up out of the mud. There were laughs now, all down the trench, and Murphy bent low, said, "Sorry. Didn't expect that."

Parker rolled up to his feet, said, "I'll help you. Don't worry about it, Murph. There's a dead boy sitting next to me who don't look older'n fifteen. I didn't expect that either."

With the new dawn came relief. The Marine Sixth Regiment, held in reserve, was now sent forward, joining up with the infantry-men of the Twenty-third and Ninth Regiments. The confusion of the day before was mostly gone, and across the ragged ground, the Second Division was to continue its push against the western face of the Soissons salient. Ultimately, the fight cost the division another four thousand casualties, but in their path, the German units showed that they were as decayed and spent as so many of the French units they had faced along this same line. Across the western flank of the Soissons salient, the combined forces of two American and one Moroccan division continued to drive the Germans back, and farther south, a combination of French and American forces completely reversed the German momentum south of Soissons. Barely six weeks before, the Germans had swept over this same ground as an unstoppable wave, charged with the confidence that would carry them into Paris. By the end of July, their gains around Soissons were erased, the German front-line troops devastated by the relentless strength of the newly energized forces that drove them back. As German prisoners poured into the hands of their Allied captors, they began to speak in a way the French had never heard before. They spoke of hunger and deprivation, began to reveal an army that had begun to collapse, and most of all, they spoke of their new enemy, the men in khaki, this new army that continued to change the war.

38

PERSHING

Chaumont—July 28, 1918

"Sir, Colonel Mitchell is here."

Pershing glanced at his watch, smiled, thought, He's early. Only man in the army who's more in a hurry than I am.

Mitchell was through the door now, stopped, saluted, said, "Morning, General."

Pershing expected some usual splash of dark humor, but Mitchell's greeting came out softly, a subdued stare from the man's tired eyes.

"Colonel, take a seat. I have some news you should appreciate."

Mitchell seemed uncertain, slid into a chair, said, "If you say so, sir. I thought you had sent for me because of what happened."

Mitchell's expression had not changed, and Pershing said, "What has happened? What are you talking about?"

Mitchell looked down for a moment, said, "So, you don't know." He looked up now. "Sir, it is my regrettable duty to inform you that on Fourteen July, Lieutenant Quentin Roosevelt, of the Ninety-fifth Aero Squadron, was shot down near Château-Thierry. He is dead, sir."

Pershing understood Mitchell's mood now, said, "I had not been informed." He let out a long breath. "Damn. Do you know if the news has been cabled to Washington?"

"I don't believe so, sir. It was decided that you might wish to offer the first word of condolence. I am aware, sir, how close you are to President Roosevelt."

"Thank you, Colonel. You handled this correctly. Teddy Roosevelt does not deserve to learn of his son's death through standard channels."

"I thought you should know, sir, that Lieutenant Roosevelt had earned his place. Since the death of Major Lufbery, only a few pilots have made a significant mark against the enemy. Lieutenant Roosevelt was among them."

"I will communicate that to his father. This will certainly be front-page news back home."

Mitchell said nothing, seemed to weigh his words.

"Something else, Colonel?"

"Since you brought up the newspapers, I suppose I should bring to your attention . . . forgive me, sir, but I am getting pretty tired of some of the garbage that is being fed to the American people."

Pershing felt his shoulders sagging. "What now?"

"George Creel, for one. Seems Mr. Creel has been overly enthusiastic in his speeches again. The Committee for Public Information has announced to one and all that several thousand American-built aircraft are currently on their way to the Western Front. The one article I saw even included photographs, taken God knows where, of a bunch of planes supposedly lined up on some airfield in New Jersey."

"Mr. Creel has accomplished a great deal, Colonel, in focusing civilian awareness on the sacrifices required to help the war effort. He is an expert at motivation, and I cannot fault the work the CPI has done. If he is somewhat rambunctious in his claims, it is only because he errs on the side of patriotism."

"General, he's lying to the American people. What you call rambunctious can also be called zealotry. He's inflammatory. Without his rabble-rousing, it's doubtful Congress could have passed the Sedition Act. Forgive my saying so, sir, but it's nearly impossible for us to know what the mood is like back home. With all respect, sir, you and I are pretty much in control of what happens around us. But the American people are finding out they're being controlled the same way. Hell, I admit it. I'm guilty of some of that stuff too. One time I smacked some loudmouthed idiot pacifist right in the mouth. But now with this Sedition Act, anyone who objects to the war, or to the president . . . hell, anybody who criticizes what you're doing over here can be put in jail for it. Most of the high brass I've talked to thinks that's a good idea, clamp all those whining mouths shut. I thought it was a good idea too, until I began to read about what's going on as a result. Hell, not just jail. People are getting beaten up, *killed* because they said something that some of Creel's self-appointed deputies thought was anti-American. I'm all for propaganda, when it serves the public good. I understand morale and patriotism. But hell, General, from what I'm hearing, it's gone way too far. I'm not sure Congress had its head on straight this time."

Pershing stared at Mitchell, had not been prepared for anything like this. "I would hope that you are exaggerating the problem, Colonel. I cannot dispute what you say. Given the events of the past few weeks, I have not paid much attention to newspaper stories from back home. George Creel is a good friend of the president. I cannot imagine that President Wilson would advocate what you're describing."

"Forgive my lack of respect, sir, but I've never been too sure just what President Wilson is thinking. It just seems to me that the government is resorting to extreme measures to convince the American people that there is a good reason for so many casualties."

"But there is, Bill. Eventually, the truth of what is happening here will be made known to the entire world. That is no small concern, not even in the States. You're right on one count. You and I will never understand how civilians see this war. We are simply too close to it. The casualty counts are horrific, even in the best of circumstances. Over the past two months, our forces were enormously successful in their efforts, and yet if the newspapers only gave the people the casualty count, it would be difficult for civilians to understand how any battle could be called a success. It is a challenge I have faced since I have been in this command, so many inquiries from congressmen, who simply mimic the doubts expressed by the people in their districts. Why is this war lasting so long? Why have we not swept the enemy aside? Why are so many men dying? We are asking the American people to offer a great deal of sacrifice. We require women to work factories, we require fathers to leave their children, young men to leave school. People react to those things that affect their own lives. To so many, this war is not much more than an inconvenience, while to others, it's a personal tragedy. They must be inspired, and, regrettably, the death of their young men is not inspiring to anyone." He paused, thought a moment. "From the moment I arrived here, I have been bombarded with doubt from our allies, whether or not America is truly as committed to this war as the president has claimed. You and I understand the depth of that commitment. Secretary Baker does as well. But our influence reaches only so far. If the American people are not committed, they will not accept sacrifice. Not everyone understands why it is so important to destroy the enemy, and why it costs so much to do so. It is far too easy to emphasize the casualties without considering the gains. That's why we need Creel. His people can go to moving-picture theaters and dance halls and town meetings, and rally the audiences. He can inspire men to enlist; he can sell war bonds. If he uses a bit too much bluster for our taste, if he paints something of an inaccurate picture, that is the kind of lie I am willing to digest."

"What about all the bull in the papers about the abuse of the Negroes?"

Pershing let out a long breath.

"I don't understand where all that has come from. How can anyone believe that this army, that my command is anything but equitable to the Negro soldiers?"

"You have enemies, sir. This entire army has enemies. Besides, one Negro gets beaten up, and you know damned well some rabble-rouser in the States is going to make hay about it."

Pershing was feeling the depression again, shook his head. "I visited the Negro divisions last week. They have both equipped themselves well in the field, and I have no doubt they will continue to do so. If there is one failing, it is in the training of their officers. Hell, the fact that they even *have* Negro officers should have gotten some attention back home. It wasn't allowed in the Civil War. All the officers were white. I just wish the War Department made some effort to train those people better. I know damned well that the problem lies in the training camps.

Some idiot instructor somewhere has decided to ignore his Negro students. Those soldiers deserve the same quality of leadership as anyone else in this army, and they're not getting it. That's one way George Creel can help this army. Encourage the Negroes to enlist, to insist on better training."

Mitchell shook his head. "Sometimes I think you're as idealistic as Woodrow Wilson. Creel has no interest in the Negroes. He's as much a rabble-rouser as anyone. If he thinks Negro soldiers will make some people uneasy, he's just as likely to preach against sending them over here in the first place."

"I cannot believe the American people would be so easily manipulated. This is a war, dammit. I would rather believe that we can come together and put aside so many different views."

"By God, you are an idealist. Right now, there are citizens being jailed because they choose to argue with men like Creel. Whether or not Negroes make good soldiers is far down on that man's list of concerns. From what I've read of the Sedition Act, it is now *illegal* to speak out against the war, or to even suggest that buying war bonds is a bad idea. A man can go to jail if he says something unkind about the president. Believe me, I'd love to tie a rope around all those loudmouth Bolsheviks who think this Russian jackass Lenin is the new messiah. But I'm just an old army mule. I can bitch about it because I know it won't really happen. If all they do is gripe, those morons are no threat to anyone. But now, the Sedition Law says they are. Now, *talk* can be treason. If this war goes on much longer, it could get real ugly back home. Vigilante justice, General. Scares the hell out of me."

"Bill, I can't do anything about civilian law. But if things are getting that bad, then the one thing I *can* do is try to end this war."

Mitchell thought a moment. "Yes, sir. I suppose that's true." He paused. "Will that be all, sir?"

Mitchell stood, and Pershing suddenly remembered why he was there.

"No, sit down. Dammit, Bill, you have a talent for leading me all over the place. If the British ever saw how you talk to me,

631

my whole command would be undermined. I sent for you for a reason. General Foulois has requested a new assignment."

Mitchell leaned forward, wide-eyed, said, "What?"

"That surprise you? Seems he's beginning to feel the heat you've been putting on his staff. I'm guessing he doesn't care for it, but—"

"But he knows that if he tries to shut me up, I'll coming running straight to you." Mitchell laughed now. "Excuse me, General. Sometimes this job does give me some satisfaction."

Pershing tried to keep his seriousness. "It's not considered especially appropriate to bypass the chain of command, Colonel."

"Certainly not, sir."

"As you may have heard, I am reorganizing the AEF. It is my intention to create an American First Army, consisting of those divisions who have already demonstrated their abilities in combat situations, along with the divisions who are now ready to join the front line. It is appropriate for me to assume command of the First Army, though, as time goes by, I hope to create a Second Army as well, and so forth. For now, General Foulois is to become the administrative assistant to the new commander of the USAAS, Mason Patrick. As you know, General Patrick has done an exceptional job in command of our construction facilities. He is quite the effective administrator."

"Yes, sir. He knows his paperwork."

Pershing ignored Mitchell's sarcasm. "It is my feeling that the First Army requires a commander of our air forces who is something of an active participant in the use of aircraft. That would be you, Colonel."

"Yes, sir. It would be."

"Try 'thank you,' Colonel."

Mitchell tried to hide his smile. "I mean no lack of respect, sir. Thank you, indeed."

"All right. You're dismissed."

Mitchell rose, made a short bow. "I am grateful, sir. I may be an army mule, but I know a compliment when I hear one. Thank you again."

"Oh, by the way, Colonel, now that the Liberty engines are

finally starting to arrive in some usable quantity, have you had the opportunity to test them?"

Mitchell closed his eyes for a second, and Pershing saw the familiar exasperation on the man's face. "I had hoped to save that bit of news for another day, sir. The engines work fine, except when they're actually placed into an aircraft. Many of the available French airframes are too light, and the Liberty has too much power. There is a danger that the aircraft will simply come apart. The problem could be remedied by the use of a propeller that is compatible with the engineering of the Liberty, however . . . um . . ."

"What, Colonel?"

"It seems, sir, that when the contracts for the Liberty were granted to the manufacturers back home, no one considered that we should also build propellers."

Chaumont—August 1, 1918

"It is entirely appropriate to offer this toast not only to the success of the American troops under General Pershing's command, but as well, I feel it essential to note that a significant milestone has been reached. I believe General Pershing will acknowledge this to be accurate. There are now something in excess of one million American soldiers on the Western Front! I raise my glass in salute!"

Pershing stood, accepted Haig's toast, said, "Thank you, Marshal Haig. Actually, we are closer to a million and a quarter, including support personnel. I have expectations that in the near future that number will be doubled."

The officers chimed in with a chorus of salutes, glasses raised all around the long table. Haig was in full bluster, and Pershing sat, waited for more.

"Gentlemen, the success that our armies have enjoyed this past month is cause enough to celebrate. But I would offer my sincerest hopes for the immediate future. In a few short weeks, the flower of the German army shall be left hanging, shriveled on the vine, perhaps only to fall among the ruins of the devastation wrought by their own hands. We should offer a toast to the destruction of their leadership, those who would grind the civilized world under the boot heel of savagery!"

The British officers raised their glasses, and Pershing caught just a bit of hesitation from the French. He raised his own glass, the cheers of the British sweeping away the puzzlement of those French officers still digesting the awkward translation of Haig's toast.

The luncheon had concluded, the various staff officers finding their counterparts, details of various operations and tasks that filled long lists. He had been surprised by Haig's buoyant mood, knew that now, with the senior commanders retiring to the meeting room, he would find out why.

Pershing had his own agenda, had anticipated pressing forward with his plan to move most of the American forces southward, spreading the battle-weary divisions along the St. Mihiel salient. It was the one sector of the front where the Germans seemed content to remain in their trenches, the one sector that could actually be described as quiet. It was, for now, the ideal place to rest his exhausted troops.

The door was closed behind them, each man's secretary seating himself along one wall. Pershing moved to one end of the long table, said, "I am anxious to know your plans, Marshal Haig."

"As well you should be, General."

Haig sat at the far end of the table, Foch and Pétain now on either side. Haig said, "General Foch and I are convinced that the enemy has considerably reduced his effective strength along the British sector, in order to compensate for the difficulties he has suffered below Soissons. We have evidence of substantial troop movements away from the Cambrai region, and the salient around Montdidier. It is a testament to the fine work of the combined Allied forces. In addition, it is my belief that the enemy in front of the British sector is weakened as well by his own decay. As I have communicated to my government, the German reserves are of such poor quality that the enemy is unable to replace what he is losing in combat. I believe it to be a certainty that within a short time, the German reserves will be entirely exhausted. I believe as well that our strength in artillery and aircraft is rapidly overtaking his, and with the addition of the American divisions, our manpower will increasingly overpower his. The most formidable weapon the German soldier has is the Maxim machine gun. We now have the tank, and in increasing numbers. It is not a fair contest."

Pershing glanced at Foch, saw a subtle nod. Of course, they have already had this discussion. A decision has already been made. Now, I shall be allowed to hear what it is.

Haig continued, "With the apparent movement of his forces away from my front, the enemy has granted us an opportunity. I am quite pleased to inform you that, commencing on August eighth, we shall launch an operation that should take full advantage of his weakness. The weather is accommodating, our troops are fit and anxious to share in the successes of their allies. And, to be frank, my men are eager to reclaim their pride and the territory that was taken from us this past March."

He looked toward Foch, who said, "The assault will take place between Amiens and Montdidier, at the farthest point west the enemy has established his position. General Pétain, because of the current position of French, American, and British divisions along the front, I have determined that the British shall engage in concert with ten French divisions now deployed in the Soissons-Montdidier sector. General Pershing, the American Thirty-third division is currently completing its training, and is positioned in reserve along the British sector. I am hopeful you will consent to allowing that division to take part in the offensive, since they are already in place. This is not a time to undergo a massive transfer of troops from one position to another. It is this very deployment that gives us the advantage of which Marshal Haig speaks."

Pershing nodded. "Under the circumstances, that is acceptable."

Haig's secretary stepped forward now, passed out maps to each of the commanders. Haig said, "I am most happy to answer any questions, gentlemen."

Pershing studied the map, the designation of the various British, Anzac, and Canadian divisions, the position of the French farther south. The American Thirty-third was designated as well, and Pershing held tightly to his reaction that the other American divisions still in training were noted on Haig's map as well.

When the massive German offensives began in the spring, American divisions had been spread out in training facilities from one end of the front to the other, from the English Channel to Lorraine. Though the Allied commanders seemed quite clear about Pershing's intentions to unite the American forces into one cohesive army, the severity of the crisis had brought various AEF forces into the fight alongside French units, under the overall authority of French corps commanders. Though the Americans had fought under their own division commanders around Château-Thierry, they fought as part of a larger French command. It was the same reason that, along the western flank of the Soissons salient, the Moroccan division had been centered between the First and Second Divisions. There was simply no time to gather every unit and place it where Pershing had ideally wanted them to be. The French generals, primarily Mangin and DeGoutte, had understood that this situation was temporary, and Pershing accepted that, in the crisis that had so threatened Paris, it was absolutely necessary. But the English had taken note. In the British sector, a total of six American divisions were undergoing training. Haig had assured Pershing that when their training was complete, they would be transferred to wherever Foch and Pershing determined the American sector to be. Now, with Haig's new offensive, Pershing felt an uneasy twitch, that it was only a matter of time before Haig, or even Foch, suggested that those American divisions remain with the British. If Haig's grand strategy failed, if his new August offensive became a repeat of the British disaster the year before, the Americans might be the only reserve strength Haig could send into the fight. Though the undertrained Americans might become little more than cannon fodder, if Haig's army found itself in desperate straits, it would be difficult for Pershing to refuse. As Pershing studied the Haig plan, he realized that if Haig was wrong about the strength of the enemy across from him, the result could be an American disaster as well.

The discussions continued, Haig's enthusiasm for certain

victory having an odd effect on Pétain. The French general kept his eyes on the map, but Pershing could see that Pétain wasn't studying anything. He was staring blankly past the paper, had said nothing for a long while.

Foch seemed to notice now, said, "General Pétain, do you wish to make inquiries? I assume this plan meets with your approval."

Pétain nodded slowly, looked up at Foch now.

"I am hopeful that Marshal Haig's confidence is appropriate. Much depends on what happens in the next few months."

Foch seemed to ignore the gloom in Pétain's words, said, "Indeed, I am quite confident that we have begun to travel along a path that will result in certain victory. By this time next year, we shall again sit together and offer our salutes. But, then, the war will be over."

Haig stood. "Agreed! It is my expectation that we have entered the final year of this conflict. General Pershing, allow me to say that the American commitment to our cause has been most beneficial. It was my prediction April a year ago, when President Wilson offered to join us, that by the summer of 1919, that tree would bear the fruits of victory. General Foch is correct. That path is right before us. The next step is mine."

As the American divisions were trained and organized, Pershing had found the need to sort through their senior officers. He had already begun weeding out officers who were physically unfit for the difficulties of their commands, a policy that echoed all the way to Washington and, naturally, created enemies. But Pershing explained his decisions to Baker, emphasizing that the AEF required men who were as energetic as the soldiers in their commands, and who were not in positions of importance simply because of seniority, or of who their friends were in Washington. As the AEF had evolved and organized, Pershing had begun a chess game of shifting men into commands suited to their talents. Some were transferred off the line into critical staff positions. Others, like Harbord and Patton, had gone from staff to line. Just prior to the assault on the Soissons salient, James Harbord had been promoted to overall command of the

Second Division, replacing Omar Bundy, who had been promoted to corps command in Pershing's new organization. In many ways, the combat experience of the fledgling army made Pershing's job easier, the commanders having no choice but to demonstrate their ability to command under pressure.

The challenges that Pershing was forced to confront were continuing to evolve as well. The latest bit of torment came not from the Western Front but from Washington. In May, General Peyton March had officially become army chief of staff. The confirmation had been strongly supported by Baker, the secretary sharing Pershing's optimism that March would be the man who would cut through the woeful lack of energy that had plagued the General Staff since the beginning of the war. Almost immediately, March attempted to put his own imprint on the General Staff, and on Pershing's command as well. Instead of increasing the efficiency of the General Staff's operations, March began to push his influence across the Atlantic, insisting that Pershing's independence be reined in. Worse, March believed he knew far more than Pershing what the AEF required in the way of supplies and equipment in France. For nearly eighteen months, Pershing's frustrations over problems with supply had usually been directed at the unwillingness of the officials in Washington to perform their jobs. Pershing knew only one man who had the temperament to confront March with Pershing's own no-nonsense aggressiveness: James Harbord. To Harbord's dismay, Pershing pulled him out of the Second Division, replacing him with General John Lejeune. Harbord was then named head of the Service of Supply, the crucial arm of the AEF that was responsible for every aspect of transporting, equipping, and supplying Pershing's army. Pershing knew that neither Baker nor President Wilson were likely to grant March as much authority as he wanted. But by manipulating the strings on the movement of men and equipment, March could have a much more meaningful and much more negative influence on the AEF than Pershing would tolerate. The one man perfectly suited to confront March at every turn was Harbord.

Paris—August 5, 1918

For several days, Pershing had escorted Harbord and the other officers on a lengthy and detailed tour of the facilities that now provided the backbone of the American operations in France, allowing Harbord to appreciate how his new responsibility far exceeded the logistics of managing one combat division. Despite Harbord's protests at being assigned to something other than a combat command, once they had made the complete tour, Pershing could see that the man was not only intrigued by the new challenge, but was already energizing himself for what lay ahead.

The SOS headquarters was located at Tours, and Harbord had been amazed that the offices there were manned by nearly seven thousand support personnel. Harbord was there now, establishing his own headquarters, familiarizing himself with the AEF's organization. His new command would oversee departments that dealt with every aspect of life in the war zone, from Medical to Construction and Forestry, from the Quartermaster to the Motor Transport service, from Aviation and Ordnance, Railroads to the Office of Records. As they visited the various facilities, Pershing had been most impressed by the extraordinary display of American engineering at the port of Nazaire. Where once the ships carrying American men and supplies had been delayed and handled with rough indifference, now, the port had been enlarged, the wharves manned with more than two thousand American stevedores. Beyond the port itself, a storage depot had been created virtually from scratch, two thousand acres of warehouses and carefully organized storage spaces, connected by two hundred miles of railroad tracks, and just beyond, a camp equipped to house sixteen thousand newly arriving American troops. As well, the facility included an enormous hospital, where wounded soldiers were gathered for their journey home. Though every commander at every facility recognized that his efforts had been made possible only by the relentless energy of the commanding general and his tireless staff, Pershing could not hide his own emotions at the monumental display of sacrifice and duty shown by the enormous number of men who would never reap any glory on the battlefield.

Pershing was exhausted, sank into the soft chair, staring at the massive arrangement of flowers that someone had placed in his room. It was customary now, the expectation of his arrival, a show of gratitude from some French official, or perhaps only the hotel manager. His senior staff officers were in the adjoining room, his new chief of staff, James McAndrew, and two of the colonels, Wilgus and Boyd. Pershing knew that they were as worn out as he was. He smiled now, closed his eyes. No, he thought, not even Jim Harbord will miss the front lines now. The SOS is an army all its own.

The telephone rang, jarring him awake. He pulled himself from the chair, raised the receiver. "What is it?"

"Sir, this is the manager. I regret the disturbance, but I must inform you. Marshal Foch has asked to see you."

Pershing was surprised, had no reason to think Foch was there at all. "Certainly. He may come up at his convenience."

He moved to the mirror, straightened his jacket. The word settled into him now. *Marshal* Foch. The announcement had just been made, Foch named a marshal of France. It had to be Clemenceau's doing, perfectly logical, the French government granting the ultimate recognition to their own man for the success against the German offensives. It was convenient for another reason as well. Now, Foch outranked Pétain, clearing up any lingering controversy between the two men. And, of course, Douglas Haig was no longer the only one among them who held the title of marshal.

He stared into the mirror, satisfied at his appearance, blinked the fog out of his eyes. There was a gentle knock on the door, and Pershing moved quickly, opened the door, saw Foch standing alone. Pershing backed away, opened the door wide.

"Welcome, sir. No staff?"

"No. Just an informal visit. I hope I am not inconveniencing you."

Pershing saw movement in the hallway, aides emerging from McAndrew's room, now McAndrew himself. McAndrew looked at Foch with surprise, said to Pershing, "Sir? Might we be of service?"

Pershing waited for Foch to move past him, held up his hand now, said to McAndrew, "Just an informal visit. If I need someone, I'll call."

He closed the door, saw Foch standing across the room, staring out through the glass doorway toward the open terrace.

"Would you care to go outside, Marshal?"

Foch turned, unsmiling, said, "No. Quite odd. I am not yet accustomed to the title. I never expected such a thing. We can sit here, if that is acceptable."

"By all means."

Pershing sat across from the wiry old man, could see Foch's mind working. Well, he thought, there must be more to this than a polite hello. Foch put a hand on his chin, rubbed slowly, said, "I understand you have received some accounting of your casualties."

"Yes."

"The cost is appalling, yes? Among the Americans alone, nearly fifty thousand men."

"The cost is always appalling. Over the past two months, we had nearly three hundred thousand troops engaged against the enemy. Nine divisions."

"There are those in the French army who do not yet grasp all that you have accomplished. It had been suggested that no American army could become effective until next year. I was quite skeptical myself, and for that, I apologize. General Pétain has been your champion for many months. I have perhaps not granted him the respect he deserves."

"General Pétain has proven to be a valuable ally. As have you, Marshal Foch."

Pershing was beginning to feel uncomfortable, thought, He didn't come here to pour syrup over me.

Foch stroked his chin for a second, said, "I have approved the troop movements, to allow your Seventy-seventh Division to retire from their position along the Vesle River. I assume you are still insisting that your troops occupy the St. Mihiel salient."

"It is the only thing I have insisted upon for many weeks, sir.

You know very well that my men require time to recuperate, to refit. We are receiving replacements to bring many of the divisions up to strength, particularly those who have given so much." He paused, studied Foch's expression, saw a slight frown. "You approved this deployment. Is there now some objection to my St. Mihiel plan?"

"Your troops have earned their rest. I do not anticipate any further enemy activity in that sector for some time, if at all. Our focus must now be on the north, on Marshal Haig."

There was no enthusiasm in Foch's words, and Pershing said, "I must ask you, sir, if you intend to press Marshal Haig to transfer the American divisions now in his sector, to unite with our forces here. The British have been reluctant to approve such a move."

Foch smiled now. "You are attempting to be diplomatic, General. It is not your most accomplished talent. I shall be blunt. It is not within my authority to order Marshal Haig to release the American divisions in his sector. That is a matter that you should address directly to him. My difficulties with Monsieur Haig go far beyond his regard for the troops under your command. He is intent on winning this war himself, at whatever cost that should require. Though I am certain the English would happily accept as much glory as he can bring them, his methods have made him enemies in his own government. Certainly it has made him the enemy of his prime minister. Mr. Lloyd George is seeking any means he can to remove Marshal Haig from his command, but thus far, the prime minister does not yet have the political power that would require. All he has been able to accomplish in his personal war with Marshal Haig is the removal of General Robertson."

Pershing sat back, was surprised by Foch's frankness, something he had seen only from Pétain. He knew that Foch was right, that Wully Robertson had been a casualty of the animosity between Lloyd George and Haig. Robertson had been named to command the British Home Forces, which no one could confuse with anything other than a demotion. Pershing understood now, with Robertson gone, Haig had lost a powerful ally in London. It was the perfect explanation why Haig seemed so overly enthusiastic about his latest strategy against the Germans. He had to be. It might be his last chance.

Foch looked down for a moment, then said, "Do you intend to pursue your plan to reduce the St. Mihiel salient?"

"I have no reason to change that plan. You have agreed that a breakthrough at the salient could open a wide doorway into the Saar Valley, and could put us in position to destroy the enemy's transportation facilities at Metz."

"We have not made a breakthrough there since the beginning of the war, General. The position was always too strongly defended."

"Marshal Foch, on this point I must agree with Marshal Haig. The enemy is not as he once was. If the American troops can be positioned in force at the salient, I have no doubt that we can succeed in eliminating it."

"You will require considerable artillery to do so. Tanks and aircraft as well, I would think. There could be difficulties in that area." Foch was staring away from him now, something Pershing had seen before, the particular habit Foch had when he did not wish a confrontation.

Pershing felt himself rising up in his chair. "Is it your intention, sir, to alter the agreement you have made with us? I do not have to explain to you that we are dependent on French artillery pieces. You have been most cooperative in furnishing our tank school and our flying squadrons with the equipment they must have."

"Cannot the English assume some of that burden, General? You know of the losses we have suffered."

Pershing gripped the arm of the chair, understood now why Foch had come alone, an informal meeting. He wanted no witnesses.

"Sir, with all respect, the British have made it clear that they place the most value on our alliance as long as it holds the potential for supplying them with infantrymen and machine-gunners. Though Marshal Haig has promised to provide us with a number of their heavy tanks, they have thus far been tightfisted with both tanks and their aircraft. Their artillery support has been provided grudgingly at best." He paused, thought, To hell with diplomacy. "Are you telling me that if I pursue my plan to deploy the American First Army at St. Mihiel, and continue to plan for the reduction of the salient, that I can count on no support from our allies?"

Foch did not respond, seemed suddenly very old. His eyes met Pershing's, and he said, "Certainly not, General. It is not necessary for you to become anxious on the matter. Much will depend on how successful the English can be against the enemy in their sector. Then we shall have to respond to the situation as it presents itself."

Foch stood, seemed shaken, frail. "I should leave, General. I have caused you distress, which was not my intention. This was to be an informal visit."

Pershing moved quickly to the door, felt his hands shaking, stared at the closed door for a moment. He turned now, said, "My apologies, sir. I have done much traveling in the past few days."

Foch seemed to welcome the opportunity for a friendly exit. He was at the door now, waited while Pershing pulled it open. "Sorry to have disturbed you, General. We shall meet again soon. Let us pray for the success of Marshal Haig and his troops."

"Certainly."

Foch was down the hallway now, and Pershing heard the adjacent door opening, faces appearing, silent questions.

"He has gone. It was just an informal visit. I'm going to get some sleep."

"Yes, sir."

"Of course, sir."

Pershing closed the door, stared across the room, was not in the mood to look at flowers. The words rolled angrily through his brain, driven hard by his own exhaustion. One word shouted itself: respond. We shall wait and *respond* to Haig's plan, just as we *responded* to the German offensives. These people are so bruised and battered, they can only think defensively. He thought of Haig, all the false bluster, the man more tormented by his own government than he was by the enemy. Well, Foch is right about one thing. We had damned well better pray for you, Sir Douglas, because if the Germans toss you back into your own defenses, and bloody you as badly as they have done before, this war is a long way from over. Foch is convinced we'll still be fighting a year from now. But the AEF didn't come over here just to make counterattacks, and our troops didn't train so damned hard just so they can sit in the damned mud. And if Foch doesn't learn to accept that, then this year and next year will come and go, and we'll all still be having these same damned arguments.

August 8, 1918

The artillery barrage began at four-twenty in the morning, across a front fourteen miles wide. Almost immediately afterward a massive wave of British, Canadian, and Anzac troops followed four hundred tanks straight into the battered German position. The Germans were caught by surprise, or, as Haig had predicted, could not mount an effective defense whether they were prepared or not. By the end of the first day, Haig's forces had plunged nine miles into German-held territory and had captured fifteen thousand prisoners. Three days later, Haig's position was held in check by gathering German resistance, but not before the Germans had lost another twelve thousand prisoners, and tens of thousands of casualties. With German resistance stiffening, Foch and Haig agreed to change fronts, and on August 15, launched a second assault farther north, near Albert, northward to the Arras River. Though the German defense was stout, Haig's attack continued to push the Germans back, until finally, two weeks after it had begun, the Germans had been forced away from most of the gains made by the spring offensives. Haig had accomplished exactly what he intended. The Germans had been driven back, with considerable losses they could not afford. While the Allies measured their reactions, and pondered what to do next, across the lines, the situation was summed up succinctly by General Ludendorff:

August 8 was the black day of the German army in the history of the war.

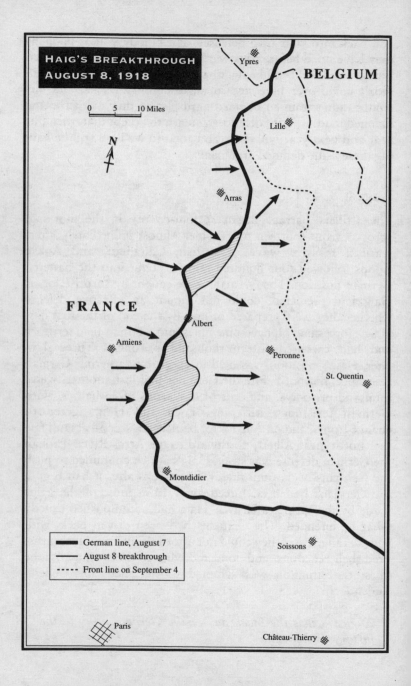

HAIG'S BREAKTHROUGH
AUGUST 8, 1918

0   5   10 Miles

N

BELGIUM

Ypres

Lille

Arras

FRANCE

Albert

Amiens

Peronne

St. Quentin

Montdidier

Soissons

——— German line, August 7
——— August 8 breakthrough
- - - - Front line on September 4

Paris

Château-Thierry

On August 10, the American First Army was officially brought into existence, and Pershing had established his new headquarters at Neufchâteau, on the Meuse River south of Verdun. Most of the American divisions were already moving south toward their new sector along the St. Mihiel salient. Pershing had put the wheels into motion. By mid-September, he would have the AEF prepared for their first full-scale attack of the war.

39

PERSHING

He had traveled almost daily, from Foch to Pétain to Haig, to most of the corps headquarters of the AEF's constantly evolving command structure. As Pershing predicted, the pressure from the British continued for the American divisions in the British sector to remain where they were. The hints were both subtle and obvious. In the North, Pershing enjoyed a chance meeting with King George, the British monarch once again offering Pershing kind words of friendship, reminders of the kinship between the two English-speaking nations, and the fervent hope that Pershing would still combine his army with the British. The cables flowed out from Lloyd George as well, but more carefully now, the prime minister making sure that Pershing was allowed to read and respond to any correspondence that was intended eventually to reach Washington. Though the substance of the requests had not changed, the style had, and Pershing realized that with Haig's enormous success, the pressure on the American divisions to serve as the British reserve might finally be silenced.

Ligny-en-Barrois, France—August 30, 1918

Pershing had moved the headquarters again, closer still to the St. Mihiel salient. He was waiting for Foch, sat at his desk, across from two of his staff officers, read through the draft of his General Order 143.

"Yes. This is exceptional. A few changes, but overall, the message is clear. I want this read to the First and Third Corps as soon as their camps are assembled." He read again, ran his finger over the line slowly: "*It fills me with pride to record in the General Orders a tribute to the service and achievements of the First and Third Corps, comprising the 1st, 2nd, 3rd, 4th, 26th, 28th, 32nd, and 42nd Divisions of the American Expeditionary Forces. . . .*"

He folded the paper, handed it to Carl Boyd, said, "Colonel, I wish I had the opportunity to recite this personally. Be sure this reaches the press. I want the American people to know that this command understands what their soldiers are accomplishing here."

"Yes, sir."

There was a knock at the open door, and Pershing looked up, saw the young Lieutenant Gray.

"Sir, Marshal Foch has arrived. He is accompanied by General Weygand. As you instructed, I have directed him to the meeting room."

"Thank you, Lieutenant. I'll be right there."

Pershing moved quickly, was out into the narrow hallway, turned in to the larger meeting room. He saw Foch, at the far end of the long table, staring down at the enormous map, Weygand standing off to one side. Pershing's own staff officers followed him, took their accustomed seats.

Foch said, "The rains are coming, you know. Marshal Haig is quite anxious that we make the best effort we can, all along the front. He feels the enemy is in a state of collapse, and has informed me of entreaties received in London. It seems the Germans are speaking of peace."

Pershing moved up to the opposite end of the table, said, "We cannot lose sight of our objectives. Of course there is talk of peace. The Germans were only too happy to encourage that kind of talk when it served their cause. If we allow our plans to be delayed, there is some hope from the pacifist element that Ludendorff will simply call off the fighting."

"I quite agree with you, General. But there are civilians who see any talk of peace as a positive thing."

"The only peace we shall reach is one where the enemy is beaten."

"Forgive me, General, but those words are easily spoken by

someone whose home is elsewhere. It is difficult for the French people to ignore the hope that somehow the devastation of their country might soon be stopped."

Pershing was growing uncomfortable now, watched Foch studying the map, the old man never once looking at him. "If we do not defeat the Germans now, the French people will enjoy only a temporary rest. Surely you must know that."

"As I said, General, I agree with you. It is perhaps why we must adopt a strategy that offers us the best hope of a rapid end to this war. Marshal Haig has suggested a large-scale offensive, to push into the enemy all along the front. He has become convinced that this war can be ended even be-fore the new year."

Pershing moved around the table, said, "Then we should not delay."

"General, are you still convinced your forces should attempt to reduce the St. Mihiel salient?"

"I have never wavered from that plan."

Foch continued to stare down, and Pershing felt the familiar heat rising inside of him. He heard a voice behind him.

"Sir? Excuse me."

Pershing was surprised to see Gray, who seemed to hesitate, and Pershing said, "What is it, Lieutenant?"

"Sir, General McAndrew has instructed me to deliver this to you with all haste."

Pershing took the envelope, tore it open, slid the fold of paper out, saw McAndrew's handwriting:

Word from Haig. British have reversed their promise of heavy tanks. Haig says he needs them for his own offensive. None to be provided AEF.

He felt like his gut had been punched, stared at the single word "None." He looked at Foch now, saw curiosity, the question rolling into Pershing's brain: Did you know about this?

"I have received some disquieting news. Apparently the British have changed their minds about providing us with heavy tanks."

He watched Foch's reaction, saw genuine surprise.

Foch seemed to anticipate Pershing's next question. "I assure you, General, I knew nothing of this. This could jeopardize your entire plan."

Pershing moved slowly to a chair, sat, put McAndrew's note in his pocket.

"Might I assume that the French will not change their minds? You were to provide us with a number of light tanks, and, of course, we still require artillery."

Foch looked at Pershing for the first time. "I did not know that Marshal Haig would do this, General. But perhaps this will encourage you to consider an alternative plan."

Pershing stood again, stepped closer to Foch, and the old man turned away, pointed to the map.

"Marshal Haig intends to press forward with his attacks. I do not believe we should allow the enemy any time to regroup. By all means, you may move forward with your strategy to reduce the salient. But, consider, General, that perhaps a limited assault there is the better option. Merely straightening the line along the St. Mihiel sector could have beneficial consequences throughout the entire front. If you were to be too successful, you might push into a salient of your own, making your forces vulnerable. I propose that you attack only along the southern face of the salient, with a limited force. The remainder of your army can be incorporated into a general assault . . . here. Two major attacks, one between the Meuse River and the Argonne Forest, executed by the French Second Army, supported by as many as six American divisions. The second attack would come farther west, from the Argonne to the Souain Road, conducted by the French Fourth Army, supported by your divisions fighting on either side of the Aisne River. Success there will crush the center of the German line, and quite probably force the enemy to withdraw from every sector of the Western Front. This will certainly assist Marshal Haig's efforts, and as I said, possibly end the war. You may still make some attempt to reduce the St. Mihiel salient, but I would think the best strategy there is a limited engagement. I understand that this presents a number of new ideas, and that you will require some time to consider

651

the details. However, I should like your first impressions."

Pershing held tightly to his fury, closed his eyes for a brief moment, then stood, stepped close to the table. "This is a very sudden change, sir. We have gone to great efforts to relocate an enormous force of men and equipment, supplies and facilities to an area that you have approved, so that we may begin an operation that you have approved as well. I have never intended the attack on the salient to be limited."

Foch continued to stare at the map. "General, the assault against the Meuse-Argonne region is scheduled to commence on September fifteenth. I do not see how your forces can be made ready to accomplish your goal at the salient before that time. Remember the rains, General. I must admit to you that the British have expressed some doubts whether the AEF is capable of reducing the salient at all. So many of the American divisions are thought to be undertrained."

"There is no such thing as perfect training. The American divisions now in the field are quite likely the most effective fighting force that confronts the enemy. Are you telling me you do not wish my original plan to be carried out? The same plan you approved less than a month ago?"

"General, it is simply that I am trying to find the most meaningful strategy to defeat the enemy. I believe a large-scale assault along both sides of the Aisne River has the greatest chance of success. And the benefits of that success will outweigh what you might accomplish at St. Mihiel."

"I disagree, sir. If my plan succeeds, it will place a sizable force of our troops in a lightly defended region, where we will cause considerable disruption to the enemy's supplies and communications. If we push through the breakthrough I have planned, we will be in open ground on the plain of Woevre, and can advance with great speed against the fortress at Metz, threaten the valuable mining region beyond, and cause the complete disruption of the enemy's communications and supply routes. The enemy can only respond by pulling forces away from other sectors, forcing them to withdraw from territory from which no one has dislodged them for four years! I would think this would be of some help to you and to Marshal

Haig!" He realized his voice had risen, and he stopped, saw quivering anger on Foch's face. "Marshal Foch, you must forgive my impatience, but surely you must see my position. Every time the AEF is ready to take the field, someone attempts to stand in the way. There is always some new plan. The president of the United States has been quite adamant. The American people and the soldiers they have sent to this war must fight as an independent army, under our own flag, under our own officers, just as the British, the Italians, the Russians, and the French have done. To disperse our army further than I have already allowed would be to crush the morale of the American soldiers. I should not have to explain this . . . yet again!"

Foch straightened, seemed to stare past him. "General Pershing, do you wish to take part in this battle?"

"Most assuredly, sir. But only as an American army."

"Then you have a choice to make. The Allied armies require the American presence along the Meuse-Argonne front, to commence an assault on September fifteenth. Regardless of how your troops may be deployed, General, you will participate in the greatest battle in all of history, a massed assault that will ultimately include the entire front from Flanders to Lorraine. If we succeed, the enemy may very well seek peace, but on terms that you and I would approve of."

"Marshal Foch, with all respect to you, sir, you do not have the authority to call upon me to yield up my command of the American army and have it scattered among the Allied forces where it will not be an American army at all."

Foch seemed surprised, and Pershing could see the man's frailty now, a slight shake in his hands. "General, I must insist upon the arrangement I have proposed."

"You may insist all you please, but I absolutely decline to agree to your plan. While our army will fight wherever you may decide, it will not fight except as an American army. I have relied upon you as an ally; I have sent American soldiers to points of crisis wherever they were needed. I have relied upon you for assistance in securing the artillery and aircraft support that my country could not yet provide. You have agreed with my plan for placing the AEF in its own sector, and you have approved my plan for what we must accomplish once we are in place. We have built roads, rail lines, hospitals. We have transported more than a half million American troops to the area you approved. In your authority as commander in chief of the Allied armies, if you now desire that the AEF be moved to another location, west of the Meuse, we will do so, despite the enormous cost in time and energy involved. I do not see how you can suggest that September fifteenth is an absolute deadline for your new plans, given all that must happen to relocate us. We are at St. Mihiel. We should attack at St. Mihiel."

"I do not see how you can hold to that proposal, General."

"If you will consent to commence your new plan at a later date, I believe the AEF could accomplish the goals we have previously agreed to. Once the St. Mihiel salient is reduced, we could begin transfer of as many divisions as practical to your proposed first line. Will you supply my army with the light tanks, artillery, and aircraft you have promised us?"

Foch tilted his head slightly, said, "What are you saying?"

"I am saying, sir, that if you will make good your promises to us, that if you delay your general attack by ten days perhaps, by September twenty-fifth, we shall take our place in line where you would have us. But first, we shall launch our attack as planned against the St. Mihiel salient."

Foch was wide-eyed, made a small laugh.

"That is not possible, General."

"We shall see."

Pétain Headquarters, Near Nettancourt—August 31, 1918

They met on a train, the railcars set up as Pétain's headquarters, allowing him far greater mobility. Pershing had arrived by midafternoon, did not have time for the usual graciousness of Pétain's hospitality, the oasis of the luxurious lunch. They were alone now, Pétain's usual habit, the staff officers left outside the one railcar that was now the general's office. There had been few formalities, neither man expecting any ceremony from what had now become frequent visits. Pershing looked forward to the meetings far more than any other official gathering, realized that Pétain had become possibly the closest friend he had in France.

Pétain poured the wine, said, "You're right, John. He does not have the authority. Once he agrees to the employment of troops, to the sectors where they shall operate, and once he coordinates the overall strategies among each of us, the details of the attack become the responsibility of each army's commander. I am quite certain Marshal Haig feels the same way."

"I believe Foch knows that. I really don't believe he has any intention of dividing up the AEF."

Pétain handed him the glass, and both men sat now. Pétain stared down at the table between them, shook his head. "No, of course not. It would be suicidal. The pressure is coming from outside."

"Clemenceau?"

Pétain shrugged. "The prime minister does not confide in me. I am no longer of sufficient rank. But, yes, I would imagine that Monsieur Clemenceau feels very much as the English do. Both are accustomed to waging a quiet little struggle with each other to see who will truly *win* this war. It is not enough to defeat the Germans. One of us must rise higher than the other."

Pétain reached out to a thick roll of paper, spread it across the table between them. "I believe my latest map is accurate as to your troop positions. Please correct any errors."

Pershing scanned the map, saw a hard blue line, the distinct U of the St. Mihiel salient, various boxed numbers, the designation of the American divisions. "Yes, this is very close." He paused. "I do not intend to alter my original plan."

"I would not, either. It is the most effective plan we have at the moment. A breakthrough at St. Mihiel gives us the most direct route into the enemy's vulnerability. A month from now, your troops could be standing at the gates of Saarbrücken. Which of course is why Marshal Foch is so insistent that it not happen."

Pershing was annoyed now, said, "Does it always come down to that? Is every strategy designed first to ensure that a victory can be credited to the proper flag?"

"This cannot be a surprise to you, John. But it's not simply glory, it's about loss and sacrifice. Some of it can be explained by mathematics. The English and the French have lost more soldiers to this war than the size of the armies they began with. The Germans as well. What you and I see on the maps here is not as important as what history will say a generation from now, or ten generations. All of them, Foch and Haig and Clemenceau, they all know what I know. Only America is capable of winning this war. But history cannot be written that way. That cannot be our legacy. Marshal Foch would likely deny this, but it is the driving force behind his strategy. He knows that dividing the AEF is a terrible tactical mistake. But it is the only means of ensuring that your president does not get to dictate the terms of the peace. That privilege is preserved for Monsieur Clemenceau and Monsieur Lloyd George. An American army cannot be allowed to march into Ludendorff's headquarters." He laughed, sipped from the wineglass. "You cannot interfere with our destiny."

Pershing felt himself draining of energy. "I have more than a million troops under my command here, and more than half of those are in position to launch the greatest assault in my country's history. I cannot accept that such a sacrifice is seen only as an inconvenience to your people."

"Not my people, John. My leaders. Never make that mistake. The French infantryman who will fight alongside you, the civilians who have lost so much in this war, they will know what you have done for them. If we prevail in this war, our leaders will make great noise about our glorious victory, but no one will be fooled."

Pershing drank from the wineglass, studied the map. "Regardless of what Foch proposes, if we launch only a limited attack on the southern flank of the salient, it could be disastrous. Any breakthrough we make there could result in my divisions becoming pressed from both flanks, even cut off. If this attack is to succeed, we must launch it against the entire salient. I cannot become so distracted by all of this political absurdity."

"No, you cannot. You have a far greater problem right in

front of you. You propose to launch sixteen divisions into the St. Mihiel salient, then, when the salient is reduced, shift the greatest part of that strength to Foch's new front sixty miles away. With very little time to rest and recuperate, those same troops will commence an assault through the Argonne Forest. Is this your notion of a compromise to Marshal Foch?"

"This is my plan to end the war."

Ligny-en-Barrois—August 31, 1918

He stood, made a short bow, caught the unmistakable scent of cologne. The French officers filed along one wall of his office, their commander stepping forward.

"General Pershing, it is my pleasure to officially remove my troops from the St. Mihiel sector, and transfer authority to you. May you enjoy considerable success against our enemy, sir."

"Thank you. We shall do our best."

"Sir, allow me to offer you . . ." The man turned, snapped his fingers, and one of the officers stepped forward with two thick books. "This first volume is our detailed plan for the assault on the St. Mihiel salient, and the other is our defensive plan. Please accept these as my gift. I hope you will find them useful."

"Certainly, General. Most useful."

There were more formal gestures, and after another minute, the Frenchmen filed out of his office. Pershing put a hand on the two books, glanced inside, saw three hundred pages. He shook his head, sat down in the chair, opened his top drawer. He pulled out a thin folder, removed the report, eight pages, his own detailed plan for the assault. Well, he thought, perhaps this explains why, four years later, they were still defending the same piece of ground.

He read the report again, the concise and specific details that had been prepared by Lieutenant Colonel George Marshall. Pershing had examined it a half dozen times, read it now with the same churning excitement that pulled him up out of his chair.

"Lieutenant Gray!"

The young man appeared, and Pershing said, "Do we know

657

the whereabouts of Colonel Marshall? Has he appeared yet?"

"Sir, I shall ask."

The young man disappeared, and Pershing heard commotion, voices in the offices. Gray returned, said, "Sir, Colonel Drum is here. He is accompanied by Colonel Marshall."

Pershing stared at the papers in his hand. "Excellent. Send them in."

Pershing had known Drum for years, one of the first selections he had made to his staff. Drum was now serving as the First Army's chief of staff, the new position Pershing himself had created. As they entered the office, Drum was smiling, seemed to know that he was not the reason for the meeting. Pershing looked at the other man, younger, tall, thin, the stiff stance, the same posture and formal demeanor that Pershing had carried his entire career.

"Sit down, gentlemen. Colonel Marshall, this is a fine piece of work. You have justified my decision in bringing you here from the First Division."

"Thank you, sir."

Marshall did not smile, seemed more relieved than grateful. Pershing could see the unmistakable signs on the young man's face that betrayed lack of sleep.

"I have been told by Marshal Foch that this plan is in fact . . . impossible. It will give me some considerable delight to inform the marshal that he is in error."

"Thank you, sir. I am not yet certain—"

"No one is certain of anything, Colonel. Marshal Foch may be correct. I believe that wars are won by those who can accomplish the impossible." Marshall seemed to grow nervous, fidgeting, and Pershing said, "You have something to add to this report, Colonel?"

"Sir, I appreciate your compliments for my work. There are contingencies which I could not address. I am apprehensive that without proper artillery support, the initial attack on the salient could prove more difficult than I have outlined."

"Too much artillery, Colonel, and we lose any element of surprise. The enemy does not yet know what our plans are. A lengthy bombardment will certainly tell him."

"Sir, there is the question of the barbed wire. I believe we should make every effort to destroy the wire with artillery before the attack begins. I estimate a barrage of eighteen hours is required."

Pershing shook his head.

"No. The men can deal with the wire firsthand. I have some thoughts on that subject that I will discuss with the engineers. Your report is precisely what I needed, to explain to Marshal Foch how we will accomplish our first mission, and then shift our divisions across the Meuse, to begin the second phase. This is no easy feat, Colonel. There are always contingencies. But thanks to your fine work, we have a road map to go by."

"Yes, sir."

He could still see the tension on Marshall's face. "Colonel, you've done your job. Leave the rest to me."

40

TEMPLE

Near Francheville, Southeast of the
St. Mihiel Salient—September 4, 1918

The camps had been prepared, some attempt at cleaning and rebuilding the run-down shacks and storage facilities. For four years now, their occupants had been French, weary and battered troops who faced an enemy across a dismal no-man's-land of wire and shell holes. But the French were gone, leaving behind the ruin and decay of the network of trenches that had been their home. Now, those same trenches had become notes on a map, with new names, new troop designations. This was now the American sector.

The Marines had marched mostly by night, on roads as congested and chaotic as any they had seen before. The traffic had been both men and machine, the familiar scene of French troops marching toward them, pulling away, vacating the position that the Second Division would now occupy. But the machines were different, none of the stinking ambulances, no wreckage of shattered wagons, disabled cannon, no signs of a fight at all. Most of the machines that rolled past them were artillery pieces, or trucks weighed down with supplies, all moving in the same direction as the Americans. There were ambulances as well, but they were clean and empty, moving in a line with trucks packed tightly with hospital supplies, some of the vehicles driven by Red Cross personnel. The Marines had tried to ignore the red crosses, avoided the glances from the medical people, medics and nurses no one ever hoped to see again. But distraction came easily, and Temple had been excited to see another kind of machine roar past. The sounds had come first, from far behind them, the rumbling of heavy steel and belching engines. As the column of tanks rolled by, the men endured the black smoke and the stink of exhaust swirling around them, watched as the steel tread churned the soft road. But there was surprise as well. These machines were nothing like the huge lumbering hulks that had led the way at the Soissons salient. These were smaller, much more compact, moving much faster than the men were walking. He heard someone, an officer, some mention of the name: Renault, someone else calling them Whippets. They had a turret, a round lump that protruded above the tapered body of the tank, one cannon barrel protruding forward. As the smaller tanks moved past, hatches had opened, men popping up from inside, the look of confidence and pride in their new machines, some giving the Marines a show, rotating the turrets, the aim of the cannon sweeping over them, the barrel itself moving up and down. There was another difference as well, another surprise that brought cheers from the Marines. This time, many of the tank crews were not French. They were American.

The mail had finally been delivered, fat canvas bags, the lieutenants standing guard while the letters were sorted by platoon. Temple sat a few feet from Scarabelli beside a large pond, muddy brown water spreading out between clusters of dead and broken trees. The camps were up above them, across the main road, spread out on a broad grassy hill.

" 'So, is it really as bad as they say?' "

"What?"

Scarabelli held the letter out toward Temple.

"That's what she writes. My sister Maria. Another dumb question. She thinks we're on vacation over here." He read again, a high-pitched whining voice. " 'I hear the worst problem you have is a shortage of cigarettes.' "

He tossed the letter aside, opened another. Temple held his solitary letter in his hand, had waited to open it, knew it was from his mother. Scarabelli had a small stack of letters, the advantage of a large family. Temple looked down toward the water's edge, saw Parker sitting alone, staring at the pages of a small book. Temple knew that when the big man wrote in his diary, he wanted solitude, would rarely talk about anything he wrote. Temple watched him for a minute, saw Parker slip the book into his shirt, then he stood, moved up toward them. Temple watched Scarabelli opening more of his mail, felt a tug of sadness as Parker moved closer. The big man had received nothing at all, did not seem surprised or particularly disappointed. But Temple knew the man well enough to know that Parker would find some excuse to go off by himself, would not participate in the enthusiasm of the others.

Scarabelli was still focused on his letters, had not seen Parker approaching. He read silently, then said, "My aunt Rosa. 'When are you going to Italy? The Italians need your help.' " Scarabelli tossed that one aside as well. "That's right, Aunt Rosa. I should go see Black Jack and tell him my family insists that the Second Division, no, the whole AEF, we go to Italy and protect my family from the Austrians. Ah, here's one from my father." He tore open the envelope, read for a few seconds, lowered the paper, shook his head, said, "Jesus." Scarabelli tossed it aside as well, a frown on his face.

"What is it?"

"Nothing."

"Gino, come on. Can I read it?"

"It's in Italian, Farm Boy. They don't speak a lot of English. Never mind. What's yours say?"

"From my mama. 'Everybody's proud of our Marine. Cousin Ida Mae wants to send you a box of her pies.' " He read silently. "A lot of news. Our neighbor has ten new cows. Another one died of the . . . influenza. The whole town is scared of it, a bunch of people in Tallahassee have died from it. What the hell's influenza?"

"It's a disease. I heard the captain talking about it. Some of the German prisoners have it. They say it's worse than getting wounded. Didn't know it was back home too." Scarabelli shuffled through his letters, opened another. "Yep. My cousin Eddie. He mentions it too. It's in New York. Got people scared to hell. People starting to wear masks."

Temple finished his mother's letter, folded it up, slipped it into his pocket. He looked at Scarabelli's growing stack, said, "You gonna keep those? You might wanna read 'em again."

"Nah. Most of 'em say the same thing. People getting married, or sick. Don't compare to yours, though. Not one of my cousins has any new cows. You're three thousand miles from home, good chance you'll get your ass shot off, and your mama makes sure you know about somebody's new cows. You come from one damned strange place, Farm Boy." He laughed, opened another letter.

Parker sat down beside him, said, "A lot of letters, Jersey."

"You'd think they'd have something more interesting to say. Mostly dumb questions. 'Have you talked to any Germans? Why are they mad?' What the hell are the newspapers telling those people?"

Temple stared at the open letters piling up beside Scarabelli, said, "Tell me what your papa said."

"All right. You wanna know?" He reached down, picked up the paper. " 'Remember what Father Moretti said. If you think you might get killed by a big cannon, stay in a hole.' "

Scarabelli tossed the letter aside again, and Temple said, "That's it? What's wrong with that? He doesn't want you to get killed."

"No, Farm Boy. You don't get it. When I left home, the priest made a big commotion. Told my father that if I was blasted all to bits, and they couldn't find my body, there'd be no way to administer last rites. I guess the priest knows something about artillery. But he had no business telling my father that. They were worried enough already. After that, my mother couldn't stop crying, was convinced if something happened to me, I'd go to hell. According to the priest, it's okay if I get killed. But just make sure it's a bullet. Something that keeps me in one piece."

Parker said, "That's how I want to go. Bullet. Like Sergeant Dugan. Quick and clean. I can't say I understand your priest, though. God don't care how many pieces you're in. Getting blown to bits don't affect your soul."

"Catholics, Mountain Man. You gotta die by the rules. My whole family goes to church so they know what the rules are."

Parker said, "Don't you?"

"I guess so. Once I joined the Corps, I stopped thinking about a lot of that. Considering how this might end over here, maybe that wasn't such a good idea. Tell you what, Mountain Man. Next time you talk to God, remind him about me. He can check in with Father Moretti, in case He's forgotten."

Parker said nothing, and Temple knew he kept his religion to himself, did not find Scarabelli's humor amusing. Temple said, "You get some writing done, Dan? I'm guessing with all that's happened, you could fill a whole diary."

Parker looked at him, shook his head. "I've given it up. Thought it would be interesting, maybe pass it along to my kids someday. Changed my mind. Nobody needs to know what's happened here, what we've seen. I wrote all about Belleau Wood, how scared I was. Wrote what it felt like to run a bayonet into a man's chest." He looked at Temple again. "Why would anyone want to tell that to his own kids?"

Temple heard the sound of an engine, and they looked across the pond, could see three men emerging from a truck. The men moved down to the edge of the water, began scooping the filthy water, filling barrels that filled the truck bed.

Scarabelli tossed a rock out into the water, said, "That's how they make our coffee. Now I know why it tastes like that. From now on, I chew my own damned coffee beans, and drink outta my canteen. Let my gut make the coffee."

Parker stood again, moved down toward the edge of the pond again.

Temple said, "Any signs of fish?"

"Nope. Funny smell in the mud. Like chemicals. Probably from gas."

Temple stood, saw Scarabelli gathering his letters, both men following Parker down toward the dark still water. Temple said, "Makes sense I guess. No reason to think fish could survive the gas any more than soldiers can."

Scarabelli had moved away, moved into a stand of tall tree trunks, said, "Hey! Look here. Somebody must think there's fish in here, and I guess they figure they belong to the French."

Temple moved that way, saw the sign now, a white plank of wood, black letters:

Parker moved up beside him, a low quiet laugh.

"Gotta be a Yankee officer. Back home, a stick of dynamite's the best fishing lure I know of. Fish'll float right up. The Huns probably dropped a few seventy-sevens here already. I'll bet the *poilus* have already had more'n one fish fry."

Scarabelli stared at Parker.

"You fish with dynamite? I can see it now. Invite the whole damned family, scoop the pond dry, fish and all, and boil it up with a hundred gallons of your homemade liquor. Mountain Man stew. See? I'm figuring out you damned southerners."

Parker laughed at Scarabelli's joke, and Temple said, "Actually, it's called moonshine. Lots of folks around the farms have their own stills for making whiskey. One neighbor close by us had one."

Scarabelli shook his head.

"A *still*? Only thing still is your brain. Both of you. Too many years living in the woods." He scratched at his shirt now. "Aagh. Cooties coming back. Hell, we just went through delousing."

Parker pointed at the pond. "There you go, Jersey. Take a bath. Drown 'em."

Scarabelli continued to scratch, and Temple could feel the itch as well, had been able to ignore it until now. Scarabelli shook his head.

"Tried that. Water just makes 'em happy. Guess the little bastards need a bath too."

Temple heard voices, could see a column of troops moving on the road above them. "We got company."

Parker began to climb the hill, looked toward the road. "They're Marines. Green uniforms. Replacements."

They all moved up to get a closer look, Scarabelli jogging out in front. They were within a few yards of the road now, and Temple could see other men gathering as well, some flowing out of the camp across the road, construction crews watching from the rooftops of the new storage sheds. The line of Marines seemed to inflate under the gaze of their audience,

665

and a sergeant gave a crisp shout, the men suddenly breaking into a discordant song.

> *"Hell's got nothing we ain't seen*
> *Hide your women if they ain't clean*
> *Army boys go back to class*
> *Marines have come to save your ass."*

The men across the road were laughing now, and Temple could see the Marines holding themselves stiff, marching with hard footsteps on the roads.

Scarabelli said, "Hey! Are you fellows really genuine Marines?"

They began to answer, competing for the chance to announce themselves.

"Damned right, army."

"You can go back to your mamas now."

Scarabelli stepped forward, close to the column, and one man moved past him, said, "Hey, army! What unit is this? You look like you can't wait to go home!"

An officer was there now, a young lieutenant, marching beside the column. "Eyes front, Private. We'll show these army boys why we're here soon enough."

Temple felt an angry explosion building in his chest, others across the road moving closer to the column, men starting to respond to the arrogance of these raw troops. He saw a sergeant coming toward them from the camp, and the man called out, "Did I hear singing? What the hell we got here?"

"Replacements, Sarge. Gonna show us how it's done."

The sergeant moved out into the road, pushed his way into the column, was suddenly in front of the lieutenant, blocking the man's way. The lieutenant stopped, and Temple saw uncertainty, questions on the man's face. The sergeant said, "Excuse me, sir, but someone should show you a proper reception. Welcome to the Fifth Marine Regiment. You boys are here because the men you're replacing have been killed."

The lieutenant seemed surprised at the sergeant's lack of formality, said, "Well, Sergeant, perhaps you can tell me where we can find Major Turrill?"

"Straight ahead, sir. Right up by the place where you'll be climbing outta those uniforms. Couple hours, you'll look just like these boys here. Like I said, sir. Welcome to the Fifth." The sergeant moved away, pushed through the column, moved back toward the camp. The lieutenant turned toward Temple, looked at the others across the road, said, "You men are Marines?"

The sergeant called out again, "One more thing. Sir. Just a piece of advice. Since your boys are trying so hard to impress these men, they should know that singing doesn't show us anything but how scared they are. If any of these boys survive, they'll learn it on their own. Veterans don't sing."

Near Remenauville—September 8, 1918

The Marines had been assigned outpost duty across the front of the entire division, manning the lookouts and communication stations once held by the French. They moved forward at night, stepping through a series of narrow trenches that zigzagged westward. As they reached the final trench, Temple had been as relieved as the men around him to see the dugouts opening up, the trenches cut deep and wide, lined with a parapet, sandbags piled high, cut by slits for the lookouts. They waited in total darkness, the unnecessary order passed along for quiet, for no light of any kind. The only words that mattered to Temple came in the brief instructions from their new lieutenant, a soft-spoken Texan named Lucas. Once they were in position, they would be within a few hundred yards of the enemy, an enemy that by all accounts did not yet know that across the barbed wire, their old adversary was gone, replaced by men who would not be content to sit quietly in the mud.

Lucas was an old-timer, had served in Cuba, seemed to come from the same stock as the old sergeants, men like Dugan, who had so terrified the new recruits at Quantico. Though Lucas had survived the fights that had claimed so many of the front-line officers, those Marines who had known him before Belleau Wood spoke now of a difference in the man, his calm and low-key demeanor charged with a frightening need to put himself in harm's way. Temple knew nothing of Lucas, could rely only on the talk that filtered through the reorganized platoon. If Lucas was carrying some dangerous need to join his lost comrades, he was still a respected officer. Throughout the platoon, the men had feared that when their new lieutenant was assigned, he might be one of the ninety-day wonders, the fresh-faced officers who came to France straight from their training classes, men who were pushed forward quickly to fill the gaping holes left by the death of so many field officers. Temple shared the same nagging concerns as the men around him, that when the attack began, if the lieutenant was not a leader, could not drive his men without wavering or hesitation, then he might as well not be there at all.

The new sergeants had appeared as well, a mix of old and young. Temple's squad had been assigned a man named Osborne, a tall angular man from the farm country of Indiana. Osborne was a surprise, had only recently arrived in France, had marched in his green uniform with the other young Marines who arrived at the camps with such casual arrogance. The squad seemed uneasy with their new leader, none more so than Parker. Temple had responded to Osborne the same as the rest of them, watching the man, the quiet search for signs of weakness. But Osborne did not seem as foolishly brazen as so many of the new replacements. Instead of bluster and crudeness, he offered the men the respect they had earned. It was appreciated, even if nothing was said. And Osborne seemed to know that if the respect was to be returned, he had to earn it.

They had not reached their position until well after midnight, and as the watch was assigned, Osborne told the rest of them to get some sleep. But Temple stayed wide-eyed, could tell that the men around him were doing the same, a silent vigil, waiting desperately for the darkness to end. He tried to calm his imagination, had tried pictur-ing the no-man's-land in front of them, desolation and carnage, all the stories they had heard. He knew that Parker was up on the parapet, Murphy as well, and he took comfort in that, good men, alert men who knew the enemy. But his confidence waged war with the fears in his mind, and Temple knew that he would get no sleep at all until he could sweep away the images and see exactly what it was they were facing.

There was movement far down the trench, small grunts, a faint clink of tin. Temple tried to calm the cold chill in his chest, saw one man rising, close to him, thought, Osborne.

"What is it, Sarge?"

The voice was a whisper, from the parapet. Temple stared up, could see faint shadows, and Osborne moved away down the trench.

Temple heard Scarabelli, a few feet away. "Maybe it's breakfast."

Temple pulled himself slowly to his feet, worked the stiffness out of his legs. He could see the men on the parapet now, soft shadows growing lighter. There was movement down the trench, and he saw a tall man coming toward him. Osborne.

"Coffee, men."

The rest of the men pulled themselves to their feet, and tin cups emerged, the odor of coffee drifting past them. Temple had learned to drink whatever they put in his cup now, waited behind Scarabelli. The orderly poured from a large fat pot, said, "More coming up soon."

Temple put a hand on Scarabelli's shoulder, said, "Hey, I thought you were gonna just eat the beans."

"You eat the beans, Farm Boy. I'll take whatever they got. The more mud the better."

Osborne moved down the trench again, and the whispers were giving way to low voices, the sergeant speaking to someone Temple couldn't see. Osborne was back now, said, "We got rations."

Temple gulped the coffee, barely warm, heard the talk begin around him, energized by thoughts of food.

"I ordered eggs."

"Me too. T-bone steak with mine."

Osborne held up a hand. "Quiet down." He looked up at the men on the parapet, said, "Anything?"

Temple saw Parker staring out through the lookout, and the big man shook his head. "All quiet, Sarge. The Huns stayed home last night."

"Okay, come on down and get some rations. The food carriers are coming now."

The men eased down off the parapet, waited with the rest of the squad. Temple saw three men moving down the trench, each man carrying a large metal can. The mess tins came out now, Temple pulling his from his belt, took another gulp of coffee, washed the crust out of his mouth. The food carriers set the cans down, large spoons appearing, and Scarabelli said, "What the hell is that smell?"

"Oh, God. It's the food."

The men with the spoons seemed oblivious, scooped out a mass of something into each of the tin plates. Temple stepped forward now, the smell curling his face, said, "What is it?"

One of the food carriers looked up at him, smiled, said, "Uncle Sam's finest. This here is cornmeal mush. And, we got a real treat to go with it. Salmon. Two pieces per man."

Temple's plate was full, and he backed away, sat down beside Scara-belli. He saw Parker, across from him, the big man stuffing the food in his mouth, ignoring the groans from the men around them.

Scarabelli said, "He calls this salmon? Salmon's a fish." He tasted it now. "Now I know why they had that sign at the pond. This is what happens to fish when you drop a bomb on it."

Temple probed the food, mashed the two mounds together, saw Parker watching him.

"That's it, Roscoe. Mix it up. Better that way. Jersey, you can gripe all you want. But where I come from, this beats a hole in your gut. Now how 'bout you shut up long enough for me to eat my breakfast."

Osborne was standing above them now, said, "Finish up quick. We need lookouts on the firing line. Temple, you're up. Scarabelli, Smith, Gruner."

Temple plunged the last mass of food into his mouth, washed it down with the last of his cold coffee. He set his tin plate on the ground, said, "I'll leave that there. Clean it later, okay, Sarge?"

"Clean it now. You might not be anywhere near here by tonight. Wipe it clean with a handful of dirt."

Temple obeyed, thought of the canteen. Nope, don't bother rinsing anything. Save your water. He packed the mess kit away, followed the others up to the parapet. He felt the familiar chill in his chest, leaned the rifle up against the sandbags, stared out through the slit. The ground in front of the trench was strangely uneven, rolling shallow pits, a vast carpet of shell holes, mostly overlapping. He stared in fascination, had expected something like this, signs of the long fight, ripped and bare earth, utter desolation. But there was nothing bare at all. Instead, the ground was a carpet of green, the shell holes fringed by small plants, the holes themselves thick with tufts of grass. He could see the barbed wire now, two hundred yards beyond the trench, vast snaking coils, extending out in both directions, several rows deep. He looked to the side, saw Scarabelli staring out.

"Hey, Gino. You expect it'd look like this?"

"I guess not. They been here four years, Farm Boy. Looks like they shelled the hell out of the place, then just left it alone. Probably fought like hell to figure out where they'd end up making their stand. How far you figure the Huns are?"

"The sarge said a few hundred yards."

"How the hell's anybody ever gonna get through that wire?"

Temple turned, saw Osborne now, said, "Hey, Sarge. How's anybody supposed to get through that stuff? Looks pretty damned tough."

Osborne climbed up on the parapet, stared out through the slit. Temple thought, It's the first he's seen it too.

"They'll find a way, Private. They been looking at that stuff for a long time. If there's a way through it, the Huns know about it."

Scarabelli was staring out again, said, "Yep. I'm guessing that too."

671

41

TEMPLE

Near Remenauville—September 10, 1918

The shot jarred him awake, movement in the darkness, hard whispers. The shot came again, echoing down through the trench. He pulled himself feetfirst out of the dugout, his helmet falling away, grabbed for his rifle, more shots, some coming from down the line, the next squad. Men were shouting now, and the shots began to blend together, a sharp chatter, flashes of light. He dropped to his knees, searched frantically for the helmet, his hand touching cold tin, the helmet up, rammed down tight on his head. He looked toward the parapet, soft gray light, the air thick and misty, saw men shooting out through the sandbags. Murphy was there, emptied his rifle, was loading quickly again. Temple felt helpless, didn't know what to do, no space on the parapet, voices all around him, high and frantic.

"How far?"

"Inside the wire!"

"Where?"

"Just to the left! Around the deep shell hole! At least a dozen of 'em!"

More men were below the parapet now, the whole squad, and Temple saw Lucas, the lieutenant staring through binoculars. Lucas shouted, "Parker! Bring the chatchat!"

Parker pushed past Temple, climbed up, one man jumping down to make room. Parker pushed the snout of the *chauchat* through the sandbags, Lucas beside him, and Lucas said, "Eleven o'clock. Watch that wide shell hole."

The rifle fire had stopped, more shouts coming from farther down the trench. Temple looked up at Parker, the big man sighting the *chauchat*, calm, scanning the ground.

Lucas still stared through the binoculars, said, "They're down in that shell hole. Sixty yards out. We got 'em trapped."

"There!"

A rifle fired, one end of the parapet, and the man pulled the rifle back, "Dammit! Jammed! I'm jammed!"

Lucas shouted, "Jump down! Somebody fill the hole!"

Temple scrambled up, the man coming down past him, and Temple put his rifle through the slit, stared out into gray mist. He saw a flicker of motion, something tumbling through the air, bouncing on the ground out in front of the sandbags. The ground in front of him exploded in a sharp blast of dirt and rock, a burst of black smoke.

Lucas shouted, "Grenade! It fell short! Keep an eye on that shell hole!"

The smoke drifted out across the open ground, and Temple saw movement at the shell hole, another grenade, arcing up, the fat stick tumbling toward him, the tin can on one end, the same kind of bomb that had killed Ballou. . . .

"Grenade!"

It fell short as well, the blast throwing dirt against the sandbags, jolting the ground beneath him. He tried to see, the smoke drifting away, no movement.

Lucas shouted, "If that shell hole was closer, those grenades would be playing hell. Keep watching. They may throw everything they've got. They can't just stay there."

Scarabelli was in the trench behind Temple, said, "What the hell are they doing here? It's daylight! What did they think they can do?"

Lucas lowered the binoculars, wiped at his eyes. "They're probably lost. Came through the wire and can't find their way back. It's the rain that brought 'em out here. They're harder to spot. Probably just a trench raid, see if they could grab a few prisoners. Sons of bitches. Watch that shell hole. Parker, you see anything move, blast hell out of the edge of that hole. Sergeant!"

"Sir!"

"I'm going down to Newman's squad, see if they have a

673

better angle. Maybe find a way to drop a grenade or two of our own."

Lucas jumped down from the parapet, disappeared down the trench. Osborne moved up onto the parapet, was beside Temple now.

"Anything, Private?"

"Not yet. I saw the Hun toss the grenade."

Parker was still hovering over the chauchat, said, "Concentrate, Roscoe. All I can do is bust up the ground. You might get a better chance. Murph, you too."

Temple blinked hard, focused through the sight of the Springfield. The shell hole was nearly ten yards across, rimmed with thick grass. He moved the sight slowly, scanning the grass, stopped, froze. There was a round black lump, between two thick tufts of green, and he stared at it for a long second, thought, *Helmet.* He let out a breath, squeezed the trigger. The Springfield jumped in his hands, and Osborne said, "What . . . ?"

The black lump was gone now, and Temple saw movement, a rifle barrel, a bayonet, another helmet slipping between the grass.

Parker said, "You stirred 'em up, Roscoe. That shell hole's gotta be shallow."

Parker fired the *chauchat*, a short burst, paused, fired again. Temple stared through his gun sight, saw movement, another black lump, fired the rifle again. He expected the helmet to disappear, but the man stood, the helmet knocked away, the man staggering up out of the hole, rifle fire now exploding down the line. The man collapsed, fell straight down into the grass. There were shouts farther down the trench, the other squad, and Murphy said, "Dumb bastards. That was your kill, Roscoe."

Temple blinked again, tried to clear the dust out of his eyes, could see the dead German clearly. My kill. The words meant nothing to him, and he stared at the man's body, felt no pride, felt nothing at all. It was not even a difficult shot.

Parker said, "Keep watching, Murph. They got nowhere to go."

The air was suddenly ripped overhead, hard smacks on the sandbags. Temple flinched, pulled back away from the slit, heard a voice, "Machine guns!"

He could hear the chatter of the Maxims now, faint, the guns back along the German lines. Of course. They figured out what's happening here. Trying to help their men. The machine guns continued, and there was rifle fire again from down the line, the other squad responding. But the firing stopped, quiet now, and Temple thought, That's Lucas, stopping them. Nothing for them to shoot at.

Parker said, "Keep watching 'em, Roscoe! They ain't aiming for you. They're just shooting blind."

Temple pushed the barrel of the rifle forward again, another burst of machine-gun fire peppering the sandbags. He pulled back again, said, "Dammit!"

The machine guns paused, and Temple peered out again, could see movement in the grass, tried to find the sight, said, "They're moving!"

The shell hole was suddenly surging with motion, the men rising up, a hard cry, the Germans up and running. Temple tried to find a target, Parker's *chauchat* now pouring out its fire, Murphy firing as well. Temple caught a dark shape in his sight, fired the rifle, jerked the bolt, fired again.

Murphy said, "They're charging!"

The rifle fire flowed out all across the line, squads on both sides of them. Temple stared in horror, frozen, watched the Germans fall away. The firing stopped, no more targets, and Lucas was in the trench now, out of breath, said, "Get 'em all?"

Parker pulled the *chauchat* back through the slit, said, "Every one of 'em."

Murphy was still aiming out, said, "I count . . . fourteen bodies."

Temple said, "There's at least one more in the hole." He turned, sat with his back against the sandbags, his heart thundering in his chest. The squad lined the trench, some climbing up, to see for themselves. Temple said, "They charged. It was stupid."

Parker stepped down into the trench now, made way for the

others, new men moving to the lookouts. He moved beside Temple, said, "It was all they could do, Roscoe."

Lucas said, "Good shooting. If one grenade makes it over these sandbags, the lot of us are ground meat." He looked at Temple, said, "Don't worry about it, Private. If they'd tried to surrender, I'm betting their own machine guns would have cut 'em down. They were better off dying than going back to their own lines. That's why we're going to win this thing."

"These are the men you picked?"

"Yes, sir. Corporal Burke, Privates Arneson, Temple, and Winkler. I'll lead them myself."

Temple stood behind Lucas, saw the captain appraising him.

"Stick close to Lieutenant Lucas, boys. He'll bring you back in one piece. It's your job to do the same for him."

"Yes, sir."

The captain slid a paper toward Lucas, said, "Don't know how much good this map of the wire will do you. The French didn't seem to worry about keeping their intelligence up to date, especially in this sector. I've heard rumors that there was so little action out here, the outposts were singing songs to each other, trading goods right through the damned wire. That's not a rumor the French officers are fond of hearing. But I've found a few empty bottles of German brandy in the officers' dugouts. Doesn't take a detective to figure out that somewhere over there, some Hun cap-tain has a sackful of something French. All right, Lieutenant, you know what you have to do. Don't start out until it's full dark. And get back by dawn."

Lucas led the men through the trenches, sharp zigzags that snaked toward the front. Temple was last in line, stayed close behind the other four, no one talking. He still didn't know why Lucas had chosen him for the patrol, had watched the lieutenant scanning the squad, searching, appraising each man for some unknown thing. The lieutenant had passed over Parker, then Scarabelli, but Temple could still see the man's long finger pointing at his face, the simple word, "You."

There would be five of them altogether, four of the riflemen, led by Lucas. The others in the squad had already started talking about what their mission might involve, all kinds of warnings about what they might expect, coming from men who had no idea what they were talking about. There was no humor, even Scarabelli unnerving Temple by speaking to him with hushed awe, as though Temple was to be part of some mysterious and heroic journey. The seriousness made Temple only more nervous, all four of the Marines glancing at each other, looking for some hint of courage in the eyes of the others. It wasn't much comfort. The only man who seemed able to calm their fear was Lucas, and Temple had paid close attention as the lieutenant gave them instructions. The captain's mission was simple enough: wait for dark, then slip out into the open ground, get close to the coils of wire, and probe, seek out some opening, some place where a man could make his way through. Then, if the wire couldn't be pulled and tied together, mark the place. They would carry a long sharp iron stake, with a small white cloth tied to one end. If the gap couldn't be closed, then the stake would be driven into the soft ground, an easily recognized marker for the Hotchkiss guns. Just like the Germans, whose Maxims would open up at random moments, the Marine gunners could spray that part of the wire often, a deadly discouragement to anyone trying to make their way through. Once the opening was found and dealt with, Lucas and his men would simply withdraw back to the outpost trench.

Lucas had been matter-of-fact about the details, and Temple sensed some edginess in the man's tone. It wasn't fear, seemed to Temple to be more like annoyance, as though Lucas himself didn't care for the captain's plan. But Temple knew not to ask, and Lucas did not speak of anything but the plan itself, and his final word of caution. There could be no noise at all, so no canteen, no mess kit. Bayonets would be fixed, gas masks tucked inside shirts. Temple felt his brain flooding with questions, saw the same uncertainty on the faces of the others. But no one asked, none of them wanting to be the one to show doubts about this seemingly simplest of missions, none of them daring to show Lucas they were afraid.

By late morning the thick mist had turned to heavy rain

again, the floor of the trench turning to soft mud. In the trenches, small landslides tumbled off the walls, trickles of water growing into small streams, gathering into pools in the low places. One dugout had simply given way, the top collapsing, the small cave now useless. It was a lesson, and the men whose turn it was to sleep stayed out in the trench itself, no one risking rest in a place that could suddenly bury him under a ton of earth. Temple sat wide-eyed, ignored the mud, the cooties, the filth that seemed to seep out of the dirt all around them. His mind held tightly to one thought, sunset, that moment when the light would slip away, the trench slowly growing dark, until nothing could be seen.

Throughout the long hours of the afternoon, the men kept their watch up on the parapet. No one expected the enemy to do anything during the day, but Lucas had been definite in his orders. Lookouts at all times. No one objected, every man remembering the grenades, falling just short, the helpless Germans who couldn't throw quite far enough, Lucas' description: *ground meat*.

The rain was suddenly harder, and above Temple, a rusted sheet of tin served as the only shelter. He saw Osborne, moving through the mud, the sergeant pointing back down the trench.

"Rations are here."

The men moved slowly, pulled themselves up from their watery seats. Temple stood, unwrapped his mess tin, his plate still crusted with dried mud. He moved to one side of the trench, held the plate under the stream of rainwater pouring from the edge of the tin.

Scarabelli was beside him now, said, "You making soup?"

Temple swirled the water out of his plate, said, "Just cleaning it."

He tossed the dirty water out, saw Scarabelli looking at him.

"You okay, Farm Boy? It was just a joke."

"Sorry. Yeah, I get it. Soup. I'm okay."

"Let's get something to eat. See what kinda treats they got for us today. Anything's better than corn mush and salmon."

The food carriers were there now, set the heavy tins into the mud, ladles appearing. Temple heard cursing, low groans.

Scarabelli moved forward, said, "What you boys brought us today?"

Temple caught the smell, heard a long groan from Scarabelli. Temple saw the tins now, held out his plate. It was corn mush and salmon.

He moved back to his seat, slid down slowly into the wetness, and beside him Parker did the same. They sat quietly for a long moment, each man working through the food on his plate, the only sound the rattle of the rain on the tin above them. Down the trench, Temple heard a voice, "Whoo! What the hell's that?"

He looked that way, heard a scattering of splashes, saw a small animal scampering toward him. It was a cat.

The animal was as wet as the men, seemed terrified, hopped up into a dugout, watching them with cold steel eyes. Men were calling to it, and Parker climbed to his feet, moved that way, said, "Shut up. You'll scare it off."

"What the hell do you care?"

Parker said, "You seen any rats since you been up here?"

The men didn't respond, and Temple thought, What's he talking about? Parker eased closer to the dugout, spoke in a low whisper, held out a piece of salmon from his plate. The cat backed away, arched its back, inched to one side, ready to make its escape out into the trench. Parker whispered again, and the cat seemed to calm, crept forward slowly. Parker set the fish down, backed away, said, "I wondered why we hadn't seen too many rats. These trenches are supposed to be full of 'em."

Scarabelli sat across from Temple, laughed. "Comforting thought, Mountain Man. You think this cat's eaten all the rats?"

"If there's one cat, there's more. This place's gotta be like heaven to 'em."

Murphy was up on the parapet, turned, said, "I wouldn't try to pick the little bastard up. Might rip your face in two."

Parker ignored him, moved back toward Temple, sat again. Temple stared at the cat, watched as it ate the salmon, still eyeing the men.

"I didn't know you liked cats, Dan."

679

"I like 'em better than rats."

Scarabelli wiped his plate out with a handful of mud, said, "One more example of how we're sitting in the lap of hell. Cats work for the devil, you know. My grandmother always said that. Little son of a bitch probably just looking us over, making note of which of us goes next."

"Shut up, Jersey."

Temple knew the tone in Parker's voice, could feel the big man tighten beside him.

Scarabelli knew it as well, said, "Sorry. I'm just getting tired of sitting up to my jewels in mud. This is where the word *mud* comes from, you know. Misery and Damnation."

Temple couldn't help laughing. "That's *mad*, you dumb Italian. I thought you spoke English."

"Okay, so it's German. Misery *und* Damnation. Hell, I just pass along the information. I don't make it up."

There was movement down the trench again, and off to one side, Osborne stood. Temple saw Lucas coming toward them.

"It's getting dark now. One more hour should be enough. Where's my volunteers?"

Temple raised his hand, the others as well.

"Clean your rifles, but no round in the chamber. You got that? Load the magazine, but leave the chamber empty. Any one of you gets jumpy and shoots at some shadow, or if your weapon fires accidentally, two dozen machine guns are gonna open up in our direction. You clear on that?"

"Yes, sir."

"Chances are, we won't be shooting at anything. If we run into anybody out there, we'll be a lot better off using the bayonet, better still, just lie still and let 'em pass. One word, men. *Quiet*. The Huns have listening posts out in front of their line. Those bastards have nothing else to do but shoot at shadows in the dark, and if they open up, the whole damned line will start shooting as well." He reached into his jacket, pulled out several small pieces of wood. "We need some kind of dry place. I guess one of the dugouts will do." He looked at Parker. "You're a country boy, right?"

"Yes, sir."

"Then I'm betting you know how to whittle."

There were low laughs, and Parker ignored them, said, "Yes, sir."

"Good. Take these, make a pile of wood shavings. Put a dry mess tin under 'em, pile 'em so they'll burn. The smaller the shavings, the less smoke they make. If we send up a plume of smoke right here, the enemy will know something's going on. It won't take long for some Huns to drop a seventy-seven in our laps. We'll use the fire to smoke our bayonets, take the shine off 'em, and we'll wipe some soot on our faces. The fire won't last long, so we'll have to be quick about it." He paused, glanced at each man. Temple saw the man's eyes, felt the cold stare. "One hour."

The rain had dissolved into thin mist, a thick fog of darkness that erased the shadows. Temple followed the faint sounds of the man in front of him, knees and boots sliding through muddy grass. The ground suddenly fell away, the man grunting, dropping down. Temple followed, could feel that they were in a hole. The men stopped, and Temple heard a faint whisper from Lucas.

"Rest. *Two minutes.*"

Temple lay flat on the wet grass, the dampness of his clothes chilling him. He began to shiver, his breaths coming in short gasps, felt a hand on his shoulder.

"Slow . . . deep . . . breaths."

Temple obeyed, rubbed his hands on the wood stock of the rifle, felt the shivers slowing. He raised his head slightly, his head filled with a strange smell, something in the ground beneath him, harsh and chemical. He pushed hard at the fear in his mind, and the questions filled his brain. But there would be no answers, no one explaining why this mission was so important, how they would know if they had found what they were looking for. He thought of Lucas. He must know. But Temple could not silence the voice, the fear filling his mind. Lucas was close beside him, and Temple tried to see his face, the lean hard Texan, the veteran. Veteran of what? He hasn't been out *here* before. He raised his head again, glanced to the side, guessed at the direction of the big shell hole, where the Germans had trapped themselves, men who were dead because they got lost in the mist. The bodies were still there, no possibility yet of burying them. The bodies brought back memories of the stories from his grandfather, what seemed now to be so much romantic foolishness, a truce on a civil war battlefield, enemies working together to bury the fallen. There was none of that here, no simple gesture of decency. His grandfather had spoken of a world that simply didn't exist now, and maybe didn't exist then. The reality seemed cruel, every man understanding that if those people across the wire see you, or they hear the shovels, the machine guns will start. So, their men will not be buried. And in a couple of days, they will start to smell. And what of us? Who will bury us?

He felt the hand tapping his shoulder, the signal, and they began to move again, crawling up and out of the hole. Lucas led the way, the others behind him in single file, feeling their way blindly. They were moving down into another hole, smaller, no cover, the men not stopping, and the jumble of thoughts was gone, his mind focusing on the only task at hand, one hand, one knee in front of the other, the rifle hanging around his neck, a pendulum, rocking slowly as he moved.

They stopped again, and Lucas tapped the ground with his palm. Temple could see a faint strip of white, the tape left by the French. It was one of the questions, no one bothering to explain to a private why they would follow the tape to the place where the French had cut the wire. That's not what the mission was. They were supposed to find the openings cut by the Germans, not the French. But they moved again, small grunts from the men, tiring, the strain of the crawl, the thick darkness, the fear pressing down on all of them. They stopped again, and Lucas moved back beside each man. Temple waited, felt the lieutenant's hand on his face, Lucas pushing Temple's head to the right. It was another signal. Right face. A ninety-degree turn. Move that way.

Lucas led the way again, and Temple caught another smell, sharp, acrid, memories of Belleau Wood. He heard a soft grunt in front of him, the man stopping. Temple crawled up beside him, heard a faint word.

"Corpse. On the wire."

The smell was overpowering now, sickening, and Temple could see a thick fat shadow on the left, realized it was the wire. He stared ahead, tried to see Lucas, and the others, heard only faint shuffling. The stench was all through him now, and he leaned close to the man, a low whisper, "Move."

The man started to crawl, suddenly vomited, the sound exploding in the dark silence. Temple froze, the fear screaming in his brain again. Move! Dammit! This is not the time! He pulled at the man's shirt now, the man responding, and Lucas was there now, faint words, "Don't stop. It's just bodies on the wire. Move! We have to probe for gaps."

Lucas moved away again, and Temple stared into the mist, the order rolling over in his brain. Probe for gaps? How? Stick our hands into the wire? The man beside him crawled forward again, some whisper of apology, and Temple let him move forward, fell in behind, could not fight the anger building inside of him. He looked to the left, into the wire, had no idea what he was supposed to do, and he heard a pop. He froze, his eyes wide, darting, listening hard, trying to judge the direction. Now there was a sharp clap, and high above them, an explosion of light, the sky bright white and blinding. He saw it all now, the wire, the men in front of him, the grass, decaying bodies hanging limp on the wire, full daylight, the scene locked in a moment of time. Lucas flattened himself on the ground and Temple did the same, his face coming down hard on the bolt of his rifle. The light began to fade, a faint hiss, a small bead of fire drifting to the ground. Now the voices came, distant, frantic, and another pop. He held tight to the ground, his face hard against the steel of the rifle, the sky exploding white again. He stared into the ground, could see the blades of grass beside him, the sharp light showing every small detail, bands of shadows from the wire. The air erupted like a thousand bees, pings and pops as the machine-gun bullets nicked the wire. The light faded again, blessed darkness, and Lucas shouted a harsh whisper, "Up! Move! Shell hole!"

Temple crawled away from the wire, blinded, had no idea where a shell hole was. The grunts of the others were all around him, and Lucas said, "Run!"

Temple stared into the darkness, the brightness of the light still blinding his eyes, terrifying shapes, blood red in his brain, sharp screams of fear. He stopped, froze for a long second, could see the air around him sliced by streaks of light, the chatter of the Maxims deafening. Run! He tried to stand, was suddenly crushed by a mass of weight, the man falling across him, sharp groans. The Maxims stopped firing, and Temple pushed his way from under the man, whispered, "You okay? Wounded?"

The man didn't respond, and Temple rose to his knees again, looked in all directions, saw no shadows, no signs of the wire, of Lucas. He wanted to call out, his voice choked away by the fear, the voice in his brain. *No. The Huns will hear!* He started to crawl again, pulled the other man behind him, slow rhythm, inches at a time. He fought through the panic, thought, Shell hole. Find a shell hole. He heard the pop again, his brain screaming: *No!* He flattened out on the ground, held his breath, heard the clap, another flood of blinding light. He could see nothing at all, his face pressed downward, but the Maxims were silent. He waited for the light to fade, closed his eyes, timed it, opened his eyes. He raised his head, stared out, could see a vast sea of shell holes, thick grass, measured the distance, the light now gone. He was up quickly, pulled at the man beside him, his fingers ripping the man's shirt. He pulled with both hands now, moving backward, frantic, in a jerking motion. The ground gave way behind him, and he stumbled backward, pulled the man into the hole. He rolled down hard, his helmet torn free, and he froze for a long moment, felt a sharp pain in his side. He tasted blood, spit, put a hand on the wetness on his face, blood coming from his nose. He felt his way around the shell hole, blessedly deep, more of the sickening smells, his hand touching a shallow pool of water, the lowest point. He moved back to the fallen man, said in a low whisper, "You okay?"

He waited, his mind racing, thought, Find a heartbeat. He put a hand on the man's chest, felt nothing, his own hands shaking.

He laid the man back against the side of the hole, felt for the man's face, motionless, cupped his hand behind the man's head, felt the wetness now, a deep bloody gash. He made a low cry, fought it. *Quiet!* He backed away, thought, Oh, God. I don't know which one he is. Lucas? I can't see his face.

He lay back on the grassy slope, held the rifle against his chest, his breathing quick and hard. There was only silence now, and the smells around him too familiar. He eased down close to the pool of water, reached out, submerged his hand, rinsed away the man's blood. His other hand was pressed into the soft dirt now, and he felt tingling, hot, tender, like sunburn, and he understood now. Gas. Doesn't matter how long ago. It's still here, some damned chemical still in the ground. That, and the gunpowder from the shell, the cordite, or whatever the hell they use. And the bodies. He closed his eyes, thought of the corpses on the wire. They said there hadn't been a fight here. A few bodies doesn't count as a fight. A patrol, just like us, some damned stupid raid that didn't work. Sure as hell nobody's gonna bury them. He looked toward the man beside him. And you. The names rolled through him: Lucas, Burke, Winkler, Arneson. Whoever you are, I hope to God we can bury you.

He lay still for long minutes, listened for any sound, any hint that the others might be close to him. They must think they got us all, or they'd be firing more of those damned star shells. Even the Maxims are quiet, and those bastards shoot just for the hell of it. He rolled over to one side, eased up to the lip of the shell hole, froze again, listened to the silence. He pushed up higher, realized he had no helmet, thought of the German he had shot that morning, the glimpse of helmet, the perfect target, the man's last mistake. He lowered his head, took a long breath, slid back down, ran his hand along the ground, found the helmet, slipped the strap under his chin. He peered up into the grass at the edge of the hole, then moved up higher again, was surprised he could see shadows. He looked straight up now, realized the rain had stopped, the mist nearly gone. He could see the wire, long low shadows, spreading out in both directions, thought, I'm maybe fifty yards back, so I'm another hundred fifty from our trenches. He felt a rush of energy. Hell, that's thirty seconds. One quick dash. The thought collapsed in his mind. So, then what? You'll run toward the sandbags and scare the hell out of the lookouts. They'll shoot you to pieces. But they know we're out here. And they gotta know we're in trouble. Dammit!

He looked up, no sign of daylight, no, that's hours away. And, at least, I'm on our side of the wire. He thought of the Maxims again, shooting so damned often whether they had targets or not. So much wasted ammunition. If they saw us moving around out here, you'd think they'd be shooting all up and down the line. They wouldn't just forget about us. He slid back up the shell hole, peered out through the grass. There was nothing to see, and he stared at the wire, thought, No more star shells, no more machine-gun fire. It makes no sense they'd just quit. The thought froze him. *Unless they have people out here too.*

He rubbed his finger along the bolt of the rifle, thought of the empty chamber. Sorry, Lieutenant, but the situation's changed. He pulled the bolt back slowly, put a hand over the magazine, muffling the sound, felt the shell pop into the breech. He touched the cartridge, made sure there was no jam, now slid the bolt closed. All right. Now I got more than a bayonet.

He kept his vigil for long minutes, his eyes growing thick, the shadows dancing. He slid down again, blinked his eyes, closed them for a few seconds, and now there was a strange sound, a dull scrape. He sat still, waited, heard a sharp whisper, the sound of a rip, torn cloth. *Barbed wire.* He slid the rifle up close beside him, up and out of the hole, rested it in the grass. He stared toward the long shadow of the wire, saw nothing, blinked hard, his vision clearing. More sounds came now, soft footsteps, breathing, shadows emerging from the wire. They began to spread out, moving toward him, and he felt the panic rising again, the shadows continuing to move forward, more of them. Many more. He slid the rifle back, pulled it close to him, slid down silently into the shell hole, the voice in his brain, too many of them! Just be quiet!

The footsteps were plain now, soft pads in the grass all around him, and he saw shadows moving past the far side of the shell hole, heard one man stumble, low whispers. They filled the darkness around him, a swarm of movement, and he thought of the lookouts, nervous fingers. Please be ready, please be alert. What can I do? There's gotta be something.

More men were stepping past him now, only a few feet from his shell hole, and he cursed to himself, no grenades. Dammit! We shoulda had grenades! He wanted to feel the cartridge belt, make sure it was still in place, saw a shadow moving slowly past the far side of the shell hole, kept still. He felt himself starting to shake, more anger than fear. He kept staring out the far side of the hole, saw no one now, thought, Maybe that's it, that's all of them. They're past me. Dammit, there's no time! Do something, just shout a warning! A word burst in his brain, some lesson from Quantico, nonsensical, so many jokes, the one word every soldier hopes to hear from the Huns, their word for surrender, the only word that might save his own life, or end it quickly. He leaned forward, took a deep breath, shouted, "*Kamarad! Kamarad!*"

He ducked low, waited, and from the trench line came shouts, pops of rifle fire. The Germans began to fire themselves, the ground shaking with the blast from a grenade. Another grenade exploded, a blinding flash of light, and he tried to see, peered up along the rim of the hole, specks of rifle fire coming from the trench line, *Marine* rifle fire. The grenades came again, each flash of light silhouetting the Germans, some dropping down, scrambling to find shell holes. He shouted again, "*Kamarad!*"

Now he heard the same word, shouted around him, "*Kamarad!*"

More men began to take up the call, a ragged chorus, the rifle fire suddenly slowing. There were lights now, faint beams from flashlights, the only light the Marines had been given. He stared toward the trench line, saw the flickers of light from the sand-bags, could see the silhouettes of the Germans, men standing, hands going up, some dropping to their knees, many hands high in the air.

"*Kamarad!*"

He heard more voices, English, "Hands in the air! Step forward! Both hands up!"

Temple watched with wide eyes, the flashlight beams holding the Germans in eerie silhouette. He looked back toward the wire, toward the Maxims, thought, Nothing, no firing! The only targets they have are their own men, but Lucas was wrong. No one over there's giving the order. The Huns won't just shoot their own men.

He stared again toward the trench, could see the Germans walking into the flashlight beam, filing past the sandbags now, hands high in the air. The voice returned to his brain, a stab of fear. Get going, Roscoe. This may be your only chance. He climbed out of the hole, focused on one flicker of light, could see the flashlight dimming, shouted, "*Marine! Marine!*"

He held the rifle high up over his head, ran down and through more of the shell holes, stumbled through water, his boots sinking into soft mud. He pulled himself forward, fire burning in his chest. The lone flashlight flickered toward him, and he shouted again, "Private Temple!"

He ran toward the speck of light, heard a sharp command, "Kill the light! You want to get him shot?"

There were men emerging from the sandbags, and he stumbled in the darkness, tried to hold the rifle up, his voice choked away, felt a hand under his arm, lifting him, pulling him, more hands grabbing him, pulling him through the cut in the sandbags. He felt his legs giving way, more hands holding him, easing him down from the parapet. He fell, his hands sinking into the mud. He was in the trench.

There was laughter, a hard grip on his shirt, pulling him up.

"What were you trying to do?"

He knew Parker's drawl, said, "We got trapped! I was in a hole. The Huns came past me. I shouted *Kamarad*. Thought it might mess 'em up, make 'em think somebody wanted to surrender."

There was more laughter, and he felt hard slaps on his back.

"You messed 'em up, all right. I though I lost you, Private. Hell of a thing."

Temple was stunned, said, "Lieutenant . . . how'd you . . ."

"We crawled back. Winkler and Burke made it with me. Haven't seen Arneson."

688

Temple thought of the man in the shell hole. Now the man had a face. Arneson.

"They got him, sir. Out by the wire. I pulled him into a hole, but he didn't have a chance. I'm sorry, sir."

"Damn it all. We got into a shell hole too. Burke took one in the leg. We wrapped it up so he could move."

"Sir, how'd you get back? I figured the lookouts would shoot us."

"Private, the lookouts knew to expect us. We got close, and when they sent up that last star shell, I waved so the lookouts could see us. All we had to do then was wait for the Maxims to stop, and just crawl in."

Men were moving toward them through the trench now, and Temple heard Osborne.

"Lieutenant, the prisoners have been handed off to the MPs. There's twenty-eight of 'em, sir. They're already talking. They started out with thirty-five. The grenades probably got the rest of 'em."

"Good. Thank you, Sergeant. Seems Private Temple wrapped 'em up for us. All we needed was the bow. Nice work, Private. Never woulda thought of that myself. Make 'em surrender by reminding 'em how. The major will get a kick out of that one. Sergeant, see to your lookouts. I'll check the other squads. Daylight in a couple hours. I need to figure out how I'm going to tell the captain how his idiotic plan didn't work."

Lucas moved away down the trench, and Osborne said, "Okay, next group up on the line. Murphy, Conrad, Vauss, Scarabelli. Same routine. I doubt the Huns will try anything else tonight, not after this little disaster. Parker, take Temple back to the first aid station, get him cleaned up. Maybe a cup of coffee." Osborne tapped him on the shoulder. "Good job, Private."

Parker had his arm around Temple's shoulders, said, "Let's go, Roscoe."

Temple followed the big man through the trench, realized now his ribs were aching. He touched his face, felt a thick crust of blood under his nose. He was suddenly dizzy, felt his legs giving way, and Parker was there, had him under the arm, said,

"Whoa. Easy. You gonna make it? I'll carry you if you want. Least I can do for our new hero."

"I'm okay. No. Dammit, stop calling me that. Everybody's all excited about what I did. Hell, I just saved my own ass, hollered out the first thing that came into my head. The Huns coulda just as easy turned around and shot me. I didn't know they'd surrender. Hell, Arneson's still out there. How we gonna bring him back? What a stupid mission, anyway. It was so damned dark, how the hell we supposed to find a gap in the wire?"

"Easy, Roscoe. How many missions we been on that ain't been stupid? How smart was it to march straight into Belleau Wood without the first clue what we were gonna find in there? It's just war, Roscoe. You ever hear of a war that wasn't stupid in the first place? Let's get you some coffee. I don't care what you say. You done real good tonight. I'm sorry about Arneson. But don't worry, we'll get him buried."

"How?"

"Hmm. While you were out there snatching up Huns, we had a little commotion our own selves. Word came down the line. Be prepared to move. Something's up, Roscoe. We're not gonna sit here much longer."

"Rumors."

"Maybe. But I been hearing rumors for long enough to know when it's more than talk. Like I said, something's up. Something big. Arneson won't have to wait long to get his burial. When we leave here, we're moving forward."

September 12, 1918

The shelling began just after midnight, three thousand artillery pieces, launching their spectacular display of light and power, dimmed and muted only by the thick clouds, the steady rain. All around the curve of the salient, the massive push would begin at five a.m., sixteen American and four French divisions, all under Pershing's command.

The Second Division occupied a compact front, its regiments positioned into a complex network of trenches behind the outposts manned by the Fifth Marines. Hours before the artillery

690

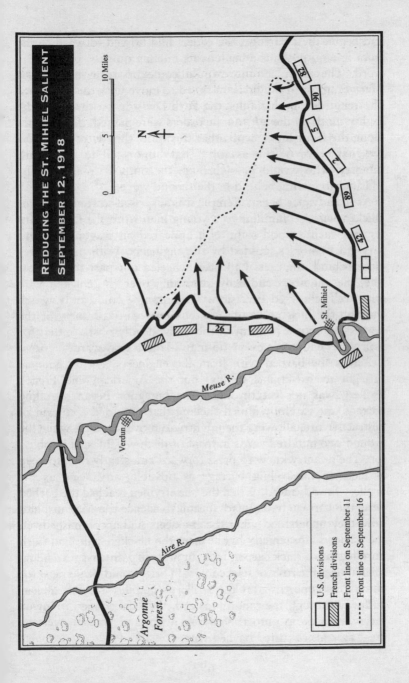

REDUCING THE ST. MIHIEL SALIENT
SEPTEMBER 12, 1918

N

10 Miles

5

0

82

90

5

2

89

42

St. Mihiel

26

Meuse R.

Verdun

Aire R.

Argonne
Forest

U.S. divisions
French divisions
Front line on September 11
Front line on September 16

had begun their barrage, the orders had flowed forward to the front-line outposts, the lieutenants moving quickly, passing the word. The main advance would come up from behind the Marines, most of the division timed to move with the vast wave of strength on both flanks, the Fifth Division on the right, the Eighty-ninth on the left. As the orders were passed, the Marines along the front line learned that this time, they were not to be the first wave of the assault. That honor fell to the Ninth Infantry, who would pass through the outpost line, with the Marines following behind in the second wave.

As the advance began, Temple was surprised to see fat rolls of chicken wire, so familiar to a young man from the farm country, but such an odd sight as it appeared on wagons brought forward by horses, guided by the engineers. With the infantry close behind, the carts had been wheeled out past the outpost line, the engineers suddenly swarming over the chicken wire with well-rehearsed precision. The infantry could only watch through the mist and rain, anxious men who all knew of the barbed-wire mass in front of them, the deadly obstacle that for four years had made every no-man's-land a graveyard.

Across the barbed wire from the engineers, enemy gunners brought their Maxims to life, but the American and French artillery was not yet through. The big guns began a rolling barrage, the carefully aimed shelling that provided a curtain of destructive fire, allowing the infantry to move forward, while the ground two hundred yards in front of them was blasted to oblivion. The infantry knew to press forward at a steady rate, to keep as close to the rolling barrage as possible, advancing as the artillery fire advanced. When the infantrymen reached the barbed wire, the barrage had already begun to silence the Maxims, and now, they understood what the engineers had accomplished. To the stunned amazement of the men, the chicken wire had been unrolled into a thick carpet, laid out in wide pathways, extending up and over the rolls of barbed wire. There would be no need for cutting, no concerns over the artillery's inability to blast a clear pathway through the tangle. Instead, the infantrymen followed their sergeants up onto the chicken wire, and walked over the great fat coils of rusted barbed wire.

* * *

By the end of the day, nearly every objective had been reached. Though the Germans had offered pockets of sharp resistance, the German High Command had known for some time that the St. Mihiel salient was not a position they could expect to hold in the face of a dedicated assault, especially against the combined force of nearly three-quarters of a million French and American troops. Even as Pershing was finalizing his own plans, and Foch was approving them, the German divisions occupying the salient had been ordered to begin a strategic withdrawal to form a stronger, less vulnerable and straighter defensive line. Though the Germans had not yet fully withdrawn, the speed with which Pershing's operation was begun caught the Germans by surprise, and many units had received the American attack unprepared for anything but retreat. Throughout the days that followed, Pershing's goal to reduce the St. Mihiel salient was fully accomplished, though the American troops had been helped by the weakened German defense. French farms and villages that had been firmly in German hands since the first great battles of the war were now back under Allied control. With their objectives realized, the Marines and the infantrymen of the Second Division were ordered away from the front, back to the rest area around Toul, a few miles south of St. Mihiel. All Temple knew was what the rumors said, rumors the lieutenants didn't dispute. Their rest period would be brief.

The essence of Colonel George Marshall's concise plan now came fully into play. Armed with Marshall's detailed instructions for shifting the American forces nearly sixty miles, Pershing communicated to Foch that the Americans were indeed prepared to satisfy Foch's insistence on a full-scale attack around the Argonne Forest, the grand assault that Foch still insisted would end the war.

42

PERSHING

Sampigny, France—September 15, 1918

He watched as Poincaré and his wife stepped down from the road. The couple moved slowly through what had once been a garden, the French president wrapping one arm around his wife's slender shoulders. The house lay shattered, the roof collapsing onto walls that were reduced to heaps of rubble. Pershing watched as the couple reached the ruins of their home, heard soft sounds, Poincaré cradling her head against his shoulder. Pershing motioned to his aides to stay behind, moved down off the road, picked his way slowly through the shell holes and debris. He stopped a few feet behind them, and Poincaré turned, a slight smile through the man's tears.

"*C'est la guerre,* General."

"I wish I could have done something to prevent this. There was no cause for the enemy to shell this place."

"No, General, you did far more than we could have hoped. I speak not for myself, but for all the people in this valley. Look before you. The Meuse River has given us the most beautiful valley in France. Now the people can return here without fear."

Pershing moved closer, and Madame Poincaré put out her hand, touched Pershing's arm. "We chose this site for the view of the valley. Look there, the forests, the farmland still green. I have so missed this place."

Pershing followed her gaze, could not turn his eye from the desolation that spread across the wide valley, blasted fields, clusters of black trees stripped bare, roads cut and broken, the wreckage of trucks and wagons. All along the horizon, there were columns of black smoke, the remains of German ammunition dumps and supply bases, destroyed in haste as the Germans pulled away. She is fortunate, he thought. She can look beyond what a soldier sees.

Madame Poincaré turned to her husband. "We can begin rebuilding immediately, yes? By next summer perhaps, the house could be ready. It has been so long."

Poincaré wrapped her with his arm again, nodded slowly. Pershing wanted to back away, leave them to their quiet moment. Poincaré stared into the wreckage of his home again, said, "General, my wife is correct. It has been so long. A civilian can only know of war what he is told by the generals. Please tell me, tell both of us, that this will end soon."

Pershing looked out across the valley, stared at the horizon, where his army was digging in, preparing to hold the ground where the enemy had been swept away.

"It will end soon."

Pétain Headquarters, Nettancourt
September 21, 1918

My Dear General,
The American First Army, under your command, on this first day has won a magnificent victory by a maneuver as skillfully prepared as it was valiantly executed. I extend to you as well as to the officers and to the troops under your command my warmest congratulations.

Marshal Foch

Pétain finished reading, and Pershing said, "I received a very kind message from Haig as well."

Pétain handed him the cable from Foch, said, "I would expect that. No one can argue with victory. Might I be honest with you?"

It was a strange question coming from Pétain.

"I would expect nothing else."

Pétain stared at him for a moment across the wide desk.

"I apologize to you, John. I am embarrassed to admit this, but for some weeks now I have had doubts about your strategy. I did not believe you could assemble your people as quickly as you did. I did not believe you could launch your assault at least until September twentieth, and even then, I anticipated that your battalions would be so badly jumbled and confused that there was the potential for disaster. I could not keep such a secret from you."

Pershing was not surprised, knew Pétain well enough to accept his gloomy predictions, a pessimism that still drifted through most of the French army. Pershing did not smile, said, "So, what do you think now?"

Pétain pointed to the paper in Pershing's hand. "I think that Marshal Foch has offered you his apology as well. He is more the politician than I am, so he does not use the word."

Pershing smiled now, thought, He is more of a politician than he admits. He didn't answer the question.

Pétain said, "I was frankly surprised when he accepted your plan. No reasonable tactician would agree to such a plan. You make your attack and then simply move most of your army to a new front. Marshal Foch had every expectation that by conceding to your stubbornness, his timetable for the general assault would be severely delayed. However, since you are deploying your troops and their support with remarkable speed, it seems there will be little delay after all."

"I do not apologize for the confidence I have in the people in my command. Call it stubbornness if you will, but I know what my officers can accomplish. The credit for the logistical plan belongs to Lieutenant Colonel Marshall. The credit for the victory at St. Mihiel belongs to the troops."

"Now who is the politician?" Pétain laughed, one hand on his round stomach.

Pershing drank from a cup of coffee, said, "I was not surprised that Foch agreed to my plan. He had no choice. You know that."

"Of course. But subordinate commanders are not to speak of

such things." Pétain laughed now. "We must oblige our superiors in their quest for the greater good."

Pershing did not share the man's humor. "I did exactly that. The greater good is to push the enemy out of France. We've merely taken the first step."

"Indeed. I hope our good fortune continues."

Pershing detected the pessimism again, Pétain's smile gone now. Pétain leaned out over the desk, looked at him with a hard stare. "Perhaps it is old age, John. Perhaps I have witnessed too many disasters. But I must share my concerns over Foch's strategy. We are about to confront the enemy at his strongest point. In your new front, between the Argonne Forest and the Meuse, he is dug into four strong defensive lines, lines that have been unmolested for nearly two years. I respect what you accomplished at St. Mihiel. But I'm sure you will agree that the enemy was taken somewhat by surprise. I mean no disrespect to your soldiers, John, but at St. Mihiel, the enemy gave way rather than make a strong stand. Ludendorff knows that between the Meuse and the Argonne, there is no giving way. If the Germans are beaten there, they risk the loss of their key rail line, which could threaten their entire front. I hope you are prepared for a difficult fight."

Pershing felt a small flash of anger, let it cool. He is my friend, he thought. And he's right. He has seen a great many disasters. He's entitled to his doubts.

"I have never been one to offer guarantees of certain victory. It is one reason the newspapers find me . . . uninteresting. I have spoken to my corps commanders, and several of my division commanders. Every one of them is energetic and eager to take the field. I have always believed that a confident commander influences the personality of his troops. The AEF no longer has anything to prove to its allies, and I will make no loud claims for instant success. Yes, this will be a difficult fight, and I believe there is no army anywhere that is capable of confronting the enemy with as much drive and dedication to victory as the men in my command."

"I cannot argue that, John. Might I ask one favor?"

Pershing was surprised to see the joviality returning to Pétain's expression. "Certainly."

"The next time you launch an attack against barbed wire, please allow me to watch how it is done."

Souilly—September 25, 1918

"I'll hand it to the French, General. They've come through for us."

Pershing had rarely seen Mitchell so positive, the man seeming to vibrate with raw energy. "How many pilots can we put in the air now?"

Mitchell pulled a piece of paper out of his pocket, slid it across the desk. "We have near six hundred ready to fly. The French have another three hundred they've placed under my command." Mitchell was smiling now. "You ever think you'd see that? I'm guessing Marshal Foch has learned something about Americans. Give us the damned tools, and we'll get the job done."

Pershing did not share Mitchell's bouncing enthusiasm, scanned the paper. "Eight hundred and fifty aircraft." He looked at Mitchell now, saw the same smile.

"Yes, sir. Eight hundred and fifty aircraft. Every damned one of 'em French. And every damned one of them under my command. It won't even be a fair fight, General. You imagine what that kind of airpower looks like? Old Fritz will see a black cloud of Nieuports and SPADs, and run like hell. Might not need the infantry at all."

Pershing slid the paper back to Mitchell, stared down at the desk for a moment, and Mitchell said, "What's wrong?"

Pershing shook his head. "It won't be that easy, Bill."

"Aw, hell, General, I know that. It's just fun to feel like things are *happening* around here. You know what I mean. The French are finally on *our* side. The enemy's in for the fight of their lives. I've never seen so many high-brass officers so enthusiastic. All the damned clerks and floor sweepers are finally out of my way. Eight hundred and fifty aircraft, General! I wish I could be up there with 'em."

Pershing looked at Mitchell now, said, "There's no chance of that, is there, Colonel?"

" 'Course not. I'm just primed for it. I wish I knew why you had the gripes. Sir."

Pershing leaned back in the chair, could not share any part of Mitchell's good mood. "A great deal depends on what happens in the next week. I wish I could look away from that. You're right. Everybody in this headquarters is ready to charge out there with the front-line troops. I don't have the luxury of that kind of enthusiasm."

"Why the hell not?"

Pershing thought a moment.

"In my whole life, there has never been anyone I admired more than Ulysses Grant. I've studied him, his strategy, what he accomplished against Lee. I'm not embarrassed to admit that Grant is a hero to me. But Grant wasn't perfect. He made mistakes, awful mistakes. I can't help thinking about Cold Harbor. His men were as enthusiastic as these men here, as you. They had pushed the rebels all the way down to Richmond, newspapers in the North predicting a quick victory, Lee's army being swept away, not capable of standing up to the might of General Grant's invincible wave. And at Cold Harbor, all that changed in one hour."

"I know my history, sir. Cold Harbor was one mistake. Grant still won the war."

"He never got over the cost, how many men died because of his mistake. He *never* got over it. Whatever happens tomorrow, there will be a price, and it will not be paid by me. It will be paid by a half million American boys. I hear officers talking all the time about their careers, making their mark on history. The French spend half their time thinking about Charlemagne, Attila, Napoleon, all the magnificent fights that took place on this same ground. But I don't fault the French. It's in all of us. How arrogant of any of us to believe our soldiers are willing to die so we can take our place in history."

"Forgive me, sir, but I think you've been around Europeans for too long. You've forgotten what these doughboys came over here for. No American soldier I know is fighting just for you. And not one of them is waiting for Joan of Arc to drop down on the damned battlefield, just so they have a cause to chase after. They're risking their lives because they believe it's the right thing to do. And it's up to you to lead them the same way. We have a good battle plan, and the right support. The men are trained and equipped. And across the way, when Fritz sees just how many American boys are coming his way, how many of my damned SPADs, and how many tanks . . . hell, the Huns won't have enough latrines. You've done your job, sir. Let the boys do theirs. And when it's done, I promise you, they'll be as proud of you as you are of them."

"Still nothing from the British, General?"

Rockenbach shook his head.

"No, sir. They are adamant that nothing can be spared. It is apparent that Marshal Haig is concerned about his own attack along the San Quentin front. I detected a considerable amount of nervousness among his subordinates."

Pershing sat back in the chair, and after a long moment, said, "General Rockenbach, is it your opinion that the tanks currently available to us will provide sufficient support to the infantry?"

"Forgive me, sir, but I don't know how to respond to that. With the latest battalions the French have made available to us, we should field over three hundred fifty light tanks, half of them piloted by our own people. I don't know how we can measure their effectiveness until the battle has concluded."

Pershing looked at the faces of the other officers, all standing behind Rockenbach.

"No, I don't suppose it is a question anyone can answer." He wanted to say more, held his words, thought, They don't need to hear my doubts. He looked up at Rockenbach again, studied the man, saw the face of an administrator, the kind of man Billy Mitchell would have little patience for. But Rockenbach had done his job, had secured as much cooperation from the French tank corps as anyone could hope for.

"You have your orders, gentlemen. I'd like to see your tanks on the streets of Berlin one day." It was a useless boast, and Pershing thought, They don't need some damned glad hand from me.

"Dismissed, gentlemen."

They began to file out, and a thought flashed into Pershing's mind. "General, one more moment."

Rockenbach turned, the others now out of the room. "Sir?"

"Tell me about Colonel Patton. You solve your, um, dispute?"

Rockenbach looked down for a brief moment. "I wasn't aware that this had reached your desk, sir. I didn't think it significant enough—"

"All right, Sam. I'm not sticking my nose into your command. I just want to know if George is going to be in the field tomorrow."

"Absolutely, sir. I believe the colonel understands my complaint with his performance at St. Mihiel. I understand he is your close acquaintance, sir—"

"Forget that, Sam. He's under your authority."

"Well, sir, if I may be blunt, he's just a bit bullheaded. He's a brigade commander, and he insists on leading the tanks himself. I have had to remind him that his place is at Corps headquarters, to coordinate the movements of his tank platoons with the infantry commanders. There were long periods during the battle when I couldn't locate him at all. I've had to contradict his order that his men carry rifles, and fight alongside the infantry if their tank is disabled. We didn't train these men so they can suddenly become foot soldiers."

Pershing nodded, suppressed the smile.

"As I said, sir, I believe we have come to an understanding. Colonel Patton knows to remain in close contact with me as much as possible. He has proposed creating a forward command center, to link up a communications line with corps headquarters. He convinced me, with admirable restraint, that a good combat leader should at least be in touch with his lead units. It was something of a compromise."

"You're in command of the tank corps, Sam. You don't have to compromise with anyone."

Rockenbach smiled. "If you say so, sir. But if I may ask, General, how would *you* handle him?"

Pershing laughed now. "I suppose, no matter what I tried to do, he'd find some way to be out there. Maybe we should just let him drive a damned tank."

43

PATTON

September 26, 1918

The lessons of St. Mihiel had been learned, and even before the artillery barrage began, he prowled among the large fuel trucks, inspecting, surprising the drivers, who had pried a few minutes' sleep from the misty darkness. The trucks would supply the gasoline for the containers on the smaller horse carts, which would be drawn forward behind the last wave of reserve tanks. It was the first great vulnerability of the tanks, something no one had predicted. In the field, under battle conditions, through muddy ground, shell holes, and shallow trenches, they gulped gasoline three times faster than they did on the parade ground. During the first day at St. Mihiel, nearly all the tanks had simply run out of fuel, some stopping just as the infantry they were supporting had needed them most. But now, with the new attack only short hours away, Patton understood the tank commander's priorities. It was no different than the cavalry. No matter how brilliant the strategy or how willing the soldiers, if you don't feed the horses, no one's going anywhere.

At St. Mihiel, he would have been just as happy driving the tank himself, a practice enjoyed by the British commanders. From their first massed fight at Cambrai, the British senior officers had refused to stay back in the headquarters, generals donning the thick leather helmets, climbing in beside the privates who worked the guns. But the British tanks were huge, had space inside for several men. The Renaults were compact, claustrophobic, room for only the driver, who sat up front, and one other man, the gunner, who manned the turret. They had no radios, no means to communicate with either headquarters or the other tanks who moved in the same formation. As the

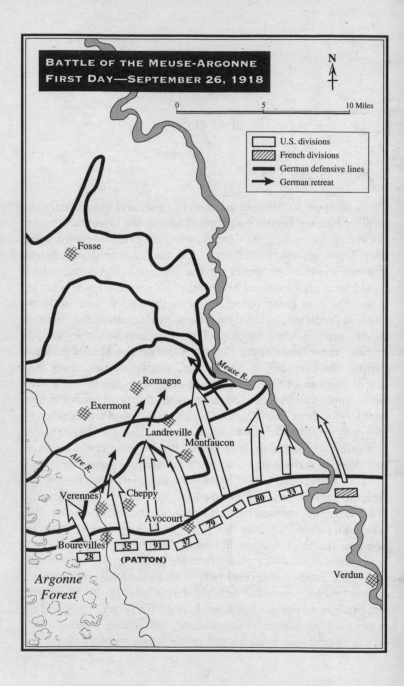

BATTLE OF THE MEUSE-ARGONNE
FIRST DAY—SEPTEMBER 26, 1918

N

☐	U.S. divisions
▨	French divisions
▬	German defensive lines
→	German retreat

0   5   10 Miles

Fosse

Meuse R.

Romagne

Exermont

Landreville

Montfaucon

Aire R.

Verennes   Cheppy

Avocourt

80   33

4

79

Bourevilles   35   91   37

28   **(PATTON)**

Argonne Forest

Verdun

number of tanks grew, so too did the experience of their commanders, and lessons had been learned from costly mistakes. In many of the early fights, the tanks had been placed directly under the command of the infantry officers, men who had no idea how the tanks should be used. Too often the tanks were driven by men with inadequate training, who sometimes tumbled their lumbering vehicles straight down into deep holes or, even if they kept their machines functioning, they ignored the needs of the infantrymen they were supposed to support. Often, the enormous firepower of the tank was negated by the lack of training by the gunners, the French in particular ignoring any emphasis on target practice. But eventually even the most reluctant generals had begun to accept what the foot soldiers already knew. Against the Maxims, and the increasingly accurate German light artillery, there could be no more comforting presence in the open field than a column of tanks.

With the increasing acceptance of the tank as a valuable tool, the French had developed the methods for maneuvering and coordinating the great machines under fire. Patton and Rockenbach had adopted many of the same practices. Each platoon of five tanks would be led by an officer on the ground, the man walking alongside, guiding the great machines, coordinating with other platoons by runner, the men the infantry called the Suicide Squad, the men who had one duty: run like hell across the battlefield carrying the messages from one commander to the other. There were four platoons to each company, two or three companies to a battalion. In the fight to come, Patton would command two battalions in the field, a total of one hundred forty tanks.

During the battle through the St. Mihiel salient, he knew that Rockenbach expected him to stay behind, and thus, to stay in direct contact with the tank brigade headquarters. But Patton had spent too many hours with these men and their amazing machines, had instead assigned an officer to remain in charge at his command post, while Patton himself advanced with the tanks. As his machines pursued the fight, he wouldn't rely on his staff of runners, had taken the fight into his own hands, darting among the tanks like some playful puppy, issuing commands to each driver. But his physical stamina could not match his enthusiasm, and finally he had climbed up, rode, surprising the driver of the Renault, as well as the foot soldiers who followed them across the narrow fields and cut ground. From his new vantage point, he could see more of the fight, guided the tanks by orders and hand signals to exhausted runners. As the tanks advanced, Patton could pick out the retreating Germans, or others who had stayed with their Maxim guns, ripe targets for the small cannon on the Renault.

From his earliest days at VMI, and then at West Point, he had nurtured the fantasy of leading a cavalry charge, that part of the army that drove the fight, that energized the foot soldiers to follow. Throughout all his training, he held tightly to the dream of being the first man across the field, the horse surging forward beneath him, being the first man to see the terror in the face of the enemy. The fantasy had been tempered by the reality of what this new war did to horses. Like so many of the infantrymen before him, the sight of the horses had been his first great shock on the battlefield, more so than the wounded men, the stretcher bearers, and ambulances. The men could be treated, healed, cared for, but no one doctored the horses, and so, if the artillery shell or the Maxim bullets didn't destroy the horse, they were left to die in slow writhing agony. The cavalryman's dream was wiped away, slowly replaced by the marvelous beauty of the tank. The big machines were not invulnerable, could be destroyed by the lucky shot from some distant artilleryman. Their clumsiness was a constant challenge, the risk of tumbling over into some unexpected chasm, bogged down into a trench that was far wider than the driver expected. They could be disabled as well by their own flaws, the engines notoriously unreliable, or, as at St. Mihiel, halted by the lack of gasoline. But when the engine ran smoothly, and the ground was firm, it was as though every horse in the world was driving across the great battlefield, invulnerable, impervious to the bullets and the deadly storm of shrapnel, a glorious, unstoppable wave. In each tank, there was one commander; every sergeant became his own general. But Patton knew there would always be the man in charge, sitting high up on the turret, leading the charge, the only place on earth where George Patton wanted to be.

After the fight at St. Mihiel, he had expected the dressing-down he received from Rockenbach. Rockenbach was not only his superior officer, but was a man who operated by the rules. Patton appreciated the necessity of the rule book, had even written his own detailed training instructions to be used at the Tank School. As an instructor, and now, as a brigade commander, Patton had built a reputation for harsh and inflexible discipline. But the rules of behavior he imposed on his subordinates were authored more by Patton himself, and it seemed perfectly logical to him that the men under his command should follow his instructions and perform their duty exactly as he would. Patton's difficulties came when the rules were handed down to him from above, someone like Rockenbach, an administrator who had his own notions of how Patton should behave.

Dawn—September 26, 1918

He told himself he would obey Rockenbach.

His command outpost was code-named "Bonehead," was little more than a protective dugout, a short trench close to the small village of Les Côtes de Forimont. For much of the night, he had hunkered down low, finding some dry place away from the misery of the weather, surrounded by other officers and a dozen runners, the men who would handle the flow of communications that Rockenbach would require him to send far behind the line. But the night would not be a long one. The shelling had begun at two-thirty, a heavy thunder that punched through the darkness, wrapping the men in silence. He had wanted to watch, enjoyed the grand display of light, flashes on both horizons, the white and gold streaks that ripped through the darkness. But the weather was still bad, and by the time the shelling had stopped, the heavy mist had given way to a steady light rain, made invisible by dense fog.

The radio had barked at five-thirty, but Patton knew the order already, knew that in front of him, alongside the banks of the Aire River, two divisions, the Twenty-eighth and the

Thirty-fifth, were in motion, nearly fifty thousand infantrymen rising up from their low places, beginning the great march northward. His tanks would move with them, spread into three lines. Patton's plan had been approved by the corps commander, the tactics carefully drawn to match the expectations of the infantry. The first line of tanks would lead the infantry far enough for the foot soldiers to get close to their first objective, to confront the German defenses that spread out from both banks of the river. The second line of tanks would move up when the first began to falter, either from enemy fire or the ever-present likelihood of mechanical and fuel problems. In the rear, the third line would serve as the reserve, pushing through if needed, or perhaps used to mop up stubborn pockets of German resistance. The first two lines were the speedy and compact Renault tanks, while the third was a combination of the Renaults and the larger French Schneider tanks, the slower and far more unreliable machines that the Renaults had rendered obsolete.

He stood up on the dugout, stared into fog, could hear the roar of the tanks, peppered by distant bursts of machine-gun and rifle fire. The field artillery was still active, some of the smaller guns rolling past the command post, moving forward into the rain and mist, disappearing on the muddy road. He was pacing, glanced at his watch, nearly six, the sounds of the fight still growing, spreading out all across the front. He jumped down from the top of the dugout, saw men watching him, said, "Anything from Brett?"

"No, sir. Not yet."

He climbed back out into the rain, could see waves of thick fog drifting over the road, more cannon rolling forward. He had confidence in Soreno Brett, the old-line infantryman and machine-gunner who now commanded his front-line battalion. No, he thought, if there's anything to tell me, he'll tell me. The second line was commanded by Captain Ranulf Compton, a man who had proven himself capable, but who did not seem to have Major Brett's sense of outright hostility to the enemy, a trait that Patton found greatly appealing. The third line was commanded by a Frenchman, Major Chanoine, a quietly competent field officer who seemed pleased to be serving with the Americans in any capacity at all.

The fight seemed to drift away in front of him, the only sound the roar of the tanks. He felt himself churning with energy, gripped his useless binoculars with one hand. There was nothing to see, no hint of what was happening. He paced along the dugout for a few long minutes, leaned out, looked down, no one coming up to meet him, no news. It was more than he could stand.

"Knowles! Edwards!"

The faces appeared in the dugout, the two officers staring up at him.

"We're moving forward! Bring the runners!"

The dugout burst into activity, and Patton walked out into the soft mud of the road, could see the wide tracks left by the tanks. The men emerged now, one struggling with several small cages, the carrier pigeons, another grappling with a coil of telephone wire, the heavy metal box that held a telephone. Patton felt the frustration bursting out of him, thought, Can't you move any faster? But he held on to the words, glanced at each of the runners, the men who might not survive the day. He saw his orderly now, Joe Angelo, the young man holding Patton's stout walking stick. Patton took it from the man's hand, stabbed it into the ground, said, "You have my compass?"

Angelo reached into a small pouch, said, "Right here, sir."

He could see the young man was shaking, nervous, took the compass from him, looked the young man in the eye, tried to calm him. "Good. Is your rifle loaded?"

Angelo held out the Springfield, a familiar routine between them, the gun offered for Patton's inspection. Patton nodded, said, "Just keep it clean, Private. You might need it." He turned, moved farther out into the road, said, "Let's move! Follow these tracks."

They fell into line behind him, Angelo and two other men moving out beside him, rifles in their hands. He glanced down at the tank tracks, probed with the walking stick, the mud not thick, the road firm, thought, Good ground. They should move quickly. We had damned well better walk fast, or this whole thing might be over before we get there.

They climbed a low hill, followed the tracks, the hill cresting, still bathed in fog. The roar from the tanks seemed scattered now, the air punched by cannon fire, most of it distant, the direction masked by the fog. Out to the right, there was machine-gun fire, a short burst, another, the men beside him crouching low. He pointed the stick forward, the silent order, the men responding. He stared out toward the sound, thought, Hell, they aren't shooting at us. Don't even know we're here. Those could be our boys, or, hell, who knows? Damned fog.

They were moving downhill now, the road turning sharply to the left, toward the river. The tank tracks continued onward, off the road now, and Patton pointed with the stick, stepped down into a muddy ditch, climbed up into a field of wet grass. He looked back, saw the men scrambling to keep up, the runners helping the men who labored to carry their gear. He would not wait for them, followed the tracks, the crushed grass, heard a harsh whisper. He turned, saw one of the runners pointing to a rough wood sign, words in German.

He moved that way, said in a whisper, "What is it? What's it say?"

"Sir, this says there's danger. I think it means . . . a minefield."

He could see more signs, several yards apart, a long row extending into the fog, parallel to the route the tanks had taken. The men had gathered close to him, and he laughed, moved close to the officer, Knowles, said, "Seems they didn't want their people to make a wrong turn. Damned nice of 'em. Probably kept a few of our boys in one piece. I guarantee there's a damned German colonel somewhere who'd be knocking heads if he knew his boys had left these signs up. Guess they weren't expecting us."

He followed the tracks again, heard another burst of machine-gun fire, the men moving quickly behind him. He didn't have the patience to calm them down, thought, Those are our guns, dammit. And if they're not, what the hell difference does it make? We're in the fog. They moved farther into the grassy field, the sound of rifle fire now meeting them, a sharp clap of thunder impacting the ground a hundred yards behind them. That's better, he thought. We're getting to where we need to be. He glanced up, saw sunlight slicing through the mist, the fog opening up in front of him. The machine guns began again, and he heard the roar of a tank out to one side, could hear the tank's cannon fire. He clenched his fists, pumped his hand in the air. That's what I want to hear, dammit! He pointed the stick toward the sound of the tank, was still following the tracks, and the men scrambled to follow. The air was still thick with mist, but the fog was breaking up now, the ground opening up, a row of trees in the distance, the field now more dirt than grass. There were ridges and low hills, and he lost sight of the tank tracks, thought, No matter. We're close. We'll see them pretty quick. They crested a low hill, and he expected to see the battle opening up in front of him, but the rifle fire was still distant, muffled. He saw them now, a half dozen tanks, pushing forward across the muddy ground. The tanks were on a road, a narrow farm lane, and he waved the men forward, began to run, waving his walking stick. The tanks were a hundred yards in front of him, and he climbed up onto the road, ran as quickly as he could, reached the first tank, his breathing in hard gasps. He rapped the stick on the tur-ret, then moved up toward the front, tapped the slits where the driver would be. The tank abruptly stopped, and Patton moved out in front, tried to speak, bent over, breathing heavily, saw the eyes of the driver staring at him through the narrow opening. The hatch opened now, and Patton saw a familiar face, a sergeant, couldn't remember the man's name, one of Compton's men.

"Sir? You okay?"

Patton saw the other men moving up behind the tank, Angelo coming up beside him, the nervous young man scanning the ridges in front of them.

"I'm just fine, Sergeant. You're Compton's battalion, right?"

"Yes, sir."

"Any idea where the fight is? Pretty calm right here."

There was no pleasantry in Patton's words, and the sergeant seemed to understand, pointed to the front, past the other tanks, said, "Sir, Lieutenant Sheeley's up ahead. There were tank tracks in this road. We were following, expected to find

711

some activity up ahead. There's not much happening right here."

"I'm aware there's nothing happening right here, Sergeant! You happy about that?"

"No, sir! Not at all, sir. You tell us where the enemy is, and we'll find them, sir!"

It was the right answer, and Patton pointed down the road, said, "The enemy's where that shooting is, Sergeant. Get going! Tell Sheeley I want him to find some damned Huns!"

The sergeant disappeared back into the tank, the engine belching smoke, the tank moving away from him.

Patton was angry now, said aloud, "Compton's sticking to the damned roads. Somebody ought to tell him these machines are made to go across terrain!"

Knowles was close to him, pointed toward a row of low hills, said, "Sir! Shells coming down. Half a mile or so."

"Well, then, that's where we need to be. We'll find a good place to sit, give these boys some rest. Brett's up there somewhere, and I want to find him!" He looked back, saw the one man sagging with the weight of the telephone wire. "Drop that, Private. There won't be any communications posts out here. We'll rely on our feet, and those damned pigeons."

The man obeyed gratefully, and they moved off the road, out into the field again.

Patton stopped, raised the binoculars, said, "There's a cut of some kind along that ridge. Let's go!"

He had climbed the long ridge, the men moving up cautiously, each one trying to gauge the direction of the fight. He scanned beyond the ridge, the ground uneven, brush and cluster of trees, narrow gullies and rocky hillsides. But there was little to see, the heavy mist fogging the binoculars, the air moving past him in clouds of thick dampness. He lowered the binoculars, felt helpless. The sounds of the fight seemed scattered, distant, disguised by the weather, bursts of machine-gun fire rattling in every direction. He turned, glanced at the man with the pigeon cages, then saw Knowles, said, "Captain! Have you determined our exact position?"

"Yes, sir. Up ahead, on the road, is the village of Cheppy. The railroad cut behind us is indicated on the maps as well."

"Good. Release a pigeon with details of my location. Rockenbach might be throwing his coffee cup against a wall about now."

The dirt in front of him was chopped, spraying him, and he heard the sound of the machine gun. Behind him, men were shouting, one hand pulling his belt, Angelo, "Sir! Get down!"

The guns came from every direction, and he saw the men scrambling, crawling back along the ridge, seeking cover. He pointed with his stick. "The railroad cut! Take cover!"

They poured over the edge, the men dropping down, the Maxims cutting the ground above their heads. He landed hard, shouted, "Where are they? Anyone see them?"

Knowles tumbled into the cut, and Patton did a quick head count, no one missing. Knowles said, "They're all over the damned place! Must have seen us coming, or they were moving through here, and we just ran right into 'em!"

Patton studied the men, terrified faces, said, "Anybody hit?"

No one responded, and he saw Angelo, only a few men with rifles.

"Private, take the flank! Corporal Hemings, the other flank! If the bastards think they have us trapped here, they may try to move around us! Keep an eye out!"

The two men moved into position, and Patton stepped past the crouching men, said, "We can't just sit here. We don't have enough guns to defend ourselves."

Angelo shouted now, "Sir! There's troops moving out across the ridge! They're ours, sir!"

Patton rose up, saw a scattering of infantry, climbed out up of the railroad cut, waved to them. "Here!"

The men responded, moved quickly toward him, began to drop into the cut. Patton looked for rank, saw only a corporal, said, "Who are you?"

"Tanner, sir! Our units are pretty messed up. We lost touch with our regiment in the fog. I hooked up with these boys. You're the first officer we've seen, sir!"

"All right, Tanner. You boys stay right here. We need your

rifles. The enemy's all over the damned place. Safest place for you is in this damned cut. Some of you spread out and watch the flanks."

The men seemed grateful for a voice of authority, and Patton scanned the faces, saw fear, the edge of panic. You're lost, so you're retreating. Not if I can help it.

The machine-gun fire had slowed, scattered bursts that seemed to drift away in the mist. Patton felt the frustration growing inside of him, said to Knowles, "Dammit, I'm not just going to sit here!"

"Sir! Listen!"

He saw one of the runners peering up along the edge of the cut, and now Patton heard the sound, the roar of tanks. He climbed up the sharp embankment, saw five Renaults, back along the base of the hill. The machine guns started again, the dirt splattering around him. He jumped back down, said, "We need those boys up this way! Captain Knowles, go down there and tell them our situation!"

Knowles looked at him for a brief moment, and Patton turned away, said under his breath, "Now, Captain."

"Yes, sir."

Knowles was up and out of the cut, and Patton began to pace, stepped past the men who lay all along the cut. The machine guns continued to fire, the men around him hunkered down. Patton climbed the embankment again, stared down toward the tanks, less than two hundred yards away, could see Knowles running, dropping down into a wide trench, then up, men around the tanks gathering to meet him. The gunfire seemed to move that way, the men suddenly disappearing into the trench, out of sight. Patton swung the walking stick, slapped the dirt hard beside his feet.

"Come on, dammit!"

He was bathed in a wet cloud of fog now, could see nothing, listened for the sound of the tank engines, heard only the uneven chatter of the guns. Hell, they're shooting all over the place. They barely know we're here! Those damned tanks could clear out this whole area! He saw more men moving over the ridge toward them, more infantry, and he waved, shouted again, "Here!"

The men ran toward him, grateful relief, slid down into the railroad cut, every face looking to him, more of the annoying fear.

"Check your rifles! We may see some Huns soon! They know we're here, but there's no better place for you to be!"

He ignored them now, strained to see the tanks, still heard no engines, shouted into the cut, "Lieutenant Edwards!"

Edwards appeared, seemed to flinch at every sound. The man was not infantry at all, had been assigned to Patton's headquarters from the Signal Corps.

"Get down there! Tell those tank drivers to get themselves up this damned hill! Those must be Compton's people. Find out where Comp-ton is!"

Edwards climbed up beside him, stared into the fog, and Patton said, "They can't see you, Lieutenant! Run like hell! You'll make it!"

Edwards was gone now, and Patton ignored him as he ran toward the tanks. Patton raised the binoculars, stared at nothing, scanned the thick air, wiped a sleeve on the lenses of the binoculars. Dammit! Somebody has to know what's happening!

The mist cleared again, and he saw the men at the tanks, Edwards there as well, could see the men gathering again, thought, Christ, they're having a damned conversation! I have to go myself!

He looked down along the cut, saw men all staring at him, edgy, nervous. I'm the only officer. And they have no fight in them. If I leave, they'll be gone.

The machine guns began again, and he realized the air was clearing. He saw a flicker of fire, a low ridgeline less than a hundred yards away, said, "There! Fire at that ridge! Those stumps!"

The men seemed to hesitate, and now the air around him was alive with the sounds of the Maxims.

"Sir! Get down!"

He saw Angelo, right below him, said, "Dammit! We need those tanks! What the hell is their problem?"

He stared down the hill, saw the men there jumping down

into low cover, the Germans guns pouring fire around the line of tanks. He felt the explosion building inside of him, the machine-gun fire cutting through the railroad cut from several directions. We can't stay here! And we need those tanks!

"Let's go! Down the hill! There's cover down there! Move!"

He waited as the men responded, Angelo beside him, and now he was moving with them, some of the foot soldiers in a mad dash for the line of tanks. He saw a wide brushy trench, blocking the path of the tanks, one big Schneider tank down in the trench, stranded. The men began to find the cover of the trench, and he pushed through it, was out the other side, moved up toward the tanks, moved past the officers without speaking, saw the hand tools, shovels and picks lashed to the side of each of the Renaults. He grabbed a shovel, yanked it free, tossed it into the trench, then another. Angelo understood, began to do the same from another tank. Knowles began to do the same, and the gunner climbed out from one of the tanks, the others following, each hatch opening, the tank crews emerging. Patton shouted at them, "Dig! Knock these sides down! Put the dirt into the trench!"

The soldiers began to help as well, helmets and bayonets scooping at the loose dirt. The machine-gun fire was increasing now, and he felt a breath of hot air on his face, bullets cracking into the tank beside him. He moved away from the tank, stared out across the open ground, the mist obscuring the view. They're right out there, he thought. Right there! Enough of this!

"Sir! We can give it a go!"

He looked at the trench, a narrow passageway caved in, shallow enough for the Renaults to cross. Slow going, he thought. And if one gets caught . . .

"Chain them together!"

The men looked at him, puzzled, then seemed to understand. Knowles was in motion, other men as well, chains unrolled from coils on the rear of each tank. In moments, the tanks were connected, and Patton stood back, pointed to the shallow trench.

"Move!"

The tanks began to rumble, coughing black smoke. The first

716

in the line lurched forward, moved down, the others close behind. The engines began to roar, each tank pulling and pushing against the other, a train of power surging through the soft earth. They were up and past the trench now, and Patton felt like laughing. Yes! Now those bastards will see what they can do with their machine guns! The tanks rolled on across the side of the hill, and Patton moved quickly across the trench, shouted to the men crowded along the bottom, "Let's go! Who's with me?"

The men began to rise, some staring up at the tanks as they moved away. They began to climb out, and Patton saw the men from his own staff, the runners, the men with the pigeon crates, few of them with rifles. He shouted to Knowles, "The unarmed men stay here. You stay with them. This is your new command post. Get word to corps headquarters of our situation."

Knowles seemed puzzled, said, "Sir, what is our situation?"

Patton turned, saw the tanks nearly up on the ridgeline, the infantry men around him waiting to follow. "Tell them . . . hell, tell them I'm still trying to find out what's going on. I'll try to get word back to you when I can. No need to mention anything about me joining the attack."

He jabbed the walking stick into the ground, began to climb the hill, the foot soldiers spreading out on both sides of him. The tanks had crested the hill, the machine-gun fire still slicing the air around him, and he pushed the stick into the ground with each step, saw Angelo on one side of him, staring up the hill.

They reached the crest, and the fight erupted across the open ground in front of them. The fire ripped the air from every cut, every cluster of brush and trees. He tried to see signs of other troops, but the thick air obscured his vision again. Around him, men began to fall, some of the infantry flattening out, seeking shelter, some hit by the fire of a dozen Maxim guns. He saw Angelo go down, the young man scrambling into a shallow depression, staring at him, shouting something, his voice drowned out by the firing all across the rough ground in front of him. Patton stared ahead, tried to see the tanks, heard a sharp blast from a Renault gun, yes, again! Pound those bastards! He looked out to both sides, most of the foot soldiers flat on the ground, and he shouted, "Let's go! Move forward! We can't stay here! Follow the tanks! Who's with me?"

He started forward, saw Angelo rising up, a few men, but only a few. He hesitated, saw most of the men staying flat on the ground, immobile, terrified. Dammit, there's no time for a speech! I'll take what I can get!

"Let's go!"

The noise was deafening, rifle fire, the Renaults still moving away, in a duel with targets Patton couldn't see. He saw a flash, barely fifty yards to one side, the wreckage of a machine gun tossed in the air, punched the air with his fist. Yes! Again! Keep firing!

There were only a half dozen men with him, and he heard a hard slap, a man suddenly collapsing close beside him. Now another man went down, the air alive with the zips of the Maxims. Two more men fell, and he looked to the front, could see open ground, pocked by shell holes, heard a hard grunt, another man curling over, his rifle clattering to the ground beside him. Angelo shouted at him, "Sir! We're alone!"

Patton glanced around, saw no one else, looked at the raw terror on Angelo's face, grabbed the man's shoulder, said, "Come on!"

He moved forward again, Angelo beside him, saw a line of low brush, heard the rush of fire from a Renault machine gun, the chatter of a Maxim, pops of rifle fire, smoke, the mist clearing again, and now he felt a hard jolt, a fist punching his left leg. He tumbled forward, fell hard on his side, heard a cry from Angelo.

"Sir! Oh God!"

He tried to stand, saw blood soaking his pants leg, a ragged hole above his knee, rolled over on his back, furious, helpless. Angelo was pulling at him now, had him by one arm, dragging him across the ground. Patton tried to say something, stop, dammit, keep going . . . but Angelo would not let go, and Patton felt himself sliding down into a hole.

Angelo was shouting at him, "Sir! Stay down!"

The young man pulled out his bayonet, cut and ripped the

cloth on Patton's pants leg. He made a bandage, tied it quickly around Patton's leg, just above the wound.

"We have to get you out of here, sir!"

The machine-gun fire continued, Angelo suddenly flattening out, the shell hole very shallow. Angelo was in motion again, slid on his belly close to him, probed the bandage, and Patton heard a new sound, another tank, closer, the sharp punch of the cannon. Angelo peered up, and Patton said, "They don't know where we are. You have to tell them!"

Angelo seemed to take a long deep breath, scrambled up out of the hole. Patton lay on his back, stared up into gray mist, felt the wetness on his face, the sting of sweat in his eyes. He reached down, felt the bandage, heard the tank gun again, the machine guns silent, voices now, men coming forward, his men, the tanks roaring ahead, the great machines still searching for targets.

They stayed close to him in the shell hole for hours after his wound, but he had ordered them not to move him, that any attempt to bring a stretcher would invite a torrent of fire from the German guns that were still dueling with the tanks. From the shell hole itself, the runners had come and gone, carrying instructions to the tank commanders as they rolled forward. Despite the wound, Patton stayed in command, his orderly tending to the bloody mess of his leg. For more than three hours, Patton worked from the shell hole with his binoculars, scanning the enemy positions, guiding the Renaults to the hottest targets. Finally, with the Germans either pushed back or their Maxim nests obliterated, Patton had allowed himself to be carried off the field.

He had been at the field hospital for two days, drifting in and out of sleep, the effects of the morphine. But the doctors had been pleasant and open with him, answering every question, details of the wound itself, how long it would take him to recover. The bullet had gone completely through, a hole punched from his thigh through his left hip. But no one seemed concerned about anything worse, and after the first day, the

719

pain had lessened, so that he might actually stay awake for more than an hour before the morphine was required.

He focused on the beds around him, the unending turmoil of movement and screams, stretcher bearers and nurses. It was the nurses who surprised him the most, women, mostly young, white uniforms stained with the blood of so many men. His brain could not hold on to the chaos, the faces a blur, the talk all of medicine and drugs. But through it all, he could see the nurses, constant motion, swarming like white birds around the beds and the men who filled them.

By the second day, they began to talk to him of moving, of evacuation to the base hospital at Allerey. The couriers came now, messages from Brett and Compton, from Knowles, many of his commanders. He sent messages of his own, replies to the kindness of his officers, mostly inquiring what was happening in the field, what kind of progress was being made in the ongoing fight. The news drifted through the hospital in waves of relief, the reports exactly what Patton hoped to hear. The tanks had led the way, and despite the loss of most of their number, mostly from mechanical exhaustion, the Americans had pressed the enemy hard, and for several days had driven him deeply into his own defenses.

The note came from Rockenbach as well, and there was no scolding, no disputing Patton's methods, no angry recitation of the rule book. Instead, Rockenbach had recommended that Lieutenant Colonel George Patton be promoted to full colonel, and as well that he be awarded the Distinguished Service Cross. Despite Patton's pride in the recognition, and the grateful thanks that he offered Rockenbach, as they moved him to the distant hospital, Patton began to focus on one goal. Heal the wound, and return to his tanks.

44

TEMPLE

October 1918

The great assault that began on September 26 had pushed the Germans back nearly ten miles. But the German defense stiffened. After four days of relentless assaults, the Americans began to suffer the same fate as so many of the troops who had pushed so hard across no-man's-land. Pershing's troops had driven themselves into complete exhaustion. Rather than watch his army destroy itself, Pershing ordered a halt to the attack, to allow time for his troops to consolidate their scattered positions, and prepare for a possible German counterattack. But the Germans were exhausted as well, and for a full day, both sides seemed willing to keep their guns silent.

As Foch's plan for the great battle unfolded all along the Western Front, the French position west of the American sector had begun to show weakness, many of the French divisions absorbing astonishing casualties as they pushed through the Argonne Forest. Foch had gone to Pershing yet again, a desperate plea for assistance for the French Fourth Army, whose divisions were grinding themselves to pulp against the German defenses. No matter how urgent Foch's needs, Pershing could not spare any American divisions from the fight that could erupt again at any time along his front. The only available force who could be sent westward quickly, to join the French Fourth Army in their struggles, was the one division resting at Toul. By September 28, the Second Division was again on the move.

Their objective was a ridge nearly two miles wide, the most prominent geographical feature for miles in all directions. It was called Blanc Mont Ridge and, at its highest point, was six hundred feet higher than the ground it dominated, the ground where the Second Division would have to begin its attack. For four years, the Germans had fortified the ridge with a network of trenches and concrete bunkers, a thick web of machine-gun nests and rifle pits. More important to the Germans, the ridge offered a perfect panoramic view of the entire Allied position, a place that served both as a magnificent reconnaissance platform and as the perfect location for the observers to direct the fire of their artillery. Behind Blanc Mont, the Germans had deployed some of the largest cannon they could use in the field, some anchored on railcars, or nestled into beds of concrete.

The ground in front of the ridge had long been in German hands as well, a network of trenches that spread over rough and uneven ground, short hills and shallow ravines, woods and brush lines. While Pershing's assault was driving northward along the eastern edge of the forest, the French had only succeeded in pushing the Germans back toward their stronghold on the ridge itself. Now, those trenches south of the great ridge were occupied by French soldiers, exhausted *poilus* who began to share the hopelessness of their officers. After days of devastating losses, most of the French commanders believed that removing the enemy from Blanc Mont Ridge was an impossible task. During the cold and rainy night of October 1, the French began to pull out, leaving the captured German trenches in the hands of the Second Division, men who did not yet know how impossible their task was supposed to be. It would be up to the Marines to sweep the Germans off Blanc Mont Ridge.

They moved into the trenches at night, protected by the heavy mist and rain that still hovered over the entire area. They stepped through rivers of soft white mud, the chalky ground pulling at their boots as the men stared ahead into wet darkness, hoping for some dry place, some kind of cover that might have been left behind by the enemy who had built these shelters. Unlike so many of the night marches, this time there were no secrets, no need for silence. Since the first attacks began, the French had been trading fire with the German forces along the base of the ridge, clusters of enemy guns and rifles along every ravine and low hillside. The machine-gun and artillery fire was constant and as the Marines slipped into place, their narrow watery pathways were made visible by the unending flashes, blasts of fire, star shells, and streaks of light that cut sharply through the thoughts of each man who marched to yet another promise of a hell like none he had ever seen.

Near Somme-Py—October 2, 1918

Temple felt the pain growing in his legs, the torment from the slow methodical steps through the chalky glue. Scarabelli was in front of him, the small man struggling even more, stopping now, a low curse, interrupted by a voice behind them.

"Keep moving! Time enough for rest up ahead!"

Temple put a hand on Scarabelli's shoulder, said, "Can't be much farther . . ."

There was a blinding flash, an explosion just behind him, and Temple was pushed hard to one side, his legs buckling. He fell forward, both hands down into the mud. The screams came now, close behind him, and he tried to pull himself upright, turned, stared into blind darkness.

"Medic! Medic here!"

He fought to see, more shells impacting around the narrow trench, caught glimpses through brief flashes. The passageway behind him was gone altogether, a smoking mound of chalky dirt, a man's arm, a helmet. He felt a hand on him, pulling him away. It was Scarabelli.

"We can't stop! They have the range. They know we're here. Come on, nothing we can do!"

Temple wiped his hands on his pants legs, checked his rifle, pulled it tight against him, mud on the shoulder strap, mud soaking through every part of him. He ran a hand over the grenades hanging from his shirt, the extra belt of ammunition, coated by a watery ooze. Scarabelli was moving ahead, and Temple followed, knew he was right, thought, It was a direct hit. Right behind me. He thought of the men who had marched behind him, but his mind kept the faces away, no names, just

Marines, the men probably dead before the dirt covered them up. Had to be a seventy-seven. Thank God. Anything bigger, and there'd be a hell of a bigger hole. I'd be in it. Temple followed Scarabelli again, ignored the mud, felt himself breath-ing hard, painful breaths, realized he was nearly running, auto-matic, hard splashes around his boots.

"File right! Dugout ahead. Another fifty yards! Frenchies coming this way, make room!"

The voice was Lucas', familiar, comforting, and Temple could see the bend in the trench, realized they were moving downhill, the trench deeper, opening up now, a wide hollow pit in the chalk, more narrow trenches feeding off in different directions. He was surprised to see a yellow light, a hole dug deep off to one side. The line was halted, and Temple stared down into a room, felt the warmth, the stale air. He glanced up, a low ceil-ing of timbers, thought, We're underground. He could still hear the shell fire, deep rumbles pulsing under his feet, echoes, the sounds distant now. He looked around, saw the men still in line, standing silently, more coming in behind him, the men who had to climb over the devastation in the trench. He ignored the faces, looked around the dugout, saw planks of wood, crude walls holding back the dirt. Men began to emerge from the far side of the dugout, *poilus*, filthy animal-like faces, moving toward them with slow deliberate steps. The Marines shifted to one side, no one speaking, the French soldiers ignoring the men who had come to replace them, too exhausted to speak, to do anything but follow the man who followed the man in front of him.

Lucas moved past Temple, dropped down the short steps into the lamp-lit room. Temple was close to the opening, could see officers, recognized the face of Major Hamilton, saw another man, a blue uniform, French. The officers were talking, and Temple saw Scarabelli lean closer to the yellow light, listening. Temple moved close up behind him, heard the major's voice.

"Who's in command here?"

"That is me. Lieutenant Bernard. There are no other officers." There was a silent moment, and Temple tried to see their faces, realized that more men had gathered close behind him. Lucas said, "How long before your men are out of here?"

"They are leaving now. There are being now ten platoons. Ninety men, perhaps less."

Temple looked around, saw the *poilus* still filing past, thought, Ninety men? Ten platoons should be near five hundred.

Hamilton said, "What are we facing? How far is the enemy?"

"A hundred meters, Major. There are four communication trenches that go forward to the next line. There are barricades thickly. The enemy is there, and cannot be moved."

"Why the hell not?"

"Major, we have tried. You will see, in the daylight. They have too strong for machine guns. Seven days we have been here."

Lucas said, "Then we'll go around. How far is the flank?"

"I do not know. We have lost too many men. Every time, they cut us down. You must know that this trench here . . . we do not hold it. The Boche are on the left flank."

Hamilton said, "What? *This* trench?"

"Oui, yes. There are heavily barricades that way. Two hundred meters."

Lucas said, "You mean this very trench? The enemy is down at the far end, just like we are here?"

"Yes. You must be careful."

The men behind Temple began to back away, a voice behind him.

"Keep moving, boys. The Frenchies are clear." Temple saw Osborne now, the tall sergeant pointing the Marines down the trench. Osborne looked at him, said, "You boys get your ears full? If the officers want you to know what the hell's going on, they'll tell you. You keep your mouth shut if you heard anything. Understand?"

Temple glanced at Scarabelli, who said, "Didn't hear anything, Sarge. Just that if we were to go off thataway, we could share rations with the enemy. They're right next to us."

Osborne glanced off to the side, smiled. "Well, then, we best put on our company manners. You'll be moving out this way a piece. And clean your damned weapon, Private. Maybe Fritz will drop by for some coffee later. Now get moving, and keep quiet."

Temple followed Scarabelli out of the wide dugout, climbed back up into the open air, the light gone now. He felt the wetness again, the rumble of artillery louder. They were in the mud again, the air cold, chilling the wetness in his uniform. He thought of the *poilus*, the words of their lieutenant . . . seven days. We stay here that long, we'll look like that too. Nope. They didn't send us up here to eat rations for seven days.

Rations. The word sent a shiver into his gut. They hadn't eaten since early that morning, cold corned beef and stale bread. Every man had said something to the food orderlies, various curses, usually involving their parenthood. Big mistake, he thought. The men with the food are not the people to yell at. I could use anything they want to bring up here. Maybe the *poilus* left something behind.

He was engulfed by a sickening odor, and his foot kicked something soft. The ground under his feet was uneven now, and he had to step carefully, his boots dropping into mud, then up again. He felt light rain on his helmet, cold misery dripping down his back, the awful smells boring into him. There was a flash of light, a shell impacting fifty yards behind the trench, and he saw now, under his feet, the bottom of the trench lined with the bodies of unburied men. He stumbled, pulled his foot back, tried to step over, was blind again, fought the horror, the sickness from the emptiness in his gut. He knew now, the French had indeed left something behind.

October 3, 1918

The rations had come up, buckets of boiled beef and potatoes, but the smell in the trench had taken most of their appetites away. The artillery had continued all night, guns on both sides throwing shells into targets that had long been destroyed. He had been put into position by Osborne, and Temple found himself on a narrow hump in the trench floor, a place to sit that was up out of the watery goo. He felt lucky, could hear the men struggling in the wetness, kept his mind away from what it was that made the hump, what might be buried underneath him.

In front of him, the walls of the trench had been carved out, the desperate work of a man long gone, a narrow slit cut into the chalk where a man could wedge himself in, sheltered from the rain. Temple had tried to take advantage, slid himself into the tight space, tried to use the makeshift bed, but the dirt walls pressed hard against him, wrapped him like a chalky hand. There would be no sleep, nothing to erase the numbing shock of the seventy-seven shell, the direct hit on the men who had marched so close behind him, the sight and smell of the men the French had no time to bury. He had stayed awake for another reason as well. In this trench there were no cats, and so in every hole, every dark place, the rats had emerged, already seeking the bodies of the *poilus*, or anything else that was available.

The French had cut parapets along the side of the trench that faced Blanc Mont, and the sergeants had posted guards, the men who would stare into the darkness toward the enemy that they now knew were only a hundred yards in front of them. They had forced themselves to be still, silent, ignoring the torment from the cooties, the water soaking through their socks. There could be no noise, nothing to distract the guards, and so the only break in the silence was the rats, scurrying through the mud, startling the man who might try to lie down. The veterans knew that if there was any sleep to be had, it was best to put your helmet over your face, to keep the rats from scratching you as they ran over you. But Temple had given up any thoughts of sleep, had crawled back out of his chalky bed, sat down on his little hump on the soggy floor of the trench.

He realized the rain had stopped, but the air was still heavy and wet. Osborne was there now, quietly relieving the guards, and Temple stood, could see down the trench, a low gray light. There was commotion, back toward the wide dugout, and he saw men moving toward him, silent, heads

727

down. Temple pulled himself back against the wall of the trench, the men filing past him, a steady flow. He understood now. They were the Sixth Marines.

At four o'clock, Lucas had come, seeking out his own platoon, giving them quiet instructions. Temple had listened hard, but the orders seemed vague, far more than Temple would need to know. The Sixth would be mostly on the right flank, but several squads would advance in a first wave from the same trench where Temple was now. With the dawn would come the first attack, and the Sixth would lead the way, would rise up quickly from the trench works, and advance toward the rough ground along the base of the great ridge. The Fifth would follow, moving in a solid line, battalion strength, would follow the Sixth to the base of Blanc Mont, then hold their position, prepared to support the Sixth as those men began the climb up through the rough hillside. Temple had wanted to ask him about the trench out in front of them, reminding the lieutenant what the French officer had said, the man's caution, the enemy dug into a place the *poilus* had simply given up trying to capture. But Lucas was gone as quickly as he had appeared, moving away, more instructions to more men, and Temple had stared into the darkness wondering if the officers had simply forgotten the caution from the French officer, or perhaps the privates didn't need to know what lay a hundred yards in front of them. In everything the lieutenant had said, there was only one mission: the ridge itself, the men simply told to do whatever it would take to get there.

The men of the Sixth continued to file past him, no one speaking, and he did not look at the faces. After St. Mihiel, both Marine regiments had been brought up to full strength, a thousand new recruits filling the gaps. At the rest camps, the veterans had been merciless, punching holes in the bravado of the new men, columns of clean-faced men whom the old sergeants referred to as warm meat. Now, in the wet dawn, there was no way to distinguish the recruit from the veteran, and there were none of the usual taunts, or the rude insults that marked the rivalry between the regiments. Today, it would be the Sixth who would go first, and they all knew that there was no special pride in that. Tomorrow, it would likely be the other way around.

He had shivered for over an hour, the air colder than anyone had expected. The trench was nearly packed with men and Temple eased past them, looked along the wall for Parker. The big man had been gone for what seemed to be an hour, had been sought out by Osborne and taken away silently toward the great wide dugout. It was curious, and Temple had wanted to ask somebody why. He knew that Murphy was up on the parapet above him, but Temple knew not to talk to him, knew that no matter what was happening down in the trench, Murphy would be doing what all the lookouts did, focusing on nothing but the ground in front of him, any movement, any sound. Whatever Parker was doing, Temple would just have to wait to find out.

The artillery fire had slowed, sporadic thumps and rumbles behind the line. Temple realized it was light enough to see his hands, and he glanced up into the heavy mist, wiped at the layer of crust on his face. The hunger growled through his stomach, and he eased his backpack off his shoulders, ignored the faces that turned toward him. He slid his hand inside, touched the cold metal, pulled out a can of emergency rations. He reached for his bayonet, felt a hand grabbing his arm, looked into the face of Osborne, heard a low whisper, "Put it away, Private. No time. You'll need it later."

"What time is it, Sarge?"

"Near six. All hell's about to break loose."

Osborne moved to the parapet, reached up, tapped the lookouts on the leg, each man turning toward him. Osborne motioned with his hand, *down*, the men stepping off the parapet. Murphy was beside him now, and Temple could hear him shivering, said in a whisper, "You okay?"

"Frozen. You got any coffee in your pocket?"

Temple's response was masked by the high shriek, a short blast, the ground out in front of the trench churned and tossed over them. The shelling then erupted behind them, a vast wave of thunder, sharp whines and ripped air. Around him, the men huddled low, and the voice in his mind shouted, It's ours! The shells blanketed the ground beyond the trench, a cascading storm of blasts that shook the dirt from the walls, choking them with burned powder. He wanted to yell, too close! They're too close! But the impacts began to move farther out now, and he understood, the rolling barrage, the great wave of fire and destruction that was designed to destroy the enemy in front of them. He thought of the unseen trench . . . out there, the place the French could not take. No, we won't take it either. We'll just blow it to hell. But that's awfully damned close. He heard a sharp shrill whistle, the familiar signal, and in one surge of motion, the men of the Sixth were up on the parapet, pushing their way out over the sandbags, moving toward the steady screaming hell of the artillery barrage. Lucas was there now, moving quickly down the trench, the same words shouted every few steps. "Up! Fix bayonets! Be ready!"

Temple felt the pounding in his chest, so familiar, the cold chill from the wet air matched by the ice inside of him. He looked down the trench, the men in motion, the bayonets, was surprised to see Parker, the big man moving quickly toward him. Temple held up his hand, *here*, and Parker stopped, leaned against the quaking walls of the trench, breathing heavily. Temple could see, he did not have the *chauchat* gun, was carrying something different, odd, a short stub of a gun. Parker held it up toward him now, and Temple could see it was a shotgun. Parker slapped at his own chest, and Temple could see bandoliers, rows of fat shotgun shells. The questions rolled through him, but the barrage swept away any talk. Parker retrieved his bayonet from his belt, twisted it into place on the barrel of the strange gun, then looked at him, a brief smile, reached out a heavy hand, patted Temple on the side of the face.

Lucas was there again, Osborne beside him, and Temple could hear the words, the artillery barrage more distant now. Lucas said, "Only one way to go, Marines! Forward!"

Lucas moved away, and Osborne glanced at the men of his squad, and pointed up to the parapet.

He braced himself for the burst of firing from the German trench, but the ground in front of them was silent, the wave of

Marines pushing past a tumble of dirt and sandbags, broken timbers and rusted heaps of barbed wire. In front of the trench, the ground was dotted with the mangled bodies of men, black shapes, draped with the shreds of French and German uniforms. The signs of the weeklong fight lay everywhere, shell holes and caved-in trenches, men and their weapons scattered through pools of deep mud and chalky water. The Marines advanced at a walk, moved past the carnage, and Temple could see that more of the bodies were German now, fresh wounds, some men still moving, the stubborn or the unlucky, caught by the artillery barrage, or cut down by the first wave, the men of the Sixth. He continued to walk with the men around him, climbed up over the short choppy hills, dropped down into uneven brushy ground. The fight was out in front of them, and Temple saw more bodies now, men in khaki, the same men who had stood beside him in dark silence. The medics were there, men running with stretchers, already tending to the wounded. He tried to ignore the cries of the wounded, stepped past a German who was sitting upright, bareheaded, talking, a meaningless chatter of words, another man lying flat beside him, most of the man's chest blown away. Temple stared ahead, heard the zip of rifle fire overhead, random, ricochets from the fight ahead.

They moved down through a line of low brush, more wounded, men from both sides, and he glanced to the side, saw Scarabelli, Parker out in front of him, holding the bizarre shotgun. They were climbing now, a low hill, the brush ending, the ground opening up into a wide clearing. He could hear machine-gun fire down to the right, where the infantry regiments were, the far right flank, and off to the left, the French, more strength pushing forward. The mist was blowing into his face now, the grass tall and wet, and as they walked out into the wide clear hillside, he could see glimpses of the horizon, the great ridge, the mass of ground that rose up, towering over them. The fight was still in front of them, and he could see movement, *Germans*, scrambling up through the gullies and thickets on the great hill itself. Men began to shout all along the clearing, cheering the work of the Sixth, the Germans giving up their defensive lines along the base of the ridge, pulling back up the hill, up to their positions of strength.

He heard the order to halt, could see the entire battalion spread along the wide sloping hillside, the officers halting them just behind the crest, the only cover they had. The men lay flat now, and Temple dropped down, listened to the rifle fire, the chatter of the Maxims, thought, Why did we stop? He felt his chest heaving against the ground beneath him, all right, we need a rest. But those boys in front of us aren't resting. He could see officers moving quickly, a group gathering behind them at the edge of the clearing, loud voices, angry men pointing out toward the flanks. He tried to hear the words, but the officers dispersed, and he looked to the front again, heard Scarabelli a few feet away.

"Something's not good. That was a pissed-off colonel."

"How you know he's a colonel?"

"Seen him before. Grouchy bastard. I bet he beats his kids."

"Shut up, Jersey."

The voice was Parker's, and Temple saw him, farther up, just below the crest of the hill.

"Hey, Dan! Why they give you a shotgun?"

Parker turned, looked back toward him, said nothing.

Temple glanced back at Scarabelli, said, "I gotta get a look at that thing."

"Jesus, Farm Boy, it's just a shotgun. You know damned well you shot your share of bluebirds with one just like it."

Temple ignored him, crawled forward on his elbows, his rifle resting in the crook of his arms. He was close to Parker now, said, "Let's see that thing, Dan. Why they give it to you?"

"Guess they figure I'll be getting a close-up look at something worth shootin'. They gave me a choice to keep the chatchat, but I decided this thing'll do more good."

Temple heard other men talking about the shotgun, some of them envious, offering Parker a trade. Temple crawled up closer still, stared at the shotgun, and he heard a loud screaming roar, louder now, the sound of a freight train, high overhead, deafening, dropping toward him. The explosion ruptured the slope behind him, punching the air out of his lungs, the shock

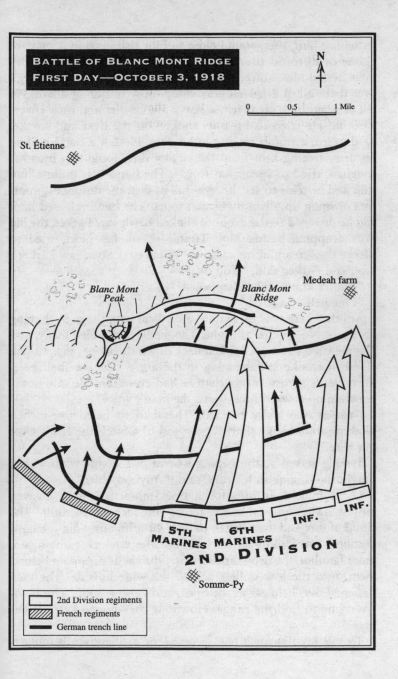

BATTLE OF BLANC MONT RIDGE
FIRST DAY—OCTOBER 3, 1918

N

0   0.5   1 Mile

St. Étienne

Blanc Mont
Peak

Blanc Mont
Ridge

Medeah farm

INF.   INF.

5TH
MARINES

6TH
MARINES

2ND DIVISION

Somme-Py

2nd Division regiments
French regiments
German trench line

flattening him, the ground close to him rising up in a massive plume of dirt and fire. He closed his eyes, pulled his arms in tight beside him, stared into darkness, the earth hanging high over them all in a frozen gray cloud, now tumbling down. He felt crushed by a great fist, a heavy pile of dirt and rock covering him. He tried to breathe, choked on the dust and smoke, hard gasps, a numb ringing in his ears. He felt a hand pulling his arm, freeing him from the chalky dirt, fought to breathe, coughed, tried to speak, no words. The hand was pulling him still, and he tried to see, his eyes full of dirt, the numbness in his ears opening up, distant voices, shouts. The hand released him, and he dropped to the ground, blinked hard, saw Parker, the big man dropping beside him. Temple shook his head, tried to silence the scream in his ears, was rolled over now, saw Parker's face, and Parker said, "You okay?"

"I don't know. What happened?"

"One hell of a shell."

Another man was there now, a medical bag, the man shaking his head, No, you're all right. The medic scrambled away, and Temple tried to sit up, looked back down the slope, saw a thick cloud of smoke still hanging in the air, a massive shell hole, thirty yards across, larger than he had ever seen. He saw Lucas crawling up toward him, heard the man's voice.

"You're one lucky bastard! That had to be a nine-incher. Nothing sounds like that. Biggest son of a bitch the Huns have out here."

Temple stared at the gaping wound in the soft white earth, fought the ringing in his ears, said, "Anybody hit?"

Lucas looked at him for a brief moment, didn't answer, moved away on his knees across the face of the hill. The cloud of dirt and dust began to drift into the misty air, the hard chemical smell rolling over him. But the screams came again, more familiar, the usual artillery fire, the shells dropping behind them, into the low gullies behind the wide hillside. The men flattened out, helpless in the open, and Parker said, "The Huns are trying to find the range. How long they gonna keep us out here?"

Temple lay flat for a few seconds, the artillery shells impacting farther away. He rolled over, looked back down the hill toward the massive crater.

"Dan . . ."

"I see it. My God, Roscoe. It took half the platoon. There were twenty or thirty men there."

Temple could see them now, bits of uniform, broken rifles, smashed helmets, ripped pieces of men. On all sides of the massive hole, men were pulling themselves together, helping hands, the medics scrambling among them, tending to the wounded. But there were not many wounded. Temple slid on his backside, moved closer to the wide smoking maw, looked at the men scattered around the crater, most crawling forward, every man putting distance between himself and this horrific wound in the earth. He saw Murphy, coated in white dirt, moving up the far side of the hole.

"Murph! You okay?"

Murphy looked toward him, nodded, then looked into the hole, stared, frozen.

"Hold on. I'll give you a hand!"

Temple started to move that way, saw Murphy still just staring, but the artillery came closer again, punching the ground just beyond the ridge in front of them. Temple saw Murphy sit up now, his eyes fixed on the shell hole, and Temple thought, He's hurt. Damn. He needs to be in cover. He slid along the ground, close to Murphy now, said, "Murph! Come on! We gotta move!"

Murphy looked at him with empty eyes, said, "They're gone. Allen, Knight. Stevie."

Temple tried to ignore the hole, pulled at Murphy. "I know, Murph. We gotta go."

The man seemed rooted, immovable, looked at him now, blinked hard. "Gino."

Temple felt a cold burst in his chest, looked into the chalky hole, wisps of smoke still rising, shredded khaki, canteens, a broken rifle. He looked back up the hill, saw Parker lying on his side, staring down at him. He scanned the other men around the hole, familiar faces, none of them the small young man from New Jersey. He was right here, he thought. I was beside him.

Oh Christ, Gino. He wanted to crawl down into the hole, something holding him back, a gray shroud, the chemical smell. The sergeants began to shout, the men moving up the slope. Temple ignored them, ignored the piercing shrieks of the shells, the blasts that punched the ground beneath him, closer now, the gunners finding the range. A medic was there, his hand on Murphy.

"It's okay, Private. I'll take care of him."

Temple looked again at Murphy, the eyes staring down past him. There was blood on Murphy's shirt, the medic pulling at him, laying him on his back, tearing the shirt open. The medic said, "Not too bad. Shrapnel wound." He looked at Temple now. "Your buddy's gonna be okay. Messed up his shoulder. You better get going. We'll get him outta here pretty quick."

Temple pointed to the shell hole, tried to speak. He flinched from a sharp whine, a shell landing in the crater, a burst of fire, the medic leaning over Murphy, shielding him from the spray of dirt.

The sergeants were shouting again, and the medic said, "Move out, Private!"

He looked at the man, wanted to explain, heard the medic's words in his mind, your *buddy*. He fought the tears, stared into the shell hole for a long moment, tried to see Scarabelli's face, gone now, like Ballou, like so many of the rest. He heard another blast, heard the whistles of shrapnel, the deadly splinters of steel, the ground rumbling under him. He rolled over, looked up the hill, saw Parker sliding down the slope toward him, the big man motioning with his hand, *lie flat*. He was there now, grabbed Temple's shoulder, pulled him over onto his stomach, flattened out beside him, said to the medic, "How's Murph?"

"He'll be okay. Busted shoulder. You guys need to go!"

The shelling was becoming more intense, consistent, the blasts erupting among the men, great gaping holes tearing through the battalion. There was a single breathless pause, and Temple heard the high scream again, the enormous roar of the freight train, shouted, "No! God, no!"

The enormous shell fell two hundred yards farther along the

hillside, another great blast, another platoon cut in half. The shouts began again, sergeants climbing to their feet, Lucas now up on the crest of the ridge, waving to them, *move*. Parker grabbed him hard, said, "Let's go!"

Temple pulled himself up, said, "Dan . . . Gino's gone."

Parker glanced at the crater, stood still for a long second, put a hand on his shoulder. "We have to go, Roscoe."

Parker started up the hill, and Temple followed, saw the wave of men flowing up and over the low crest, heard Parker say, "God bless you, Jersey."

45

TEMPLE

Blanc Mont Ridge—October 4, 1918

By dark, the Sixth Marines had topped the eastern end of Blanc Mont Ridge, and had driven the Germans completely off that part of the high ground. But to the west, the Germans still held tightly to the ridge's highest point. As the Marines pushed up and over their objective, the French forces who began the day on their left flank attempted to clear the Germans out of their trenches, but the attacks had bogged down, the Germans holding firm. As night fell, the French were still back on the south side of the great ridge, had failed to match the progress of the Marines, and so had failed to protect the Americans' left flank.

On the Marines' right, the Second Division's infantry regiments, the Ninth and Twenty-third, had skirted past the northern edge of the ridge, had nearly reached their objective, pushing the Germans back to their defensive lines north of the Medeah farm. But the Marines had pressed their success too far. As the Sixth drove down the north side of the ridge, they had far outpaced not only the French but their own infantry support. Though much of Blanc Mont was in their hands, the result was a deep bulge pushed into the German defenses. As darkness settled over the ground, the Fifth Marines moved up and relieved the Sixth, the proud, exhausted men who believed that they accomplished the goal the French had said was impossible. In the darkness, the men of the Fifth protected themselves as best they could from continuous artillery attacks, completely unaware that their flanks were in the air. With the new dawn only hours away, it was the officers who first began to understand that the Marines were now facing the enemy on three sides. And if the Germans took advantage, and sliced across

738

the rear of the American salient, the entire regiment would be surrounded.

The battalion was now spread along a narrow ravine, a natural trench that gave the men cover from the sporadic shelling. Temple had carved a soft place for himself in the dirt, a depression protected on the uphill side by a fat rock. Parker was close to him, had dug out a shelter of his own, the same muffled sounds repeated all through the cut in the earth. They had no idea what lay out in front of them, had found their place in the line only by following Lucas. There had been talk again of French guides, the furious officers cursing the absurdly unreliable men who never seemed to appear. Lucas had simply followed a compass, aided by runners scrambling through the dark. All along the battalion front the officers had spent much of the night trying to find each other, to pull their units into some kind of cohesive line. In the shadowy darkness Temple could see the great hulking shape of Blanc Mont Ridge, behind them now. Despite the success of the Sixth, Temple shared the uncomfortable feeling with the men around him that there had been an enormous price for that success. The Fifth had paid a price as well. Back on that gentle sloping hillside, the open ground on the far side of the ridge, the German artillery had been brutally accurate. As they moved up to support the men who fought on the hill itself, the Fifth had left several hundred casualties behind, entire platoons gone, several companies now faint skeletons of their strength. Temple knew little of what had truly happened, knew nothing of maps and mistakes. But the rumors had already found their way through the darkness, grumbles about confusion, angry talk of the failure of the French.

The German guns that had done such deadly work had been positioned where the Marines now dug in. But those guns were gone, pulled back to some new vantage point, someplace where the German observers who still huddled on the western half of Blanc Mont Ridge could again direct their fire.

Temple lay on his back, wrapped in his thin wool blanket, staring up into stars, the first clear sky he had seen for a week. His stomach churned in a noisy grumble, made worse by the emergency rations, the only rations anyone had. He still hated the grotesque beef in the small cans, what Scarabelli had called "monkey meat." Temple had always laughed at the small Italian's peculiar view of the world around him, the vivid descriptions, his amazing talent for reading conspiracy into every annoyance. Temple had his own vivid description now, his mind carrying him back to the extraordinary shell hole, the impact of the mammoth artillery shell, what the lieutenant said was nine inches thick. In the quiet darkness he could not help thinking of Scarabelli's devout father, the man so concerned how his son would die. Temple had already started a letter in his mind, would not let Scarabelli's family know of their boy's death only from some War Department formality. All he knew of them were Scarabelli's descriptions, the large, emotional family, newly transplanted Americans, so proud of their Marine, so proud to offer their own to this war. He had first thought of writing to Scarabelli's mother, tried to imagine his own mother's reaction to word of her son's death. He imagined his mother, the strong woman who was so prone to emotion, sitting in her single chair on the wide porch of the farmhouse, unstoppable tears. It sickened him, knowing her pride in her son could be replaced by stunning grief. She had written him of her hopes for his safe return, apologizing for a mother's concerns. Now, he imagined her receiving the cold impersonal regrets of her government, a woman whose life would be changed in such a horrible way, losing her only son to a war she knew so little about. How many mothers had been through this already, women who watched their sons board the trains or the great ships, pride tempered by tears, scolded by the men in their lives not to embarrass their sons with a mother's fawning. He had to believe that Scarabelli's mother would react to the awful news the same way. An Italian woman in New Jersey would certainly grieve as deeply as the straight-backed woman who worked the farm in Florida. No, he thought, I will write to the father. Easier to tell this to a man, to explain, convince him that his priest was wrong. I'm sorry for you, sir. But if it was God's decision to take your boy, He will not explain why, not to you, not to your priest. The words flowed through Temple's mind now: Tell your priest that your boy died fighting, that he died doing the right thing. Surely that is what matters to God. And if someone tries to tell you that God punished him for something, you must know that Gino never felt . . . anything. He never knew what happened. There was no suffering, no pain, no horrible wound. The best way to go. All that idiotic talk about the clean bullet wound, less pain. No, there is nothing *clean* about a bullet in your body. It should happen the way it happened to Gino. One big damned shell falls right on your head, blows you to dust, nothing left, nothing to bury, no blood, no *pieces*, no horrible memories to torture your friends. That's the gift God gives the rest of us. Let us remember Gino as he was.

He was suddenly awake, was still on his back, stared into dull light, the stars gone. The air was cold, and he shivered, glanced to the side, saw men moving slowly, some looking up, pointing. He heard the sound now, a low hum, realized it was an aero-plane, the droning growing louder. He sat up, tried to see a reflection, some glimmer of metal from the faint glow of sunrise.

"Nobody move! They're looking for our position!"

The voice was Lucas, and Temple understood, of course, they know we're here, but they don't know how many of us or where we spent the night. The calls echoed down through the ravine, and Temple turned his head slowly toward the front, tried to see past the rock, could see only that their shelter was not much of a shelter at all, the ravine shallow, opening quickly up to a flat grassy field. He was shivering now, angry at himself. You fell asleep on your *back*. Your face exposed. Stupid.

The plane was coming toward them, the hum growing louder, and he looked out along the low ground, saw men spread in all directions, clusters of dark blankets and khaki against the white dirt. The plane was overhead now, and he couldn't hold still, looked up, the plane not more than three hundred feet above them. The plane moved quickly, parallel to their lines, spun away to the side, seemed to waggle its wings. The faint daylight showed the detail, the pair of black crosses on the bottom wing.

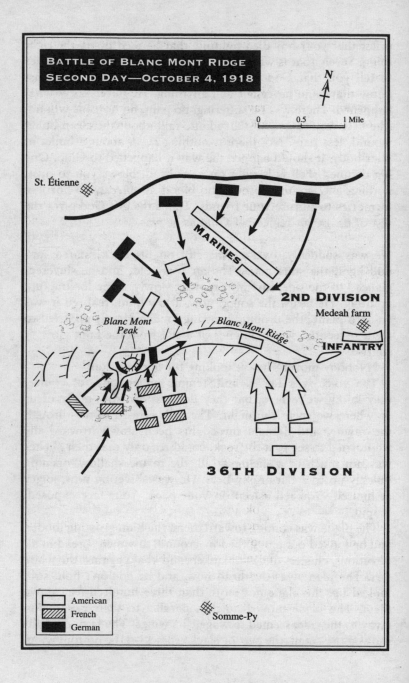

BATTLE OF BLANC MONT RIDGE
SECOND DAY—OCTOBER 4, 1918

N

0   0.5   1 Mile

St. Étienne

MARINES

2ND DIVISION

Medeah farm

Blanc Mont Ridge

Blanc Mont Peak

INFANTRY

36TH DIVISION

American
French
German

Somme-Py

The plane made a sharp turn, came right above them again, and Lucas said, "Dammit! Artillery spotter! Get ready to move out fast!"

The shells came now, a single blast, then four more, punching the ground along the ravine. Temple rolled the blanket quickly, grabbed his pack, glanced out in all directions, any signs of cover, the shells falling faster, a steady rhythm to it, some landing directly into the narrow cut. Lucas was up, running along the ravine, shouted, "This way!"

Men seemed to boil up out of the low ground, the smoke and blasts punching through them, and Temple followed, saw Parker up, running in front of him. Lucas led them into a stand of blasted trees and the men flattened out, other officers running through them, shouts, confusion, the shelling coming down behind them. Temple dropped down beside a fat tree trunk, raised his head, tried to see through the blackened timber, a vast patch of devastated forest, uneven ground. The shelling had stopped as quickly as it had begun, and Lucas shouted, "Get ready to move! They're not done!"

He heard low talk, frantic voices, saw a runner, the man moving quickly, darting through the burned trees. More voices drifted over, officers from other companies, sergeants, useless orders to men who had nowhere else to go.

He could hear the plane again, but different now, and he rolled over, stared up, searched the sky. He saw them, counted four, looping in a wide arc, one banking hard. There were scattered cheers from the men, and he saw, Yes, they're French! No, not all of them. He saw the black crosses again, said aloud, "Three of ours! Get the bastard!"

Others near him took up the call, cheering on the French pilots, their voices punctuated by the faint chattering of the machine guns high above. The German plane seemed to flip over, and Temple saw smoke, the men around him silent for a brief second, everyone staring hard, hoping. The German plane dipped low, the others swarming behind it, and suddenly the plane nosed down, thick black smoke, dove straight down, crashed into the ground a hundred yards from where Temple lay. The men cheered again, the French planes swooping low, verifying their kill, hands waving, new shouts from the officers, "Let's go! On your feet!"

Temple looked around, spotted Lucas, the lieutenant moving through the burned stumps, pulling the men up. Parker rose up from behind a fat log, pointed the way with the shotgun, said, "Get ready, Roscoe. Looks like we're going back up the hill."

Temple could see the officers leading the men toward the great ridge, the same place they had come down the evening before. But it wasn't the same place. It was nothing like he had imagined in the dark. He could see the whole ridge now, the sunlight revealing the hillside. They had come over the eastern crest, vague hints in the darkness of German earthworks, scattered debris, bodies of men in gray and khaki. But he realized now how large the ridge was, saw that down to the west, the hill rose up to a peak, and all along the crest there were huts and small buildings, a network of shelters and bunkers, trench lines clearly visible. Toward the far peak of the hill, the flashes and flickers of fire began, machine guns, rifle fire. The air was alive with the sounds, men dropping down again, finding cover. Temple crawled down behind another blackened stump, his mind racing, furious thoughts. What the hell is going on? How did the Huns get back up there? He thought of the men of the Sixth, so happy to see their replacements, exhausted and smiling. Smiling for what? They were supposed to push the Huns off the hill. Where the hell are the French? Weren't they supposed to be up there?

He curled up tightly, listened to the smack and thump of the bullets, the sharp whiz and zips above him. Now what? We have to go back up there? All of us? He peered around the stumps, saw muddy boots protruding from behind a fallen tree.

"Dan! You see the lieutenant? You tell what's going on?"

The stump above his head was suddenly splintered, and he ducked low, the firing coming from another direction, closer. He jerked his head around, saw streaks of fire coming from the opposite direction, the sound of machine guns. He felt a burst of panic, the fire coming from the low ground to the north. There was a shout, a single word, "Crossfire!"

There was nowhere for him to move, no shelter, the pops and thumps of rifle fire finding the men in their cover. Around him, the Marines began to return fire, blind, men shooting in different directions. There were angry shouts from men he couldn't see: "Hold your fire! No targets!"

Beyond the stump, Temple heard movement, Parker crawling quickly, the big man moving up close, lying flat beside him. "We're in trouble, Roscoe."

"What the hell happened?"

"Don't know. Feels like we're in a box. I'm guessing we're about to get the order to attack. Either that, or the Huns'll just mop us up. I'd rather go after 'em than just wait here."

The order came now, the tall frame of Osborne suddenly rising up close to Temple.

"Marines! Up! Pull back toward the ridge! Let's go!"

Osborne began to move through the timber, and Temple took a long deep breath, the stump above him splattering again from machine-gun fire. He waited, another breath, saw Parker pull himself up, and Temple rose as well, followed the wave of men toward the hill.

They moved over low hills and brushy ravines, the same kind of ground they had fought through so many times before. But they could not stay in the short cover. The Germans high on the ridge had perfect targets, and the new sounds came, sharp blasts, mortar shells coming straight down off the crest. Temple ran as hard as he could, ducked low into a narrow ditch, then up again, pushing through brush. The ground around him was peppered with machine-gun fire, the familiar sickening chatter of the Maxims. Men were falling all around him, one man a few feet in front of him suddenly rolling over. Temple wanted to stop, help the man, but the voice in his head was screaming, No, keep moving!

They were on the steeper slope now, and he saw a narrow hole between two rocks, fell into the gap, stopped, gasping, turned, saw the men swarming up around him. He could see out across the base of the ridge, the entire battalion, all of them in motion. Far to the north, there was movement as well, a wave of gray, Germans moving in line, coming toward them. To the west, there were flickers of fire, the enemy moving closer along the base of the ridge, firing into the Marines from the flank. A bullet smacked the rock close to him, and he ducked, looked up the hill, saw men crawling up through the thickets, more shouts. Lucas rose up, crawled up onto a fat rock, waving his arm, pointing the way. Temple watched the man for a long second, felt a dark place suddenly burst open inside of him, no, dammit, get down. . . .

Lucas fell now, tumbled off the rock, the wave of men pushing past him, not stopping. Temple felt the panic again, slid out from between the rocks, moved up the hill, saw a body, bareheaded, a bullet through the man's forehead. But it was not Lucas, and Temple searched frantically, moved beyond the rock, saw another body. He moved closer, the familiar face, blood on the man's leg, and Temple ducked low, a spray of machine-gun fire cutting the brush above him. He knelt beside Lucas, the lieutenant rolling over, his hand gripping the shattered leg.

"I got you, sir! Come on!"

"Get the hell out of here, Private! Find cover. They're hitting us from every direction! Find Osborne, any officer! Tell them to pull the men into a defensive position! We have to get up as high on the hill as we can!"

"I can't leave you here, sir! Let me wrap your leg!"

"I'll do it, Private! Go! Find an officer!"

Temple stared at the man's leg, blood streaming out in a pool on the ground. Lucas pulled his knife, sliced his blanket. He glanced up at Temple, his hands never stopping, said, "Private! Get up that damned hill!"

The men sought any kind of cover, helmets and bayonets ripping the ground, many digging shallow one-man trenches. Temple worked his way up the hill, saw bodies in every open place, others firing down at the enemy pressing them from below. Out to one side, others were lining up to fire up along the crest of the hill. There had been only sporadic artillery, the Marines too close to the enemy positions for the German gunners to draw a clear field of fire. The worst danger was still the Maxims, many firing from concrete bunkers, or the occasional mortar shell lobbed down from the west end of the ridge.

Temple had found Osborne, had given him Lucas' order, the lanky sergeant passing the word to a desperately frightened runner, who disappeared into the brush. Osborne was close to him now, Parker as well, others working with them to carve out some kind of shallow ditch, a vantage point to put up some kind of fire line toward the enemy down below the hill. Temple was exhausted, sweating, lay on his stomach, peering down. He had positioned himself where he could see an opening in a line of brush, a trail that he had followed up the hill. All across the slope, men were finding someplace to make a fight, others moving farther up, strengthening the ridgeline itself, a desperate stand to keep the enemy from moving straight across the high ground behind them.

He stared down the barrel of the Springfield, then raised his head, slid the rifle straight out, then back toward him again, seating it firmly into a soft cradle of dirt. The ground erupted off to one side, another mortar shell, the men responding with low curses. The mortar shells gave no warning, dropped too slowly to make the whine or scream of the artillery shell. In the open ground, you could see the mortar shells coming, the high arcing dot, might even have time to move out of the way. But there was nothing to see now, the shells falling on them by pure chance, finding men who had no time even to flinch.

As the Germans below tried to push up the hill toward them, the Marines had made good use of their grenades, deadly bombs that were as effective as well-aimed rifle fire at holding the Germans at bay. Thrown from the slope of the hill, the grenades could go a long way, falling into the scattered clusters of the enemy with the same silent effect as the mortar shells. Parker had the reputation as the man with the strong arm, several of the men passing their bombs to him, cheering the big man who threw the grenades like a baseball pitcher. Parker had never done it correctly, had infuriated the training officers by never following the correct procedure. But there were no officers now, no one to judge him but the men grateful for his gift of strength. More men were gathering around Temple now, some still digging, the firing growing more scattered, quieting down. Parker slid along the makeshift trench, moving closer to him, and Temple saw that he was carrying two guns, the shot-gun and a Springfield.

Parker crawled up close to him, laid the Springfield up on the edge of the dirt pile, said, "Shotgun not much good unless they charge right on us. Figured I better find a rifle. Plenty of 'em to be found. How much ammo you got left?"

Temple ran a hand over the ammo belt, said, "Not much. A dozen rounds. Two grenades."

Parker looked down at the scattering of men, said, "How much ammo?"

The answers came back, most of them the same.

"Not much."

"Damned near out."

Parker looked behind them, stared up toward the top of the ridge.

"We should make our way to the top. Join up with those boys there. What do you think, Sarge?"

Temple looked toward Osborne, who said, "Sit tight for now. Those boys are in no better shape than we are. They're keeping our backs clear. We have to do the same for them. Awfully damned quiet."

No one spoke for a long moment, eyes straining to see move-ment down the hill, out on the flat ground.

"There! Look! To the left!"

Temple saw what they all saw now, a wave of gray, several lines of enemy troops suddenly appearing in the burned timber, another thick line coming up from behind the low hills in the flat ground farther north. Across the base of the hill, there was another wave, enemy troops who were close to the cover down below, where Lucas was wounded. There were dull pops of rifle fire, Springfields, from Marines farther down the slope. After a silent moment, Parker said, "Hey, Sarge. How many men in the Hun army?"

"Hell, I don't know."

"Well, we're about to find out. 'Cause they're all coming."

Temple felt the cold shiver, stared down the rifle barrel again, focused on the gap in the brush. He tried not to see what the others were watching, heavy lines of enemy troops moving at a steady pace toward them, the great masses converging, like a monstrous gray pincer. Temple said, "Sarge? I don't have enough ammo to do much good. We can't hold 'em back for long."

Osborne said nothing, and Temple looked toward him, saw Osborne with his head down. The sergeant looked at him now, said, "They didn't teach me how to retreat, Private."

Parker said, "Well, Sarge, maybe it's time you learned. We sit here, we're dead in a half hour. And that ain't gonna help those boys up top. We get up there with 'em, we can pool our ammo, make our stand on the high ground. The higher up we are, the harder it'll be for the Huns. My granddaddy learned that the hard way at Gettysburg."

Osborne stared down, scanned the open ground where the gray waves were rolling closer. He pulled himself to his knees now, said, "Pass the word. Everybody to the top of the ridge. Pick up whatever ammo you can."

Temple looked down at the rocks where Lucas had gone down.

"Sarge, what do we do about the wounded?"

Osborne didn't answer, stood, began to move up the hill. The others began to follow, men rising up all along the side of the hill, the word passing. Temple grabbed his rifle, and beside him, Parker said, "We'll get 'em later, Roscoe."

They had formed a defensive line in three directions, most of the movable cover placed to the west, blocking the fire from the Maxim guns on the high part of the ridge. The rifles mostly pointed down, the Marines seeking a field of fire, waiting in cold silence for the enemy to come into range on the wide hillside. There were no officers, and the few sergeants who remained had made a quick count of the available ammo, barely twenty rounds per man, and altogether no more than thirty grenades among them. They could hear sounds of a fight to the east, the division's infantry regiments battling on the low ground near the Medeah farm. Far down behind the ridge, from the French positions, another fight had broken out. The French seemed to be fighting their way past the old German trench works, were pressing an attack against the far end of Blanc Mont Ridge. But both fights were far away, and the Marines could focus only on what lay right in front of them. They were about to be swallowed up.

The rifle fire began down to Temple's right, men shouting out, targets finally appearing close below them. The Germans were returning fire, a rolling chatter that spread all down to the east. Below him, the open patches of hillside were suddenly alive with men, the lines of gray pressing up the hill. He tried to calm the quivering in his hands, aimed the rifle as he had done so many times, picked his target, a patch of gray, the helmet, the man's bayonet pointing forward, and he pulled the trigger.

Around him, the men chose their shots carefully, the first wave of Germans punched back, men tumbling away on the hillside. But the Germans did not stop, and Temple fired again, saw the man fall forward, another man right behind him filling the same gap. He fired again, the rattling of the Springfields around him deafening, someone tossing a grenade, a blast of dirt down below, more gray uniforms pushing through it. The firing continued down to the right, louder now, no more than fifty men holding the flank. He heard shouts, glanced that way, a sergeant running toward him, a dozen men following, enemy troops suddenly appearing on the crest a hundred yards behind them. Men were falling, the Germans stopping to fire, more gray uniforms rolling up the hill in front of him. Temple tried to focus, aimed the Springfield, the Germans now pushing up to the flat ground. The gray wave began to flow right into the Marines, and Temple saw a man running straight toward him, the bayonet high over the German's head. Temple saw the man's face, the eyes, tried to lift the rifle, heard a hard blast close beside him. It was Parker's shotgun, and the German folded over, collapsing facedown in front of him. The enemy was swarming up all along the ridgeline, hand-to-hand fighting, no time to aim, targets rising up in all directions. Temple fired the rifle into a mass of gray. He jerked the bolt, the magazine empty, grabbed for cartridges at his belt, Parker's shotgun erupting again. Some Marines were rising up, confronting the Germans with their bayonets. Temple's fingers fumbled with the bullets, and he stuffed one into the breech of the rifle, closed the bolt, another man rushing toward him. He fired, the man twisting, falling to the side, but not dead, rising again. Temple was up now, pulled the rifle in close to him, saw the man's bayonet, high, arcing toward him, a hard shout, the blade coming toward him in a hard thrust. Temple slapped at the bayonet with his rifle, the man stumbling, and Temple lunged his own bayonet hard, caught the man in the side, drove the bayonet deep. The man went down, the rifle jerked from Temple's hands. He saw more gray, coming closer, another blast from the shotgun, smoke, men falling, a vast storm of rifle fire now roaring behind him. The firing came in a rolling wave that seemed to spread all down behind them. He reached for the rifle, the bayonet still lodged in the man's ribs, no time, turned, expected to see the enemy, more bayonets, felt his knees buckle, dropped down, pulling hard on the rifle, *no time*, and now he saw them, another surging wave of men. But the uniforms were not gray. They were khaki. They were Americans.

Pershing had sent the Thirty-sixth Division to support the trapped Marines on Blanc Mont Ridge. The fresh infantrymen had made the hard march through the old trench lines, had pushed out through the brush, across the open clearings, past the ripped ground where so many of the Marines still lay. As the battle rolled in on the Marines from three directions, the first companies of the Thirty-sixth reached the crest of the ridge. The Germans who pushed their fight so close were suddenly confronted by waves of fresh infantry, and by late in the afternoon, the reinforcements helped the Marines to roll the exhausted Germans back. By nighttime, the combined forces had strengthened the position the Marines had fought to gain the day before. The one task that still lay before the Americans on Blanc Mont Ridge was to sweep the last German stronghold off the highest point at the western end of the ridge. With the French finally pressing their attack from the south, the Germans realized their position was untenable. By the evening of the following day, the Germans pulled most of their troops out of their fortified strongholds. Those who could not escape surrendered, the Americans capturing nearly three thousand prisoners. Blanc Mont Ridge was completely in Allied hands.

Within a few days, the Second and Thirty-sixth Divisions pushed northward again, and with the added pressure from the French, they captured the town of St. Étienne. By October 10, the Thirty-sixth Division took the lead in holding the newly won position, while the Second was pulled back to recuperate. As the numbers became known, the shock echoed through the entire AEF. The battalion of the Fifth Marines that had been trapped in the "box" north of Blanc Mont Ridge had numbered a thousand men. By the end of the fighting, one hundred thirty-four marched out.

To the east of the Argonne forest, Pershing's army continued their unrelenting assault northward through the long-established German defenses. No fight was easy, no resistance passive, but as had happened at Blanc Mont Ridge, the Americans had the benefit of reinforcements, of reserves who could be shifted to the most dangerous fronts on the field. The cost to both sides had become appalling, and despite staggering losses to many of the American divisions, the toll inflicted on their German counterparts was far worse. With the French Fourth Army linked to the American left flank, the push continued, until, by October 16, the Argonne Forest was cleared of German troops. The fight now swung more to the northeast, the Germans gradually giving ground as the Allied divisions pressed them close to their last great defensive barrier along the Meuse River. As the generals worked to gather and reorganize their commands, the Second Division was reunited with Pershing's First Army, was made ready yet again to confront an enemy now fighting for his very survival.

46

VON HINDENBURG

October 24, 1918

With a view to avoiding further bloodshed, the German Government requests the immediate conclusion of an armistice. . . .

The cable had been sent to Washington on October 6, signed by the new chancellor, Prince Max von Baden, the fourth man to hold that position in the last twelve months.

Von Hindenburg knew that the entire civilian government was poised to champion any overture that President Wilson was likely to make. Wilson was the logical choice to be the recipient of Germany's request for a halt to the war, since the American president had long advocated a far more lenient peace than what France or England would certainly insist upon. It was the one belief that the German military shared with their civilian ministers. If the war was to be decided on the battlefield, no general, no matter what country he fought for, would be pleased with anything short of total surrender. It was simply their nature. But as harsh as the generals might be, the German government had to believe that both Clemenceau and Lloyd George would be equally as harsh. If Foch could secure victory on the battlefields, in both London and Paris, any talk of peace would include victory of another kind, absolute and devastating not only to Germany's military, but to her government, her economy, and her people.

A peace overture had become inevitable with the collapse of Ludendorff's spring offensives. Though German troops had occupied more French soil than at any time in the war, the army had been too exhausted to take full advantage of any major breakthrough. Worse, with the Americans now pouring into the front lines, Foch's grand strategy had reclaimed nearly every swath of ground the Germans had captured that spring. With the success of the British assaults in August, Ludendorff had to concede that his great strategy had simply failed. Not only the army, but the nation that supported it was too exhausted, too drained of manpower and supplies to hold back what was becoming an inevitable collapse.

Von Hindenburg had stayed on his train, mostly immobile now, no place where he really needed to be. He had long accepted what everyone in the High Command knew, that Ludendorff was truly in command and that this fat old man was only the symbol of something that had once been, and now might never be again. Von Hindenburg knew they spoke of him that way, and it was not insulting, no great wound to his pride. The pride was all inside of Ludendorff, the perpetually angry man, railing at the failure of his government, the failure of so many subordinates, the failure of the front-line troops to carry out the genius of Ludendorff's plan. There had been rumors of Ludendorff's collapse, some sort of mental or physical breakdown. But von Hindenburg would hear none of it, was still close enough to Ludendorff to understand what had happened to him. The failures were many and more costly than anyone could have predicted and Ludendorff could no longer energize the army by the fire of his will. Von Hindenburg knew that Ludendorff had used all his strength to combat the defeatism that was spreading through the entire army, through all of Germany. It was a struggle between what should have been and what was, the ideal against the practical. For over a year von Hindenburg had watched the ideal fall away, replaced by the consequences of so many mistakes, some of them made by Ludendorff himself. Ludendorff had never pushed for a German tank building program, did not ever believe that the British and French armor would be of any real consequence in the field. His troops told him differently. On the oceans, the convoy system used by the Allies had virtually eliminated the U-boat as Germany's most powerful weapon, and with the German admirals too timid to confront the British navy, the control of the oceans was firmly in Allied hands.

The optimism from the scattered fronts of the war had collapsed along with Ludendorff's spring offensives. In Italy, the enormous success of the Austrians at Caporetto the autumn before had been entirely reversed. The Austrians had taken their success one step too far, had extended their forces unwisely, and the new Italian commander, Armando Diaz, had taken full advantage. By mid-June, the Austrians had suffered an enormously costly defeat along the Piave River. The losses had so devastated the Austrians and their commander that von Hindenburg was convinced the Austrians would never again be able to mount any kind of offensive.

In the Middle East, the British had made consistent gains against the Turks for more than a year. Von Hindenburg had never regarded the Turkish leadership as a faithful ally, but the enormous benefit of tying up massive British forces in that region had clearly made the alliance worthwhile for Germany. But now, the Turks were in danger of a total collapse. The Bulgarians were already defeated, and the fighting in the Balkans had dwindled to scattered battles that added nothing to Germany's efforts. With the growing inevitability of the failure of Germany's allies, it was clear that in time, the enemy, particularly the British, could eventually retrieve their scattered armies, and feed them into the offensives now driving the Germans back along the entire Western Front.

For more than a year, the High Command had been elated by the overthrow of the Russian czarist government. Lenin's revolution had thrown that country into total chaos, and had thus taken them completely out of the war. The inevitable result of the Russian collapse was a theme loudly voiced by every observer on both sides of the Western Front. It was a certainty that the enormous influx of German troops shifting from the Eastern Front to France would so add to German power that they could crush anything the Allied armies could put before them. In the spring, it had nearly worked. But there were forces at work in the ranks of the German army that Ludendorff had ignored, and even now von Hindenburg didn't fully understand. The proximity of so many German divisions to the turmoil of the Russian Revolution had infected many of those troops with the stain of Bolshevism. By the time many of those troops reached France, they had passed through the heart of a depressed Germany, had seen too much of what the war had done to the home front, to the German people, to their own families. Even as Ludendorff's great offensives were rolling forward, there was talk in the army of mutiny and revolt, rumors planted by supporters of a Marxist revolution that would restore Germany to a peaceful glory, instead of the brutal suffering of the people from the policies of their military, or the whimsical vanity of their kaiser. The talk had grown louder by August, when the British crushed their way through the German lines. Entire companies of German troops had simply quit, massive surrenders, desertions, open defiance of officers. Von Hindenburg had been shocked, appalled at the news. Ludendorff had reacted with fury, but there was no one to blame, no ringleader to execute.

For four years, the Belgian frontier had been a death trap for the British, had swallowed up so many casualties that von Hindenburg had long expected that the British government might simply give up, and abandon their allies. But since August, the combination of British, Anzac, Canadian, and Belgian forces had been too much for the worn-out German army to hold back. With so many of the reserve units sent to the Argonne to face the Americans, in Flanders, there was virtually no reserve left at all. The combined efforts of the American, French, and British forces had driven the Germans back to the Hindenburg Line. But the great defensive barrier, once so impenetrable, was weakened far more than Germany's enemies knew. All across the Western Front, from Flanders to the Meuse River, Foch's grand strategy of a massive general assault had been costly but effective. While Foch had cautiously celebrated the victories of the Allied armies, the German High Command knew that his success was due as much to the deterioration of the German army as any superiority Foch had on the battlefield. In the face of the Allies' devastating pressure, Ludendorff's field commanders had finally convinced their leader that the Hindenburg Line might not be so impenetrable after all. The battered German army was coming apart from the inside out, and Ludendorff was forced to accept what von Hindenburg already knew. Unless there was an armistice, and very soon, Germany wouldn't have an army left to put into the field. If the French and British had their way, they might press their armies all the way across the Rhine River. It would not be just the defeat of the German army. It would be the end of the Fatherland.

Von Hindenburg had decided to go to Berlin, a necessity now with the growing pressure from the Reichstag to pursue some form of armistice. His train rolled across bleak farmlands, empty fields, through quiet villages where churches still offered comfort to the misery of the people. The roads that ran parallel to the tracks were empty. There were no cars, gasoline severely restricted, tires and oil nonexistent. He stared out the window, saw an old man tending to a small garden. There was no horse, no livestock in the man's fields at all. It was the most common sight now. What the army had not taken, the people had consumed themselves. Horses were a luxury no farmer could afford. Von Hindenburg watched the man for as long as he could see him, a man too old for war, whose grandsons might be facing the enemy somewhere to the west. He turned away from the window, the sights too familiar. He was too tired for work, for the numbing details of troop positions, and the chaotic calls from senior officers who each faced the same kind of crisis. Ludendorff kept him dutifully informed, fed him copies of the significant orders, the reports from the field of casualties and troop movements. But von Hindenburg rarely offered any comment, had not issued his own orders for some time. He understood more than ever that Ludendorff needed him to be a buffer between the army and the kaiser. Von Hindenburg had no argument with that role, had known for some time that it was Ludendorff's war. He glanced again out the window, thought, Should it have been any other way? If I was younger and had his energy, his fire, would I have done anything so differently? What did I know of tanks? Without von Hoeppner making such a nuisance of himself, we likely wouldn't have relied on the Air Service. No, this was never my war. I am here because my country expected me to be here. What do they expect now?

There was the soft sound of a teacup, and von Hindenburg ignored the orderly who set the tea on his desk, was thinking now of Ludendorff. Did they expect too much of him? No, I think not. An army needs a strong leader, *one* strong leader. He will be the last soldier in the army, the last man to surrender, the last man to accept that everything we have believed in and everything we have worked for has been taken away. All those nagging voices in the Reichstag, all those civilians who seek the more comfortable way out of any crisis, those men have no grasp of what the Fatherland means to a soldier. While they cower in their offices, seeking any shameful rescue from our difficulties, it is Ludendorff who would stand in front of the Reichstag, who would defend Germany even if he is the last man to hold a sword. And for that, they would label him a dangerous fool.

He looked now at the letters on his desk, copies of all the correspondence that had flowed back and forth between the Reichstag and Washington. So now we crawl to President Wilson like a child who seeks favors of the most gullible of our parents. We place our faith in this man because he is thought to vacillate, to be soft. And right now, *soft* is the only hope we have. He closed his eyes, took a deep breath. How ironic. The American president who sent his army across the ocean, the same army that has taken victory away from us . . . he is the man we believe to be the most forgiving. Months ago we spoke of peace, a quiet suggestion that the English and French could not ignore. But then, we were in a position of strength. The advantages were all ours. If not for the Americans, the French and English people would have forced their governments to seek some end to this war. But now, everything is different. A year ago, it was our enemies who needed the Americans. Now, it is us.

He had no energy for diplomacy, knew that the cables had gone both ways since the first suggestion of an armistice that the chancellor had put forth. Now the *language* begins, he thought, the posturing, the careful phrases, the perfect wording. We must not offer too much, show we are too eager, and they cannot offer us too much hope, or lead us down some path that will infuriate their allies. What hope is there anyway? Does anyone in Berlin believe that Clemenceau or Lloyd George will simply roll over like Wilson's house pets and accept the terms the Americans find acceptable? No, that is a poor description. They are not house pets. They are two braying asses, spouting their diatribes, each one grabbing for his place in history, each one spitting and clawing at the other to see who can lay claim to the obliteration of the German people. They may not even listen to Wilson at all. When the history of this is written, no Englishman, no Frenchman will allow himself to admit that without the Americans, this war would be over. If Mr. Wilson's army had never arrived, the kaiser would be turning the palace at Versailles into his summer residence.

He noticed the tea now, cradled the cup with a thick hand. Cold. He thought of calling the orderly, but had no strength even for that now. Enjoy your quiet moment, he thought. This evening is not likely to be so . . . calm.

Bellevue Palace, Berlin—October 24, 1918

He and Ludendorff had been summoned to meet with Kaiser Wilhelm, word coming to the High Command of another cable from Woodrow Wilson. The long-distance discussion of the possibilities of an armistice had unfolded exactly as von Hindenburg had expected. It had been an exercise in precision, perfect clarity, no possibility of any vague pronouncement or misunderstanding that could suddenly erupt into a verbal sparring match that would toss away hope of the kind of peace that would benefit anyone.

He and Ludendorff arrived together at the kaiser's palace, a show of unity that would at least offer a symbolic gesture that command of the army was still in the hands of the two men who had given the kaiser so much loyalty. The show was fragile at best, something von Hindenburg accepted with calm. He wasn't certain that Ludendorff accepted it at all.

The Kaiser sat back in his lush chair, seemed tired, gazed past them as the aides handed each man a copy of Wilson's cable. Von Hindenburg took the paper, adjusted his glasses, read.

Feeling that the whole peace of the world depends now on plain speaking and straightforward action, the President deems it his duty to say, without any attempt to soften what may seem harsh words, that the nations of the world do not and cannot trust the word of those who have hitherto been the masters of German policy, and to point out once more that in concluding peace and attempting to undo the infinite injuries and injustices of this war the Government of the United States cannot deal with any but veritable representatives of the German people, who have been assured of a genuine constitutional standing as the real rulers of Germany.

If it must deal with the military masters and the monarchial autocrats of Germany . . . it must demand not peace negotiations, but surrender. . . .

Ludendorff tossed the paper onto the table in front of him, said, "Unconditional surrender. This is the price we pay for placing our faith in such a man. This is utterly unacceptable to any soldier. It proves that our cause has been just from the very beginning. The president of the United States uncloaks the pretense, strips bare the rhetoric. Our enemies desire nothing more than our total destruction." He looked at von Hindenburg. "We must tell the army of this. All those cowardly officers who whimper and crawl to us for inspiration will now find it right here. If they cannot give their own soldiers a reason to fight, then we shall. What son of Germany can fail to rise to this challenge? Here it is, for all the world to see! If we do not fight, we will perish!" Ludendorff was shaking, his hands gripping the arms of the chair.

Von Hindenburg studied him for a moment, saw sweat on the man's brow. He looked now at the kaiser, who seemed lost in thought, and von Hindenburg said, "Your Excellency, I must agree in large part with General Ludendorff. If we tell our army what the Americans propose, they will share our outrage. It will energize their fight. It may be the only means to prolong this war so that we can achieve the kind of armistice that will guarantee that our enemies do not abuse our people."

Ludendorff said, "What armistice may we expect now? If the Americans are willing to succumb to the pressures of the British and French, we have no future left to us. Look at this letter. The American president refuses to recognize that we lead this nation! Your Excellency, he insults you directly! He says plainly that he will only deal with a leader of his own choosing!"

Wilhelm seemed to focus now, said in a quiet voice, "Then what would you have me do?"

Ludendorff said, "Fight to the death! If we show such resolve, the enemy will understand that we will never be dictated to in such a way! It matters not where the front may be, it matters not where the enemy places his troops. Prolonging the war will exhaust our enemies to the point where they will succumb to a peace that *we* dictate! Your Excellency, a fortress that surrenders without defending itself to the last is dishonored."

The kaiser stared at the desk, and von Hindenburg could see that Wilhelm never looked at Ludendorff at all. Wilhelm said, "You would allow this war to be brought into our own streets?"

"Excellency, what else can we do? We use the word *armistice*. They use the word *surrender*. What they mean is punishment. Destruction. Obliteration. Is that not worth fighting for?"

Von Hindenburg put a hand on Ludendorff's arm, could feel the man's boiling fury. He tightened his grip and Ludendorff looked at him, responded to the old man's silent order. *Calm.* Von Hindenburg said, "Your Excellency, I do not wish to see our nation suffer the ravages of war, but if we are to survive, that may be inevitable. We have enemies on this continent who would celebrate our extinction. We had all hoped that the Americans would prevent such a catastrophe, would respond to our desire for peace by holding to President Wilson's own declaration of fairness and justice. By this response, I fear it will not be so. We do not know what pressures have been placed upon him. It is possible that Herr Clemenceau and Herr Lloyd George have convinced him that a just peace is not an acceptable option. Our armies are in retreat. That has inspired a bloodlust in our enemies we cannot underestimate."

Wilhelm still stared at the desktop in front of him. There was a silent moment, and von Hindenburg could hear Ludendorff's breathing, short and urgent. Wilhelm said, "If you believe it is our only option, then prepare your proclamation for the army. Tell them what the Americans propose. A copy shall be given to the chancellor. The civilian ministers will hear it as well. They have opposed me for so long . . . this will show them what I am faced with." He looked up now, tired eyes looking past von Hindenburg. "The president of the United States does not wish to negotiate with me. I *am* insulted. I cannot ignore that."

Berlin—October 26, 1918

The statement was prepared, and communicated to the headquarters of every division on the Western Front. It was made public the same night to the civilians in the Reichstag. The essence of the message was simple. The Americans might offer any terms they pleased. The German army intended to fight to the last man.

Von Hindenburg had returned to his train, but would not yet leave Berlin. The night passed like so many before, an old man's dreams of great battles, horsemen riding under bright flags, silver swords reflecting the sunlight. But the dreams were interrupted, a soft knock at the door, the soft apologies of his orderly.

"Field Marshal, an urgent message has come from General Ludendorff. He was most insistent that you come to his office, sir."

General Staff Headquarters, Berlin
October 26, 1918

Ludendorff was behind his desk, watched him as he entered. Von Hindenburg moved to his usual chair, sat, saw a single piece of paper on the desk, a handwritten note.

"Thank you for responding, Field Marshal. I hope I did not wake you too early."

There was a quiet formality to Ludendorff's words, unusual, a soft edge to his voice that von Hindenburg had rarely heard before.

"I am always at your service, General, when I can be."

"I have learned that the Reichstag did not receive our proclamation in the patriotic spirit that we had intended. Apparently there was considerable debate on the matter. As has become regrettably commonplace, there are opportunists in the government who have used our current crisis as a sounding board for their personal ambitions. The traitors have revealed themselves." Von Hindenburg said nothing, watched Ludendorff carefully, the man's hands fidgeting, his eyes black, sleepless. "The civilian government has deserted us. It seems President Wilson has found allies among our own ministers for his blatant attempt to destroy the Imperial German government."

Von Hindenburg looked again at the handwritten note on the desk, said, "May I inquire?"

Ludendorff pushed it toward him. "I have prepared my resignation. I shall abide by your wishes as to when this should become effective. And of course, the wishes of His Imperial Majesty."

Von Hindenburg ignored the paper, said, "There will be none of this. The Fatherland still calls upon its warriors. I know of nothing that should change your resolve to continue this fight. Civilian ministers will never control the army, and will never convince their country to lie down beneath the boots of our enemies."

There was a faint knock at the door, and Ludendorff said, "Enter."

An aide appeared, snapped to attention, said, "Sir, a messenger has just delivered this."

He stepped forward, placed a white envelope on the desk. Ludendorff said, "Dismissed, Captain."

The man was gone, the door quickly closed, and both men stared at the envelope for a long moment, the eloquence of the gold border, the official seal of His Imperial Majesty, Kaiser

Wilhelm II. Ludendorff picked it up, opened it slowly, read, then tossed it across the desk.

"We have been summoned to the palace."

Bellevue Palace, Berlin—October 26, 1918

"I am outraged that my own commanders would dare to submit this proclamation to our soldiers. Indeed, all of Germany is outraged! I do not require excuses, nor do I intend to hear explanations. General Ludendorff, have you any other response to offer?"

Ludendorff sat stiffly, no expression, said, "Your Excellency, it is clear to me that I no longer enjoy your confidence. I beg most humbly to be relieved of my office."

"I accept your resignation. General Ludendorff, as of this moment, you are relieved of all duties with the Imperial German Army."

Von Hindenburg absorbed the shock of the kaiser's abrupt change of attitude, had seen too much of it before. Ludendorff stood, snapped to attention, and marched quickly out of the office. There was a heavy silence in the room, and von Hindenburg watched Wilhelm's face, saw the coldness in the man's eyes soften. Von Hindenburg said, "Your Excellency, forgive me, but under the circumstances, I must offer my resignation as well."

The kaiser seemed surprised, smiled now. "Nonsense! You have my full confidence, Field Marshal. And, I might add, the chancellor feels the same way. We must have our strong pillars in a time of crisis. Even the gloomiest night gives way to the dawn. The German people require a unifying symbol to show us the way out of the darkness. I'm sure you have much work to do."

Von Hindenburg knew the sign. The meeting was over. He rose, made a short bow, said simply, "Your Excellency."

He moved outside the office, no sign of Ludendorff. No, he would not wait. It is not in his nature to sit quietly while others discuss anything that does not concern him, not even the kaiser. He has no place here.

All the maneuvering that had taken place was clear to him now. The chancellor was the civilian leader, who functioned as the kaiser's link to the Reichstag. Von Hindenburg thought of the kaiser granting permission to issue the proclamation, so conveniently forgotten. No, now he succumbs to the pressure from the civilians, has heard too much despair of the people that he possibly fears for his own safety. After all, the Russian czar and his entire family have been executed, and Wilhelm must surely know that his control of both the army and the people is becoming tenuous. His Majesty never trusted Ludendorff, and now every voice in the Reichstag is convincing him he was right. They have lost all faith in the army. For four years they resisted the power and the influence we held over them, over the kaiser himself. And now we have failed them. General Ludendorff has made many enemies, and now they can strike back at him. And so they have.

He was furious now, moved slowly through the hallways of the grand palace, ignored the attention from the people who stood aside as he passed. The fools! They fear us? The army is all they have ever been able to rely on, and they can rely on us now! We are the only means this country has of preventing our enemies from destroying us in their own fashion! So the ministers believe they must make a choice. Fight for their country or accept the demands of President Wilson and his allies. And if the kaiser is convinced he cannot rely on his own army, then he must rely on the chancellor. And so, he concedes his power. Without his army, Kaiser Wilhelm is a toothless monarch. And that is precisely what our enemies seek.

He moved out into the street, saw the car waiting for him, the limousine that would carry him back to his headquarters, where the reports would be waiting, the continuing news of disaster from the Western Front.

47

TEMPLE

Near Landreville—November 1, 1918

The replacements had come once again, more fresh-faced men, more protests as they were ordered to leave behind the distinctive green uniforms. As they marched into the ranks of the veterans, the scenes played out as they had before, proud, boastful boys announcing their arrival with loud bravado. But the veterans had seen too much of it by now. Anyone who had lost their friends or their entire platoons at Belleau Wood or the Soissons salient or Blanc Mont Ridge knew that, in a week's time, many of these boys would be gone as well.

The faces around Temple were mostly familiar, mainly veterans. The company had been reorganized again, the men assembled into new platoons, new squads, with new sergeants, and a new lieutenant, a man fresh from officer training. To Temple's enormous relief, Lieutenant Lucas had indeed survived Blanc Mont Ridge, had been discovered among the rocks by the medics of the Thirty-sixth. But he was in the hospital now, a message coming to the platoon that he had lost the leg, would be on his way home before Christmas. The new man was named Yancey, a small splinter of a man who spoke in a high reedy voice; despite the best hopes and prayers of the men, Yancey was, by all accounts, a Ninety-Day Wonder. But the grousing was minor. By now, the veterans knew what they would find on the battlefield, and if Yancey could not lead them, they would find a way to lead themselves.

The Second Division was back home with the First Army, and it was surprising to no one that Pershing had chosen them to lead the new attack. In all, twenty-two American divisions were

prepared to renew their drive northw[...]
out of their last strongholds west of t[...]
predawn hours of November 1, the artille[...]
another three hours of continuous bombard[...]
battered German positions. At five-thirty, th[...]
surge forward in a front over ten miles wide. In t[...]
line, the Second Division was placed beside the [...]
the same men they had fought beside at St. Mihie[...] [...]wo
divisions now comprised the Fifth Corps, commanded [...] one of
Pershing's most trusted subordinates, Major General Charles
Summerall. As the army resumed its massed assault on the
German lines, the Second Division was in the center of the
entire line, the point of the spear.

As the Marines advanced, there was nothing new, nothing
they had not already experienced in every major fight. No matter the artillery barrage that preceded them, the troops
advanced into the withering fire of the Maxim guns, manned by
the die-hard men who somehow always survived the shelling,
the machine-gunners who hunkered down in their hidden nests.

The Maxim gunners were a different kind of soldier, who
manned their posts with a dedication that rivaled anything the
Marines brought to the field. They were chosen not by chance,
and not just because they could handle a machine gun. The duty
called for more than obedience and training, more than pride.
The gunners had been selected by their officers because they had
shown a grim dedication to the job they had to do, that no
matter the opposition, they would hold their ground to the last.
There were fewer of them now, but not so few that the
Americans wouldn't feel the effect of their guns. The machine-
gunners were as veteran as any Marine, had survived tank
assaults and artillery barrages, had survived four years of
assaults by the French. They knew nothing of the political
turmoil behind their own lines, knew nothing of the despair
and diplomatic outrage that rolled through Berlin. Despite the
collapse of so many of the German units that had once made
the Hindenburg Line the impenetrable fortress, here, in the
rolling hills west of the Meuse River, the men at the Maxim
guns knew only that across the way, there would be another

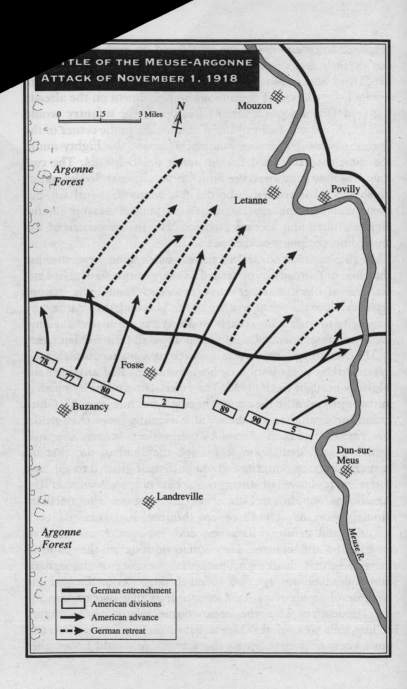

BATTLE OF THE MEUSE-ARGONNE
ATTACK OF NOVEMBER 1, 1918

0   1.5   3 Miles

N

Argonne
Forest

Mouzon

Letanne

Povilly

78

77

80

Fosse

2

Buzancy

89

90

5

Landreville

Dun-sur-
Meus

Argonne
Forest

Meuse R.

German entrenchment
American divisions
American advance
German retreat

attack, another great wave of men sent out to confront them. Every man carried the tradition: before any man surrendered, or abandoned his machine gun, he was supposed to die.

Near Fosse—November 1, 1918

The fight had been as so many fights before, men pressing ahead through the mist and fog, across grassy fields and sloping hillsides. The enemy lay in every thicket, every line of brush, old trenches that had become a part of the landscape.

Temple crested yet another low rise, the sounds of the fight echoing around him from all directions. The battalion had made its way quickly to the first great trench line, what the maps showed was called Kriemhilde. After a sharp fight, the Germans began to pull out, were flowing back to the next heavy line of earthworks, the final line that put their backs to the Meuse River.

The men around him worked methodically, some of them survivors of Blanc Mont Ridge, men who knew how to use the land, how to find the cover, how to work their way close enough to throw the grenades. For most of the day, the fog and rain had sheltered them in the wide fields, but by midafternoon, the wet air began to clear, and so the rifles became the most effective weapon. Temple had made good use of the Springfield, the others in the squad already knowing that this farm boy was a crack marksman. As they climbed each ridge, they would move carefully, making sure there was no ambush beyond, no cluster of the enemy waiting to spring a deadly trap. The Maxim guns were there, as they were always there, and the best response the company had were the marksmen like Roscoe Temple. From field to valley, the conditions of the ground and the positions of the machine guns had driven the Marines to a routine in their assault. From each low place, they would crawl slowly to the crests of the next rise, would scan the distant cover, drawing fire any way they could, forcing the Maxims to reveal themselves. The other men in Temple's squad would spot for him, picking out the flickers of fire, while he settled himself into a comfortable place, resting the rifle on a firm bed, the careful aim, the precise shot. Each man contributed cartridges, and after Temple had emptied the rifle three or four times, the task had been accomplished. Usually the Marines would see the enemy falling back, the German foot soldiers escaping from the terrifying accuracy of the enemy they couldn't see, the Maxim guns falling silent as their crews were struck down one by one. With the ground in front of them clear, the squad would move forward again.

They were close to the main German trench line now, a long ridge that was pockmarked by concrete bunkers, behind acres of barbed wire. The division had moved forward piecemeal, each battalion pressing the attack along its own front, backed up by another battalion a quarter mile to its rear. Each platoon was ordered to maintain some contact with the units on both flanks, but the uneven ground kept the men in small pockets, out of sight of each other, hidden whenever possible from the enemy in front of them. What they couldn't see, they could hear, bursts of fire from machine-gun nests, from the concrete bunkers, small field cannon blasting glimpses of targets.

Temple hadn't seen the new lieutenant for over an hour, the platoon scattered, a sudden firefight breaking out to the right, men scrambling from that way, bringing word to Osborne of a close fight with a perfectly concealed machine-gun nest. The men who escaped were following Osborne now, the only sergeant left among them.

As they approached the barbed wire, they could see the ridge-line clearly, and the enemy in their concrete bunkers obliged them with withering machine-gun fire. Osborne divided the men, left a dozen rifles back in the field, who had dug themselves into some kind of protection. Those men would make some attempt at covering fire, while Osborne led the rest of the men in a frantic dash through the barbed wire. The artillery gunners far behind them had given the Marines an extraordinary gift, a gap in the wire blown open by the perfect strike of an artillery shell. Beyond the wire, the grounds dropped off into a ravine, another blessing, a stretch of ground below the field of fire of the enemy gunners in their concrete shelters.

They jumped and darted from shell hole to shell hole, freshly churned dirt from the work of the artillery hours before. The wire was only yards in front of them, the blessed gap looming wide. Temple crouched low, ran his hand over the ammo belt, a silent count, twenty . . . thirty. Enough for now. He touched the grenades on his chest, something the men were never without now, a lesson that had taken the officers far too long to learn. The ground in front of the shell hole sprayed over him, relentless fire from the Maxims. He pulled himself low, glanced at the others in the hole, four men, nameless, helmets covering their faces. He heard a shout, Osborne, a few yards away, another shell hole.

"On my signal, charge through the wire! Get to that damned ditch! Rifles! Covering fire!"

From a depression back behind them, the Springfields began to rattle, pops of fire directed at the bunkers, no more than two hundred yards in front of them. The Maxims answered, overwhelming, the air humming with a thousand bees. Osborne shouted again, "Let's go!"

Temple closed his eyes, wanted to say something to God, a prayer, have mercy. But his mind was empty, his body in motion now, the men beside him rising as well. He burst up out of the shell hole, ran toward the gap in the wire, the air ripped around him, fire going both ways, a man falling, another, the wire on both sides of him. Men were passing him, the faster runners, Osborne, the ravine close now, another man hit, the ravine there now, Temple jumping down, tumbling into soft white dirt. The others came down all around him, soft cries, grunts, Parker, landing hard, rolling, on his knees, breathing hard.

"You okay, Roscoe?"

"Yeah."

The men gathered, moved close to the base of the ridge, the fire from the Maxims slowing, the Springfields still popping, smacks of lead on the concrete above them. Osborne was there now, a hard whisper. "Everybody all right? Anybody hit?"

One man pointed out toward the wire, panic in the man's voice. "Tucker's out there. I saw him fall. We gotta go back—"

"Shut up! Nobody's going back out there!"

Parker moved close to the man, said, "They'll get him later. We got a job to do first." He looked at Osborne now. "At least four went down in the wire. There's a dozen of us here. We better keep moving."

Osborne looked down to the right, said, "Lower ground down that way. Keep an eye behind us. Huns may decide to come down here and get us. I'm surprised there's none here now. They probably got out of here when the artillery started. Let's go."

There were signs that the ravine had been used as a natural trench, the ground churned and trampled, bits of equipment, backpacks, ration tins scattered, dropped by men who had now pulled out. Osborne led them through the soft white dirt, the men moving blind, sweating in the chilly dampness. Temple glanced up, nothing to see, the edges of the ravine blanketed by thick brush and vines. He looked out away from the slope, could see the coils of wire, more shell holes, one close to the edge of the ravine, thought, No, this isn't a good place to soak up shell fire. He glanced at the men behind him, most of them veterans, and a few whose eyes betrayed the terror, the men who had begun this day on their first battlefield.

They could see nothing but the brush above them, the ravine winding along the base of the ridge. He knew the concrete bunkers were right above them, at least three, in a widely spaced row. The rifle fire still peppered the air above them, mostly Springfields, the men back behind the wire doing their job, taking aim from dangerous hiding places, their shots answered by short blasts from the machine guns twenty feet above Temple's head. They must know we're here, he thought. They must know. What do we do now? He looked ahead to Parker, following closely behind Osborne, wanted to ask him, Where the hell are we going?

The fire from the machine guns had stopped, deathly quiet now, and Parker tapped Osborne on the shoulder, pointing up. They all stopped, and Temple could hear the voices, German, felt a hard chill.

Osborne looked back, pointed to three men, motioned to the corporal, Burke, said in a low whisper, "Climb up right here. If they try to come down, you'll surprise the hell out of 'em. And it'll warn us they're coming. Otherwise, wait ten minutes, long enough for us to get up close. If we start shooting, get your asses up the hill. If we're lucky, one of us will draw their fire, while the other gets to 'em."

Temple watched the faces of the three men, saw no emotion, Burke looking at the other two, quick nods. They moved to the slope, Burke testing the soft earth, pulling himself up. The others followed, and Temple looked up, the concrete wall still not visible. *Draw their fire.* He had heard the phrase too many times, never considered what it truly meant. Give them a target. On purpose. How do you do that? The men climbed up farther, slid silently into the low brush, climbed carefully up the hill, their backs concealed by the vines.

There was a sudden blast, thirty yards behind them, the soft dirt tossed in the air. Now another, whistles of shrapnel, the men dropping to their knees, flattening out along the base of the slope. The voices were above them now, and Temple saw the grenade coming down, a soft thump in the dirt, twenty yards, the blast throwing the dirt high. There were pops of rifle fire now, the Springfields, the German voices loud, orders, one sharp cry. He felt a hand on him, Parker pulling him up, Osborne now waving frantically, the silent order, *move!* They jogged ahead, the rifle fire now silent, no targets for the Marines, the Germans withdrawing back into their cover. Temple was breathing in short gasps, thought, Yep, they know we're here! Thank God for those men out there. Thank God for Springfields! He looked at Osborne, grateful, the man with no more experience than any of them, thought, *Covering fire.* Damn! I wouldn't have thought of that. Maybe none of us would have. Thank God for sergeants! He saw Osborne looking back, scanning the side of the slope, and Temple saw now, a single hand, emerging from the brush halfway up the slope, a slow wave. Burke! They're still okay. Osborne looked at each of them, focused on the new men, wide-eyed fear, the men who might panic, do something supremely stupid. He put a finger to his lips, *quiet*, held out both hands, a gesture of calm. The voices came again, straight above them, and Temple looked up, felt a bolt of ice in his chest. The ravine was more shallow now, a concrete bunker no more than ten feet above them. The men leaned flat against the brushy slope, and Temple slid up beside Parker who gripped the shotgun close to his chest. Parker seemed to be having a silent talk with Osborne, pointed a finger up the hill. Osborne nodded, made the sign with his fingers: two. He put a hand on Temple's shoulder, then did the same to Parker, and Temple understood. It's the two of us. Temple glanced at his bayonet, the muzzle of his rifle, his mind focused, fixed on the muffled voices just a few feet above them. The Germans were suddenly quiet, and now the Maxim exploded to life. The burst cut the air right above them, the Marines holding tight to the slope, frozen. The Maxim was silent again, and he heard a man laughing, the click of metal, reloading, more talk now. Parker moved away, and Temple followed, kept his eyes up on the concrete wall, could see the openings, a row of round holes, one narrow rectangle. Parker jerked his arm forward, pointed, a trail leading up through the brush, the trail the Germans had used to climb the hill. Parker started up through the narrow gap, the ground not as steep now, pulled himself up by the thick bases of the vines. Temple crouched low, followed, the voice in his head, stay low! Parker was flat against the slope, lying on his belly, pulled himself up to the top of the hill, an avalanche of soft sand falling into Temple's face. Parker disappeared up over the top, and Temple stared up for a moment, waited for Parker's legs to clear the space, now climbed up after him. The concrete wall was on their left, and he could see that the bunker was circular, maybe twenty feet across, more openings all along the front, a round hole not more than four feet above them. There was open ground behind the bunker, a low wall, no movement. He scanned the open ground, thought, Where are the foot soldiers? Are they . . . inside? The Maxim fired again, out to the far side, toward the barbed wire, and Temple flattened on the ground, the sound piercing his brain, thundering chatter, silent again. The German voices came again, one man with authority, instructions, the voice of an officer. Parker was close against the wall, staring back at him with black silent eyes. He pointed to the rear of the bunker, then crooked his finger, *this way*, began to crawl again. Temple followed, slow deliberate movements, felt the cold pounding in his chest, thought, Where are we going? They continued along the curving concrete, and Parker froze. Temple could see past him, the backside of the bunker, realized there was a depression in the ground, steps, leading down to a wooden door. The Maxim fired again, and Temple could see past the bunker, more just like it, heard more bursts of fire farther away. Parker crawled forward, slid down into the stairway, made room for Temple, motioned for him to follow. Temple was there now, the voices of the men distinct through thedoor. Parker pointed to Temple's chest, touched two of the grenades and Temple nodded, yes, two. He set the rifle down slowly, pulled a grenade free of his shirt, saw a leather strap attached to the door, the handle. Parker grabbed it, the shotgun in one hand, and looked at him again, the cold stare. Temple's heart was pounding, and he hooked a finger through the pin of the first grenade, held it tightly in his hand, nodded to Parker now, and the big man pulled on the strap. The door didn't move. Parker tugged, looked at Temple, furious, shook his head. Temple stared at the door, his brain screaming the words: It's locked!

Parker's expression didn't change, and he peered up out of the depression, crawled up, looked back at Temple, pointed to the door, the silent command. *Stay here*. He slid away, and Temple felt the panic coming, stepped back from the door, thought, What are you going to do? The voice in his head was chattering in a manic stream of words, the bayonet? What if they rush out? The voice in his brain was silenced by a sharp blast. Temple peered out around the edge of the bunker, saw Parker reloading the shotgun, then firing again, straight into a hole in the concrete. Temple stuffed the

775

grenade into his pocket, grabbed the rifle, pointed it at the door, heard another shot from Parker. Inside the bunker, the voices returned, the single word, "*Kamarad!*"

The door didn't open, and Temple's hands shook, the bayonet poised, the word again, "*Kamarad!*"

Parker fired again, and now more Marines burst up out of the brush, more firing into the slits in the bunker. "*Kamarad!*"

Temple stared at the door, furious now. Come on out! Dammit! He pulled the trigger, punched a hole in the wooden door, fired again, men beside him now, Parker's voice, "Ready grenades!"

The shotgun erupted close to Temple's ear, the door splintering, and now another man jumped down beside Temple, kicked at the door, the timbers cracking, the door coming apart. Temple pointed the rifle inside, smoke and darkness, the thick smell of gunpowder, silence. Parker pushed his way past him, snatched a grenade from Temple's shirt, yanked on the pin, tossed it into the bunker. They all ducked away, the bunker bursting from inside, thick gray smoke rolling out through the shattered door. Parker kicked his way through the door, plunged into the bunker, disappeared, and Temple stared blindly, heard the thick punch of the bayonet, another, the big man finishing the job.

Osborne was there now, knelt low beside the stairwell, said, "Spread out! Advance to the next bunker! Let's move!"

The machine-gun fire rolled across the ridge, more rifle fire from down below, more Marines pushing through the wire, climbing the ridge. They came up in a steady wave now, the Maxim guns falling silent, shouts farther down the ridge, "Surrender!"

"*Kamarad!*"

"They're coming out!"

"*Kamarad!*"

But the voices faded, and Temple watched as Parker emerged from the smoky concrete, blood on the bayonet. He looked at Temple, the hard glare still in his eyes, and Temple backed away, felt an odd fear, something cold and animal in Parker's stare.

"Dan, they were trying to surrender."

Parker moved past him, climbed up out of the depression, said quietly, "You don't capture machine-gunners. You kill them."

48

TEMPLE

November 2, 1918

The Marines still pushed forward, careful, deliberate, probing the trenches and the dugouts. The fighting was scattered, small pockets of the enemy crouched in bunkers, stragglers making a stand, the Maxim gunners slipping into deeper cover, until they exhausted their ammunition.

Temple still followed Parker, the other survivors of the platoon treading lightly through a German encampment, concrete shelters dug low in the ground, covered by bundles of brush and camouflaged tin. They moved slowly, the men silent, listening for any sound of wounded men in the deep pits that spread out from the camp, long rows of trenches that were mostly abandoned now, the enemy pulling out or captured. The artillery had done its work, many of the shelters blown open, some by the bombs dropped from the massed squadrons of Billy Mitchell's aircraft. There was smoke still, thick plumes, drifting up from holes deep in the ground.

The squad spread out in a circle around a gaping shell hole, and Temple could see now, it wasn't a shell hole at all. It was a vast underground room, the roof caved in, the perfect strike from one of the big guns. Temple moved close, watched as one of the men heaved on a long timber, a thick log that had once supported the roof. The man motioned with his hand, waved them close, pointed down. Temple could see stairs, what had once been the door, and the man began to move down, pushing more timbers aside, descending into the smoky darkness. Osborne was there now, said in a low voice, "Take it slow. Check every bit of cover, any place a man can hide."

They moved down in single file, and Temple caught the odors

now, a sickening mix of death and churned earth. They reached the bottom, the men spreading out, Temple's eyes adjusting to the dim light. There were short tunnels, leading to more rooms, and he realized now, he was walking on concrete.

"Here!"

He followed the voice, saw Parker pointing the shotgun downward, Osborne moving past him. There were bodies, a broken table, china plates in pieces on the floor. Parker moved into the smoky darkness, probed the bodies with the point of his bayonet, said, "Nobody been alive here for a while."

Osborne said, "Direct hit. Trapped 'em in here. Concussion got 'em. Or they suffocated. They're all officers."

Parker had stepped past the bodies, and Temple could see the dead men now, three of them, one older, gray hair, a medal on the man's chest. There was no blood, no terrible wound, and he thought of Osborne's word, suffocated. His mind held it away, and he followed Parker down into the darkness, heard the click of a matchstick, a flicker of light. Parker was standing over a bed, said, "They weren't all officers."

Temple moved up beside him, the match giving off a soft yellow glow. There were two beds, a small space between them, and on each bed the body of a woman. Temple stared wide-eyed, said, "Good God. What the hell are they doing here?"

Osborne was there now, put a hand on Temple's shoulder. "You're too young, Private. Jesus, they're in nightgowns. I can still smell their perfume."

Parker probed one body with the bayonet, said, "Senior officers' quarters, I'm guessing. Soft beds, good food. *Entertainment.*"

Osborne looked up, a lightbulb on the ceiling, said, "They had electricity. The shelling must have wrecked the wiring. These people have been here for a long time. They never expected the enemy would come busting through here."

Parker struck another match, and Temple stared at the woman closest to him, dark hair, and very young. He closed his eyes, could not look at her face, caught the smell of the perfume, sickening, his stomach twisting. He backed away, turned toward the light at the doorway, heard a voice outside. "Hey, Sarge."

Osborne moved that way and Temple followed, saw the man holding a bundle of maps.

"Lots more of these, Sarge. Looks like a meeting room over this way. A dozen chairs. Ritchie found a box of cigars."

Another man emerged from the room holding an armful of artifacts.

"Yep. Havanas too. All kinds of good stuff here, Sarge. Damned nice set of binoculars."

Osborne said, "All right, drop that garbage right here. This isn't a looting party. You want souvenirs, come back when the war's over. We got work to do."

There were low grumbles, and the men obeyed. Parker said, "Sarge, we need to tell the lieutenant to check every one of these fancy dugouts. There could still be people hiding out."

Osborne moved to the stairway, said, "Yep. Let's move. Daylight for a couple hours yet."

The men filed up the stairs, and Temple could not erase the image of the women from his mind. Women in the trenches? Were they prostitutes? Why in hell would somebody bring a woman out here? Did they have any idea where they were going? The questions rolled through his brain, a disgusting mystery. He glanced ahead to Osborne, the sergeant waiting for them at the top of the stairway, wanted to ask more, but Osborne was looking away, said, "This way. Let's go."

Other squads were sifting through the wreckage of the buildings, some calling out with word of some kind of find. Temple saw a column of men moving toward them, prisoners, guarded by a half dozen Marines. The Germans were filthy, no helmets, the same look Temple had seen before on the faces of the retreating *poilus*. They passed by, one of the Marine guards making some lewd comment for the benefit of his new audience. Temple ignored the man, saw one of the prisoners staring at him, dark and desperate eyes. Temple tried to ignore the man's stare, thought, Nothing I can do for you, Fritz. You lived through it. Count your damned blessings.

The prisoners were past him now, and Temple continued forward, saw that the ground was falling away, a wide sloping hillside, more buildings, concrete and tin. Osborne was moving down the hill, and Temple could see men gathering down below, around a low square building, undamaged, small windows, the glass still intact. Temple was surprised to see Yancey, the first time he had seen the lieutenant for many hours. Yancey seemed not to recognize Osborne, stood in front of the door to the building, shouted, "Come out of there! We have you surrounded!"

There was silence, Temple moving closer, and Yancey scanned the faces around him, said, "Well, I suppose no one's inside. We need to break down the door."

Parker moved past Temple, said, "Excuse me, sir. But if no one's inside, the door should be open."

Parker moved to the door, the shotgun pointed out in front of him, pressed the bayonet into the wood. The door opened slowly, and Parker stepped back, said, "We oughta toss a grenade or two, sir. Anybody's hiding out, it'll discourage 'em."

Yancey looked at Osborne, seemed uncertain, said, "No, there could be things we might want to see. Papers and such. The major wants us to find any information we can."

Parker said, "Whatever you say, sir. Would you like some of us to go inside first?"

"Yes. Proceed, Private."

Parker nodded to Osborne, who said, "Surround the building. Somebody may try to go out a window." He looked at Temple, pointed to two other men. "You three stand back from the door, and be ready for somebody besides us to come out. They might be in a hurry. The rest of you stay ready. If we holler, you come quick."

Temple obeyed, saw Yancey moving away to one side, nervous, staring at the door.

Osborne said to Parker, "Let's go."

The two men slipped into the building, and Temple stared into the dark opening, his heart pounding, saw a flicker of light, and Osborne shouted, "All clear!"

The men gathered at the door, and Yancey moved past them, was inside now, the others filing in. Temple was engulfed by the smells, the magnificent odor of cooked meat, and Osborne said, "The chef's been here. Left a pot of beans on the stove. Must be twenty gallons. Look at the chunks of meat in there. Damn! Reminds me how hungry I am!"

Temple's eyes adjusted to the dim light, and he could see a long table, many chairs, a countertop. It was a mess kitchen, the smell of the meat and beans overwhelming him. He moved to the stove, saw a huge metal pot.

Osborne said, "Somebody left us his dinner. What do you say, Lieutenant? Mind if these boys grab a cupful? Beats the hell out of monkey meat."

Yancey seemed unsure, said, "Uh, well, I don't see the harm. We shouldn't advance any farther until we receive instructions from Major Hamilton. I suppose we can wait here."

Osborne opened a row of cabinet doors, said, "Here we go. Coffee cups, bowls. Grab one, boys. Give everybody a chance. We got any left over, we'll share with some of those boys outside."

The men gathered around the stove, the cups dipping into the thick brown stew. Temple filled his own cup, made room for the others, moved out toward the door. He slurped at the beans, chewed a thick chunk of soft salty meat. Behind him, Osborne said, "Temple! Give a holler to those other boys out there. We got plenty here. Might as well share."

"Okay, Sarge."

He stepped outside, heard Parker say, "They got a woodstove here, all packed full, and ready to go. Let's warm the place up. I'm outta matches. Somebody give me one."

Temple looked out across the open hillside, saw a dozen men sifting through the wreckage of a bunker. He moved that way, raised his hand, shouted, "Hey! We got food here—"

Behind him, the building erupted with a thunderous blast, a flash of fire and smoke, a fist punching Temple hard to the ground. He tried to move, the debris of the concrete now tumbling down on him, thick black smoke blinding him, burning his throat. He tried to crawl, his mind screaming, Move, cover! He expected more blasts, the air coming alive with the horrible screams of artillery, but there was only a hard numbing

782

roar in his ears. He tried to rise up, saw men running toward him, could see pieces of the building scattered all around him, the smoke clearing, hands on him now, loud voices:

"What happened?"

"Anybody inside?"

"*How many inside?*"

He tried to pull away from the hands, stared back into the thick cloud of dust and smoke, saw what was left of the concrete building, the walls cracked and shattered, the roof blown apart. He stared for a long moment, more men around him now, a man's face, leaning close, a medic.

"Lie back. You'll be okay."

He ignored the man, sat up, stared at the wrecked building, said aloud, "Dan . . ."

"How many men were inside, Private?" He was drawn to the voice, deep, older, saw an officer, recognized Major Hamilton. "What happened, Private?"

"Artillery shell, sir."

"No. It wasn't a shell, son. No warning. The building just blew up. What were you doing?"

"Sir!"

The shout came from the smoking wreckage, and Temple saw them crawling through the debris, some pulling bodies out, and the man said, "There's an officer here, sir! A lieutenant. Looks like maybe eight more besides him. They're all dead, sir. It's not pretty."

Hamilton leaned close to his face now.

"What were they doing, Private? What's the last thing you remember?"

"I walked outside and Dan was gonna . . . light the stove."

Hamilton straightened up now, said, "Son of a bitch! Another one!"

Temple wiped at the grit in his eyes, could see more clearly now, men swarming through the debris. He tried to stand, his legs unsteady, sat again, the medic close beside him. Hamilton said, "He all right, Corporal? Any wounds?"

"Doesn't appear so, sir. Pretty shook up. Looks like he lost a bunch of his buddies."

783

Hamilton said, "That damned lieutenant should have known better."

Temple said, "I don't understand. What happened, sir?"

"You know what a booby trap is, son? The Huns left 'em all over the place. They probably packed the stove with gun cotton or a powder charge. Bastards."

Temple stood now, the medic supporting him under one arm. The Marines were dragging bodies out of the debris.

Hamilton moved away, said to an aide, "Get a burial party up here! The rest of you, keep moving! Gather up with Lieutenant Hawkins. We've gone farther than anyone expected us to. There may not be much else happening today." Temple stared at the smoking rubble, the crushed bodies dragged out, laid in a gruesome row. He counted five, closed his eyes, wouldn't see it, knew why the rest weren't there. Dan . . . there wouldn't be a body at all. The tears came now, but he curled a hard fist around his brain, shut it down. He tried to close the icy hole in his chest, his mind clearing. Time for that later, he thought. The medic released his arm, said, "You okay now? We're gonna make camp soon. Just take it easy. I'll tell Lieutenant Hawkins about you. I'm sorry about your buddies."

Temple nodded, stared at the rubble, said, "Yeah. Thanks."

He thought of Hamilton's words, *booby trap*. This was somebody's plan, some clever officer, tempting hungry soldiers. Men died . . . for a cup of beans. But not me. Why the hell am I still alive?

He looked down, saw his rifle coated with a thick layer of gray dust. He picked it up, pulled on the bayonet, made sure it was tight, blew a sharp breath into the breech. He stared again at the wreckage, wanted to see, a last glimpse, but the hard fist in his mind held him away. Let him be, he thought. If Dan was here, if he had come outside with me, you know what he'd say now, what he always said. Let's go.

By late afternoon, the Second Division had pushed forward nearly six miles, had reached their objectives, the Heights of Barricourt, which placed them so deep into the German position that they directly threatened the German artillery batteries. But

784

the Germans responded by backing their troops into their strongest positions yet, had gathered as much reserve strength as the High Command could send to that part of the line. With the certainty of appalling casualties, the senior American officers met to design a new strategy, some way to neutralize the power of the German defensive position.

As the sun set on the field, the Americans could count their assault as another overwhelming success. Men on both sides settled into their routine, rations, sleep, guards and lookouts posted. But as the orders from headquarters reached the front lines, the Marines began to realize that their routine was about to change completely.

Near Barricourt—November 5, 1918

After so many night marches, they had become used to the dark, had begun to expect rain as well, just another part of the job. But there were no guides now, no signposts, no headquarters or maps to mark their way. They marched along narrow pathways that cut through patches of woods, through gullies and low valleys. In front of each company, the lieutenants had their compasses, tried as much as possible to keep the men moving north. Unlike so many night marches before, they were not simply moving to a new deployment, some field where the dawn would bring the grand assault. The night march now was slow and silent and dangerous. And it wasn't a march at all. It was an attack.

Lieutenant Hawkins passed along the instructions. The attack was to be made by the Twenty-third Regiment, with one battalion of Marines in support. Their mission was simply to march into the German lines until they found something, taking advantage of the hurried deployment of the retreating Germans, capturing as many men as possible, causing chaos in their new position.

Temple followed the man in front of him, climbed up out of a muddy ditch, felt the ground hard under his boots, knew they were on some kind of road. There were no sounds but the steady spatter of rain, the men able to move more quickly now.

They stayed on the road for another hundred yards, and the men in front of Temple began to stop, gathering, moving off to the side of the road. He stared into the darkness, tried to see shapes, the rain different now, an odd echo, louder. He moved up close to the men in front of him, heard a soft whisper. "Tin."

It was a building, the rain bouncing off a tin roof. He strained to see, a large hulking shadow beside the road, the men moving, easing down into the mud, closer. They stopped again, listening, bayonets ready, and he heard it now, the sound of voices.

They moved again, one man, the lieutenant, guiding each man past him. They flowed out slowly into the open ground around the building, two dozen men standing motionless for a long moment. The lieutenant moved up close now, a handful of men following him, and suddenly the darkness was blasted by light from inside the building, the door punched open, the Marines rushing inside. Temple was at the door now, heard the sharp cry of surprise, the voices muffled quickly by filthy hands, hard whispers, bayonets pointing at the half dozen men who sat around a square table. They were German officers, wide-eyed with terror, each man pulled quickly out of his chair, shoved flat on the floor, a bayonet pressed against the back of his neck.

For three nights, the silent attacks continued, the Marines capturing men in their tents, soldiers sleeping in blankets, camps of entire platoons. Most of the captives were taken without a shot being fired, no alerting the units who might have come to their aid. As the night began to give way to the sunrise, the German artillery began their predawn routine, firing into the American positions along their front. But the gunners had no idea that even as the big guns did their work, squads of American soldiers were surrounding them, the gunners suddenly gobbled up by the quick strike, their gun now silent.

With the sunrise, the Americans would be pulled back, their prisoners in tow, more than two thousand men swept right out of the German defenses. When the daylight attacks began, the morale of the German defenders had been devastated by the surprise raids and the sudden depletion of so many front-line units. By November 7, the American offensive had driven the Germans up and out of their final major entrenchment. To avoid the complete destruction of the last units who could still mount an effective defense, the German High Command ordered them to pull back again, to regroup and strengthen their lines, putting the natural barrier of the Meuse River between themselves and the pursuing Americans.

In front of the Second Division, the river was narrow and deep, and the far bank was a high bluff, the perfect kind of ground for a defense. All along the west bank of the river, the Americans pressed closer, and several miles to the south, the Fifth Division had already established a crossing. The area of the river confronted by the Second consisted of two sharp S curves that combined to form a W. At this particular sector of the line, the engineers who attempted to float their bridges across the twisting river could be caught in a perfect cross fire. The only possible way to push anyone across would be, of course, at night.

Near Letanne—November 10, 1918

The faces were unfamiliar, but even among strangers, Temple could pick out the veterans from the men who had not yet lost a friend. The veterans were mostly quiet, mostly alone, hard men who stared into coffee cups, who ate the corned beef and gnawed at the dry bread without complaints. Even as they gathered to hear the instructions from the lieutenant, their thoughts were somewhere else, manic and restless behind silent eyes. Temple had felt it himself, sitting among squads of men he didn't know, gathering to learn their new mission. But the lieutenant's words simply drifted past him, and unlike the new men, he had learned that no matter the mission, the job would be the same. The officers always spoke of maps, and Temple knew that a man crawling through brush under the muzzles of the Maxim guns had no need for maps. The whole world was what you could see in your gun sight, and no matter how closely the replacements listened to the officer's instructions, Temple's mind pulled him back to those other missions, crawling through

787

brush, sliding up beside concrete, the sound of Maxim guns and screaming men and the deafening punch of grenades.

If there was humor in the camps now, it came only from the replacements, the men who were still ignorant of the horror. They tormented each other with the same teasing insults, laughing at the men who slipped and fell into hidden shell holes, who gagged on the muddy coffee poured from filthy pots. To the veterans, the jokes had become wearying, too familiar, and if they tried to share the humor of the others, it was forced, uneasy laughter from men who knew too much about the war. If the humor was directed away from the veterans, the curiosity was not, and at every bivouac, the nervous newcomers had sought out the silent men, seeking answers to questions none of the veterans wanted to hear.

Unlike the veterans, the new men listened breathlessly to the officers, the sergeants. With the mission explained, the bravado would begin again, so many of them caught up in the celebration of the success of those men before them who had done the work, none of the replacements understanding the horror, the cost, and none of them believing that after the next mission, it might be their buddy who didn't come back, or, as Temple relived now in his own violent nightmare, if you came back, it just increased the chance that your buddy didn't.

The rations had come forward, a brief rest, the entire division drawing up close to the river. Temple probed the meat on his plate, drank from the canteen, ignored the low talk that drifted through the darkness around him. He stared out, guessed at the direction of the river, had seen a glimpse of it in the last glow of sunset, the water narrow and swift, the ground beyond a high curving ridge. The engineers had tried to build some kind of crossing to the north, up near the village of Mouzon, but the German artillery had been placed in perfect position to shell every possible location. Down to the right flank, the Eighty-ninth Division was in place, and the Marines were shifted down close to their front, the officers talking about better ground, better cover. No one seemed to ask why the Eighty-ninth wouldn't lead the crossing in front of their own sector. Temple knew, as they all did. The plan was for footbridges and wading through black water, to an invisible shore beyond. That wasn't a job for infantry. It was a job for the Marines.

He finished the salty beef, another long swig from the canteen. He looked back through the darkness, heard the sound of tin plates, knew the water wagon was out on the road, behind a small hill. He stood, slid the rifle up on his shoulder, stepped past silent men, heard a low voice, "I heard it from some MPs. They say word's going out to every division headquarters."

"Bull. Never believe it."

"Well, hell, I don't believe it either, but the MPs were real excited."

Temple moved past them, made his way to the road. Men were gathered, filling canteens, and the talk came again.

"I heard Major Hamilton say he knows nothing about it. Rumors, all it is."

"Some damned Hun trick. Put out the word of an armistice so we stop fighting. Give 'em one day to regroup, hell, no telling what they can do."

Temple pushed forward, the mess sergeant directing the men toward the spout.

"Keep moving, you grunts. Hurry it up. This one's about empty. May not be another one. Careful, you jackass. Don't spill it."

His canteen was full now, and Temple moved away, felt the dull rumble in his gut, the usual response to the oily corned beef. He saw a small tent, thought, Major Hamilton, saw a cluster of officers standing beside it. There was more of the low talk, words finding him, ". . . no way to know for certain."

"I heard it came from Lejeune himself."

"I'll hear it from him before I believe it."

He stopped, listened, could tell that others were doing the same. The MPs were there now, moving men away, one man standing in front of Temple. "Get moving, grunt. You got some other place to be."

Temple backed away, had no energy for arguing with a man who stood a head taller than him. He climbed up off the road, moved toward the camp, familiar steps toward another platoon, another squad, another sergeant who would lead them toward the next walk into hell.

The night had turned colder, the men shuffling through the darkness, fighting the hard chill that stiffened and numbed their fingers. Temple followed a man he didn't know, could hear short whispers as they passed by guides, spaced every few yards. They were dropping downhill now, a winding trail that seemed to cut deep into the ground, dirt embankments close on either side, the smell of muddy earth and filthy men. He felt the wetness now, looked up, the mist on his face, the smells changing. He knew the feel of fog, cold dampness in his nose, could hear the footsteps turning wetter, soft mud, felt his boots slipping now. There was a ditch, the men dropping down suddenly, another guide, no sounds but the slipping and tumbling of men sliding on their backsides, landing into watery grass. He splashed down, felt water inside his boots now, cursed to himself, was climbing up again, heard a whisper behind him, "Not much of a river."

There was low laughter farther back, and Temple ignored it, continued to climb, crested the hill, was surprised to step onto railroad tracks. There was another guide, the man moving them to the left, the Marines walking down the center of the tracks. He looked to the right, nothing to see, the darkness and the fog wrapping around all of them. The river, he thought. Fog like this means water. This railroad must run alongside it.

The sounds startled them all, a chattering of a machine gun, coming from the right, from across the river. The men were moving more quickly now on the tracks, more guides, a man every twenty yards or so. The machine gun opened up again, sharp cries in front of him. Now another gun started, the bullets tearing through the fog above his head. Of course. They know where we are. Hell, they're right across the river. What? Two hundred yards?

The Maxim guns kept up their fire, and he stumbled on a body on the tracks. He stopped, whispered to the man behind him, "Help me! Get him off the tracks!"

More men tumbled down off the tracks, groans, men splashing

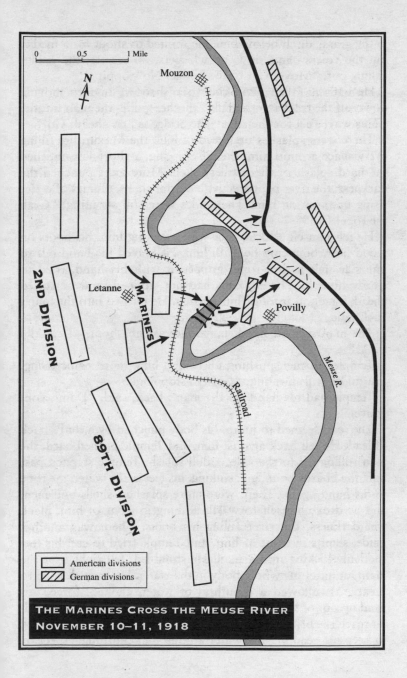

Mouzon

2ND DIVISION

Letanne

MARINES

Povilly

Meuse R.

Railroad

89TH DIVISION

0   0.5   1 Mile

N

☐ American divisions
▨ German divisions

THE MARINES CROSS THE MEUSE RIVER
NOVEMBER 10–11, 1918

in the grassy ditch below him. He wanted to shout for a medic, but the voices came now, no whispers, no secrets, the guides calling out, "Move! Get to the bridge! No stopping!"

He left the fallen man, could see shadows of men moving down off the tracks to the right, another guide, the man frantic. "This way! Feel for the rope! The bridge is just ahead! Go!"

There were splashes up ahead of him, the Maxim fire filling every space around him, the air erupting, a short scream, then the hard splash of the artillery shell. More guns punched the darkness, the river peppered with mortar shells, plumes of water rising up, soaking him. The guides were still shouting, "Grab the rope! Go!"

He felt himself shaking, the water soaking him, his boots on wood now, bouncing beneath him. He waved his hand out to one side, felt a thin rope, gripped it with his hand, tried to steady himself. The Maxims had not stopped, and he stared ahead, a man in front of him, frozen. He pushed into the man's back, said, "Move!"

The man seemed fixed, immobile, a high shout, "I can't! I can't!"

Temple felt men pushing up behind him, more panic rising, the guides still shouting, "Go! No stopping!"

Temple had his hand on the man's back, said, "Damn you! Move!"

The man seemed to jump, his body punched by a dull smack of lead. He fell back against him, and Temple pushed hard, the man rolling off to the side, a dull splash. Temple stepped past him, the boards bouncing, sinking, his feet in the water, the rope in his hand again. There were more splashes, shells and men, and he drove himself forward, nothing in front of him, black wet darkness, the river filling his boots. There was another guide, shouts in front of him, and Temple tried to see, his feet suddenly kicking into a man. He stumbled, fell right over the man, hit hard, his whole body in the water. He gasped, tried to breathe, swallowed a mouthful of water, choked, forced his head up out of the water. He gasped again, more voices, couldn't reach the bridge. He started to move his arms, frantic, trying to keep his head up, the water around him churning, shell fire, more men falling from the bridge. His arms were rubber, and he felt himself sinking, held his breath, put his feet down. He touched something hard, stood, realized the water was only up to his chest. He took a hard breath, coughed, the air singing above him, boots on the wooden bridge, splashes again, a flash of light, the sharp blast of a shell behind him. He tried to step forward, the river bottom sloping up, pushed himself through the water, shallower now, voices in front of him, more flashes of light. He was in mud now, out of the water, drove his legs forward, aching exhaustion, his lungs searing pain, was stepping on rocks, tripped again, his hands out, a hard fall. The pain rolled through his knees, his arms, and he pulled himself up, the hard chatter of the Maxims in front of him, soft specks of light in the fog. He dropped back down, lay flat for a long moment, the screaming blasts behind him, the river still churned and splashed, the Maxim gun close in front of him. He tried to focus, fought through the pain in his lungs, his hand coming up to his chest, gripping the grenade. He snatched it from his shirt, jerked the pin, stared into the darkness, waited for the glimpse of light, the gun bursting into life again. He had no idea of the distance, took a deep breath, pulled himself to his knees, blinded by the water in his eyes, the darkness and fog, saw the image of Parker, the big man throwing the grenade like a baseball pitcher. No, Dan, not this time. He straightened his arm behind him, another breath, saw the flickers from the Maxim again, his shoulder now uncoiling like a spring, his arm arcing up and over his head, the grenade tossed high. He dropped flat, his face on rock, long unending seconds, and the blast came now, the Maxim silent. He pulled himself up, stared blindly, crawled forward, the rifle gripped in one hand. He crouched low, moved forward quickly, blindly, the rocks giving way to grass, a sloping hill, soft dirt. He could smell the powder, the smoke from his own grenade, dropped down again, crawled into a small crevice, pulled his bayonet from his belt, and began to dig.

The East Bank of the Meuse River—
November 11, 1918

The fog was still thick, hiding the far bank of the river, but there was light now, and he could see what was left of the bridge, shattered planks of wood, drifting down the near shore, strung together with short pieces of shredded rope. It had been the extraordinary work of the engineers, men kneeling on buoyant bundles of wood, paddling themselves across a river in total darkness. They were linked to the shore behind them by a thin strand of rope, had probed and felt their way to the far bank, within yards of the enemy whose guns had a perfect field of fire. With the rope secured, the bridge had come to life, flat boards that sagged into the water under the weight of the engineers who survived the enemy fire long enough to anchor it, just enough so that the Marines could move across. Many of the engineers had died around the bridges, some dying as they guided the Marines to the ropes. Even the wounded had little chance, so many falling into the river, death by drowning, the same as so many of the Marines who lost their footing, some shot down by the Maxims, or jolted by the shock of the artillery shells. But they had continued to come, and when the bridge was cut by the impact of a shell, the engineers had done their work again, another man paddling another rope across the black water. All night the Marines crossed as quickly as the bridges would allow, pushing into the fire of the enemy. Now, with the daylight the Maxims continued their assault, the Germans on the bluffs above them seeking targets in the fog, peppering the far bank with a constant storm of fire. The bridge was useless now, and as long as the Germans held the heights above them, the engineers could only wait for the darkness before trying again.

Temple had hollowed out a depression in the side of the hill, was protected from any kind of fire from above. From first light, he had seen the riverbank, only a few yards from where he sat now, could see a carpet of bodies, some partially in the water, some tangled in the ruins of the bridge, slow movement as the current brushed past them. But he had seen the others as well, the men who had made it across, who huddled in their cover along the base of the high bluff, dozens, perhaps hundreds of men waiting for someone to give the order, someone who knew what might be above them, and how they might make their way up and off the edge of the river. He had been tempted to crawl out, find a vantage point, a way to use the rifle. But the fog was a blessing, and as long as the Germans made no attempt to come down the hill, there was no reason to do anything but wait.

The Meuse River—Mid-Morning, November 11, 1918

He followed the lieutenant, a stocky bear of a man named Hopper. There were a dozen men behind him, pulling themselves up through the thick grass, using the choppy unevenness of the hillside as cover. They moved along the side of a deep crevasse, almost directly above the wrecked Maxim gun, the work of Temple's grenade. If there had been other Maxims along the riverbank, they had been silenced as well, their dugouts and thickets now used by the Marines. The machine guns on the bluffs above had been quiet for a while now, and Temple had been as curious as so many of the others, the men along the river starting to gather, seeking someone in command. Temple was surprised to see how many men had made it across, more than three hundred, the few lieutenants now organizing squads to probe upward, to scout the bluffs, to find out why the German guns had grown silent.

The lieutenant stopped right above him, and Temple saw him crouching low, then raising his head slowly. Hopper made a sound, a quick wave of his hand, then crawled up quickly, and Temple followed, the men behind him keeping pace. He was suddenly in the open, the ground flattening out, the crest of the bluffs extending out to both sides, all along the river, a quarter mile across. The crest of the bluff was as cut up and ragged as the slope itself, pockets of brush and timber. He stood beside the lieutenant, saw the aftermath of the fight, ammo boxes, empty belts, all the debris of a retreating army. Hopper said, "Where the hell did they go?"

795

The other men were up beside them now, began to spread out, and Temple heard the shots, a single pop, then more.

Hopper said, "Get down!" Temple dropped down flat in the grass, heard Hopper shout, "Back to the slope! Pull back!"

Temple slid on his belly, reached the edge of the cliff, rolled over the side, tumbled into hard clumps of dirt and grass. He caught himself, his feet digging hard, the other men sliding down beside him. Hopper was a few feet away, said, "They were just waiting for us! They pulled back from the edge so the boys across the river couldn't see 'em! We can't do any good here. Let's get back down to the river."

The descent took only a few seconds, the men down below reacting to the shots, expectant stares upward. Hopper moved out onto the riverbank, officers gathering around him. Temple could see across the river now, the fog burning away, a thick column of men huddled low along the bank. Other men were moving quickly along the edge of the river, the engineers, carrying coils of rope, men hauling stacks of planks to the water's edge. Temple heard Hopper shout, "Rifles! Back up the hill. We need to keep the Huns back! The men who were with me, let's get back up there!"

Temple heard grumbles, one man said simply, "Officers."

Temple followed Hopper to the slope, thought, Yeah, well I guess we could have stayed up there. Hopper began to climb, the others as well, and Temple could see more squads pushing up the hill as well, streams of men all along the hillsides. His legs were aching, hard breaths, sweat, the men around him all making the same sounds. After several painful minutes, they reached the top, Hopper's words coming through hard gasps.

"Find a good place to shoot. Watch the ground out there as best you can. Keep your damned heads down. Wish we had a damned periscope."

Temple settled against the soft dirt, sat on a thick clump of grass, peered up over the edge. The ragged fields were still empty, and he turned, looked out across the river. There was movement in every direction, artillery and trucks, columns of marching troops. No wonder the Huns want to hold this ground. If we stay over there, we have no place to hide. There was a low voice, a few yards away.

"They're in that cut . . . two hundred yards, sir, maybe two fifty. I saw helmets."

Hopper said, "Be ready. They may be drawing up for a counterattack, try to drive us back across the river."

Temple glanced down at the river, thought, No bridges. We supposed to swim?

The air screamed above them, the shell coming down squarely in the river. Temple saw the sharp plume of water, said, "I think you're right, sir."

He could see the streaks arcing over them, the shells falling on the far side of the river, some in the river itself. The engineers were still working, bridges slowly stringing across the river, more riflemen starting to cross. But the artillery had no precision, the shells falling without any kind of pattern, scattered, distant and close, guns firing without spotters. Temple hugged tightly to the hillside, nothing else to do, could hear new sounds, artillery shells flying the other way, the American gunners responding. The ground shook beneath him, a hard shock, one shell impacting on the flat ground a few yards out in front of him. There were smaller blasts now, mortar shells coming down along the river itself, the only way for the enemy to reach the men on the near side of the river. The sounds thundered in his ears, the ground pulsing beneath him, more men climbing the hill now, fresh men just now coming across the river. The hillside was swarming with Marines, some going up and over onto the flat ground. One man climbed up behind Temple, shouted above the roar of the artillery, "Lieutenant!"

Hopper waved to the man, who climbed up closer, and Temple could hear bits of the man's words.

"Go . . . advance . . ."

The men around Hopper were all watching him and he waved up toward the open ground, yelled out, "Let's go! Form up with the squads on the flank. We're going after them!"

Temple could hear Maxim guns again, targets now, the Marines surging up, massing on the flat ground. He felt a hard shiver, sickness in his gut, had done this too many times now,

797

too many men going down around him. Hopper hadn't given the order, but Temple knew the routine too well. He pulled the bayonet from his belt, pulled it tight on the muzzle of the rifle. Across the top of the bluff, the American guns were finding the range, the cuts and thickets now blasted into tall plumes of dirt and rock. The machine guns continued to fire, the Marines mostly flat on the ground, waiting for the final order, the signal to move forward. Temple stayed flat against the side of the hill, the ground above him chopped by a burst of machine-gun fire, the screams of the artillery shells deafening.

And then, it stopped.

Hopper was up, began to wave them forward, other officers as well, their shouts now cutting the air, voices calling their men to the attack. Temple scanned the ground out in front of them, expected to see the enemy in motion, retreating perhaps, but there was nothing, no movement, no sound. Hopper seemed to freeze, stared out toward the German position, no Maxim fire, no mortars, no fire at all. The Marines were rising now, men staring ahead, rifles pointed forward, waiting for the signal, low voices drifting along the line of men. Temple looked back across the river, the guns silent, a steady stream of men on the bridges, still crossing the river. Hopper said, "What the hell . . . ?"

Temple heard it now, from across the river, the column of troops along the riverbank yelling, hands and helmets in the air, cheers and screams. He saw men pushing quickly past the foot soldiers on the narrow bridges, arms in the air, calls to the men who were still spread out all across the slope. The word came up the hill now, passed from runner to officer to the men who carried the rifle. Temple saw an officer coming up the slope toward him, the man climbing quickly past the riflemen who moved aside.

The man was only a few yards down the hillside, called out, "Lieutenant! Order your men to withdraw! Pass the order! There's an armistice! You are to withdraw to your position along the riverbank!"

Hopper was just above Temple now, said, "On whose authority?"

"Orders from General Lejeune."

Hopper stood quietly for a long moment, but the men around him began to pass the word on their own. More officers reached the flat ground, the commotion spreading, the men beginning to cheer. Temple climbed up, stood on the flat ground, frozen. He thought of the rumors, the talk he had heard the night before. Now, the rumors had become orders, the attack halted even as it began, the artillery and the mortars and the machine-gun fire on both sides suddenly silent.

Hopper was talking to the officer on the slope, said, "Are you certain of this?"

"Orders from General Lejeune, Lieutenant. Your men are to withdraw to the position they had reached as of eleven o'clock. There is no discretion, Lieutenant."

Hopper stood, said, "All right. Back down the hill! Let's move!"

The men began to flow past Temple, boisterous talk, chattering men sliding back down the hill, obeying the order Temple still didn't understand. Hopper said, "Let's go, Private. Back to the river. There's an armistice. Somebody thinks this is over."

Hopper moved away, passing the order to the men along the flat ground, waving them back. Temple walked out away from the edge of the slope, stared toward the German position, saw men emerging from their cover, standing in plain sight, staring across the open ground at the Americans who only moments ago were bringing the rifles and the bayonets, the men who would be cut down by the deadly fire of the German guns. Temple walked out a few steps farther, saw men in gray doing the same. He wasn't curious, didn't want to speak to them, didn't want to know them at all. He turned, looked along the edge of the bluff, saw dozens of men standing as he was, numb, silent. He knew what they shared, that they were the veterans, the men who had seen too much of the horror, who could not just set aside all they had seen and all they had lost. They did not cheer, could not yet feel the joy, could not yet share in any celebration. They carried wounds in some deep place, wounds that might never heal. Like so many nightmares on so many fields, this was just another dream, unreal, a cruel joke. Temple still pointed the bayonet, stared now at the men in gray, the men he was destined to kill, the faceless enemy who had taken so much from him. The cheering behind him became a faint echo now, and he thought, How can this be true? How can this just . . . end? He felt the taut spring in his mind slowly loosening, the hate and the horror and the images of so much death starting to move inside him. He looked to the side, saw some of the Marines dropping to their knees, and Temple felt it now, the utter exhaustion, was kneeling as well, the rifle falling from his hands, so many nightmares, so much sadness, the numbness starting to wear away. In the soft silence, he lowered his head, and began to cry.

49

PERSHING

November 11, 1918

The delegates had met on a railroad siding in the Compiègne forest, forty miles northeast of Paris, two railcars perched beside each other beneath the skeletal limbs of windblown trees. The ground was French, and the man who hosted the meeting was not only the most symbolic representative the Allies could offer, he was the man who held the reins on the forces that were driving the German army toward oblivion: Marshal Ferdinand Foch.

The German delegation was headed by Matthias Erzberger, a man who had long made enemies among German military leaders by daring to speak out against Ludendorff's prosecution of the war. For more than a year, Erzberger had been the champion of efforts to end the war by any means that would preserve Germany's pride, even if it meant withdrawing from those foreign lands the German army now occupied. His growing influence had been completely ignored by Ludendorff. But the despair of the German people gave energy to Erzberger's cause, and his view had gained considerable strength in the Reichstag, one cause of the wide rift between Germany's civilian and military leaders. Blunt opposition to the kaiser had always been politically unwise, and with the military controlling so much of Germany's policies, that opposition could be dangerous as well. But the tides of war had changed Germany in a way even Erzberger could not have predicted.

In many of Germany's larger cities, riots had broken out, workers loudly echoing the sentiments of the Russian Bolsheviks. The growing anarchy had infected the military as well, the port cities to the north seething with violence from sailors who had abandoned their ships. The mutinies and mass desertions had now spread to the army's security forces that guarded the cities. From Cologne to Munich, and finally, to Berlin itself, the despair of the German people had exploded into desperation, made worse by the news of the retreat of their army. The failure of the kaiser to control his own country had given his enemies more ammunition for their protests, the kind of violence that was rapidly drawing the country into a civil war. Though the kaiser clung mightily to the fantasy that his army would still support him, his own generals finally convinced him that the reality was far different. As Erzberger and Foch endured the contentious atmosphere of their meetings, a wire was received from Berlin. On November 10, as the mobs in Berlin threatened to invade the Reichstag itself, Kaiser Wilhelm escaped their wrath by discreetly boarding a train bound for Holland. The kaiser had abdicated his throne.

The kaiser's sudden absence made little difference to the negotiators. What remained of an organized German government was now in the hands of the chancellor, Max von Baden, the man who had given Erzberger the authority to negotiate the armistice in the first place. The German delegation had come to Compiègne with hopes of an immediate cease-fire, which might help restore order inside of Germany, and as well, provide their army with the opportunity to organize its forces. Foch realized immediately that the German delegation had no leverage to push the negotiations their own way. Erzberger had to concede that Foch was right.

The terms of the armistice were severe and absolute. All foreign territory occupied by German forces was to be abandoned, and as the German troops pulled away, they would be closely followed by Allied forces, who would eventually occupy the western bank of the Rhine River. Germany would turn over most of its remaining artillery pieces, machine guns, aircraft, railway cars and locomotives, and all submarines and naval vessels would be disarmed and held captive in German ports. Erzberger could not agree to the terms on his own authority, and the response from Berlin was entirely predictable. Von Baden and Erzberger might protest, but Germany was in no position to dictate anything. At five-ten a.m., on November 11, the German delegates signed the armistice. Foch's order had been transmitted immediately afterward:

> *Hostilities will cease on the entire front at 11 o'clock, November 11th (French hour). The allied troops will not go beyond the line reached at that hour on that date until further orders.*
> *Marshal Foch, 5:45 a.m.*

Pershing knew why the Germans had approached Woodrow Wilson with their peace overtures. For nearly a year, the American president had been championing his "Fourteen Points," Wilson's clear-cut solution to ending the war, with terms that would satisfy Wilson's idealistic view of how the world should be. The terms were inarguably fair to the Germans, and to American interests. But the French and British had other ideas. In all of Pershing's discussions with Foch or Haig, Clemenceau or Lloyd George, there was no hint that anyone was interested in what was *fair*. For the first time since he had set foot in France, Pershing felt more aligned with their views than he did with his own president. But Pershing didn't share what he saw as the Allies' burning need for revenge. His focus was on military necessity, on the importance of utterly defeating the enemy, something that didn't seem to concern Woodrow Wilson. Pershing shared the fire that drove his troops forward on every field of battle, the courage of facing the guns, the courage that allowed a commander to send young men to their deaths. He could not simply allow the fire that drove his army to be extinguished by diplomacy. Pershing had made his protests to Washington, voiced his disagreements to the men who brought Wilson's terms to Europe. But the president's determination to have his way gave the Allied leaders an uncomfortable choice. If Wilson's proposals weren't agreed to, the Americans might make their own separate peace with Germany. It was a poorly disguised form of blackmail. If the Americans had signed their own treaty with Germany, and suddenly withdrew from the war, the leverage that Foch had enjoyed at Compiègne would have been a mirage. Neither the British nor the French armies had the strength left to enforce an armistice, or demand anything of the Germans.

Across the Meuse River, the Germans were beginning their pullback, starting their march home. They still flew their flags, and despite the mutinies that had spread through so much of the German army, a significant number of troops still marched behind their officers, and would return to their homes still believing they were soldiers. They had marched away from the battlefields knowing that though they had been pushed, they had not been beaten, they had not *surrendered*. And if they were called upon again, Pershing had no doubt that the German army, in some form, would again take to the field.

Wilson's Fourteen Points had on first appearance seemed perfectly rational, dealing with specific ways to end territorial disputes from Belgium to Turkey, Russia to the Middle East. The document had been widely hailed in diplomatic circles all over the world. But the cheering did not extend to either London or Paris, or the headquarters of the AEF. Two words were missing from Wilson's document. The first was *reparations*, what the Allies considered among their first priorities, placing heavy pressure on Germany to repay the Allies for damages, thus guaranteeing a crippling of the German economy for years to come. With the German economy in shambles, it would be impossible for that nation to rebuild its war machine, ending the threat of German militarism that had caused decades of misery, particularly in France. The second word was *surrender*. It was the burning stake that drove hard into Pershing's instincts as a military commander. To Pershing, it seemed that Wilson was satisfied that if the shooting stopped and both sides simply took their armies home, then the war had come to an appropriate end. Pershing was furious that the president was denying his army the victory they had earned. Without the unconditional surrender of the German army, there was no victory. The armistice included one specific term. If the Germans did not obey every clause in the armistice, the Allies reserved the right to begin the fighting all over again. Pershing knew that Foch had inserted that clause as a gesture of power, a fist to back up the demands the Germans would have to accept. But the reality was that the only army capable of enforcing such a clause was American. Anyone who expected the Allied armies, especially the French, to simply rush to arms again might find themselves confronting a mutiny as severe as what Pétain had to defuse in 1917. But without a formal German surrender, Foch had no choice but to include such a clause. It was for this one reason that Pershing believed the armistice to be a disastrous mistake.

Paris—November 12, 1918

Pershing's headquarters was on a railway car now, giving him the same mobility enjoyed by Pétain. He had come to the city to meet with Foch, to present the Allied commander with the Distinguished Service Medal, a symbolic and diplomatic gesture suggested by President Wilson. Before the ceremony, Foch's staff had made a more formal visit to Pershing's headquarters, to present Foch's lengthy list of expectations for the AEF. There would be logistical problems, the assignments to the specific routes that the Americans would take eastward, how the transfer of German equipment would occur, what would happen to the extraordinary number of German prisoners now held behind the Allied lines. Pershing was used to this kind of nightmare of detail, but now, the nightmare was made worse by the fog of uncertainty that he felt about the armistice itself. The focus now was on the careful adherence to the terms of the armistice, keeping his army within their proper boundaries, making sure the Germans did the same. No matter how important it was to enforce every term of the armistice, Pershing could not avoid a dull aching depression.

Pershing's initial reaction to the armistice order had been the same as many of his men, exhausted disbelief. But he shared none of the giddiness of the men around his headquarters, would not shout out some mindless salute to victory. As much as he yearned for the end of the war, he had always believed that the end could only come about by the absolute defeat of the enemy. The armistice was a halt to the shooting. But the enemy was still out there, and was still capable of making a fight.

The ceremony had been brief and emotional, a show of respect that Foch received with words of gratitude for America's role in the war. The ceremonies were repeated in the various headquarters, the medal awarded to Douglas Haig and Henri Pétain as well. Each of the commanders hosted Pershing with luncheons and music, and the perfect dress uniforms of honor guards, all the signs of respect and dignity, bestowing solemn gravity to the ceremonies that Pershing knew were utterly meaningless. Though the medals were simply gestures, the words that passed between the men did have meaning, toasts of respect that gave way to surprising displays of emotion. Even Foch's formal rigidity had been shaken, the stoic Frenchman offering Pershing what every American soldier knew to be true: without the Americans, there would be no armistice.

There would be one more medal awarded, something Pershing had insisted upon, something he did not mention to Foch. Pershing understood the realities of politics, what was acceptable protocol, who should first receive the glad-handed salutes. The final ceremony would be without fanfare, no bands, no honor guard, would take place in the quiet surroundings of an office that had seen little activity in the long weeks of the final campaign. As much as Pershing had to respect Foch, as close as he felt to Pétain, this final ceremony was the one Pershing looked forward to most of all. With President Wilson's reluctant approval, Pershing would present the Distinguished Service Medal to Marshal Joseph Joffre.

The drive through the wide avenues of Paris had been as chaotic as any experience he had endured along the front lines. With the announcement of the armistice, the city had erupted in a celebration that filled every public square with raucous enthusiasm, great throngs of people who blocked every route. As his limousine became engulfed by the joyous mobs, he had been recognized, word spreading, the people climbing up on his car, some tumbling right into the seat with him. He had been rescued by a small group of American soldiers, who had been part of the celebration themselves, men who had just enough sobriety to understand the necessity of moving their commander on his way.

Joffre had maintained an office in the French National War College, the École de Guerre, knew to expect the visit only because Pershing's staff had relayed word of his arrival. Pershing was accompanied by three of his staff, including James Harbord, whose extraordinary performance in his position as head of the Service of Supply had completely justified Pershing's faith in the man's abilities. Under Harbord's command, the flow of equipment and provisions to the front lines had been one of the primary tools that had allowed the Americans to achieve their success on the battlefield. It seemed entirely appropriate to Pershing that Harbord had earned the honor of accompanying him to see Joffre.

"Marshal Joffre, I have been authorized by the President of the United States to bestow upon you one of my country's highest military honors. I am honored to present you, sir, with the Distinguished Service Medal."

Pershing removed the medal from the box, pinned it on the man's coat. There was a silent moment, no boisterous toasts, the two men looking into each other's eyes. Pershing was suddenly emotional, felt a tightness in his throat, unexpected, embarrassing.

After a long pause, Joffre said, "Your recognition is gratefully accepted, General, and that of your president. I have always appreciated that you are a man who holds to his beliefs in what is right, and then performs accordingly. That is a valuable part of being a general. It is not always so useful for a politician. I admit to some regret that these days, I am neither."

"You will always be a soldier, sir."

Joffre laughed. "There you are, once again. Trying to sound like a politician. I assure you, General, at my age, one does not think in terms of what will *always* be."

Pershing saw the frailty in the old man now, watched as Joffre moved to his chair. Joffre sat, motioned to Pershing's officers. "Please, gentlemen. Do not be so formal. Your ceremony has concluded. We may become friends again."

Harbord said, "Marshal Joffre, perhaps it would be best if we waited outside. I should enjoy speaking with your chief of staff. I have not seen him in some time."

Pershing appreciated Harbord's gesture, and Joffre said, "Certainly, General Harbord. Colonel Fabre was looking forward to seeing you again."

Harbord leaned down toward Pershing, said, "Sir. If you will permit—"

"Go on, General. I'll be along shortly."

The door closed, and Pershing was alone with the old man now, noticed that Joffre seemed to be somewhat thinner. Pershing said, "I hope you are well, sir."

"You cannot do it, can you? You cannot bring yourself to call me by my name. Is that what they did to you at your West Point? You are not allowed ever to be relaxed?"

Pershing smiled. "Perhaps not. I apologize. I am accustomed to meetings with Marshal Foch. He does not relax, either."

"Nor should he. He bears the weight of history on his shoulders. He has civilians barking at him from behind, and a German army crouching low in front of him like some wounded beast. I would imagine he has not known a comfortable night's sleep in a long time."

Pershing measured his words, and after a pause said, "I cannot say I have, either."

Joffre shook his head. "I expected so. Are you not pleased with all that has happened? Well, no, of course you're not."

"Is Marshal Foch pleased?"

Joffre seemed puzzled. "What an interesting question. He is certainly reaping the fruits of his efforts. He has assured himself a prominent place in French history. Every Frenchman now believes him to be a great hero. To the soldiers, Marshal Foch is the face of victory, the very backbone of our success. Why would he not be pleased?"

"You said yourself, he does not sleep well."

"Ah, but that is merely the cost. Even he would say it is a fair price."

"I cannot believe he was completely in favor of the armistice."

Joffre cocked his head to the side, looked at him with a slight smile. "What difference does that make now? The armistice is a fact. Whether or not Foch agreed with the terms, he convinced the Germans that he did. He eliminated any discussion, any leverage they thought they might have. The Germans had to believe that we would continue to fight if they did not succumb to the terms of the armistice."

Pershing said nothing, looked down, and Joffre said, "Ah, yes, I see. So, what would you have done differently, John? You would have ignored your president? Ignored the inevitable? The Germans were in complete disarray, completely exhausted, no reserves, limited supplies. Their ranks are suffering the devastation of influenza. So you would have pursued them further, pressed the attack, yes?"

"I should like to have seen my troops marching into Berlin."

"You would have taken the war into Germany? At what cost? A million American lives? Two or three more years of war? Forgive me, my friend, but you are being naïve. You would suggest that we continue this war until there is some conclusion that is satisfactory only to generals? Who would have gone with you? France and England are as defeated as the Germans, have suffered as much. I should not have to instruct you on basic military wisdom, John. Never underestimate your enemy. The Germans would have defended their homeland with far greater passion than they defended the lands they had conquered from us. If Foch would have sent all of our troops across the Rhine, then all those political factions that still threaten to destroy the German government would have suddenly had a reason to unite. Instead of the kaiser, they would have had a new enemy. You. The German people would have rallied around their troops. The workers would have returned to their factories. There would have been snipers on every rooftop, mines on every roadway."

Pershing appreciated Joffre's candor, was feeling embarrassed now. "I cannot argue with what you say. But it still frustrates me. How else is a general to see it? We had them defeated on every front, but we were not allowed to complete the task. There may be a price to pay for that. A price for *you* to pay.

Germany still believes France to be her enemy, and no matter how many years pass, you will still have your common border, and you must still maintain a military presence there."

"That is not your problem, John. It is time for you and Pétain and Haig to step aside, and hand the world over to the men with the papers, the men who redraw the maps and write the treaties. It has always been, and it will always be. Soldiers make terrible diplomats, and you know very well that when peace comes to a free land, soldiers are simply in the way. Men like you are an uncomfortable reminder that peace is fragile, temporary, that even in the best of times, prosperity must be protected by men with guns."

"If the peace is temporary, it will be because we were not allowed to eliminate the enemy's ability to make war."

"You must step back, John. You must see this war as the civilians see it. Strategy and tactics mean nothing to people who have lost their sons, their homes, their villages. The woman who has seen her husband's mutilated body will care very little which political principle is worth standing up for. Do not forget, John. Nations fight wars, not armies. It is the leaders who start wars, whether they are civilian or military, whether they be presidents or kings or dictators. You and I are merely the tools they use. Your president is an idealist, a man who sees the world as he wishes it to be. Is not a world without war better than one with such a horror? It matters not to the idealist who prevails on the battlefield. President Wilson believes he has a duty to change our world so that it is a better place for all mankind. I doubt he will succeed, but I applaud him for believing it is possible."

"So who is more naïve? He is my president and I obey him, and I suppose I even respect him. But I don't believe he understands war. I don't believe he understands that to some people, war is the preferred state, the only means to an end. Germany caused this war for no other reason than it was their desire to do so. How many wars have begun for no greater purpose than hatred of a neighbor, or a desire to grab a piece of land?"

"John, perhaps your president understands the lessons of *this* war, lessons that we should all have learned. The world has never seen anything like this before. The suffering and the destruction went far beyond what anyone could predict, what any nation has ever endured. We must hope that this time the leaders have been sufficiently horrified by the price of their arguments, that they have learned a lesson from what it can cost to have an enemy. I cannot imagine in my worst nightmares that the world will allow this to happen again."

Pershing nodded slowly and Joffre said, "John, it is time for you to stand aside. You and I made their war. We must trust others to make the peace."

"It would have been better if they had allowed us to finish the job."

50

TEMPLE

La Rochette, Luxembourg—December 1, 1918

It was one more march through the misery of the freezing rain. The division had been ordered to move north, passing through the southeastern corner of Belgium, establishing camp on the Sauer River, which divided Luxembourg and Germany. There they would wait a week, while the entire army of occupation made ready to cross as one unified mass into German territory.

Temple's feet were more than sore. He suffered from deep blisters, bandaged and smeared thick with ointment from the medical wagon. Most of the men were footsore. It was only one of the aftereffects of the bloody crossing of the footbridges over the Meuse River, every uniform soaked, every boot filled with muddy water. In the days that followed the armistice, the weather had been as bad as any they had seen before, made worse by the sharp cold that often turned the rain to sleet. There was no dry place, few meals that were much warmer than the men who suffered through them, more corned beef and salmon and cornmeal mush.

When the order came, Temple had awakened to a new chorus of cursing, an outpouring of misery voiced by too many of the men who had only recently arrived. The replacements were coming still, even after the armistice, rebuilding the division back to full strength, a reminder that no matter the celebrations, an armistice was not, after all, a peace treaty. Despite the low tolerance for discomfort shown by the new men, the veterans saw the march for what it was. For the first time, the infantrymen and Marines would march to some new place knowing that this time, no one would be shooting at them.

Near Ahrweiler, Germany—December 8, 1918

The Second Division was to man one of the three primary bridgeheads across the Rhine River, alongside the First and Thirty-second Divisions. The bridgeheads had been defined by the terms of the armistice, each one a zone of occupation that extended in an arc twenty miles east of the river. The American sector was the crossing at Koblenz, a picturesque city perched alongside the great river, which would be their home for as long as it took for a final peace treaty to be signed.

They marched again through rain that Temple believed might never stop. The wide road was coated with an oozing pool of slippery mud, aggravating the pain in his feet, torturing the sore legs of every man in the column. He had limped along with the men around him, the exhaustion in each of them increased by the burden they carried. Besides their backpacks and blankets, they had been ordered to carry extra bandoliers of ammunition, an order born of caution, the senior command's uncertainty that here, in the towns and villages where the enemy might suddenly make a stand, the men had best be prepared. As the Second Division marched deeper into Germany, they knew that not so far in front of them, the enemy was moving in the same direction, heading for home. The roadsides gave hints of the condition of the German soldiers, scattered heaps of cast-off equipment, rags that had once been coats, the occasional carcass of a horse that had been starved and driven to death. But the villages showed no sign of the war, no shell holes peppering the roads, no shattered houses or blasted orchards. The people gathered in small crowds, stoic, unsmiling, but there were no outcries or hostile displays, no displays at all. The German civilians seemed thin, underfed, their mood as despairing as the French refugees Temple had seen so many times before. The fields were empty of life, brown and barren. There were almost no young men, something else these people had in common with the French, the faces of the women mostly sad and empty, the old people bent and fragile. But in every village, Temple was surprised to see children, a great many children, many as subdued as their mothers, drawn out to the roadside to watch this weary ragged parade, as curious about the Americans as the Americans were of them. There was talk, some effort by the Marines to inspire a smile, some of the men making idiotic faces to wide-eyed toddlers, some of whom responded by making idiotic faces of their own. Temple could feel the effect of the children, not only on the Marines, but on the landscape itself. No matter the bleak despair of the adults, the children were still children, who knew little of the war, who had not suffered as much from the loss and deprivation, the younger ones already beginning to forget the father who had been dead for a month, a year, four years. Temple wanted to feel something of hope from them, a new generation that would learn from the mistakes of their fathers, who would work to rebuild their country and all of Europe alongside the fatherless children of France. But as the Marines marched through yet another village, Temple began to sense something different. His fantasy was dissolved by the cynicism of some of the veterans around him, men who began to see something else. The children were a symbol after all, that Germany was still alive and still had a future. As much as Temple wanted to believe that so much innocence could be preserved, he knew how brutally his own innocence had been drained away. If there was no guiding hand to pass on the horrible lessons of this war, then they would grow up knowing only what their leaders told them. There might be nothing to prevent them from repeating the horrific mistakes of their fathers.

Along the Rhine River—Spring 1919

They were billeted in houses all through the countryside, the same living arrangements they had once seen in France. Some of the men around Temple had been in Europe now for more than twenty months, and Temple had celebrated his first year away from home by enduring the silent misery of a snowstorm. As the weather grew warmer, the troops had changed along with the landscape. The commanders had cautioned against allowing the men to become too comfortable, too soft for a sudden return to action. Reports came frequently of hostility and controversy at the conference tables where the peace treaty was being engineered. There had been alerts, rumors that the Germans were suddenly arming again, the officers scrambling to assemble the men into formations, preparation for combat, as though any moment might bring artillery fire from German positions no one could see. The Marines took the rumors seriously, only a few of them questioning whether German gunners would be so likely to shell their own towns. In the absence of any real threat, the officers had ordered the men back into training, drills and marches designed to keep them fit and sharp. To the veterans, it was as ridiculous as any order they had ever received, men who had survived the worst combat in American history asked to respect the need for mindless drills on a parade ground. The more experienced commanders understood that assigning the men useless exercise was more likely to destroy morale than build it, and the parade grounds were transformed into venues for all manner of sporting events. From football and baseball to horsemanship and marksmanship, the competitions pitted battalion against battalion, regiment against regiment, and finally, at the urging of the more ambitious division commanders, the Second Division began to field teams in every sport against other divisions both in and beyond their sector. The veterans who had faced the enemy alongside men like Roscoe Temple were not surprised that when it came to marksmanship, no one could compete with the Marines.

As the weeks stretched into months, the morale of the men could not be shielded from the awareness that no matter the activities, the improvement in their food and billets, they were still in a foreign land. The order finally came on July 3, 1919. The Treaty of Versailles had been signed. Now they could go home.

The North Atlantic—August 7, 1919

The ship was the *George Washington*, the same ship that had transported President Wilson to France. On this voyage westward, the cargo was five thousand infantrymen and Marines of the Second Division, and their commander, Major General John Lejeune.

There had been nothing unusual about the journey, no particularly rough seas, no disciplinary problems to cause anyone concern. Temple was housed in a cabin with fifteen other men, his bunk the lowest of four, just enough space above him for him to roll his body out sideways. For the first few days at sea the mood had been boisterous, the men boiling with noisy enthusiasm for all that would happen once they were home. But it had been a week now, and the talk had grown quiet, the men settling into the boredom of the journey. There were card games, letters written, the newer men seeking out the veterans, prodding them for the stories that would be heard by grandchildren one day, whether or not the story belonged to the men telling the tale.

Temple had stayed mostly by himself, had noticed many of the familiar faces doing the same. For most of the trip, he had thought less of home than of what was left behind. The worst time was the night, and he had begun to hate the order for *lights out*. If there was any sleep at all, it was ripped apart by the nightmares, his mind filling with the constant chatter of Maxim guns. When the nightmares would leave him, his sleep would be jarred by the creaks and groans of the ship, haunting echoes of artillery fire, screams from the shells, or the men they destroyed. More often he had passed the night by staring into darkness, unable to hold closed those awful places in his mind, the bodies of so many men, the faces of the friends who would not come home. Already the corpses were being gathered by grim burial details, pulled out of the ground from their haphazard graves on every field the division had crossed. The official graveyards were not yet completed, those massive patches of quiet land that would serve as a permanent memorial to the fallen. But the work had begun, and already the remains of so many were being laid into French soil beneath white crosses, some with names engraved, some bearing the simple tragic word: *unknown*. Every unit in the AEF would have someplace their men could return to, some reminder of what was lost. But none more than the men who had fought with Temple. The Second Division had suffered more than twenty-three thousand casualties, nearly six thousand dead, the worst losses of any division in the AEF.

The word had been passed to expect landfall in the morning, and after the evening mess, the men had seemed to drift toward the bow of the ship, gathering in the darkness, many more up on every deck, peering forward, all of them trying to catch the first glimpse of the lights of New York. Temple had stayed back, moved now toward the stern, leaned on the thickly painted railing staring toward the open sea. Above him, the trail of black smoke clouded out the stars, the black water beneath his feet churning in hard swirls.

He had not sent the letter to Scarabelli's father. It annoyed him even now, a dark sense of shame, his lack of courage to confront the man's pain. As he stared into darkness, he tried to see his friend's face, could only conjure up the voice, unmistakably New Jersey, the ridiculous claims, stories no one believed were true. That's what we bring home, he thought. Ridiculous stories. What do I truly have to offer Gino's father? Do I seek him out, find their home, knock on their door and announce myself as the man who saw his son die? What of my own mother? Do I wander back to the farm with a smile, so relieved, so grateful to be home? How can any of us be grateful to be the survivors of something that so many others died for?

He had tried to keep the faces in his mind, had even thought of making a list, all the men he had known who were now buried in France, making sure no one was forgotten. But the exercise was futile, frustrating, only made him angrier at himself. He had fought against all the clichés, how all would be healed with the passing of time, the awful memories taken away. The images were more than important to him, they were a part of who he had become. He felt a responsibility to every one of them, to remember, to tell their stories. There hadn't been time for the men to really know each other, and it gnawed at him now. He had known so little about Ballou, the cowboy who never rode a horse, knew nothing of the man's parents, of anyone he had left behind. Parker was the same, the soft-spoken giant of a man who had been so changed by the war. Temple could only describe him now as the uneducated backwoodsman with the slow drawl, who had become the most efficient killer in the platoon. Dan should have been a sergeant, he thought. Maybe even a lieutenant. He had the natural instinct for it. Hell, the sergeants followed *him*. What would have happened to him when he got home? Would he have gone back to the mountains? Who would have been there for him? He thought of Scarabelli now, so different, so much fun. Temple could not help smiling, knew that he could never go to New York without hearing the voice of Scarabelli. Gino would have never left the city, that's for certain. And he would have loved showing this farm boy around, scaring the hell out of me with tales of, what? Crime and loose women.

He stared out for a moment, a swirl of wind wrapping him in the smoke. He closed his eyes, waited for it to pass, breathed the cold salty air again. What about you, Farm Boy? What will you do? He had asked the question too many times, and every possible answer terrified him. The Corps? What use are Marines now? Will there be another war? Years from now maybe, some jackass in some foreign country does something incredibly stupid, and so, the Marines will go do their job. But I won't be there. Look at all the men on this ship, so many of them so inexperienced. New wars are for new men. How many of the veterans will stay in the Corps? They won't need so many of us now.

So, what about you, Farm Boy? How will they treat you now? What kind of hero will you be back home? Or, will they be scared of you? He had put aside the questions for many days, was angry now, angry at his friends as much as the war, angry at being the one to go home.

He turned away from the open water, stared at the flickering lights of the great ocean liner, realized there was a damp mist in the air now. A pair of sailors emerged from a doorway, ignored him, climbed a ladder to some place Temple knew nothing about. He watched them until they disappeared, closed his eyes, asked the silent question again. So, what the hell is waiting for you? He leaned back against the railing, tried to see the farm, the creek, the woods, his grandfather's old cabin. Home. Where nothing happens. What will they expect you to do there? Tell all

818

the awful stories to people who'll think you're lying? And even if they believed you, why would anyone want to hear about a man being blown to dust, about arms ripped away, faces torn from a man's head? That's what I'm bringing home. That's what I'll be good for, scaring children. How do I plow a field without thinking of turning up bodies? It's a damned good thing we don't grow wheat. How the hell could I look at another wheat field and not . . . remember?

He felt his hands shaking, felt the familiar terror. He stared out into the darkness again, thought of Scarabelli. It should have been you. You should be here now. You were the one who knew how to make a place for yourself. You could go back home and tell your stories and no one would be scared of you. You would love the attention. One day you'd be the crazy old man your grandchildren would love to tease behind your back. And tomorrow, your family would be there on that dock waiting for you, proud of their son. The Marine. The hero.

He thought of his mother now. So, what will you think of me? All you know of the world is what you can touch in your hands, soil and feathers and homespun cloth. Will you be proud of the son who learned how to kill a man with his hands? How much have you already read about this war? No matter how awful the stories, all of them are true. And now your son brings it all home with him. The son who survived while all of his friends died. The man who hears machine-gun fire in his sleep. The man who didn't have the courage to tell a father what kind of man his son was. Goddamn this war. God help the men who cannot escape it. God help me.

He had gone below just long enough to gather his back-pack. The officers had not ordered the men to their bunks, and like so many, Temple stayed out on deck all night, the gray mist soaking him. The ship had slipped quietly into New York Harbor at dawn, and all along the rails of the ship they had cheered, passing close to the Statue of Liberty, deep emotions rising up in so many of the men. Temple had tried to feel their mood, share their tears, so many men so grateful to be coming home. It made him miss Scarabelli again, knew that the magnificent statue would inspire something deep and meaning-ful in the small Italian, something he would share with his whole family. As the ship drew closer to the Hoboken docks, Temple began to feel the fear again, terrified of what home would mean, of what he would find, terrified of losing all that he had left behind him.

The tugs had come, the ship pushed gently to its mooring, the ropes securing her to the pier. He stayed against the far rail, waited while the men were lined up, the long procession now marching slowly from the ship. He stared instead out toward the New York skyline, tried to focus on the tall buildings, the marvels of engineering, the voice in his head nervously chatter-ing, distracting him.

"All ashore, Private!"

He turned, saw an MP, felt paralyzed by the cold in his gut. He forced himself away from the rail, hoisted his backpack up on his shoulders, moved to the end of the column. He saw now that the pier below was filled with people, small clusters of fam-ily gathered around men in uniform. They were drifting away now, happy crying people, the pier slowly emptying. He reached the gangplank, the men in front of him mostly officers, and as they stepped down onto the dock there were more cries, wives and small children coming forward, arms out, the men moving down as quickly as the line would allow. The gangplank ended, and he stepped onto the hard wood of the pier, stood for a moment, felt utterly lost. He moved past officers holding chil-dren, couples locked in hard embraces, saw the sign directing the men away from the pier, toward the billets, where the men who had no one to meet them would find a temporary base. There was a voice now, a high shout.

"*Temple!*"

He stopped, heard it again, "*Temple!*"

He looked toward the thin crowd that still lined the ropes to one side, saw a man with his hand in the air, waving.

"*Temple!*"

He moved that way, stared at the man, curious, saw now he was in a suit, a size too small, a small round man, dark, the man now smiling at him through tear-filled eyes.

820

"You are Temple!"

"Yes. Roscoe Temple."

"My son wrote me so much about you! I am Gino's father. I am Scarabelli."

Temple was suddenly frozen, confused, thought, Doesn't he know? My God . . .

"You were Gino's best friend. You were with him, yes? Will you tell us about him? What kind of soldier he was? I want to know everything about my boy."

"How did you know me . . . ?"

The man stood to one side, and Temple saw her, the rail-thin woman, the simple dress, a wide hat. She stepped forward, and Temple stared for a long silent moment, then said, "How . . ."

"Mr. Scarabelli sent me a train ticket. We weren't sure which ship you would be on."

Temple moved past the ropes, close to her, "Mama . . ."

He saw her soft smile now, took her hands in his, felt her strength, the tears coming to both of them, the quiet words flowing deep inside of him, pushing the fear away.

"Welcome home, Roscoe."

The questions rose up, how they found her, why she had come. But he had no words, it was not the time. She held tightly to his arm, and he saw more of Scarabelli's family, older women, a boy, sadness and smiles, tears and welcoming hands. All of his fear was a memory now, pushed aside with all the other memories, replaced by the welcome, the warmth, her comforting smile. Now he could go home.

THE END

AFTERWORD

*The war ended on the eleventh hour of the eleventh
day of the eleventh month of 1918. It had meant
nothing, solved nothing and proved nothing.*
—LEON WOLFF, historian

*The wars are not over. . . . There will be the Devil
to pay all around the world.*
—GENERAL TASKER BLISS, 1919

The Treaty of Versailles

The negotiations begin in January 1919, in Paris. Almost
immediately, the contest becomes not so much a test of wills
between the Allies and the Germans, but between the Allies
themselves. The meetings are chaired by Clemenceau, who
presses hard for reparations and a more punitive treaty, and
Woodrow Wilson comes to understand for the first time the
political motivation that drives the Allies. Though Wilson
insists that the first clause of the treaty should outline the
foundation of his cherished "League of Nations," Clemenceau
and David Lloyd George are far less interested in the future
of the world at large than they are of the future of Germany's
ability to ever make war. But Clemenceau and Lloyd
George have very different views of how punishing the treaty
should be, and there are long weeks of rancorous debates.
While Clemenceau pushes for a far more punitive treaty
than the British, Lloyd George expresses fear that the more
brutal the terms, the more German resentment might be fueled,

resulting in some possible difficulty in the future.

The final draft of the treaty, consisting of more than four hundred specific clauses, is completed in April 1919, at which time it is simply handed to the Germans for signature. The German delegates, who have expected to be directly involved in the point-by-point negotiation of the treaty, are shocked to learn that the Allies will entertain no discussion with them at all. The German government protests the severity of the terms, claiming the terms are "intolerable for any nation." But the protests are largely ignored. Faced with no power base from which to enforce their concerns, the Germans have no choice but to accept the treaty virtually as written. On June 28, the new German chancellor, Friedrich Ebert, authorizes his delegation to sign the treaty.

Germany loses nearly fifteen percent of its landmass, much of which is granted to Poland, including the valuable seaport of Danzig (now Gdansk). The long disputed lands of Alsace and Lorraine are returned to French control, and additional territory is ceded to Czechoslovakia, Belgium, Denmark, and Lithuania. In addition, the critical mining regions of the Saar Valley are to be occupied by Allied armies until 1935, with the raw materials produced there being given to France as part of Germany's reparations.

The German military virtually ceases to exist. The army is reduced to no more than one hundred thousand men, who are allowed no heavy artillery, aircraft, or tanks, and very few machine guns. Poison gas is outlawed as well. The German navy is gutted the same way, including the complete elimination of submarines.

The issue of reparations continues to be controversial even after the treaty is signed. Forced to agree to a blanket admission of guilt for causing the war, the Germans are therefore obliged to pay out funds for the entire estimated cost of the war, based on each injured nation's claims, a figure that eventually exceeds thirty billion dollars. More than any other clause of the treaty, the issue of reparations ensures that the German economy cannot recover, and that Germany will not enjoy economic prosperity for decades to come.

Woodrow Wilson reluctantly accepts the treaty as a necessary evil, believing the harshest terms might be amended later by the League of Nations. But the treaty is never ratified by the United States Congress. The refusal is a hard blow to Wilson's prestige, and is a testament not only to Wilson's diminishing political power, but to the surge in isolationist sentiment that begins to sweep across America.

Though the treaty is criticized in Washington as being too harsh and in France as being too lenient, the most emotional reaction to its terms is in Germany itself. Though the German government is mired in political chaos, a power struggle between the different factions who seek control of the country, the German people look beyond their own borders and unite behind one distinctive view: the terms of the treaty are brutally humiliating and a permanent assault on German national pride. With the German economy in shambles, starvation breeds fear, which breeds increasing violence. The people begin to unify, driven by their collective anger toward the enemies who have stripped Germany of her kaiser, her military, and her national identity. All that is missing is a voice, a single figure who can channel that anger into a rallying cry, the kind of response that the toothless German government is unable to provide.

As the American troops sail for home, those who had served the German army now look to their futures as well, a future that to many, seems devoid of hope. One man, a corporal, an Austrian serving with the Bavarian reserves, returns home carrying the same despair as so many of the men he has served alongside, a personal despair that festers into a furious cry for vengeance. The cry will come in September 1922, the man issuing a challenge for his nation to fight back, to throw off the abuses of the Treaty of Versailles. The cry will be heard by a desperate people, the man's gift for oratory inflaming the nation not just toward a path of revenge, but toward the utter destruction of its enemies. His name is Adolf Hitler.

John J. Pershing

His outspoken opposition to the armistice is seen by Woodrow

Wilson and his deputies as an obstacle to their delicate position at the peace conference, and Pershing is never allowed to participate. He returns to the States in September 1919, and is welcomed as a national hero. He is promoted to "General of the Armies," which makes him the nation's first commander of that rank since George Washington. He is appointed army chief of staff in 1921, spends much of his time modernizing the army's systems and organization. He retires in 1924, enjoys counseling troubled soldiers, and uses his considerable influence to assist veterans of the American Expeditionary Force to find their way into civilian life. Always dedicated to the proper recognition of his soldiers, he serves on the American Battle Monuments Commission, ensuring that appropriate attention is given to memorializing the efforts of the American army in France.

He is approached by friends who believe he should run for president, but Pershing refuses, freely acknowledges that he is not a man whose temperament is suited for the realities of politics.

In 1931, he publishes his memoirs, titled *My Experiences in the World War*, which is awarded the Pulitzer Prize.

Though Pershing maintains a lifelong friendship with George Patton, when the war concludes, Pershing and Patton's sister Nita do not resume their romance. Pershing's romantic interests lie with a considerably younger woman named Micheline Resco, whom he meets in France. The relationship carries hints of scandal, and Pershing guards her privacy and his own with zealous secrecy. In the years after the war, he visits her periodically, and they eventually marry. But the couple maintain their privacy, and "Michette" is rarely visible among the social whirlwind that some try to surround him with in Washington.

With the outbreak of the Second World War, President Franklin Roosevelt calls upon Pershing as a trusted adviser, and Pershing recommends that Roosevelt appoint General George C. Marshall to the post of chief of staff. It is one of Roosevelt's, and the nation's most fortunate decisions.

Pershing is disappointed when his surviving son, Warren, does not pursue a military career. But with the outbreak of the Second World War, Warren appreciates the nation's need for a

Pershing in uniform, and he joins the army, rising eventually to the rank of major, and participates in the Normandy invasion.

Throughout the war, the elder Pershing settles into a fitful old age, lives in a men's club in Washington, follows news of the war as best as his failing faculties will allow. On July 15, 1948, Pershing dies at Walter Reed Army Hospital. He is eighty-eight. President Truman orders that Pershing's body lie in state in the rotunda of the Capitol, and after an extraordinary funeral procession of old soldiers and admirers, he is buried in Arlington National Cemetery.

> *Thus passed a man—a remarkable figure in*
> *American military tradition . . . one of our*
> *country's greatest soldiers every hour of his military*
> *life. No other could have taken his place or carried*
> *out his assignment.*
> —ARCH WHITEHOUSE, historian

Roscoe Temple

He returns with his mother to the farm in north Florida, assumes his role as the man of the house, and of the farm. In 1922, he marries Ruthann Culp, a woman he has known all his life. They have one son. Though Temple makes every effort to find peace in the quiet surroundings of the rural landscape, the war is never far from his thoughts, and when his mother dies in 1928, he leaves the farm in the hands of tenants and moves to Atlanta. He attempts to find work as a teacher at a small military school, but he is plagued by the incessant curiosity of youth, and instead of teaching, he becomes obsessed with turning his students toward the future instead of the past. It is not a realistic solution, and more than ever, Temple is unable to escape the haunting memories of his experiences in France. In 1930, while eating dinner with a group of friends, he reacts to the sound of an airplane by suddenly jumping through an open window; he can never tolerate a Fourth of July fireworks celebration.

His health begins to deteriorate, and, diagnosed with a heart ailment, he returns to Monticello and the farm. But the Great Depression destroys the prospects of many small farmers, and Temple is barely able to provide for his family from the meager yields of his land. In 1938, he attends a twentieth-anniversary reunion of the Second Division, reunites with Brian Murphy, who offers him an opportunity to join a tractor manufacturing company in Chicago. Temple accepts, plans an abrupt change in his life, but Ruthann will not leave her family behind in Florida. Unable to convince her, a distraught Temple files for divorce, but before the marriage is ended, he dies suddenly of a heart attack in June 1939. He is forty-one. In 1943, his son, Mark, is killed in North Africa, serving under General George Patton.

The Legacy of the Red Baron

There is immediate controversy as to who is responsible for Richthofen's death. The Camel that pursued him is piloted by Canadian captain Roy Brown, who insists to his dying day that it was his guns that sent the Fokker down. On the ground, the Australians are as vigorous in their claims, several machine-gunners stating officially that they observed the effects of their fire on the red triplane and its pilot. From the nature of Richthofen's wounds, which are from the side and not behind, the verdict points to the Australians.

Upon confirmation of Richthofen's death, the Air Service names a new commander to JG-1, a young captain named Hermann Goering. But unlike Goering, who later commands Hitler's Luftwaffe, the legacy of Richthofen will suffer none of the stain associated with the rise of the Nazis. Even those who place such harsh judgment on the brutal German militarism that gave rise to the horrors of World War I cannot legitimately diminish the accomplishments of their most accomplished pilot. In death, as in life, Richthofen's name is revered in Germany like no other.

On April 22, 1918, Richthofen is buried by the British in a massive military graveyard in Fricourt, France. In 1925, after considerable petitioning by his family, Richthofen's body is moved to Invaliden Cemetery in Berlin, where he is reburied in a ceremony that is one of the largest of its kind in German history. The first man who tosses dirt on the casket is the aged German commander, now president of the German Republic, Paul von Hindenburg. The grave site is regarded as one of Germany's most revered national shrines, but it suffers from another horror of history, is nearly destroyed in 1961 by the construction of the Berlin Wall, and for twenty-eight years, is cut off from visitors by its close proximity to the Soviet side of the wall.

Until her death, Richthofen's mother maintains the house at Schweidnitz (today known as Swidnica, Poland) as a museum to her fallen son, but when the Soviets occupy the region in 1945, the museum and its artifacts are either looted by soldiers, or shipped to Russia. Many of the items are never recovered.

As the war ends, JG-1 is demobilized, its roster of pilots so decimated that nearly all who remain never actually served with Richthofen. In the 1930s, as Adolf Hitler rebuilds the might of the German war machine, Richthofen's name is called upon again for inspiration: one wing of Goering's Luftwaffe, JG-2, is now called the "Richthofen Wing." After the war, Richthofen's name survives the ash heap of Nazi Germany, and in 1955, with Germany now a part of NATO, the German air force is reestablished. To this day, Jagdgeschwader 71 is known as the Richthofen wing.

The pop-culture appeal of Richthofen's legacy is not confined to Germany. Among many examples, the most graphic and entertaining begins in 1965; when cartoonist Charles Schulz introduces a story line in his *Peanuts* comic strip, in which Snoopy begins a lengthy and frustrating series of duels with his nemesis, the Red Baron.

Though historians continue to debate whether or not Manfred von Richthofen is deserving of his reputation as Germany's finest flying ace, or whether the man is simply the beneficiary of the kaiser's desperate need for propaganda, one undeniable fact remains. Manfred von Richthofen shot down eighty Allied fighter planes, including a significant number of the finest and most technically advanced planes of the day. No one else on either side came close.

Lothar von Richthofen

He learns of his brother's death while still in the hospital in Dusseldorf, his recuperation eventually requiring a four-month stay. But the Air Service remains desperate for heroes, and though General von Hoeppner suggests he serve behind a desk, Lothar insists he once again be allowed to fly. His wish is granted, and he returns to JG-1, where, on August 12, 1918, he scores his fortieth and final kill. The next day, he is seriously wounded in combat, and he spends the remainder of the war recuperating yet again.

As the war ends, he returns home to Schweidnitz, and in 1920, upon the death of his father, becomes master of the Richthofen estate. He marries that same year and has one son, but Lothar is not a man who adapts to peacetime, and those who know him for his boisterous personality see a changed man, who finds no enjoyment in life. His marriage soon dissolves. In the disastrous postwar climate of Germany, jobs for former soldiers are virtually nonexistent, but trained pilots are an asset, and Lothar accepts a position flying cargo planes. But his recklessness catches up to him, and on July 4, 1921, he crashes near Hamburg, and dies the same day. He is twenty-six.

The Legacy of the Lafayette Escadrille

From its formation in April 1916, until it is officially brought into the American Air Service in February 1918, the Lafayette Escadrille brings to the American people more awareness of the Great War than any other single factor. From newspapers to magazines, to an enormous volume of individual fan mail, the pilots of the escadrille are celebrated, ironically, like national heroes. From the German point of view, the escadrille is the single most effective tool of French propaganda at work in the United States.

For decades after the escadrille's final flights, hundreds of men make claim to having served on its roster. Though a large number of American pilots fly in various French squadrons, there is no other unit that is as uniquely and distinctly

American. Throughout its existence, its roster includes a total of only thirty-eight Americans. Among these, nine are killed in combat, and one, Clyde Balsley, is wounded so severely that he never returns to service. One is captured, and held prisoner until the armistice. He is James Norman "Jimmy" Hall, who, despite the worst fears of his squadron, does not die when his plane crashes in May 1918.

The escadrille is credited with fifty-seven confirmed kills. Raoul Lufbery receives confirmation of sixteen of them, yet not one of his victims hits the ground on the French side of the lines. Like so many French and British pilots, most of their confrontations occur over German-held territory. Since confirmations are granted only when ground observers witness the outcome of the duel, Lufbery is denied what many believe to be his rightful place among the most accomplished aces of the war, a distinction that means far more to his fellow pilots than to him. Everyone who serves with him records many instances of enemy planes going down under his guns, including one memorable day in September 1917, when he engages six German fighters, and shoots down five of them. Estimates of Lufbery's actual number of victories range from thirty-five to as many as sixty.

On July 4, 1928, a permanent memorial is dedicated to all the American pilots who flew for France in the Great War. Financed by private donations from thousands of American and French citizens, the Mémorial de L'Escadrille Lafayette stands in the park of Villeneuve L'Étang, in St. Cloud, between Paris and Versailles. Intended as a tomb to house the remains of every American pilot who gave his life to the Allied cause, the monument remains mostly empty. Among the six escadrille pilots who are buried there is Raoul Lufbery.

After his death, Lufbery continues to be an inspiration to the "Hat in the Ring" Ninety-fourth Aero Squadron, which becomes the most celebrated flying wing in the history of the American Air Service, known now, of course, as the United States Air Force.

Bill Thaw

He continues to lead the 103rd Pursuit Squadron for the AEF until August 1918, when he is promoted to group commander in the newly created First Army Air Service. On November 12, 1918, the day after the armistice is signed, he is promoted to lieutenant colonel. He returns to the States, and is given command of Rockwell Field, near San Diego, California, named for his friend Kiffin Rockwell. He seeks and is granted discharge from the army in July 1919, pursues the commercial use of balloons as recreation, a business that founders.

He is married in 1921 to Marjorie Priest, of St. Louis. They have no children.

In 1924, Thaw is contacted by Dr. Edmund Gros, who is seeking the means to construct the monument to the Lafayette Escadrille outside of Paris. Thaw enthusiastically supports the idea, though he is confronted by the influential father of fallen pilot Norman "Nimmie" Prince, who expends considerable energy to place himself and his late son at the center of the escadrille's glory. After considerable controversy and bad blood between Thaw and Frederick Prince, Thaw receives the support of several escadrille families, and the elder Prince, one of America's wealthiest and most powerful men, is forced to admit publicly that his son was not the sole shining star of the Lafayette Escadrille.

Thaw pursues the growing sport of air racing, but in September 1928, he is nearly killed when his racing plane crashes in Indiana. The crash only adds to the considerable damage his body suffers from his activities in the war, and he considers the crash to be a warning that his flying days are past. Though still a young man, his health begins to fail, and among other ailments, he suffers from Bright's disease. Though he travels a great deal, and continues his passionate quest for fishing, his health drains the spirit out of the man who could always be relied on for a hearty laugh.

The Great Depression takes a serious toll on the Thaw family businesses, and the family mansion in Pittsburgh falls into ruin. Returning there in 1934, Thaw is stricken with pneumonia and after a brief coma, he dies. He is forty years old. Though great effort is made to move his remains to Paris, to rest within the crypt of the Lafayette Escadrille Memorial, his widow refuses, and so, Thaw is buried in Pittsburgh.

Edwin "Ted" Parsons

After the termination of the Lafayette Escadrille, Parsons chooses to remain in the French Air Service, and is assigned to Escadrille SPA.3, and by the fall of that year, he commands the squadron. After the armistice, he returns to the States, but still carries his commission in the Aeronautique Militaire, and thus, finds himself serving as a liaison in the French High Commission in Washington. After his discharge in 1920, he applies to serve in the newly formed Federal Bureau of Investigation, and graduates in the FBI's first training class for special agents. He is assigned to Los Angeles, but in 1923, he tires of the structure of government service, and resigns. He becomes a private investigator, but meets Hollywood film director William Wellman, who offers Parsons a position at Paramount Studios. Wellman discovers Parsons to be a talented writer, and in 1926, Parsons produces screenplays, as well as serving as the technical adviser to a number of aviation films. He eventually works for Howard Hughes, where he contributes to the production of *Hell's Angels*, considered by many at the time to be Hughes' best film.

Parsons continues to pursue a talent for writing, and in 1937, he publishes his memoirs, *I Flew with the Lafayette Escadrille*, considered to be the most complete and finest account of the pilots' experiences in the escadrille, as well as the most entertaining.

He joins the United States Naval Reserve, but in 1939, the political neutrality of the United States infuriates him, and he attempts to re-create the formation of the escadrille by assembling a group of pilots who will again serve the French effort against the threats from Germany. But the American government is considerably less tolerant of such efforts than it had been in 1916, and Parsons abandons the attempt. In 1940, as America begins the process of rebuilding its military for what many see as the inevitability of another war with Germany, Parsons goes to Pensacola, Florida, where he serves as a flight instructor.

With the outbreak of war, now—Lieutenant Commander Parsons serves in the Pacific theater, and commands an amphibious assault unit, where he receives considerable praise for his handling of operations in both the Philippines and Okinawa. He retires from the navy in 1954, having achieved the rank of rear admiral. He settles near Sarasota, Florida, and, in 1957, marries for the first time.

Along with Paul Rockwell (Kiffin's older brother), Parsons' efforts are critical to the preservation of much of the history and records of the escadrille. He remains active in reunions with the few remaining pilots, and dies in 1968, at age seventy-five. He is buried in Arlington National Cemetery.

Georges Thenault

After the Lafayette Escadrille is absorbed by the American Air Service, the squadron's sole commanding officer remains in service to the Aeronautique Militaire. In February 1918, he is assigned to the training facility at Pau, France, where he serves until the armistice. After the war, he travels to the United States for the first time, where he becomes the French military attaché to his nation's embassy in Washington. As efforts to fund the monument to the escadrille take shape, Thenault finds himself involved with the influential Frederick Prince, in the same kinds of controversies that plague Bill Thaw. Thenault writes his memoirs, which he naïvely submits to a patronizing Prince, who translates Thenault's work by incorporating considerable added material that makes it appear that Thenault himself credits Nimmie Prince for the escadrille's successes. When the book is published in the States, Thenault finds himself the target of considerable wrath from surviving escadrille members. Furious, he works through the difficult process of altering and revising his work.

Thenault remains in the United States, and in 1925, like Bill Thaw, he marries a woman from St. Louis. They have two children.

Still serving the French Air Service, he is promoted to colonel, and is recalled to France in 1933 to command yet another flying squadron. But seeking to remain close to his growing family, he chooses to retire, and in 1935, his service to France concludes.

He dies in Paris, in 1948, at age fifty-nine. He is buried in the Lafayette Escadrille Memorial.

Billy Mitchell

The man most responsible for the creation of an effective flying arm of the United States military returns home to confront the never-ending bureaucratic obstacles to his ideas of a continuously modernizing air force. Through Pershing's help, Mitchell's air force is given considerable status in the Army Reorganization Act of 1920, but Mitchell is not satisfied, and his aggressive and unyielding style makes enemies. In 1925, his harassment of his superiors over their failure to give priority to his arm of the service brings about his court-martial, for "conduct prejudicial to good order and military discipline." In response, Mitchell resigns from the army. He dies in 1936, at age fifty-six. It is only after his death that his enthusiasm for the value of aircraft is accepted as standard policy in the American armed forces.

Edward "Eddie" Rickenbacker

On May 30, 1918, he becomes an official ace by claiming his fifth victory. His verified total of kills by the end of the war totals twenty-six, which makes him, officially, the most successful American ace of the war. After Lufbery's death, Rickenbacker is named to command the Ninety-fourth Aero Squadron, which, under his leadership, shoots down more enemy aircraft than any other American squadron.

He returns home a celebrated hero, and his memoirs, *Fighting the Flying Circus*, are published in 1919. Using his considerable skills as both a writer and public speaker, he skillfully promotes and romanticizes the exploits of America's flying aces, including, of course, himself. The former race-car driver founds Rickenbacker Motors, becomes the first president of Eastern Airlines, and in 1930 receives the Medal of Honor. He lives the flamboyant life of a national hero until his death in 1973. Throughout his life, those who seek out his tales of air combat in the Great War learn firsthand that Eddie Rickenbacker never fails to give credit to the one man who taught him how to fight and defeat the enemy in the air: Raoul Lufbery.

Erich Ludendorff

With the abdication of the kaiser, Ludendorff escapes the wrath of the German mobs by traveling first to Denmark, and then to Sweden. He immediately begins work on his memoirs, driven by the belief that he must expose the damaging effects of Bolshevism, which he believes to be the cause of the violent unrest in Germany. By February 1919, when civil order begins to quiet Berlin, Ludendorff discreetly returns, protected by many who still regard him as an important national hero. He is infuriated by the terms of the armistice, and begins to speak openly that Germany's defeat came not so much at the hands of the Allies but from the "back-stabbing" of the civilian politicians in Berlin. It is a philosophy that finds sympathy with a great many former soldiers. In March 1920, he is one of the leaders of a march on Berlin that intimidates the civilian ministers, including the chancellor, Friedrich Ebert, into leaving their posts. But the would-be coup has no real muscle, and the chaos in Berlin erupts into fighting between factions loyal to all sides of the issue. Ludendorff wisely escapes the conflicts, and seeks refuge in Bavaria. Though he stays out of the public eye for nearly two years, he begins to follow the rise of the National Socialist German Worker's Party, whose most vocal leader is Adolf Hitler. Hitler speaks to Ludendorff's own increasing obsession with identifying the enemies of Germany. In December 1921, Ludendorff writes: "I see the work of the Bolsheviks in the writings of the Jews."

In May 1923, he meets Hitler face-to-face, is impressed by the young man's zeal, not to mention his unflagging compliments toward Ludendorff as a true hero of Germany. In November 1923, Ludendorff stands beside Hitler during the Nazis' attempt to take control of the city of Munich (the Munich Putsch), and marches through a parade of bullets as Hitler's attempted coup collapses into violence. Hitler himself is captured and imprisoned. Ludendorff is arrested as well, but he is acquitted of all charges. With Hitler in prison, Ludendorff begins to separate himself from the Nazis, believing that Hitler is more interested in his own interests than in the greater good of Germany. But when Hitler is released, he courts Ludendorff again, insists that Ludendorff vie for the position of president of the new Weimar Republic. But Ludendorff's day has passed, and the public virtually ignores his candidacy. Hitler is quick to perceive that Ludendorff is no longer an asset, and so, the Nazis throw their support instead to the aging hero Paul von Hindenburg.

In 1926, Ludendorff divorces his wife, and marries a woman whose radical ideas play on Ludendorff's crumbling sanity. He develops a fanatical hatred of various ethnic groups, including Jews, Christians, Jesuits, Freemasons, and Catholics, and begins to rely on astrology and the occult to govern his daily life. Despite his mental decay, he continues to write articles expressing his views, particularly regarding the absolute necessity of a military dictatorship as the only reliable means of governing a nation, particularly the German nation. He dies in Munich in 1937, at age seventy-two.

Paul von Hindenburg

He survives the violence that rolls through Germany, and attempts to become a voice of reason, even as the terms of the armistice galvanize the German people. In 1925, at the urging of several political groups, he reluctantly agrees to run for the office of president, and to his surprise, he wins. But von Hindenburg cannot prevent Hitler's rise to power, and, as he had done with Ludendorff, von Hindenburg takes a more passive role as the titular head of the nation that Hitler in fact controls. In 1933, von Hindenburg bows to the inevitable, and names Hitler chancellor of Germany, which cements Hitler's position as absolute dictator. Von Hindenburg dies in 1934, at age eighty-seven.

Henri-Philippe Pétain

Among the men he commanded, Pétain is arguably France's most popular military leader. Promoted to marshal of France after the armistice, he continues to serve in the army. He is named minister of war in 1936, and two years later, is named France's minister to Spain.

In 1940, when France cannot hold back the German occupation of Paris, the aging Pétain signs the armistice documents that signify France's defeat. The documents are signed in the presence of Hitler himself, which, by no accident, takes place in the same railcars Foch had used in 1918. Instead of retiring, and thus preserving some of his dignity, Pétain inexplicably accepts control of the Vichy government, whose function is to serve Nazi interests in unoccupied France, thus assuming the role as the ultimate French collaborator. Astonishingly, Pétain serves Hitler by providing the Nazis with lists of French Jews, who are then arrested and sent to concentration camps. At the war's end, Pétain is charged with treason and sentenced to be executed. But the new French leader, Charles de Gaulle, will not allow France to forget Pétain's earlier legacy, and the sentence is commuted. Pétain serves out the remaining years of his life in exile, on an island off the French coast. He dies in 1951, at age ninety-five.

Ferdinand Foch

Unlike Pershing, Foch takes an active role in the contentious negotiations over the Treaty of Versailles, as the primary representative of the French military. He is an outspoken critic of the treaty, believing it to be far too lenient, but performs his duty as one of the administrators who oversees German compliance. His criticism of the Treaty of Versailles results in a feud with Georges Clemenceau that continues even after his death. Foch's memoirs, published posthumously, attacks Clemenceau, which causes Clemenceau to respond in his own memoirs, also published posthumously, which of course neither man can ever argue.

Though Foch is regarded as France's most celebrated hero of the Great War, he refuses all offers to pursue a career in politics. He dies in 1929, at age seventy-eight.

Foch is the first French leader to have a statue erected to him in London.

Marshal Joseph Joffre

Though he serves as titular chairman of the Supreme War Council, he is keenly aware that any role assigned to him is more ceremonial than meaningful. Once the Treaty of Versailles is signed, he retires. Joffre is a realist, and he understands that the failures of the French army to hold back the German invasion, and the subsequent agony of the four years of bloodletting, must be placed at someone's feet. Joffre accepts his assigned place as France's military scapegoat.

He is still much admired by the French people, who are consistently more forgiving than their politicians, and bowing to public pressure, the Ministry of War allows him to maintain a position and an office there, though again, Joffre knows he has no real authority. He is elected to the French Academy, a testament to the esteem he receives in many prominent social circles, and spends the rest of his life in quiet retirement. He dies in 1931, at age seventy-nine.

Sir Douglas Haig

After the armistice, he eventually returns to London and finds that he is a commander without a command. Having lost the battle of wills to David Lloyd George, Haig finds he has no allies in the British government, and settles into bored retirement at his home in Edinburgh, Scotland. He is granted peerage, given the title of Baron Haig of Bemersyde, and Parliament awards him a gift of one hundred thousand pounds.

Various attempts to place him in some prestigious position come to nothing, including a campaign to have him named Viceroy of India. He settles miserably into a life of leisure, plays golf, hunts, and lunches at various clubs, which consider him an honored member.

As is typical of a commander who was popular with his troops, he receives a considerable amount of mail, is distressed to learn of the misery of so many of his men who are struggling to find their way in the civilian world. Haig begins to work with charity hospitals, drawing attention to the extraordinary number of invalid soldiers, and offers aid to counseling organizations, an effort to make life easier for the men who had fought so valiantly under his command.

Despite ongoing criticism of his ability in the field, including scathing assaults on him in Lloyd George's memoirs, Haig makes no effort to state his own case, is confident that history will vindicate him. To this day he has his rabid supporters as well as equally passionate detractors. He dies in 1928 of a heart attack, at age seventy-seven.

The Legacy of the "War to End All Wars"

The numbers tell the tale. In four years of the most brutal combat the world has ever seen, nearly ten million men die on the battlefield or in the hospitals nearby. The cost in human life can be translated to the loss of more than five thousand men every day the war was fought. Thus an entire generation of young men is erased from the future of humanity.

In all, fifty-seven countries participate on some level in the Great War. The war, and the subsequent treaties that follow, radically alter the map of Europe and the Middle East. Where once were kings and empires, from Germany to Austria-Hungary, Turkey to Russia, new governments arise, new leaders place their names in the history books.

In the United States, the cost of the war is horrifying in its own way. Over fifty thousand men die, a number that pales in comparison to the losses of the other major participants. But the American deaths occur in the relatively brief period from May to November 1918. The number is eerily similar to the losses suffered in the Vietnam War, losses that occur over a period of *fourteen years*. Other numbers are appalling as well. In the fledgling American Air Service, *one-third* of all pilots who report for duty in Europe are killed.

In all countries, heroes emerge, and in America, the public's need to cherish and embellish some positive side of the war results in the rise of legends, men like Eddie Rickenbacker and Alvin York. But for every Sergeant York, there are men whose names are much less celebrated, and for the most part remain unknown to this day: Samuel Woodfill, Ulysses Grant McAlexander, Jesse Wooldridge, Charles Whittlesey, Henry Hulbert, Harry Adams. And Raoul Lufbery.

For every veteran of the Great War who rises to extraordinary notoriety in the Second World War, for every George Patton, George Marshall, or Douglas MacArthur, there are thousands more who will serve again, enlisted men and junior officers who rise to command, all of whom are better soldiers because of their experiences in 1918.

Though historians continue to debate the overall impact of the American military's role, the economic impact of America's exports to England and France had been felt long before the first soldiers of the AEF ever landed in France. From wheat and textiles to steel and lumber, American goods become a lifeblood of survival, particularly for Great Britain. It was this aid that gives rise to considerable protest in Germany, and ammunition to critics of Woodrow Wilson, who realizes that the United States was never truly a neutral party to the war. Once Wilson declares war, America begins to contribute enormous quantities of munitions and chemicals for high explosives (including gas), which eventually give the Allies an enormous advantage on the battlefield.

Throughout history, wars are often decided by technology, and in no event in modern history is this more evident than in the First World War, which of course explains the enormous cost in human life. For the first time, nations bring to combat the submarine and the airplane, the machine gun and the flamethrower, poison gas, portable trench mortars, and the grenade, plus the development of far more efficient artillery and small arms. Yet through much of the war, the commanders continue to march their men in slow formations, attacking headlong into an entrenched enemy.

During Christmas, 1914, the soldiers who faced each other along many stretches of the Western Front violated the orders of their officers and began a spontaneous celebration of the holiday. British, French, and German soldiers gathered in no-man's-land and traded goods or saluted each other with greetings painted on huge wooden signs. Christmas trees were placed by German troops on the parapets of trenches. In some instances, games of soccer were played, the spirit of innocence still spread throughout the armies on both sides. After that first Christmas of the war, it never happened again.

The men who return home in 1918 bring with them the horrible memories and the lessons of their experience that inspire numerous articles and books, all insisting with perfect certainty that no war of this magnitude could ever occur again. The view is one of hope, of optimism, that man's worst instincts have been extinguished. Today, nearly a century later, the world knows that to be regretfully untrue.

To this day historians continue to write from both sides of the fence regarding the impact of the American army on the outcome of the war. For decades after the Treaty of Versailles, many British and French historians completely dismiss America's role, some even describing the American effort as nothing more than a quick grab at glory by entering the war when it was all but over. Regardless of the ongoing debates, many of which echo the sentiments of what is currently fashionable, the facts and the documented words of so many of the Allied (and German) leaders indicate a clear consensus. If the United States Army had not arrived when it did and had not fought the way it did, the Allies would have lost the war.

American Comrades: I am grateful to you for the blood so generously spilled on the soil of my country. I am

proud . . . to have fought with you for the deliverance of the world.
—GENERAL CHARLES MANGIN
Commander, French Tenth Army

Nobody among us will ever forget what America did.
—FIELD MARSHAL FERDINAND FOCH

GALLIPOLI
By L. A. Carlyon

'*Because it was fought so close to his old home ground, Homer might have seen this war on the Gallipoli Peninsula as an epic. Brief by his standards, but essentially heroic. Shakespeare might have seen it as a tragedy with splendid bit-parts for buffoons and brigands and lots of graveyard scenes. Those thigh bones you occasionally see rearing out of the yellow earth of Gully ravine, snapped open so that they look like pumice, belong to a generation of young men who on this peninsula first lost their innocence and then their lives, and maybe something else as well . . .*'

Gallipoli remains one of the most poignant battlefronts of the First World War and L. A. Carlyon's monumental account of that campaign has been rightfully acclaimed and a massive bestseller in Australia. Brilliantly told, supremely readable and deeply moving, *Gallipoli* brings this epic tragedy to life and stands as both a landmark chapter in the history of the war and a salutary reminder of all that is fine and all that is foolish in the human condition.

'Incisive, emotionally-charged and visceral . . . blends a real feel for the fighting soldier with a firm grasp of the strangely beautiful countryside which saw such a bewildering mix of tragedy, missed opportunity and wasted heroism. A hard-hitting and heart-breaking book'
Richard Holmes

'Superb . . . Carlyon's writing is so vivid that you almost imagine yourself present. A stunning achievement'   Saul David, *Daily Telegraph*

'Carlyon is a gifted writer . . . his book deserves to take its place alongside other classic accounts of Gallipoli. He conveys the beauty of the place and its ugliness 90 years ago'   John Keegan, *Daily Telegraph*

'A brilliantly managed narrative and remarkably even-handed . . . a superb account'   Trevor Royle, *Glasgow Herald*

'Massively researched . . . an enthralling account of an appalling fiasco'   Peter Porter, *Spectator*

'The book of the year . . . the most stunning account of the Anzac boneyard'   Alan Ramsey, *Sydney Morning Herald*

0 553 81506 7

BANTAM BOOKS

AN ACT OF COURAGE
By Allan Mallinson

THE SEVENTH GRIPPING MATTHEW HERVEY ADVENTURE

Christmas 1826, and Captain Matthew Hervey of the 6th Light Dragoons is a prisoner of the Spanish, incarcerated in the infamous fortress of Badajoz. As he plans his escape, his thoughts return to the year 1812 when he was a cornet in Wellington's Peninsular Army. He and the Sixth had survived Corunna to endure three more years of brutal fighting that would culminate in one of the most vital, and vicious, confrontations of the campaign: the siege of Badajoz . . .

And while Hervey paces his prison cell and relives the bloodshed of battles past, friends from unexpected quarters are rushing to his aid . . .

'What a pleasure . . . concentrating on the battle of Talavara and the investment of Badajoz, both sparklingly described, he plays to his undoubted strengths'
Observer

'Most impressive . . . Mallinson reinforces his position as a master of narrative military history'
The Times

'Mallinson's descriptions of what it is like to be on campaign are as compelling, vivid and plausible as in any war novel I have ever read'
Daily Telegraph

0 553 81674 8

BANTAM BOOKS

WHERE THEY LAY
By Earl Swift

The US government has an unspoken pledge with every man and woman it sends into battle: you may be wounded doing your duty, you may even be killed, but you'll come home. You won't be left behind . . .

On 20 March 1971, during the largest helicopter battle in history, an American chopper exploded in the skies over Laos. Its scorched remains fell onto terrain about which the allied forces knew little except that it was hostile, so dense with North Vietnamese that going in search of the downed crew was out of the question. And so they were left where they lay – four among the 2,583 servicemen whose bodies remained unrecovered at war's end.

Thirty years on and a team of soldiers and scientists is returning to that battlefield. Their mission – one of dozens conducted every year – is to dig among the unexploded bombs, in ground slick from monsoon rains, in jungle infested with foot-long centipedes, leeches and snakes, to find these lost men, to bring them home and to put a name – the right name – on each headstone.

Telling the enthralling and little-known story of these recovery teams and their elusive employer: the US Army's Central Identification Laboratory – the world's largest forensic science lab, *Where They Lay* is a classic of modern warfare and its aftermath.

'A poignant tale of one war and four lost lives. And the story of all who never came back'
James Bradley, author of *Flags of Our Fathers*

0 553 81444 3

BANTAM BOOKS

A SELECTED LIST OF FINE WRITING
AVAILABLE FROM TRANSWORLD PUBLISHERS

15108 4	WITNESS TO WAR: DIARIES OF THE SECOND WORLD WAR IN EUROPE	Richard Aldrich	£9.99
81672 1	GWEILO: MEMORIES OF A HONG KONG CHILDHOOD	Martin Booth	£7.99
81506 7	GALLIPOLI	L. A. Carlyon	£9.99
77288 7	A THREAD OF GRACE	Mary Doria Russell	£7.99
99986 5	A MOTH AT THE GLASS	Mogue Doyle	£6.99
81447 8	INTO AFRICA	Martin Dugard	£8.99
15094 0	IN THE COMPANY OF HEROES	Michael J. Durant	£6.99
77206 2	PEACETIME	Robert Edric	£6.99
99987 3	NO-ONE THINKS OF GREENLAND	John Griesemer	£6.99
81521 0	ARBELLA: ENGLAND'S LOST QUEEN	Sarah Gristwood	£9.99
81445 1	HIMMLER'S CRUSADE	Christopher Hale	£7.99
81485 0	THE AIR LOOM GANG	Mike Jay	£7.99
81353 6	THE DEVIL IN THE WHITE CITY	Erik Larson	£7.99
81642 X	ANCIENT MARINER	Ken McGoogan	£7.99
81674 8	AN ACT OF COURAGE	Allan Mallinson	£6.99
81498 2	GENGHIS KHAN	John Man	£7.99
81522 9	1421: THE YEAR CHINA DISCOVERED THE WORLD	Gavin Menzies	£9.99
81460 5	THE WAR AND UNCLE WALTER	Walter Musto	£7.99
81554 7	DAD'S WAR	Howard Reid	£6.99
99810 9	THE JUKEBOX QUEEN OF MALTA	Nicholas Rinaldi	£6.99
81610 1	THE LAST MISSION	Jim Smith and Malcolm McConnell	£7.99
81444 3	WHERE THEY LAY	Earl Swift	£7.99
99864 8	A DESERT IN BOHEMIA	Jill Paton Walsh	£6.99
81539 3	THE MAPMAKER'S WIFE: A TRUE TALE OF LOVE, MURDER AND SURVIVAL IN THE AMAZON	Robert Whitaker	£7.99